大中华文库
LIBRARY
OF CHINESE CLASSICS

学术顾问委员会：(按姓氏笔画排序)

丁望道　叶水夫　任继愈　刘重德
汤博文　李学勤　李赋宁　杨宪益
沙博理　季羡林　林戊荪　金开诚
胡文仲　徐公持　袁行霈　梁良兴
韩素音　戴文葆

Academic Consulting Committee:

Dai Wenbao, Ding Wangdao,
Han Suyin, Hu Wenzhong, Ji Xianlin,
Jin Kaicheng, Li Funing, Li Xueqin,
Liang Liangxing, Lin Wusun,
Liu Zhongde, Ren Jiyu, Sidney Shapiro,
Tang Bowen, Xu Gongchi, Yang Xianyi,
Ye Shuifu, Yuan Xingpei

总　监　纂：于友先
副总监纂：杨正泉　刘杲
　　　　　陈满之

Compilation Supervisor: Yu Youxian
Compilation Co-Supervisors:
Yang Zhengquan, Liu Gao,
Chen Manzhi

工作委员会：
主　　　任：杨牧之
副　主　任：黄友义　阎晓宏
　　　　　　张光华
委　　　员：(按姓氏笔画排序)
　　　　　　王显臣　李朋义
　　　　　　李振国　李景端
　　　　　　陈万雄　周洪力
　　　　　　凌　原　熊治祁

Working Committee:

Chairman: Yang Muzhi
Vice-Chairmen:
Huang Youyi, Yan Xiaohong,
Zhang Guanghua
Members:
Chan Man-hung, Li Jingduan,
Li Pengyi, Li Zhenguo, Ling Yuan,
Wang Xianchen, Xiong Zhiqi,
Zhou Hongli

编辑委员会：
总　编　辑：杨牧之
副总编辑：(按姓氏笔画排序)
　　　　　　马欣来　尹飞舟
　　　　　　徐明强　黄友义

Editorial Committee:

Chief-Editor: Yang Muzhi
Deputy Chief-Editors:
Huang Youyi, Ma Xinlai,
Xu Mingqiang, Yin Feizhou

装帧设计：廖铁　蔡荣
　　　　　李伯红
印装监制：李坦　黄国斌

Designers: Liao Tie, Cai Rong,
Li Bohong
Production Controllers:
Li Tan, Huang Guobin

大中华文库
汉英对照
LIBRARY OF CHINESE CLASSICS
Chinese-English

牡 丹 亭
The Poeny Pavilion
I

［明］汤显祖　著
汪榕培　英译
徐朔方　杨笑梅　点校

Written by Tang Xianzu

Translated by Wang Rongpei

Punctuated and Revised by Xu Shuofang and Yang Xiaomei

湖南人民出版社
Hunan People's Publishing House

外文出版社
Foreign Languages Press

First Edition 2000

All rights reserved. No part of this publication may be reproduced or transmitted in any form or by any means, electronic or mechanical, now known or to be invented, without permission in writing from the publishers, except for brief quotations by reviewers.

ISBN 7-5438-2534-1 / I • 320
©2000 Hunan People's Publishing House

Published by
Hunan People's Publishing House
  78 Yin Pen South Road, Changsha 410006, Hunan, China
Foreign Languages Press
  24 Baiwanzhuang Road, Beijing 100037, China
  http: // www. flp. com. cn
Printed by
Donnelley Bright Sun Printing Co., Shenzhen, China

Printed in the People's Republic of China

总　　序

《大中华文库》终于出版了。我们为之高兴，为之鼓舞，但也倍感压力。

当此之际，我们愿将郁积在我们心底的话，向读者倾诉。

一

中华民族有着悠久的历史和灿烂的文化，系统、准确地将中华民族的文化经典翻译成外文，编辑出版，介绍给全世界，是几代中国人的愿望。早在几十年前，西方一位学者翻译《红楼梦》，书名译成《一个红楼上的梦》，将林黛玉译为"黑色的玉"。我们一方面对外国学者将中国的名著介绍到世界上去表示由衷的感谢，一方面为祖国的名著还不被完全认识，甚而受到曲解，而感到深深的遗憾。还有西方学者翻译《金瓶梅》，专门摘选其中自然主义描述最为突出的篇章加以译介。一时间，西方学者好像发现了奇迹，掀起了《金瓶梅》热，说中国是"性开放的源头"，公开地在报刊上鼓吹中国要"发扬开放之传统"。还有许多资深、友善的汉学家译介中国古代的哲学著作，在把中华民族文化介绍给全世界的工作方面作出了重大贡献，但或囿于理解有误，或缘于对中国文字认识的局限，质量上乘的并不多，常常是隔靴搔痒，说不到点子上。大哲学家黑格尔曾经说过：中国有最完备的国史。但他认为中国古代没有真正意义上的哲学，还处在哲学史前状态。这么了不起的哲学家竟然作出这样大失水准的评论，何其不幸。正如任何哲学家都要受时间、地点、条件的制约一样，黑格尔也离不开这一规律。当时他也只能从上述水平的汉学家译过去的文字去分析、理解，所以，黑格尔先生对中国古代社会的认识水平是什么状态，也就不难想象了。

中国离不开世界，世界也缺少不了中国。中国文化摄取外域的新成分，丰富了自己，又以自己的新成就输送给别人，贡献于世界。从公元5世纪开始到公元15世纪，大约有一千年，中国走在世界的前列。在这一千多年的时间里，她的光辉照耀全世界。人类要前进，怎么能不全面认识中国，怎么能不认真研究中国的历史呢？

二

中华民族是伟大的，曾经辉煌过，蓝天、白云、阳光灿烂，和平而兴旺；也有过黑暗的、想起来就让人战栗的日子，但中华民族从来是充满理想，不断追求，不断学习，渴望和平与友谊的。

中国古代伟大的思想家孔子曾经说过："三人行，必有我师焉。择其善者而从之，其不善者而改之。"孔子的话就是要人们向别人学习。这段话正是概括了整个中华民族与人交往的原则。人与人之间交往如此，在与周边的国家交往中也是如此。

秦始皇第一个统一了中国，可惜在位只有十几年，来不及作更多的事情。汉朝继秦而继续强大，便开始走出去，了解自己周边的世界。公元前138年，汉武帝派张骞出使西域。他带着一万头牛羊，总值一万万钱的金帛货物，作为礼物，开始西行，最远到过"安息"（即波斯）。公元前36年，班超又率36人出使西域。36个人按今天的话说，也只有一个排，显然是为了拜访未曾见过面的邻居，是去交朋友。到了西域，班超派遣甘英作为使者继续西行，往更远处的大秦国（即罗马）去访问，"乃抵条支而历安息，临西海以望大秦"（《后汉书·西域传》）。"条支"在"安息"以西，即今天的伊拉克、叙利亚一带，"西海"应是今天的地中海。也就是说甘英已经到达地中海边上，与罗马帝国隔海相望，"临大海欲渡"，却被人劝阻而未成行，这在历史上留下了遗恨。可以想见班超、甘英沟通友谊的无比勇气和强烈愿望。接下来是唐代的玄奘，历经千难万险，到"西天"印度取经，带回了南亚国家的古老文化。归国后，他把带回的佛教经典组织人翻译，到后来很多经典印度失传了，但中国却保存完好，以至于今天，没有玄奘的《大唐西域记》，印度人很难编写印度古代史。明代郑和"七下西洋"，把中华文化传到东南亚一带。鸦片战争以后，一代又一代先进的中国人，为了振兴中华，又前赴后继，向西方国家学习先进的科学思想和文明成果。这中间有我们的领导人朱德、周恩来、邓小平；有许许多多大科学家、文学家、艺术家，如郭沫若、李四光、钱学森、冼星海、徐悲鸿等。他们的追求、奋斗，他们的博大胸怀，兼收并蓄的精神，为人类社会增添了光彩。

中国文化的形成和发展过程，就是一个以众为师，以各国人民为师，不断学习和创造的过程。中华民族曾经向周边国家和民族学习过许多东西，假如没有这些学习，中华民族决不可能创造出昔日的辉煌。回顾历史，我们怎么能够不对伟大的古埃及文明、古希腊文明、古印度文明满怀深深的感激?怎么能够不对伟大的欧洲文明、非洲文明、美洲文明、澳洲文明,以及中国周围的亚洲文明充满温情与敬意?

中华民族为人类社会曾作出过独特的贡献。在15世纪以前,中国的科学技术一直处于世界遥遥领先的地位。英国科学家李约瑟说:"中国在公元3世纪到13世纪之间,保持着一个西方所望尘莫及的科学知识水平。"美国耶鲁大学教授、《大国的兴衰》的作者保罗·肯尼迪坦言:"在近代以前时期的所有文明中,没有一个国家的文明比中国更发达,更先进。"

世界各国的有识之士千里迢迢来中国观光、学习。在这个过程中,中国唐朝的长安城渐渐发展成为国际大都市。西方的波斯、东罗马,东亚的高丽、新罗、百济、南天竺、北天竺,频繁前来。外国的王侯、留学生,在长安供职的外国官员、商贾、乐工和舞士,总有几十个国家,几万人之多。日本派出"遣唐使"更是一批接一批。传为美谈的日本人阿部仲麻吕(晁衡)在长安留学的故事,很能说明外国人与中国的交往。晁衡学成仕于唐朝,前后历时五十余年。晁衡与中国的知识分子结下了深厚的友情。他归国时,传说在海中遇难身亡。大诗人李白作诗哭悼:"日本晁卿辞帝都,征帆一片远蓬壶。明月不归沉碧海,白云愁色满苍梧。"晁衡遇险是误传,但由此可见中外学者之间在中国长安交往的情谊。

后来,不断有外国人到中国来探寻秘密,所见所闻,常常让他们目瞪口呆。《希腊纪事》(希腊人波桑尼阿著)记载公元2世纪时,希腊人在中国的见闻。书中写道:"赛里斯人用小米和青芦喂一种类似蜘蛛的昆虫,喂到第五年,虫肚子胀裂开,便从里面取出丝来。"从这段对中国古代养蚕技术的描述,可见当时欧洲人与中国人的差距。公元9世纪中叶,阿拉伯人来到中国。一位阿拉伯作家在他所著的《中国印度闻见录》中记载了曾旅居中国的阿拉伯商人的见闻：

——一天，一个外商去拜见驻守广州的中国官吏。会见时，外商总盯着官吏的胸部，官吏很奇怪，便问："你好像总盯着我的胸，这是怎么回事？"那位外商回答说："透过你穿的丝绸衣服，我隐约看到你胸口上长着一个黑痣，这是什么丝绸，我感到十分惊奇。"官吏听后，失声大笑，伸出胳膊，说："请你数数吧，看我穿了几件衣服？"那商人数过，竟然穿了五件之多，黑痣正是透过这五层丝绸衣服显现出来的。外商惊得目瞪口呆，官吏说："我穿的丝绸还不算是最好的，总督穿的要更精美。"

——书中关于茶（他们叫干草叶子）的记载，可见阿拉伯国家当时还没有喝茶的习惯。书中记述："中国国王本人的收入主要靠盐税和泡开水喝的一种干草税。在各个城市里，这种干草叶售价都很高，中国人称这种草叶叫'茶'，这种干草叶比苜蓿的叶子还多，也略比它香，稍有苦味，用开水冲喝，治百病。"

——他们对中国的医疗条件十分羡慕，书中记载道："中国人医疗条件很好，穷人可以从国库中得到药费。"还说："城市里，很多地方立一石碑，高10肘，上面刻有各种疾病和药物，写明某种病用某种药医治。"

——关于当时中国的京城，书中作了生动的描述：中国的京城很大，人口众多，一条宽阔的长街把全城分为两半，大街右边的东区，住着皇帝、宰相、禁军及皇家的总管、奴婢。在这个区域，沿街开凿了小河，流水潺潺；路旁，葱茏的树木整然有序，一幢幢宅邸鳞次栉比。大街左边的西区，住着庶民和商人。这里有货栈和商店，每当清晨，人们可以看到,皇室的总管、宫廷的仆役,或骑马或步行,到这里来采购。

此后的史籍对西人来华的记载,渐渐多了起来。13世纪意大利旅行家马可·波罗,尽管有人对他是否真的到过中国持怀疑态度,但他留下一部记述元代事件的《马可·波罗游记》却是确凿无疑的。这部游记中的一些关于当时中国的描述使得西方人认为是"天方夜谭"。总之,从中西文化交流史来说,这以前的时期还是一个想象和臆测的时代,相互之间充满了好奇与幻想。

从16世纪末开始,由于航海技术的发展,东西方航路的开通,随着一批批传教士来华,中国与西方开始了直接的交流。沟通中西的使命在意大利传教士利玛窦那里有了充分的体现。利玛窦于1582年来华,1610年病逝于北京,在华20余年。除了传教以外,做了两件具有历史象征意义的事,一是1594年前后在韶州用拉丁文翻译《四书》,并作了注释;二是与明代学者徐光启合作,用中文翻译了《几何原本》。

西方传教士对《四书》等中国经典的粗略翻译,以及杜赫德的《中华帝国志》等书对中国的介绍,在西方读者的眼前展现了一个异域文明,在当时及稍后一段时期引起了一场"中国热",许多西方大思想家的眼光都曾注目中国文化。有的推崇中华文明,如莱布尼兹、伏尔泰、魁奈等,有的对中华文明持批评态度,如孟德斯鸠、黑格尔等。莱布尼兹认识到中国文化的某些思想与他的观念相近,如周易的卦象与他发明的二进制相契合,对中国文化给予了热情的礼赞;黑格尔则从他整个哲学体系的推演出发,认为中国没有真正意义上的哲学,还处在哲学史前的状态。但是,不论是推崇还是批评,是吸纳还是排斥,中西文化的交流产生了巨大的影响。随着先进的中国科学技术的西传，特别是中国的造纸、火药、印刷术和指南针四大发明的问世，大大改变了世界的面貌。马克思说："中国的火药把骑士阶层炸得粉碎，指南针打开了世界市场并建立了殖民地，而印刷术则变成了新教的工具，变成对精神发展创造必要前提的最强大的杠杆。"英国的哲学家培根说：中国的四大发明"改变了全世界的面貌和一切事物的状态"。

三

大千世界，潮起潮落。云散云聚，万象更新。中国古代产生了无数伟大科学家：祖冲之、李时珍、孙思邈、张衡、沈括、毕升……，产生了无数科技成果：《齐民要术》、《九章算术》、《伤寒杂病论》、《本草纲目》……，以及保存至今的世界奇迹：浑天仪、地动仪、都江堰、敦煌石窟、大运河、万里长城……。但从15世纪下半叶起，风水似乎从东方转到了西方，落后的欧洲只经过400年便成为世界瞩目的文明中心。英国的牛顿、波兰的哥白尼、德国的伦琴、法国的居里、德国的爱因斯坦、意大利的伽利略、俄国的门捷列夫、美国的费米和爱迪生……，光芒四射，令人敬仰。

中华民族开始思考了。潮起潮落究竟是什么原因？中国人发明的火药，传到欧洲，转眼之间反成为欧洲列强轰击中国大门的炮弹，又是因为什么？

鸦片战争终于催醒了中国人沉睡的迷梦，最先"睁眼看世界"的一代精英林则徐、魏源迈出了威武雄壮的一步。曾国藩、李鸿章搞起了洋务运动。中国的知识分子喊出"民主与科学"的口号。中国是落后了，中国的志士仁人在苦苦探索。但落后中饱含着变革的动力，探索中孕育着崛起的希望。"向科学进军"，中华民族终于又迎来了科学的春天。

今天，世界毕竟来到了21世纪的门槛。分散隔绝的世界，逐渐变成联系为一体的世界。现在，全球一体化趋势日益明显，人类历史也就在愈来愈大的程度上成为全世界的历史。当今，任何一种文化的发展都离不开对其它优秀文化的汲取，都以其它优秀文化的发展为前提。在近现代，西方文化汲取中国文化，不仅是中国文化的传播，更是西方文化自身的创新和发展；正如中国文化对西方文化的汲取一样，既是西方文化在中国的传播，同时也是中国文化在近代的转型和发展。地球上所有的人类文化，都是我们共同的宝贵遗产。既然我们生活的各个大陆，在地球史上曾经是连成一气的"泛大陆"，或者说是一个完整的"地球村"，那么，我们同样可以在这个以知识和学习为特征的网络时代，走上相互学习、共同发展的大路，建设和开拓我们人类崭新的"地球村"。

西学仍在东渐，中学也将西传。各国人民的优秀文化正日益迅速地为中国文化所汲取，而无论西方和东方，也都需要从中国文化中汲取养分。正是基于这一认识，我们组织出版汉英对照版《大中华文库》，全面系统地翻译介绍中国传统文化典籍。我们试图通过《大中华文库》，向全世界展示，中华民族五千年的追求，五千年的梦想，正在新的历史时期重放光芒。中国人民就像火后的凤凰，万众一心，迎接新世纪文明的太阳。

杨牧之

1999年8月　北京

PREFACE TO THE
LIBRARY OF CHINESE CLASSICS

The publication of the *Library of Chinese Classics* is a matter of great satisfaction to all of us who have been involved in the production of this monumental work. At the same time, we feel a weighty sense of responsibility, and take this opportunity to explain to our readers the motivation for undertaking this cross-century task.

1

The Chinese nation has a long history and a glorious culture, and it has been the aspiration of several generations of Chinese scholars to translate, edit and publish the whole corpus of the Chinese literary classics so that the nation's greatest cultural achievements can be introduced to people all over the world. There have been many translations of the Chinese classics done by foreign scholars. A few dozen years ago, a Western scholar translated the title of *A Dream of Red Mansions* into "A Dream of Red Chambers" and Lin Daiyu, the heroine in the novel, into "Black Jade." But while their endeavours have been laudable, the results of their labours have been less than satisfactory. Lack of knowledge of Chinese culture and an inadequate grasp of the Chinese written language have led the translators into many errors. As a consequence, not only are Chinese classical writings widely misunderstood in the rest of the world, in some cases their content has actually been distorted. At one time, there was a "*Jin Ping Mei* craze" among Western scholars, who thought that they had uncovered a miraculous phenomenon, and published theories claiming that China was the "fountainhead of eroticism," and that a Chinese "tradition of permissiveness" was about to be laid bare. This distorted view came about due to the translators of the *Jin Ping Mei (Plum in the Golden Vase)* putting one-sided stress on the raw elements in that novel, to the neglect of its overall literary value. Meanwhile, there have been many distinguished and well-intentioned

Sinologists who have attempted to make the culture of the Chinese nation more widely known by translating works of ancient Chinese philosophy. However, the quality of such work, in many cases, is unsatisfactory, often missing the point entirely. The great philosopher Hegel considered that ancient China had no philosophy in the real sense of the word, being stuck in philosophical "prehistory." For such an eminent authority to make such a colossal error of judgment is truly regrettable. But, of course, Hegel was just as subject to the constraints of time, space and other objective conditions as anyone else, and since he had to rely for his knowledge of Chinese philosophy on inadequate translations it is not difficult to imagine why he went so far off the mark.

China cannot be separated from the rest of the world; and the rest of the world cannot ignore China. Throughout its history, Chinese civilization has enriched itself by absorbing new elements from the outside world, and in turn has contributed to the progress of world civilization as a whole by transmitting to other peoples its own cultural achievements. From the 5th to the 15th centuries, China marched in the front ranks of world civilization. If mankind wishes to advance, how can it afford to ignore China? How can it afford not to make a thoroughgoing study of its history?

2

Despite the ups and downs in their fortunes, the Chinese people have always been idealistic, and have never ceased to forge ahead and learn from others, eager to strengthen ties of peace and friendship.

The great ancient Chinese philosopher Confucius once said, "Wherever three persons come together, one of them will surely be able to teach me something. I will pick out his good points and emulate them; his bad points I will reform." Confucius meant by this that we should always be ready to learn from others. This maxim encapsulates the principle the Chinese people have always followed in their dealings with other peoples, not only on an individual basis but also at the level of state-to-state relations.

After generations of internecine strife, China was unified by Emperor Qin Shi Huang (the First Emperor of the Qin Dynasty) in 221 B.C. The Han Dynasty, which succeeded that of the short-lived Qin, waxed powerful, and for the first time brought China into contact with the outside world. In 138 B.C., Emperor Wu dispatched Zhang Qian to the western regions, i.e. Central Asia. Zhang, who traveled as far as what is now Iran, took with him as presents for the rulers he visited on the way 10,000 head of sheep and cattle, as well as gold and silks worth a fabulous amount. In 36 B.C., Ban Chao headed a 36-man legation to the western regions. These were missions of friendship to visit neighbours the Chinese people had never met before and to learn from them. Ban Chao sent Gan Ying to explore further toward the west. According to the "Western Regions Section" in the *Book of Later Han*, Gan Ying traveled across the territories of present-day Iraq and Syria, and reached the Mediterranean Sea, an expedition which brought him within the confines of the Roman Empire. Later, during the Tang Dynasty, the monk Xuan Zang made a journey fraught with danger to reach India and seek the knowledge of that land. Upon his return, he organized a team of scholars to translate the Buddhist scriptures, which he had brought back with him. As a result, many of these scriptural classics which were later lost in India have been preserved in China. In fact, it would have been difficult for the people of India to reconstruct their own ancient history if it had not been for Xuan Zang's *A Record of a Journey to the West in the Time of the Great Tang Dynasty*. In the Ming Dynasty, Zheng He transmitted Chinese culture to Southeast Asia during his seven voyages. Following the Opium Wars in the mid-19th century, progressive Chinese, generation after generation, went to study the advanced scientific thought and cultural achievements of the Western countries. Their aim was to revive the fortunes of their own country. Among them were people who were later to become leaders of China, including Zhu De, Zhou Enlai and Deng Xiaoping. In addition, there were people who were to become leading scientists, literary figures and artists, such as Guo Moruo, Li Siguang, Qian Xuesen, Xian Xinghai and Xu Beihong. Their spirit of ambition, their struggles and their breadth of vision were an inspiration not only to the Chinese people but to people all over the world.

Indeed, it is true that if the Chinese people had not learned many things from the surrounding countries they would never have been able to produce the splendid achievements of former days. When we look back upon history, how can we not feel profoundly grateful for the legacies of the civilizations of ancient Egypt, Greece and India? How can we not feel fondness and respect for the cultures of Europe, Africa, America and Oceania?

The Chinese nation, in turn, has made unique contributions to the community of mankind. Prior to the 15th century, China led the world in science and technology. The British scientist Joseph Needham once said, "From the third century B.C. to the 13th century A.D. China was far ahead of the West in the level of its scientific knowledge." Paul Kennedy, of Yale University in the U.S., author of *The Rise and Fall of the Great Powers*, said, "Of all the civilizations of the pre-modern period, none was as well-developed or as progressive as that of China."

Foreigners who came to China were often astonished at what they saw and heard. The Greek geographer Pausanias in the second century A.D. gave the first account in the West of the technique of silk production in China: "The Chinese feed a spider-like insect with millet and reeds. After five years the insect's stomach splits open, and silk is extracted therefrom." From this extract, we can see that the Europeans at that time did not know the art of silk manufacture. In the middle of the 9th century A.D., an Arabian writer includes the following anecdote in his *Account of China and India*:

"One day, an Arabian merchant called upon the military governor of Guangzhou. Throughout the meeting, the visitor could not keep his eyes off the governor's chest. Noticing this, the latter asked the Arab merchant what he was staring at. The merchant replied, 'Through the silk robe you are wearing, I can faintly see a black mole on your chest. Your robe must be made out of very fine silk indeed!' The governor burst out laughing, and holding out his sleeve invited the merchant to count how many garments he was wearing. The merchant did so, and discovered that the governor was actually wearing five silk robes, one on top of the other, and they were made of such fine material that a tiny mole could be seen through them all! Moreover, the governor explained that the robes he was wearing were not made of the finest silk at all; silk of the highest grade was reserved for the garments worn by the provincial governor."

The references to tea in this book (the author calls it "dried grass") reveal that the custom of drinking tea was unknown in the Arab countries at that time: "The king of China's revenue comes mainly from taxes on salt and the dry leaves of a kind of grass which is drunk after boiled water is poured on it. This dried grass is sold at a high price in every city in the country. The Chinese call it 'cha.' The bush is like alfalfa, except that it bears more leaves, which are also more fragrant than alfalfa. It has a slightly bitter taste, and when it is infused in boiling water it is said to have medicinal properties."

Foreign visitors showed especial admiration for Chinese medicine. One wrote, "China has very good medical conditions. Poor people are given money to buy medicines by the government."

In this period, when Chinese culture was in full bloom, scholars flocked from all over the world to China for sightseeing and for study. Chang'an, the capital of the Tang Dynasty was host to visitors from as far away as the Byzantine Empire, not to mention the neighboring countries of Asia. Chang'an, at that time the world's greatest metropolis, was packed with thousands of foreign dignitaries, students, diplomats, merchants, artisans and entertainers. Japan especially sent contingent after contingent of envoys to the Tang court. Worthy of note are the accounts of life in Chang'an written by Abeno Nakamaro, a Japanese scholar who studied in China and had close friendships with ministers of the Tang court and many Chinese scholars in a period of over 50 years. The description throws light on the exchanges between Chinese and foreigners in this period. When Abeno was supposedly lost at sea on his way back home, the leading poet of the time, Li Bai, wrote a eulogy for him.

The following centuries saw a steady increase in the accounts of China written by Western visitors. The Italian Marco Polo described conditions in China during the Yuan Dynasty in his *Travels*. However, until advances in the science of navigation led to the opening of east-west shipping routes at the beginning of the 16th century Sino-Western cultural exchanges were coloured by fantasy and conjecture. Concrete progress was made when a contingent of religious missionaries, men well versed in Western science and technology, made their way to China, ushering in an era of direct contacts between China and the West. The experience of this era was embodied in the career of the Italian Jesuit Matteo Ricci. Arriving in

China in 1582, Ricci died in Beijing in 1610. Apart from his missionary work, Ricci accomplished two historically symbolic tasks — one was the translation into Latin of the "Four Books," together with annotations, in 1594; the other was the translation into Chinese of Euclid's *Elements*.

The rough translations of the "Four Books" and other Chinese classical works by Western missionaries, and the publication of Père du Halde's *Description Geographique, Historique, Chronologique, Politique, et Physique de l'Empire de la Chine* revealed an exotic culture to Western readers, and sparked a "China fever," during which the eyes of many Western intellectuals were fixed on China. Some of these intellectuals, including Leibniz, held China in high esteem; others, such as Hegel, nursed a critical attitude toward Chinese culture. Leibniz considered that some aspects of Chinese thought were close to his own views, such as the philosophy of the *Book of Changes* and his own binary system. Hegel, on the other hand, as mentioned above, considered that China had developed no proper philosophy of its own. Nevertheless, no matter whether the reaction was one of admiration, criticism, acceptance or rejection, Sino-Western exchanges were of great significance. The transmission of advanced Chinese science and technology to the West, especially the Chinese inventions of paper-making, gunpowder, printing and the compass, greatly changed the face of the whole world. Karl Marx said, "Chinese gunpowder blew the feudal class of knights to smithereens; the compass opened up world markets and built colonies; and printing became an implement of Protestantism and the most powerful lever and necessary precondition for intellectual development and creation." The English philosopher Roger Bacon said that China's four great inventions had "changed the face of the whole world and the state of affairs of everything."

3

Ancient China gave birth to a large number of eminent scientists, such as Zu Chongzhi, Li Shizhen, Sun Simiao, Zhang Heng, Shen Kuo and Bi Sheng. They produced numerous treatises on scientific subjects, including *The Manual of Important Arts for the People's Welfare, Nine*

Chapters on the Mathematical Art, A Treatise on Febrile Diseases and *Compendium of Materia Medica*. Their accomplishments included ones whose influence has been felt right down to modern times, such as the armillary sphere, seismograph, Dujiangyan water conservancy project, Dunhuang Grottoes, Grand Canal and Great Wall. But from the latter part of the 15th century, and for the next 400 years, Europe gradually became the cultural centre upon which the world's eyes were fixed. The world's most outstanding scientists then were England's Isaac Newton, Poland's Copernicus, France's Marie Curie, Germany's Rontgen and Einstein, Italy's Galileo, Russia's Mendelev and America's Edison.

The Chinese people then began to think: What is the cause of the rise and fall of nations? Moreover, how did it happen that gunpowder, invented in China and transmitted to the West, in no time at all made Europe powerful enough to batter down the gates of China herself?

It took the Opium War to wake China from its reverie. The first generation to make the bold step of "turning our eyes once again to the rest of the world" was represented by Lin Zexu and Wei Yuan. Zeng Guofan and Li Hongzhang started the Westernization Movement, and later intellectuals raised the slogan of "Democracy and Science." Noble-minded patriots, realizing that China had fallen behind in the race for modernization, set out on a painful quest. But in backwardness lay the motivation for change, and the quest produced the embryo of a towering hope, and the Chinese people finally gathered under a banner proclaiming a "March Toward Science."

On the threshold of the 21st century, the world is moving in the direction of becoming an integrated entity. This trend is becoming clearer by the day. In fact, the history of the various peoples of the world is also becoming the history of mankind as a whole. Today, it is impossible for any nation's culture to develop without absorbing the excellent aspects of the cultures of other peoples. When Western culture absorbs aspects of Chinese culture, this is not just because it has come into contact with Chinese culture, but also because of the active creativity and development of Western culture itself; and vice versa. The various cultures of the world's peoples are a precious heritage which we all share. Mankind no longer lives on different continents, but on one big continent, or in a "global village." And so, in this era characterized by an all-encompassing network of knowledge and information we should learn from each other and march in step along the highway of development to construct a brand-new "global village."

Western learning is still being transmitted to the East, and vice versa. China is accelerating its pace of absorption of the best parts of the cultures of other countries, and there is no doubt that both the West and the East need the nourishment of Chinese culture. Based on this recognition, we have edited and published the *Library of Chinese Classics* in a Chinese-English format as an introduction to the corpus of traditional Chinese culture in a comprehensive and systematic translation. Through this collection, our aim is to reveal to the world the aspirations and dreams of the Chinese people over the past 5,000 years and the splendour of the new historical era in China. Like a phoenix rising from the ashes, the Chinese people in unison are welcoming the cultural sunrise of the new century.

Yang Muzhi

August 1999, Beijing

前　　言

1. 关于汤显祖

1.1. 汤显祖的生平及影响

汤显祖是联合国教科文组织指定的100名国际文化名人之一，是中国明代末年一个富有传奇色彩的、具有浓厚的思想家气质的伟大文学家、戏曲家，字义仍，号若士，亦号海若，别署清远道人和玉茗堂山人。他于明世宗嘉靖二十九年八月十四日（公元1550年9月24日）出生于临川的一个书香人家，早有才名，12岁时诗作即已显露才华，14岁进学，21岁中举，34岁中进士，在南京先后任太常寺博士、詹事府主簿和礼部祠祭司主事。万历十九年（公元1591年），作著名的《论辅臣科臣疏》，批评神宗朱翊钧即位后的朝政，抨击宰辅张居正和申时行，因而被贬广东徐闻任典史，次年调任浙江遂昌知县，和劳动人民有了较直接的接触，实行了一些开明的措施。他在任职5年后告归故里，逐渐打消仕进之念，专事写作，于万历四十四年六月十六日（公元1616年7月29日）在临川玉茗堂逝世。

汤显祖一生留下2200多篇诗、文、赋，主要创作成就在戏曲方面，代表作是《牡丹亭》（又名《还魂记》），它和《邯郸记》、《南柯记》、《紫钗记》合称"玉茗堂四梦"。他的作品《红泉逸草》、《问棘邮草》、《玉茗堂全集》，以及《紫箫记》和"四梦"，都有明清刻本传世。中华人民共和国成立后，

1962年出版了钱南扬和徐朔方整理的《汤显祖集》，1999年出版了徐朔方笺校的《汤显祖全集》。汤显祖的代表作传奇《牡丹亭》于1598年写成以后，先以抄本形式流传，然后有数十种刻本流传。作为文学本，有明代的文林阁本、石林居士本、朱墨本、清晖阁本等，清代的竹林堂本、自娱斋本、芥子园本、冰丝馆本、暖红室本等。在明清时期，《牡丹亭》的各种评点本和改编本也应运而生。其中比较著名的评点本有茅瑛评本、王思任评本、吴吴山三妇合评本、杨葆光的手批本等；比较著名的改编本有沈璟的《同梦记》、臧懋循的《牡丹亭》（删改本）、冯梦龙的《风流梦》、徐日曦的《牡丹亭》（硕园本）、徐肃颖的《丹青记》等。

　　汤显祖在当时就已产生很大影响。尤其是他的《牡丹亭》问世后，盛行一时，许多人为之倾倒。与他同时代的评论家几乎无一不称赞《牡丹亭》，如吕天成在《曲品》一书中推崇汤显祖为"绝代奇才、冠世博学"和"千秋之词匠"，称赞他的《牡丹亭》是"巧妙迭出，无境不新，真堪千古矣"。又如沈德符说"汤义仍《牡丹亭》梦一出，家传户诵，几令《西厢》减价"，又说他"才情自足不朽"。戏曲理论家王骥德在《曲律》一书中写道，汤显祖如果没有"当置法字无论"等弱点，"可令前无作者，后鲜来哲，二百年来，一人而已"。王思任则在《评点玉茗堂牡丹亭叙》中评论了《牡丹亭》中人物刻画之生动："杜丽娘之妖也，柳梦梅之痴也，老夫人之软也，杜安抚之古执也，陈最良之雾也，春香之贼牢也：无不从筋节窍髓，以探其七情生动之微也。"在清代，评论更是屡见不鲜，大多采取赞美的态度，孟称舜、吴炳、阮大铖、洪升、孔尚任等人在剧作的思想、情节、语言等方面都从

《牡丹亭》汲取了不少营养。

尽管汤显祖一直受到文学界和戏剧界的重视，然而"汤学"的逐渐形成却是20世纪的事情。我国本世纪的汤学研究(尤其是对《牡丹亭》的研究)大致可以分为前半世纪和后半世纪两个阶段。前半世纪的研究较多地继承了明清以来考辨本事、制曲度曲、曲辞鉴赏的传统，较少有观念的更新和理论的说明，研究者仅有少数曲学专家和文学史家，前期有王国维、吴梅、王季烈、卢前等人，后期有俞平伯、郑振铎、赵景深、张友鸾、江寄萍、吴重翰等人。后半世纪的研究虽然曾经受到庸俗社会学和极左思潮的影响，但是在1957年前后围绕纪念汤显祖逝世340周年纪念，还是形成了一个研究的小高潮。70年代后期以来，汤显祖研究逐步深入和发展。全国学术界在1982年以纪念汤显祖逝世366周年为契机，在汤显祖的故乡举行了隆重的纪念活动，并随之将汤显祖研究推上一个新阶段，论文和著作的数量都有大幅度的增加。2000年在大连和临川分别举行的汤显祖诞生450周年国际学术讨论会和纪念会，以其规模之大和论文之多标志着汤学研究已经达到一个崭新的高度。

最近20年出版的汤学研究著作主要有：徐朔方的《汤显祖年谱》(1980)、《论汤显祖及其他》(1983)、《汤显祖评传》(1993)和《汤显祖全集》(1999)，黄文锡和吴凤雏的《汤显祖传》(1983)，毛效同的《汤显祖研究资料汇编》(1984)，江西文学研究所的《汤显祖研究论文集》(1984)，龚重谟等的《汤显祖传》(1986)，周育德的《汤显祖论稿》(1991)，徐扶明的《牡丹亭研究资料考释》(1987)和《汤显祖与牡丹亭》(1985)，项兆丰的《汤显祖遂昌诗文全编》(2000)，邹元江的《汤显祖的情与梦》（1998）等。最值得一提的是，在世纪末出版的《汤显祖全集》（1999），全书4册2627页，新收录"制艺"一卷和多篇佚文，是目前为止内容覆盖最完整的汤显祖著作全集。这本书出自汤显祖研究的耆老、现年76岁的徐朔方先生，它把汤学研究推向了一个新的高峰。《汤显祖的情与梦》（1998）把汤显祖的生平、思想、人格、艺术、美学联系起来，作全方位的研究，甚为准确而全面地概括了汤显祖思想与艺术的基本特征。这本书出自武汉大学哲学系的青年学者邹元江先生，着重分析和阐述了汤显祖的理学著作，为汤显祖研究开辟了新的方向。由此可见，参加汤显祖研究的人员已经形成一支老中青结合的梯队，而研究的范围也有了新的拓展，包括汤显祖的生平、剧本的蓝本探讨、思想意义和社会价值的评估、艺术形式和演出情况等诸多方面，并开始从哲学、历史、美学等新的角度对汤显祖进行研究。正如叶长海先生提出的那样，汤显祖研究已经名副其实地形成了"汤学"。

1.2. 汤显祖在国外

对于国外读者来说，汤显祖的名字跟他的剧作《牡丹亭》是分不开的。早在17世纪初年，《牡丹亭》已经东传日本。据日本《御文库目录》所载，1636年御文库即已收藏明刊本《牡丹亭记》（臧懋循改本）六本。岸春风楼翻译的《牡丹亭还魂记》于1916年由文教社出版；宫原民平译注的《还魂记》由东京国民文库刊行会出版，收入《国译汉文大成》第10卷（1920-1924）；铃木彦次郎和佐佐木静光合译的《牡丹亭还魂记》由东京支那大学大观刊行会出版，收入《支那文学大观》（1926-1927）。另外，还有岩城秀夫的《还魂记》。

《牡丹亭》最早译成的西方文字是德文。1929年，徐道灵撰写的《中国的爱情故事》一文中，有关于《牡丹亭》的摘译和介绍，该文载于《中国学》杂志第4卷。北京大学德文系教授洪涛生翻译的《牡丹亭》摘译本于1933年由北京出版社出版，全译本于1937年分别由苏黎士与莱比锡的拉舍尔出版社出版。法文译本有徐仲年翻译的《牡丹亭·惊梦》及评价文字，载《中国诗文选》，1933年由巴黎德拉格拉夫书局出版；最新的译本是安德里·莱维的法文全译本《牡丹亭》，于2000年在巴黎出版。俄文译本有孟烈夫于1976年翻译出版的《牡丹亭》片断，并收入《东方古典戏剧·印度·中国·日本》。

《牡丹亭》最早的英译本是阿克顿选译的《牡丹亭·春香闹学》，载《天下月刊》第8卷1939年4月号。白之于1965年在《中国文学选读》中选译了《牡丹亭》的部分场次，并于1980年在印地安那大学出版社出版了全译本。张光前的英语全译本于1994年由旅游教育出版社出版，汪榕培的英语韵体全译本于2000年由上海外语教育出版社首次出版。

《牡丹亭》在中国已被多次改编为小说（例如，1995年山西古籍出版社出版的潘慎、张裔改编本，1997年吉林文史出版社的赵清阁改编本等），1999年又有了小说的英文版。一种是陈美林的改编本，由新世界出版社出版，另一种改编本由美国新泽西州海马图书公司出版。

在90年代末期，《牡丹亭》的四个演出本分别以现代人的精神对这部古典名著进行了全新的诠释，在国内外引起了轰动。1999年上海昆剧团排演了新版昆剧《牡丹亭》，作为国庆50周年献礼演出，于1999年10月12日至17日首次公演，于1999年11月19日至21日在上海国际艺术节再次上演。这个演出本以汤显祖原著为依据,经过删改,基本上保持了原来的艺术框架,体现了昆剧融诗、文、歌、舞于一体的特色。新排的《牡丹亭》本着"取其菁华、去其枝蔓"的精神,将原著精心缩编为上、中、下三本34出,演出时间约7个小时。以白之的译文为基础,由谭盾作曲、彼得·塞拉斯导演的歌剧《牡丹亭》长达四个半小时,该剧由华文猗、黄英等主演,于1998年5月12日在维也那首演,接着在巴黎、罗马、伦敦、旧金山相继上演。这个歌剧把东方与西方、古代与现代、现实主义与浪漫主义有机地结合起来,引起了西方观众的兴趣。由美籍华人陈士争执导的55出全本《牡丹亭》,分为6集,用三个下午和三个晚上演完,6集的标题分别为"惊梦"、"寻梦"、"幽媾"、"回生"、"责寇"和"圆驾"。1999年7月在林肯中心艺术节时上演了三轮,演出地点是纽约拉瓜底亚中学的多功能音乐厅。2000年2月24日到3月12日,美国的中国戏剧工作坊以昆剧演员和玩偶交错演出的方式,在纽约多罗茜剧场上演了由冯光玉和史蒂芬·卡普林导演的玩偶剧场《牡丹亭》,一小时的演出受到了观众的欢迎和好评。

  国外对汤显祖的研究早在20世纪初即已开始,日本著名戏曲史专家青本正儿在1916年出版的《中国近世戏曲史》中首次将汤显祖与莎士比亚相提并论。在70和80年代,日本的岩成秀夫撰写了长达411页的论文《汤显祖研究》,美国的白之撰写了论文《〈牡丹亭〉或〈还魂记〉》(1974)和《〈牡丹亭〉结构》(1980),另外还有J. Y. H. Hu的论文《从冥府到人间:〈牡丹亭〉结构分析》(1980)和夏志清的论文《汤显祖剧作的自我与社会》(1970)等。俄罗斯学者索罗金·马努辛也发表了不少研究汤显祖的论文，例如，1974年发表的《论汤显祖的〈紫箫记〉》、《汤显祖的戏曲〈紫钗记〉》。

以博士论文而言，1974年汉堡大学商棠的博士论文《汤显祖的四梦》出版，1975年明尼苏达大学陈旺的博士论文《〈邯郸梦记〉的讽刺艺术》出版，90年代有华玮的博士论文《寻求"和"：汤显祖戏剧艺术研究》(1991)、荣赛星的《〈邯郸记〉评析》(1992)，陈佳梅的博士论文《犯相思病的少女的梦幻世界：妇女对〈牡丹亭〉的反映(1598－1795)研究》(1996)等。此外，王益春的博士论文《梦与戏剧：16－17世纪之交中、英、西班牙之剧作》(1986)亦述及汤显祖之作，卡塞林·斯瓦特克的博士论文《冯梦龙的"浪漫之梦"：〈牡丹亭〉的改编里抑遏的策略》(1990)则论及汤剧的流传。

1.3. 汤学研究的展望

在21世纪已经来临的时候，我们可以满怀信心地期待汤显祖和他的戏剧和诗文将在世界范围内引起更大的重视，研究汤显祖的个人以及出版和发行的研究汤显祖的论文和著作必然会有增无减，研究汤显祖的团体、机构、期刊必然会出现，汤学研究成为显学是情理中的事情。

我们至少可以预测新世纪的汤学研究会有以下几个方面的发展。

第一，汤学研究的广度和深度会有新的拓展。从20世纪末发表的汤学研究的著作和论文中已经可以初见端倪，前面提到的邹元江先生的专著《汤显祖的情和梦》就是一个例子。以前两年发表的若干论文为例，江巨荣先生的《〈牡丹亭〉演出小史》和《二十世纪〈牡丹亭〉研究综述》是归纳总结性的论文，赵山林先生《汤显祖与魏晋风度》、杨忠先生的《论汤显祖的历史观及其史学成就》、龚国光先生的《忽闻歌古调，偏惊物候新——汤显祖戏剧创作理论与审美意识探因》、刘彦君女士的《论汤学的自由生命意识》、汪榕培先生的《〈牡丹亭〉的集唐诗及其英译》、华玮女士的《〈牡丹亭〉的人物设计》、邹元江先生的《我们该如何纪念汤显祖》等文章已经把汤显祖的研究范围向各个领域开拓，新世纪的汤学研究范围必然会有更大的拓展。

第二，汤学研究将被置于世界文学的大范围内。把汤显祖跟英国的莎士比亚相提并论已经有将近一个世纪的历史了，已经出现了许多把汤显祖与莎士比亚进行比较研究的论文。汤显祖的《牡丹亭》经常跟莎士比亚的《罗密欧与朱丽叶》和《冬天的故事》相比较，最近我们也见到了徐顺生先生把汤显祖的《牡丹亭》与雨果的《艾那尼》相比较的文章。在世界文学的大范围内进行比较，通过各国学者的比较和研究，从不同的文化背景来理解，汤显祖的剧作和诗文将更加显出他的特色和不同凡响之处。

把汤显祖的艺术思想跟西方的某些文学思潮相对比，也会对汤显祖有一些新的认识，成为一个饶有兴趣的课题。例如，法国的超现实主义诗人勃勒东，第一次世界大战战争期间在精神病院服役，接触到弗洛伊德心理分析的理论，后来又受到与传统决裂的同时代诗人阿波利奈尔的影响，便设法将对潜意识的探索运用到诗歌艺术中去。1924年他发表的《超现实主义宣言》强调潜意识，强调梦幻，提倡写"事物的巧合"。汤显祖把自己的剧作统称为"玉茗堂四梦"，多次在著作中提到"梦"。把汤显祖关于"梦"的认识与超现实主义的认识乃至弗洛伊德关于梦的理论相对比,我们可以吃惊地看到,汤显祖比他们早300多年就已经成为"新潮派"或"先锋派"呢!

第三,汤显祖剧本的各种译本会在世界范围内得到更加广泛的传播。在20世纪末,《牡丹亭》已经享誉海内外,并且已经译成日语,译成欧洲的多种文字,但是汤显祖的其他剧本还没有译成英语,更不用说其他欧洲文字了。我相信,在不久的将来,汤显祖的其他剧本都会被译成英语和其他文字,至少我也会成为译者之一,在有生之年把"玉茗堂四梦"全部译成英语。全世界的读者对汤显祖的其他剧本同样会感兴趣的。

第四,汤显祖的剧本会在世界范围内更多地演出。《牡丹亭》在20世纪末的四个演出本都已染上了现代的气息。古典戏剧的现代化尝试是无可非议的,原汁原味的古典演出和彻底现代化的改编是可以并行不悖的。莎士比亚的《罗密欧与朱丽叶》依然在英国伊丽莎白时代风格的舞台上演出,可是在现代改编本的电影里,小流氓在马路上骑摩托车打仗,罗密欧和朱丽叶在游泳池里谈恋爱!古典的艺术形式要保留下去,新的艺术形式会不断出现,昆剧《牡丹亭》已经在中国拍成电视连续剧,新改编的电影《牡丹亭》早晚也会被搬上银幕。

第五,研究汤学的团体、机构、期刊必然会出现。部分同志已经在酝酿成立全国性组织"汤显祖研究会",全国性的汤显祖研究会和国际性的汤显祖研究会是早晚会成立的,将来也许还会出现许多地区性的分会。这些研究会早晚也会出版自己的期刊或不定期刊物,到那时候汤学研究者就会有自己的学术阵地和学术出版物了。

2. 关于《牡丹亭》

2.1. 《牡丹亭》的剧情梗概

《牡丹亭》共 55 出，描写杜丽娘和柳梦梅之间的爱情故事，是充满浪漫主义色彩的悲喜剧。《牡丹亭》的不少情节取自明代话本《杜丽娘慕色还魂》，然而跟话本相比，不仅在情节和描写上作了较大改动，而且主题思想有极大的提高。在小说中，杜丽娘还魂后，门当户对的婚姻顺利缔成；而在戏曲中，传说故事同明代社会的现实生活有机地结合起来了。杜丽娘死而复生的故事看起来荒诞不经，却强烈地表达了与封建礼教对立的人文主义思想萌芽和对自由爱情的执着追求，甚至生死的境界都可以超越。

南宋初，南安太守杜宝夫妇有个独生女杜丽娘，老人家十分爱惜她，聘请了一个迂腐的老教师陈最良来教她古代诗文。杜丽娘的侍女春香百般淘气，不但跟老先生开玩笑，而且引杜丽娘到后花园去游览。正当一个春天的困人季节，杜丽娘前去游玩花园，惹起了她的情思，在花园里牡丹亭旁小睡了一会，并且做了一个离奇的梦，梦见了她理想中的情人——一个风度翩翩的书生，两下产生了融洽的感情。杜丽娘得了这个梦以后，念念不忘梦中情景，因而成病。病中，她自己画了一幅小像，作为对书生的留念。虽然经过她母亲的细心照料，可是她终究因相思忧郁而死。

杜宝因为李全作乱，朝廷派他做安抚使到扬州去坐镇。杜宝走了以后，杜家人依据杜丽娘临死时的话，把她葬到后花园的一棵梅树底下，还造了一所梅花观，由石道姑伴守着她的灵柩。石道姑进梅花观住了没多久,来了一个游学的青年柳梦梅。他租借了梅花观的空房暂时住下。一天,他在随意游玩后花园时,碰巧拾取了杜丽娘生前画的那张画;他仔细看了一会,对画中的美人很觉有情,当晚也做了个梦,梦见杜丽娘告诉他可以想法使她重新活在人世。第二天,他就和石道姑设法祈祷,开了墓穴,救转了死去已久的杜丽娘,两下大喜。但是柳梦梅恐怕这件事要被人发觉而声扬出来,于是就偷偷地带了杜丽娘避到京城临安去。

那时杜宝已经移镇淮安,叫他的妻子和春香也住到临安去。杜母在路上凑巧遇见了再生的杜丽娘,惊喜之余,丽娘也知道了父亲的音讯。等待柳梦梅在京应试后,杜丽娘叫他去探问杜宝的情况。杜宝起先虽被敌人围困,但在柳梦梅去探问期间,却已解围而调升回京,碰到了来路不明的女婿,以为柳梦梅是个说谎的无赖,带回临安进行审问。这时,柳梦梅已经中了状元,在金殿上经过杜丽娘的详尽解释,皇帝颁下旨意,柳梦梅和杜丽娘奉旨完婚,有情人终成眷属。

2.2. 《牡丹亭》的人物刻画

《牡丹亭》全本 55 出,情节恍惚迷离,结构宏大辉煌,尤以刻画人物为佳。剧中出现的各种各样的人物有 160 个之多,有名有姓的主要人物有 30 多个,尤其是杜丽娘、柳梦梅、杜宝、陈最良、春香、石道姑等人物无不栩栩如生。剧中的人物上至文武官员,下至地痞妓女,外有番王番使,更有判官花神,各色人物"笑者真笑,笑即有声;啼者真啼,啼即有泪;叹者真叹,叹即有气",俨然是一幅活生生的明代风物全景画。

《牡丹亭》中描写得最成功的人物当数杜丽娘,她是古典戏曲中最可爱的少女形象之一。追求爱情的缠绵而执著，是杜丽娘的一种性格特点，但杜丽娘还有她的思想特点。在《牡丹亭》以前，戏曲、小说中描写女子执著、坚定地追求爱情，不乏其例，但像杜丽娘这样表现了要求个性自由发展思想的却很罕见。《牡丹亭》写杜丽娘的性格发展和心理活动，层次鲜明、细致熨帖，而写杜丽娘的思想与行动的同步，是杜丽娘形象塑造中最有光彩之处。下面我们来看一下剧本是如何用诗化的语言来刻画杜丽娘这一形象的。

杜丽娘在"娇莺如语，眼见春如许"的大好时光，终日身居绣房，"刚打的秋千画图，闲榻着鸳鸯绣谱"，却不时"白日而眠"。内心蕴藏着隐隐的苦闷，因为"儒门旧家数"没有给"一生儿爱好是天然"的她带来生活的情趣。

杜宝夫妇为了女儿"他日到人家，知书知礼，父母光辉"，请来腐儒陈最良坐馆教书。尽管陈最良在讲解《关雎》诗的时候，把《诗经》曲解为"《诗》三百，一言以蔽之，没多些，只'无邪'两字，付与儿家"，杜丽娘却在诵读"关关雎鸠，在河之洲。窈窕淑女，君子好逑"的时候，却意识到《关雎》的爱情主题，骚动的情欲油然而生："'关'了的雎鸠，尚然有洲渚之兴，何以人而不如鸟乎？"从此以后她在"梦回莺转，乱煞年光遍。人立小庭深院"的时候，"剪不断，理还乱，闷无端"，为的是"袅晴丝吹来闲庭院，摇漾春如线"。使她心绪不安的正是春天的柳丝——春天的"晴丝"（情丝、情思）。

杜丽娘趁父亲下乡劝农的时机，来到了春光明媚的后花园。"原来姹紫嫣红开遍，似这般都付与断井颓垣。良辰美景奈何天，赏心乐事谁家院？"她由春色易去联想到红颜难久，感到自己幽处深闺，未免太辜负了这大好春光："朝飞暮卷，云霞翠轩；雨丝风片，烟波画船——锦屏人忒看的这韶光贱！"在深闺看到的柳丝（晴丝）"荼䕷外烟丝醉软"，万条烟罩，加深了她的迷茫心情。她为自己还未找到如意郎君而叹息："吾生于宦族，长在名门。年已及笄，不得早成佳配，诚为虚度青春，光阴如过隙耳。"想到这里，杜丽娘不禁潸然泪下，陷入深深的郁闷之中："可惜妾身颜色如花，岂料命如一叶乎！"

杜丽娘在这种郁闷之中，"身子困乏了，且自隐几而眠"，进入了没有任何人为制约的自由自在的精神境界。她在睡梦中，隐约见到一名书生手执柳枝翩翩而来。那位书生与她虽然素昧平生，却"是那处曾相见，相看俨然，早难道这好处相逢无一言"，两人在花神的保护下，在"牡丹亭畔、芍药栏边，共成云雨之欢"。杜丽娘美梦醒来，发现是不可理解自己的母亲站在眼前。从此以后，那梦境一直萦绕在她的心头，"困春心游赏倦，也不索熏香绣被眠。天呵，有心情那梦还去不远"。

第二天，杜丽娘平添了新愁，"独坐思量，情殊怅怏"，更觉得"真个可怜人也"。她茶饭不思，回忆昨日的梦境："昨日所梦，池亭俨然。只图旧梦重来，其奈新愁一段。寻思展转，竟夜无眠。咱待乘此空闲，背却春香，悄向花园寻看。"她来到后花园寻梦，景色依旧，但是"寻来寻去，都不见了。牡丹亭、芍药栏怎生这般凄凉冷落，杳无人迹？好不伤心也。"她看到一棵"梅树依依可人"，冒出"我杜丽娘若死后得葬于此，幸矣"的想法。她看到"这花花草草由人恋，生生死死随人愿，便酸酸楚楚无人怨"，立誓要"待打并香魂一片，阴雨梅天，守的个梅根相见"。

从后花园寻梦归来以后，杜丽娘整日里"泪花儿打迸着梦魂飘"，"瘦到九分九了"，心想"若不趁此时自行描画，流在人间，一旦无常，谁知西蜀杜丽娘，有如此之美貌乎"，于是自描真容，并题诗一首："近睹分明似俨然，远观自在若飞仙。他年得傍蟾宫客，不在梅边在柳边。"她不胜感慨地叹道："也有古今美女，早嫁了丈夫相爱，替他描模画样；也有美人自家写照，寄与情人。似我杜丽娘，寄谁呵？"

杜丽娘"自春游一梦，卧病如今。不痒不疼，如痴如醉"，病情日趋严重，不时魇语"我的人那"。她"拜月堂空，行云径拥。骨冷怕成秋梦。世间何物似情浓？整一片断魂心痛"。"人去难逢，须不是神挑鬼弄。在眉峰，心坎里别是一半疼痛。"她自知不久人世，在中秋夜央告母亲在死后葬在"后园梅树之下"，"怕树头树底不到的五更风，和俺小坟边立断魂碑一统"。她最后的遗言是："禁了这一夜雨，怎能够月落重生灯再红！"就这样，杜丽娘在忧郁之中伤春而死。

汤显祖在本剧《题词》中写道："如丽娘者，乃可谓之有情人耳。情不知所起，一往而深，生者可以死，死可以生。生而不可与死，死而不可复生者，皆非情之至也。"汤显祖所说的"情"，指人们的真正感情，在《牡丹亭》里表现为青年男女对自由的爱情生活的追求，跟封建道德观念中的"理"是截然相对的。这种明确的创作指导思想，与当时的进步思潮一脉相通，使《牡丹亭》比同时代的爱情剧高出一筹。剧中关于杜丽娘、柳梦梅在梦中第一次见面就相好幽会，杜丽娘鬼魂和情人同居，还魂后才正式"拜告天地"成婚的描写，关于杜丽娘不是死于爱情的被破坏，而是由于梦中获得的爱情在现实中难以寻觅，一时感伤而死，也即所谓"慕色而亡"的描写，都使它别具一格，显示了要求个性解放的思想倾向和浪漫夸张的艺术手法。

汤显祖在《牡丹亭还魂记题辞》中写道："天下女子有情，宁有如杜丽娘者乎！梦其人即病，病即弥连，至手画形容，传于世而后死。"这段话归纳了杜丽娘忧郁而死的过程——思春、探春、感春、伤春，反映了汤显祖的人文主义思想。宋明理学家强调"情"与"理"的融合，以"理"取"情"，"存天理、灭人欲"，汤显祖的"情至"观是对程朱理学的反动。杜丽娘潜意识中的情欲，在游园前体现为莫名的苦闷，在游园的过程中由袅袅"晴丝"勾起缕缕"情丝"，升华为梦中与书生幽会，种下郁郁的"情思"，在现实中寻梦不成，独处深闺，积郁成病，终于忧郁而死。由此，《牡丹亭》开创了中国浪漫主义剧作的先河，奠定了汤显祖作为世界级文化巨人的基础。

2.3.《牡丹亭》的艺术魅力

《牡丹亭》问世后，盛行一时，使许多人为之倾倒。杜丽娘作为一个艺术形象之所以感人肺腑，重要的原因之一在于她在追求爱情时所产生的忧郁情结引起了封建时代青年女子的强烈共鸣，具有强烈的艺术感染力，她几乎成为闺阁妇女追求情爱自由的偶像。400年来，《牡丹亭》在中国的舞台上久演不衰，多少青年女子为之心灵震撼，为杜丽娘的命运洒下了一掬掬同情之泪。

娄江女子俞二娘，"酷嗜《牡丹亭》传奇，蝇头细字，批注其侧，有痛于本词者。十七惋愤而死"。扬州女子金凤钿，"时《牡丹亭》书方出，因读而成癖，至于日夕把卷，吟玩不辍"。"临死，遗命于婢曰：'惟我命薄，不得见一才人，虽死，目难瞑，我死，须以《牡丹亭》曲殉，无违我志也。'"广陵女子冯小青，"自幼娴习翰墨。年十六，嫁杭州冯生为妾"。在忧郁而死之际，留下绝句一首："冷雨幽窗不可听，挑灯闲看《牡丹亭》，人间亦有痴如我，岂独伤心是小青？"

一代代演员的心血使《牡丹亭》由案头剧本转化为动人心弦的舞台演出，具有振人心魄的艺术力量。杭州女子商小玲，"以色艺称，于《还魂记》尤擅场。尝有所属意，而势不得通，遂郁郁成疾。每作杜丽娘《寻梦》、《闹殇》诸剧，真若身其事者，缠绵凄婉，泪痕盈目。一日演《寻梦》，唱至'待打并香魂一片，阴雨梅天，梅根相见'，盈盈界面，随声倚地。春香上视之，已气绝矣"。在新版昆剧《牡丹亭》中扮演柳梦梅的一位年轻演员张军同样动情地说："从小到大，不知演过多少次《游园惊梦》，《牡丹亭》的故事，犹如昆剧人的人生，为自己所爱，魂牵梦绕，从一而终。"

当代昆剧名家俞振飞的弟子岳美缇谈到她和华文漪合演这一段戏的体会，足以反映中国艺术的文化底蕴："昆剧的表演特色，是通过水袖、身段和脚步生发出高尚而虚幻的境界，而不是通过'脱衣解带'之类的办法，去造成一种紧迫的生活实感。比如，柳唱到'和你把领扣松'时，正好是我和华文漪转身之时，打着水袖'双翻'。这本身就是很美的舞蹈动作，笼统地看，也能表现郎才女貌气氛中的一种'自得'之感；如果进一步研究，就更能解析出其中的深意，这就是男孩子用水袖向女孩子身上'扑'，女孩子则用水袖来'推'。等唱到'袖稍儿揾着牙儿苦也'时，我们的动作没有去图解词义，甚至可以说，这词义根本无法用动作表达。

女孩子用袖子挡住脸，害羞，男孩子则用手拉住女孩子的袖尖(注意，柳在全剧中从不碰杜的手)，轻轻把挡脸的手曳下来。二人相视，欲笑又不肯轻笑，脸上不笑心里却分明在笑——这是二人心中的感觉，反映到形体动作上来，就是两人相互曳着衣袖，一顺边地晃起来又晃下去，我出右脚右手，文漪出左脚左手。我们这样晃啊晃啊，心中充满了幸福的感觉，观众想必也受到感染。"

3. 《牡丹亭》的英译

3.1. 白之的译本

　　《牡丹亭》的第一个英文全译本是由白之于1980年由美国印第安那大学出版社出版的。白之是美国当代著名的汉学家，美国加州大学伯克莱校区东亚文学系名誉教授，现已退休。他除了翻译《牡丹亭》以外，还翻译了《中国神怪志异》、《明代故事选》、《中国明代戏剧选》等作品，并且编辑了《中国文学选读》、《中国文学类型研究》等书籍。他有关《牡丹亭》的论文有《〈牡丹亭〉或〈还魂记〉》、《〈牡丹亭〉结构》和《〈冬天的故事〉与〈牡丹亭〉》等。

　　白之的英译以流畅的现代英语再现了原著的风貌，从总体上说是忠实于原文的，唱词部分和诗体部分都采用了自由诗的形式，以第十出"惊梦"的一段著名唱词为例：

　　"原来姹紫嫣红开遍，似这般都付与断井颓垣。良辰美景奈何天，赏心乐事谁家院！"

　　白之的译文是：

See how deepest purple, brightest scarlet

open their beauty only to dry well crumbling.

"Bright the morn, lovely the scene,"
listless and lost the heart
—— where is the garden "gay with joyous cries"?

这段译文基本上是忠实于原文的，通顺流畅，节奏感也很强。值得一说的是，在1972年出版的他主编的《中国文学选读》中，已经有了这段文字：

See how deepest purple, brightest scarlet
open their beauty only to dry well's crumbling parapet.
"Bright the morn, lovely the scene,"
listless and lost the heart
—— where is the garden "gay with joyous cries"?

从修改后的文字来看，第二行更精练了，第三行分成两行，更富有诗意。

接下去的几行唱词是完全改写了，原文是："朝飞暮卷，云霞翠轩；云丝风片，烟波画船——锦屏人忒看的这韶光贱！"

白之1972年的译文是：

Flying clouds of dawn, rolling storm at dusk
pavilion in emerald shade against the sunset glow
fine threads of rain, petals borne on breeze
gilded pleasure-boat in waves of mist:
sights little treasured by the cloistered maid
who sees them only on a painted screen.

1980年的译文是：

Streaking the dawn, close-curled at dusk,
rosy clouds frame emerald pavilion;
fine threads of rain, petals borne on breeze,

gilded pleasure boat in waves of mist:

glories of spring but little treasured

by screen-secluded maid.

从以上两个文本可以看出：第一，白之的学术态度是严谨的，对自己的译文进行了认真的修改；第二，白之的译文不是一蹴而就的，从最早的翻译到最后全书完成，至少经历了七八年时间。

白之英译的《牡丹亭》基本没有采用传统的格律，也没有押韵，只有为了取得滑稽的效果时才采用韵脚。

在西方演出的《牡丹亭》都是以白之的译本为基础，他的译本确实为《牡丹亭》从中国走向世界起了不可磨灭的重要作用。

3.2. 张光前的译本

《牡丹亭》的第一个由中国译者独立完成的英语全译本是张光前教授于1994年由旅游教育出版社出版的。张光前先生是合肥中国科技大学的教授，他在繁重的教学工作之余，历时多年将这一巨著率先在中国译成英语，是功不可没的。

跟白之的译本相比，张光前先生的译本最大的优点是在传达原著的意思方面更加准确，这是中国译者翻译中国古典名著的一个明显的强项。从译文可以看出，张光前先生的古文功底是非常扎实的。他在翻译唱词和诗句的时候，多数场合使用了素体诗的格式，以抑扬格为基本节奏，偶尔也有顺其自然而押韵的地方。还是以第十出"惊梦"的一段著名唱词为例："原来姹紫嫣红开遍，似这般都付与断井颓垣。良辰美景奈何天，赏心乐事谁家院！"张光前先生的译文是：

So the garden is all abloom in pink and red,

yet all abandoned to dry wells and crumbling walls.

　　The best of seasons won't forever last,

　　can any household claim undying joy?

这段译文的前两行是整齐的六音步抑扬格，后两行是整齐的五音步抑扬格，没有拘泥于原文的字面意义，而传达的意境是基本准确的。

接下去的几行唱词，"朝飞暮卷，云霞翠轩；云丝风片，烟波画船——锦屏人忒看的这韶光贱！"张光前先生的译文是：

　　Clouds that scud southward at the break of day

　　bring back evening showers in the western hills.

　　Rosy clouds, verdant cots,

　　threads of rain, sheets of wind,

　　misty waves, painted boats

　　—— spring's splendour has escaped the chambered girls.

这几行唱词的译文同样是不押韵的，以五音步抑扬格为基础，但是破格的地方较多，而三、四、五行出现四个重音，内容与原文略有出入，但总体的意境是表达出来了。

总体来说，张光前先生的译文是成功的，在不少地方比白之的译文还要准确和更精练。

3.3. 我的译文

我从1996年开始翻译《牡丹亭》，前后历时三年有余。我在翻译的过程中，为汤显祖所展示的艺术魅力深深打动，又经常因他引经据典所体现出来的文化底蕴，而自感功力不足。

为了对汤显祖的生平和创作有一点感性认识，我在1999

年3月到他的故乡江西省抚州(临川)市去考察了一次。汤显祖的陵墓坐落在市中心美丽的人民公园里，陵墓的两边是青翠的树木，后方还建了一座"牡丹亭"，亭子两边的对联是"文章越海内，品节冠临川"，寄托了后人对他的崇敬和赞扬。地处抚州近郊的"汤显祖纪念馆"还在扩建之中，占地二十余亩，进得院去迎面见到汤显祖的高大塑像，背后是玉茗堂四梦的浮雕。纪念馆里展览了汤显祖的生平，院内桃花绽开，一片春意盎然。"牡丹亭"矗立在一个高冈上，不远处竟然还有座杜丽娘墓，墓碑上故意留下裂纹，后面是破碎的坟墓，杜丽娘和柳梦梅含情脉脉地偎倚在墓前。分外显目的是毛泽东的手书，"惊梦"中的精彩唱词："原来姹紫嫣红开遍，似这般都付与断井颓垣。良辰美景奈何天，赏心乐事谁家院！朝飞暮卷，云霞翠轩，雨丝风片，烟波画船——锦屏人忒看的这韶光贱！"再往前走是"梅花观"，正面供奉着杜丽娘和柳梦梅的塑像，上悬"姻缘如意"的匾额，雕像前三个小香炉里香烟缭绕。我仿佛置身于《牡丹亭》的情景之中，一幕幕场景活生生地展现眼前，产生了更加强烈的翻译愿望。

有了这番经历以后，我的翻译速度出乎意料地加快了，两个月内鬼使神差似地完成了最后15出戏。如果全剧都是以这个速度来翻译的话，根本用不了一年时间——我却整整用了三年！

我在翻译《牡丹亭》的过程中，文字方面遇到不少难题，总算一个一个啃下来了。有的地方则字相识而意不明，最典型的是剧中276句集唐诗，许多诗句似懂非懂。总不能以其昏昏使人昭昭，于是我在译完初稿以后，索性一句一句地找出典。结果，除了对诗句的原意有所了解，便于准确地体现在译文中以外，最后竟然还有一点有趣的发现，写了一篇中国文学专题研究的短文。

我为自己的译文制定了"传神达意"的目标，假如没有特色和新意，复译也就没有意义了。

第一，我的译文应该是创造性地准确再现原著的风采。字对字的翻译当然不等于忠实于原文，"妙趣横生"不能译成"The interest flows horizontally"，"年已二八"不能译成"at the double eight"，"折桂之夫"不能译成"scholar to break the cassia bough"，连"laurel holder"似乎也有点勉强。但是，如果把原文中的形象说法都改成大白话，自然也不能说是再现了原著的风采。所以，我在翻译的过程中，把散体对话或独白部分尽量译成明白易懂的英文，例如把"吾今年已二八，未逢折桂之夫"译成"I've turned sixteen now, but no one has come to ask for my hand"。与此同时，在翻译唱词和诗句的时候，在不影响英语读者理解的前提下，尽可能地保持作者原有的意象，否则就宁肯牺牲原有的意象而用英语的相应表达方式来取代。我在唱词和诗句的部分是下了一番苦心的。我当然没有能力把所有的唱词和诗句都译成莎士比亚《罗密欧与朱丽叶》里的美丽抒情诗，但是我努力用英语进行再创作，以体现原著文字的优美。当然，语言是随着时代的变化而变化的，当代的中国读者对汤显祖的语言也有点陌生了，当代的英美读者对莎士比亚的语言也有点陌生了。但是如果能够带点古色古香的味道，却又没有离开当代英语的规范，则大功告成矣。

第二，对于原文的诗体部分及唱词部分，我在一定程度上采用了英语传统格律诗的若干形式。由于汤显祖的《牡丹亭》的唱词是有严格的曲调的，诗体的部分也是采用了格律诗的形式，所以，我在翻译唱词和诗句的时候，以抑扬格为基本格式，音步则可能有差异，因为唱词原文的字数就是长短不等的。原著的唱词在每一出戏中基本上一韵到底，英语无法做到这一点，我采用了多种不同的韵式。对于译诗是不是押韵的问题，在中国和在西方都有不同的看法，更不用说译一个可演出22个小时的长篇剧本了。我的译本可能会引起争议，可能有的地方确实"因音损义"了，也可能有的地方显得"滑稽可笑"，不过我可以于心无愧地说，我已经尽了我的努力进行了一次尝试，评论只能留给读者（尤其是专家）了。

下面以前面已经引用过的几段唱词，敬请读者来予以评判，我自己就不加评论了。先是第十出"惊梦"的那段著名唱词："原来姹紫嫣红开遍，似这般都付与断井颓垣。良辰美景奈何天，赏心乐事谁家院！"我的译文是：

The flowers glitter in the air,
Around the wells and walls deserted here and there.
Where is the "pleasant day and pretty night"?
Who can enjoy "contentment and delight"?

接下去的几行唱词，"朝飞暮卷，云霞翠轩；雨丝风片，烟波画船——锦屏人忒看的这韶光贱！"我的译文是：

The mist at dawn and rain at dusk,
The bowers in the evening rays,
The threads of clouds in gales of wind,
The painted boat and hazy sprays:
All are foreign to secluded maids.

我为自己的翻译定出这些具体目标以后，也有后悔的时候，尤其是用韵体来翻译全剧，因为费的功夫太大了，而且很可能会吃力不讨好。不过，我愿意使我的英译成为《牡丹亭》走向世界的新的一步，为最终出现一个真正传神达意的译本提供又一层肩膀。中国的戏曲是一门高度综合的艺术，融文字、音乐、舞蹈、美术、武术、杂技于一体，具有独特的表演程式。汤显祖的《牡丹亭》是世界文化中的瑰宝，理应将最好的英译本献给英语世界，以使它在英语世界得以更好的传播。

在本书翻译过程中，浙江大学的徐朔方教授给予了多次具体指教，华东师范大学的赵山林教授和中国科技大学的张光前教授不吝赐教，复旦大学的江巨荣教授以他的大作给本书提供了他的最新研究成果，上海外语教育出版社的王彤福教授为全书的编排提出了建设性的意见，中国京剧院的京剧著名表演艺术家袁世海先生和上海昆剧团的昆剧著名表演艺术家蔡正仁先生对本书的出版给予了鼓励和支持，台北中央研究院的华玮女士和加利福尼亚大学的白之先生给予了很大的鼓励，我的研究生李茜、吴春晓和赵冬逐词逐句地通读了校样，我在此谨向诸位表示由衷的感谢。

本书于2000年由上海外语教育出版社以极其精美的开本出版。在《大中华文库》需要收录的时候，上海外语教育出版社不顾本社可能遭受的损失，给予了全力的支持，我谨向上海外语教育出版社（尤其是向庄智象社长和王彤福总编）表示衷心的感谢。

汪榕培
2001年2月28日

INTRODUCTION

1. About Tang Xianzu

1.1. Tang Xianzu's Life and Influence

Tang Xianzu, alias Yireng, one of the 100 International Cultural Celebrities nominated by the UNESCO, was a great writer and dramatist with a legendary life and the quality of a profound thinker at the end of China's Ming Dynasty. He styled himself Ruoshi, Hairuo, Qingyuan Taoist and Hermit of the Jade Tea Studio. Born in an intellectual family in Linchuan on September 24, 1550, he was known for his intelligence in his childhood. At the age of 12, he made his poems known; when he reached 14, he passed the imperial examination at the county level; while he was 21, he passed the imperial examination at the provincial level ; not until he was 34 did he pass the imperial examination at the national level. He served in Nanjing successively as adviser of the Court of Imperial Sacrifices, secretary of the Office of Tuition, and administrative aide in the Sacrifice Bureau in the Ministry of Rites. In 1591, he wrote the famous *Memorial to Impeach the Ministers and Supervisors*, criticizing the court's misadministration since the ascendance of Emperor Shenzong and impeaching the Prime Minister Zhang Juzheng and Shen Shixing. As a result he was demoted to the position of a clerk in Xuwen County, Guangdong Province. In the next year he was transferred to be the magistrate of Suichang County, Zhejiang Province, where he formed some direct contact with the common people and took some enlightened measures. After five years in office, he returned to his hometown, gradually gave up any idea of an official career and devoted himself to writing. On July 29, 1616, he died in the Jade Tea Studio in Linchuan.

Tang Xianzu has left behind him 2200 odd poems, essays and verse essays, with his chief achievement in drama. His masterpiece *The Peony Pavilion* (also entitled *The Return of the Soul*), *The Handan Dream*, *The Nanke Dream* and *The Purple Hairpin* are known as the "four dreams of the Jade Tea Studio". His *Leisurely Poems from the Red Spring Studio, Collected Poems Sent by Tang Xianzu, The Complete Works of Jade Tea Studio, The Purple Flute* and the "four dreams" have passed down through printings in Ming and Qing dynasties. After the founding of the People's Republic of China, *Collected Works of Tang Xianzu* edited by Qian Nanyang and Xu Shuofang was published in 1962 and *The Complete Works of Tang Xianzu* annotated by Xu Shuofang was published in 1999. Written in 1598, Tang Xianzu's legendary drama *The Peony Pavilion* was first circulated in handwritten copies and then in dozens of printings. As literary versions, in the Ming Dynasty there was the Literary Pavilion version, the Retired Scholar Stone-Forest version, the Cinnabar and Ink version, the Bright Light Pavilion version and so on; in the Qing Dynasty, there was the Bamboo Forest Pavilion version, the Self-Recreation Room version, the Mustard-Seed Garden version, the Silk House version, the Warm and Red Room version, and so on. In the Ming and Qing dynasties, there appeared various annotated versions and adopted versions. Among the better known annotated versions were the Mao Ying's version with commentary, the Wang Siren's version with commentary, the commentated version by Three Ladies of Wushan in Wu County, the Yang Baoguang hand-commentated annotated version, and so on; among the better known adopted versions were

Shen Jing's *A Shared Dream*, Zang Maoxun's *The Peony Pavilion* (abbreviated version), Feng Menglong's *An Amorous Dream*, Xu Rixi's *The Peony Pavilion* (the Noble Garden version), Xu Suying's *A Lady's Painting*, and so on.

Tang Xianzu began to enjoy great fame in his lifetime, especially for his *The Peony Pavilion*, which became popular when it was written and overwhelmed many people. Nearly all the contemporary critics made high estimations for *The Peony Pavilion*. For example, Lu Tianchen wrote in his book *Comments on Drama* that Tang Xianzu was "an unprecedented genius with top knowledge" and "a poet for generations" and that his *The Peony Pavilion* was "for the future generations for its numerous wits and new inventions". Shen Defu wrote that "Since its publication, Tang Yireng's *The Peony Pavilion* has been passing from door to door and nearly outshines *Romance of the Western Bower*" and that his "profound intelligence will live forever". Another dramatic theorist Wang Jide wrote in his book *Dramatic Versification* that but for his defects in the "violation of versification rules, Tang Xianzu is the only writer in 200 years with no precedent and few successors". Wang Siren commented on the vivid character portrayal of *The Peony Pavilion* in his *Preface to the Commentated The Peony Pavilion of Jade Tea Studio*: "Du Liniang's attraction, Liu Mengmei's infatuation, the Madam's frailty, Magistrate Du's stubbornness, Chen Zuiliang's confusion and Chunxiang's smartness: all these characteristics are penetrating insights into the characters." For the comments in the Qing Dynasty, most of the critics adapted a praising inclination. Meng Chengshun, Wu Bing, Ruan Dacheng, Hong Sheng, Kong Shangren and many others drew much nutrition from *The Peony Pavilion*.

Although Tang Xianzu had won high esteem in the literary and dramatic circles, "Tang Xianzu Studies" gradually came into being only in the 20th century. China's studies in Tang Xianzu, especially in *The Peony Pavilion*, can be roughly divided into two stages (the first half of the 20th century and the second half of the 20th century). The studies in the first half of the 20th century inherited the tradition of Ming and Qing dynasties in tracing the origin of the story, composing and singing the tunes, appreciating the lines, but lacking renovation in ideas and elucidation in theories. The researchers were confined to certain experts in drama and literary history, including Wang Guowei, Wu Mei, Wang Jilie and Lu Qian in the early period and Yu Pingbo, Zhao Jingchen, Zhang Youluan, Jiang Jiping and Wu Zhonghan in the later period. The studies in the second half of the 20th century, in spite of the interference of vulgar sociology and ultra-left ideology, saw a small high tide around 1957 in commemorating the 340th anniversary of Tang Xianzu's death. Since the end of the 70s, Tang Xianzu Studies have been developing in depth. In commemorating the 366th anniversary of Tang Xianzu's death, China's academic circles held grand ceremonies in his native town and published a number of thesis and works, thus pushing the Tang Xianzu Studies into a new era. The international symposium and commemorative meeting held in Dalian and Linchuan in 2000 marked a new height in Tang Xianzu Studies.

Among the books on Tang Xianzu Studies published in the past 20 years, the most noteworthy are Xu Shuofang's *Tang Xianzu's Chronology* (1980), *Essays on Tang Xianzu and Other* (1983), *A Critical Biography of Tang Xianzu* (1993), and *The Complete Works of Tang Xianzu* (1999), Huang Wenxi and Wu Fengchu's *A Biography of Tang Xianzu* (1983), Mao Xiaotong's *A Collection of Reference Materials on Tang Xianzu Studies* (1984), Jiangxi Institute of Literature's *Collected Essays on Tang Xianzu Studies* (1984), Gong Zhongmo's *A Bi-*

ography of Tang Xianzu (1986), Zhou Yude's *Essays on Tang Xianzu* (1991), Xu Fuming's *Annotated Reference Materials on Tang Xianzu Studies* (1987) and *Tang Xianzu and The Peony Pavilion* (1985), Xiang Zhaofeng's *A Complete Collection of Tang Xianzu's Poems and Essays Written in Suichang* (2000), Zou Yuanjiang's *Tang Xianzu's Sentiments and Dreams* (1998) and so on. What deserves special mention is that the 2,627 pages of four volumes of *The Complete Works of Tang Xianzu* (1999) constitute a comprehensive collection of all Tang Xianzu's works, including the addition of "penmanship" section and a number of newly discovered essays. This collection, edited by Xu Shuofang, the senior expert of Tang Xianzu Studies at the age of 76, is a fresh milestone in Tang Xianzu Studies. *Tang Xianzu's Sentiments and Dreams* (1998) is a comprehensive research on Tang Xianzu's life, thoughts, personality, art and aesthetics, presenting an accurate summary of the basic characteristics of Tang Xianzu's thought and art. This book, written by Zou Yuanjing, a young scholar in the department of philosophy in Wuhan University, breaks a new trail in Tang Xianzu Studies by analyzing and elucidating Tang Xianzu's essays on ethics. Therefore, Tang Xianzu Studies have attracted old, middle-aged and young researchers and have covered such new fields as Tang Xianzu's life, the sources of his plays, ideological significance, social value, art form, and performances, to be viewed from such new angles as philosophy, history and aesthetics. In Mr Ye Changhai's words, studies in Tang Xianzu have become "Tang Xianzu Studies" in its real sense.

1.2. Tang Xianzu's International Fame

To the readers outside China, Tang Xianzu's name is inseparable with his play *The Peony Pavilion*, which reached Japan at the beginning of the 17th century. According to *The Catalogue of the Royal Library*, six copies of *The Peony Pavilion* (Zang Maoxun's adapted version) published in the Ming Dynasty were stored in the royal library. *The Return of the Soul in the Peony Pavilion* translated by Kishi Shunpulo was published by the Culture and Education Press in 1916; *The Return of the Soul* translated and annotated by Miyahara Minpei was published by the Tokyo National Library Publishing Association, contained in Volume 10 of *Collection of Chinese Works Translated into Japanese* (1920-1924); *The Return of the Soul in the Peony Pavilion* translated by Suzuki Hikojiro and Sasaki Shizumitsu was published by the Collection Publishing Association of the China University in Tokyo, contained in *Collection of Chinese Literature* (1926 -1927); Yiwashiro Shideo also translated *The Return of the Soul* into Japanese.

The earliest western version of *The Peony Pavilion* was in the German language. A selected translation of and an introduction to *The Peony Pavilion* was contained in an essay entitled *China's Love Stories* written by Xu Daolin, published in volume 4 of the journal *Sinology*. German professor Vincenz Hundhausen in Beijing University translated *The Peony Pavilion* into German, a selected translation being published by Beijing Publishing House in 1933 and a complete translation being published by Lacherre Publishing House in Zurich and Leipzig in 1937. Xu Zhongnian's French translation of "A Surprising Dream" from *The Peony Pavilion* and a commentary was contained in *An Anthology of Chinese Poems and Essays*, published by the Delagraphe Publishing House in Paris in 1933; the latest complete French translation of *The Peony Pavilion* by Andre Levy went into publication in Paris in 2000. L. N. Menshkov translated scenes from *The Peony Pavilion* into Russian, contained in *Oriental Classic Drama*: *India, China and Japan* in 1976.

The earliest English version of *The Peony Pavilion* was the scene

"Chunxiang Makes a Row at School" translated by H. Acton, contained in Volume 8 of *T'ien Hsia Monthly* in April 1939. Cyril Birch translated scenes of *The Peony Pavilion* and collected them in his *Anthology of Chinese Literature* (1965) and published a complete translation in Indiana University Press in 1980. Zhang Guangqian's complete translation was published by Tourism Education Press in 1994 and Wang Rongpei's complete versified translation was first published by Shanghai Foreign Language Education Press in 2000.

The Peony Pavilion has been time and again adapted into novels, e.g. Pan Shen and Zhang Yi's adaptation published by Shanxi Classic Press in 1995, Zhao Qingge's adaptation published by Jilin Literature and History Press in 1997. Two English adaptations were published in 1999, Chen Meilin's adaptation published by New World Press in Beijing and Yan Xiaoping's adaptation published by Moma and Sekey Press in New Jersey.

By the end of the 20th century, four different productions of *The Peony Pavilion* shook the stage at home and abroad, explicating this Chinese classic with a modern spirit. In 1999, Shanghai Kunju Troupe performed a new version of *The Peony Pavilion* in the *kunju* form to celebrate the 50th anniversary of the founding of PRC. As condensation of the original play, this new version retains the original art framework and gives full play to the *kunju* features of melting poetry, speech, song and dance into an organic whole. In the spirit of "adopting the essence and removing the side issues", it is condensed into three parts of 34 scenes to be staged for seven hours. *The Peony Pavilion* in the opera form is based on Cyril Birch's English translation, which lasts for four hours and a half, with Tan Dun as the composer, Peter Sellars as the director, Hua Wenyi and Huang Ying as the actresses, was staged first in Vienna on May 12, 1998 and then in Paris, Rome, London and San Francisco. This opera is a combination of the east and the west, the ancient and the modern, realism and romanticism, thus rousing the interest of the western audience. Directed by the Chinese American Chen Shizheng, the complete version of 55 scenes of *The Peony Pavilion*, which includes the six episodes of "The Interrupted Dream", "The Pursuit of the Dream", "Making Love to a Ghost", "Resurrection", "War Against the Bandits" and "Reunion", was staged in La Guardia Concert Hall in July, 1999 during the Lincoln Center Festival. From February 24 to March 12, 2000, the Chinese Theater Workshop staged the puppet *The Peony Pavilion* in Dorothy Williams Theatre, directed by Kuang-yu Fong and Stephen Kaplin. Performed by the *kunju* actors and the puppets in turns, this one-hour performance was welcomed by the audience.

Tang Xianzu Studies abroad started as early as the beginning of the 20th century. In his *History of Modern Chinese Drama* published in 1916, the famous Japanese historian of drama Aomoto Masako first placed Tang Xianzu on a par with William Shakespeare. The Japanese scholar Yiwashiro Shideo published the 411-page long thesis *Studies in Tang Xianzu* in 1986. The American scholar Cyril Birch published *The Peony Pavilion or The Return of the Soul* in 1974 and *The Structure of The Peony Pavilion* in 1980. Other theses include J. Y. H. Hu's *From the Netherworld to the Human World: An Analysis of the Structure of The Peony Pavilion* (1980) and Xia Zhiqing's *The Self and the Society in Tang Xianzu's Drama* (1970). The Russian scholar V. S. Manucine also published a number of theses on Tang Xianzu Studies, e.g. *On Tang Xianzu's The Purple Flute and Tang Xianzu's Drama The Purple Hairpin*, both published in 1974.

As far as PhD monographs are concerned, Lily Tang Shang's *The*

Four Dreams of T'ang Hien-Tsu was published in Hamburg University in 1974 and C.Wang Chen's *The Art of Satire in The Handan Dream* was published in Minnesota University in 1975. In the 90s PhD monographs include Hua Wei's *The Search for Great Harmony: A Study of Tang Xianzu's Dramatic Art* (1991), Sai-sing Yung's *A Critical Analysis of The Handan Dream* (1992), Chen Jiamei's *The Dream World of Love-sick Maidens: A Study of Women's Responses to the Peony Pavilion, 1598–1795* (1996). Besides, Wang I-chun's *Dream and Drama: In Late Sixteenth Century and Early Seventeenth Century China, England and Spain Theatre* (1986) also mentions Tang Xianzu's works; Catherine Crutchfield Swatek's *Feng Menglung's "Romantic Dream": Strategies of Containment in His Revision of The Peony Pavilion* touches upon the spread of Tang Xianzu's plays.

1.3. Prospects for Tang Xianzu Studies

On entering the 21st century, we are full of confidence that Tang Xianzu with his plays, poems and essays will gain worldwide attention, more people will be engaged in Tang Xianzu Studies, more theses and monographs will be published, organizations, associations and periodicals devoted to Tang Xianzu Studies will come into being. It is only natural that Tang Xianzu Studies will become a popular subject in the new century.

In regard to the growth of Tang Xianzu Studies in the new century, we can at least make the following predictions.

Firstly, Tang Xianzu Studies will develop in breadth and depth, as can be witnessed from the books and theses published at the end of the 20th century, the above-mentioned monograph *Tang Xianzu's Sentiments and Dreams* by Zou Yuanjiang being a ready proof. Take some theses published in the previous two years for example, Jiang Jurong's *A Short History of the Performances of The Peony Pavilion* and *A Summary of 20th-Century Studies in The Peony Pavilion* are summarizing theses. Zhao Shanlin's *Tang Xianzu and the Manners in Wei and Jin Dynasties,* Yang Zhong's *On Tang Xianzu's Historical Views and His Achievements in History Studies,* Gong Guoguang's *When I hear Old Tunes, I Am Surprised at Their New Bearings: Tang Xianzu's Theories in Dramatic Creations and His Aesthetic Consciousness,* Liu Yanjun's *On the Consciousness of Free Life in Tang Xianzu Studies,* Wang Rongpei's *The Lines from Tang Poems in The Peony Pavilion and Their Translations,* Hua Wei's *The Character Design in The Peony Pavilion,* Zou Yuanjiang's *In What Way Are We to Commemorate Tang Xianzu* and many other articles have already expanded the scope of Tang Xianzu Studies, which is bound to have further expansion.

Secondly, Tang Xianzu Studies will be placed within the range of world literature. It has been nearly a century since Tang Xianzu was ranked with William Shakespeare in Britain. Many theses to compare Tang Xianzu with William Shakespeare have been published, for instance, Tang Xianzu's *The Peony Pavilion* has been compared with William Shakespeare's *Romeo and Juliet* and *The Winter's Tale*. Recently Xu Shunsheng has written an article to compare Tang Xianzu's *The Peony Pavilion* with Victor Hugo's *Hernani*. A comparison in the sphere of world literature by scholars of various nationalities against different cultural backgrounds will give prominence to what is characteristic of and extraordinary for Tang Xianzu's plays, poems and essays.

We will gain some new insight into Tang Xianzu if we compare his artistic thought with certain literary trends in the west. This kind of comparison will become an interesting subject for research. One example is the French surrealistic poet André Breton, who served in a lunatic asylum during World War I and had some contact with Freud's theory of psychological analysis. Under the influence of the contemporary poet Guillame Apollinaire, he succeeded in transplanting the search for the subconscious into the poetry. In 1924 he published *The Surrealist Manifesto*, in which he stressed the subconscious and the dream and advocated the writing of "coincidence". Tang Xianzu labeled his plays as "the four dreams of the Jade Tea Studio" and mentioned "dreams" many times in his writings. If we compare Tang Xianzu's idea of "dream" with the surrealist conceptions and Freud's theories of the dream, we will be surprised to realize that Tang Xianzu became a "herald" or "vanguard" over 300 years earlier than these French surrealists!

Thirdly, Tang Xianzu's plays in various languages will spread over the world. Up to the end of the 20th century, *The Peony Pavilion* has gained popularity in China and abroad. Although it has been translated into Japanese and many European languages, Tang Xianzu's other plays have not been translated into English, let alone other European languages. I believe that these plays will be translated into English and other languages in the near future. At least I shall be one of the translators. If I succeed in translating all the "four dreams of the Jade Tea Studio" into English, the readers all over the world will be interested in them as well.

Fourthly, Tang Xianzu's plays will be staged more often all over the world. The four stage versions of *The Peony Pavilion* have all been modernized to an extent. It is beyond reproach to modernize the classic dramas. A classic performance in the original style and a completely modernized adaptation are not mutually exclusive. William Shakespeare's *Romeo and Juliet* is still performed on the Elizabethan stages, but in the modernized film version, the hooligans are fighting in the street by riding the motors while Romeo and Juliet are dating in the swimming pool. The classic forms of art will live on and new forms of art will come into being.

Now that *The Peony Pavilion* in *the kunju* form has been adapted into TV series, new film versions will be shown on the screen sooner or later.

Fifthly, organizations, associations and periodicals devoted to Tang Xianzu Studies are bound to come into existence. We are bound to see a national or international association of Tang Xianzu Studies with its local branches, which might have their own periodicals. By then the researchers in Tang Xianzu will have their own academic field and their own academic publications.

2. About *The Peony Pavilion*

2.1. A Synopsis of *The Peony Pavilion*

The Peony Pavilion in 55 scenes, is a romantic tragicomedy which describes the love story between Du Liniang and Liu Mengmei. Although it draws its plot largely from the short story *Du Liniang Revives for Love* published in the Ming Dynasty, there are major alternations in its plot and narration and there is a great enhancement in its themes. In the short story, after Du Liniang has been revived, a marriage well matched in social status naturally follows. In Tang Xianzu's play, the legendary story is melted into the real life of the Ming Dynasty. The story of Du Liniang's revival seems to be absurd, but in fact reflects the germs of humanism, the persistent aspiration for free love, which transcends life and death.

In the early days of the Southern Song Dynasty, the magistrate Du Bao of Nan'an has a pampered single daughter Du Liniang and employs an old pedagogue Chen Zuiliang as the tutor to teach her ancient classics. Du Liniang's naughty maid Chunxiang makes fun with the tutor and persuades Du Liniang to have a stroll in the back garden. The stroll in the garden in the bright spring day rouses Du Liniang's aspiration for love.

She takes a nap near the Peony Pavilion and dreams a strange dream, in which she meets her ideal lover a romantic scholar and falls in love with her. Haunted by the dream, she falls ill and draws a self-portrait in her illness as a keepsake for the scholar. In spite of the care of her mother, she dies in lovesickness.

Because of Li Quan's rebellion, Du Bao is sent to station in Yangzhou as the imperial envoy. After Du Bao's departure, Du Liniang is buried under the plum tree in the back garden according to her last wishes. A Taoist temple is built with Sister Stone as the guardian of her coffin. Not long afterwards, the young scholar Liu Mengmei from afar comes and stops over in a room in the temple. When he strolls in the garden one day, he happens to pick up Du Liniang's self-portrait. He scrutinizes the portrait and falls in love with the beauty in the portrait. He dreams a dream that night, in which Du Liniang says that she can be revived. On the second day, he prays with Sister Stone, opens the grave and revives Du Liniang. They are very happy but afraid that the secret will leak out. Therefore, they leave for the capital Lin'an.

At that time, Du Bao has been moved to Huai'an and tells his wife and Chunxiang to go to Lin'an. On their way to Lin'an, they meet with the revived Du Liniang. On hearing about the news of her father, Du Liniang tells Liu Mengmei to learn more about her father when Liu Mengmei is waiting for the outcome of the imperial examination. After the enclosure has been relieved, Du Bao is about to return to Lin'an when he meets his son-in-law and thinks that he is a liar. Liu Mengmei is brought to Lin'an and is being interrogated when report comes that he has been selected as the Number-one Scholar. Du Liniang explains everything in the court and the couple is happily reunited by imperial decree.

2.2. The Character Portrayals in *The Peony Pavilion*

With its complicated plot and magnificent structure, *The Peony Pavilion* in 55 scenes is particularly known for its excellent character portrayals. Among its 160 odd characters in the play, its 30 odd main characters are vividly presented, especially Du Liniang, Liu Mengmei, Du Bao, Chen Zuiliang, Chunxiang, and Sister Stone. From the ministers and generals to the ruffians and whores, from the Tartar king and missionaries to the infernal judge and flower gods, all the characters who laugh, weep and sigh at the right occasion provide a panoramic picture of the social life in the Ming Dynasty.

The best-depicted character is of course Du Liniang, one of the most loving female characters in ancient Chinese drama. Besides her lingering and persistent love, a common theme in traditional Chinese drama and fiction, she is characterized by her aspiration for free individual development, which is indeed a rare case. In *The Peony Pavilion*, the evolvement of her personal character and her psychology is distinct and minute. The description of her mind in pace with her action is an excellent part of her character portrayal. Now let's have a taste of how the playwright uses poetic language to create the character of Du Liniang.

In days when "the oriole is fond to sing at such a lovely time of spring", Du Liniang stays in her chamber, "now drawing a picture of the swing, then weaving the lovebirds on the wing" and often "takes a nap during the day". She feels unhappy because she has to "act properly in front of all", but love of beauty is her natural design.

As her parents hope that she will be learned and know the rites when some day she is married, they employs the pedagogue Chen Zuiliang as her tutor. In explaining "The Waterfowl", Chen Zuiliang distorts the poem by saying that "In a word, of the three hundred poems in *The Book of*

Poetry the mere phrase 'without evil thought' is of great import." Upon reading the lines "The waterfowl would coo upon an islet in the brook. A lad would like to woo a lass with a pretty look," Du Liniang is aware of the love theme and is stirred in her inner mind: "Now that a caged waterfowl would like to coo upon an islet in the brook, how could a human being be less passionate!" After the lessons, "when she is awakened by the orioles' songs and finds the springtime beauty all around, she stands in deep thought on the courtyard ground." "That which scissors cannot sever, and, sorted out, is tangled again, makes me bored than ever", because "in the courtyard drifts the willow-threads, torn by spring breeze into flimsy shreds." It is the willow-threads that upset her — the willow-threads are nothing but the love-threads in her heart.

When her father is on an inspection to the farms, Du Liniang goes to the back garden which is bathed in springtime sunshine: "The flowers glitter brightly in the air, around the wells and walls deserted here and there. Where is the pleasant day and pretty sight? Who can enjoy contentment and delight?" She links the swift passage of spring to the swift passage of her youth and regrets that she is wasting her youth in her chamber: "The clouds at dawn and rain at dusk, the bowers in the evening rays, the threads of shower in gales of wind, the painted boat in hazy sprays: all are foreign to secluded maids." When she sees "the willow-threads (love-threads) cling upon the roseleaf raspberries", she is much depressed. She sighs because she has not found her lover yet: "Born and brought up in a renowned family of high officialdom, I've come of age but haven't found a fiancé yet. I'm wasting my youth that will soon pass." At the thought of this, she weeps and sinks into deeper sorrow: "What a pity that my face is as pretty as a flower but my fate is as dreary as a leaf!"

In deep sorrow, Du Liniang "feels dizzy, leans on the table and takes a short nap", thus entering a free spiritual world. In her dream, she seems to see a scholar coming toward her with a willow-twig in his hand. Although the scholar is a total stranger to her, "is it absurd that they seem to meet somewhere before but stand here face to face without a word?" Under the protection of the flower god, they "make love near the Peony Pavilion beside the peonies". When she awakes from her dream, she sees her mother standing in front of her. Ever since then, the dreamland has always lingered in her mind: "As springtime tour has tired me out, there is no need to sent my quilt. Good heavens, I wishes that pleasant dreams would soon sprout."

On the second day, Du Liniang "sits alone thinking over the dream, feels depressed and thinks how piteous she is." She hates to eat or drink when she recalls yesterday's dream: "Oh heavens, the lake and the pavilion in yesterday's dream were real enough. I tried to relive the old dream but new disappointment ensued. I tossed and turned all night without a moment's sleep. Now that Chunxiang is gone, I'll take this opportunity to sneak into the garden and have a look." When she tries to retrace the dream in the back garden, the sights are the same. However, here and there she seeks her dream but she's found nothing. The Peony Pavilion, the rose grove, how can they be so desolate! How can they be so lifeless! How the sight breaks her heart! When she sees that "the plum tree is lovely indeed", an idea comes across her mind: "I would be lucky enough if I could be buried underneath." She thinks that if she were free to pick her bloom or grass, if she were free to choose to live or die, she would resign to fate without a sigh. She vows that she'll risk her life and weather raging storms to be his faithful wife.

After she returns from the back garden, Du Liniang "sheds large drops of tears in dreams" all night long and "is utterly worn out". She says, "If I don't paint a picture of myself now to live in the world, who will ever know of my beauty once I pass away?" She draws a self-portrait and writes an inscription on it: "A close inspection shows her as her self; / A distant look displays her as an elf. / Her future spouse who shares the pillow / Will be found by the plum or willow." She sighs with emotion and says, "In the past and at present, beauties married early have pictures drawn by their husbands or draw their own pictures as gifts to their lovers. But to whom shall I present this picture?"

Du Liniang "has been laid in bed since her dream during the spring stroll. Although she is not afflicted by pain or itches, she feels dizzy all the time." As her illness becomes more serious, she cries "Oh my dear" all the time in a trance. "There is no moonlight in the hall, when floating clouds conceal the sky. Her chilly dream is bitter as gall. Earth has not anything to show more smart than her affection in her broken heart." "When he has left, he is hard to see again; I blames the god and ghost for this in vain. On my brow and in my heart, waves of sorrow start." Du Liniang knows that she will not live long and begs her mother to bury her under a plum tree and to erect a stone before her tomb when she loses life as dropping bloom. Her last words are:"It has been raining all through the night. When the moon is set, I'll meet my doom!" Thus, Du Liniang dies in deep lovesickness.

In his inscription to *The Peony Pavilion*, Tang Xianzu writes, "To be as Du Liniang is truly to have known love. Love is of source unknown, yet it grows ever deeper. The living may die of it, by its power the dead live again. Love is not love at its fullest if one who lives is unwilling to die for it; or if it cannot restore to life the one who has so died." The "love" in Tang Xianzu's sense is the genuine affection of human beings, in direct opposition to the "ethics" in feudalist morality. This guiding principle keeps in steps with the progressive ideology of the time and thus makes *The Peony Pavilion* above par with other plays of love of the time. Du Liniang makes rendezvous with Liu Mengmei on their first meeting, her ghost form makes love with her lover and holds the wedding after she has revived. Du Liniang does not die because her love is interrupted but because her dreamland love cannot come true in real life. In other words, she "dies of love". All these details are extraordinary in the tendency of seeking after personal freedom and in the artistic technique of romantic exaggeration.

Tang Xianzu also writes in his inscription, "Has the world ever seen a woman's love to rival that of Du Liniang? Dreaming of a lover she fell sick; once sick she became ever worse; and finally, after painting her own portrait as a legacy to the world, she died." These words are a summary of the process of Du Liniang's death (desire for love, search for love, sentiments for love and sorrow for love) and a reflection of Tang Xianzu's humanist ideas. The Song and Ming ethnics lay stress on the melting of the heart and mind and the conquest of the mind over the heart (the preservation of the heavenly ethics instead of human desires) while Tang Xianzu's view on "utmost love" is a reaction to the ethics. Du Liniang's subconscious sexual desire is unnamed sorrow before her stroll in the back garden, growing desire for love during her stroll in the garden, dreamland encounter with the scholar and death for unrealized love after her illness. Therefore, *The Peony Pavilion* can be regarded as the beginning of romantic Chinese drama and lays the foundation for Tang Xianzu as a giant in world literature.

2.3. The Artistic Charm of *The Peony Pavilion*

The Peony Pavilion became popular and appealing as soon as it went on stage. Du Liniang has enchanted the young women in the feudalist society by her melancholy and has become their idol for free love. In the past four centuries, *The Peony Pavilion* has shocked the hearts of numerous young women, who shed floods of tears for Du Liniang.

Yu Erniang in Loujiang "was particularly fond of *The Peony Pavilion*. She wrote notes on the margins in fine letters and was deeply moved by the play. She died of sorrow at the age of seventeen." Jin Fengdian in Yangzhou "was so fond of *The Peony Pavilion* upon its publication that she kept it in hand day and night and was absolutely absolved in it. On her deathbed, she said to her maidservant, 'I am so unfortunate that I fail to meet an ideal husband. I won't close my eyes after my death. When I am dead, see to it that bury the book *The Peony Pavilion* with me.'" Feng Xiaoqing in Guanglin "knew how to read and write when she was a child. She was married to Feng Sheng when she was sixteen. When she died in melancholy, she left a poem behind her: 'I hate to face the rain with windows so damp, /But read *The Peony Pavilion* under the lamp./ There must be people as crazy as me; /Xiaoqing is not the only one you can see.'"

The painstaking efforts of performers for generations have turned *The Peony Pavilion* from a desktop drama into stirring stage performances with touching artistic charm. Shang Xiaoling in Hangzhou "was a charming actress known for her acting in *The Return of the Soul*. As she failed to find her man, she grew sick out of melancholy. Whenever she staged the scenes of 'Seeking the Dream' or 'Premature Death', she felt sad and shed floods of tears as if she were experiencing the tragedy by herself. When she was staging the scene 'Seeking the Dream' one day, singing the aria 'I'll risk my life and weather raging storm to be your faithful wife', she cried and fell on the stage. When Chunxiang came to see what happened to her, she had lost her breath." Zhang Jun, a young actor in the new *kunju* edition of *The Peony Pavilion*, said with emotion, "I have staged *The Peony Pavilion* for many times since I was very young. As an actor, I love *kunju* so much that I am willing to die for it."

Yue Meiti, student of the famous *kunju* artist Yu Zhenfei, once wrote about her experience to stage the scene "An Amazing Dream" with Hua Wenyi. Her words fully reflect the profound cultural content of Chinese art: "In *kunju* performances, the real life is embodied in the movements of sleeves, figures and steps instead of 'removing the clothes'. For instance, when we come to Liu Mengmei's lines 'I shall unbutton your gown and strip it down', Hua Wenyi and I turn round, flapping our long sleeves. The dancing movements are pretty in themselves, expressing the contentment of the lovers. A further analysis will show that 'he' is 'rushing' towards her while 'she' is 'pushing' him aside. With the lines 'You'll bite your sleeve-top with your teeth', we do not try to interpret the words with our actions. In fact, these words are un-interpretable. 'She' covers her face with her sleeves in bashfulness while 'he' grasps the top of her sleeves and pull down her hands lightly (they never touch hands during the performance). 'He' and 'she' look at each other and smile in their hearts, not on their faces. The feelings are reflected in their actions: flapping their long sleeves with happiness in their hearts. The audience must be deeply affected."

3. English Versions of *The Peony Pavilion*

3.1. Cyril Birch's Version

The first complete English version of *The Peony Pavilion* by Cyril Birch was published by the Indiana University Press in 1980. Cyril Birch is a distinguished Sinologist, retired professor emeritus of the California

University at Berkley. Besides *The Peony Pavilion*, he has also translated *Chinese Myths and Fantasies, Stories from a Ming Collection, Scenes for Mandarins and Edited Anthology of Chinese Literature, Studies in Chinese Literary Genres*. Besides *The Peony Pavilion or The Return of the Soul and The Structure of The Peony Pavilion*, he has also written the essay *Winter's Tale and The Peony Pavilion*.

In his translation, Cyril Birch reproduces *The Peony Pavilion* in fluent English. On the whole, his version is truthful to the original, with arias and poems rendered into free verse.

Let's take the famous aria in Scene Ten "An Amazing Dream" for example:

"See how deepest purple, brightest scarlet

open their beauty only to dry well crumbling.

'Bright the morn, lovely the scene,'

Listless and lost the heart

— where is the garden 'gay with joyous cries'?"

This aria is basically truthful to the original, fluent and rhythmical. What is worth mentioning here is that this aria also appears in his *Anthology of Chinese Literature* (1972):

"See how deepest purple, brightest scarlet

open their beauty only to dry well's crumbling parapet.

'Bright the morn, lovely the scene,' listless and lost the heart

— where is the garden 'gay with joyous cries'?"

The following lines of the aria are completely rewritten. His 1972 version reads as follows:

"Flying clouds of dawn, rolling storm at dusk

pavilion in emerald shade against the sunset glow

fine threads of rain, petals borne on breeze

gilded pleasure-boat in waves of mist:

sights little treasured by the cloistered maid

who sees them only on a painted screen."

His 1980 version reads as follows:

"Streaking the dawn, close-curled at dusk,

rosy clouds frame emerald pavilion;

fine threads of rain, petals borne on breeze,

gilded pleasure boat in waves of mist:

glories of spring but little treasured

by screen-secluded maid."

From the above two versions we can get two conclusions. First, Cyril Birch is very serious in his academic attitude in that he does serious revisions to his own translations. Second, his translation is not done in a single day. It takes at least seven years for him to do the translation from beginning to end.

In his translation, Cyril Birch neither follows the traditional way of versification nor uses rhymes in most cases except in certain cases to achieve comic effect.

The current performances in the west have mostly adapted Cyril Birch's version, which has played an undeniably important role in bringing *The Peony Pavilion* to the world.

3.2. Zhang Guangqian's Version

The first Chinese translator who translates the complete play of *The Peony Pavilion* into English is Professor Zhang Guangqian, whose version was published by the Tourism Education Press in 1994. As professor in China Science and Technology University in Hefei, he makes great contributions by spending his spare time for several years translating this magnum opus into English.

Compared with Cyril Birch's version, Zhang Guangqian's version is more accurate on interpreting the original ideas. As a Chinese translator, he has a firm grasp of the English language and a good understanding of the original work. In translating the arias and the poems in the play, he uses blank verse in most cases and employs rhymes when occasion arises. Here is the famous aria cited above:

"So the garden is all abloom in pink and red,

yet all abandoned to dry wells and crumbling walls.

The best of seasons won't forever last,

can any household claim undying joy?"

The first two lines are in regular iambic hexameters while the next two lines are in regular iambic pentameters. The wording is not restricted to the literal meaning of the Chinese words, but has conveyed the basic mood of the original work. The next lines are:

"Clouds that scud southward at the break of day

bring back evening showers in the western hills.

Rosy clouds, verdant cots,

threads of rain, sheets of wind,

misty waves, painted boats

——spring's splendour has escaped the chambered girls."

These lines are not rhymed, but take the iambic pentameter as the basic pattern, with many exceptions. The third, fourth and fifth lines have four stresses each and the general ideas are conveyed to the readers.

Generally speaking, Zhang Guangqian's version is successful and it is more accurate and concise in certain places than Cyril Birch's version.

3.3. My Version

I spent over three years in translating *The Peony Pavilion* into English from 1996. During this process, I was often moved by his artistic attractions and was disturbed by his profound learning.

In order to get some on-the-spot knowledge of Tang Xianzu's life and creations, I went on an inspection to his hometown Linchuan. Tang Xianzu's tomb was located in the People's Park in the center of the city and surrounded by verdant trees. Behind the tomb was a "Peony Pavilion" with two scrolls of eulogy on the pillars: "His articles top all; his integrity towers over Linchuan." The Tang Xianzu Memorial Hall situated in the outskirts of Linchuan was still under construction, occupying several hectors of land. Right inside the gate stood the giant statue of Tang Xianzu, behind which were the relief sculptures of the four dreams of the Jade Tea Studio. In the exhibition hall was exhibited the life of Tang Xianzu. Peach flowers blossomed in the yard, full of spring vitality. "The Peony Pavilion" was erected on a hilltop beside which was the tomb of Du Liniang with a deliberately cracked tombstone, behind which Du Liniang and Liu Mengmei standing hugged together. On a huge stone wall was inscribed Mao Zedong's calligraphy, an aria from the scene "An Amazing Dream": "The flowers glitter brightly in the air, around the wells and walls deserted here and there. Where is the 'pleasant day and pretty sight'? Who can enjoy 'contentment and delight'? The clouds at dawn and rain at dusk, the bowers in the evening rays, the threads of shower in the gales of wind, the painted boat in hazy sprays: all are foreign to secluded maids." When I went on, I saw the Plum Blossom Temple, where stood the statues of Du Liniang and Liu Mengmei. A horizontal board with the words "A Happy Marriage" was hanging above and joss-stick coils were rising from an incense furnace. I seemed to be living through the scenes of *The Peony Pavilion* and was greatly encouraged for my efforts in doing the translation.

After that experience, I did much more quickly in my translation and finished the last fifteen scenes within two months. If I had been working like this, I could have completed the whole play within a year, but I had spent three whole years on it.

When I translated *The Peony Pavilion*, I overcame one difficulty after another in comprehension. Some words looked like familiar strangers, the most typical example being the 276 lines of collected Tang poems in the play. I had only a vague notion for some lines, but I could not make other people understand the lines if I myself did not fully understand them. When I had completed my first draft, I looked up one line after another. As a result, I not only made clear the original meaning of these lines so that I could make a better translation, but also wrote a short thesis on this subject on Chinese literature.

I set for myself the objective of "vivid in description and faithful in meaning". If there were nothing special or new, there would not be the need to translate this play again.

Firstly, my version must be a recreation of the original charm. A word-for-word translation of course does not mean a faithful translation. Such literal renderings as "The interest flows horizontally", "at the double eight" and "scholar to break the cassia bough" are not regular English at all, but plain words cannot always convey the original charms. Therefore, I have turned the dialogues or monologues into daily English, e.g. "I've turned sixteen now, but no one has come to ask for my hand." When I translate the arias or the poems, I have tried to keep the original images if they are within reach of the western readers; otherwise, I would use equivalent English phrases at the sacrifice of the original images. I have spent much efforts translating the arias and poems in the play. It is natural that I am not capable of translating them into such lyrical poems as in Shakespeare's

Romeo and Juliet, but I have tried my best to recreate the arias and poems in the English language. Language changes with times. As the present-day Chinese readers are no longer familiar with Tang Xianzu's language, so the present-day English readers are no longer familiar with Shakespeare's language. However, if my translation contains the flavour of the far away and the long ago yet never really archaic to be intelligible, I have succeeded.

Secondly, I have tried to employ the traditional English versification and rhyming to translate the arias and poems in the play. As Tang Xianzu employed the traditional Chinese versification and rhyming, I have employed the iamb as the basis and various patterns of rhyming although the same rhyme may be used in a whole scene in the original Chinese play. Of course, views differ on whether to employ rhymes in translating poems, let alone in translating a play which lasts as long as 22 hours. My version may rouse arguments and some parts may "miss the meaning because of the rhymes". But I can say with a calm mind that I have done my best to make a trial and that I shall leave the comments to the readers.

What follows is my version for the above quotations. I sincerely welcome the comments and criticisms from the readers. For the first quotation, my version reads as follows:

"The flowers glitter in the air,

Around the wells and walls deserted here and there.

Where is the 'pleasant day and pretty night'"?

Who can enjoy 'contentment and delight'?"

For the second quotation, my version reads as follows:

"The mist at dawn and rain at dusk,

The bowers in the evening rays,

The threads of clouds in gales of wind,

The painted boat and hazy sprays:

All are foreign to secluded maids."

After I set the concrete objectives (especially for the versified translation), I have felt regretful at times. It is too painstaking and too risky to employ the rhymes, because it may prove to be tough and unrewarding. The Chinese drama is a highly synthetic form of art, combining literature with music, dance, fine arts, martial arts and acrobatics. It has a singular pattern of performance. However, I do hope that my English version will become another step forward to bring *The Peony Pavilion* nearer to the world and another "shoulder" for the climbers toward a perfect English version of the play. As a gem in the treasure house of world culture, Tang Xianzu's *The Peony Pavilion* will be more popular in the English-speaking world if there is a perfect translation in the real sense.

When I was doing the translation, Professor Xu Shuofang from Zhejiang University gave me many detailed instructions. Pofessor Zhao Shanlin from East China Normal University and Professor Zhang Guangqian from China Science and Technology University expressed their precious views. Professor Jiang Jurong from Fudan University offered his thesis, Professor Wang Tongfu from Shanghai Foreign Language Education Press gave constructive suggestions for the layout of the book, the famous actor Mr Yuan Shihai from Chinese Jingju Troupe and the famous actor Mr Cai Zhengren from Shanghai Kunju Troupe contributed their share, Madam Hua Wei from the Academia Sinica in Taipei and Mr Cyril Birch from California University gave me much encouragement, my graduate students Li Qian, Wu Chunxiao and Zhao Dong did the proofreading word by word. I would like to express my heartfelt thanks to all those who have given me generous assistance in bringing my translation into publication.

A deluxe edition of my versified English version of *The Peony Pavilion* was published by the Shanghai Foreign Language Education Press in 2000. When this book is to be included in the *Library of Chinese Classics*, the Shanghai Foreign Language Education Press gives full support at the sacrifice of its own financial interests. I am deeply indebted to the Shanghai Foreign Language Education Press, especially to director Zhuang Zhixiang and editor-in-chief Wang Tongfu.

Wang Rongpei
February 28, 2001

目 录

第一出 标目	2
第二出 言怀	6
第三出 训女	12
第四出 腐叹	26
第五出 延师	34
第六出 怅眺	48
第七出 闺塾	60
第八出 劝农	82
第九出 肃苑	104
第十出 惊梦	118
第十一出 慈戒	144
第十二出 寻梦	150
第十三出 诀谒	174

CONTENTS

Scene One   3
Prelude

Scene Two   7
A Scholar's Ambition

Scene Three   13
Admonishing His Daughter

Scene Four   27
A Pedagogue's Complaints

Scene Five   35
Employing the Tutor

Scene Six   49
An Out-skirting

Scene Seven   61
Studying at Home

Scene Eight   83
Inspecting the Farms

Scene Nine   105
Cleaning the Garden

Scene Ten   119
An Amazing Dream

Scene Eleven   145
Madam's Admonishment

Scene Twelve   151
Seeking the Dream

Scene Thirteen   175
Leaving Home

第十四出 写 真	182
第十五出 虏 谍	198
第十六出 诘 病	204
第十七出 道 觋	218
第十八出 诊 祟	242
第十九出 牝 贼	264
第二十出 闹 殇	270
第二十一出 谒 遇	302
第二十二出 旅 寄	320
第二十三出 冥 判	330
第二十四出 拾 画	378
第二十五出 忆 女	388
第二十六出 玩 真	398
第二十七出 魂 游	408
第二十八出 幽 媾	430

Scene Fourteen Drawing Her Own Image	183
Scene Fifteen Brooding on an Invasion	199
Scene Sixteen Inquiring about the Disease	205
Scene Seventeen A Taoist Nun	219
Scene Eighteen Making Diagnoses	243
Scene Nineteen The Female Chieftain	265
Scene Twenty Premature Death	271
Scene Twenty-one An Audience with the Envoy	303
Scene Twenty-two A Hard Journey	321
Scene Twenty-three The Judgement in Hell	331
Scene Twenty-four Picking up the Portrait	379
Scene Twenty-five Recalling Her Daughter	389
Scene Twenty-six Cherishing the Portrait	399
Scene Twenty-seven The Roaming Soul	409
Scene Twenty-eight Union with the Ghost	431

第一出　　标　目

【蝶恋花】
　　[末上]忙处抛人闲处住，
　　百计思量，
　　没个为欢处。
　　白日消磨肠断句，
　　世间只有情难诉。
　　玉茗堂前朝复暮，
　　红烛迎人，
　　俊得江山助。
　　但是相思莫相负，
　　牡丹亭上三生路。
　　杜宝黄堂，生丽娘小姐，爱踏春阳。感梦书生折柳，竟为情伤。写真留记，葬梅花道院凄凉。三年上，有梦梅柳子，于此赴高唐。果尔回生定配。赴

Scene One
Prelude

(*Enter Announcer*)

Announcer:
(*To the tune of Dielianhua*)
All the men prefer remaining free;
Yet howe'er they try,
They are as worried as can be.
Among the sentimental tales I write,
Love is as mysterious as the sea.
I write the tale from morning till night,
With candles burning bright,
Enlightening me in the brightest ray.
When a beauty falls in love with a man,
The Peony Pavilion sees her ardent way.
"Du Bao, the magistrate,
Has a daughter by the name of Liniang,
Who strolls in a sunny springtime date.
When she dreams of a scholar breaking willows,
She's thrown into a grievous state.
She draws a self-portrait
And pines away lamenting o'er her fate.
When three years have passed by,
Liu Mengmei comes along
To meet her in the garden once again.
Du Liniang gains her second life.

临安取试，寇起淮扬。正把杜公围困，小姐惊惶。教柳郎行探，反遭疑激恼平章。风流况，施行正苦，报中状元郎。

杜丽娘梦写丹青记。
陈教授说下梨花枪。
柳秀才偷载回生女。
杜平章刁打状元郎。

When Liu is about to seek office in Lin'an,
There arrives a mob of rebellious men.
As Du Bao is besieged inside the town,
His daughter is in a panic then.
Liu Mengmei goes to seek information,
But his good will is beyond Du's ken.
When his love affair is in great trouble,
News comes that Liu is allotted office
And Liu at last fulfills his yen."

Du Liniang draws a portrait true to life;
Chen Zuiliang brings about the peace once more;
Liu Mengmei meets his resurrected wife;
Du Bao gives tortures to his son-in-law.

第二出　　言　怀

【真珠帘】
　　[生上]河东旧族、柳氏名门最。
论星宿，连张带鬼。
几叶到寒儒，
受雨打风吹。
谩说书中能富贵，
颜如玉，和黄金那里？
贫薄把人灰，
且养就这浩然之气。
"刮尽鲸鳌背上霜，寒儒偏喜住炎方。凭依造化三分福，绍接诗书一脉香。能凿壁，会悬梁，偷天妙手绣文章。必须砍得蟾宫桂，始信人间玉斧长。"小生姓柳，名梦梅，表字春卿。原系唐朝柳州司马

Scene Two
A Scholar's Ambition

(*Enter Liu Mengmei*)

Liu Mengmei:

(*To the tune of* *Zhenzhulian*)

Among the houses of distinction in Hedong,
The most renowned has been the house of Liu.
In astrologic terms,
The fortune star is due.
As their descendants are poor scholars,
They do not have a brilliant sight in view.
The saying goes that studies bring the wealth,
But where is pretty lady
And where is gold?
Although wretched poverty may discourage me,
I am as honest as of old.
"I've studied hard but have made no success,
A southern scholar in the deepest stress.
Howe'er, endowed with favours from above,
Profoundest learning is what I possess.
Because I study hard till late at night,
I can write essays with far-reaching sight.
When I win the laurel in the future days,
I'll prove that I am really smart and bright."

My name is Liu Mengmei, also called Chunqing. A descendant of Liu Zongyuan, poet and Prefect of Liuzhou in the Tang

柳宗元之后,留家岭南。父亲朝散之职,母亲县君之封。[叹介]所恨俺自小孤单,生事微渺。喜的是今日成人长大,二十过头,志慧聪明,三场得手。只恨未遭时势,不免饥寒。赖有始祖柳州公,带下郭橐驼,柳州衙舍,栽接花果。橐驼遗下一个驼孙,也跟随俺广州种树,相依过活。虽然如此,不是男儿结果之场。每日情思昏昏,忽然半月之前,做下一梦。梦到一园,梅花树下,立着个美人,不长不短,如送如迎。说道:"柳生,柳生,遇俺方有姻缘之分,发迹之期。"因此改名梦梅,春卿为字。正是:"梦短梦长俱是梦,年来年去是何年!"

【九回肠】
虽则俺改名换字,
俏魂儿未卜先知?
定佳期盼煞蟾宫桂,
柳梦梅不卖查梨。
还则怕嫦娥妒色花颓气,

dynasty, I have lived with my family in Lingnan. My father was a minister without portmanteau and my mother was conferred the title of County Lady.

(*With a sigh*)

As an orphan since my early childhood, I have scraped a bare living. Now that I have grown up to be over twenty, I am intelligent enough to pass the county examination. Unfortunately, as I haven't got the right opportunity to hold an office, I'm still living in cold and hunger. My ancestor Prefect Liu had a servant Hunchback Guo, a gardener for his official residence in Liuzhou. This man has a hunchback descendant who works as a gardener here in Guangzhou and helps me with my daily life. However, this is not the right way for a worthy man to live through his life. Day by day I am in a melancholy mood. It happens that I had a strange dream half a month ago. I dreamed of a belle standing under a plum tree in a garden. She was of medium height and looked at me in a coy manner. She said, "Sir, sir, you are destined to meet me as your love and then start your career." That is why I change my name to Mengmei which literally means "dreaming of the plums" and also call myself Chunqing which literally means "spring lord". Truly,

"Long dream or short, it is anyway a dream;
Year in year out, time and tide moves like a stream."

(*To the tune of Jiuhuichang*)

"Although I've changed my name offhand,
Does the beauty know in her dreamland?
Although I long to wed and get a post,
I Liu Mengmei will never make a boast.
For fear that beauty fades away too soon,

等的俺梅子酸心柳皱眉,
浑如醉。
无萤凿遍了邻家壁,
甚东墙不许人窥!
有一日春光暗度黄金柳,
雪意冲开了白玉梅。
那时节走马在章台内,
丝儿翠、笼定个百花魁。
虽然这般说,有个朋友韩子才,是韩昌黎之后,寄居赵佗王台。他虽是香火秀才,却有些谈吐,不免随喜一会。

门前梅柳烂春晖,
梦见君王觉后疑。
心似百花开未得,
托身须上万年枝。

I seem to sit on pins and needles

And cry for the moon."

"I use no fireflies when I read and learn;

Beyond the east wall stays the girl I yearn.

The lucky star will shine on me someday

And I'll no longer fidget in dismay."

"By then I'll ride across the streets,

Accept the hearty greetings

And pick from beauties on their seats."

Let me forget about it. I have a friend by the name of Han Zicai. As a descendant of Han Yu, he stops over at the Terrace of Prince Zhao Tuo. He is tending to his ancestral shrines, but he is an eloquent speaker. I'd like to pay a visit to his place.

When plums and willows grow before the gate,
I see the king but doubts arise when dreams abate.
My heart contains a hundred blooms in buds,
But as to find a branch, I have to wait.

第三出　　训　女

【满庭芳】

[外扮杜太守上]西蜀名儒，
南安太守，
几番廊庙江湖。
紫袍金带，
功业未全无。
华发不堪回首。
意抽簪万里桥西，
还只怕君恩未许，
五马欲踟蹰。

"一生名宦守南安，莫作寻常太守看。到来只饮官中水，归去惟看屋外山。"自家南安太守杜宝，表字子充，乃唐朝杜子美之后。流落巴蜀，年过五旬。想廿岁登科，三年出守，清名惠政，播在人间。内有夫人甄氏，乃魏朝甄皇后嫡派。此家峨眉山，见世出贤德。夫人单生小女，才貌端妍，唤名

Scene Three
Admonishing His Daughter

(*Enter Du Bao*)

Du Bao:

(*To the tune of* **Mantingfang**)

A well-known scholar from Sichuan
And now the prefect of Nan'an,
In and out of office, I've done what I can.
In robes and golden belt I'm dressed,
Which shows my ranking higher than the rest.
As my hair is turning grey degree by degree,
I'd like to retire and have time free,
But I'm afraid the emperor will not agree
And I still have to wait and see.

"*All my life an honoured official in Nan'an,
I do much better than the ordinary man.
I serve my term of office with clean hands;
When I retire, I'll stay in my native lands.*"

I am Du Bao, Prefect of Nan'an, also called Zichong and descended from Du Fu of the Tang dynasty. I have lived with my family in Sichuan and now I am past fifty. I passed the imperial examination when I was twenty and became a prefect three years afterwards. I have been renowned for my clean government. My wife is Zhen, a descendent of Empress Zhen of the Wei dynasty. Her family has been living near Mount Emei and has enjoyed a good reputation for generations. My

丽娘，未议婚配。看起自来淑女，无不知书。今日政有余闲，不免请出夫人，商议此事。正是："中郎学富单传女，伯道官贫更少儿。"

【绕池游】
［老旦上］甄妃洛浦，
嫡派来西蜀，
封大郡南安杜母。
［见介］
［外］"老拜名邦无甚德，
［老旦］妾沾封诰有何功！
［外］春来闺阁闲多少？
［老旦］也长向花阴课女工。"
［外］女工一事，想女儿精巧过人。看来古今贤淑，多晓诗书。他日嫁一书生，不枉了谈吐相称。你意

wife has given birth to a daughter only, a gifted and pretty girl by the name of Liniang. I have not made any arrangements for her marriage yet. It is universally acknowledged that a virtuous girl should be well educated. As I have some time free from my office, I'll call my wife and discuss it with her. As the saying goes,

"Well learned, Cai Yong had a daughter of good fame;
A poor official, Deng You lost his son but earned his name."

(*Enter Zhen*)

Zhen:

(*To the tune of* **Raochiyou**)

A descendent from Princess Zhen

And a resident in Sichuan,

I've been conferred the title Lady of Nan'an.

(*She greets her husband*)

Du Bao:

"Without much worth, I serve the court although I'm aged;

Zhen:

Without much work, I've got a title from the king.

Du Bao:

How does Liniang pass her time in spring?

Zhen:

In needlework alone is she engaged."

Du Bao:

Our daughter is good at needlework. In the past and at present, virtuous girls should be well educated. When she marries a scholar, she can share a talk with him. What do you think

下如何?

[老旦]但凭尊意。

【前腔】

[贴持酒台,随旦上]娇莺欲语,

眼见春如许。

寸草心,

怎报的春光一二!

[见介]爹娘万福。

[外]孩儿,后面捧着酒肴,是何主意?

[旦跪介]今日春光明媚,爹娘宽坐后堂,女孩儿敢进三爵之觞,少效千春之祝。

[外笑介]生受你。

【玉山颓】

[旦进酒介]爹娘万福,

女孩儿无限欢娱。

坐黄堂百岁春光,

进美酒一家天禄。

about it?

Zhen:

I agree with you.

(*Enter Du Liniang, followed by her servant maid Chunxiang carrying a tray of wine vessels*)

Du Liniang:

(*To the previous tune*)

The oriole is fond to sing

At such a lovely time of spring.

How can I e'er requite

My parents for their caressing light?

(*Greets her parents*)

Bliss on you, Dad and Mom.

Du Bao:

Why do you tell your maid to bring the wine here, child?

Du Liniang:

(*Kneels*)

In such a fine spring day, you are taking a rest in the rear hall. I'd like to offer you three cups of wine with my best wishes to you in the spring.

Du Bao:

(*With a smile*)

Thank you very much.

Du Liniang:

(*To the tune of Yushantui*)

With bliss on you, my dad and mom,

That is where all my joy comes from.

With everlasting spring air in the hall,

You drink the wine and bring joy to all.

祝萱花椿树,
虽则是子生迟暮,
守得见这蟠桃熟。
[合]且提壶,花间竹下长引着凤凰雏。
[外]春香,酌小姐一杯。

【前腔】
吾家杜甫,
为飘零老愧妻孥。
[泪介]夫人,我比子美公公更可怜也。
他还有念老夫诗句男儿,
俺则有学母氏画眉娇女。
[老旦]相公休焦,倘然招得好女婿,与儿子一般。
[外笑介]可一般呢!
[老旦]"做门楣"古语,
为甚的这叨叨絮絮,才到中年路。
[合前]

Oh father dear, oh mother dear!

I wish you'd have a son this year

To stay with you and bring you cheer.

Du Bao, Zhen:

Fill high the cups with vernal wine

For our dear son and daughter fine!

Du Bao:

Fill in a cup for your mistress, Chunxiang.

(*To the previous tune*)

My ancestor Du Fu wandered all his life

And felt ashamed to face his son and wife.

(*Weeps*)

My lady, I am more pitiable than my ancestor Du Fu.

He could yet write about his lovely son

While I have my daughter as my only fun.

Zhen:

Don't get worried, my lord. If we find a good son-in-law, he will be as good as a son.

Du Bao:

(*Smiles*)

Yes, indeed!

Zhen:

A daughter brings the same bliss as a son.

There is no need to make the grudge

When only half of your life-course is run.

Du Bao, Zhen:

Fill high the cups with vernal wine

For our dear son and daughter fine!

Du Bao:

[外]女孩儿,把台盏收去。
[旦下介]
[外]叫春香。俺问你小姐终日绣房,有何生活?
[贴]绣房中则是绣。
[外]绣的许多?
[贴]绣了打绵。
[外]甚么绵?
[贴]睡眠。
[外]好哩,好哩。夫人,你才说"长向花阴课女工",却纵容女孩儿闲眠,是何家教?叫女孩儿。
[旦上]爹爹有何分付?
[外]适问春香,你白日眠睡,是何道理?假如刺绣余闲,有架上图书,可以寓目。他日到人家,知书知礼,父母光辉。这都是你娘亲失教也。

Take the wine vessels away, my child.

(*Exit Du Liniang*)

Du Bao:

Chunxiang, tell me what your young mistress does by the day in her bower.

Chunxiang:

She does embroidery in her bower.

Du Bao:

How much embroidery does she do?

Chunxiang:

She does her embroidery with a nap.

Du Bao:

What do you mean by "nap"?

Chunxiang:

A brief sleep.

Du Bao:

So, so! Madam, you just said that she was engaged in needlework alone, and you went as far as to allow her to take naps! How are you teaching your daughter! Call the girl back!

(*Enter Du Liniang*)

Du Liniang:

What can I do for you, Dad?

Du Bao:

Just now I asked Chunxiang about you. How can you be taking naps during the day? After you've finished your embroidery, you have plenty of books to read on the shelves. When some day you are married, you will be learned and know the rites. In this way, your dad and mom will feel honoured. Your mom has not done her duty to teach you.

【玉抱肚】
　　宦囊清苦，
　　也不曾诗书误儒。
　　你好些时做客为儿，
　　有一日把家当户。
　　是为爹的疏散不儿拘，
　　道的个为娘是女模。
【前腔】
　　[老旦]眼前儿女，
　　俺为娘心苏体劬。
　　娇养他掌上明珠，
　　出落的人中美玉。
　　儿呵，爹三分说话你自心模，
　　难道八字梳头做目呼。
【前腔】
　　[旦]黄堂父母，
　　倚娇痴惯习如愚。
　　刚打的秋千画图，
　　闲榻着鸳鸯绣谱。
　　从今后茶余饭饱破工夫，
　　玉镜台前插架书。
　　[老旦]虽然如此，要个女先生讲解才好。
　　[外]不能够。

(*To the tune of Yubaodu*)

Although I always live a meagre life,

I've ne'er neglected learning in my strife.

In my home as my daughter you have grown,

But very soon you'll stand upon your own.

As I'm too busy to teach you every day,

You should follow your mom in every way.

Zhen:

(*To the previous tune*)

Liniang, although you're not a boy,

You've brought me all the joy.

I look upon you as the pearl of pearls

And you are really now the girl of girls.

My dear, please keep your father's words in mind,

You must be of the intelligent kind.

Du Liniang:

I've grown up in a prefect's home,

Indulging myself in the paint and comb.

Now I draw a picture of the swing,

Then I weave the lovebirds on the wing.

From now on I'll make full use of my time,

Reading all the books sublime.

Zhen:

That's good indeed, but you'd better have a lady tutor to teach you.

Du Bao:

That won't do.

(*To the previous tune*)

In my official residence,

【前腔】
　　后堂公所，
　　请先生则是黉门腐儒。
　　[老旦]女儿呵，怎念遍的孔子诗书，
　　但略识周公礼数。
　　[合]不枉了银娘玉姐只做个纺砖儿，
　　谢女班姬女校书。
　　[外]请先生不难，则要好生管待。
【尾声】
　　说与你夫人爱女休禽犊，
　　馆明师茶饭须清楚。
　　你看俺治国齐家、也则是数卷书。

　　往年何事乞西宾？
　　主领春风只在君。
　　伯道暮年无嗣子，
　　女中谁是卫夫人？

Her tutor ought to be a scholar with common sense.

Zhen:

My daughter does not have to read all the books,

But she should know something about the rites.

Du Bao, Zhen:

In this way she will not only know how to spin,

But also be an intelligent virgin.

Du Bao:

It's not difficult to find her a tutor, but he must be well treated.

(*To the tune of **Coda***)

Madam, as you love your daughter, grudge no expense

And give the tutor tasty food from hence.

When I do anything with creed,

The books are all I need.

Why is a tutor summoned to the house?

He is to teach my daughter under age.

As I have not a son born by my spouse,

Can my daughter be a genuine sage?

第四出　腐　叹

【双劝酒】
　　[末扮老儒上]灯窗苦吟，
　　寒酸撒吞。
　　科场苦禁，
　　蹉跎直恁！
　　可怜辜负看书心。
　　吼儿病年来进侵。
　　"咳嗽病多疏酒盏，村童俸薄减厨烟。争知天上无人住，吊下春愁鹤发仙。"自家南安府儒学生员陈最良，表字伯粹。祖父行医。小子自幼习儒。十二岁进学，超增补廪。观场一十五次。不幸前任宗师，考居劣等停廪。兼且两年失馆，衣食单薄。这些后生都顺口叫我"陈绝粮"。因我医、卜、地

Scene Four
A Pedagogue's Complaints

(*Enter Chen Zuiliang*)
Chen Zuiliang:
(*To the tune of* **Shuangquanjiu**)
Perusing books by night and day,
I'm poor but always wait and wait.
As lucky star ne'er shines my way,
I am reduced to this sad state.
To add pain to my deep distress,
The asthma gets me in a mess.
"*I drink less for my bad disease;*
I cook less for my scanty fees.
While no one lives high in the sky,
A grey-haired sage on earth would sigh."

I am Chen Zuiliang, also called Bocui, student of the Confucian Academy in the Prefecture of Nan'an. I came from a doctor's family but have pursued the Confucian learning since early childhood. I entered the academy at the age of twelve and received stipend from the government. In these forty-five years I sat for examinations fifteen times without success. Unfortunately, I turned out to be the last in the previous examination and was deprived of my stipend by the supervisor. To make things worse, out of work as a tutor for two years, I only scraped a meagre existence. Therefore, those young fellow students mockingly changed my name from Chen Zuiliang to

理，所事皆知，又改我表字伯粹做"百杂碎"。明年是第六个旬头，也不想甚的了。有个祖父药店，依然开张在此。"儒变医，菜变齑"，这都不在话下。昨日听见本府杜太守，有个小姐，要请先生。好些奔竞的钻去。他可为甚的？乡邦好说话，一也；通关节，二也；撞太岁，三也；穿他门子管家，改窜文卷，四也；别处吹嘘进身，五也；下头官儿怕他，六也；家里骗人，七也。为此七事，没了头要去。他们都不知官衙可是好踏的！况且女学生一发难教，轻不得，重不得。倘然间体面有些不臻，啼不得，笑不得。似我老人家罢了。"正是有书遮老眼，不妨无药散闲愁。"

［丑扮府学门子上］"天下秀才穷到底，学中门子老成精。"

Chen Jueliang, which literally means "Devoid of Food". Besides, as I am well versed in medicine, prophecy and geomancy, they have changed my other name from Bocui to Baizasui, which literally means "Jack of All Trades". Now that I shall arrive at the age of sixty by next year, I do not cherish any more hope. I am now running the pharmacy handed down from my grandfather. As the saying goes, "A Confucian scholar becomes a doctor, just as the vegetable becomes the pickles."—Forget about it. Yesterday I heard that our Prefect Du was looking for a tutor for his daughter. A lot of people vie with each other for the post. But why? First, to have something to show off to their kith and kin; second, to make some connections in the government office; third, to earn some money; fourth, to alter the archives through the help of the servants and butlers; fifth, to prepare for posts somewhere else; sixth, to scare the inferior officials; seventh, to cheat their family members. These seven considerations drive them to vie with each other for the post. However, they have not realised that official residence is a hazardous place. Besides, a girl student is even more difficult to deal with. Neither soft words nor hard words will do with her. If I get into some trouble with her, I'll really be in a dilemma. As an old man, I'd better follow the saying,

> "Nowhere am I to fix my look
> But bury my head in the book."

(*Enter the janitor*)

Janitor:

> "The scholars in the world are poor
> While janitors are smart for sure."

[见介]陈斋长报喜。
[末]何喜？
[丑]杜太爷要请个先生教小姐，掌教老爷开了十数名去都不中，说要老成的。我去掌教老爷处禀上了你，太爷有请帖在此。
[末]"人之患在好为人师"。
[丑]人之饭，有得你吃哩。
[末]这等便行。[行介]

【洞仙歌】
[末]咱头巾破了修，
靴头绽了兜。
[丑]你坐老斋头，
衫襟没了后头。
[合]砚水漱净口，
去承官饭溲，
剔牙杖敢黄虀臭。

(*Greets Chen Zuiliang*)

Congratulations, Sir.

Chen Zuiliang:

For what?

Janitor:

Prefect Du would like to find a tutor for his daughter, but is not satisfied with anyone recommended by the director of the Prefectural Academy because he wants an experienced tutor. I spoke to the director and recommended you. Here is the letter of invitation from Prefect Du.

Chen Zuiliang:

Mencius teaches us, "Man's anxieties begin when he would like to teach others."

Janitor:

But man's hunger is more tormenting than man's anxieties. You don't have to worry about your stomach at least.

Chen Zuiliang:

In this case, let's go now.

(*They begin to leave*)

(*To the tune of* ***Dongxiange***)

I sew my scarf when it is torn

And mend my shoes when they are worn.

Janitor:

When you take the tutor's post,

You'll share the honour of the host.

Chen Zuiliang, Janitor:

Rinse with water from the writing tray

Before the tasty dinners every day

And use toothpicks to keep the stink away.

【前腔】
　　[丑]咱门儿寻事头，
　　你斋长干罢休？
　　[末]要我谢酬，
　　知那里留不留？
　　[合]不论端阳九，
　　但逢出府游，
　　则捻着衫儿袖。
　　[丑]望见府门了。

　　[丑]世间荣乐本逡巡，
　　[末]谁睬髭须白似银？
　　[丑]风流太守容闲坐，
　　[合]便有无边求福人。

Janitor:

> (*To the previous tune*)
>
> I have found such a precious job for you;
>
> Don't you forget to give me a gift or two!

Chen Zuiliang:

> I know you want me to repay,
>
> But I don't know if I can stay.

Chen Zuiliang, Janitor:

> On festivals when days are fair,
>
> Be sure to go out in the air
>
> And bring something for us to share.

Janitor:

The prefect's gate is in sight now.

The worldly honour comes and goes,

Chen Zuiliang:

But who cares for old men for their woes?

Janitor:

When prefects sit at home in ease,

Chen Zuiliang, Janitor:

The favour-curriers come in rows.

第五出　　延　师

【浣纱溪】

[外引贴扮门子，丑扮皂隶上]山色好，
讼庭稀。
朝看飞鸟暮飞回。
印床花落帘垂地。
"杜母高风不可攀，甘棠游憩在南安。虽然为政多阴德，尚少阶前玉树兰。"我杜宝出守此间，只有夫人一女。寻个老儒教训他。昨日府学开送一名廪生陈最良。年可六旬，从来饱学。一来可以教授小女，二来可以陪伴老夫。今日放了衙参，分付安排礼酒，叫门子伺候。[众应介]

【前腔】

[末儒巾蓝衫上]须抖擞，
要拳奇。

Scene Five
Employing the Tutor

(*Enter Du Bao with his butler and attendant*)

Du Bao:

(*To the tune of* **Huanshaxi**)

The mountains look their best;

The court now takes a rest.

The birds come and go above the hall;

The petals cover my seal stand and curtains fall.

"Although Du Shi exceeds me in esteem,

I've earned a good reputation in Nan'an.

For all my contributions so supreme,

I have begot no male heir to my clan."

As Prefect of Nan'an, I only have my wife and my daughter on my side. I intend to find a tutor for my daughter. Yesterday, the Confucian Academy of the prefecture recommended to me a scholar by the name of Chen Zuiliang, a learned man about sixty years old. He can teach my daughter and also chat with me. Today I have laid off official duties so that I can entertain him with a dinner. Butler, get ready for the guest.

(*The butler and the attendant answer the order*)

(*Enter Chen Zuiliang in a blue robe and a scholar's cap*)

Chen Zuiliang:

(*To the previous tune*)

I'll do away with fear

And put on my best cheer.

衣冠欠整老而衰。
养浩然分庭还抗礼。
〔丑禀介〕陈斋长到门。
〔外〕就请衙内相见。
〔丑唱门介〕南安府学生员进。〔下〕
〔末跪，起揖，又跪介〕生员陈最良禀拜。〔拜介〕
〔末〕"讲学开书院，
〔外〕崇儒引席珍。
〔末〕献酬樽俎列，
〔外〕宾主位班陈。"叫左右，陈斋长在此清叙，着门役散回，家丁伺候。
〔众应下〕〔净扮家童上〕
〔外〕久闻先生饱学。敢问尊年有几，祖上可也习儒？

In shabby coats for my old age,

I'll face my master like a sage.

Attendant:

(*Announces*)

Mr Chen is at the gate.

Du Bao:

Invite him to come in.

Attendant:

(*Announces*)

Here comes the scholar from the prefectural academy.

(*Exit Attendant*)

Chen Zuiliang:

(*Kneels, rises to his feet, bows and kneels again*)

Chen Zuiliang from the prefectural academy kowtows to Your Excellency.

(*Kowtows*)

"After schools are set up in the town,

Du Bao:

A scholar is deemed of high renown.

Chen Zuiliang:

Toasts after toasts are now exchanged,

Du Bao:

When host and guest are properly arranged."

Now all the attendants may go home since I shall have a chat with Mr Chen. Tell the servants to attend on us.

(*The attendants answer the order and withdraw*)

(*Enter the servant boy*)

I've long heard that you are well learned. May I ask how old you are and whether you come from a Confucian family?

［末］容禀。

【锁南枝】
　　将耳顺，
　　望古稀，
　　儒冠误人霜鬓丝。
　　［外］近来？
　　［末］君子要知医，
　　悬壶旧家世。
　　［外］原来世医。还有他长？
　　［末］凡杂作，可试为；
　　但诸家，略通的。
　　［外］这等一发有用。

【前腔】
　　闻名久，
　　识面初，
　　果然大邦生大儒。
　　［末］不敢。
　　［外］有女颇知书，
　　先生长训诂。
　　［末］当得。则怕做不得小姐之师。

Chen Zuiliang:

    Yes, of course.

    (*To the tune of Suonanzhi*)

    I'm over sixty years of age,

    On my way toward three score and ten,

    A scholar whose youth will ne'er come again.

Du Bao:

    And now?

Chen Zuiliang:

    I practise medicine to earn some pay,

    A practice passed down from the ancient day.

Du Bao:

    So medicine is your family heritage. What else do you know?

Chen Zuiliang:

    I can do prophecy for men;

    And geomancy is within my ken.

Du Bao:

    These skills are all the more useful.

    (*To the previous tune*)

    I've heard of your name for many years,

    But it's the first time for me to meet

    A scholar of enormous feat.

Chen Zuiliang:

    You're over-praising me.

Du Bao:

    My daughter knows how to read and write

    And will surely learn from you with delight.

Chen Zuiliang:

    I'll do my best, but I'm not sure whether I can teach her well

[外]那女学士，你做的班大姑。
今日选良辰，
叫他拜师傅。
[外]院子，敲云板，请小姐出来。

【前腔】
[旦引贴上]添眉翠，
摇佩珠，
绣屏中生成士女图。
莲步鲤庭趋，
儒门旧家数。
[贴]先生来了怎好？
[旦]那少不得去。
丫头，那贤达女，
都是些古镜模。
你便略知书，
也做好奴仆。
[净报介]小姐到。[见介]
[外]我儿过来。"玉不琢，不成器；人不学，不知道。"今日吉辰，来拜了先生。
[内鼓吹介]

enough.

Du Bao:

>Lucky is my daughter
>
>To have you as her tutor.
>
>As this is a day of bliss
>
>For my daughter to meet her tutor.

Butler, strike the summoning plate to call the young mistress.

>(*Enter Du Liniang with Chunxiang*)

Du Liniang:

>(*To the previous tune*)
>
>With eyebrows craven-black
>
>And pendants emerald-green,
>
>A beauty steps from behind the screen.
>
>In buoyant footsteps to the hall,
>
>I act properly in front of all.

Chunxiang:

Now that the tutor has arrived, what shall we do?

Du Liniang:

I have to meet him anyway, Chunxiang.

>The names of virtuous ladies never fade;
>
>A little learning makes you a better maid.

Butler:

Here comes the young mistress.

>(*Du Liniang bows to her father*)

Du Bao:

Come forward, my child. As *The Book of Rites* says, "Uncarved jade is unfit for use; uneducated men are unaware of Tao." As today is a day of bliss, come and meet your tutor.

>(*Sounds of drums and music within*)

[旦拜]学生自愧蒲柳之姿，敢烦桃李之教。

[末]愚老恭承捧珠之爱，谬加琢玉之功。

[外]春香丫头，向陈师父叩头。着他伴读。[贴叩头介]

[末]敢问小姐所读何书？

[外]男、女《四书》，他都成诵了。则看些经旨罢。《易经》以道阴阳，义理深奥；《书》以道政事，与妇女没相干；《春秋》、《礼记》，又是孤经；则《诗经》开首便是后妃之德，四个字儿顺口，且是学生家传，习《诗》罢。其余书史尽有，则可惜他是个女儿。

【前腔】

我年将半，

性喜书，

牙签插架三万余。

Du Liniang:

(*Makes obeisance*)

I'm an unworthy student for an experienced teacher.

Chen Zuiliang:

It's an honour for an old man like me to teach a talented student.

Du Bao:

Chunxiang, come and kowtow to Mr Chen. This servant maid will accompany my daughter in her studies.

(*Chunxiang kowtows*)

Chen Zuiliang:

May I ask what books the mistress has studied?

Du Bao:

She's able to memorise the *Four Books* both for men and for women, and now she'd better read something from the *Five Classics*. *The Book of Changes* deals with the duality of *yin* and *yang*; that's too profound for her. *The Book of History* deals with political affairs; that's of no concern for women. *The Spring and Autumn Annals* and *The Book of Rites* are too fragmented. *The Book of Poetry*, however, starts with eulogy of the virtue of queens and consorts and is easy to remember with its four-syllabic verse. Moreover, poetry conforms with my family tradition. It's better for her to study *The Book of Poetry*. I have all kinds of books and histories, but the pity is that she is a girl.

(*To the previous tune*)

At fifty years of age,

I'm fond of books myself,

With thirty thousand on the shelf.

[叹介]我伯道恐无儿,
中郎有谁付?
先生,他要看的书尽看。有不臻的所在,打丫头。
[贴]哎哟!
[外]冠儿下,
他做个女秘书。
小梅香,要防护。
[末]谨领。
[外]春香伴小姐进衙,我陪先生酒去。
[旦拜介]"酒是先生馔,女为君子儒。"[下]
[外]请先生后花园饮酒。

[外]门馆无私白日闲,
[末]百年粗粝腐儒餐。
[外]左家弄玉惟娇女,

(*Sighs*)

What's the use of my great name,

If I have not a son to carry on the fame?

Mr Chen, my daughter has all the books at her disposal. If she's done anything wrong, just punish the maid.

Chunxiang:

Alas!

Du Bao:

I hope that you will make my daughter

A worthy scholar of the topmost grade.

Meanwhile, just watch out

For the naughty maid.

Chen Zuiliang:

Yes, I'll do my best.

Du Bao:

Chunxiang, see your young mistress to her room while I have a drink with Mr Chen.

Du Liniang:

(*Makes obeisance*)

"The tutor has his wine to drink;

The daughter has her books to think."

(*Exit Du Liniang with Chunxiang*)

Du Bao:

Mr Chen, let's have a drink in the back garden.

A tutor teaches pupils in the day,

Chen Zuiliang:

Poor scholars have but rice upon the tray.

Du Bao:

A loving daughter as my single heir,

[合]花里寻师到杏坛。

Chen Zuiliang, Du Bao:

She has a tutor now to guide her way.

第六出　怅眺

【番卜算】

[丑扮韩秀才上]家世大唐年，
寄籍潮阳县。
越王台上海连天，
可是鹏程便？

"榕树梢头访古台，下看甲子海门开。越王歌舞今何在？时有鹧鸪飞去来。"自家韩子才。俺公公唐朝韩退之，为上了《破佛骨表》，贬落潮州。一出门蓝关雪阻，马不能前。先祖心里暗暗道，第一程采头罢了。正苦中间，忽然有个湘子侄儿，乃下八洞神仙，蓝缕相见。俺退之公公一发心里不快。呵融冻笔，题一首诗在蓝关草驿之上。末二句单指着湘子说道："知汝远来应有意，好收吾骨瘴江边。"湘子袖了这诗，长笑一声，腾空而去。果然后来退之公公潮州瘴死，举目无亲。那湘子恰在云端看

Scene Six
An Out-skirting

(*Enter Han Zicai*)

Han Zicai:

(*To the tune of* ***Fanbusuan***)
With family name tracing back to Tang,
I now dwell in the town Chaoyang.
Now that I watch the boundless roaring sea,
Will my career be promising for me?
"On Ancient Terrace under banyan trees,
I watch the Jiazi Bay below in breeze.
Without a trace of former song and dance,
I see a partridge come and go at ease."

I am Han Zicai. My ancestor Han Yu was banished to Chaozhou in the south because he wrote the essay *On the Bones of Buddha*. As soon as he arrived at the Languan Pass, his horse was unable to go on because of heavy snow. He thought that this was an ill omen. In distress, he saw his nephew Han Xiangzi, one of the eight immortals, approach him in rags. All the more distressed, he thawed his frozen brush and wrote a poem in the hostel. The last two lines read:

"I know that you have come to me
To take my relics to the sea."

Han Xiangzi thrust the poem in his sleeves and soared into the sky with a prolonged laugh. It so happened that my ancestor Han Yu died of malaria in Chaozhou with no relatives beside

见，想起前诗，按下云头，收其骨殖。到得衙中，四顾无人，单单则有湘子原妻一个在衙。四目相视，把湘子一点凡心顿起。当时生下一支，留在水潮，传了宗祀。小生乃其嫡派苗裔也。因乱流来广城。官府念是先贤之后，表请敕封小生为昌黎祠香火秀才。寄居赵佗王台子之上。正是："虽然乞相寒儒，却是仙风道骨。"呀，早一位朋友上来。谁也？

【前腔】
　　[生上]经史腹便便，
　　昼梦人还倦。
　　欲寻高耸看云烟，
　　海色光平面。
　　[相见介]
　　[丑]是柳春卿，甚风儿吹的老兄来？
　　[生]偶尔孤游上此台。
　　[丑]这台上风光尽可矣。
　　[生]则无奈登临不快哉。

his deathbed. Han Xiangzi witnessed all this up in the clouds. As he recalled the poem, he lowered his clouds and collected the remains. When he came to the official residence, he saw no one but his former wife. As they looked at each other, his mortal instinct was aroused. A son was born in Shuichao to carry on the family line and I am descended from this line. In times of turmoil, I moved here to Guangzhou and was assigned as an assistant to the Temple of Han Yu because I was his descendant. And so I'm now living near the Terrace of Prince Zhao Tuo. As the poem goes,

"A scholar of the poorest kind
May have the loftiest mind."

Here comes a friend of mine. Who can it be?

(*Enter Liu Mengmei*)

Liu Mengmei:

(*To the previous tune*)

With learning and experience

Behind an inconspicuous appearance,

I'd like to mount the hills to watch the cloud

Above the flat sea like a shroud.

(*Exchanges greetings with Han Zicai*)

Han Zicai:

Hi, Liu Mengmei! What wind has brought you here?

Liu Mengmei:

I'm wandering alone and happen to climb to this terrace.

Han Zicai:

This terrace commands an excellent view.

Liu Mengmei:

But it's not easy to climb such a height.

[丑]小弟此间受用也。
[生]小弟想起来，到是不读书的人受用。
[丑]谁？
[生]赵佗王便是。

【锁寒窗】
　　祖龙飞、鹿走中原，
　　尉佗呵，他倚定着摩崖半壁天。
　　称孤道寡，
　　是他英雄本然。
　　白占了江山，
　　猛起些宫殿。
　　似吾侪读尽万卷书，可有半块土么？
　　那半部上山河不见。
　　[合]由天，那攀今吊古也徒然，
　　荒台古树寒烟。
[丑]小弟看兄气象言谈，似有无聊之叹。先祖昌黎公有云："不患有司之不明，只患文章之不精；不患有司之不公，只患经书之不通。"老兄，还则怕工

Han Zicai:

I'm having a good time here.

Liu Mengmei:

It suddenly occurs to me that the illiterate have the best time.

Han Zicai:

Whom do you mean?

Liu Mengmei:

Prince Zhao.

(*To the tune of Suohanchuang*)

When Qin's First Emperor was dead,
Across the land the turmoil spread.
Prince Zhao usurped a stretch of land
And thus became a sovereign head.
A hero without any dread,
With people under his command,
He built a palace tall and grand.

But for scholars like you and me, do we have a single bit of land?

Confucian books bring no land to our hand.

Liu Mengmei, Han Zicai:

Oh, Gracious Heaven,
It's no use dwelling on the past;
The terrace alone will stand and last.

Han Zicai:

You look as if you were upset. My ancestor Han Yu wrote,

"Never mind whether the official is bright,
But mind whether your essay is right;
Never mind whether the official is fair,
But mind whether your knowledge is there."

夫有不到处。

[生]这话休提。比如我公公柳宗元,与你公公韩退之,他都是饱学才子,却也时运不济。你公公错题了《佛骨表》,贬职潮阳。我公公则为在朝阳殿与王叔文丞相下棋子,惊了圣驾,直贬做柳州司马。都是边海烟瘴地方。那时两公一路而来,旅舍之中,两个挑灯细论。你公公说道:"宗元,宗元,我和你两人文章,三六九比势:我有《王泥水传》,你便有《梓人传》;我有《毛中书传》,你便有《郭驼子传》;我有《祭鳄鱼文》,你便有《捕蛇者说》。这也罢了。则我进《平淮西碑》,取奉取奉朝廷,你却又进个平淮西的雅。一篇一篇,你都放俺不过。恰如今贬窜烟方,也合着一处。岂非时乎,运乎,命乎!"韩兄,这长远的事休提了。假如俺和你论如常,难道便应这等寒落。因何俺公公造下一篇《乞巧文》,到俺二十八代元孙,再不曾乞得一些巧来?便是你公公立意做下《送穷文》,

Brother, I'm afraid we still have something to learn.

Liu Mengmei:

Let's forget about it. Both my ancestor Liu Zongyuan and your ancestor Han Yu were men of great learning, but they were born under the wrong star. Your ancestor was banished to Chaozhou — he should not have written *On the Bones of Buddha*; my ancestor was banished to Liuzhou — he should not have played chess with Prime Minister Wang Shuwen in the Chaoyang Hall of the palace and thus disturbed the Emperor. Both Chaozhou and Liuzhou were located in the foggy coastal areas. While they travelled together to the south, they chatted under the lamp in the hostel. "Zongyuan, Zongyuan," said Han Yu, "your essays are as good as mine. I wrote *A Biography of Wang Chengfu, the Bricklayer* and you wrote *A Biography of a Carpenter*; I wrote *A Biography of Minister Mao Yin* and you wrote *A Biography of Hunchback Guo, the Gardener*; I wrote *A Funeral Oration to the Crocodile* and you wrote *Reminiscences of a Snake-Catcher.* So far so good. When I submitted *An Epigraph on the Pacification of Huaixi* to curry favour with the throne, you wrote in your turn *Ode to the Pacification of Huaixi*. You competed with me essay by essay. Now that we are banished to the remote regions, we are in the same boat. What has brought us together, the time, the chance or the fate?" Brother, let's forget about things in the distant past but comment on you and me. Should we deserve such destitution? Why hasn't my ancestor's essay *Pursuit for Fortune* brought any fortune to the twenty-eight generations of my family? Why hasn't your ancestor's essay *Farewell to Poverty* bid farewell to poverty

到老兄二十几辈了,还不曾送的个穷去?算来都则为时运二字所亏。

[丑]是也。春卿兄,

【前腔】

你费家资制买书田,

怎知他卖向明时不值钱。

虽然如此,你看赵佗王当时,也是个秀才陆贾,拜为奉使中大夫到此。赵佗王多少尊重他。

他归朝燕,

黄金累千。

那时汉高皇厌见读书之人,但有个带儒巾的,都拿来溺尿。这陆贾秀才,端然带了四方巾,深衣大摆,去见汉高皇。那高皇望见,这又是个掉尿鳖子的来了。便迎着陆贾骂道:"你老子用马上得天下,何用诗书?"那陆生有趣,不多应他,只回他一句:"陛下马上取天下,能以马上治之乎?"汉高皇听了,哑然一笑,说道:"便依你说。不管什么文字,念了与寡人听之。"陆大夫不慌不忙,袖里出一卷文字,恰是平日灯窗下纂集的《新语》一十三篇,高声奏上。那高皇才听了一篇,龙颜大喜。后来一篇一篇,都喝彩称善。立封他做个关内侯。那一日好不气象!休道汉高皇,便是那两班文武,见者皆呼万岁。

一言掷地,

all through the twenty-odd generations of your family? The time and the chance seem to be the only answer.

Han Zicai:

Exactly. Chunqing,

(*To the previous tune*)

You buy the books to enrich your mind,

But oft-times knowledge may be left behind.

However, Lu Jia, a scholar in Prince Zhao's times, came here on an imperial errand and was entitled a high-ranking official. How well he was received by Prince Zhao!

In honour he returned to court,

With treasures of various sorts.

Emperor Gaozu in the Han dynasty detested scholars. Whenever he saw a Confucian cap, he would piss on it. One day Lu Jia went for an audience in his square cap and dark robe. On seeing Lu Jia, Emperor Gaozu said to himself, "Another piss pot for me!" and shouted at Lu Jia, "I won my empire on horseback; what's the use of poems and books?" Lu Jia was witty enough to retort: "Your Majesty has won the empire on horseback, but can you rule over the empire on horseback?" The emperor smiled at these words and said, "True as you are, let me hear a passage." Lu Jia took his time and drew from his sleeves a scroll of *Latest Remarks*, thirteen essays written at home. The emperor was delighted when he heard the first essay, and praised each essay when they were read out. Lu Jia was immediately entitled Interior Marquis. What a glory for him! Not only the emperor but also the ministers and generals gave high credit to him.

A word of wisdom from the learned man

万岁喧天。
[生叹介]则俺连篇累牍无人见。
[合前]
[丑]再问春卿,在家何以为生?
[生]寄食园公。
[丑]依小弟说,不如干谒些须,可图前进。
[生]你不知,今人少趣哩。
[丑]老兄可知?有个钦差识宝中郎苗老先生,到是个知趣人。今秋任满,例于香山嶴多宝寺中赛宝。那时一往何如?
[生]领教。

应念愁中恨索居,
青云器业俺全疏。
越王自指高台笑,
刘项原来不读书。

Roused applause from whole clan.

Liu Mengmei:

(*Heaves a sigh*)

As for my essays, no one would like to scan.

Liu Mengmei, Han Zicai:

Oh, Gracious Heaven,

It's no use dwelling on the past;

The terrace alone will stand and last.

Han Zicai:

Chunqing, may I ask how you manage to make a living?

Liu Mengmei:

I'm living with my gardener.

Han Zicai:

In my opinion, you'd better find a patron to help you out.

Liu Mengmei:

You know, nowadays very few people care for men of learning.

Han Zicai:

Haven't you heard that Miao Shunbin, Imperial Envoy for treasure appraisal, cares for men of learning? Before his term of office ends this autumn, he will go as usual to assess treasures in the Treasure Temple near Xiangshan Bay in Macao. Shall we go and try to see him at that time?

Liu Mengmei:

I'll be glad to.

A man of sorrow fears to live alone,

Who never hopes to make himself well known.

The prince takes pride in his own terrace

While men who never read ascend the throne.

第七出　　闺　塾

[末上]"吟余改抹前春句,饭后寻思午晌茶。蚁上案头沿砚水,蜂穿窗眼咂瓶花。"我陈最良杜衙设帐,杜小姐家传《毛诗》。极承老夫人管待。今日早膳已过,我且把毛注潜玩一遍。[念介]"关关雎鸠,在河之洲。窈窕淑女,君子好逑。"好者好也,逑者求也。[看介]这早晚了,还不见女学生进馆。却也娇养的凶。待我敲三声云板。[敲云板介]春香,请小姐解书。

【绕池游】

[旦引贴捧书上]素妆才罢,

Scene Seven
Studying at Home

(*Enter Chen Zuiliang*)

Chen Zuiliang:

"I read and copy poems I wrote last spring;
After meals I guess what tea to bring.
An ant is creeping to the ink-slab pool;
A bee is sucking at blooms with its sting."

I, Chen Zuiliang, am a tutor in the prefect's residence, to teach Miss Du *The Book of Poetry*, following her family tradition. Madam Du has treated me very well. Now that breakfast is over, I'm going to review the notes on *The Book of Poetry*.

(*Reads*)

"The waterfowl would coo
Upon an islet in the brooks.
A lad would like to woo
A lass with pretty looks."

"Like" means "love" while "woo" means "seek after".

(*Looks around*)

At this late hour, there's yet no sign of my pupil. She must have been pampered badly. I have to strike the summoning plate.

(*Strikes the summoning plate*)

Chunxiang, ask Miss Du to come to class.

(*Enter Du Liniang, followed by Chunxiang with books in her hands*)

缓步书堂下。
对净几明窗潇洒。
[贴]《昔氏贤文》,
把人禁杀,
恁时节则好教鹦哥唤茶。
[见介]
[旦]先生万福。
[贴]先生少怪。
[末]凡为女子,鸡初鸣,咸盥、漱、栉、笄,问安于父母。日出之后,各供其事。如今女学生以读书为事,须要早起。
[旦]以后不敢了。
[贴]知道了。今夜不睡,三更时分,请先生上书。
[末]昨日上的《毛诗》,可温习?
[旦]温习了。则待讲解。

Du Liniang:

(*To the tune of* **Raochiyou**)

I've made up for the day

And come into my study,

A room so bright and full of ray.

Chunxiang:

Wise Sayings from the Ancient Times

Really bothers me;

It's only fit to make the parrots cry for tea.

(*Du Liniang and Chunxiang greet Mr Chen*)

Du Liniang:

I wish you happiness, respected tutor.

Chunxiang:

I wish you kindness, respected tutor.

Chen Zuiliang:

According to *The Book of Rites*, it is proper for a young mistress to get up at the first cockcrow, wash her hands, rinse her mouth, brush and comb her hair, and then pay respects to her parents. After sunrise, each will attend to her own work. And now your work is to study. You must get up early.

Du Liniang:

I won't be late from now on.

Chunxiang:

I see. I won't go to bed tonight and I shall ask you to give us lessons at midnight.

Chen Zuiliang:

Have you gone over the poem I taught yesterday?

Du Liniang:

Yes, I have. I'm expecting your interpretation today.

[末]你念来。

[旦念书介]"关关雎鸠,在河之洲。窈窕淑女,君子好逑。"

[末]听讲。"关关雎鸠",雎鸠是个鸟,关关鸟声也。

[贴]怎样声儿?

[末作鸠声][贴学鸠声诨介]

[末]此鸟性喜幽静,在河之洲。

[贴]是了。不是昨日是前日,不是今年是去年,俺衙内关着个斑鸠儿,被小姐放去,一去去在何知州家。

[末]胡说,这是兴。

[贴]兴个甚的那?

[末]兴者起也。起那下头窈窕淑女,是幽闲女子,有那等君子好好的来求他。

Chen Zuiliang:

Please read the poem.

Du Liniang:

(*Reads*)

"The waterfowl would coo

Upon an islet in the brooks.

A lad would like to woo

A lass with pretty looks."

Chen Zuiliang:

Now listen to me. "The waterfowl would coo." "Waterfowl" is a bird and "coo" describes the birdcall.

Chunxiang:

What kind of call is it?

(*Chen Zuiliang imitates the birdcall*)

(*Chunxiang imitates Chen's birdcall*)

Chen Zuiliang:

This kind of bird is fond of the quietness "upon an islet in the brooks".

Chunxiang:

That's it. It happened yesterday or the day before yesterday, this year or last year. When my young mistress set free the waterfowl in the cage, it flew to the house of Mr Brooks.

Chen Zuiliang:

Nonsense! This is an analogy.

Chunxiang:

What does it analogise?

Chen Zuiliang:

An analogy is the beginning of a poem. It leads to the pretty lass, a quiet girl wooed by a lad.

[贴]为甚好好的求他?

[末]多嘴哩。

[旦]师父,依注解书,学生自会。但把《诗经》大意,敷演一番。

【掉角色】

[末]论《六经》,《诗经》最葩,

闺门内许多风雅:

有指证,姜嫄产哇;

不嫉妒,后妃贤达。

更有那咏鸡鸣,

伤燕羽,

泣江皋,

思汉广,

洗净铅华。

有风有化,

宜室宜家。

[旦]这经文偌多?

[末]《诗》三百,一言以蔽之,

没多些,只"无邪"两字,

Chunxiang:

    Why should he give her wood?

Chen Zuiliang:

    Shut up!

Du Liniang:

    Mr Chen, I can follow the notes by myself, but will you tell me the general idea of the book?

Chen Zuiliang:

    (*To the tune of Diaojuese*)

    Among the Six Classics,

    The Book of Poetry is the best

    To tell about ladies who are blessed:

    About the life in the wild,

    There's Jiang Yuan who conceived a child;

    Against jealousy,

    There're consorts who were e'er carefree.

In other poems,

    The roosters crow at break of day;

    The swallows sadden travellers on the way;

    The river rouses great dismay;

    The streams are where the lovers stay.

    The poems in plain and simple style

    Teach the people all the while

    And build their homes in smile.

Du Liniang:

    How can it contain so many things?

Chen Zuiliang:

    In a word, of the three hundred poems in *The Book of Poetry*,

        For you, the mere short phrase

付与儿家。

书讲了。春香取文房四宝来模字。

[贴下取上]纸、墨、笔、砚在此。

[末]这什么墨?

[旦]丫头错拿了,这是螺子黛,画眉的。

[末]这什么笔?

[旦作笑介]这便是画眉细笔。

[末]俺从不曾见。拿去,拿去!这是什么纸?

[旦]薛涛笺。

[末]拿去,拿去。只拿那蔡伦造的来。这是什么砚?是一个是两个?

[旦]鸳鸯砚。

[末]许多眼?

"Without evil thought"

Is of great import.

So much for the poems. Chunxiang, fetch the stationery set for calligraphy.

Chunxiang:

Here's the paper, the ink, the brush and the ink-slab.

Chen Zuiliang:

What kind of ink is this?

Du Liniang:

She's fetched the wrong kind of ink. It's the paint for the brows.

Chen Zuiliang:

What kind of brush is this?

Du Liniang:

(*Smiles*)

It's a kind of brush to paint the brows with.

Chen Zuiliang:

I've never seen these things. Take them away! Take them away! And what kind of paper is this?

Du Liniang:

It's ladies' writing paper.

Chen Zuiliang:

Take it away! Take it away! Fetch the writing paper for the gentleman. And what kind of ink-slab is this? Is it single or double?

Du Liniang:

It's a mandarin-duck ink-slab.

Chen Zuiliang:

Why are there so many eyes on the slab?

[旦]泪眼。
[末]哭什么子?一发换了来。
[贴背介]好个标老儿!待换去。
[下换上]这可好?
[末看介]着。
[旦]学生自会临书。春香还劳把笔。
[末]看你临。
[旦写字介]
[末看惊介]我从不曾见这样好字。这什么格?
[旦]是卫夫人传下美女簪花之格。
[贴]待俺写个奴婢学夫人。
[旦]还早哩。
[贴]先生,学生领出恭牌。[下]

Du Liniang:

They are called "weeping eyes".

Chen Zuiliang:

What are they weeping for? Go and change the whole set.

Chunxiang:

(*Aside*)

What a boorish old man! I'll go and change them.

(*Exit and re-enter with a new set*)

Will these things do?

Chen Zuiliang:

(*Examines the writing-set*)

Yes.

Du Liniang:

I know how to copy the characters, but Chunxiang needs your help.

Chen Zuiliang:

I'll watch how you copy the characters.

(*Du Liniang copies*)

(*Chen Zuiliang is surprised*)

I've never seen such fine writing. What style is it?

Du Liniang:

It's the beauty-bloom style, invented by Lady Wei.

Chunxiang:

I'll imitate my young mistress.

Du Liniang:

It's too early for you to do that.

Chunxiang:

May I ask permission to wash my hands?

(*Exit Chunxiang*)

[旦]敢问师母尊年?
[末]目下平头六十。
[旦]学生待绣对鞋儿上寿,请个样儿。
[末]生受了。依《孟子》上样儿,做个"不知足而为履"罢了。
[旦]还不见春香来。
[末]要唤他么?[末叫三度介]
[贴上]害淋的。
[旦作恼介]劣丫头那里来?
[贴笑介]溺尿去来。原来有座大花园。花明柳绿,好耍子哩。
[末]哎也,不攻书,花园去。待俺取荆条来。

Du Liniang:

May I venture to ask the age of your wife?

Chen Zuiliang:

She's just reached sixty.

Du Liniang:

I'll embroider a pair of shoes for her if you tell me the pattern she likes.

Chen Zuiliang:

Thanks. As for the pattern, you can follow the teaching of *Mencius:* "Make shoes without knowing the feet."

Du Liniang:

What's the matter with Chunxiang?

Chen Zuiliang:

Shall I call her back?

(*Calls Chunxiang three times*)

(*Re-enter Chunxiang*)

Chunxiang:

Old rascal!

Du Liniang:

(*Angrily*)

Where have you been, nasty maid?

Chunxiang:

(*Smiles*)

I've been to the toilet. I went by a big garden overgrown with flowers and willows. It's fun over there.

Chen Zuiliang:

Alas! Instead of studying, you played in the garden! I'll get a cane.

Chunxiang:

[贴]荆条做什么?

【前腔】
女郎行那里应文科判衙?
止不过识字儿书涂嫩鸦。[起介]
[末]古人读书,有囊萤的,趁月亮的。
[贴]待映月,耀蟾蜍眼花;
待囊萤,把虫蚁儿活支煞。
[末]悬梁、刺股呢?
[贴]比似你悬了梁,损头发;
刺了股,添疤痆。
有甚光华!
[内叫卖花介]
[贴]小姐,你听一声声卖花,
把读书声差。
[末]又引逗小姐哩。待俺当真打一下。[末做打介]

What do you need a cane for?

(*To the previous tune*)

How can a maid

Become a scholar of the topmost grade?

It's but a literary game she played.

Chen Zuiliang:

(*Stands up*)

There were students in ancient times, who read by the light of the fireflies and the moon.

Chunxiang:

The moonlight glares the eye

While fireflies burn and die.

Chen Zuiliang:

How about the student who tied his hair to the beam to keep awake and the student who stabbed his thighs?

Chunxiang:

You hang on the beam and hurt your hair;

You stab in the thigh and leave a scar there.

What's the use even if you dare!

(*A flower-peddler's cry within*)

Listen, mistress,

A flower-peddler's cries

Distract my reading eyes.

Chen Zuiliang:

You're again diverting the attention of your mistress. I'll give you a sound beating.

(*Raises the cane*)

Chunxiang:

(*Dodges*)

[贴闪介]你待打、打这哇哇,
桃李门墙,
崄把负荆人唬煞。[贴抢荆条投地介]
[旦]死丫头,唐突了师父,快跪下。
[贴跪介]
[旦]师父看他初犯,容学生责认一遭儿。

【前腔】
手不许把秋千索拿,
脚不许把花园路踏。
[贴]则瞧罢。
[旦]还嘴,这招风嘴,
把香头来绰疤;
招花眼,
把绣针儿签瞎。
[贴]瞎了中甚用?
[旦]则要你守砚台,
跟书案,
伴"诗云",
陪"子曰",
没的争差。
[贴]争差些罢。
[旦扌尹贴发介]则问你几丝儿头发,

Oh, dear me,

A tutor beats a maid

In spite of her plea.

(*Grabs the cane and throws it to the ground*)

Du Liniang:

You naughty maid! As you have offended the tutor, down on your knees!

(*Chunxiang kneels*)

Mr Chen, as this is her first offence, it'll be enough to give her a scolding.

(*To the previous tune*)

Keep your hands off the garden swing

And keep your feet off the garden ring.

Chunxiang:

It all depends.

Du Liniang:

You're talking back!

I'll scorch your wicked mouth with incense-stick

And give your wicked eyes a needle-prick.

Chunxiang:

What can I do for you if I'm blind?

Du Liniang:

You'll hold the slab beside the desk,

Recite the poems and read the lines

And never do anything grotesque.

Chunxiang:

Please pardon me for something grotesque.

Du Liniang:

(*Seizes Chunxiang's hair*)

几条背花?
敢也怕些些夫人堂上那些家法。
[贴]再不敢了。
[旦]可知道?
[末]也罢,松这一遭儿。起来。
[贴起介]

【尾声】
[末]女弟子则争个不求闻达,
和男学生一般儿教法。
你们工课完了,方可回衙。咱和公相陪话去。
[合]怎辜负的这一弄明窗新绛纱。
[末下]
[贴作背后指末骂介]村老牛,痴老狗,一些趣也不知。
[旦作扯介]死丫头,"一日为师,终身为父",他打不的你?俺且问你那花园在那里?

How many hairs will you lack?

How many welts will be on your back?

My mother keeps whips on the stack!

Chunxiang:

I'll never do it again.

Du Liniang:

Now you understand?

Chen Zuiliang:

Well, I'll spare you this time. Stand up!

(*Chunxiang rises to her feet*)

Chen Zuiliang:

(*To the tune of Coda*)

A girl just learns for joy;

Otherwise, she's like a boy.

You may go back when your homework is done. I'll have a chat with your father.

Chen Zuiliang, Du Liniang, Chunxiang:

It is indeed a shame

To waste the time as in a game.

(*Exit Chen Zuiliang*)

Chunxiang:

(*Points scornfully at Chen's back*)

A bull! A silly old dog! He's an out-and-out boor!

Du Liniang:

(*Pulls at Chunxiang*)

You naughty maid! "Your teacher for a day is your father for a lifetime." Hasn't he got the right to beat you? By the way, where's the garden?

Chunxiang:

[贴做不说][旦做笑问介][贴指介]兀那不是!
[旦]可有什么景致?
[贴]景致么,有亭台六七座,秋千一两架。绕的流觞曲水,面着太湖山石。名花异草,委实华丽。
[旦]原来有这等一个所在,且回衙去。

[旦]也曾飞絮谢家庭,
[贴]欲化西园蝶未成。
[旦]无限春愁莫相问,
[合]绿阴终借暂时行。

(*Feigns to ignore, but points when Du Liniang asks a second time with a smile*)

Over there!

Du Liniang:

What are the sights?

Chunxiang:

As for the sights, there are half a dozen of pavilions and a couple of swings. There's a meandering stream and an artificial hill, plus beautiful flowers and grass.

Du Liniang:

I didn't know there's such a wonderful place. But let's go back to my room for the moment.

I can sing poems just as a lark;

Chunxiang:

A pity that we miss the park.

Du Liniang:

With boundless sorrows in my heart,

Du Liniang, Chunxiang:

We'll walk on lawns before it's dark.

第八出　　劝　农

【夜游朝】

[外引净扮皂隶，贴扮门子同上]何处行春开五马？
采邠风物候秾华。
竹宇闻鸠，
朱幡引鹿。
且留憩甘棠之下。
"时节时节，过了春三二月。乍晴膏雨烟浓，太守春深劝农。农重农重，缓理征徭词讼。"俺南安府在江广之间，春事颇早。想俺为太守的，深居府堂，那远乡僻坞，有抛荒游懒的，何由得知？昨已分付该县置买花酒，待本府亲自劝农。想已齐备。
[丑扮县吏上]"承行无令史，带办有农民。"禀爷

Scene Eight
Inspecting the Farms

(*Enter Du Bao, followed by his attendants and butler*)

Du Bao:

(*To the tune of* ***Yeyouchao***)

Where shall I go inspecting the farm?

I'll gather poems of springtime charm.

The turtledove's song I hear;

Behind my carriage runs the deer.

Under trees I'll take a rest in good cheer.

"The season, the season

Is now in the middle of the spring.

After timely rain the fog is thick

When I go around to check everything.

As farm-work takes the foremost place,

Peace and order I shall bring."

Spring comes early to the Nan'an Prefecture, which is located between the Yangtze River and the Guangdong Province. As a prefect, I spend most of the time in my mansion and know little about what is happening in the remote villages and who is neglecting his farm-work. Yesterday I ordered that sweet wine be prepared to reward the farmers. I believe everything is ready by now.

(*Enter the county official*)

County Official:

"I carry out the order from above

爷，劝农花酒，俱已齐备。

[外]分付起行。近乡之处，不许多人啰唣。

[众应，喝道起行介]

[外]正是："为乘阳气行春令，不是闲游玩物华。"

[下]

【前腔】

[生、末扮父老上]白发年来公事寡。

听儿童笑语喧哗。

太守巡游，

春风满马。

敢借着这务农宣化？

俺等乃是南安府清乐乡中父老。恭喜本府杜太爷，管治三年，慈祥端正，弊绝风清。凡各村乡约保甲，义仓社学，无不举行，极是地方有福。现今亲自各乡劝农，不免官亭伺候。那祗候们扛抬花酒到来也。

And have it done by villagers I love."

Your Excellency, the sweet wine for your inspection is ready.

Du Bao:

Get ready to set out. See to it that when we approach the village, people should be kept in order.

(*The attendants answer the order and the party set off*)

Du Bao:

As the poem goes,

"I'm on a tour to make sure the yields,
Not to see the sights in the fields."

(*Exeunt all*)
(*Enter village elders*)

Village Elders:

(*To the previous tune*)

Grey-hairs care less for daily strife;
The children's games enrich our life.
Here comes the prefect on his tour,
With his horse trotting slow and sure.
Will he meet the farmers, rich and poor?

We are village elders from Qingle Township of the Nan'an Prefecture. We are glad to have Prefect Du in office for three years. Kind and honest, he gets rid of evil practice and promotes virtue. In all the villages, rules and regulations are established, local organisations are set up, public granaries and village schools are in operation. It's indeed our blessing. Now he's on a tour to inspect the farms, and so we'll go and greet him in the official pavilion. Here come the bailiffs carrying sweet wine.

(*Enter the bailiffs carrying sweet wine*)

【普贤歌】

[丑、老旦扮公人,扛酒提花上]俺天生的快手贼无过。
衙舍里消消没的睃,
扛酒去前坡。
[做跌介]几乎破了哥,
摔破了花花你赖不的我。
[生、末]列位祗候哥到来。
[老旦、丑]便是这酒埕子漏了,则怕酒少,烦老官儿遮盖些。
[生、末]不妨。且抬过一边,村务里嗑酒去。
[老旦、丑下]
[生、末]地方端正坐椅,太爷到来。
[虚下]

【排歌】

[外引众上]红杏深花,
菖蒲浅芽。
春畴渐暖年华。
竹篱茅舍酒旗儿叉。
雨过炊烟一缕斜。
[生、末接介]

Bailiffs:

> (*To the tune of* **Puxiange**)
>
> We outrun thieves in chasing race;
>
> Today we leave the office without a trace,
>
> Bearing sweet wine at quick pace.
>
> (*Stumble*)
>
> We nearly spilt the wine,
>
> But the fault is not mine.

Village Elders:

Welcome to our village.

Bailiffs:

As the jar is cracked and some wine is leaking, please find some excuse for us.

Village Elders:

No problem. Put the jars aside and then have a drink in the village tavern.

> (*Step aside*)
>
> (*Exeunt the bailiffs*)

Community chiefs, put the chair in the proper place. Prefect Du is coming.

> (*Enter Du Bao with his attendants*)

Du Bao:

> (*To the tune of* **Paige**)
>
> The apricot flowers turn red
>
> And green sweet sedges spread —
>
> It's getting warmer day by day.
>
> Above the fence the tavern flags float high;
>
> While chimney smoke spirals to the sky.
>
> (*Village elders come forward to welcome Du Bao*)

[合]提壶叫,
布谷喳。
行看几日免排衙。
休头踏,
省喧哗,
怕惊他林外野人家。
[皂禀介]禀爷,到官亭。
[生、末见介]
[外]众父老,此为何乡何都?
[生、末]南安县第一都清乐乡。
[外]待我一观。[望介]
[外]美哉此乡,真个清而可乐也。你看山也清,水也清,人在山阴道上行。春云处处生。
[生、末]正是。官也清,吏也清,村民无事到公

All:

> The pelicans sing;
>
> The cuckoo songs ring;
>
> The office closes for the spring.
>
> Bring no guards;
>
> Make no clamour;
>
> Don't disturb farmers in the yards.

Attendant:

Your Excellency, here we are at the official pavilion.

(*Village elders greet Du Bao*)

Du Bao:

Respected elders, what's the name of this village and township?

Village Elders:

This is the Number One Township Qingle.

Du Bao:

Let me have a good look.

(*Looks around*)

A pretty place with a pretty name Qingle — tranquil and happy. Just look,

> "The hills are clear;
>
> The rills are clear.
>
> When you walk in the wilds,
>
> Spring clouds appear."

Village Elders:

Indeed,

> "The officials are clear;
>
> Their followers are clear.
>
> When lawsuits decrease,

庭。农歌三两声。

[外]父老，知我春游之意乎？

【八声甘州】
　　平原麦洒，
　　翠波摇翦翦，
　　绿畴如画。
　　如酥嫩雨，
　　绕塍春色蟇苴。
　　趁江南土疏田脉佳。
　　怕人户们抛荒力不加。
　　还怕，有那无头官事，
　　误了你好生涯。

[生、末]以前昼有公差，夜有盗警。老爷到后呵，

【前腔】
　　千村转岁华。
　　愚父老香盆，
　　儿童竹马。
　　阳春有脚，
　　经过百姓人家。
　　月明无犬吠黄花，
　　雨过有人耕绿野。
　　真个，村村雨露桑麻。

[内歌《泥滑喇》介]

The pastorals appear."

Du Bao:

Respected elders, do you know the purpose of my spring inspection?

(*To the tune of* **Bashengganzhou**)

When wheat grows lush in the fields,

Green waves rise and fall,

Predicting bumper yields.

Gentle is the rain

That moistens the plain.

As the fields are richly spaced,

I hate to have them lie in waste.

I also fear that pointless feud

Delays the work you've pursued.

Village Elders:

In the old days, we were harassed by the officials during the day and by the burglars during the night, but since Your Excellency took office,

(*To the previous tune*)

Our life is turning better day by day.

That's why we elders greet you on the way

And children hail you while they play.

Like spring sunshine from above,

You shower us with endless love.

When dogs no longer bark at night

And farmers plough the fields with might,

The country life presents a thriving sight.

(*The song "The Slippery Track" is heard from within*)

Du Bao:

[外]前村田歌可听。

【孝白歌】

[净扮田夫上]泥滑喇,
脚支沙,
短耙长犁滑律的拿。
夜雨撒菇麻,
天晴出粪渣,
香风馣鲊。

[外]歌的好。"夜雨撒菇麻,天晴出粪渣,香风馣鲊",是说那粪臭。父老呵,他却不知这粪是香的。有诗为证:"焚香列鼎奉君王,馔玉炊金饱即妨。直到饥时闻饭过,龙涎不及粪渣香。"与他插花赏酒。

[净插花赏酒,笑介]好老爷,好酒。

[合]官里醉流霞,
风前笑插花,

Listen, there rings a village song.

(*Enter a farmer*)

Farmer:

(*To the tune of* **Xiaobaige**)

Along the slippery track

I glide my way,

With a rake and a plough upon my back.

I sow the seedlings after nightly rain

And spread manure in sunny weather,

With stinky smell across the plain.

Du Bao:

It's indeed a good song.

"I sow the seedlings after nightly rain

And spread manure in sunny weather,

With stinky smell across the plain."

He's referring to the stink of the manure, but respected elders, he fails to realise that the manure can be fragrant. As is said in a poem,

"While sumptuous dinners scarcely bring

Delicious savour to a king,

The smell of rice in hungry times

Is better than a fragrant thing."

Give him flowers to wear and some wine to drink.

Farmer:

(*Smiles as he puts on the flowers and drinks the wine*)

Thank you, my good lord, the wine tastes good.

All:

The tasty wine from gracious lord

And flowers on my head

把农夫们俊煞。[下]

[门子禀介]一个小厮唱的来也。

【前腔】

[丑扮牧童拿笛上]春鞭打,
笛儿吵,
倒牛背斜阳闪暮鸦。
[笛指门子介]他一样小腰抱,
一般双髻丫,
能骑大马。
[外]歌的好。怎生指着门子唱"一样小腰抱,一般双髻丫,能骑大马"?父老,他怎知骑牛的到稳。有诗为证:"常羡人间万户侯,只知骑马胜骑牛。今朝马上看山色,争似骑牛得自由。"赏他酒,插花去。

[丑插花饮酒介]

Are farmers' best reward.

(*Exit the farmer*)

Butler:

(*Reports*)

Here comes a cowboy singing.

(*Enter a cowboy with a flute in his hand*)

Cowboy:

(*To the previous tune*)

A whip in hand,

A flute on lips,

I ride an ox upon its hips.

(*Points his flute at the butler*)

He's of my size

And wears my hair,

But rides a mighty mare!

Du Bao:

He sings a good song, but why should he point at the butler and sing,

"*He's of my size*

And wears my hair,

But rides a mighty mare?"

Respected elders, he fails to know that an ox provides a steadier ride. As is said in a poem,

"*I used to envy wealthy men,*

Who ride the horses now and then.

Yet when I ride a horse in hills,

I'd rather ride an ox again."

Give him flowers to wear and some wine to drink.

(*The cowboy puts on the flowers and drinks the wine*)

[合]官里醉流霞，
风前笑插花，
村童们俊煞。[下]
[门子禀介]一对妇人歌的来也。

【前腔】
[旦、老旦采桑上]那桑阴下，
柳篓儿搓，
顺手腰身翦一丫。
呀，什么官员在此？
俺罗敷自有家，
便秋胡怎认他，
提金下马？
[外]歌的好。说与他，不是鲁国秋胡，不是秦家使君，是本府太爷劝农。见此勤劬采桑，可敬也。有诗为证："一般桃李听笙歌，此地桑阴十亩多。不比世间闲草木，丝丝叶叶是绫罗。"领酒，插花去。

All:
>The tasty wine from the gracious lord
>
>And flowers on my head
>
>Are cowboys' best reward.
>
>(*Exit the cowboy*)

Butler:
>(*Reports*)
>
>Here come two women singing.
>
>(*Enter a young woman and an old woman, picking mulberry leaves*)

Two Women:
>(*To the previous tune*)
>
>Under mulberry trees,
>
>With baskets on our backs
>
>We pick the leaves at ease.
>
>Oh, who is the official over there?
>
>Like Luo Fu who had her man,
>
>We'll not be tempted as of old
>
>By silver or expensive gold.

Du Bao:
>They sing a good song. Tell them that I'm not a man who flirts with women in the old days. I am the prefect inspecting the farms. I respect them for they work hard picking mulberry leaves. As is said in a poem,
>
>>"The peach and plum inspire the song,
>>
>>But mulberry trees here are ten acres strong.
>>
>>Unlike the useless plants that grow around,
>>
>>They turn out silk that will prolong."
>
>Give them flowers to wear and some wine to drink.

[二旦背插花，饮酒介]
[合]官里醉流霞，
风前笑插花，
采桑人俊煞。[下]
[门子禀介]又一对妇人唱的来也。

【前腔】
[老旦、丑持筐采茶上]乘谷雨，
采新茶，
一旗半枪金缕芽。
呀，什么官员在此？
学士雪炊他，
书生困想他，
竹烟新瓦。
[外]歌的好。说与他，不是邮亭学士，不是阳羡书生，是本府太爷劝农。看你妇女们采桑采茶，胜如采花。有诗为证："只因天上少茶星，地下先开百草精。闲煞女郎贪斗草，风光不似斗茶清。"领了酒，插花去。

(*The women put on the flowers and drink the wine*)

All:

The tasty wine from gracious lord

And flowers on our heads

Are mulberry pickers' best reward.

(*Exeunt the two women*)

Butler:

(*Reports*)

Here come two more women singing.

(*Enter two women, carrying baskets and plucking tea-leaves*)

Two Women:

(*To the previous tune*)

In late spring days

We pluck the fresh tea-leaves,

Leaves of topmost tea on trays.

Oh, who is the official over there?

A scholar brews the tea with snow;

A weary student longs for tea —

They both make tea with fire aglow.

Du Bao:

They sing a good song. Tell them that I'm not the famous scholar or weary student in the old days. I am the prefect inspecting the farms. I admire them for they work hard plucking tea-leaves. As is said in a poem,

"*As there's no tea-star in the sky,*

The young tea-nymph on earth is sly.

When girls engage in bets for tea,

In grander games the men would vie."

Give them flowers to wear and some wine to drink.

[老旦、丑插花，饮酒介]
[合]官里醉流霞，
风前笑插花，
采茶人俊煞。[下]
[生、末跪介]禀老爷，众父老茶饭伺候。
[外]不消。余花余酒，父老们领去，给散小乡村，也见官府劝农之意。叫祗候们起马。
[生、末做攀留不许介]
[起叫介]村中男妇领了花赏了酒的，都来送太爷。

【清江引】
[前各众插花上]黄堂春游韵潇洒，
身骑五花马。
村务里有光华，
花酒藏风雅。
男女们请了，你德政碑随路打。[下]

(*The women put on the flowers and drink the wine*)

All:

The tasty wine from gracious lord

And flowers on our heads

Are tea-leaf pluckers' best reward.

(*Exeunt the two women*)

Village Elders:

(*Kneel*)

Your Excellency, the villagers have set the table for dinner in your honour.

Du Bao:

There's no need for the trouble. Just take the flowers and wine that remain to share with people in smaller villages as a token for the government's concern for farming. Tell the attendants to get ready to start.

Village Elders:

(*Rise to their feet and call out loudly when they fail to detain Du Bao*)

Those who have received the flowers and the wine, come forward to see His Excellency off.

(*Enter Farmer, Cowboy, Four women, wearing flowers*)

Farmer, Cowboy, Four Women:

(*To the tune of* **Qingjiangyin**)

On his grand inspection tour,

The prefect rides a horse that looks so fine.

He brings to us his deep concern

With his flowers and wine.

Come along, villagers,

We'll sing of deeds that'll always shine.

间阎缭绕接山巅,
春草青青万顷田。
日暮不辞停五马,
桃花红近竹林边。

(*Exeunt*)

Du Bao:
> The houses wind their way uphill,
> With verdant fields along the rill.
> When I halt my horse at dusk,
> I see peach blossoms glowing still.

第九出　　肃　苑

【一江风】
　　[贴上]小春香,
　　一种在人奴上,
　　画阁里从娇养。
　　侍娘行,
　　弄粉调朱,
　　贴翠拈花,
　　惯向妆台傍。
　　陪他理绣床,
　　陪他烧夜香。
　　小苗条吃的是夫人杖。
"花面丫头十三四,春来绰约省人事。终须等着个助情花,处处相随步步觑。"俺春香日夜跟随小姐。看他名为国色,实守家声。嫩脸娇羞,老成尊重。只因老爷延师教授,读到《毛诗》第一章:"窈窕淑女,君子好逑。"悄然废书而叹曰:"圣人之

Scene Nine
Cleaning the Garden

(*Enter Chunxiang*)

Chunxiang:

(*To the tune of* **Yijiangfeng**)

I am Chunxiang, a little maid;

Long favoured by my miss,

Within her rooms I've stayed.

I wait on her,

Make up for her,

Dress up for her,

And stand by her.

I do silk-work with care

And listen to her prayer,

But Madam gives me punishment unfair.

"*A pretty lass in early teens*

Has sensed the female ways and means.

A young man of the proper kind

Will wholly occupy her mind."

I've been attending on my young mistress day and night. Beautiful as she is, she places her family honour in the first place. Gentle and shy as she is, she is in fact sombre and elegant. Her father has engaged a tutor for her. When she read the first poem in *The Book of Poetry* and came across the lines

"*A lad would like to woo*

A lass with pretty looks",

情,尽见于此矣。今古同怀,岂不然乎?"春香因而进言:"小姐读书困闷,怎生消遣则个?"小姐一会沉吟,逡巡而起。便问道:"春香,你教我怎生消遣那?"俺便应道:"小姐,也没个甚法儿,后花园走走罢。"小姐说:"死丫头,老爷闻知怎好?"春香应说:"老爷下乡,有几日了。"小姐低回不语者久之,方才取过历书选看。说明日不佳,后日欠好,除大后日,是个小游神吉期。预唤花郎,扫清花径。我一时应了,则怕老夫人知道。却也由他。且自叫那小花郎分付去。呀,回廊那厢,陈师父来了。正是:"年光到处皆堪赏,说与痴翁总不知。"

【前腔】

[末上]老书堂,
　暂借扶风帐。
　日暖钩帘荡。

she quietly laid down the book and sighed, "In these lines are revealed the passions of the sage to the fullest extent. Isn't it true that people in ancient times and in modern times share the same passions?" On hearing her words, I suggested, "If you're tired of reading the books, why don't you try to have some fun?" After a few moments of hesitation, she rose to her feet and asked, "Chunxiang, what fun would you suggest that I have?" I replied, "Well, my mistress, as far as I can see, why don't we take a stroll in the back garden?" She said, "Nonsense, what if my father should find it out?" I answered, "Lord Du has been to the countryside for several days." She walked up and down the room without a word for quite a few moments before she began to consult a calendar. "Tomorrow's no good," she said, "The day after tomorrow is little better, and only the next day will be auspicious because it is the day of the god of minor trips." She told me to order the gardener to clean the garden paths. I said yes but I'm afraid that Madam will find it out. I have to wait and see. For the moment I'll go and tell the gardener. Alas, here comes Tutor Chen along the corridor. As the poem goes,

"The springtime here is full of glee;
Old fools alone will fail to see."
(*Enter Chen Zuiliang*)

Chen Zuiliang:

(*To the previous tune*)
The scholar in old age
Is teaching here to earn some wage,
With classroom curtains flapping in the sun.
Now,

呀，那回廊，
小立双鬟，
似语无言，
近看如何相？
是春香，问你恩官在那厢？
夫人在那厢？
女书生怎不把书来上？
[贴]原来是陈师父。俺小姐这几日没工夫上书。
[末]为甚？
[贴]听呵，

【前腔】
甚年光！
忒煞通明相，
所事关情况。
[末]有什么情况？
[贴]老师父还不知，老爷怪你哩。
[末]何事？
[贴]说你讲《毛诗》，毛的忒精了。小姐呵，

On the corridor

   Stands a young girl with coiled hair,

   Who seems to murmur something.

   I'll go and see who's staying there.

 Oh, it's Chunxiang. Tell me,

   Where is the gracious master?

   Where is the madam?

   What keeps my pupil from attending class?

Chunxiang:

   Hello, Mr Chen. My young mistress has no time to attend class these days.

Chen Zuiliang:

   What's she doing now?

Chunxiang:

   Let me tell you.

   (*To the previous tune*)

   In this time of the year,

   You should be smart enough to know

   That there is something severe.

Chen Zuiliang:

   What is it?

Chunxiang:

   Don't you know, Mr Chen, that the master is angry with you?

Chen Zuiliang:

   What is he angry for?

Chunxiang:

   He says that your exposition of *The Book of Poetry* goes way too far. For the young mistress,

   These poems of ancient art

为诗章,讲动情肠。
[末]则讲了个"关关雎鸠"。
[贴]故此了。小姐说,关了的雎鸠,尚然有洲渚之兴,可以人而不如鸟乎!
书要埋头,那景致则抬头望。
如今分付,明后日游后花园。
[末]为甚去游?
[贴]他平白地为春伤。
因春去的忙,
后花园要把春愁漾。
[末]一发不该了。
【前腔】
论娘行,
出入人观望,
步起须屏障。
春香,你师父靠天也六十来岁,从不晓得伤个春,从不曾游个花园。
[贴]为甚?

Have touched her to the heart.

Chen Zuiliang:

I've just started with the very first line "The waterfowl would coo".

Chunxiang:

That's it. The young mistress said, "Now that a caged waterfowl would like to coo upon an islet in the brooks, how could a human being be less passionate!"

Delve deep in books by all means,

And raise your head to view the scenes.

She's told me to get ready for a stroll to the back garden in a day or two.

Chen Zuiliang:

What's her intent for the visit?

Chunxiang:

With spirits low when spring is on the way,

She fears that spring would leave too soon,

And in the back garden,

She'll try to cast her woe away.

Chen Zuiliang:

How can she do that!

(*To the previous tune*)

When a girl proceeds from place to place,

She has to wear a veil

Lest man should see her face.

I'm over sixty, but I've never worried about the hasty passage of spring nor been sightseeing in a garden.

Chunxiang:

Why?

Chen Zuiliang:

[末]你不知,孟夫子说的好,圣人千言万语,则要人"收其放心"。
但如常,
着甚春伤?
要甚春游?
你放春归,怎把心儿放?
小姐既不上书,我且告归几日。春香呵,
你寻常到讲堂,
时常向琐窗,
怕燕泥香点涴在琴书上。
我去了。"绣户女郎闲斗草,下帷老子不窥园。"
[下]
[贴吊场]且喜陈师父去了。叫花郎在么?
[叫介]花郎!

【普贤歌】
[丑扮小花郎醉上]一生花里小随衙,
偷去街头学卖花。
令史们将我揸,
祗候们将我搭,
狠烧刀、险把我嫩盘肠生灌杀。

Haven't you heard that the sage Mencius' sayings can be boiled down to this: men should "restrain his strayed heart"?

    If you stick to the normal state of mind,

    Why do you feel depressed in spring?

    Why do you need spring tour of any kind?

Upon your return from the sightseeing,

    Nothing but disquiet you'll bring.

Since the young mistress is not going to class, I'll leave for home for a few days. Chunxiang,

    Please often go to the classroom

    And check the windows with looped hooks,

    Lest the swallows soil the books.

I'm leaving now.

    "Young ladies play grass games to waste their prime;

    Old scholars read the classics all the time."

    (*Exit Chen Zuiliang*)

Chunxiang:

    (*To herself*)

Mr Chen is gone at last. Where on earth is the gardener?

    (*Calls out*)

Gardener!

    (*Enter the young gardener, in a tipsy state*)

Young Gardener:

    (*To the tune of* ***Puxiange***)

    Tending flowers is what I do,

    But sometimes I sell a few.

    The sheriffs may catch me,

    The sergeants may grab me,

    And now strong liquor nearly kills me.

［见介］春姐在此。
［贴］好打。私出衙前骗酒,这几日菜也不送。
［丑］有菜夫。
［贴］水也不视。
［丑］有水夫。
［贴］花也不送。
［丑］每早送花,夫人一分,小姐一分。
［贴］还有一分哩?
［丑］这该打。
［贴］你叫什么名字?
［丑］花郎。
［贴］你把花郎的意思,挡个曲儿俺听。挡的好,饶打。
［丑］使得。

(*Greets Chunxiang*)

Hi, Chunxiang.

Chunxiang:

You deserve a sound beating, sneaking out to the streets and wining around. And you haven't delivered vegetables for days.

Young Gardener:

That's the greengrocer's business.

Chunxiang:

And you haven't carried the water yet.

Young Gardener:

That's the water carrier's business.

Chunxiang:

And you haven't delivered the flowers yet.

Young Gardener:

I deliver the flowers every morning, one bunch for the madam and another bunch for the young mistress.

Chunxiang:

And yet another bunch for me?

Young Gardener:

Oh, I'm to blame.

Chunxiang:

What's your name?

Young Gardener:

They just call me Gardener.

Chunxiang:

Well, just make up a song to explain your name. If I like the song, I'll spare the rod.

Young Gardener:

Please listen,

【梨花儿】
　　小花郎看尽了花成浪，
　　则春姐花沁的水洸浪。
　　和你这日高头偷眼眼，
　　嗏，好花枝干鳖了作么朗！
　　[贴]待俺还你也哥。
【前腔】
　　小花郎做尽花儿浪，
　　小郎当夹细的大当郎？
　　[丑]哎哟，
　　[贴]俺待到老爷回时说一浪，
　　[采丑发介]嗏，敢几个小榔头把你分的朗。
　　[丑倒介]罢了，姐姐为甚事光降小园？
　　[贴]小姐大后日来瞧花园，好些扫除花径。
　　[丑]知道了。

　　东郊风物正薰馨，
　　应喜家山接女星。
　　莫遣儿童触红粉，
　　便教莺语太丁宁。

(*To the tune of Lihuaer*)

I've seen so many flowers surge and surge,

But from the flowers you emerge.

Let's go and seek for pleasure in the day;

Ah,

At dusk a morning bud may sing its dirge!

Chunxiang:

Now it's my turn,

(*To the previous tune*)

You've seen too many flowers surge and surge,

But can you have me now that I emerge?

Young Gardener:

Oops!

Chunxiang:

When I report to Master of your words,

(*Grasps the Young Gardener by the hair*)

I'm sure you'll have a pleasant scourge.

Young Gardener:

(*Topples*)

Now I give up. Well, what has brought you here to the garden?

Chunxiang:

The young mistress is coming to visit the garden in two days.

So be sure to clean the garden paths.

Young Gardener:

Yes, I see.

In eastern suburbs flowers are at their best;

By Lady Star is hometown fully blessed.

Once lads and lasses are aware of love,

Their youthful hearts can hardly be suppressed.

第十出　惊　梦

【绕池游】
　　[旦上]梦回莺啭,
　　乱煞年光遍。
　　人立小庭深院。
　　[贴]炷尽沉烟,
　　抛残绣线,
　　恁今春关情似去年?
　　[旦]"晓来望断梅关,宿妆残。
　　[贴]你侧着宜春髻子恰凭阑。
　　[旦]翦不断,理还乱,闷无端。
　　[贴]已分付催花莺燕借春看。"

Scene Ten
An Amazing Dream

(*Enter Du Liniang with Chunxiang*)

Du Liniang:

(*To the tune of* **Raochiyou**)

When I'm awakened by the orioles' songs

And find the springtime beauty all around,

I stand in deep thought on the courtyard ground.

Chunxiang:

With burnt incense

And silk yarns scattered here and there,

This spring no longer holds back maidens fair.

Du Liniang:

"With the distant pass in view at dawn,

In my night-gown I stand forlorn.

Chunxiang:

In spring-style braid,

You lean against the balustrade.

Du Liniang:

That which scissors cannot sever,

And, sorted out, is tangled again,

Makes me bored than ever.

Chunxiang:

I've told the early birds

To meet the spring and send your words."

Du Liniang:

[旦]春香,可曾叫人扫除花径?
[贴]分付了。
[旦]取镜台衣服来。
[贴取镜台衣服上]"云髻罢梳还对镜,罗衣欲换更添香。"镜台衣服在此。

【步步娇】
[旦]袅晴丝吹来闲庭院,
摇漾春如线。
停半晌、整花钿。
没揣菱花,
偷人半面,
迤逗的彩云偏。
[行介]步香闺怎便把全身现!
[贴]今日穿插的好。

【醉扶归】
[旦]你道翠生生出落的裙衫儿茜,
艳晶晶花簪八宝填,
可知我常一生儿爱好是天然。

Have you ordered the garden paths to be cleaned, Chunxiang?

Chunxiang:

Yes, I have.

Du Liniang:

Bring my mirror and gowns.

(*Exit and re-enter Chunxiang with the mirror and gowns*)

Chunxiang:

"Face the mirror when she's done her hairs;

Perfume the gowns once more before she wears."

Here's the mirror and gowns.

Du Liniang:

(*To the tune of Bubujiao*)

In the courtyard drifts the willow-threads,

Torn by spring breeze into flimsy shreds.

I pause awhile

To do my hairstyle.

When all at once

The mirror glances at my face,

I tremble and my hair slips out of lace.

(*Walks in the room*)

As I pace the room,

How can anyone see me in full bloom!

Chunxiang:

You're so pretty today.

Du Liniang:

(*To the tune of Zuifugui*)

You say my dress is fine

And hairpins shine,

But love of beauty is my natural design.

恰三春好处无人见。
不提防沉鱼落雁鸟惊喧,
则怕的羞花闭月花愁颤。
[贴]早茶时了,请行。
[行介]你看:"画廊金粉半零星,池馆苍苔一片青。
踏草怕泥新绣袜,惜花疼煞小金铃。"
[旦]不到园林,怎知春色如许!

【皂罗袍】
原来姹紫嫣红开遍,
似这般都付与断井颓垣。
良辰美景奈何天,
赏心乐事谁家院!
恁般景致,我老爷和奶奶再不提起。
[合]朝飞暮卷,
云霞翠轩;
雨丝风片,
烟波画船
——锦屏人忒看的这韶光贱!
[贴]是花都放了,那牡丹还早。

My beauty is concealed in the hall,

But it'll make fish delve and birds fall

And outshine blooms, the moon and all.

Chunxiang:

It's time for breakfast. Let's go.

(*Begins to move*)

Look,

"How the painted corridor shines!

How green the moss appears in endless lines!

To walk on grass I fear to soil my socks;

To love the blooms I want to keep them under locks."

Du Liniang:

If I had not come to the garden, how could I have tasted the beauty of spring!

(*To the tune of* **Zaoluopao**)

The flowers glitter brightly in the air,

Around the wells and walls deserted here and there.

Where is the "pleasant day and pretty sight"?

Who can enjoy "contentment and delight"?

Mom and Dad have never mentioned such pretty sights.

Du Liniang, Chunxiang:

The clouds at dawn and rain at dusk,

The bowers in the evening rays,

The threads of shower in gales of wind,

The painted boat in hazy sprays:

All are foreign to secluded maids.

Chunxiang:

All the seasonal flowers are in full blossom, but it's still too early for the peony.

【好姐姐】
　　[旦]遍青山啼红了杜鹃，
　　荼蘼外烟丝醉软。
　　春香呵，牡丹虽好，
　　他春归怎占的先！
　　[贴]成对儿莺燕呵。
　　[合]闲凝眄，
　　生生燕语明如翦，
　　呖呖莺歌溜的圆。
　　[旦]去罢。
　　[贴]这园子委是观之不足也。
　　[旦]提他怎的！[行介]
【隔尾】
　　观之不足由他缱，
　　便赏遍了十二亭台是枉然。
　　到不如兴尽回家闲过遣。
　　[作到介]
　　[贴]"开我西阁门，展我东阁床。瓶插映山紫，炉

Du Liniang:

(*To the tune of* **Haojiejie**)

Amid the red azaleas cuckoos sing;

Upon roseleaf raspberries willow-threads cling.

Oh, Chunxiang,

The peony is fair indeed,

But comes the latest on the mead.

Chunxiang:

Look at the orioles and swallows in pairs!

Du Liniang, Chunxiang:

When we cast a casual eye,

The swallows chatter and swiftly fly

While orioles sing their way across the sky.

Du Liniang:

It's time to leave.

Chunxiang:

There's more than enough to be seen in the garden.

Du Liniang:

No more about it.

(*Du Liniang and Chunxiang begin to leave*)

(*To the tune of* **Quasi-coda**)

It's true that there's more than enough to be seen,

But what though we visit all the scenic spots?

We'd better find more fun behind the screen.

(*They arrive at the chamber*)

Chunxiang:

"I open doors of chambers east and west

And sit on my own bed to take a rest.

I put azalea in the earthen vase

添沉水香。"小姐,你歇息片时,俺瞧老夫人去也。[下]

[旦叹介]"默地游春转,小试宜春面。"春呵,得和你两留连,春去如何遣?咳,恁般天气,好困人也。春香那里?[作左右瞧介][又低首沉吟介]天呵,春色恼人,信有之乎!常观诗词乐府,古之女子,因春感情,遇秋成恨,诚不谬矣。吾今年已二八,未逢折桂之夫;忽慕春情,怎得蟾宫之客?昔日韩夫人得遇于郎,张生偶逢崔氏,曾有《题红记》、《崔徽传》二书。此佳人才子,前以密约偷期,后皆得成秦晋。[长叹介]吾生于宦族,长在名门。年已及笄,不得早成佳配,诚为虚度青春,光阴如过隙耳。[泪介]可惜妾身颜色如花,岂料命如一叶乎!

And add incense unto the proper place."

Mistress, please take a rest now and I'll go and see the madam.

(*Exit*)

Du Liniang:

(*Sighs*)

"Back from a brief spring tour,
I know my beauty now for sure."

Oh spring, now that I love you so much, what shall I do when you are gone? How dizzy I feel in such weather! Where's Chunxiang?

(*Looks around and lowers her head again, murmuring*)

Oh heavens! Now I do believe that spring is annoying. It is true indeed what is written in various kinds of poems about maidens in ancient times, who felt passionate in spring and grieved in autumn. I've turned sixteen now, but no one has come to ask for my hand. Stirred by the spring passion, where can I come across one who will go after me? In the past Lady Han met a scholar named Yu, and Scholar Zhang came across Miss Cui. Their love stories have been recorded in the books *The Story of the Maple Leaves* and *The Life of Cui Hui*. These lovely ladies and talented scholars started with furtive dating but ended in happy reunion.

(*Heaves a long sigh*)

Born and brought up in a renowned family of high officialdom, I've come of age but haven't found a fiancé yet. I'm wasting my youth that will soon pass.

(*Weeps*)

What a pity that my face is as pretty as a flower but my fate is as dreary as a leaf!

【山坡羊】
没乱里春情难遣,
蓦地里怀人幽怨。
则为俺生小婵娟,
拣名门一例、一例里神仙眷。
甚良缘,
把青春抛的远!
俺的睡情谁见?
则索因循腼腆。
想幽梦谁边,
和春光暗流转?
迁延,
这衷怀那处言!
淹煎,
泼残生,
除问天!
身子困乏了,且自隐几而眠。[睡介][梦生介]
[生持柳枝上]"莺逢日暖歌声滑,人遇风情笑口开。一径落花随水入,今朝阮肇到天台。"小生顺路儿跟着杜小姐回来,怎生不见?[回看介]呀,小姐,小姐!

(*To the tune of* **Shanpoyang**)

Indulged in springtime passion of all sorts,

I'm all of a sudden roused to plaintive thoughts.

I have a pretty face

And so my spouse must be as good,

With a noble place.

What is there to meet my fate

That I must waste my youth to wait!

When I go to bed, who'll peep

At my shyness in my sleep?

With whom shall I lie in my secret dream,

Drifting down the springtime stream?

Tormented day by day,

To whom can I say

About my woe,

About my wretched fate?

Only the heavens know!

I feel dizzy. I'll lean on the table and take a short nap.

(*Falls asleep and begins to dream*)

(*Enter Liu Mengmei with a willow-twig in his hand*)

Liu Mengmei:

"In warm days oriole's songs ring apace

While man in deep affection has a smiling face.

I chase the fragrant petals in the stream,

To find the fair lady in my dream."

I follow the footsteps of Miss Du along the path, but how is it that I lose sight of her now?

(*Looks back*)

Hi, Miss Du! Hi, Miss Du!

[旦作惊起介][相见介]

[生]小生那一处不寻访小姐来,却在这里!

[旦作斜视不语介]

[生]恰好花园内,折取垂柳半枝。姐姐,你既淹通书史,可作诗以赏此柳枝乎?

[旦惊喜,欲言又止介][背想]这生素昧平生,何因到此?

[生笑介]小姐,咱爱杀你哩!

【山桃红】则为你如花美眷,

　　似水流年,

　　是答儿闲寻遍。

　　在幽闺自怜。

　　小姐,和你那答儿讲话去。

[旦作含笑不行][生作牵衣介]

[旦低问]那边去?

[生]转过这芍药栏前,紧靠着湖山石边。

(*Du Liniang rises in astonishment and greets Liu Mengmei*)

I've been looking for you here and there. Now I find you at last.

(*Du Liniang looks aside without a word*)

I just snapped a willow-twig in the garden. Miss Du, as you are well versed in classics, why don't you write a poem to honour the twig?

(*In happy astonishment, Du Liniang is about to speak but holds back her tongue*)

Du Liniang:

(*Aside*)

I've never seen this young man before. Why does he come here?

Liu Mengmei:

(*With a smile*)

I'm up to the neck in love with you, Miss Du!

(*To the tune of **Shantaohong***)

For you, a maiden fair,

With beauty that will soon fade,

I've been searching here and there,

But alone in chamber you have stayed.

Come with me and let's have a chat over there, Miss Du.

(*Du Liniang smiles but does not move*)

(*Liu Mengmei pulls her by the sleeve*)

Du Liniang:

(*In a subdued voice*)

Where to?

Liu Mengmei:

Beyond the rose grove,

[旦低问]秀才,去怎的?
[生低答]和你把领扣松,衣带宽,
袖梢儿揾着牙儿苫也,
则待你忍耐温存一晌眠。
[旦作羞][生前抱][旦推介]
[合]是那处曾相见,
相看俨然,
早难道这好处相逢无一言?
[生强抱旦下]
[末扮花神束发冠,红衣插花上]"催花御史惜花天,检点春工又一年。蘸客伤心红雨下,勾人悬梦彩云边。"吾乃掌管南安府后花园花神是也。因杜知府小姐丽娘,与柳梦梅秀才,后日有姻缘之分。杜小姐游春感伤,致使柳秀才入梦。咱花神专掌惜玉怜

Beside the mount we'll rove.

Du Liniang:

(*In a subdued voice*)

What to do, sir?

Liu Mengmei:

(*Also in a subdued voice*)

I shall unbutton your gown

And strip it down.

You'll bite your sleeve-top with your teeth,

Then make a hug and lie beneath.

(*Du Liniang is shy, but Liu Mengmei comes forward to embrace her. She feigns to push him away*)

Liu Mengmei, Du Liniang:

Is it absurd

That we seem to meet somewhere before

But stand here face to face without a word?

(*Exit Liu Mengmei, holding Du Liniang in his arms*)

(*Enter Flower God with bundled hair, dressed in red and strewn with flowers*)

Flower God:

"The flower god looks after flowers here

And keeps the springtime busy year by year.

When petals fall from flowers in a rain,

The flower gazer starts to dream in vain."

I am the flower god in charge of the prefect's back garden in Nan'an. As the prefect's daughter Du Liniang and the scholar Liu Mengmei are predestined to get married, Miss Du is so affected by her spring tour that she has enticed Liu Mengmei into her dream. I am a flower god to take care of all the beau-

香,竟来保护他,要他云雨十分欢幸也。

【鲍老催】

[末]单则是混阳蒸变,
看他似虫儿般蠢动把风情扇。
一般儿娇凝翠绽魂儿颤。
这是景上缘,
想内成,因中见。
呀,淫邪展污了花台殿。
咱待拈片落花儿惊醒他。[向鬼门丢花介]
他梦酣春透了怎留连?
拈花闪碎的红如片。
秀才才到的半梦儿;梦毕之时,好送杜小姐仍归香阁。吾神去也。[下]

【山桃红】

[生、旦携手上]
[生]这一霎天留人便,
草藉花眠。
小姐可好?
[旦低头介]
[生]则把云鬟点,
红松翠偏。
小姐休忘了呵,见了你紧相偎,
慢厮连,

ties in this area, and so I've come here to protect her in order that she will enjoy herself to the full.

(*To the tune of Baolaocui*)

In the surge of earth and sky,

He swirls like a busy bee

And glares the flowery maiden's eye.

That is a meeting in the dream,

A wedding in the mind,

An outcome of the fate

That brings defilement of the foulest kind.

I'll drop a flower petal to wake her up.

(*Scatters some petals to the entrance of the stage*)

How can they tear themselves away from dream?

They'll wake up when the petals gleam.

The scholar is still indulged in his dream, but when he wakes up, he'll see Miss Du to her chamber. I've got to go now.

(*Exit*)

(*Enter Liu Mengmei and Du Liniang, hand in hand*)

Liu Mengmei:

(*To the tune of Shantaohong*)

With heaven and earth as our bridal room,

We sleep on grass and bloom.

Are you all right, my dear?

(*Du Liniang lowers her head*)

Look at her pretty hair,

Loosened here and there.

Please never forget the day when we

Lie together side by side,

Make love for hours and hours,

恨不得肉儿般团成片也,
逗的个日下胭脂雨上鲜。
[旦]秀才,你可去呵?
[合]是那处曾相见,
相看俨然,
早难道这好处相逢无一言?
[生]姐姐,你身子乏了,将息,将息。[送旦依前作睡介][轻拍旦介]姐姐,俺去了。[作回顾介]姐姐,你可十分将息,我再来瞧你那。"行来春色三分雨,睡去巫山一片云。"[下]
[旦作惊醒,低叫介]秀才,秀才,你去了也?[又作痴睡介]
[老旦上]"夫婿坐黄堂,娇娃立绣窗。怪他裙衩上,花鸟绣双双。"孩儿,孩儿,你为甚瞌睡在此?

And hug as man and bride,

With your face red as flowers.

Du Liniang:

Are you leaving now, my love?

Liu Mengmei, Du Liniang:

Is it absurd

That we seem to meet somewhere before

But stand here face to face without a word?

Liu Mengmei:

You must be tired, my dear. Sleep awhile, sleep awhile!

(*Sees Du Liniang to her sleeping position, and pats her on the back*)

I'm going, my dear.

(*Looks back*)

Please sleep awhile, my dear, and I'll come and see you again.

"She comes like gentle rain in spring

And wets me like clouds on the wing."

(*Exit*)

Du Liniang:

(*Wakes up with a start and murmurs*)

Are you leaving, my love?

(*Dozes off again*)

(*Enter Zhen*)

Zhen:

"*My husband holds high office here;*

My daughter stays without much cheer.

Her worry comes from skirts she wears,

With blooms and birds adorned in pairs."

How can you doze off like this, my child?

[旦作醒，叫秀才介]咳也。

[老旦]孩儿怎的来？

[旦作惊起介]奶奶到此！

[老旦]我儿，何不做些针指，或观玩书史，舒展情怀？因何昼寝于此？

[旦]孩儿适花园中闲玩，忽值春暄恼人，故此回房。无可消遣，不觉困倦少息。有失迎接，望母亲恕儿之罪。

[老旦]孩儿，这后花园中冷静，少去闲行。

[旦]领母亲严命。

[老旦]孩儿，学堂看书去。

[旦]先生不在，且自消停。

Du Liniang:

(*Wakes and calls the scholar*)

Oh! Oh!

Zhen:

What's wrong with you, my child?

Du Liniang:

(*Stands up with a start*)

Oh, it's you, Mom!

Zhen:

Why don't you, my child, enjoy yourself by doing some needlework or reading some books? Why are you dozing off like this?

Du Liniang:

Just now I took a stroll in the back garden, but I was annoyed by the noise of the birds and so I came back to my chamber. As I could not find a way to while away the time, I dozed off for a moment. Please forgive me for having not greeted you at the door.

Zhen:

As the back garden is a desolate place, my child, don't go there again.

Du Liniang:

I'll follow your advice, Mom.

Zhen:

Go and study in the classroom, my child.

Du Liniang:

As the tutor is on leave, I have a few days off.

Zhen:

(*Sighs*)

[老旦叹介]女孩儿长成，自有许多情态，且自由他。正是："宛转随儿女，辛勤做老娘。"[下]

[旦长叹介][看老旦下介]哎也，天那，今日杜丽娘有些侥幸也。偶到后花园中，百花开遍，睹景伤情。没兴而回，昼眠香阁。忽见一生，年可弱冠，丰姿俊妍。于园中折得柳丝一枝，笑对奴家说："姐姐既淹通书史，何不将柳枝题赏一篇？"那时待要应他一声，心中自忖，素昧平生，不知名姓，何得轻与交言。正如此想间，只见那生向前说了几句伤心话儿，将奴搂抱去牡丹亭畔，芍药阑边，共成云雨之欢。两情和合，真个是千般爱惜，万种温存。欢毕之时，又送我睡眠，几声"将息"。正待自送那生出门，忽值母亲来到，唤醒将来。我一身冷汗，乃是南柯一梦。忙身参礼母亲，又被母亲絮了许多闲话。奴家口虽无言答应，心内思想梦中之事，何曾放怀。行坐不宁，自觉如有所失。娘呵，你教我学堂看书去，知他看那一种书消闷也。[作掩泪介]

A girl has her own emotions when she has come of age. I'd better leave her alone. As the saying goes,

"Busy for the children all her life,

A mother always has her strife."

(*Exit Zhen*)

Du Liniang:

(*Sighs deeply and watches Zhen leave*)

Alas, heavens! I'm lucky enough today. A whimsical stroll to the back garden made me pathetic in spite of the beautiful scenery. After I came back in low spirits, I took a nap in my chamber. In my dream I saw a handsome scholar by the age of twenty. He broke a willow-twig in the garden and said to me with a smile, "Miss Du, as you are well versed in classics, why don't you write a poem to honour the twig?" I was about to reply when it occurred to me that I should not speak to him because he was a total stranger and I did not know his name yet. When I was hesitating, he came forward, spoke a few melancholy words and carried me to the Peony Pavilion. We made love there beside the peonies. With mutual passion, we stuck to each other in tenderness. When it was all over, he brought me back and said time and again, "Sleep awhile." I was about to see the scholar to the door when my mother came and startled me out of my dream. I was wet in cold sweat from my daydream. I made haste to greet my mother and then had to listen to her talk. I kept silent but was still troubled in my heart. I seemed to be sitting on pins and needles, utterly at a loss. Oh, Mother, you told me to go back to my classroom, but what kind of books can bring me relief?

(*Covers her eyes with her sleeve and weeps*)

【绵搭絮】
　　雨香云片，
　　才到梦儿边。
　　无奈高堂，唤醒纱窗睡不便。
　　泼新鲜冷汗粘煎，
　　闪的俺心悠步䪨，
　　意软鬟偏。
　　不争多费尽神情，
　　坐起谁忺？
　　则待去眠。
　　[贴上]"晚妆销粉印，春润费香篝。"小姐，薰了被窝睡罢。
【尾声】
　　[旦]困春心游赏倦，
　　也不索香薰绣被眠。
　　天呵，有心情那梦儿还去不远。

　　春望逍遥出画堂，
　　间梅遮柳不胜芳。
　　可知刘阮逢人处？
　　回首东风一断肠。

(*To the tune of* **Miandaxu**)

The youthful joy in love regime

Had reached the verge of dream

When Mother came into the room

And woke me back to my deep gloom.

With cold sweat that soaked my dress,

I was simply rooted to the ground,

My mind and hair in utter mess.

In a sunken mood,

Not knowing how to sit or stand,

I'd go and sleep in solitude.

(*Enter Chunxiang*)

Chunxiang:

"My make-up is undone at night,

With only incense burning bright."

Your quilts have been scented, Mistress. It's time to go to bed.

Du Liniang:

(*To the tune of* **Coda**)

As springtime tour has tired me out,

There is no need to scent my quilts.

Good heavens,

I wish that pleasant dreams would soon sprout.

A springtime tour from painted halls

Brings near the scent of bloom that falls.

If you should ask where lovers meet,

I say that hearts break where they greet.

第十一出　　慈　戒

[老旦上]"昨日胜今日,今年老去年。可怜小儿女,长自绣窗前。"几日不到女孩儿房中,午晌去瞧他,只见情思无聊,独眠香阁。问知他在后花园回,身子困倦。他年幼不知:凡少年女子,最不宜艳妆戏游空冷无人之处。这都是春香贱材逗引他。春香那里?
[贴上]"闺中图一睡,堂上有千呼。"奶奶,怎夜分时节,还未安寝?
[老旦]小姐在那里?
[贴]陪过夫人到香阁中,自言自语,淹淹春睡去了。敢在做梦也。

Scene Eleven
Madam's Admonishment

(*Enter Zhen*)

Zhen:

> "Each day becomes worse than the last;
> Each year grows older than the past.
> My daughter is deprived of weal,
> Who stands before the window seal."

I had not been to my daughter's chamber for several days. When I went to see her at noontime, I found her listless and dozing alone in her room. She told me that she felt tired because she had just returned from the back garden. She's too young to realise that girls should never visit a deserted place in full make-up. That must be all Chunxiang's fault to give her the temptation. Where's Chunxiang?

(*Enter Chunxiang*)

Chunxiang:

> "A maid who wants a moment's sleep
> Will soon be called to clean and sweep."

How is it that you haven't gone to bed at such late hours?

Zhen:

Where's your young mistress?

Chunxiang:

After you left her chamber, Madam, she kept murmuring to herself and gradually fell asleep. She must be dreaming now.

Zhen:

[老旦]你这贱材,引逗小姐后花园去。倘有疏虞,怎生是了!

[贴]以后再不敢了。

[老旦]听俺分付:

【征胡兵】
女孩儿只合香闺坐,
拈花翦朵。
问绣窗针指如何?
逗工夫一线多。
更昼长闲不过,
琴书外自有好腾那。
去花园怎么?

[贴]花园好景。

[老旦]丫头,不说你不知:

【前腔】
后花园窅静无边阔,
亭台半倒落。
便我中年人要去时节,
尚兀自里打个磨陀。
女儿家甚做作?
星辰高犹自可。

[贴]不高怎的?

You good-for-nothing! You tempted the young mistress to the back garden. What if something should happen to her?

Chunxiang:

I won't any more.

Zhen:

Now mark my words,

(*To the tune of Zhenghubing*)

A girl should stay in her own room,

To work with hands or at the loom.

As far as sewing is concerned,

A stitch more is a moment earned.

In summer when daytime is slow,

There're lutes to play and books to read;

The garden isn't the place to go.

Chunxiang:

There're pretty things to see in the garden.

Zhen:

Let me tell you, ignorant maid,

(*To the previous tune*)

The garden is a lonely place by day,

With terraces and pavilions in decay.

Even when a mature lady like me has to go there,

I have to hesitate.

What are you girls to do o'er there?

Her luck depends upon her fate.

Chunxiang:

What if she's ill-fated?

Zhen:

If it comes true

[老旦唱]厮撞着,有甚不着科,
教娘怎么?
小姐不曾晚餐,早饭要早。你说与他。

[老旦]风雨林中有鬼神,
[贴]寂寥未是采花人。
[老旦]素娥毕竟难防备,
[贴]似有微词动绛唇。

That something should go wrong,

What can her mother do?

As she didn't have supper today, get her an early breakfast tomorrow. Tell her what I said to you.

In stormy woods the ghosts and demons groan,

Chunxiang:

But flower pickers seldom stay alone.

Zhen:

As pretty maidens have their way of life,

Chunxiang:

There are admonishments from Prefect's wife.

第十二出　寻　梦

【夜游宫】
[贴上]腻脸朝云罢盥，
倒犀簪斜插双鬟。
侍香闺起早，
睡意阑珊：
衣桁前，妆阁畔，画屏间。

伏侍千金小姐，丫环一位春香。请过猫儿师父，不许老鼠放光。侥幸《毛诗》感动，小姐吉日时良。拖带春香遣闷，后花园里游芳。谁知小姐瞌睡，恰遇着夫人问当。絮了小姐一会，要与春香一场。春香无言知罪，以后劝止娘行。夫人还是不放，少不得发咒禁当。

[内介]春香姐，发个甚咒来？
[贴]敢再跟娘胡撞，教春香即世里不见儿郎。虽然一时抵对，乌鸦管的凤凰？一夜小姐焦躁，起来促

Scene Twelve
Seeking the Dream

(*Enter Chunxiang*)

Chunxiang:

(*To the tune of* **Yeyougong**)

I wash my face at early dawn

And put on hairpins in the morn.

I serve the miss from morn till night

With drowsy eyes in candlelight:

Before the wardrobe,

Beside the dressing-table,

Between the painted screens.

I'm Chunxiang, maid to serve Miss Du. Miss Du has a tutor, who is like a cat watching over the mice. It happens that she was affected by *The Book of Poetry* and thus chose an auspicious day to have a walk in the back garden to while away the time. Miss Du was just dozing off when the madam dropped in. She scolded Miss Du and laid the blame on me. I kept silent and then promised never to do that again, but the madam would not let me off and I had to vow and swear.

Voice Within:

What did you vow and swear, Sister Chunxiang?

Chunxiang:

"If I should make trouble again," I said, "I would never be able to get married." Although I answered like that, how can a crow control a phoenix? Miss Du tossed and turned all night.

水朝妆。由他自言自语,日高花影纱窗。
[内介]快请小姐早膳。
[贴]"报道官厨饭热,且去传递茶汤。"[下]
【月儿高】
[旦上]几曲屏山展,
残眉黛深浅。
为甚衾儿里不住的柔肠转?
这憔悴非关爱月眠迟倦,
可为惜花,朝起庭院?
"忽忽花间起梦情,女儿心性未分明。无眠一夜灯明灭,分煞梅香唤不醒。"昨日偶尔春游,何人见梦。绸缪顾盼,如遇平生。独坐思量,情殊怅怳。真个可怜人也。[闷介]

She got up early this morning and urged me to fetch water for her to make up. She has been talking to herself all the time till now the sun is shining over the flowers and windows.

Voice Within:

Hurry up! It's time for Miss Du to have breakfast.

Chunxiang:

> *"The cook has word for me*
>
> *To fetch the soup and tea."*
>
> (*Exit Chunxiang*)
>
> (*Enter Du Liniang*)

Du Liniang:

> (*To the tune of* **Yueergao**)
>
> Like arching hills on painted screens,
>
> My brows are drawn by various means.
>
> Why couldn't quilts conceal my care?
>
> The moon is not the thing I'd stare.
>
> Isn't it the fallen bloom
>
> That draws me from my room?
>
> *"Among the flowers rose a dream*
>
> *That drove my thoughts to riotous stream.*
>
> *I stayed awake with candlelight,*
>
> *To watch my maid sleep well all night."*

A random spring stroll yesterday brought me face to face with someone in the dream. I fixed my eyes on him as if he had been my true lover. When I sit alone thinking over the dream, I feel depressed. How piteous I am!

> (*In a depressed mood*)
>
> (*Enter Chunxiang with tea and food*)

Chunxiang:

[贴捧茶食上]"香饭盛来鹦鹉粒,清茶擎出鹧鸪斑。"小姐早膳哩。
[旦]咱有甚心情也!

【前腔】
梳洗了才匀面,
照台儿未收展。
睡起无滋味,
茶饭怎生咽?
[贴]夫人分付,早饭要早。
[旦]你猛说夫人,则待把饥人劝。
你说为人在世,怎生叫做吃饭?
[贴]一日三餐。
[旦]咳,甚瓯儿气力与擎拳!
生生的了前件。
你自拿去吃便了。
[贴]"受用余杯冷炙,胜如剩粉残膏。"[下]
[旦]春香已去。天呵,昨日所梦,池亭俨然。只图

> *"The tray contains pearl-like rice*
> *And fragrant tea of costly price."*

Breakfast is ready, Mistress.

Du Liniang:

I'm not in a mood for breakfast.

(*To the previous tune*)

I have just washed and done my face

And left the glass not yet in place.

I see life as a total waste;

How can I have a pleasant taste?

Chunxiang:

Orders from Madam that you have an early breakfast.

Du Liniang:

For you to use my mother's word

To push a hungry soul appears absurd.

Do you know how people eat to keep alive?

Chunxiang:

Three meals a day.

Du Liniang:

Alas,

Not strong enough to hold the bowl,

I've had enough as a hungry soul.

Take the breakfast away and have it by yourself.

Chunxiang:

> *"I would prefer the leftover food*
> *To paints and rouge that is no good."*

(*Exit Chunxiang*)

Du Liniang:

Chunxiang is gone at last. Oh heavens, the lake and the pavil-

旧梦重来，其奈新愁一段。寻思展转，竟夜无眠。咱待乘此空闲，背却春香，悄向花园寻看。[悲介]哎也，似咱这般，正是："梦无彩凤双飞翼，心有灵犀一点通。"[行介]一径行来，喜的园门洞开，守花的都不在。则这残红满地呵!

【懒画眉】
　　最撩人春色是今年。
　　少什么低就高来粉画垣，
　　元来春心无处不飞悬。
　　[绊介]哎，睡荼蘼抓住裙衩线，
　　恰便是花似人心好处牵。
　　这一湾流水呵!

【前腔】
　　为甚呵，玉真重溯武陵源？
　　也则为水点花飞在眼前。
　　是天公不费买花钱，
　　则咱人心上有啼红怨。
　　咳，辜负了春三二月天。

ion in yesterday's dream were real enough. I tried to relive the old dream but new disappointment ensued. I tossed and turned all night without a moment's sleep. Now that Chunxiang is gone, I'll take this opportunity to sneak into the garden and have a look.

(*In a sad mood*)

Oops, I feel as if

"*The dream displays no phoenix on the wing,*
But links the yearning hearts with one tough string."

(*Walks*)

Here's the garden. As luck has it, the gate is left open and the gardener is not here. How the ground is scattered with fallen petals!

(*To the tune of* **Lanhuamei**)

This spring has strongly stirred my heart.

High above the garden walls,

The blooms and branches stretch and dart.

(*Stumbles*)

Oh, the raspberries are pulling at my skirt,

As if they tried to grasp my heart and flirt.

How the streamlet flows!

(*To the previous tune*)

Why should lovers try to find the same old place?

The blooms and streams must have left trace.

For flowers, the heavens need not pay a cent

But people cried o'er fallen petals

As lovely spring thus came and went.

(*Enter Chunxiang*)

Chunxiang:

[贴上]吃饭去,不见了小姐,则得一径寻来。呀,小姐,你在这里!

【不是路】
何意婵娟,
小立在垂垂花树边。
才朝膳,
个人无伴怎游园?
[旦]画廊前,
深深蓦见衔泥燕,
随步名园是偶然。
[贴]娘回转,
幽闺窣地教人见,
"那些儿闲串?
那些儿闲串?"

【前腔】
[旦作恼介]咦,偶尔来前,道的咱偷闲学少年。
[贴]咳,不偷闲,偷淡。
[旦]欺奴善,把护春台都猜做谎桃源。
[贴]敢胡言,这是夫人命,

When I came back from breakfast, I lost sight of Miss Du. I have to look for her here and there. Oh, here you are, Mistress!

(*To the tune of Bushilu*)

How come my pretty mistress stands

By plum trees with a twig in hands?

What brings you to this zone

So early in the morn alone?

Du Liniang:

On the corridor,

I saw the swallows build a nest

And followed them without a rest.

Chunxiang:

If Madam comes to you

And finds you out of view,

She'll say, "Where's she fooling around?

Where's she fooling around?"

Du Liniang:

(*Feigns to be annoyed*)

(*To the previous tune*)

I came here all by chance,

But you suggest I seek after leisure.

Chunxiang:

Well, you're not seeking after leisure, but after pleasure.

Du Liniang:

Don't treat me as a child

And say the garden's wild.

Chunxiang:

I dare not be so bold,

道春多刺绣宜添线,
润逼炉香好腻笺。
[旦]还说甚来?
[贴]这荒园堑,
怕花妖木客寻常见。
去小庭深院,
去小庭深院!
[旦]知道了。你好生答应夫人去,俺随后便来。
[贴]"闲花傍砌如依主,娇鸟嫌笼会骂人。"[下]
[旦]丫头去了,正好寻梦。
【忒忒令】
那一答可是湖山石边,
这一答似牡丹亭畔。
嵌雕阑芍药芽儿浅,
一丝丝垂杨线,
一丢丢榆荚钱。
线儿春甚金钱吊转!
呀,昨日那书生将柳枝要我题咏,强我欢会之时。
好不话长!

But Madam gave the order that

You do more needlework in spring

And scent the paper twofold.

Du Liniang:

What else did she say?

Chunxiang:

This garden is a haunted place,

With ghosts and demons all apace.

Back to your secluded chambers!

Back to your secluded chambers!

Du Liniang:

Yes, I see. You go first and make promise for me to my mother and I'll be back in no time.

Chunxiang:

"Wild flowers lie unstirred

While caged birds utter foul word."

(*Exit Chunxiang*)

Du Liniang:

Now that Chunxiang is gone, it's time for me to seek my dream.

(*To the tune of* **Teteling**)

Here the lakeside rocks are piled,

With Peony Pavilion lying wild.

There the peonies dot the way;

The twigs of willows sway;

The elm fruits dangling from the trees

Are mourning in the springtime breeze!

Oh, this is the place where the scholar asked me to write a poem in the name of willow twigs and forced me to make love with him. It's a long, long story!

【嘉庆子】
　　是谁家少俊来近远,
　　敢迤逗这香闺去沁园?
　　话到其间腼腆。
　　他捏这眼,奈烦也天;
　　咱嚥这口,待酬言。
【尹令】
　　那书生可意呵,咱不是前生爱眷,
　　又素乏平生半面。
　　则道来生出现,
　　乍便今生梦见。
　　生就个书生,
　　恰恰生生抱咱去眠。
　　那些好不动人春意也。
【品令】
　　他倚太湖石,
　　立着咱玉婵娟。
　　待把俺玉山推倒,
　　便日暖玉生烟。
　　捱过雕阑,转过秋千,
　　揹着裙花展。
　　敢席着地,怕天瞧见。
　　好一会分明,
　　美满幽香不可言。
　　梦到正好时节,甚花片儿吊下来也!

(*To the tune of Jiaqingzi*)

Who was the handsome man

That lured me through the garden tour?

I felt ashamed for sure.

He stroked me, my eyes blurred;

I tried to speak, but without a word.

(*To the tune of Yinling*)

How enticing the scholar is!

In my previous life I had not been his wife

And never saw him in this life.

In my afterlife I shall be his wife

And dream appears first in this life.

Overcome by his enticing charms,

I left myself in his strong arms.

What a splendid moment!

(*To the tune of Pinling*)

He leaned against the rocks and stones;

I stood beside him with faint groans.

He pulled me softly to the ground,

Permeated with springtime warmth around.

Above the fence,

Across the swing,

My skirt spread out from hence.

We lay on grass and faced the sky,

But what if heavens should spy?

It was eternal time

When we enjoyed life's prime.

At the best time of the dream, some petals dropped from the flowers!

【豆叶黄】
　　他兴心儿紧咽咽，
　　鸣着咱香肩。
　　俺可也慢揸揸做意儿周旋。
　　等闲间把一个照人儿昏善，
　　那般形现，
　　那般软绵。
　　忑一片撒花心的红影儿吊将来半天。
　　敢是咱梦魂儿厮缠？
　　咳，寻来寻去，都不见了。牡丹亭，芍药阑，怎生这般凄凉冷落，杳无人迹？好不伤心也！
【玉交枝】
　　[泪介]是这等荒凉地面，
　　没多半亭台靠边，
　　好是咱眯瞑色眼寻难见。
　　明放着白日青天，
　　猛教人抓不到魂梦前。
　　霎时间有如活现，
　　打方旋再得俄延，
　　呀，是这答儿压黄金钏匾。
　　要再见那书生呵，
【月上海棠】
　　怎赚骗，
　　依稀想像人儿见。
　　那来时荏苒，
　　去也迁延。

(*To the tune of* **Douyehuang**)

He grew much bolder

And kissed my shoulder.

I played with him in little haste,

But soon became less graced,

Soft and tender

With a sensual taste.

But floral rains that gleam

Bewildered me in my sweet dream.

Alas, here and there I seek my dream, but I've found nothing. The Peony Pavilion, the rose grove, how can they be so desolate! How can they be so lifeless! How the sight breaks my heart!

(*Weeps*)

(*To the tune of* **Yujiaozhi**)

In a place forlorn,

Without pavilions far and near,

How is it that I can neither see nor hear?

In the broad daylight,

I fail to find the dreamland sight.

The visions flash before my eye

And would not linger though I try.

Well, it's here that we meet and sigh.

Oh that I see my man again!

(*To the tune of* **Yueshanghaitang**)

How can I explain

Why he appears again?

Here he comes at leisured pace;

There he leaves without a trace.

非远,那雨迹云踪才一转,
敢依花傍柳还重现。
昨日今朝,
眼下心前,
阳台一座登时变。
再消停一番。[望介]呀,无人之处,忽然大梅树一株,梅子磊磊可爱。

【二犯幺令】
偏则他暗香清远,
伞儿般盖的周全。
他趁这,他趁这春三月红绽雨肥天,
叶儿青,
偏迸着苦仁儿里撒圆。
爱杀这昼阴便,
再得到罗浮梦边。
罢了,这梅树依依可人,我杜丽娘若死后,得葬于此,幸矣。

【江儿水】
偶然间心似缱,
梅树边。
这般花花草草由人恋,
生生死死随人愿,
便酸酸楚楚无人怨。
待打并香魂一片,
阴雨梅天,
守的个梅根相见。

He is not far away —

Before the rain and cloud disperse,

Behind the blooms I see him stay.

At this time yesterday,

On this very spot,

I was transformed and went astray.

I'll stay here for another moment.

(*Looks around*)

Why! In this lonely place where no one comes, a huge plum tree stands before me, hanging with lovely fruits.

(*To the tune of* **Erfanyaoling**)

How can its fragrance spread

And its leaves crown like a shed?

When plums are ripe and rain is clean,

The vernal leaves are thriving green.

How can the plum contain a bitter heart?

I love the shade provided by the tree,

For in my dream I'll play another part.

Well, the plum tree is lovely indeed. After my death, I would be lucky enough if I could be buried underneath.

(*To the tune of* **Jiangershui**)

All of a sudden my heart is drawn

Toward this plum tree by the lawn.

If I were free to pick my bloom or grass,

If I were free to choose to live or die,

I would resign to fate without a sigh.

I'll risk my life

And weather raging storms

To be your faithful wife.

[倦坐介]

[贴上]"佳人拾翠春亭远,侍女添香午院清。"咳,小姐走乏了,梅树下盹。

【川拨棹】

　　你游花院,

　　怎靠着梅树偃?

　　[旦]一时间望,一时间望眼连天,

　　忽忽地伤心自怜。

　　[泣介]

　　[合]知怎生情怅然,

　　知怎生泪暗悬?

　　[贴]小姐甚意儿?

【前腔】

　　[旦]春归人面,

　　整相看无一言,

　　我待要折,我待要折的那柳枝儿问天,

　　我如今悔,我如今悔不与题笺。

(*Sits down on the ground wearily*)

(*Enter Chunxiang*)

Chunxiang:

"She tours the garden in spring days;

Her maid burns incense in court maze."

Well, Miss Du is dossing off under the plum tree as she is tired from the garden tour.

(*To the tune of Chuanbozhao*)

How does the plum tree allure

You to end the garden tour?

Du Liniang:

When I gaze,

When I gaze at the endless skies,

Woe and sorrow moist my eyes.

(*In tears*)

Du Liniang, Chunxiang:

Who knows from where the woe arises?

Who knows from where the tear arises?

Chunxiang:

What's weighing on your mind, Mistress?

Du Liniang:

(*To the previous tune*)

How absurd

That we gazed without a word!

I should have held,

I should have held the twig and yelled.

Now I regret,

Now I regret that not a word he did get.

Chunxiang:

[贴]这一句猜头儿是怎言?
[合前]
[贴]去罢。
[旦作行又住介]

【前腔】
为我慢归休,
缓留连。
[内鸟啼介]听,听这不如归春暮天,
难道我再,难道我再到这亭园,
则挣的个长眠和短眠!
[合前]
[贴]到了,和小姐瞧奶奶去。
[旦]罢了。

【意不尽】
软咍咍刚扶到画阑偏,
报堂上夫人稳便。
咱杜丽娘呵,
少不得楼上花枝也则是照独眠。

What is the riddle you have set?

Du Liniang, Chunxiang:

Who knows from where the woe arises?

Who knows from where the tear arises?

Chunxiang:

We'd better go back now.

Du Liniang:

(*Starts to move but stops again*)

(*To the previous tune*)

Spring, stay a while

And linger in exile.

(*Birds sing within*)

Listen,

Listen to the cuckoo's song.

Is it true that I can only come—

Come here to see the plum—

In dream or death that will prolong?

Du Liniang, Chunxiang:

Who knows from where the woe arises?

Who knows from where the tear arises?

Chunxiang:

Here we are. Let's go and see Madam, Mistress.

Du Liniang:

Not now.

(*To the tune of Yibujin*)

I dragged my weary steps to my own room,

About to greet my mom,

But I alone sleep with bedside bloom.

Du Liniang:

［旦］武陵何处访仙郎？
［贴］只怪游人思易忘。
［旦］从此时时春梦里，
［贴］一生遗恨系心肠。

Where on earth can fairy love be found?

Chunxiang:

The tourist's zeal can hardly be profound.

Du Liniang:

In dreams my man will show up off and on;

Chunxiang:

Eternal woe will ne'er be dead and gone.

第十三出　　诀　谒

【杏花天】
　　[生上]虽然是饱学名儒，
　　腹中饥，
　　峥嵘胀气。
　　梦魂中紫阁丹墀，
　　猛抬头、破屋半间而已。
　　"蛟龙失水砚池枯，狡兔腾天笔势孤。百事不成真画虎，一枝难稳又惊乌。"我柳梦梅在广州学里，也是个数一数二的秀才，捱了些数伏数九的日子。于今藏身荒圃，寄口髯奴。思之，思之，惶愧，惶愧。想起韩友之谈，不如外县傍州，寻觅活计。正是："家徒四壁求杨意，树少千头愧木奴。"老园公那里？

Scene Thirteen
Leaving Home

(*Enter Liu Mengmei*)

Liu Mengmei:

(*To the tune of* **Xinghuatian**)

Although my learning is beyond compare,

My stomach is empty most of the time,

Filled with dismal air.

In dreams I stalk in the splendid court,

But when I wake up in the hut,

My vision quickly thaws.

"When dragons leave, ink-slabs are dry;

When hares are gone, pen-brushes are bare.

I've tried in vain to find a way,

Like a bird that hovers here and there."

I'm Liu Mengmei, an outstanding scholar in the Guangzhou academy. I have studied hard there for several winters and summers, but now I still have to live in a desolate garden and depend on my gardener for a living. The more I think about it, the more ashamed I feel. I'd better follow Han Zicai's advice to move to some other county to seek a better living. As the saying goes,

"An empty house provides no food;

The scanty trees don't brood good mood."

Where are you, gardener?

(*Enter Hunchback Guo*)

Hunchback Guo:

【字字双】
　　[净扮郭驼上]前山低坬后山堆，驼背；
　　牵弓射弩做人儿，把势；
　　一连十个偌来回，漏地；
　　有时跌做绣球儿，滚气。
　　自家种园的郭驼子是也。祖公公郭橐驼，从唐朝柳员外来柳州。我因兵乱，跟随他二十八代玄孙柳梦梅秀才的父亲，流转到广，又是若干年矣。卖果子回来，看秀才去。[见介]秀才，读书辛苦。
　　[生]园公，正待商量一事。我读书过了廿岁，并无发迹之期。思想起来，前路多长，岂能郁郁居此。搬柴运水，多有劳累。园中果树，都判与伊。听我道来：

【桂花锁南枝】
　　俺有身如寄，
　　无人似你。
　　俺吃尽了黄淡酸甜，
　　费你老人家浇培接植。

(*To the tune of Zizishuang*)

With a curved front, a humped back,

I'm a hunchback.

Like fully stretched bows,

I pose.

To walk with bumble, tumble, stumble,

I'm humble.

To roll down the street like a ball,

I fall.

I am Hunchback Guo, the gardener. My ancestor who followed Prefect Liu to Liuzhou in the Tang dynasty was also a hunchback. It's been quite a few years since I followed his twenty-eighth generation descendant, Liu Mengmei's father, to escape the war and settle down in Guangzhou. Now that I have sold the fruit, I'll go and greet my master.

(*Greets Liu Mengmei*)

Hello, Master, how hard you've been working on your books!

Liu Mengmei:

Well, gardener, I've something to discuss with you. After twenty years of studies, I still have no hope of getting into office. I think I'm still young, and how can I idle away my time here like this! Thank you for all you've done for me: carrying the firewood and the water for me. Now, all the fruit trees in the garden are yours. Listen to what I have to say:

(*To the tune of Guihuasuonanzhi*)

All these years I have relied on you;

Such faithful men like you are very few.

The life is hard and food is plain,

But I should owe all this to you.

你道俺像甚的来?
镇日里似醉汉扶头。
甚日的和老驼伸背?
自株守,教怨谁?
让荒园,你存济。

【前腔】
　　[净]俺橐驼风味,种园家世。
　　[揖介]不能够展脚伸腰,
也和你鞠躬尽力。
秀才,你贴了俺果园那里去?
　　[生]坐食三餐,不如走空一棍。
　　[净]怎生叫做一棍?
　　[生]混名打秋风哩!
　　[净]咳,你费工夫去撞府穿州,
不如依本分登科及第。

What am I like in your eyes?

    I sit and daydream like a fool all day,

    And never give you help in any way.

    My very daydream is a shame;

    Who else am I to blame?

    I'll leave the garden trees to you;

    That is all I can do.

Hunchback Guo:

    (*To the previous tune*)

    For years with you I've stayed

    And gardening is my family trade.

    (*Makes a bow*)

    As a hunchback I'm not of much use,

    But I shall do my best without excuse.

By the way, may I ask where you're going now that you've given me the garden?

Liu Mengmei:

I'd rather go begging with a stick than sit idle and wait to eat at home.

Hunchback Guo:

What do you mean by "go begging with a stick"?

Liu Mengmei:

That's another term for "going with the autumn wind", that is, seeking favour from the rich.

Hunchback Guo:

Good Gracious,

    Rather than go begging from town to town,

    You'd better study hard to win renown.

Liu Mengmei:

[生]你说打秋风不好?"茂陵刘郎秋风客",到大来做了皇帝。
[净]秀才,不要攀今吊古的。你待秋风谁?
你道滕王阁,风顺随;
则怕鲁颜碑,响雷碎。
[生]俺干谒之兴甚浓,休的阻挡。
[净]也整理些衣服去。

【尾声】
把破衫衿彻骨捶挑洗。
[生]学干谒黉门一布衣。
[净]秀才,则要你衣锦还乡俺还见的你。

[生]此身飘泊苦西东,
[净]笑指生涯树树红。
[生]欲尽出游那可得?
[净]秋风还不及春风。

Do you mean that "going with the autumn wind" is no good? Have you ever heard of the poem "Emperor Wu Went with the Autumn Wind"? Life is short indeed, but he became the emperor in the end.

Hunchback Guo:

No more of your allusions, Master. Which wind are you going with?

When luck is with you,

The wind will go with you.

When luck is against you,

The wind will go against you.

Liu Mengmei:

As I've made up my mind, don't try to stop me.

Hunchback Guo:

I'll pack some dress for you.

(*To the tune of* Coda)

I'll wash and pack your shabby dress;

Liu Mengmei:

A scholar is a beggar in distress.

Hunchback Guo:

Good-bye, master,

I hope to see you come back with success.

Liu Mengmei:

I have to wander east and west,

Hunchback Guo:

When blooms on trees are at their best.

Liu Mengmei:

Where am I to seek the "autumn wind"?

Hunchback Guo:

In spring you'd better pass the imperial test.

第十四出　　写　真

【破齐阵】
　　[旦上]径曲梦回人杳，
　　闺深珮冷魂销。
　　似雾濛花，
　　如云漏月，
　　一点幽情动早。
　　[贴上]怕待寻芳迷翠蝶，
　　倦起临妆听伯劳。
　　春归红袖招。
　　[旦]"不经人事意相关，牡丹亭梦残。
　　[贴]断肠春色在眉弯，倩谁临远山？
　　[旦]排恨叠，怯衣单，花枝红泪弹。

Scene Fourteen
Drawing Her Own Image

(*Enter Du Liniang*)

Du Liniang:

(*To the tune of* **Poqizhen**)

The man fades with the garden dream;

The gems in chambers hear my soul scream.

Like blooms seen through the mist,

Like moonlight piercing through the cloud,

My precocious emotions will persist.

(*Enter Chunxiang*)

Chunxiang:

My mistress seems to get a troubled heart

And lends her ear to songs of shrikes;

With spring it's hard for her to part.

Du Liniang:

"*Entangled in affairs I see and hear,*

I linger in the dreamland now and here.

Chunxiang:

With sorrow painted on her brow,

She knows not where it comes and how.

Du Liniang:

With endless grief,

In flimsy dress,

I shed teardrops in distress.

Du Liniang, Chunxiang:

[合]蜀妆晴雨画来难,高唐云影间。"
[贴]小姐,你自花园游后,寝食悠悠,敢为春伤,顿成消瘦?春香愚不谏贤,那花园以后再不可行走了。
[旦]你怎知就里?这是:"春梦暗随三月景,晓寒瘦减一分花。"

【刷子序犯】
　　[旦低唱]春归恁寒悄,
　　都来几日意懒心乔,
　　竟妆成熏香独坐无聊。
　　逍遥,
　　怎划尽助愁芳草,
　　甚法儿点活心苗!
　　真情强笑为谁娇?
　　泪花儿打迸着梦魂飘。

【朱奴儿犯】
　　[贴]小姐,你热性儿怎不冰着,
　　冷泪儿几曾干燥?
　　这两度春游忒分晓,
　　是禁不的燕抄莺闹。

The fairy on Mount Wu is hard to depict,
Her fate still harder to predict."

Chunxiang:

Mistress, since your stroll to the back garden, you have never had enough food or sleep. Is it your spring thoughts that make you pine away? Although I am not in a position to give you any advice, I'd venture to suggest that you never go to the back garden again.

Du Liniang:

How can you get to know my mind! As the poem goes,

"A dream in spring contains the season's flight;
The morning chill destroys the vernal sight."

(*To the tune of* **Shuazixufan**)

(*In a low voice*)

When spring departs with chilly pace,

For days I keep a weary face

And sit alone with thoughts in a race.

I'd not have peace of mind

Unless the troubled thoughts declined

And way of life gets realigned!

For him I smiled with hearty cheers;

In dreams I shed large drops of tears.

Chunxiang:

(*To the tune of* **Zhunuerfan**)

Mistress,

Why has your passion not yet died?

Why have your cold tears not been dried?

It's clear that the recent garden-tour

Has worn you out with songs of birds for sure.

你自窨约,
敢夫人见焦。
再愁烦,
十分容貌怕不上九分瞧。
[旦作惊介]咳,听春香言话,俺丽娘瘦到九分九了。俺且镜前一照,委是如何?[照介][悲介]哎也,俺往日艳冶轻盈,奈何一瘦至此!若不趁此时自行描画,流在人间,一旦无常,谁知西蜀杜丽娘有如此之美貌乎!春香,取素绢、丹青,看我描画。
[贴下取绢、笔上]"三分春色描来易,一段伤心画出难。"绢幅、丹青,俱已齐备。
[旦泣介]杜丽娘二八春容,怎生便是杜丽娘自手生描也呵!

【普天乐】
这些时把少年人如花貌,
不多时憔悴了。
不因他福分难销,
可甚的红颜易老?
论人间绝色偏不少,
等把风光丢抹早。

Just think,

How you will make Madam's heart sink!

If you retain this downcast mood,

Your beauty will become platitude.

Du Liniang:

(*In surprise*)

Oh, do you mean that I'm utterly worn out? I'll have a look in the mirror to see what has happened to me.

(*Looks in the mirror and feels sad*)

Where's my former beauty! How can I be so haggard! If I don't paint a picture of myself now to live in the world, who will ever know of my beauty once I pass away? Chunxiang, fetch me some silk, ink and pen, and then watch how I paint.

Chunxiang:

(*Goes off and re-enters with silk, ink and pen*)

"It's easy to paint a scene in springs,

But hard to paint how her heart stings."

Here's the silk, ink and pen.

Du Liniang:

(*In tears*)

I'm painting a picture of myself at the age of sixteen. Why should things come to this!

(*To the tune of **Putianle***)

My beauty in its fullest prime

Is spent within a few days' time.

It's true that youth can hardly last,

But why does it dissolve so fast?

There have been beauties in the world

Who pined away at early age, I've heard.

打灭起离魂舍欲火三焦，
摆列着昭容阁文房四宝，
待画出西子湖眉月双高。
【雁过声】
[照镜叹介]轻绡，
把镜儿擘掠。
笔花尖淡扫轻描。
影儿呵，和你细评度：
你腮斗儿恁喜谑，
则待注樱桃，
染柳条，
渲云鬟烟霭飘萧；
眉梢青未了，
个中人全在秋波妙，
可可的淡春山钿翠小。
【倾杯序】
[贴]宜笑，
淡东风立细腰，
又以被春愁着。
[旦]谢半点江山，
三分门户，
一种人才，
小小行乐，
捻青梅闲厮调。
倚湖山梦晓，

I'll calm my burning soul

And wield the drawing pen

To paint my beauty on a scroll.

(*Looks in the mirror and sighs*)

(*To the tune of Yanguosheng*)

With silken cloth,

I wipe the mirror clean

And move my pen to paint the scene.

Oh, my image,

This is how you look like:

Two dimpled cheeks,

A cherry mouth,

Two thin brow-streaks,

The hair-locks floating north and south.

My eyebrows stretch to the hair

Above my eyes that talk

And shine with ornaments I wear.

Chunxiang:

(*To the tune of Qingbeixu*)

With a pleasant smile,

The slender mistress stands against the eastern breeze,

But feels depressed when springtime flees.

Du Liniang:

Against the background of hills,

With huts beside the rills,

I paint a picture of a maid,

A maid who wanders in the shade,

Fumbles plums and feels dismayed.

She leans against a rocky seat,

对垂杨风袅。
忒苗条,
斜添他几叶翠芭蕉。
春香,憻起来,可厮像也?

【玉芙蓉】
[贴]丹青女易描,
真色人难学。
似空花水月,
影儿相照。
[旦喜介]画的来可爱人也。
咳,情知画到中间好,
再有似生成别样娇。
[贴]只少个姐夫在身旁。
若是姻缘早,
把风流婿招,
少什么美夫妻图画在碧云高!
[旦]春香,咱不瞒你,花园游玩之时,咱也有个人儿。
[贴惊介]小姐,怎的有这等方便呵?
[旦]梦哩!

Beside the willow-tree retreat.

With palm-tree leaves the picture is complete.

Chunxiang, hold up the picture. Does the maid in the picture look like me?

Chunxiang:

(*To the tune of* **Yufurong**)

It's easy to paint a picture of a maid,

But hard to show her inner trait.

You see in the picture you prepare

As the moon upon the lake or flower in the air.

Du Liniang:

(*Cheers up*)

What a lovely picture! Oh,

I know full well how I look like;

Additional strokes will spoil my psyche.

Chunxiang:

It's a pity that you do not have a husband by your side.

If you become a bride

At an early date,

The pair will feel elated side by side!

Du Liniang:

Tell you the truth, Chunxiang, I met a man during my garden stroll.

Chunxiang:

(*In surprise*)

How was it possible, Mistress?

Du Liniang:

It was a dream!

(*To the tune of* **Shantaofan**)

【山桃犯】
　　有一个曾同笑，
　　待想像生描着，
　　再消详邈入其中妙，
　　则女孩家怕漏泄风情稿。
　　这春容呵，似孤秋片月离云峤，
　　甚蟾宫贵客傍的云霄？
　　春香，记起来了。那梦里书生，曾折柳一枝赠我。此莫非他日所适之夫姓柳乎？故有此警报耳。偶成一诗，暗藏春色，题于帧首之上何如？
　　[贴]却好。
　　[旦题吟介]"近睹分明似俨然，远观自在若飞仙。他年得傍蟾宫客，不在梅边在柳边。"[放笔叹介]春香，也有古今美女，早嫁了丈夫相爱，替他描模画样；也有美人自家写照，寄与情人。似我杜丽娘寄谁呵！
【尾犯序】
　　心喜转心焦。
　　喜的明妆俨雅，
　　仙珮飘飖。

I had a merry time with the man;

I'll search my mind and do what I can

To add him in the picture here,

But that'll reveal my secret love, I fear.

My delicate figure in the picture

Is like the lonely autumn moon;

Which handsome man will join me soon?

It occurs to me, Chunxiang, that the scholar in my dream snapped off a willow-twig as a gift for me. Is it an omen that my would-be husband is a Mr Liu, which means "willow"? I've composed an occasional poem that alludes to my yearning. What about inscribing it at the top of the picture?

Chunxiang:

A good idea!

Du Liniang:

(*Recites the poem when she inscribes it*)

"*A close inspection shows her as her self;*

A distant look displays her as an elf.

Her future spouse who shares the pillow

Will be found by the plum or willow."

(*Puts down the pen and sighs*)

Chunxiang, in the past and at present, beauties married early have pictures drawn by their husbands or draw their own pictures as gifts to their lovers. But to whom shall I present this picture?

(*To the tune of* **Weifanxu**)

My heart is filled with weal and woe:

A joy to see her dress shine bright

And her pendants glow;

则怕呵,把俺年深色浅,
当了个金屋藏娇。
虚劳,
寄春容教谁泪落,
做真真无人唤叫。
[泪介]堪愁夭,
精神出现留与后人标。
春香,悄悄唤那花郎分付他。
[贴叫介]
[丑扮花郎上]"秦宫一生花里活,崔徽不似卷中人。"小姐有何分付?
[旦]这一幅行乐图,向行家裱去。叫人家收拾好些。

【鲍老催】
这本色人儿妙,
助美的谁家裱?
要练花绡帘儿莹、边阑小,
教他有人问着休胡嘌。
日炙风吹悬衬的好,
怕好物不坚牢。
把咱巧丹青休涴了。
[丑]小姐,裱完了,安奉在那里?

A grief to see her pine away

As time and tide relentlessly flow.

Love's labour's lost!

Who will shed his tears for her?

Who will ever call for her?

(*In tears*)

What ill fate

That she must wait to see her mate.

Chunxiang, bring the gardener quietly.

(*Chunxiang calls for the gardener. Enter the young gardener*)

Young Gardener:

"I live among the flowers all my days;

The mistress loses her brilliant rays."

What can I do for you, Mistress?

Du Liniang:

Have this picture mounted by the scroll-maker. Make sure that the job is well done.

(*To the tune of **Baolaocui***)

Who will mount this picture here

To make a better souvenir?

The silk material must be white

While margins must not be wide.

To keep secret, you must keep your mouth shut tight.

In sunny days, the scroll must be well dried

Lest it decay in the broad daylight

And my painting be vilified.

Young Gardener:

When the picture is mounted, where shall I hang it, Mistress?

Du Liniang:

【尾声】
　　[旦]尽香闺赏玩无人到,
　　[贴]这形模则合挂巫山庙。
　　[合]又怕为雨为云飞去了。

　　[贴]眼前珠翠与心违,
　　[旦]却向花前痛哭归。
　　[贴]好写妖娆与教看,
　　[旦]令人评泊画杨妃。

(*To the tune of* **Coda**)

In my chamber it shall be displayed;

Chunxiang:

It fits much better in the fairy temple.

Du Liniang, Chunxiang:

But with the rain and wind it'll fade.

Chunxiang:

As pearls and jewels go against her bent;

Du Liniang:

She weeps for flowers to her heart's content.

Chunxiang:

When it reveals its genuine worth,

Du Liniang:

It pales the prettiest maid on earth.

第十五出　虏　谍

【一枝花】
[净扮番王引众上]天心起灭了辽，
世界平分了赵。
静鞭儿替了胡筘哨。
擂鼓鸣钟，
看文武班齐到。
骨碌碌南人笑，
则个鼻凹儿跻，
脸皮儿鲍，
毛梢儿魈。

"万里江山万里尘。一朝天子一朝臣。俺北地怎禁沙日月，南人偏占锦乾坤。"自家大金皇帝完颜亮是也。身为夷虏，性爱风骚。俺祖公阿骨都，抢了南朝天下，赵康王走去杭州，今又三十余年矣。听得他妆点杭州，胜似汴梁风景。一座西湖，朝欢暮乐。有个曲儿，说他："三秋桂子，十里荷花。"便

Scene Fifteen
Brooding on an Invasion

(*Enter the Jin Emperor, followed by his attendants*)

Jin Emperor:

(*To the tune of Yizhihua*)

At heaven's will we overthrew the Liao
And share the world with House of Zhao;
The ceremonies at court have altered now.
With beat of drums and sound of bells,
The ministers arrive with northern smells.
Our countenances make the southerners laugh:
Our beaked noses,
Our freckled faces,
Our curls of hair.

"*Upon our vast terrain of land and dust,*
New ministers enjoy the new king's trust.
Why should we northerners put up with the sands?
Why should they southerners live on fertile lands?"

I'm Dignai, emperor of the great Jin dynasty. Although I am a barbarian, I love to read poems. It's over thirty years since my grandfather Ogda grabbed the northern part of the Song dynasty, Emperor Zhao Gou fled and made Hangzhou the new capital. It's said that he has built Hangzhou into a city more beautiful than Bianliang, the former capital. He and his followers make merry day and night on the West Lake. As a *ci* poem has it,

待起兵百万，吞取何难？兵法虚虚实实，俺待用个南人，为我乡导。喜他淮扬贼汉李全，有万夫不当之勇。他心顺溜于俺，俺先封他为溜金王之职。限他三年内招兵买马，骚扰淮扬地方。相机而行，以开征进之路。哎哟，俺巴不到西湖上散闷儿也！

【北二犯江儿水】
平分天道，
虽则是平分天道，
高头偏俺照。
俺司天台标着那南朝，
标着他那答儿好。
[众]那答里好？
[净笑介]你说西子怎娇娆，
向西湖上笑倚着兰桡。
[众]西湖有俺这南海子、北海子大么？

> "Osmanthus blossoms during autumn days
> And lotus flowers bloom along the bays."

So I can easily raise a million troops and occupy that part of the land. According to military strategy, I'd better employ a southerner as my guide. It happens that Li Quan, a bandit chief in Huaiyang, is brave enough to fight ten thousand men. As he is loyal to me, I have bestowed him the title of Gilded Prince. I've told him to raise his own troops in three years and to cause trouble in his area. At the same time, he should look for the opportunity for me to start my military excursion. How I wish I could find some fun on the West Lake!

(*To the tune of* **Beierfanjiangershui**)

Share and share alike,

Share and share alike,

But I have made a lucky strike.

The arrow on my map is pointed to the south,

To the best dominion in the south.

Jin Attendants:

What's good over there?

Jin Emperor:

(*With a laugh*)

Have you heard of

The charming maiden on the shore,

Who smiles and leans against the oar?

Jin Attendants:

Is the West Lake as large as our Beihai Lake and the Nanhai Lake in Beijing?

Jin Emperor:

[净]周围三百里。
波上花摇,
云外香飘。
无明夜、锦笙歌围醉绕。
[众]万岁爷,借他来耍耍。
[净]已潜遣画工,偷将他全景来了。那湖上有吴山第一峰,画俺立马其上。俺好不狠也!
吴山最高,
俺立马在吴山最高。
江南低小,
也看见了江南低小。
[舞介]俺怕不占场儿砌一个《锦西湖上马娇》。
[众]奏万岁爷,怕急不能够到西湖,何方驻驾?

【北尾】
[净]呀,急切要画图中匹马把西湖哨,
且迤递的看花向洛阳道。
我呵,少不的把赵康王剩水残山都占了。

线大长江扇大天,
旌旗遥拂雁行偏。
可胜饮尽江南酒?
交割山川直到燕。

The lake is over a hundred miles in circumference.

Upon the waves the flowers dance in crowds

And send their scent beyond the clouds.

All through the endless nights,

The songs and music ring around.

Jin Attendants:

Your Majesty, let's borrow it and have some fun.

Jin Emperor:

I've sent some painters in disguise and made a sketch of the whole scene. I am painted as riding a horse on the highest peak of Mount Wu by the lake. How mighty and powerful I am!

Mount Wu is unique,

But I ride atop the peak.

The southern land is low

And I have seen it lie below.

(*Dances for joy*)

Look, how I make the show!

Jin Attendants:

Your Majesty, as we can't reach the West Lake at once, where will you stay over the night?

Jin Emperor:

(*To the tune of Beiwei*)

Before I ride my horse around West Lake,

I'll march toward Luoyang and take a break.

The rest of Zhao's realm will soon be at stake.

Narrow is the river, small the sky;

How our military flags float high!

Can we drink up all the southern wine

When all the southern land is mine?

第十六出　　诘　病

【三登乐】
[老旦上]今生怎生？
偏则是红颜薄命，
眼见的孤苦仃俜。
[泣介]掌上珍，
心头肉，
泪珠儿暗倾。
天呵，偏人家七子团圆，
一个女孩儿厮病。
"如花娇怯，合得天饶借。风雨于花生分岁，作意十分凌藉。止堪深阁重帘，谁教月榭风檐。我发短回肠寸断，眼昏眵泪双淹。"老身年将半百，单生一女丽娘。因何一病，起倒半年？看他举止容谈，

Scene Sixteen
Inquiring about the Disease

(*Enter Zhen*)

Zhen:
(*To the tune of* **Sandengle**)
What does this life mean to me?
My daughter has not many days to see
And I'll be childless, like a lonely tree.
(*In tears*)
Like a pearl held on my palm,
Like flesh torn from my heart,
For my daughter I weep and lose my calm.
Oh heavens!
Why should health stay with others
While illness strikes my daughter who has no brothers?
"Delicate as bloom,
She should be blessed, I presume.
Yet cruel wind and rain
Torment her with grave pain.
She should have stayed in her room,
Instead of watching the moon and bloom.
Filled with sorrow in my growing years,
I feel so dizzy with large drops of tears."

Now that I am approaching fifty years of age, I've got my only daughter Liniang. What disease is it that has laid her down for half a year? Judging from her appearance and behaviour,

不似风寒暑湿。中间缘故,春香必知,则问他便了。春香贱才那里?

[贴上]有哩。我"眼里不逢乖小使,掌中擎着个病多娇。得知堂上夫人召,剩酒残脂要咱消"。春香叩头。

[老旦]小姐闲常好好的,才着你贱才伏侍他,不上半年,偏是病害。可恼,可恼!且问近日茶饭多少?

【驻马听】

[贴]他茶饭何曾,
所事儿休提、叫懒应。
看他娇啼隐忍,
笑谵迷厮,
睡眼憕憕。

[老旦]早早禀请太医了。

[贴]则除是八法针针断软绵情。
怕九还丹丹不的腌臜证。

her disease does not seem to have come from cold or heat. I'll question Chunxiang as she must know something about the reason. Where's the mischievous Chunxiang?

(*Enter Chunxiang*)

Chunxiang:

I'm coming.

"*Without a clever boy to help me out,*
I serve a miss who can't be up and about.
When I hear the madam call my name,
I know I have to bear the scold and blame."

Zhen:

Your young mistress used to be in perfect health, but she has been ill since you became her maid half a year ago. I'm really distressed, distressed! Now tell me about her appetite these days.

Chunxiang:

(*To the tune of Zhumating*)

Little does she eat,

Nothing does she do,

And nobody does she meet.

She weeps by herself,

She laughs by herself

And thinks by herself.

Zhen:

She's seen the doctor.

Chunxiang:

No doctor can put her at ease;

No pills can cure her disease.

Zhen:

[老旦]是什么病?
[贴]春香不知,道他一枕秋清,
却怎生还害的是春前病。
[老旦哭介]怎生了。

【前腔】
他一搦身形,
瘦的庞儿没了四星。
都是小奴才逗他。
大古是烟花惹事,
莺燕成招,
云月知情。
贱才还不跪!取家法来。
[贴跪介]春香实不知道。
[老旦]因何瘦坏了玉娉婷,
你怎生触损了他娇情性?
[贴]小姐好好的拈花弄柳,不知因甚病了。
[老旦恼,打贴介]打你这牢承,
嘴骨棱的胡遮映。

What is she suffering from?

Chunxiang:

I don't know.

She lies in bed in autumn days,

But caught the illness in spring days.

Zhen:

(*Sobs*)

What's the matter with her?

(*To the previous tune*)

Her slender form

Grows thinner than the norm.

It must be your fault!

She was tempted by spring flowers,

Enticed by flighty birds

And lured by frivolous words!

On your knees, you devil! Hand me the rod!

Chunxiang:

(*Kneels on the ground*)

I really don't know.

Zhen:

How do you make her pine away?

How do you lead her astray?

Chunxiang:

My young mistress went to the garden, picking flowers and playing with willows, but I don't know how she got ill.

Zhen:

(*Gets irritated and beats Chunxiang*)

I beat you for your artful tongue

And honeyed tunes you've sung!

[贴]夫人休闪了手。容春香诉来。便是那一日游花园回来,夫人撞到时节,说个秀才手里折的柳枝儿,要小姐题诗。小姐说这秀才素昧平生,也不和他题了。
[老旦]不题罢了。后来?
[贴]后来那、那、那秀才就一拍手把小姐端端正正抱在牡丹亭上去了。
[老旦]去怎的?
[贴]春香怎得知?小姐做梦哩。
[老旦惊介]是梦么?
[贴]是梦。
[老旦]这等着鬼了。快请老爷商议。
[贴请介]老爷有请。
[外上]"肘后印嫌金带重,掌中珠怕玉盘轻。"

Chunxiang:

Please pardon me, Madam, and I'll tell you the whole story. It happened on the day when we visited the back garden and you came across us on our way back. She told me about a young scholar who snapped off a willow-twig and asked her to write a poem. She said she did not write anything because he was a stranger.

Zhen:

Well, so far so good. And what happened then?

Chunxiang:

Then, then the scholar came forward and carried my young mistress straight to the Peony Pavilion.

Zhen:

What for?

Chunxiang:

How can I know? It's just her dream.

Zhen:

Her dream?

Chunxiang:

Yes, her dream.

Zhen:

She must be haunted. Ask the master to come here and I'll talk it over with him.

Chunxiang:

Master, please come here.

   (*Enter Du Bao*)

Du Bao:

   "An aged man cares not for the title of earl,
   But for his daughter precious as a pearl."

夫人，女儿病体因何？

[老旦泣介]老爷听讲：

【前腔】
说起心疼，
这病知他是怎生！
看他长眠短起，
似笑如啼，
有影无形。
原来女儿到后花园游了。梦见一人手执柳枝，闪了他去。[作叹介]
怕腰身触污了柳精灵，
虚嚣侧犯了花神圣。
老爷呵，急与禳星，
怕流星赶月相刑迸。

[外]却还来。我请陈斋长教书，要他拘束身心。你为母亲的，倒纵他闲游。[笑介]则是些日炙风吹，伤寒流转。便要禳解，不用师巫，则叫紫阳宫石道婆诵些经卷可矣。古语云："信巫不信医，一不治也。"我已请过陈斋长看他脉息去了。

Madam, how's our daughter like this?

Zhen:

　　(*In tears*)

　　Listen to what I have to say, my lord,

　　　　(*To the previous tune*)

　　　　It gives me pain to speak

　　　　About what ails her and makes her weak.

　　　　Confined in bed most of the time,

　　　　Now she smiles, now she weeps;

　　　　Her illness comes without reason or rhyme.

It so happened that when Liniang visited the back garden, she dreamt of a man holding a willow-twig and carrying her away.

　　(*With a sigh*)

　　She smeared the willow sprite with sod

　　Or maybe upset the flower god.

My lord,

　　Invite a Taoist priest to use his charms

　　Lest ill fate should do her harms.

Du Bao:

No more of your nonsense! I've engaged Mr Chen as her tutor to teach her proper manners, but you as her mother allows her to take spring strolls.

　　(*With a smile*)

She's been exposed to the sun and wind and has caught a cold. There's no need for Taoist charms. If you like, you can ask Sister Stone from the Purple Sunlight Temple to chant a few scriptures. As the ancient saying goes, "To prefer the witch to the doctor is one way to avoid cure." I've told Mr Chen to feel her pulse.

[老旦]看甚脉息。若早有了人家,敢没这病。

[外]咳,古者男子三十而娶,女子二十而嫁。女儿点点年纪,知道个什么呢?

【前腔】
忒恁憨生,
一个哇儿甚七情?
则不过往来潮热,
大小伤寒,
急慢风惊。
则是你为母的呵,
真珠不放在掌中擎,
因此娇花不奈这心头病。[泣介]
[合]两口丁零,
告天天,半边儿是咱全家命。
[丑扮院公上]"人来大庾岭,船去郁孤台。"禀老爷,有使客到。

【尾声】
[外]俺为官公事有期程。
夫人,好看惜女儿身命,
少不的人向秋风病骨轻。

Zhen:

What's the use of feeling her pulse! If she had been engaged, she would not have caught the disease.

Du Bao:

Well, in ancient times, man married at thirty and woman married at twenty. Liniang is too young to know anything about it.

(*To the previous tune*)

Innocent as a dove,

How can she know such things as love?

It's just a fever,

Or a cold,

Or a disease untold.

As her mother, you

Neglect your pearl upon your palm

And for her illness you cannot keep calm.

(*In tears*)

Du Bao, Zhen:

For man and wife,

Oh heavens above,

The daughter means our life.

(*Enter Steward*)

Steward:

"The visitor comes from the hills;

The vessel sails down the rills."

Du Bao:

(*To the tune of* **Coda**)

With official work to do,

I'll leave the daughter unto you:

In autumn chills her illness cannot subdue.

[外、丑下]

[老旦、贴吊场介]

[老旦]"无官一身轻,有子万事足。"我看老相公则为往来使客,把女儿病都不瞧。好伤怀也。[泣介]想起来一边叫石道婆禳解,一边教陈教授下药。知他效验如何?正是:"世间只有娘怜女,天下能无卜与医!"[下]

(*Exit Du Bao with the steward, leaving Zhen and Chunxiang on the stage*)

Zhen:

"*Man is free when official work is done;*
Man is snug when he has a son."

My man ignores his daughter when a messenger comes. How sad it is!

(*Weeps*)

Now I'll ask Sister Stone to chant the scriptures and ask Mr Chen to prescribe some medicine, but I don't know what will come out of all this. It is true indeed

"*A mother is the dearest to her daughter,*
But all the same requires the witch and doctor!"

第十七出　　道　觋

【风入松】

[净扮老道姑上]人间嫁娶苦奔忙，
只为有阴阳。
问天天从来不具人身相，
只得来道扮男妆，
屈指有四旬之上。
当人生，
梦一场。

"紫府空歌碧落寒，竹石如山不敢安。长恨人心不如石，每逢佳处便开看。"贫道紫阳宫石道姑是也。俗家原不姓石，则因生为石女，为人所弃，故号"石姑"。思想起来：要还俗，《百家姓》上有俺一家；论出身，《千字文》中有俺数句。天呵，非是俺"求古寻论"，恰正是"史鱼秉直"。俺因何

Scene Seventeen
A Taoist Nun

(*Enter Sister Stone*)

Sister Stone:

(*To the tune of* **Fengrusong**)

The world is busy getting wed
With *yin* and *yang* as linking thread.
Resigned to my destined fate,
I wore a Taoist robe from early date.
For over forty years,
I've lived a tasteless life,
A dream without the slightest cheers.
"The Taoist temple stands upon the earth,
Near where the rocks and bamboo idly lie.
I grieve that human heart is even worse
And runs wild when temptation chances by."

I am Sister Stone in the Purple Sunlight Nunnery. Stone was not my surname, but I've got the title Sister Stone because I was born sterile and was thus deserted by my husband. Come to think of it: if I want to return to secular life, "Stone" is contained in *Hundred Surnames* and my personal life is described in *The Thousand Character Text*. Oh heavens, I do not want to

"find proof from ancient texts",

but, on the contrary, I just want to be

"as straightforward as the historian Shi Yu".

住在这"楼观飞惊",打并的"劳谦谨敕"?看修行似"福缘善庆",论因果是"祸因恶积"。有什么"荣业所基"?几辈儿"林皋幸即"。生下俺"形端表正",那些"性静情逸"。大便孔似"园莽抽条",小净处也"渠荷滴沥"。只那些儿正好叉着口,"钜野洞庭";偏和你灭了缝,"昆池碣石"。虽则石路上可以"路侠槐卿",石田中怎生"我艺

Why have I been living in this
   "magnificent nunnery"
and striving to be
   "diligent and strict with myself"?
It is because the Taoist practice is like
   "virtue which leads to bliss"
while retribution means that
   "vices add up to misfortune".
What is the
   "prestigious foundation of my family"?
For generations my ancestors have
   "lived in retirement".
When I was born, I had
   "a good shape and good manners",
with an aptitude for
   "peace and tranquillity".
My shit was like
   "twigs of the chaste tree",
and my piss was like
   "drips from the lotus leaves".
At the delta where there should have been
   "a vast lake or swamp",
there was only a stretch of land, which is
   "a dried pond with an arid rock".
Although the pebbled path could
   "clutch the scholar-trees",
how could the barren land
   "grow corns and millets"?
Who would marry me for

黍稷"?难道嫁人家"空谷传声"?则好守娘家"孝当竭力"。可奈不由人"诸姑伯叔",聒噪俺"入奉母仪"。母亲说你内才儿虽然"守真志满",外像儿"毛施淑姿",是人家有个"上和下睦",偏你石二姐没个"夫唱妇随"?便请了个有口齿的媒人,"信使可覆"。许了个大鼻子的女婿,"器欲难量"。则见不多时,那人家下定了。说道选择了一年上"日月盈昃",配定了八字儿"辰宿列张"。他过的礼,"金生丽水",俺上了轿,"玉

"unproductive echoes in the empty valley"?
I had to stay by mother's side and
"do my filial duties".
However, there were those
"aunts and uncles",
who babbled about
"getting married and bearing children".
My mother said that although I would
"remain chaste all my life",
I look like
"the fairest of the fairest".
Since all the other women could live
"a harmonious family life",
Why shouldn't I have
"a husband to accompany me"?
So she hired a matchmaker with a glib tongue to
"pass on words of honour"
and had me engaged to a licentious man with a big nose, whose
"lust was insatiable".
All was fixed very soon. The bridegroom picked a day of good omen with
"the sun and the moon in the best phase"
and checked the horoscope to see to it that
"the two stars were aligned in good order".
He sent me betrothal money of
"pure gold from River Li"
and I stepped on the bridal sedan chair as
"genuine jade from Mount Kungang".
I covered my face with

出崑冈"。遮脸的"纨扇圆洁",引路的"银烛辉煌"。那新郎好不打扮的头直上"高冠陪辇"。咱新人一般排比了腰儿下"束带矜庄"。请了些"亲戚故旧",半路上"接杯举觞"。请新人"升阶纳陛",叫女伴们"侍巾帷房"。合卺的"弦歌酒燕",撒帐的"诗赞羔羊"。把俺做新人嘴脸儿一寸寸"鉴貌辨色",将俺那宝妆奁一件件都"寓目囊箱"。早是二更时分,新郎紧上来了。替俺说,俺两口儿活像"鸣凤在竹",一时间就要"白驹食场"。则见被窝儿"盖此身发",灯影里褪尽了这

"a round silk fan"

and went in a procession with

"candles burning bright".

The bridegroom in his holiday best

"sat on my right in a high hat"

and I the bride was also well dressed

"with an elegant air".

We invited some

"kith and kin"

to greet us on the way

"with goblets and wine".

I was led

"up the stairs and into the hall",

with bridesmaids

"waiting on me in the nuptial chamber".

We drank our wedding drink amidst

"songs and music in the feast"

and scattered coins and candies to the children from the nuptial bed amidst

"chants and hymns in praise of the lamb".

Inch by inch the guests

"examined my figure and countenance";

item by item the guests

"assessed my precious dowry".

In the deep of night, the bridegroom came forward and sat close to me, saying that we were like

"phoenixes echoing in the bamboo groves"

and that we would soon

"graze like snow-white colts".

几件"乃服衣裳"。天呵,瞧了他那"驴骡犊特";教俺好一会"悚惧恐惶"。那新郎见我害怕,说道:新人,你年纪不少了,"闰余成岁"。俺可也不使狠,和你慢慢的"律吕调阳"。俺听了口不应,心儿里笑着。新郎,新郎,任你"矫手顿足",你可也"靡恃己长"。三更四更了,他则待阳台上"云腾致雨",怎生巫峡内"露结为霜"?他一时摸不出路数儿,道是怎的?快取亮来。侧着脑要"右通广内",踏着眼在"篮笋象床"。那时节俺口不说,心下好不冷笑。新郎,新郎,俺这件东西,则许你"徘徊瞻眺",怎许你"适口充肠"。如此者几度了,恼的他气不分的嘴唠叨"俊

With a quilt
   "covering our body and hair",
we removed
   "our last shreds of clothing".
Oh heavens, on seeing his
   "beastly male organ",
I went through a moment of
   "fright and fear".
When he saw how nervous I was, he said that I had
   "grown in years"
and that he would take his time to
   "tune in with me".
I made no reply but smiled to myself, thinking that however hard he was
   "busy with his hands and feet",
he'd better
   "refrain from overconfidence in his strength".
When night grew deeper, he was still
   "pushing and thrusting",
but how could he break through
   "the frozen land"?
For a moment he was confused and wondered what the matter was. He asked for a lamp and leaned his head, trying to
   "find his way to the right spot",
and fixed his eyes on
   "the ivory bed".
I said nothing but grinned to myself, thinking that my private parts were for him to
   "look and see",

乂密勿"，累的他凿不窍皮混沌的"天地玄黄"。和他整夜价则是"寸阴是竞"。待讲起，丑煞那"属耳垣墙"。几番待悬梁，待投河，"免其指斥"。若还用刀钻，用线药，"岂敢毁伤"？便拼做赳了交"索居闲处"，甚法儿取他意"悦豫且康"？有了，有了。他没奈何央及煞后庭花"背邙面洛"，俺也则得且随顺干荷叶，和他"秋收冬藏"。哎哟，对面儿做的个"女慕贞洁"，转腰儿到做了"男效才良"。虽则暂时间"释纷利俗"，

but not for him to

"taste and satiate his desire".

After he tried in vain several more times, he was so annoyed that he mumbled about

"practice makes perfect",

and he was tired out before he made a hole in

"the chaos of heaven and earth".

All through the night, he

"grabbed every minute";

and, to speak of what he did, it would put to shame

"the walls that had ears".

On several occasions I would like to hang myself or drown myself so as to

"escape from his blame",

and if I were to drill a hole or burn a hole, how could I violate the commandment

"Thou shalt not hurt yourself"?

I would even rather run away and

"live a solitary life",

but how could I make him

"feel satisfied"?

Yes, there was a way out. In the end he had to take

"the back position"

while I had to comply with him by

"storing what he offered".

Alas, when we were face to face, I acted as if I

"had striven to keep chaste",

but when I turned round, I acted as a

"male partner".

毕竟情意儿"四大五常"。要留俺怕误了他"嫡后嗣续",要嫁了俺怕人笑"饥厌糟糠"。这时节俺也索劝他了:官人,官人,少不得请一房"妾御绩纺",省你气那"鸟官人皇"。俺情愿"推位让国",则要你"得能莫忘"。后来当真讨一个了。没多时做小的"宠增抗极",反捻去俺为正的"率宾归王"。不怨他,只"省躬讥诫"。出了家罢,俺则"垂拱平章"。若论这道院里,昔年也不甚"宫殿盘郁";到老身,才开辟了"宇宙洪荒"。

Although for the moment I
> "satisfied his desire",

I knew the meaning of
> "nuptial love".

If he kept me as his wife, he would
> "have no sons and heirs"

and if he divorced me, he would be denounced as
> "betraying his former wife".

So I tried to persuade him to wed a concubine to
> "weave and spin"

lest he should feel annoyed to be
> "a husband in name only".

I would like to
> "resign from my post as a genuine wife"

if only he did not
> "forget his first lady".

Later he did get a concubine. Not long afterwards his concubine
> "won greater favour and challenged my authority",

and deprived me of my position as
> "the rooster of the house".

Bearing no grudge against her, I
> "engaged myself in introspection"

and decided to leave the family and become a nun,
> "living in seclusion".

My nunnery had never been
> "a magnificent edifice",

and it was me that
> "brought chaos in order".

画真武"剑号巨阙",步北斗"珠称夜光"。奉香供"果珍李柰",把斋素也是"菜重芥姜"。世间味识得破"海咸河淡",人中网逃得出"鳞潜羽翔"。俺这出了家呵,把那几年前做新郎的臭粘涎"骸垢想浴",将俺即世里做老婆的干柴火"执热愿凉"。则可惜做观主"游鹍独运",也要知观的"顾答审详"。赴会的都要"具膳餐饭",行脚的也要"老少异粮"。怎生观中再没个人儿?也都则是"沉默寂寥",全不会"笺牒简要"。俺老将来

I had a picture painted of the Taoist immortal king
>   "weaving his mighty sword"

and started to make pills of immortality
>   "under the starry sky".

I offered to the immortals
>   "fruits and cakes",

and ate vegetables
>   "with mustard and ginger seasonings".

I no longer cared about the worldly affairs
>   "with its ups and downs",

having escaped from the human bondage,
>   "scot-free".

Since I converted to Taoism several years ago, the fluid from my husband
>   "has been washed away"

and my lust as a wife has dropped
>   "from the boiling point to the freezing point".

It is a pity that as the head of the nunnery I,
>   "living all alone",

have to
>   "take pains to give consultations".

Those who come for the service must be
>   "provided with meals"

and those travelling nuns must be
>   "provided with grains".

How is it that there are no other nuns in the nunnery? I live
>   "a secluded life"

and have no one to
>   "write to for alms".

"年矢每催",镜儿里"晦魄环照"。硬配不上仕女图"驰誉丹青",也要接得着仙真传"坚持雅操"。懒云游"东西二京",端一味"坐朝问道"。女冠子有几个"同气连枝",骚道士不与他"工颦妍笑"。怕了他暗地虎"布射辽丸",则守着寒水鱼"钧巧任钓"。使唤的只一个"犹子比儿",叫做癞头鼋"愚蒙等诮"。

[内]姑娘骂俺哩。俺是个妙人儿。

[净]好不羞。"殆辱近耻",到夸奖你"并皆佳妙"。

When I grow old
>"with passing years",

my beauty fades
>"like the waning moon".

Although I am not as beautiful as those ladies
>"who will forever live in the portraits",

I hope to live among the immortals
>"who are pious and chaste".

Too lazy to
>"wander around the world",

I spend all the time
>"sitting in deep contemplation".

Few nuns
>"share my views"

while few monks are worthy of my
>"coy smiles".

For fear of their
>"underhand means",

I'm like a fish in cold waters that
>"does not bite the bait".

My only attendant is my
>"nephew who is treated as my son",

who is called Scabby Turtle,
>"ridiculed as an ignorant man".

Voice Within:

Why are you calling names, Auntie? I'm a lovely boy.

Sister Stone:

Shame on you! Don't you know
>"loss of sense of shame is a disgrace"?

[内]杜太爷皂隶拿姑娘哩。
[净]为什么?
[内]说你是个贼道。
[净]咳,便道那府牌来"杜藁钟隶",把俺做女妖看"诛斩贼盗"。俺可也"散虑逍遥",不用你这般"虚辉朗耀"。
[丑扮府差上]"承差府堂上,提名仙观中。"[见介]
[净]府牌哥为何而来?

【大迓鼓】
　　[丑]府主坐黄堂,
　　夫人传示,
　　衙内敲梆。

Do you really think that you are
> "lovely and attractive"?

Voice Within:
A bailiff from Prefect Du is coming to arrest you.

Sister Stone:
Why?

Voice Within:
He says that you are a witch of a Taoist nun.

Sister Stone:
Oh, those bailiffs are
> "runners from the office",

taking me as a witch
> "on the wanted list".

I may well
> "stay at ease"

and care nothing for their
> "intimidations".

(*Enter Bailiff*)

Bailiff:
> "A bailiff from the office hall,
> On the Taoist nun I call."

Sister Stone:
(*Greets the bailiff*)
What can I do for you, Mr bailiff?

Bailiff:
(*To the tune of* **Dayagu**)
> The prefect stays in office;
> His wife has sent her word
> To cure some pain absurd.

知他小姐年多长,
染一疾,
半年光。
[净]俺不是女科。
[丑]请你修斋,
一会祈禳。

【前腔】
[净]俺仙家有禁方。
小小灵符,
带在身旁。
教他刻下人无恙。
[丑]有这等灵符!快行动些。
[行介]
[净]叫童儿。
[内应介]
[净]好看守,卧云房。
殿上无人,仔细灯香。
[内]知道了。

[净]紫微宫女夜焚香,

Her dainty daughter

Has caught a strange disease,

And half a year now flees.

Sister Stone:

I'm not a gynaecologist.

Bailiff:

You'll hold a service for her,

Then pray for her and see what will occur.

Sister Stone:

(*To the previous tune*)

We Taoists have our secret way:

Use tiny talismans to pray

Beside her bed

And illness will flee from her head.

Bailiff:

As you have such magic talismans, let's hurry!

(*They start to move*)

Sister Stone:

Boy!

(*Response from within*)

Take good care

And stay o'er there.

As no one is in the hall,

Watch the lights and all.

Voice Within:

Yes, I see.

Sister Stone:

While fairy ladies burn incense at night,

Bailiff:

[丑]古观云根路已荒。
[净]犹有真妃长命缕,
[丑]九天无事莫推忙。

The mountain nunnery hides itself from sight.

Sister Stone:

Since Goddess carries remedies of life,

Bailiff:

Make no excuse or rush in for the strife!

第十八出　　诊　祟

【一江风】
　　[贴扶病旦上]
　　[旦]病迷厮。
　　为甚轻憔悴？
　　打不破愁魂谜。
　　梦初回，
　　燕尾翻风，
　　乱飐起湘帘翠。
　　春去偌多时，
　　春去偌多时，
　　花容只顾衰。
　　井梧声刮的我心儿碎。
　　春香呵，我"楚楚精神，叶叶腰身，能禁多病逡巡！
　　[贴]你星星措与，种种生成，有许多娇，许多韵，许多情。

Scene Eighteen
Making Diagnoses

(*Enter Du Liniang in illness, supported by Chunxiang*)

Du Liniang:

(*To the tune of* **Yijiangfeng**)

I feel so dizzy in disease.

Why am I not feeling well?

The reason is hard to tell.

When I woke up from my dream,

I saw the swallows in the sky

And bamboo blinds nearby.

I watch the spring depart,

I watch the spring depart.

While flowers fall apart,

The rustling tree-leaves break my heart.

Well, Chunxiang,

"*How can a dreary lass,*

Like a leaf in breeze,

Endure the long disease?

Chunxiang:

In every act

And every deed,

You show your charm,

Your noble breed

And lofty creed.

Du Liniang:

[旦]咳,咱弄梅心事,那折柳情人,梦淹渐暗老残春。

[贴]正好篝炉香午,枕扇风清。知为谁颦,为谁瘦,为谁疼?"

[旦]春香,我自春游一梦,卧病如今。不痒不疼,如痴如醉。知他怎生?

[贴]小姐,梦儿里事,想他则甚!

[旦]你教我怎生不想呵!

【金落索】
贪他半晌痴,
赚了多情泥。
待不思量,
怎不思量得?
就里暗销肌,
怕人知。
嗽腔腔嫩喘微。
哎哟,我这惯淹煎的样子谁怜惜?
自噤窄的春心怎的支?

> *My longing for plum bloom*
> *And man with willow-twigs*
> *Vanish with the spring in gloom.*

Chunxiang:

> *When incense burns at noon*
> *And tranquil air is known,*
> *Who makes you groan?*
> *Who makes you pine?*
> *Who makes you feel alone?"*

Du Liniang:

Chunxiang, I've been laid in bed since my dream during the spring stroll. Although I'm not afflicted by pain or itches, I feel dizzy all the time. What's the matter with me?

Chunxiang:

Mistress, a dream is a dream. Forget about it!

Du Liniang:

How can I forget about it!

> (*To the tune of* Jinluosuo)
>
> For a moment's joy,
> I'm entangled with the boy.
> I'd like to stop recalling him,
> But how can I stop recalling him?
> I pine away
> And live in fear from day to day,
> Coughing all the way.

Alas!

> Who will feel for me?
> Who will share my woe with me?
> How I regret,

心儿悔,
悔当初一觉留春睡。
[贴]老夫人替小姐冲喜。
[旦]信他冲的个甚喜?
到的年时,敢犯杀花园内?

【前腔】
[贴]看他春归何处归,
春睡何曾睡?
气丝儿怎度的长天日?
把心儿捧凑眉,
病西施。
小姐,梦去知他实实谁?
病来只送的个虚虚的你。
做行云先渴倒在巫阳会。
全无谓,
把单相思害得忒明昧。
又不是困人天气,
中酒心期,
魆魆地常如醉。
[末上]"日下晒书嫌鸟迹,月中捣药要蟾酥。"我

How I regret for dreamland fret!

Chunxiang:

Madam has arranged a Taoist service to rid you of the evil spell.

Du Liniang:

What's the point to rid me of the spell?

Was it in the garden

That I met the evil spirit from the hell?

Chunxiang:

(*To the previous tune*)

When spring has left, does she think so?

When bedtime comes, does she think so?

Can she retain her breath as seasons flow?

She frowns in stress,

Like a beauty in distress.

My dear mistress,

Is the dreamland man your genuine wealth

That damages your fragile health?

You pine away before you wed your man.

What's the use

Of unrequited love in your life-span?

There is no sultry heat,

But you seem to be drunk by chance,

Always in a trance.

(*Enter Chen Zuiliang*)

Chen Zuiliang:

"To air the books, I fear the birds on roads;

To make the medicine, I need the fluid of toads."

I am instructed by the prefect to make a diagnosis for the

陈最良承公相命,来诊视小姐脉息。到此后堂,不免打叫一声。春香贤弟有么?
[贴见介]是陈师父。小姐睡哩。
[末]免惊动他。我自进去。[见介]小姐。
[旦作惊介]谁?
[贴]陈师父哩。
[旦扶起介][旦]师父,我学生患病。久失敬了。
[末]学生,学生,古书有云:"学精于勤,荒于嬉。"你因为后花园汤风冒日,感下这疾,荒废书工。我为师的在外,寝食不安。幸喜老公相请来看病。也不料你清减至此。似这般样,几时能够起来读书?早则端阳节哩。

young mistress. Here I am in the inner court. I'll call for someone to show me the way. Where's my pupil Chunxiang?

Chunxiang:

(*Greets Chen*)

Mr Chen, Miss Du is now sleeping.

Chen Zuiliang:

Don't disturb her. I'll enter the room by myself.

(*Greets Du Liniang*)

Mistress!

Du Liniang:

(*Startled*)

Who is it?

Chunxiang:

It's Mr Chen.

Du Liniang:

(*Sits up on bed*)

Mr Chen, as I'm confined to bed, I haven't paid respects to you for some time.

Chen Zuiliang:

Mistress, as the saying goes in the classics, "Studies start from diligence and ends in negligence." Since you were exposed to the sun and the wind in the backgarden the other day, you have been taken ill and have neglected your studies. I've been worried about your health although I did not come to see you. And so I'm delighted to see you and make a diagnosis for you when orders come from the prefect. But I have not expected to see that you are so frail. In this case, when will you be able to get up and go on with your studies? I'm afraid the Dragon-Boat Festival is the earliest.

[贴]师父，端节有你的。

[末]我说端阳，难道要你粽子？小姐，望闻问切，我且问你病症因何？

[贴]师父问什么！只因你讲《毛诗》，这病便是"君子好求"上来的。

[末]是那一位君子？

[贴]知他是那一位君子。

[末]这般说，《毛诗》病用《毛诗》去医。那头一卷就有女科圣惠方在里。

[贴]师父，可记的《毛诗》上方儿？

[末]便依他处方。小姐害了"君子"的病，用的史君子。《毛诗》："既见君子，云胡不瘳？"这病有了君子抽一抽，就抽好了。

Chunxiang:

You'll have your share for the festival, Mr Chen.

Chen Zuiliang:

When I speak of the Dragon-Boat Festival, I don't mean to ask for my share of the gift. As part of the diagnosis, may I ask how you got ill?

Chunxiang:

There's no need to ask. It must have come from *The Book of Poetry*, especially from the line "*A lad would like to woo*".

Chen Zuiliang:

Which lad do you mean?

Chunxiang:

Who knows!

Chen Zuiliang:

If that is the case, I'll use *The Book of Poetry* to cure a disease contracted from it. There is a magic prescription for women's diseases in the first volume.

Chunxiang:

Do you remember the prescription in *The Book of Poetry*, Mr Chen?

Chen Zuiliang:

According to the prescription, the young mistress should take a lad as she is sick for the lad.

As *The Book of Poetry* has it,

"*As I have seen my dear,*

Why shouldn't I rejoice?"

If the lad gives her a few thrusts, the disease will be thrust out of her at once.

Du Liniang:

[旦羞介]哎也!
[贴]还有甚药?
[末]酸梅十个。《诗》云:"摽有梅,其实七兮",又说:"其实三兮。"三个打七个,是十个。此方单医男女过时思酸之病。
[旦叹介]
[贴]还有呢?
[末]天南星三个。
[贴]可少?
[末]再添些。《诗》云:"三星在天。"专医男女及时之病。
[贴]还有呢?
[末]俺看小姐一肚子火,你可抹净一个大马桶,待

(*Embarrassed*)

Oh!

Chunxiang:

What else would you prescribe?

Chen Zuiliang:

Ten sour plums. As *The Book of Poetry* has it,

"You see seven plums drop

From the tree, lying on the way."

There is also the line

"You see three plums drop from the tree".

Three and seven makes ten. That is a good cure for sour memory of lovesickness between men and women.

(*Du Liniang sighs*)

Chunxiang:

What else?

Chen Zuiliang:

Three southern stars.

Chunxiang:

Will three be enough?

Chen Zuiliang:

Add a few more if you like. It's said in *The Book of Poetry,*

"I see three stars of Orion rise."

This is a good cure for acute lovesickness between men and women.

Chunxiang:

What else?

Chen Zuiliang:

I can see that the young mistress has much internal heat. You go and get a closet-stool ready and I'll feed her with some

我用栀子仁、当归，泻下他火来。这也是依方："之子于归，言秣其马。"

[贴]师父，这马不同那"其马"。

[末]一样髀揪窟洞下。

[旦]好个伤风切药陈先生。

[贴]做的按月通经陈妈妈。

[旦]师父不可执方，还是诊脉为稳。

[末看脉，错按旦手背介]

[贴]师父，讨个转手。

[末]女人反此背看之，正是王叔和《脉诀》。也罢，顺手看是。[诊脉介]呀，小姐脉息，到这个分际了。

【金索挂梧桐】
　　他人才忒整齐，
　　脉息恁微细。
　　小小香闺，
　　为甚伤憔悴？

purgatives. This is part of the prescription:

"If you are married to me,
I'll feed your horse for thee."

Chunxiang:

Feeding the mistress is quite different from feeding the horse.

Chen Zuiliang:

In both cases, you are feeding somebody with something.

Du Liniang:

Mr Chen proves to be a quack doctor.

Chunxiang:

Experienced like an elderly lady in her monthly periods.

Du Liniang:

Don't stick to your prescriptions, Mr Chen. You'd better start by feeling my pulse.

Chen Zuiliang:

(*Tries to feel her pulse on the back of her hand*)

Chunxiang:

Please turn over her hand, Mr Chen.

Chen Zuiliang:

According to the *Pulse Know-how* by the famous doctor Wang Shuhe, you must feel the female pulse upside down. Well, for the time being, I'll turn her hand over.

(*Feels her pulse*)

Good Gracious, her pulse is so weak!

(*To the tune of* **Jinsuoguawutong**)

Her mind is meek;

Her pulse is weak.

In the prime of her day,

What makes her pine away?

[起介]春香呵,似他这伤春怯夏肌,
好扶持。
病烦人容易伤秋意。
小姐,我去咀药来。
[旦叹介]师父,少不得情栽了窍髓针难入,
病躲在烟花你药怎知?
[泣介]承尊觑,
何时何日来看这女颜回?
[合]病中身怕的是惊疑。
且将息,
休烦絮。
[旦]师父且自在。送不得你了。可曾把俺八字推算么?
[末]算来要过中秋好。"当生止有八个字,起死曾
无三世医。"[下]
[贴]一个道姑走来了。

(*Rises to his feet*)

Listen to me, Chunxiang,

Sick in spring and summer days,

Your mistress needs more care

When autumn brings despair.

I'll go and prepare your medicine, Mistress.

Du Liniang:

(*With a sigh*)

Well, Mr Chen,

Deep-rooted out of amour,

My lovesickness is beyond cure.

(*Weeps*)

You try to cure me but in vain;

When will you come to see me again?

Chen Zuiliang, Chunxiang:

As patients cannot bear alarm,

You'd better take a rest

And keep away from harm.

Du Liniang:

Take your time, Mr Chen, I'm afraid I can't see you off. By the way, have you made a divination for me?

Chen Zuiliang:

Yes, you'll turn for the better after the Mid-Autumn Festival.

"*From fate no one has ever fled;*

No doctor can revive the dead."

(*Exit Chen Zuiliang*)

Chunxiang:

Here comes a Taoist nun.

(*Enter Sister Stone*)

[净上]"不闻弄玉吹箫去,又见嫦娥窃药来。"自家紫阳宫石道姑便是。承杜老夫人呼唤,替小姐禳解。[见贴介]

[贴]姑姑为何而来?

[净]吾乃紫阳宫石道姑。承夫人命,替小姐禳解。不知害的甚病?

[贴]尴尬病。

[净]为谁来?

[贴]后花园耍来。

[净举三指,贴摇头介][净举五指,贴又摇头介]

[净]咳,你说是三是五,与他做主。

[贴]你自问他去。

[净见旦介]小姐,小姐,道姑稽首那。

[旦作惊介]那里道姑?

[净]紫阳宫石道姑。夫人有召,替小姐保禳。闻说小姐在后花园着魅,我不信。

Sister Stone:

"While no fairy is heard to give salute,
Another lady tastes forbidden fruit."

I'm Sister Stone from the Purple Sunlight Nunnery. I've received order from the Madam to pray for Miss Du. What is she suffering from?

Chunxiang:

She's suffering from lovesickness.

Sister Stone:

Who is her lover?

Chunxiang:

Someone in the back garden.

(*Sister Stone raises three fingers and Chunxiang shakes her head. Then Sister Stone raises five fingers and Chunxiang shakes her head again*)

Sister Stone:

Well, tell me whether it is three or five and I'll pray for her.

Chunxiang:

Go and ask her by yourself.

Sister Stone:

(*Greets Du Liniang*)

Good morning, Miss Du. I'm a Taoist nun!

Du Liniang:

(*Taken aback*)

Where are you from?

Sister Stone:

I'm Sister Stone from the Purple Sunlight Nunnery. I've received orders from the madam to pray for you. It's said that you were haunted in the back garden, but I don't believe it.

【前腔】
你惺惺的怎着迷？
设设的浑如魅。
[旦作魇语介]我的人那。
[净、贴背介]你听他念念呢呢，
作的风风势。
是了，身边带有个小符儿。
[取旦钗挂小符，作咒介]"赫赫扬扬，日出东方。此符屏却恶梦，辟除不祥。急急如律令敕。"
[插钗介]这钗头小篆符，
眠坐莫教离。
把闲神野梦都回避。
[旦醒介]咳，这符敢不中？我那人呵，
须不是依花附木廉纤鬼，
咱做的弄影团风抹媚痴。
[净]再痴时，请个五雷打他。

(*To the previous tune*)

For a maiden as smart as you,

Can your distracted state be true?

Du Liniang:

(*In a trance*)

Oh my dear!

Sister Stone, Chunxiang:

(*Aside*)

In a trance she said,

As if she'd lost her head.

Sister Stone:

(*Takes a hairpin from Du Liniang and hangs a talisman on it, enchanting an incantation*)

"Beaming bright, beaming bright,

The sun is shedding light.

This talisman dispels the spell

And drives the evils to the hell.

Going, going, gone!"

(*Puts the hairpin back onto Du Liniang's head*)

Keep this talisman

When you sit and sleep

To keep the wild thoughts under ban.

Du Liniang:

(*Comes to her senses*)

Well, is this talisman effective? Isn't my lover

A sprite among the trees

That puts me ill at ease!

Sister Stone:

If she loses her senses again, I'll strike her with a thunderbolt

[旦]些儿意,正待携云握雨,
你却用掌心雷。
[合前]
[净]还分明说与,起个三丈高咒幡儿。
[旦]待说个什么子好?

【尾声】
依稀则记的个柳和梅。
姑姑,你也不索打符桩挂竹枝,
则待我冷思量,
一星星咒向梦儿里。
[贴扶旦下]

[贴]绿惨双蛾不自持,
[净]道家妆束厌禳时。
[旦]如今不在花红处,
[合]为报东风且莫吹。

from my palm.

Du Liniang:

    It makes just little sense

    That while I weather the wind and rain,

    You add a thunder to my pain.

Sister Stone, Chunxiang:

    In a trance she said,

    As if she'd lost her head.

Sister Stone:

    If she goes on like this, I'll hoist a magic flag ten feet high.

Du Liniang:

    What can I say to a nun like this!

    (*To the tune of* **Coda**)

    With the handsome man dim in my mind,

    Oh, Sister Stone,

    You have no need for flags of any kind.

    When I'm in a pensive mood,

    I will be in my dreams confined.

Chunxiang:

    (*Supports Du Liniang and goes off stage*)

    My mistress is too weak to lift an eye;

Sister Stone:

    As a Taoist nun I pray and lie.

Du Liniang:

    I stay away from crimson bloom

All:

    To stop the east wind in its gloom.

第十九出　　牝　贼

【北点绛唇】

[净扮李全引众上]世扰羶风,

家传杂种。

刀兵动,

这贼英雄,

比不的穿墙洞。

"野马千蹄合一群,眼看江海尽风尘。汉儿学得胡儿语,又替胡儿骂汉人。"自家李全是也。本贯楚州人氏。身有万夫不当之勇。南朝不用,去而为盗。以五百人出没江淮之间,正无归着。所幸大金皇帝,遥封俺为溜金王。央我骚扰淮扬,看机进取。奈我多勇少谋。所喜妻子杨氏娘娘,能使一条梨花枪,万人无敌。夫妻上阵,大有威风。则是娘娘有些吃酸,但是掳的妇人,都要送他帐下。便是

Scene Nineteen
The Female Chieftain

(*Enter Li Quan with his men*)

Li Quan:

(*To the tune of* **Beidianjiangchun**)
A smell of mutton struck the land
While aliens dashed and hurled.
Against the winds of war,
We bandit heroes
Outshine the burglars who break the door.
"*The army of a thousand hoofs*
Raises dust and ashes o'er the roofs.
When Hans acquire an alien tongue,
They curse their natives old and young."

I'm Li Quan, a native of Chuzhou. As a warrior brave enough to fight ten thousand men, I was neglected by the southern dynasty and so I became a bandit chieftain of five hundred men, roaming in the Huaiyang area. At a time when I did not know where to turn to, the emperor of the great Jin dynasty bestowed me the title of Gilded Prince, told me to cause trouble in this area and try to find the opportunity to start a military excursion. To tell the truth, I have more courage than wisdom, but my wife Yang helps a lot. With a pear-blossom spear in hand, she has no match among ten thousand men. What a valiant couple we are on the battlefield! The only pity is that my wife is a bit jealous — all the women captives must be

军士们，都只畏惧他。正是："山妻独霸蛇吞象，海贼封王鱼变龙。"

【番卜算】

[丑扮杨婆持枪上]百战惹雌雄，

血映燕支重。

[舞介]一枝枪洒落花风，

点点梨花弄。

[见举手介]大王千岁。奴家介胄在身，不拜了。

[净]娘娘，你可知大金皇帝，封俺做溜金王？

[丑]怎么叫做溜金王？

[净]溜者顺也。

[丑]封你何事？

[净]央俺骚扰淮扬三年。待俺兵粮齐集，一举渡江，灭了赵宋。那时还封俺为帝哩！

handed over to her at once. All my men are more afraid of her than me. It's true that

"A snake of a wife swallows the elephant;
A prince of a bandit is the dragon."

(*Enter Lady Yang, carrying a spear*)

Lady Yang:

(*To the tune of* **Fanbusuan**)

A bandit's wife with spear and shield

Adds blood to rouge on battlefield.

(*Wields her spear*)

With swirls of wind I wield my spear

And sparkles of pear-blooms appear.

(*Raises her hand as a sign of salutation*)

Your Highness, as I'm fully armoured, I won't do the formal greeting.

Li Quan:

Do you know, Madam, that the emperor of the great Jin dynasty has bestowed me the title of Gilded Prince?

Lady Yang:

What's Gilded Prince?

Li Quan:

"Gilded" means "brilliant".

Lady Yang:

Why did he bestow you the title?

Li Quan:

He asked me to cause trouble in Huaiyang for three years. Then when we have amassed a large troop with ample provisions, we'll cross the river and overthrow the Song dynasty. If we succeed, I'll be crowned the king.

[丑]有这等事！恭喜了。借此号令，买马招军。

【六幺令】
　　如雷喧哄，
　　紧辕门画鼓冬冬。
　　哨尖儿飞过海云东。
　　[合]好男女，坐当中，
　　淮扬草木都惊动。

【前腔】
　　取粮收众。
　　选高蹄战马青骢。
　　闪盔缨斜簇玉钗红。
　　[合前]

　　[净]群雄竞起向前朝，
　　[丑]折戟沉沙铁未销。
　　　　平原好牧无人放，
　　　　白草连天野火烧。

Lady Yang:

What a wonder! Congratulations! We'll take this opportunity to buy horses and enrol soldiers.

(*To the tune of Liuyaoling*)

Like thunders in the sky,

In the camps the battle drums will roar

While spies are sent across the eastern shore.

All:

A valiant pair

Sit within the camp

And threaten people everywhere.

Lady Yang:

(*To the previous tune*)

Amass the grain, enrol the men,

And buy the battle steeds.

My hairpins glitter now and then.

All:

A valiant pair

Sit within the camp

And threaten people everywhere.

Li Quan:

Rebellions start all o'er the land,

Lady Yang:

With broken swords stuck in the sand.

No cattle graze on fertile grass

When wildfire spreads afield, alas!

第二十出　　闹　殇

【金珑璁】
[贴上]连宵风雨重，
多娇多病愁中。
仙少效，
药无功。
"颦有为颦，笑有为笑。不颦不笑，哀哉年少。"春香侍奉小姐，伤春病到深秋。今夕中秋佳节，风雨萧条。小姐病转沉吟，待我扶他消遣。正是："从来雨打中秋月，更值风摇长命灯。"[下]

【鹊桥仙】
[贴扶病旦上]拜月堂空，
行云径拥。

Scene Twenty
Premature Death

(*Enter Chunxiang*)

Chunxiang:

(*To the tune of Jinlongcong*)

In nightly storm

Endless woes reduce her form.

No Taoist magic will prevail;

No medicine is of avail.

"You frown when you should frown;

You smile when you should smile.

If you can't smile or frown,

You will die in a while."

I've done my best to wait on Miss Du, for she has been ill from early spring till late autumn. Today is the Mid-Autumn Festival, but it is blowing and raining hard outside. Miss Du is growing from bad to worse, and still I'll bring her here to idle away the time. Yes,

"A heavy rain enshrouds the autumn moon

While prayer lamps will die out soon."

(*Exit Chunxiang*)

(*Enter the sickly Du Liniang supported by Chunxiang*)

Chunxiang:

(*To the tune of Queqiaoxian*)

There is no moonlight in the hall,

When floating clouds conceal the sky.

骨冷怕成秋梦。
世间何物似情浓？
整一片断魂心痛。
[旦]"枕函敲破漏声残，似醉如呆死不难。一段暗香迷夜雨，十分清瘦怯秋寒。"春香，病境沉沉，不知今夕何夕？
[贴]八月半了。
[旦]哎也，是中秋佳节哩。老爷，奶奶，都为我愁烦，不曾玩赏了？
[贴]这都不在话下了。
[旦]听见陈师父替我推命，要过中秋。看看病势转沉，今宵欠好。你为我开轩一望，月色如何？
[贴开窗，旦望介]

【集贤宾】
[旦]海天悠、问冰蟾何处涌？
玉杵秋空，

Her chilly dream is bitter as gall.

Earth has not anything to show more smart

Than her affection in her broken heart.

Du Liniang:

"The water clock drips weaker than my breath

While I still linger on the verge of death.

Amid the fragrance in the nightly rain,

With autumn chill my strength is on the wane."

In my serious illness, Chunxiang, I don't know what day today is.

Chunxiang:

It's the fifteen of the eighth month.

Du Liniang:

Oh, it's the Mid-Autumn Festival! Are my parents too distressed to enjoy the moon?

Chunxiang:

Never mind about that.

Du Liniang:

Mr Chen made the prophecy that I'd get better after the Mid-Autumn Festival. However, my health is going from bad to worse and I don't feel too well this evening. Open the window and I'll have a look at the moon.

(*Chunxiang opens the window and Du Liniang looks at the moon*)

Du Liniang:

(*To the tune of **Jixianbin***)

In the boundless skies,

From where does the moon arise?

In the autumn skies,

凭谁窃药把嫦娥奉?
甚西风吹梦无踪!
人去难逢,
须不是神挑鬼弄。
在眉峰,
心坎里别是一般疼痛。
[旦闷介]

【前腔】
[贴]甚春归无端厮和哄,
雾和烟两不玲珑。
算来人命关天重,
会消详、直恁匆匆!
为着谁侬,
俏样子等闲抛送?
待我谎他。姐姐,月上了。
月轮空,
敢蘸破你一床幽梦。
[旦望叹介]"轮时盼节想中秋,人到中秋不自由。奴命不中孤月照,残生今夜雨中休。"

【前腔】
你便好中秋月儿谁受用?
剪西风泪雨梧桐。

Who helps the fairy arise?

Does the west wind make the dream vaporise?

When he has left, he is hard to see again;

I blame the god and ghost for this in vain.

On my brows and in my heart,

Waves of sorrow start.

(*In a depressed mood*)

Chunxiang:

(*To the previous tune*)

Spring fancy made her in a trance;

Spring fog and smoke aroused romance.

As human life is not a joke,

It starts and ceases in due time;

Who knows her life recedes like smoke!

For whom, for whom

Has she pined away in gloom?

I'll try to give her a little cheer. Mistress, the moon is hanging in the sky.

The silvery moon o'er there

Will send your gloomy dreams into the air.

Du Liniang:

(*Looks up to the sky and sighs*)

"*I've yearned for this Mid-Autumn Day,*

But festive day has filled me with dismay.

Just like the solitary moon,

I'll vanish in the rain too soon."

(*To the previous tune*)

Whom does the autumn moonlight please?

The rain and west wind hurt the trees.

楞生瘦骨加沉重。
趱程期是那天外哀鸿。
草际寒蛩，
撒剌剌纸条窗缝。
[旦惊作昏介]冷松松，
软兀剌四梢难动。
[贴惊介]小姐冷厥了。夫人有请。
[老旦上]"百岁少忧夫主贵，一生多病女儿娇。"
我的儿，病体怎生了？
[贴]奶奶，欠好，欠好。
[老旦]可怎了！

【前腔】
不提防你后花园闲梦铳，
不分明再不惺松，
睡临侵打不起头梢重。
[泣介]恨不呵早早乘龙。
夜夜孤鸿，
活害杀俺翠娟娟雏凤。
一场空，
是这答里把娘儿命送。

I'm growing thinner on sick bed,

　　Like a wild goose hurrying to its shed.

　　I hear the crickets chirrup on the plains

　　And fierce wind whistle through the window-panes.

　　(*Shivers, about to faint*)

　　I feel so chilly in a fit;

　　My limbs can hardly move a bit.

Chunxiang:

　　(*Alarmed*)

　　Miss Du has fainted. Come please, Madam!

　　(*Enter Zhen*)

Zhen:

　　"My husband is so rich in wealth;

　　My daughter is so poor in health."

　　How are you feeling now, my dear daughter?

Chunxiang:

　　She's not feeling well, Madam, she's not feeling well.

Zhen:

　　What's to be done!

　　(*To the previous tune*)

　　The dream in your last garden tour

　　Has put you in a trance;

　　There is no way of any cure.

　　(*Weeps*)

　　How I wish she find a spouse!

　　If she's alone like this,

　　She'll soon die in the house.

　　Everything is null and void;

　　Our lives will be destroyed.

【啭林莺】
　　[旦醒介]甚飞丝缱的阳神动，
　　弄悠扬风马叮咚。
　　[泣介]娘，儿拜谢你了。
　　[拜跌介]从小来觑的千金重，
　　不孝女孝顺无终。
　　娘呵，此乃天之数也。
　　当今生花开一红，
　　愿来生把萱椿再奉。
　　[众泣介]
　　[合]恨西风，一霎无端碎绿摧红。
【前腔】
　　[老旦]并无儿、荡得个娇香种，
　　绕娘前笑眼欢容。
　　但成人索把俺高堂送。
　　恨天涯老运孤穷。
　　儿呵，暂时间月直年空，
　　返将息你这心烦意冗。
　　[合前]

Du Liniang:
>(*Comes to senses again*)
>(*To the tune of Zhuanlinying*)
>What has brought my soul out of the hell?
>I am awakened by the tinkling bell.
>(*Weeps*)

Thank you for coming, Mom.
>(*Falls on her knees in a shaky way*)
>You've treasured me since early days,
>But I can't serve you in my filial ways.

Oh Mom, it's fate!
>I bloom and pine before my prime,
>And so I'll serve you in my next lifetime.

Du Liniang, Zhen, Chunxiang:
>(*Weep*)
>O wild West Wind, why should you
>Strike me like a bolt out of the blue!

Zhen:
>(*To the previous tune*)
>With no sons by my side,
>I only have a dainty daughter,
>Who plays with joy and pride.
>We hoped we'd have her all the time,
>But now she's dying before her prime.

My child,
>As evil omens do suggest,
>Your weary heart will go to rest.

Du Liniang, Zhen, Chunxiang:
>O wild West Wind, why should you

[旦]娘，你女儿不幸，作何处置？

[老旦]奔你回去也。儿!

【玉莺儿】

[旦泣介]旅榇梦魂中，

盼家山千万重。

[老旦]便远也去。

[旦]是不是，听女孩儿一言。这后园中一株梅树，儿心所爱。但葬我梅树之下可矣。

[老旦]这是怎的来？

[旦]做不的病婵娟桂窟里长生，

则分的粉骷髅向梅花古洞。

[老旦泣介]看他强扶头泪濛，

冷淋心汗倾，

不如我先他一命无常用。

[合]恨苍穹，

妒花风雨，

偏在月明中。

Strike me like a bolt out of the blue!

Du Liniang:

If the worst comes to the worst, Mom, what are you going to do with my remains?

Zhen:

We'll send you back to our ancestral burying ground.

Du Liniang:

(*Weeps*)

(*To the tune of* **Yuyinger**)

In the coffin I shall stay,

For fear of hills on homeward way.

Zhen:

We'll send you home although it's a long way.

Du Liniang:

However, I have but one request to make. In the back garden there's a plum tree, which I love very much. Will you bury me under that tree?

Zhen:

How do you come across this idea?

Du Liniang:

As I can't become a fairy queen,

I'll lie beneath a tree that's fresh and green.

Zhen:

(*Weeps*)

She bends her head and sheds large drops of tear,

Soaked with sweat that chills her heart;

At sight of this, I'd give my life for my dear.

Du Liniang, Zhen, Chunxiang:

Oh, relentless heaven,

[老旦]还去与爹讲,广做道场也。儿,"银蟾谩捣君臣药,纸马重烧子母钱。"[下]

[旦]春香,咱可有回生之日否?

【前腔】

[叹介]你生小事依从,

我情中你意中。

春香,你小心奉事老爷奶奶。

[贴]这是当的了。

[旦]春香,我记起一事来。我那春容,题诗在上,外观不雅。葬我之后,盛着紫檀匣儿,藏在太湖石底。

[贴]这是主何意儿?

[旦]有心灵翰墨春容,

倘直那人知重。

Why should flowers suffer from the blight

While the moon is full and bright?

Zhen:

I'll have to go now and prepare with your father for a Taoist service, my child.

"When medicine becomes of little use,

A Taoist service we shall introduce."

(*Exit*)

Du Liniang:

Do you think, Chunxiang, that I may revive someday?

(*Sighs*)

(*To the previous tune*)

You've always been servile to me;

All the time our thoughts agree.

From now on, Chunxiang, be sure to take good care of my parents.

Chunxiang:

Of course I will.

Du Liniang:

Chunxiang, one thing comes to my mind. My portrait, with a poem inscribed on it, should not be exposed to others. When I'm buried, put it in a red sandalwood case and conceal it under a Taihu rock.

Chunxiang:

What for?

Du Liniang:

My portrait, by a maiden fair and smart,

May find an echo in another heart.

Chunxiang:

[贴]姐姐宽心。你如今不幸,坟孤独影。肯将息起来,禀过老爷,但是姓梅姓柳秀才,招选一个,同生同死,可不美哉!

[旦]怕等不得了。哎哟,哎哟!

[贴]这病根儿怎攻,

心上医怎逢?

[旦]春香,我亡后,你常向灵位前叫唤我一声儿。

[贴]他一星星说向咱伤情重。

[合前][旦昏介]

[贴]不好了,不好了,老爷奶奶快来!

【忆莺儿】

[外、老旦上]鼓三冬,

愁万重。

冷雨幽窗灯不红。

听侍儿传言女病凶。

Please rest at ease, Mistress. If you should pass away, you would stay in the grave all by yourself. But if you take a good rest and get recovered, I'll beg your father to find a scholar by the name of Plum Mei or Willow Liu as your life companion. Wouldn't that be wonderful?

Du Liniang:

I'm afraid there's no time for me to wait. Oops, Oops!

Chunxiang:

How can we lessen her disease?

How can we make her heart at ease?

Du Liniang:

After my death, Chunxiang, come and stand before my memorial tablet from time to time, calling aloud to me.

Chunxiang:

Her murmur makes my feeling freeze.

Du Liniang, Chunxiang:

Oh, relentless heaven,

Why should flowers suffer from the blight

While the moon is full and bright?

(*Du Liniang faints away*)

Chunxiang:

Help, help! Hurry up, Master, Madam!

(*Enter Du Bao and Zhen*)

Du Bao, Zhen:

(*To the tune of* Yiyinger)

The night is deep;

The woe is deep.

The gloomy window is wet with rain;

Our daughter fills our hearts with pain.

[贴泣介]我的小姐,小姐!
[外、老旦同泣介]我的儿呵,你舍的命终,
抛的我途穷。
当初只望把爹娘送。
[合]恨匆匆,
萍踪浪影,
风剪了玉芙蓉。
[旦作醒介]
[外]快苏醒!儿,爹在此。
[旦作看外介]哎哟,爹爹扶我中堂去罢。
[外]扶你也,儿。[扶介]
【尾声】
[旦]怕树头树底不到的五更风,
和俺小坟边立断肠碑一统。
爹,今夜是中秋。
[外]是中秋也,儿。

Chunxiang:

(*Weeps*)

Mistress! My dear mistress!

Du Bao, Zhen:

(*Weep*)

Oh, our dear daughter!

When you pass away

And leave us far behind,

Which heir can we then find?

Du Bao, Zhen, Chunxiang:

Alas, alas! The human life is brief,

As a floating dandelion or fading wave,

As a lonely wind-borne lotus leaf.

(*Du Liniang regains senses*)

Du Bao:

Come on, my child! Your dad is here.

Du Liniang:

(*Looks at Du Bao*)

Oh, Dad, help me to the middle hall.

Du Bao:

Lean on me, my child.

(*Supports Du Liniang*)

Du Liniang:

(*To the tune of* Coda)

When I lose life as a dropping bloom,

Please erect a stone before my tomb.

Dad, is it the Mid-Autumn Festival tonight?

Du Bao:

Yes, it is, my child.

[旦]禁了这一夜雨。

[叹介]怎能够月落重生灯再红![并下]

[贴哭上]我的小姐,我的小姐,"天有不测之风云,人有无常之祸福。"我小姐一病伤春死了。痛杀了我家老爷、我家奶奶。列位看官们,怎了也!待我哭他一会。

【红衲袄】
　　小姐,再不叫咱把领头香心字烧,
　　再不叫咱把剔花灯红泪缴,
　　再不叫咱拈花侧眼调歌鸟,
　　再不叫咱转镜移肩和你点绛桃。
　　想着你夜深深放剪刀,
　　晓清清临画稿。
　　提起那春容,被老爷看见了,怕奶奶伤情,分付殉了葬罢。俺想小姐临终之言,
　　依旧向湖山石儿靠也,
　　怕等得个拾翠人来把画粉销。
　　老姑姑,你也来了。

[净上]你哭得好,我也来帮你。

Du Liniang:

    It has been raining all through the night.

    When the moon is set, I'll meet my doom!

    (*Exeunt all*)

    (*Re-enter Chunxiang, in tears*)

Chunxiang:

Mistress, my dear mistress!

    "In nature there are unexpected storms;

    In life there are ill lucks of various forms."

Miss Du died of sorrow for the brevity of spring. My master and madam are deep in grief over her death. Dear audience, what can I do but have a good cry? Mistress, no more will you ask me

    (*To the tune of **Hongnaao***)

    To burn the incense sticks,

    Remove the candle drips,

    Entice the whistling birds,

    Or paint your tender lips.

I still remember the sight when you

    Laid down your scissors late at night

    And drew your portrait till daylight.

Well, speaking of the portrait, my master saw it and told me to bury it with the coffin lest it should make the madam sad. However, I'll follow my mistress' last wish to

    Conceal it under Taihu rock, but fear

    That colours fade before her man comes here.

Oh, here comes Sister Stone.

    (*Enter Sister Stone*)

Sister Stone:

【前腔】
　　春香姐，再不教你暖朱唇学弄箫。
　　[贴]为此。
　　[净]再不和你荡湘裙闲斗草。
　　[贴]便是。
　　[净]小姐不在，春香姐也松泛多少。
　　[贴]怎见得？
　　[净]再不要你冷温存热絮叨，
　　再不要你夜眠迟、朝起的早。
　　[贴]这也惯了。
　　[净]还有省气的所在。
　　鸡眼睛不用你做嘴儿挑，
　　马子儿不用你随鼻儿倒。
　　[贴啐介]
　　[净]还一件，小姐青春有了，没时间做出些儿也，
　　那老夫人呵，少不的把你后花园打折腰。

You're having a good cry and I'll join you. Chunxiang, no more will your mistress

(*To the previous tune*)

Teach you how to play the flute,

Chunxiang:

True.

Sister Stone:

Or stamp on grass and pick the fruit.

Chunxiang:

Naturally.

Sister Stone:

Now that your mistress is dead and gone, life is easier for you.

Chunxiang:

What do you mean?

Sister Stone:

You don't have to

Chat with your young mistress,

Stay up late at night

Or get up before the day is bright.

Chunxiang:

I've got used to it.

Sister Stone:

There's less trouble for you, too. You don't have to

Pout your lips when you pick her corn,

Or clean the night-stool in the morn.

(*Chunxiang spits with scorn*)

What's more, when your mistress has come of age, she might

Have a rendezvous off the track,

And then her mom will break your back.

[贴]休胡说！老夫人来也。
[老旦哭介]我的亲儿，

【前腔】
每日绕娘身有百十遭，
并不见你向人前轻一笑。
他背熟的班姬《四诫》从头学，
不要得孟母三迁把气淘。
也愁他软苗条忒恁娇，
谁料他病淹煎真不好。
[哭介]从今后谁把亲娘叫也，
一寸肝肠做了百寸焦。
[老旦闷倒，贴惊叫介]老爷，痛杀了奶奶也。快来，快来！
[外哭上]我的儿也，呀，原来夫人闷倒在此。

【前腔】
夫人，不是你坐孤辰把子宿嚣，
则是我坐公堂冤业报。
较不似老仓公多女好。
撞不着赛卢医他一病跻。
天，天，似俺头白中年呵，
便做了大家缘何处消？

Chunxiang:

None of your nonsense! Here comes the madam.

Zhen:

(*In tears*)

My dear child!

(*To the previous tune*)

You stayed around me from day to day

And never smiled to men nor went astray.

You learned the maiden classics from the start

And I had not a worry in my heart.

Indeed I had been worried about your health

But never thought that death would strike by stealth.

(*Sobs*)

I'll have no daughter in my future days;

This thought inflicts me in a thousand ways.

(*Falls in a swoon*)

Chunxiang:

(*In alarm*)

Madam has fainted, Master! Hurry, hurry!

(*Enter Du Bao, in tears*)

Du Bao:

My poor child! Alas, here lies my lady in a faint. My lady,

(*To the previous tune*)

Had you not been fated to be without an heir,

I must have made mistakes without compare.

It's best to have more daughters by our side,

When we haven't well-known doctors as our guide.

Oh, heavens, heavens! At my age when my hair turns grey,

What's the use of having massive wealth,

见放着小门楣生折倒!
夫人,你且自保重。
便做你寸肠千断了也,
则怕女儿呵,
他望帝魂归不可招。
〔丑扮院公上〕"人间旧恨惊鸦去,天上新恩喜鹊来。"禀老爷,朝报高升。
〔外看报介〕吏部一本,奉圣旨:"金寇南窥,南安知府杜宝,可升安抚使,镇守淮扬,即日起程,不得违误。钦此。"〔叹介〕夫人,朝旨催人北往,女丧不便西归。院子,请陈斋长讲话。
〔丑〕老相公有请。
〔末上〕"彭殇真一壑,吊贺每同堂。"〔见介〕

When our daughter dies of broken health?
Take care of yourself, my lady. Even if you
Are filled with woe and pain,
Your daughter won't
Come back to life again.

(*Enter the butler*)

Butler:

"*The scared crow flies away with worldly woes;
The magpie brings in bliss the king bestows.*"

My lord, here's the government bulletin on your promotion.

Du Bao:

(*Reads the government bulletin*)

The Ministry of Personnel issues the following imperial decree: "In view of the intended southward invasion by the bandits from the Jin dynasty, Du Bao, Prefect of Nan'an, is promoted to the Envoy of Appeasement in charge of the defence of Huaiyang. Du Bao is to go to his new office without delay. So much for the imperial command."

(*With sighs*)

As the imperial decree impels me to go north, my lady, I won't be able to send Liniang's remains to the west. Butler, send for Tutor Chen at once.

Butler:

His Excellency wants to see you, Mr Chen.

(*Enter Chen Zuiliang*)

Chen Zuiliang:

"*Long life, short life, a grave contains them all;
For weal, for woe, the guests meet in the selfsame hall.*"

(*Greets Du Bao*)

[外]陈先生，小女长谢你了。
[末哭介]正是。苦伤小姐仙逝，陈最良四顾无门。所喜老公相乔迁，陈最良一发失所。
[众哭介]
[外]陈先生有事商量。学生奉旨，不得久停。因小女遗言，就葬后园梅树之下，又恐不便后官居住，已分付割取后园，起座梅花庵观，安置小女神位。就着这石道姑焚修看守。那道姑可承应的来？
[净跪介]老道婆添香换水。但往来看顾，还得一人。
[老旦]就烦陈斋长为便。
[末]老夫人有命，情愿效劳。
[老旦]老爷，须置些祭田才好。

Du Bao:

Mr Chen, my daughter has left you for good.

Chen Zuiliang:

(*Weeps*)

I know. I'm deeply grieved at the passing away of Miss Du, which has left me out of a job. I'm glad that you have been promoted, but I have nowhere to dwell in.

(*All weep*)

Du Bao:

I've something to talk over with you, Mr Chen. I've received the imperial decree to go to my new office immediately. My daughter will be buried under a plum tree in the back garden according to her last wish. As I'm afraid that there might be inconvenience for my successor, I've ordered that the back garden be exclusively separated and be named the Plum Blossom Taoist Nunnery, where my daughter's memorial tablet will be placed. I'd like to ask Sister Stone to tend to the shrine. Sister Stone, do you agree?

Sister Stone:

(*Kneels*)

I'll burn incense and add fresh water to the shrine, but I need someone else to take charge of other duties.

Zhen:

Will you be so kind as to do this, Mr Chen?

Chen Zuiliang:

I'll be glad at your service.

Zhen:

My lord, we'd better assign some land to cover the expenses for the maintenance.

[外]有漏泽院二顷虚田,拨资香火。
[末]这漏泽院田,就漏在生员身上。
[净]咱号道姑,堪收稻谷。你是陈绝粮,漏不到你。
[末]秀才口吃十一方,你是姑姑,我还是孤老,偏不该我收粮?
[外]不消争,陈先生收给。陈先生,我在此数年,优待学校。
[末]都知道。便是老公相高升,旧规有诸生遗爱记、生祠碑文,到京伴礼送人为妙。
[净]陈绝粮,遗爱记是老爷遗下与令爱作表记么?

Du Bao:

There are two hectors of uncultivated land in the public cemetery. The yield from the land can be used to cover the expenses for the nunnery.

Chen Zuiliang:

I'll take care of the land.

Sister Stone:

As I'm the nun of the nunnery, naturally I'll take care of it. As you're nicknamed Chen Jueliang, which means "Devoid of Food", how can you take care of it?

Chen Zuiliang:

A scholar can find food everywhere, including the nunnery. You are the nun of the nunnery, but I am an elderly scholar. Why shouldn't I take care of the land and reap the harvest?

Du Bao:

You don't have to argue. Mr Chen will take care of the land. Mr Chen, in my term of office here, I've always favoured the schools.

Chen Zuiliang:

This is known to all. According to the time-honoured practice, at the time of your promotion, I'll have the local scholars write a eulogy on the love you've left behind for the people and erect an inscribed monument in the memorial hall. Copies of the eulogy and the inscriptions go well with the gifts to your superiors when you arrive in the capital.

Sister Stone:

Mr "Devoid of Food", is the eulogy on the love of your mistress?

Chen Zuiliang:

[末]是老公相政迹歌谣。什么"令爱"!
[净]怎么叫做生祠?
[末]大祠宇塑老爷像供养,门上写着"杜公之祠"。
[净]这等不如就塑小姐在傍,我普同供养。
[外恼介]胡说!但是旧规,我通不用了。

【意不尽】
 陈先生,老道姑,
 咱女坟儿三尺暮云高,
 老夫妻一言相靠。
 不敢望时时看守,
 则清明寒食一碗饭儿浇。

[外]魂归冥漠魄归泉,
[老旦]使汝悠悠十八年。
[末]一叫一回肠一断,
[合]如今重说恨绵绵。

It's a eulogy on the prefect's love for the people. It has nothing to do with the mistress.

Sister Stone:

And what is a memorial hall?

Chen Zuiliang:

It's a large worshipping hall with a statue of the prefect in it. Above the door there is a horizontal board with the inscription "Memorial Hall for Lord Du".

Sister Stone:

In this case, why not have a statue of the young mistress too and we'll take care of them both?

Du Bao:

(*Annoyed*)

None of your nonsense! Although this is a time-honoured practice, I'll do away with it. Mr Chen, Sister Stone,

(*To the tune of Yibujin*)

Our daughter's grave mounts three feet high;

My wife and I entrust it to you hereby.

We do not expect you to watch over it all the time, but we hope that on festivals

A bowl of rice for her you will supply.

Du Bao:

Her soul and spirit have gained eternal life,

Zhen:

After eighteen years of earthly strife.

Chen Zuiliang:

As sorrow for her will forever last,

Du Bao, Zhen, Chen Zuiliang, Sister Stone:

We feel deep grief when we retrace her past.

第二十一出　　谒　遇

【光光乍】
　　[老旦扮僧上]一领破袈裟，
　　香山嶴里巴。
　　多生多宝多菩萨，
　　多多照证光光乍。
　　小僧广州府香山嶴多宝寺一个住持。这寺原是番鬼们建造。以便迎接收宝官员。兹有钦差苗爷任满，祭宝于多宝菩萨位前，不免迎接。
【挂真儿】
　　[净扮苗舜宾，末扮通事，外、贴扮皂卒，丑扮番鬼上]半壁天南开海汊，
　　向真珠窟里排衙。
　　[僧接介]
　　[合]广利神王，
　　善财天女，
　　听梵放海潮音下。

Scene Twenty-one
An Audience with the Envoy

(*Enter the monk*)

Monk:

(*To the tune of* **Guangguangzha**)

In a ragged sakaya here and now,

I am a Buddhist monk in Macao.

With bodhisattvas of abundant wealth

Live many monks of soundest health.

I'm the head monk of the Treasure Temple near the Xiangshan Bay, Guangzhou Prefecture. This temple was built by the foreign merchants to receive the officials of treasure appraisal. The Imperial Envoy Lord Miao, whose term of office has just ended, will display his treasures before the Treasure Bodhisattva. Here I am to welcome him.

(*Enter the imperial envoy Miao Shunbin, followed by the interpreter, two attendants and a foreign merchant*)

Miao Shunbin:

(*To the tune of* **Guazhener**)

As Southern Song begins its foreign trade,

My men approach the Pearl House in a parade.

(*The monk welcomes Miao Shunbin*)

All:

The God of Southern Sea,

Treasure Boy and Virgin Maid

Listen to bodhisattva's decree.

[净]"铜柱珠崖道路难,伏波横海旧登坛。越人自贡珊瑚树,汉使何劳獬豸冠?"自家钦差识宝使臣苗舜宾便是。三年任满,例当祭赛多宝菩萨。通事那里?
[末见介]
[丑见介]伽喇喇。
[老旦见介]
[净]叫通事,分付番回献宝。
[末]俱已陈设。
[净起看宝介]奇哉宝也。真乃磊落山川,精荧日月。多宝寺不虚名矣!看香。[内鸣钟,净礼拜介]

【亭前柳】
　[净]三宝唱三多,
七宝妙无过。
庄严成世界,
光彩遍娑婆。

Miao Shunbin:
> *"Although the traffic to the cliff was hard,*
> *The marshal marched to the sea in disregard.*
> *As the Vietnamese sent corals of their free will,*
> *The envoy need not go through hills and rills."*

I am Miao Shunbin, Imperial Envoy for treasure appraisal. Now that my three years' term of office is over, I'm going to pay my last tribute to the Treasure Bodhisattva. Interpreter!

(*The interpreter greets Miao Shunbin*)

Foreign Merchant:
(*Greets Miao Shunbin*)

Galala ...

(*The monk greets Miao Shunbin*)

Miao Shunbin:
Interpreter, tell the foreign merchant to present his treasures.

Interpreter:
All the treasures are ready for your inspection.

Miao Shunbin:
(*Rises to his feet and inspects the treasures*)

What rare treasures! They are as crystal as mountain torrents and as brilliant as the sun and the moon. This Treasure Temple indeed deserves its name! Offer incense to the Bodhisattva.

(*With ringing of bells within, Miao Shunbin kowtows*)

Miao Shunbin:
(*To the tune of* **Tingqianliu**)

While the monks chant of three virtuous deeds,
I watch the seven treasures none exceeds.
They make the earthly world sedate and bright
And bathe the universe with brilliant light.

甚多，功德无边阔。
[合]领拜南无，多得宝，宝多罗多罗。
[净]和尚，替番回海商，祝赞一番。

【前腔】
[老旦]大海宝藏多，
船舫遇风波。
商人持重宝，
险路怕经过。
刹那，念彼观音脱。
[合前]

【挂真儿】
[生上]望长安西日下，
偏吾生海角天涯。
爱宝的喇嘛，
抽珠的佛法，
滑琉璃两下难拿。
自笑柳梦梅，一贫无赖，弃家而游。幸遇钦差寺中

By displaying this,

The Bodhisattva showers his bliss.

All:

Oh, Bodhisattva,

Give us a great store,

And much makes more.

Miao Shunbin:

Monk, chant a blessing for the foreign merchant.

Monk:

(*To the previous tune*)

The sea abounds in treasures of all kinds,

But waves may toss the ships and minds.

The merchants with their treasure hoard

Fear to brave the wind and waves aboard.

Bodhisattva Guanyin,

Your name brings bliss through thick and thin.

All:

Oh, Bodhisattva,

Give us a great store,

And much makes more.

(*Enter Liu Mengmei*)

Liu Mengmei:

(*To the tune of* **Guazhener**)

The capital lies in the westernmost,

But I was born beside the southern coast.

The treasure-loving lamas

And bead-reckoning monks

Are worthless as the junks.

I often sneer at myself, a penniless loafer without home. As

祭宝,托词进见。倘言语中间,可以打动,得其赈援,亦未可知。
[见外介]
[生]烦大哥通报一声。广州府学生员柳梦梅,来求看宝。
[报介]
[净]朝廷禁物,那许人观。既系斯文,权请相见。
[见介]
[生]"南海开珠殿。
[净]西方掩玉门。
[生]剖怀俟知己。
[净]照乘接贤人。"敢问秀才以何至此?
[生]小生贫苦无聊。闻得老大人在此赛宝,愿求一观,以开怀抱。

chance would have it, the imperial envoy is inspecting the treasures in the temple and I'll try to obtain an audience with him. I don't know whether I can move him into giving me some help.

(*Greets the attendant*)

Sir, will you be kind to announce that Liu Mengmei, student of the Confucian Academy in the Prefecture of Guangzhou, would like to ask permission to have a look at the treasures.

(*The attendant announces*)

Miao Shunbin:

These treasures are gifts to the emperor, not for public display. However, as he's a Confucian scholar, let him come in and have a look.

Liu Mengmei:

(*Greets Miao Shunbin*)

"As pearls in southern palace are the best,

Miao Shunbin:

There is no need to have jade from the west.

Liu Mengmei:

Here I am to bare my thoughts to you,

Miao Shunbin:

And I am glad to meet a brilliant guest."

May I ask why you come to this temple?

Liu Mengmei:

I am a poor scholar. Hearing of your inspection of the treasures, I've come here to ask your permission to let me have a look at the treasures so that I can be enlightened.

Miao Shunbin:

(*With a smile*)

[净笑介]既逢南土之珍,何惜西崑之秘。请试一观。[净引生看宝介]

[生]明珠美玉,小生见而知之。其间数种,未委何名?烦老大人一一指教。

【驻云飞】

[净]这是星汉神砂,
这是煮海金丹和铁树花。
少什么猫眼精光射,
母碌通明差。
嗏,这是靺鞨柳金芽,
这是温凉玉斝,
这是吸月的蟾蜍,
和阳燧冰盘化。
[生]我广南有明月珠,珊瑚树。
[净]径寸明珠等让他,
便是几尺珊瑚碎了他。
[生]小生不游大方之门,何因睹此!

As you are a pearl of a man from the south, I don't have to conceal the western jade from you. Feel free to have a look round.

(*Shows Liu Mengmei around to inspect the treasures*)

Liu Mengmei:

I thought I knew the names of precious jewels and jades, but I cannot recognise some specimens here. Your Excellency, will you be kind to enlighten on me?

Miao Shunbin:

Here you see

(*To the tune of Zhuyunfei*)

The Divine Pebbles of the Milky Way,

The Pills of Gold, the Iron Tree Bloom,

The Cat's-eyes that emit the brilliant ray,

And Emeralds that dispel the gloom.

Look, there you see

The Rubies from the foreign land,

The Magic goblet from the west,

The Toad of Jade that sucks moon-sand,

The Sun-flint Pearls and Ice-plate blest.

Liu Mengmei:

In southern Guangzhou, we have moonlight pearls and coral trees.

Miao Shunbin:

The inch-wide pearls will have no place to stay;

The three-feet corals will all be thrown away.

Liu Mengmei:

If I had not come to this sacred place, how could I have witnessed such miracles!

【前腔】
　　天地精华,
　　偏出在番回到帝子家。
　　禀问老大人,这宝来路多远?
[净]有远三万里的,至少也有一万多程。
[生]这般远,可是飞来、走来?
[净笑介]那有飞走而至之理。都因朝廷重价购求,自来贡献。
[生叹介]老大人,这宝物蠢尔无知,三万里之外,尚然无足而至;生员柳梦梅,满胸奇异,到长安三千里之近,倒无一人购取,有脚不能飞!
　　他重价高悬下,
　　那市舶能奸诈,
　　嗏,浪把宝船划。
[净]疑惑这宝物欠真么?
[生]老大人,便是真,饥不可食,寒不可衣,

(*To the previous tune*)

The rarest treasures come from foreign lands

And in the end will reach imperial hands.

Your Excellency, may I ask how far away these treasures came from?

Miao Shunbin:

Some came from thirty thousand *li* away and the others at least ten thousand *li* away.

Liu Mengmei:

Is that possible? Did they fly here or did they walk here?

Miao Shunbin:

(*Laughs*)

How could they fly or walk! The foreign merchants have brought them here as the court has offered a high price.

Liu Mengmei:

(*With a sigh*)

Your Excellency, these insensible and footless treasures can reach the emperor from thirty thousand *li* away, while a competent scholar like me cannot reach the emperor from three thousand *li* away. I have feet but I cannot fly!

Attracted by alluring prices,

The crafty merchants came by ship;

Alas!

The waves have lent wings to the trip.

Miao Shunbin:

Do you suspect that these treasures are all shams?

Liu Mengmei:

Your Excellency, even if they are genuine, you can't eat them when you are hungry and you can't wear them when you are

看他似虚舟飘瓦。
[净]依秀才说,何为真宝?
[生]不欺,小生到是个真正献世宝。
我若载宝而朝,
世上应无价。
[净笑介]则怕朝廷之上,这样献世宝也多着。
[生]但献宝龙宫笑杀他,
便斗宝临潼也赛得他。
[净]这等便好献与圣天子了。
[生]寒儒薄相,要伺候官府,尚不能够。怎见的圣天子?
[净]你不知到是圣天子好见。
[生]则三千里路资难处。
[净]一发不难。古人黄金赠壮士,我将衙门常例银两,助君远行。

cold. They are but

    Useless small devices!

Miao Shunbin:

Then, what is your idea of genuine treasures?

Liu Mengmei:

To be frank, I am a piece of genuine treasure.

    At court I'll prove my worth,

    The rarest treasure here on earth.

Miao Shunbin:

    (*Laughs*)

I'm afraid that there are too many rare birds at court now.

Liu Mengmei:

    I'm better than the treasures in the sea

    Or all the treasures people ever see.

Miao Shunbin:

In that case, you should be presented to His Majesty.

Liu Mengmei:

As a poor scholar, I'm unable to serve the officials; how am I in a position to see His Majesty?

Miao Shunbin:

You see, it's easier to see the emperor than the officials.

Liu Mengmei:

But the travel expenses for three thousand *li* are more than I can provide.

Miao Shunbin:

That won't be a problem at all. As the ancients gave pieces of gold to valiant men, I will give you pieces of silver from the official revenue to cover your travel expenses.

Liu Mengmei:

[生]果尔,小生无父母妻子之累,就此拜辞。
[净]左右,取书仪,看酒。
[丑上]"广南爱吃荔枝酒,直北偏飞榆荚钱。"酒到,书仪在此。
[净]路费先生收下。
[生]谢了。
[净送酒介]

【三学士】
你带微醺走出这香山罅,
向长安有路荣华。
[生]无过献宝当今驾,
撒去收来再似他。
[合]骤金鞭及早把荷衣挂,
望归来锦上花。

【前腔】
[生]则怕呵,重瞳有眼苍天瞎,

With your help I'll set off at once because I have no family burden.

Miao Shunbin:

Attendants, get some silver for the scholar and prepare some wine.

(*Enter the attendant*)

Attendant:

"*The Guangzhou folk prefer the litchi wine;*
The north-bound scholar meets a patron benign."

The wine is ready and here's the silver.

Miao Shunbin:

Sir, please accept the silver for your travel expenses.

Liu Mengmei:

Thank you very much.

Miao Shunbin:

(*Offers the wine*)

(*To the tune of* **Sanxueshi**)

When you leave here with wine on your lips,

You'll make fair progress on your trips.

Liu Mengmei:

When emperor offers lofty price,

I'll serve him with my sound advice.

Miao Shunbin, Liu Mengmei:

Make haste to shed the scholar's gown;

Become a high official with renown.

Liu Mengmei:

I'm really afraid that

(*To the previous tune*)

Although the emperor has discerning eyes,

似波斯赏鉴无差。
[净]由来宝色无真假,
只在淘金的会拣沙。
[合前]
[生]告行了。
【尾声】
你赠壮士黄金气色佳。
[净]一杯酒酸寒奋发,
则愿的你呵,
宝气冲天海上槎。

[生]乌纱巾上是青天,
[净]俊骨英才气俨然。
[生]闻道金门堪济美,
[净]临行赠汝绕朝鞭。

The heaven may be blind.

Oh that I be a gem the Persians find!

Miao Shunbin:

As the gold is always there,

The panner is aware of what to spare.

Miao Shunbin, Liu Mengmei:

Make haste to shed the scholar's gown;

Become a high official with renown.

Liu Mengmei:

I'm leaving now.

(*To the tune of* Coda)

It's kind of you to give me gold.

Miao Shunbin:

A cup of wine has made you bold.

I wish you

A brilliant future ahead of you!

Liu Mengmei:

Above my black silk hat is lucid air;

Miao Shunbin:

You are a man with noble grace and wit.

Liu Mengmei:

I hear that the imperial court is just and fair;

Miao Shunbin:

I've helped you make your journey there.

第二十二出　　旅　寄

【捣练子】
[生伞、袱，病容上]人出路，鸟离巢。
[内风声介]搅天风雪梦牢骚。
这几日精神寒冻倒。
"香山㠗里打包来，三水船儿到岸开。要寄乡心值寒岁，岭南南上半枝梅。"我柳梦梅。秋风拜别中郎，因循亲友辞饯。离船过岭，早是暮冬。不提防岭北风严，感了寒疾，又无扫兴而回之理。一天风雪，望见南安。好苦也！
【山坡羊】
树槎牙饿鸢惊叫，
岭迢遥病魂孤吊。
破头巾雹打风筛，

Scene Twenty-two
A Hard Journey

(*Enter Liu Mengmei, with an umbrella and a bundle, looking sick*)

Liu Mengmei:
(*To the tune of* **Daolianzi**)
A man en route without a rest
Is like a bird out of its nest.
(*Howling wind within*)
I brave the dreadful wind and snow,
Feeling cold and thus depressed.
"*I packed my bundle in the south*
And took a boat toward the north.
With homesick thoughts in chilly days,
I see plum blossoms bursting forth."
The autumn wind was blowing when I left Envoy Miao Shunbin and had farewell dinner with my kith and kin. Winter has now been well under way when I get off the boat and climb over the Plum Ridge. As the wind north of the ridge is unexpectedly bitter, I've caught a cold but do not want to turn back. After one day's trudge in the wind and snow, now I see Nan'an in the distance. What a wretched journey!
(*To the tune of* **Shanpoyang**)
With hungry vultures howling in the trees,
Alone the sick man leaves the ridge behind.
The hailstones hit my head and make me freeze;

透衣单伞做张儿哨。
路斜抄,
急没个店儿捎。
雪儿呵,偏则把白面书生奚落。
怎生冰凌断桥,
步高低蹬着。
好了。有一株柳,酬将过去。
方便处柳跎腰。
[扶柳过介]虚嚣,
尽枯杨命一条。
蹊跷,
滑喇沙跌一交。[跌介]

【步步娇】
[末上]俺是个卧雪先生没烦恼。
背上驴儿笑,
心知第五桥。
那里开年有斋村学!
[生作哎呀介]
[末]怎生来人怨语声高?
[看介]呀,甚城南破瓦窑,
闪下个精寒料。

The whistling umbrella stirs my mind.

A shortcut I take,

But no inns can I find.

Alas, snow,

Why do you play tricks on me flake by flake?

Look, there's a broken bridge across the stream!

My footsteps shake.

Well, here's a willow tree. I'll hold onto it and walk across the bridge.

It is a hunchback friend, I deem.

(*Holds onto the willow tree and walks across the bridge*)

Snap,

It is a withered tree I've found.

Thump,

I slip and fall flat on the ground.

(*Falls to the ground*)

(*Enter Chen Zuiliang*)

Chen Zuiliang:

(*To the tune of* ***Bubujiao***)

Free from care, free from woe,

On a donkey I ride,

Toward a bridge I go.

To find a tutor's job I've tried.

(*Liu Mengmei groans*)

Why is there such a groan?

(*Looks around*)

Well, from which broken kiln

Comes such a man of skin and bone?

Liu Mengmei:

[生]救人,救人!
[末]我陈最良,为求馆冲寒到此。彩头儿恰遇着吊水之人,且由他去。
[生又叫介]救人!
[末]听说救人,那里不是积福处。俺试问他。
[问介]你是何等之人。失脚在此?
[生]俺是读书之人。
[末]委是读书之人,待俺扶起你来。
[末扶生,相跌,诨介]
[末]请问何方至此?

【风入松】
[生]五羊城一叶过南韶,
柳梦梅来献宝。
[末]有何宝货?
[生]我孤身取试长安道,
犯严寒少衾单病了。

Help! Help!

Chen Zuiliang:

I, Chen Zuiliang, have come out in the cold weather to look for a tutor's job. As my luck would have it, the first thing I meet is someone who falls in the stream. It's none of my business.

Liu Mengmei:

(*Cries again*)

Help!

Chen Zuiliang:

Help? A good deed is always a double blessing. I'll ask him what's happened.

(*Asks Liu Mengmei*)

Who are you and how did you have a fall here?

Liu Mengmei:

I'm a scholar.

Chen Zuiliang:

As you are a scholar, let me help you to your feet.

(*Slips when he tries to help Liu Mengmei to his feet. They make fun at each other*)

May I ask where you come from?

Liu Mengmei:

(*To the tune of* ***Fenrusong***)

From Guangzhou I've come by boat

To offer treasures I can boast.

Chen Zuiliang:

What are your treasures?

Liu Mengmei:

On my way to take imperial tests,

I've caught a cold in flimsy coat.

没揣的逗着断桥溪道,
险跌折柳郎腰。
[末]你自揣高中的,方可去受这等辛苦。
[生]不瞒说,小生是个擎天柱,架海梁。
[末笑介]却怎生冻折了擎天柱,扑倒了紫金梁?这也罢了,老夫颇谙医理。边近有梅花观,权将息度岁而行。

【前腔】
[末]尾生般抱柱正题桥,
做倒地文星佳兆。
论草包似俺堪调药,
暂将息梅花观好。
[生]此去多远?
[末指介]看一树雪垂垂如笑,
墙直上绣幡飘。
[生]这等望先生引进。

[生]三十无家作路人,

When I tried to cross the bridge,

I nearly broke my back and throat.

Chen Zuiliang:

It seems to me that you are fully confident of your success, otherwise you won't be going through all the hardships.

Liu Mengmei:

As a matter of fact, I'm a jade pillar that holds up the sky and a gold bridge that runs across the sea.

Chen Zuiliang:

(*Laughs*)

How comes that the pillar cracks with the cold weather and that the bridge collapses in the middle? Well, so much so. I'm quite well versed in medicine. There is a Plum Blossom Nunnery nearby, where you can stop over till spring comes.

(*To the previous tune*)

A scholar came across the bridge,

A blissful sign to have a fall.

I'll get you medicine on the ridge,

For you to take in nunnery best of all.

Liu Mengmei:

How far is the nunnery away from here?

Chen Zuiliang:

(*Points the way*)

Over there where snow-white blossoms smile

And silken banners wave above the wall.

Liu Mengmei:

Will you please lead the way?

At thirty still without a home,

Chen Zuiliang:

[末]与君相见即相亲。
[生]华阳洞里仙坛上,
[合]似近东风别有因。

>   I saw you at first sight a friend.

Liu Mengmei:

>   In holy places where the fairies roam,

Liu Mengmei, Chen Zuiliang:

>   The east wind escorts them to a good end.

第二十三出　　冥　判

【北点绛唇】

[净扮判官，丑扮鬼持笔、簿上]十地宣差，
一天封拜。
阎浮界，
阳世栽埋，
又把俺这里门楗迈。

自家十地阎罗王殿下一个胡判官是也。原有十位殿下，因阳世赵大郎家，和金达子争占江山，损折众生，十停去了一停，因此玉皇上帝，照见人民稀少，钦奉裁减事例。九州九个殿下，单减了俺十殿下之位，印无归着。玉帝可怜见下官正直聪明，着权管十地狱印信。今日走马到任，鬼卒夜叉，两傍刀剑，非同容易也。

[丑捧笔介]新官到任，都要这笔判刑名，押花字。请

Scene Twenty-three
The Judgement in Hell

(*Enter the infernal judge, followed by a ghost carrying a writing-brush and a register-book*)

Infernal Judge:

(*To the tune of Beidianjiangchun*)

I did my service well

For Prince of Tenth Hell.

The human beings,

When they are no more,

Will be led into our door.

I am Judge Hu under Prince of Tenth Hell. There had been ten princes in the hell, but when the population dwindled due to the wars between the house of Zhao and the house of Jin, the Jade Emperor in the heaven decreed to cut the staff. One prince was to take charge of one of the nine territories, and only the tenth prince was dismissed from his office. As there was no one to take care of the official seal, the Jade Emperor placed it in my charge as a reward to my honesty and intelligence. Today is my first day to be in office. At the sight of the lines of ghosts and yakshas with knives and swords in their hands, I can sense that this is no small occasion.

Ghost:

(*Presents the writing-brush*)

Every new official on his inauguration day will use this brush to allot the punishment and sign his name. Will Your Lordship

新官喝彩他一番。

[净看笔介]鬼使,捧了这笔,好不干系也。

【混江龙】

这笔架在那落迦山外,
肉莲花高耸案前排。
捧的是功曹令史,
识字当该。

[丑]笔管儿?

[净]笔管儿是手想骨、脚想骨,
竹筒般剉的圆滴溜。

[丑]笔毫?

[净]笔毫呵,是牛头须、夜叉发,
铁丝儿揉定赤支毸。

[丑]判爷上的选哩?

[净]这笔头公,是遮须国选的人才。

[丑]有甚名号?

[净]这管城子,在夜郎城受了封拜。

sing praise of the brush?

Infernal Judge:

(*Examines the brush*)

You see, ghost, this writing-brush is of great significance.

(*To the tune of* **Hunjianglong**)

This brush is resting on the rack,

Made of human flesh.

The clerks and copyists at the back

Are always smart and fresh.

Ghost:

What's the brush-shaft made of?

Infernal Judge:

It's made of an arm-bone or a shin-bone,

As round as a bamboo pole.

Ghost:

What about the brush-hairs?

Infernal Judge:

They are hairs from the heads of the ox-head ghosts and the yakshas,

Or scarlet beard encircled by the wire.

Ghost:

Who selected the hairs?

Infernal Judge:

The hairs were picked

According to the special desire.

Ghost:

What is the name of this writing-brush?

Infernal Judge:

This tube of a pen

[丑]判爷兴哩?
[净作笑舞介]啸一声,支兀另汉钟馗其冠不正。
舞一回,疏喇沙斗河魁近墨者黑。
[丑]喜哩?
[净]喜时节,溱河桥题笔儿耍去。
[丑]闷呵?
[净]闷时节,鬼门关投笔归来。
[丑]判爷可上榜来?
[净]俺也曾考神祇,朔望旦名题天榜。
[丑]可会书来?
[净]摄星辰,井鬼宿,
俺可也文会书斋。

Is honoured by the sire.

Ghost:

What would you do if you are in high spirits?

Infernal Judge:

(*Laughs and then dances*)

I'll make a whistle

To scare away the evil force,

Or start a dance

To track the heavenly course.

Ghost:

What if you are merry?

Infernal Judge:

When I'm merry,

I'll bring my brush toward the bridge to hell.

Ghost:

What if you are bored?

Infernal Judge:

When I'm bored,

I'll throw my brush toward the door to hell.

Ghost:

Did you succeed in the celestial examination?

Infernal Judge:

When I took the test for gods,

My name was listed on the top.

Ghost:

Are you good at writing poems?

Infernal Judge:

With the help of literary stars,

My flow of poems will never stop.

[丑]判爷高才。
[净]做弗迭鬼仙才,
白玉楼摩空作赋;
陪得过风月主,
芙蓉城遇晚书怀。
便写不尽四大洲转轮日月,
也差的着五瘟使号令风雷。
[丑]判爷见有地分?
[净]有地分,则合北斗司、阎浮殿,立俺边傍;
没衙门,却怎生东岳观、城隍庙,也塑人左侧。
[丑]让谁?
[净]便百里城高捧手,
让大菩萨,好相庄严乘坐位。
[丑]恼谁?
[净]怎三尺土,低分气,

Ghost:

You are a highly gifted scholar.

Infernal Judge:

    Although I'm no match with Li He

    Whose songs resounded to a height,

    I'm on a par with Shi Manqing

    Who wrote his poems at night.

    Although I can't depict the whole wild world,

    I can well stir up trouble with all might.

Ghost:

What position are you holding now?

Infernal Judge:

    You ask about my position?

    In Polaris' hall, in Yama's palace,

    I stand erect with pride.

    You say I've no office?

    In temples of mountain gods and city gods,

    My statue stands on the left-hand side.

Ghost:

Is there anyone whom you respect?

Infernal Judge:

    With upraised hands I stand there in my place,

    And let the Buddha sit in solemn grace.

Ghost:

Is there anyone who annoys you?

Infernal Judge:

Well, a statue of mine less than three feet tall is by no means majestic. I have to face

    Inferior ghosts of various kinds

对小鬼卒，清奇古怪立基阶。
[丑]纱帽古气些。
[净]但站脚，
一管笔、一本簿，尘泥轩冕。
[丑]笔干了。
[净]要润笔，
十锭金、十贯钞，纸陌钱财。
[丑]点鬼簿在此。
[净]则见没揸三展花分鱼尾册，
无赏一挂日子虎头牌。
真乃是鬼董狐落了款，
《春秋传》某年某月某日下，
崩薨葬卒大注脚。
假如他支祈兽上了样，
把禹王鼎各山各水各路上，
魍魍魑魅细分腮。
[丑]待俺磨墨。
[净]看他子时砚，
忔忔察察，

With grotesque shapes and minds.

Ghost:

Your official hat is somewhat outworn.

Infernal Judge:

As I stand all day,

With a writing-brush and a register-book in hand,

My hat is stained with dust and clay.

Ghost:

There's no ink on your writing-brush.

Infernal Judge:

To moisten the brush,

If you give me gold, silver or money,

I will not blush.

Ghost:

Here's the register-book of the dead.

Infernal Judge:

To find the names I take a casual look

And fetch the dead men at the proper date.

I'll make a tick and sign my name

Behind one man or another

According to his destined fate.

In the register-book

Is recorded every name,

Be it small or great.

Ghost:

I'll prepare the ink for you.

Infernal Judge:

On the slab he prepares the ink;

Scritch-scratch, scritch-scratch,

乌龙蘸眼显精神。
[丑]鸡唱了。
[净]听丁字牌，冬冬登登，
金鸡觉梦追魂魄。
[丑]禀爷点卷。
[净]但点上格子眼，
串出四万八千三界，
有漏人名，乌星炮粲。
怎按下笔尖头，
插入一百四十二重，
无间地狱铁树花开。
[丑]大押花。
[净]哎也，押花字，止不过发落簿刲、烧、舂、磨一灵儿。
[丑]少一个请字。
[净]登请书，左则是那虚无堂，
瘫、痨、蛊、膈四正客。
[丑]吊起称竿来。
[众卒应介]

The ink is black and is filled to the brink.

Ghost:

The cock is crowing.

Infernal Judge:

The death-knell tolls,

Ding-dong, ding-dong,

While cocks invoke the wandering souls.

Ghost:

Will you please tick the names now?

Infernal Judge:

When I tick some names,

These souls will enter samsara,

A multitude of weal and woe.

When I tick the other names,

Those souls will enter bottomless hell,

To suffer endless torments down below.

Ghost:

Your signature, please.

Infernal Judge:

Alas, with my signature,

They will go through severe ordeal.

Ghost:

What about "invitations"?

Infernal Judge:

As for invitations,

They're for the sick that cannot heal.

Ghost:

Hang up the scales!

(*Petty ghosts respond in chorus*)

[净]发称竿,看业重身轻,
衡石程书秦狱吏。
[内作"哎哟",叫"饶也,苦也"介]
[丑]隔壁九殿下拷鬼。
[净]肉鼓吹,听神啼鬼哭,
毛钳刀笔汉乔才。
这时节呵,你便是没关节包待制、"人厌其笑"。
[内哭介]
恁风景,谁听的无棺椁颜修文、"子哭之哀"!
[丑]判爷害怕哩。
[净恼介]哎,《楼炭经》,是俺六科五判。
刀花树,是俺九棘三槐。
脸娄搜风髯赴赴。
眉剔竖电目崖崖。
少不得中书鬼考,
录事神差。

Infernal Judge:
> With a pair of scales hanging on hair,
>
> We find their bodies lighter than their crime,
>
> And so we'll finish with them in no time.
>
> (*Cries of pain and begging for mercy are heard from within*)

Ghost:
The Ninth Prince is torturing the dead souls next door.

Infernal Judge:
The torture is music of the flesh.
> The wails and howls of those dead souls
>
> Are masterpieces of pain.
>
> At this time,
>
> The slightest smile is thought to be insane.
>
> (*Wails are heard from within*)
>
> In this place,
>
> The faintest moan is held in rein.

Ghost:
So you are afraid!

Infernal Judge:
> (*Annoyed*)

Oops!
> By infernal law
>
> I mete out different awards.
>
> In the dreadful hell,
>
> I wield my judicial swords.
>
> My bearded face is fierce and stern;
>
> My uplift eyes are burning bright.
>
> I've got recorders on my left
>
> And secretaries on my right.

比着阳世那金州判、银府判、铜司判、铁院判,
白虎临官,
一样价打贴刑名催伍作;
实则俺阴府里注湿生,牒化生,准胎生,照卵生,
青蝇报赦,
十分的磊齐功德转三阶。
威凛凛人间掌命,
颤巍巍天上消灾。
叫掌案的,这簿上开除都也明白。还有几宗人犯,应该发落了?
[贴扮吏上]"人间勾令史,地下列功曹。"禀爷,因缺了殿下,地狱空虚三年。则有枉死城中轻罪男子四名,赵大、钱十五、孙心、李猴儿;女囚一名,杜丽娘:未经发落。
[净]先取男犯四名。

Like the gold county judge,
Like the silver prefectural judge,
Like the copper provincial judge,
Like the iron ministerial judge —
Like all the judges in the earthly courts,
I make my judgements according to laws.
With a humidity samsara,
With a universe samsara,
With a womb samsara,
With a shell samsara —
With different samsara forms,
I've been promoted because I have norms.
In dignity I rule the fate of men;
In majesty I fulfil the godly yen.

Send for the secretary. As is recorded in the register-book, how many cases are to be dispatched today?

(*Enter the secretary*)

Secretary:

"*A secretary in the human world*
Becomes a secretary in the nether world."

Your Lordship, since the Tenth Prince was dismissed, his office has been vacant for three years. In the City of Innocent Deaths, there are four males of minor offences Zhao Da, Qian Shiwu, Sun Xin and Li Houer, in addition to a female Du Liniang. They haven't been sentenced yet.

Infernal Judge:

Bring in the four male offenders first.

(*The ghost leads in the four male offenders: Zhao Da, Qian Shiwu, Sun Xin and Li Houer*)

[生、末、外、老旦扮四犯,丑押上]

[丑]男犯带到。

[净点名介]赵大有何罪业,脱在枉死城?

[生]鬼犯没甚罪。生前喜歌唱些。

[净]一边去。叫钱十五。

[末]鬼犯无罪。则是做了一个小小房儿,沉香泥壁。

[净]一边去。叫孙心。

[老旦]鬼犯些小年纪,好使些花粉钱。

[净]叫李猴儿。

[外]鬼犯是有些罪,好男风。

[丑]是真。便在地狱里,还勾上这小孙儿。

[净恼介]谁叫你插嘴!起去伺候。

Ghost:

Here are the male offenders.

Infernal Judge:

(*Calls the roll*)

For what offence, Zhao Da, are you detained in the City of Innocent Death?

Zhao Da:

I'm not guilty. When I was alive, I would like to sing some songs.

Infernal Judge:

Step aside. What about you, Qian Shiwu?

Qian Shiwu:

I'm not guilty. When I built a small hut, I mixed some allalloch eaglewood in the mud.

Infernal Judge:

Step aside. And you, Sun Xin?

Sun Xin:

When I was young, I used to spend some money in the brothel.

Infernal Judge:

And you, Li Houer?

Li Houer:

I committed a minor offence. I'm homosexual.

Ghost:

That's true. Even here in the hell he seduced a little monkey of a man.

Infernal Judge:

(*Annoyed*)

Shut up! Stand back and mind your own business!

(*Writes on the register-book*)

[做写簿介]叫鬼犯听发落。[四犯同跪介]
[净]俺初权印,且不用刑。赦你们卵生去罢。
[外]鬼犯们禀问恩爷,这个卵是什么卵?若是回回卵,又生在边方去了。
[净]咦,还想人身?向蛋壳里走去。
[四犯泣介]哎。被人宰了!
[净]也罢,不教阳间宰吃你。赵大喜歌唱,贬做黄莺儿。
[生]好了。做莺莺小姐去。
[净]钱十五住香泥房子。也罢,准你去燕窠里受用,做个小小燕儿。
[末]恰好做飞燕娘娘哩。
[净]孙心使花粉钱,做个蝴蝶儿。
[外]鬼犯便和孙心同做蝴蝶去。

Now listen carefully to the verdicts.

(*The four male offenders kneel on the ground*)

As I have just come into office, I'm not going to put you to tortures. You are remitted and allowed to have a shell samsara.

Li Houer:

Would Your Lordship tell us what shells you mean? If they are of Arabian eggs, we'll be reborn in the remote border-area.

Infernal Judge:

Pooh, do you want to be reborn a man? You'll enter the egg-shells.

Zhao Da, Qian Shiwu, Sun Xin, Li Houer:

(*Wail loudly*)

Oh, we'll be devoured by men!

Infernal Judge:

All right, I won't have men devour you. Zhao Da, as you were fond of singing, you shall be reborn as an oriole.

Zhao Da:

It's nice of you. I shall be Miss Oriole in my next life!

Infernal Judge:

Qian Shiwu, as you used to live in a spiced mud hut, you shall be reborn as a swallow to enjoy your next life in a swallow's nest.

Qian Shiwu:

I'll be glad to be Empress Swallow in my next life!

Infernal Judge:

Sun Xin, as you used to spend money in the brothel, you shall be reborn as a butterfly.

Li Houer:

I'd like to go with Sun Xin and be a butterfly too.

[净]你是那好男风的李猴,着你做蜜蜂儿去,屁窟里长拖一个针。

[外]哎哟,叫俺钉谁去?

[净]四位虫儿听分付:

【油葫芦】
　　蝴蝶呵,你粉版花衣胜剪裁;
　　蜂儿呵,你忒利害,甜口儿咋着细腰捱;
　　燕儿呵,斩香泥弄影钩帘内;
　　莺儿呵,溜笙歌警梦纱窗外:
　　恰好个花间四友无拘碍。
　　则阳世里孩子们轻薄,
　　怕弹珠儿打的呆,
　　扇梢儿扑的坏,
　　不枉了你宜题入画高人爱,
　　则教你翅挪儿展将春色闹场来。

[外]俺做蜂儿的不来,再来钉肿你个判官脑。

[净]讨打。

[外]可怜见小性命。

Infernal Judge:

    Li Houer, as you used to be a homosexual, you shall be reborn as a bee with a needle in your ass-hole.

Li Houer:

    Why, whom am I to sting?

Infernal Judge:

    Now you four insects, listen to me.

        (*To the tune of Youhulu*)

    Oh Butterfly,

    How pretty is your powdered coat!

    Oh Bee,

    How bitter is your biting sting!

    Oh Swallow,

    How fragrant is your mudded nest!

    Oh Oriole,

    How pleasant is the song you sing!

    You friends will fly among the blooms abreast.

    In the earthly world, the lads and lasses may

    Pelt you oriole all around,

    Or strike you butterfly with a perfume fan.

    At the same time,

    In paintings you swallow is found;

    In spring you bee will buzz as hard as you can.

Li Houer:

    When I come here again as a bee, I'll sting your head.

Infernal Judge:

    You're asking for a sound beating.

Li Houer:

    Oh, pity on me!

[净]罢了。顺风儿放去,快走快走。
[净噗气介][四人做各色飞下]
[净做向鬼门嘘气呎声介]
[丑带旦上]"天台有路难逢俺,地狱无情欲恨谁?"女鬼见。
[净抬头背介]这女鬼到有几分颜色!

【天下乐】
　　猛见了荡地惊天女俊才,
　　哈也么哈,来俺里来。
　　[旦叫苦介]
　　[净]血盆中叫苦观自在。
　　[丑耳语介]判爷权收做个后房夫人。
　　[净]咳,有天条,擅用囚妇者斩。
　　则你那小鬼头胡乱筛,
　　俺判官头何处买?
　　[旦叫哎介]

Infernal Judge:

All right, be gone with the wind! Get out at once!

(*The Infernal Judge puffs at the four males. Exeunt the four, each flying in his own manner. The Infernal Judge whistles towards the exit. Enter the ghost, ushering in Du Liniang*)

Ghost:

"You won't meet me on Heaven's path;

I'm not to blame for Hell's fierce wrath."

Here's the female offender.

Infernal Judge:

(*Raises his head. Aside*)

What a fair lady-ghost!

(*To the tune of **Tianxiale***)

A fairy of a ghost is standing here,

Heigh-ho, heigh-ho,

Come near, please come near.

(*Du Liniang complains*)

Infernal Judge:

Bodhisattva Guanyin's cry in hell, I hear.

Ghost:

(*Whispers in Infernal Judge's ear*)

Why don't you take her as your concubine?

Infernal Judge:

Pooh, according to the celestial law, those who flirt with women prisoners will be beheaded.

"You may go on with your wild talk,

But without my head, how can I walk?"

(*Du Liniang moans*)

Infernal Judge:

[净回身]是不曾见他粉油头忒弄色。
叫那女鬼上来。

【那吒令】
瞧了你润风风粉腮,
到花台、酒台?
溜些些短钗,
过歌台、舞台?
笑微微美怀,
住秦台、楚台?
因甚的病患来?
是谁家嫡支派?
这颜色不像似在泉台。

[旦]女囚不曾过人家,也不曾饮酒,是这般颜色。则为在南安府后花园梅树之下,梦见一秀才,折柳一枝,要奴题咏。留连婉转,甚是多情。梦醒来沉吟,题诗一首:"他年若傍蟾宫客,不是梅边是柳边。"为此感伤,坏了一命。

[净]谎也。世有一梦而亡之理?

【鹊踏枝】
一溜溜女婴孩,
梦儿里能宁耐!
谁曾挂圆梦招牌,

(*Turns back*)

Doesn't she seem to flirt with me?

Bring her forward!

(*To the tune of Nuozhaling*)

With rosy cheeks,

Are you going to a garden or a pub?

With pretty hairpins,

Are you going to a concert or a club?

With honey smiles,

Are you going to a date?

Of what illness did you die?

Where is your family estate?

Your colour is alien to hell at any rate.

Du Liniang:

I've neither married nor drunk any wine. My skin has looked like this since I was born. Under a plum tree in the back garden of Nan'an Prefect's residence, I dreamed of a scholar who snapped off a willow-twig and asked me to write a poem about it. He was gentle and affectionate. When I woke up, I wrote a poem, saying,

> "*Her future spouse who shares the pillow*
> *Will be found by the plum or willow.*"

As a matter of fact, I died of lovesickness.

Infernal Judge:

You liar! How can anyone die as a result of a dream?

(*To the tune of Quetazhi*)

Young and tiny as you look,

You cling so strongly to your dream.

Who can read your dream?

谁和你拆字道白?
哈也么哈,
那秀才何在?
梦魂中曾见谁来?
[旦]不曾见谁。则见朵花儿闪下来,好一惊。
[净]唤取南安府后花园花神勘问。
[丑叫介]
[末扮花神上]"红雨数番春落魄,山香一曲女消魂。"老判大人请了。[举手介]
[净]花神,这女鬼说是后花园一梦,为花飞惊闪而亡。可是?
[末]是也。他与秀才梦的绵缠,偶尔落花惊醒。这女子慕色而亡。
[净]敢便是你花神假充秀才,迷误人家女子?
[末]你说俺着甚迷他来?

Who can guess the theme?

Heigh-ho, heigh-ho,

Where is this young scholar?

Who else did you see in your dream?

Du Liniang:

I didn't see anyone else. When a flower dropped off, I was frightened.

Infernal Judge:

Send for the flower god in charge of the prefect's back garden in Nan'an.

(*The ghost repeats the order*)

(*Enter Flower God*)

Flower God:

"The flowers drop with springtime rain;

A moment's joy is mixed with pain."

How do you do, Your Excellency!

(*Salutes the Infernal Judge*)

Infernal Judge:

Flower God, she says that she had a dream in the back garden and died of a startle caused by a fallen flower. Is that true?

Flower God:

Yes. She was dreaming of a rendezvous with a young scholar when she was wakened by a fallen flower. She died of lovesickness.

Infernal Judge:

Were you dressed as a young scholar to allure her?

Flower God:

Do you mean that I allured her?

Infernal Judge:

[净]你说俺阴司里不知道呵!

【后庭花滚】
　　但寻常春自在,
　　恁司花忒弄乖。
　　眨眼儿偷元气艳楼台。
　　克性子费春工淹酒债。
　　恰好九分态,
　　你要做十分颜色。
　　数着你那胡弄的花色儿来。
　　[末]便数来。碧桃花。
　　[净]他惹天台。
　　[末]红梨花。
　　[净]扇妖怪。
　　[末]金钱花。
　　[净]下的财。
　　[末]绣球花。
　　[净]结得彩。
　　[末]芍药花。
　　[净]心事谐。

Do you think that we are all fools in the nether world?

(*To the tune of* **Houtinghuagun**)

Spring is a carefree time for all,

But you disturb the peace of mind.

With flowers you decorate the hall;

You should have left your lust behind.

With blossoms at your beck and call,

An overabundance glares mankind.

Now, enumerate the flowers you find.

Flower God:

I'll enumerate for you. The peach blossom —

Infernal Judge:

Leads to a lover's tryst;

Flower God:

The pear blossom —

Infernal Judge:

Gives love a twist.

Flower God:

The gold-coin blossom —

Infernal Judge:

Is a wedding gift;

Flower God:

The seven-barks blossom —

Infernal Judge:

Serves as a wooing shift.

Flower God:

The peony blossom —

Infernal Judge:

Links the hearts;

［末］木笔花。
［净］写明白。
［末］水菱花。
［净］宜镜台。
［末］玉簪花。
［净］堪插戴。
［末］蔷薇花。
［净］露渲腮。
［末］腊梅花。
［净］春点额。
［末］翦春花。
［净］罗袂裁。
［末］水仙花。
［净］把绫袜踹。

Flower God:

    The brush-pen blossom —

Infernal Judge:

    Practices the writing arts.

Flower God:

    The water chestnut blossom —

Infernal Judge:

    Stands on the dressing-table there;

Flower God:

    The plantain lily blossom —

Infernal Judge:

    Adorns the hair.

Flower God:

    The rose blossom —

Infernal Judge:

    Applies to the face;

Flower God:

    The winter-sweet blossom —

Infernal Judge:

    Paints the forehead with grace.

Flower God:

    The mullein blossom —

Infernal Judge:

    Decorates the skirt;

Flower God:

    The narcissus blossom —

Infernal Judge:

    Looks like a fairy shirt.

Flower God:

[末]灯笼花。
[净]红影筛。
[末]酴醿花。
[净]春醉态。
[末]金盏花。
[净]做合卺杯。
[末]锦带花。
[净]做裙褶带。
[末]合欢花。
[净]头懒抬。
[末]杨柳花。
[净]腰恁摆。
[末]凌霄花。
[净]阳壮的咍。
[末]辣椒花。

The lantern blossom —
Infernal Judge:
> Is shining bright;

Flower God:
> The roseleaf raspberry blossom —

Infernal Judge:
> Causes a drunken sight.

Flower God:
> The pot marigold blossom —

Infernal Judge:
> Serves for a wedding cup;

Flower God:
> The ribbon blossom —

Infernal Judge:
> Ties the skirt up.

Flower God:
> The mulga blossom —

Infernal Judge:
> Hangs her head in taste;

Flower God:
> The willow blossom —

Infernal Judge:
> Sways like slender waist.

Flower God:
> The trumpet-vine blossom —

Infernal Judge:
> Blows like a cock;

Flower God:
> The hot-pepper blossom —

[净]把阴热窄。
[末]含笑花。
[净]情要来。
[末]红葵花。
[净]日得他爱。
[末]女萝花。
[净]缠的歪。
[末]紫薇花。
[净]痒的怪。
[末]宜男花。
[净]人美怀。
[末]丁香花。
[净]结半躧。
[末]豆蔻花。

Infernal Judge:
>Removes her block.

Flower God:
>The Michelia figo blossom —

Infernal Judge:
>Expects her love;

Flower God:
>The red sunflower blossom —

Infernal Judge:
>Turns to her face above.

Flower God:
>The liana blossom —

Infernal Judge:
>Twines like a bitch;

Flower God:
>The crape myrtle blossom —

Infernal Judge:
>Fears the itch.

Flower God:
>The day lily blossom —

Infernal Judge:
>Prophesies a son;

Flower God:
>The lilac blossom —

Infernal Judge:
>Blooms in the sun.

Flower God:
>The cardamum blossom —

Infernal Judge:

［净］含着胎。
［末］奶子花。
［净］摸着奶。
［末］栀子花。
［净］知趣乖。
［末］柰子花。
［净］恣情奈。
［末］枳壳花。
［净］好处揩。
［末］海棠花。
［净］春困怠。
［末］孩儿花。
［净］呆笑孩。
［末］姊妹花。
［净］偏妒色。

Is pregnant with seeds;
Flower God:
The milk blossom —
Infernal Judge:
Is sufficient for needs.
Flower God:
The gardenia blossom —
Infernal Judge:
Is discrete beyond compare;
Flower God:
The wild-apple blossom —
Infernal Judge:
Is free from any care.
Flower God:
The citrus blossom —
Infernal Judge:
Leans against the fence;
Flower God:
The crabapple blossom —
Infernal Judge:
Has a drowsy sense.
Flower God:
The boy blossom —
Infernal Judge:
Is a smiling lad;
Flower God:
The sister blossom —
Infernal Judge:
Is a jealous lass.

[末]水红花。
[净]了不开。
[末]瑞香花。
[净]谁要采。
[末]旱莲花。
[净]怜再来。
[末]石榴花。
[净]可留得在?几桩儿你自猜。
哎,把天公无计策。
你道为什么流动了女裙钗,
划地里牡丹亭又把他杜鹃花魂魄洒?
[末]这花色花样,都是天公定下来的。小神不过遵奉钦依,岂有故意勾人之理?且看多少女色,那有玩花而亡。
[净]你说自来女色,没有玩花而亡。数你听着。

Flower God:

The knotweed blossom —

Infernal Judge:

Is reluctant to bud;

Flower God:

The winter daphne blossom —

Infernal Judge:

Sleeps in the mud.

Flower God:

The dryland lotus blossom —

Infernal Judge:

Attracts her spouse to come again;

Flower God:

The pomegranate blossom —

Infernal Judge:

Is kept in vain.

There are more riddles for you to guess,

Riddles that put the heaven in stress.

What made her take bated breath?

Why did she die an early death?

Flower God:

It is the heaven that predestines the colours and shapes of flowers. I do nothing but carry out the heaven's decrees. How dare I tempt anyone? I've never heard of any beautiful lady dying of love for flowers.

Infernal Judge:

You say that no beautiful ladies died of love for flowers? I'll name a few for you.

(*To the tune of **Jishengcao***)

【寄生草】
　　花把青春卖，
　　花生锦绣灾。
　　有一个夜舒莲，
　　扯不住留仙带；
　　一个海棠丝翦不断香囊怪；
　　一个瑞香风赶不上非烟在。
　　你道花容那个玩花亡？
　　可不道你这花神罪业随花败。
[末]花神知罪，今后再不开花了。
[净]花神，俺这里已发落过花间四友，付你收管。这女囚慕色而亡，也贬在燕莺队里去罢。
[末]禀老判，此女犯乃梦中之罪，如晓风残月。且他父亲为官清正，单生一女，可以耽饶。
[净]父亲是何人？
[旦]父亲杜宝知府，今升淮扬总制之职。

The flowers make the maidens in a mess;
The flowers make the maidens in distress.
There was a lotus that bloomed at night,
And Empress Feiyan died on the site.
There was a crabapple that never quit,
And Lady Yang was buried with it.
There was a winter daphne that caught man's breath,
And Concubine Feiyan was flogged to death.
How can you say that flowers bring no harm?
You Flower God roused all the alarm!

Flower God:

I know I'm guilty. From now on I'll allow no blooming.

Infernal Judge:

I've just given verdicts to the four friends among the flowers. You are now to watch over them. Since this female offender died of lovesickness, she'll go with them as a swallow or an oriole.

Flower God:

Your Excellency, this female offender committed a crime in her dream, which is as invisible as the morning breeze. Besides, as her father is an upright official and she is his only child, I think she should be remitted.

Infernal Judge:

Who is your father?

Du Liniang:

My father was the Prefect of Nan'an, and is now promoted to be Envoy of Appeasement in charge of the defence of Huaiyang.

Infernal Judge:

[净]千金小姐哩。也罢,杜老先生分上,当奏过天庭,再行议处。
[旦]就烦恩官替女犯查查,怎生有此伤感之事?
[净]这事情注在断肠簿上。
[旦]劳再查女犯的丈夫,还是姓柳姓梅?
[净]取婚姻簿查来。[作背查介]是。有个柳梦梅,乃新科状元也。妻杜丽娘,前系幽欢,后成明配。相会在红梅观中。不可泄漏。[回介]有此人和你姻缘之分。我今放你出了枉死城,随风游戏,跟寻此人。
[末]杜小姐,拜了老判。
[旦叩头介]拜谢恩官,重生父母。则俺那爹娘在扬州,可能够一见?

So you're a maiden with blue blood. Well, on account of Prefect Du, I'll report your case to the celestial emperor before I pass a sentence on you.

Du Liniang:

Will you be so kind as to check why I was reduced to such misery?

Infernal Judge:

It must have been recorded in the Book of Heartbreaks.

Du Liniang:

Will you do me another favour by checking the name of my husband? Is he Liu or Mei? Has he anything to do with Willow or Plum?

Infernal Judge:

Get me the Marriage Book.

(*Turns aside and looks up the Marriage Book*)

Yes, here is Liu Mengmei, the new Number One Scholar. Wife, Du Liniang. A secret love at first, official wedding in the end. Destined to meet in the Red Plum Blossom Nunnery. Top secret.

(*Turns round*)

You are destined to marry this man. I'll release you from the City of Innocent Deaths so that you can float with the wind and look for this man.

Flower God:

Miss Du, kowtow to the Judge!

Du Liniang:

(*Kowtows*)

Thank you for giving me a second life. However, as my parents are in Yangzhou, may I see them again?

[净]使得。

【幺篇】
他阳禄还长在,
阴司数未该。
禁烟花一种春无赖,
近柳梅一处情无外。
望椿萱一带天无碍。
则这水玻璃,堆起望乡台,
可哨见纸铜钱,夜市扬州界?
花神,可引他望乡台随意观玩。
[旦随末登台,望扬州哭介]那是扬州,俺爹爹奶奶呵,待飞将去。
[末扯住介]还不是你去的时节。
[净]下来听分付。功曹给一纸游魂路引去,花神休坏了他的肉身也。
[旦]谢恩官。

【赚尾】
[净]欲火近干柴,
且留的青山在,
不可被雨打风吹日晒。

Infernal Judge:

Yes.

(*To the tune of **Yaopian***)

With many years of human life ahead,

You should not have come here yet.

While wanton love shall be what you dread,

The plum and willow shall be what you get.

To stare at parents now that the sky is clear,

You mount the Home-gazing Terrace to see

Night scenes of mourning in Yangzhou from here.

Flower God, show her around the Home-gazing Terrace.

Du Liniang:

(*Mounts the terrace with Flower God and wails in the direction of Yangzhou*)

Yangzhou is over there! Dear Dad, dear Mom! How I wish to fly to you at once!

Flower God:

(*Stops her*)

It's not the time for you to go yet.

Infernal Judge:

Come back and listen to me. Attendant, prepare a passport for her. Flower God, take care to protect her body of flesh.

Du Liniang:

Thank you very much, Your Excellency.

Infernal Judge:

(*To the tune of **Semi-coda***)

Remember to keep your passion in control,

As where there're hills there's wood.

Keep away from rain and sunshine when you stroll.

则许你傍月依星将天地拜,
一任你魂魄来回。
脱了狱省的勾牌,
接着活免的投胎。
那花间四友你差排,
叫莺窥燕猜,倩蜂媒蝶采,
敢守的那破棺星圆梦那人来。
[净下]
[末]小姐回后花园去来。

[末]醉斜乌帽发如丝,
[旦]尽日灵风不满旗。
[净]年年检点人间事,
[合]为待萧何作判司。

You'll be allowed to wed your lover,

And free to come and go will be your soul.

Now that you are released,

You will resume your human role.

Four friends among the flowers are at your command:

The butterfly and bee, the swallow and oriole.

You'll wait for the man who digs the grave,

To fulfil your dream and console your soul.

(*Exit the infernal judge*)

Flower God:

Come, Miss, let's return to the back garden.

I wear my hat awry in drunken state;

Du Liniang:

By day the flags keep still in breathless air.

Infernal Judge:

Year by year I check the human fate;

Flower God, Du Liniang, Infernal Judge:

We all await a judge who's just and fair.

第二十四出 拾 画

【金珑璁】
　　[生上]惊春谁似我?
　　客途中都不问其他。
　　风吹绽蒲桃褐,
　　雨淋殷杏子罗。
　　今日晴和,
　　晒衾单兀自有残云涴。
　　"脉脉梨花春院香,一年愁事费商量。不知柳思能多少?打叠腰肢斗沈郎。"小生卧病梅花观中,喜得陈友知医,调理痊可。则这几日间春怀郁闷,何处忘忧?早是老姑姑到也。
【一落索】
　　[净上]无奈女冠何,
　　识的书生破。

Scene Twenty-four
Picking up the Portrait

(*Enter Liu Mengmei*)

Liu Mengmei:

(*To the tune of Jinlongcong*)

Who cares more for spring days than I?

To stormy weather I am on alert.

The wind has pierced my shabby gown;

The rain has soaked my yellow shirt.

When I woke to a day without rains,

I found my bed-sheets wet with dreamland stains.

"The yard in spring is fragrant with pear bloom,

But still my by-gone worries can be traced.

How come that spring is casting endless gloom?

I am appalled to see my slimming waist."

My illness has confined me to the Plum Blossom Nunnery. I'm lucky to get acquainted with a Mr Chen who is good at medicine, and I'm feeling much better now. However, the spring weather makes me bored and depressed these days. I don't know where I can go to kill some time. Well, here comes Sister Stone.

(*Enter Sister Stone*)

Sister Stone:

(*To the tune of Yiluosuo*)

A nun may have discerning eyes

To read a scholar's deep dismay.

知他何处梦儿多?
每日价欠伸千个。
秀才安稳!
[生]日来病患较些,闷坐不过。偌大梅花观,少甚园亭消遣。
[净]此后有花园一座,虽然亭榭荒芜,颇有闲花点缀。则留散闷,不许伤心。
[生]怎的得伤心也!
[净作叹介]是这般说。你自去游便了。从西廊转画墙而去,百步之外,便是篱门。三里之遥,都为池馆。你尽情玩赏,竟日消停,不索老身陪去也。"名园随客到,幽恨少人知。"[下]
[生]既有后花园,就此迤逦而去。[行介]这是西廊下了。[行介]好个葱翠的篱门,倒了半架。[叹介]"凭

From where does endless daydream rise

That he keeps yawning all the day?

How are you feeling now, young scholar?

Liu Mengmei:

I'm feeling much better these days, but I feel a little bored sitting idly all the time. In such a big nunnery, there must be a garden or some pavilions where I can walk around.

Sister Stone:

There is a garden in the back. Although it has been deserted, you can find some flowers here and there. You can while away some time there, but don't get sentimental.

Liu Mengmei:

Why should I get sentimental!

Sister Stone:

(*With a sigh*)

Forget about it. Go ahead and enjoy yourself. Follow the corridor and turn around the painted wall. In a hundred yards you will find a wicket gate. There are ponds and pavilions for three *li* around. You can enjoy yourself as much as you please and as long as you like. There's no need for me to go with you.

"The tourists come and go,

But who will know such woe!"

(*Exit*)

Liu Mengmei:

As there's such a back garden, I'll take a leisurely stroll there.

(*Walks*)

Here is the west corridor.

(*Walks on*)

What a green wicket gate! A pity that half of it is collapsed.

阑仍是玉阑干,四面墙垣不忍看。想得当时好风月,万条烟罩一时干。"[到介]呀,偌大一个园子也。

【好事近】
　　则见风月暗消磨,
　　画墙西正南侧左。
　　[跌介]苍苔滑擦,
　　倚逗着断垣低垛,
　　因何蝴蝶门儿落合?
　　原来以前游客颇盛,题名在竹林之上。
　　客来过,
　　年月偏多,
　　刻画尽琅玕千个。
　　咳,早则是寒花绕砌,
　　荒草成窠。
　　怪哉,一个梅花观,女冠之流,怎起的这座大园子?好疑惑也。便是这湾流水呵!

【锦缠道】
　　门儿锁,
　　放着这武陵源一座。
　　恁好处教颓堕!

(*With a sigh*)

"While marble balustrades as yet stand there,
The painted garden walls have lacked repair.
Where pleasant scenery used to glare the eyes,
The withered willows dangle in the air."

(*Arrives at the garden*)

Oh, what a spacious garden!

(*To the tune of* **Haoshijin**)

With years of constant wear and tear,

The painted walls remain in bad repair.

(*Slips*)

Now that the slippery moss

Intrudes the broken wall,

Why should the door be closed to all?

This garden must have been haunted by many visitors, judging from the numerous names inscribed on the bamboo stems.

This is a place where tourists used to come,

And as years went by,

Only names on bamboo stems defy the sky.

Alas, what I see now is nothing but

Wild flowers overgrowing the path,

With weeds and bushes as an aftermath.

Isn't it curious that a Taoist nun in the Peach Blossom Nunnery could have built such a magnificent garden? It's puzzling indeed. Just look at the meandering stream:

(*To the tune of* **Jinchandao**)

Behind bolted gates

There lies a fairyland;

Why is it in such decay?

断烟中见水阁摧残，
画船抛躲，
冷秋千尚挂下裙拖。
又不是曾经兵火，
似这般狼籍呵，
敢断肠人远、伤心事多？
待不关情么，
恰湖山石畔留着你打磨陀。
好一座山子哩。[窥介]呀，就里一个小匣儿。待把左侧一峰靠着，看是何物？[作石倒介]呀，是个檀香匣儿。[开匣看画介]呀。一幅观世音喜相。善哉，善哉！待小生捧到书馆，顶礼供养，强如埋在此中。

【千秋岁】
[捧匣回介]小嵯峨，
压的旃檀合，
便做了好相观音俏楼阁。
片石峰前，那片石峰前，
多则是飞来石，
三生因果。
请将去炉烟上过，

Beside the lake are misty estates

And painted boats stuck in the sand,

While swings would never sway.

But for the fire or war,

Why is it in such a wretched state?

Does it contain a mournful lore

Or people with a doleful fate?

Although I try to think of it no more,

The lakeside rocks have made me hesitate.

What a hill of mounted rocks!

(*Looks around the hill*)

Oh, there's a little box in the crevice. I'll lean against the left side in order to see what it is.

(*A rock slides down*)

Why, it's a red sandalwood case.

(*Opens the case to find a portrait*)

Well, it's a portrait of Bodhisattva Guanyin. Bliss on me! I'll take it to my study and pay my homage to her, rather than have it buried here.

(*Walks back, holding the case in his hand*)

(*To the tune of* **Qianqiusui**)

Under cragged rocks

Is a case of sandalwood,

Where Bodhisattva Guanyin is enshrined.

The peak of rocks,

The peak of rocks

Seems to fly across from foreign lands —

A wonder of the fate destined.

I shall perfume the portrait with incense

头纳地,
添灯火,
照的他慈悲我。
俺这里尽情供养,
他于意云何?
[到介]到了观中,且安置阁儿上,择日展礼。
[净上]柳相公多早了!

【尾声】
[生]姑姑,一生为客恨情多,
过冷澹园林日午矬。
老姑姑,你道不许伤心,
你为俺再寻一个定不伤心何处可。

[生]僻居虽爱近林泉,
[净]早是伤春梦雨天。
[生]何处邈将归画府?
[合]三峰花半碧堂悬。

And kowtow on the ground;

I'll add oil to the lamp from hence

To be endowed with bliss profound.

I'll pay my homage here,

But will she ever hear?

(*Arrives at the nunnery*)

Now that I'm back in the nunnery, I'll shelve the portrait till an auspicious day to do the service.

(*Enter Sister Stone*)

Sister Stone:

So you are back already, Mr Liu!

Liu Mengmei:

(*To the tune of* **Coda**)

Sister Stone,

A stroller can hardly find relief,

And daytime in the garden seems so brief.

You told me not to be sentimental, but you'd better show me

A place without regret or grief.

Liu Mengmei:

Although I love to live near hills and rills,

Sister Stone:

I can't escape from dreamy thrills.

Liu Mengmei:

Where shall I hang the portrait in the hall?

Liu Mengmei, Sister Stone:

The flowery maid is smiling on the wall.

第二十五出　忆　女

【玩仙灯】
　　[贴上]睹物怀人，
人去物华销尽。
道的个"仙果难成，名花易陨"。
　　[叹介]恨兰昌殉葬无因，
收拾起烛灰香烬。
自家杜府春香是也。跟随公相夫人到扬州。小姐去世，将次三年。俺看老夫人那一日不作念，那一日不悲啼。纵然老公相暂时宽解，怎散真愁？莫说老夫人，便是俺春香想起小姐平常恩养，病里言词，好不伤心也。今乃小姐生忌之辰，老夫人分付香灯，遥望南安浇奠。早已安排。夫人，有请。

【前腔】
　　[老旦上]地老天昏，

Scene Twenty-five
Recalling Her Daughter

(*Enter Chunxiang*)

Chunxiang:

(*To the tune of Wanxiandeng*)

At sight of things their owner comes to my mind;
Once the owner dies, things lose their charm.
It's true that "fairy fruits are hard to find
While precious blooms are prone to serious harm".

(*With a sigh*)

Dear Miss Du, I couldn't die with you;
To clear the incense ash is what I do.

I, Chunxiang, am maid to the Du family, with whom I came to Yangzhou. It's been about three years since my young mistress died. Every day Madam wept at the thought of her daughter. My old master tries hard to console her, but can hardly reduce her sorrow. Even I, the maid, feel sad when I recall the kindness of Miss Du and her words on her deathbed. As today is Miss Du's birthday, Madam orders me to prepare incense sticks and candles for a memorial service in the direction of Nan'an. Now everything is ready. Madam, will you come for the service?

(*Enter Zhen*)

Zhen:

(*To the previous tune*)

Between the heaven and earth,

没处把老娘安顿。
思量起举目无亲,
招魂有尽。
[哭介]我的丽娘儿也!
在天涯老命难存,
割断的肝肠寸寸。
"岭云沉,关树杳。
[贴]春思无凭,断送人年少。
[老旦]子母千回肠断绕。绣夹书囊,尚带余香袅。
[贴]瑞烟清,银烛皎。
[老旦]绣佛灵辰,血泪风前祷。[哭介]
[合]万里招魂魂可到?则愿的人天净处超生早。"
[老旦]春香,自从小姐亡过,俺皮骨空存,肝肠痛尽。但见他读残书本,绣罢花枝,断粉零香,余簪

> There is no place to rest my bones.
>
> I can't see my daughter on the day of her birth;
>
> Her soul is now in unknown zones.
>
> (*Weeps*)

Oh Liniang, my dear daughter!

> My life on earth has but limited lease,
>
> As my heart is torn apart piece by piece.
>
> "The clouds loom o'er the ridge,
>
> The dense trees veil the distant pass.

Chunxiang:

> *The dreams in spring are groundless,*
>
> *Yet they deprived the life of a lass.*

Zhen:

> *Close to her mother's heart,*
>
> *My daughter is dead and gone,*
>
> *But her scents won't depart.*

Chunxiang:

> *Incense smoke rises to the sky*
>
> *While silver candles burn bright.*

Zhen:

> *I pray to Buddha on her birthday,*
>
> *And shed my tears of blood upon the rite.*
>
> (*Wails*)

Zhen, Chunxiang:

> *Can her soul return?*
>
> *Her second birth is what we yearn."*

Zhen:

Chunxiang, since Liniang died, I've been like a living corpse tormented by sorrow all the time. The books she read, the

弃履，触处无非泪眼，见之总是伤心。算来一去三年，又是生辰之日。心香奉佛，泪烛浇天。分付安排，想已齐备。

[贴]夫人，就此望空顶礼。

[老旦拜介]"微香冉冉泪涓涓，酒滴灰香似去年。四尺孤坟何处是？南方归去再生天。"杜安抚之妻甄氏，敬为亡女生辰，顶礼佛爷。愿得杜丽娘皈依佛力，早早生天。[起介]春香，祷告了佛爷，不免将此茶饭，浇奠小姐。

【香罗带】

[老旦]丽娘何处坟？

问天难问。

梦中相见得眼儿昏，

则听的叫娘的声和韵也，

惊跳起，猛回身，

则见阴风几阵残灯晕。

flowers she embroidered, the powder and perfume she used, the hairpins and shoes she wore — the sight of all these things would bring tears to my eyes and break my heart. It's been three years now since she passed away, and today is her birthday again. The incense seems to burn from my heart, and the candles seem to shed tears from my eyes. I've told you to prepare for a service. I suppose everything is ready by now.

Chunxiang:

Yes, Madam, everything's ready. Will you start the service?

Zhen:

(*Kowtows*)

"Incense smoke swirls and candles weep;
I sprinkle wine and burn incense as last year.
Where lies her lonely tomb of cloddy heap?
Her soul flies south toward eternal sphere."

I, wife of Envoy Du, pray to great Buddha that my daughter Du Liniang be blessed by his mighty power and ascend to heaven in no time.

(*Rises to her feet*)

Chunxiang, now that I've prayed to the Buddha, it's time to offer some tea and rice to Liniang.

(*To the tune of* ***Xiangluodai***)

Where is Liniang's grave?

The heaven will not answer me.

Her shape in dreams I cannot clearly see;

Her voice alone rings wave on wave.

I raise myself on bed

And turn my head

To find flickering lamp instead.

[哭介]俺的丽娘人儿也,
你怎抛下的万里无儿白发亲!

【前腔】
[贴拜介]名香叩玉真,
受恩无尽,
赏春香还是你旧罗裙。
[起介]小姐临去之时,分付春香,长叫唤一声。今日叫他,"小姐,小姐呵",
叫的一声声小姐可曾闻也?
[老旦、贴哭介]
[合]想他那情切,那伤神,
恨天天生割断俺娘儿直恁忍!
[贴回介]俺的小姐人儿也,
你可还向旧宅里重生何处身?
[贴跪介]禀老夫人,人到中年,不堪哀毁。小姐难以生易死,夫人无以死伤生。且自调养尊年,与老相公同享富贵。

(*Weeps*)

Oh Liniang my dear,

How can you bear to leave me here!

Chunxiang:

(*Kowtows*)

(*To the previous tune*)

With fragrant stick I kowtow to you

To show my gratitude for you,

Wearing coats I got from you.

(*Rises to her feet*)

On your deathbed, you told me to call out for you from time to time. Now I'm calling you, "Mistress! Mistress!"

Can I get response from you?

Chunxiang, Zhen:

(*Wail*)

With all her tender love

And boundless woe,

Why should she be doomed by heaven above?

Chunxiang:

(*Turns to the memorial tablet again*)

Oh my mistress dear,

Will you go back to your old house from here?

(*Kneels*)

At your age, Madam, you can't sustain too much grief. As Miss Du can't come to life again, it's worthless to hurt yourself by grieving over the dead. Take good care of yourself so that you can enjoy lasting wealth and honour with the master.

Zhen:

(*Weeps*)

[老旦哭介]春香,你可知老相公年来因少男儿,常有娶小之意?止因小姐承欢膝下,百事因循。如今小姐丧亡,家门无托。俺与老相公闷怀相对,何以为情?天呵!
[贴]老夫人,春香愚不谏贤,依夫人所言,既然老相公有娶小之意,不如顺他,收下一房,生子为便。
[老旦]春香,你见人家庶出之子,可如亲生?
[贴]春香但蒙夫人收养,尚且非亲是亲,夫人肯将庶出看成,岂不无子有子?
[老旦]好话,好话。

[老旦]曾伴残蛾到女儿,
[贴]白杨今日几人悲。
[老旦]须知此恨消难得,
[合]泪滴寒塘蕙草时。

Did you know, Chunxiang, that my lord had been considering to have a concubine as he did not have a son? His love for Liniang alone made him drop the idea. Now that Liniang is dead, we are left without an heir. What can I say to console him when we sit facing each other? Oh, good gracious!

Chunxiang:

Madam, I'm not in a position to give any advice, but from what you have said, I get to know that the master would like to have a concubine. In that case, you'd better let him have one so that he'll beget a son.

Zhen:

Chunxiang, do you suppose that a concubine's son will be as good as my own son?

Chunxiang:

Madam, I'm lucky to be brought up by you and I treat you as my own parent although we have no blood ties at all. If you treat the concubine's son as your own, he'll treat you as his own mother, I'm sure.

Zhen:

Well said! Well said!

My daughter perished like the waning moon;

Chunxiang:

My moans resound like wailing poplar trees.

Zhen:

Our sorrows cannot fade and vanish soon;

Chunxiang, Zhen:

Tears fall into the wintry pond and freeze.

第二十六出　　玩　真

[生上]"芭蕉叶上雨难留，芍药梢头风欲收。画意无明偏着眼，春光有路暗抬头。"小生客中孤闷，闲游后园。湖山之下，拾得一轴小画，似是观音大士，宝匣庄严。风雨淹旬，未能展视。且喜今日晴和，瞻礼一会。[开匣，展画介]

【黄莺儿】
秋影挂银河，
展天身，自在波。
诸般好相能停妥。
他真身在补陀，
咱海南人遇他。
[想介]甚威光不上莲花座？
再延俄，

Scene Twenty-six
Cherishing the Portrait

(*Enter Liu Mengmei*)

Liu Mengmei:

"The palm leaves seldom hold the drops of rain;
The tips of peony stop the wind in vain.
Although the portrait itself throws no light,
The vernal sight illuminates the brain."

When I felt bored for my sojourn at the nunnery, I took a leisurely walk in the back garden. Under the Taihu rocks, I picked up a scroll of a painting. It seems to be a portrait of Bodhisattva Guanyin, concealed in a precious case. As it has been raining for the past ten days, I didn't think it fit to open the case. It happens that today is bright and clear. I'll open the case and pay my homage to the portrait.

(*Opens the case and unscrolls the portrait*)

(*To the tune of* **Huangyinger**)

Like the autumn moon upon the Milky Way,

She stretches herself as a virgin,

Oh, Bodhisattva Guanyin

With her magnificence in full display!

An image of the goddess in Putuo

Reveals herself before me in full glow.

(*Meditates*)

But why doesn't she sit on the lotus seat?

Wait, there's something wrong:

怎湘裙直下一对小凌波？

是观音，怎一对小脚儿？待俺端详一会。

【二郎神慢】

些儿个，画图中影儿则度。

着了，敢谁书馆中吊下幅小嫦娥，

画的这俜停倭妥。

是嫦娥，一发该顶戴了。

问嫦娥折桂人有我？

可是嫦娥，

怎影儿外没半朵祥云托？

树皱儿又不似桂丛花琐？

不是观音，又不是嫦娥，人间那得有此？

成惊愕，

似曾相识，

向俺心头摸。

待俺瞧，是画工临的，还是美人自手描的？

【莺啼序】

问丹青何处娇娥，

片月影光生豪末？

似恁般一个人儿，

早见了百花低躲。

总天然意态难模，

谁近得把春云淡破？

Why does the skirt reveal a pair of tiny feet?
How can Bodhisattva Guanyin have a pair of tiny feet? Let me look more closely.

(*To the tune of* **Erlangshenman**)

Once more,

Let me have a closer look soon.

Well, I've got it.

This must be the portrait of Chang E,

A fairy lady dwelling in the moon.

If it's Chang E, I'll pay more homage to her.

I'd like to ask Chang E

Whether I shall break the bough for her?

But if it is Chang E,

Why is there no cloud to uphold her?

Why is there no laurel surrounding her?

If it's neither Bodhisattva Guanyin nor Chang E, who on earth could look like this?

To my surprise,

I seem to know this maid.

Who is this maid of such fair size?

Let me have another look. Is this portrait done by a painter or by the fair maid herself?

(*To the tune of* **Yingtixu**)

Tell me, fair maid, where you were born,

And who has drawn your pretty form.

A maid with such a pretty form

Makes all the flowers feel forlorn.

A piece of nature as its norm,

Who could have got so close to her?

想来画工怎能到此!
多敢他自己能描会脱。
且住,细观他帧首之上,小字数行。[看介]呀,原来绝句一首。[念介]"近睹分明似俨然,远观自在若飞仙。他年得傍蟾宫客,不在梅边在柳边。"呀,此乃人间女子行乐图也。何言"不在梅边在柳边"?奇哉怪事哩!

【集贤宾】
望关山梅岭天一抹,
怎知俺柳梦梅过?
得傍蟾宫知怎么?
待喜呵,
端详停和,
俺姓名儿直么费嫦娥定夺?
打么诃,
敢则是梦魂中真个。
好不回盼小生!

【黄莺儿】
空影落纤娥,
动春蕉,
散绮罗。
春心只在眉间锁,
春山翠拖,

It's impossible for a painter to get so close to her.

    She must have painted her own form!

Wait, here at the top of the scroll, a few lines are inscribed in fine characters.

    (*Looks*)

    Why, it's a quatrain!

    (*Reads*)

    "A close inspection shows her as her self;
    A distant look displays her as an elf.
    Her future spouse who shares the pillow
    Will be found by the plum or willow."

Oh, it's the self-portrait of a fair lady. But why did she say "Will be found by the plum or willow"? It's really fantastic!

    (*To the tune of* **Jixianbin**)

    Across the hill and rill, across the sky,

    How could she know that I'll come by?

    Does it mean that I'll gain fame?

    I'll wait, wait all the same

    And have a closer look.

    How could she know my name?

    Let me think anew!

    Has my dream come true?

How I long to see her!

    (*To the tune of* **Huangyinger**)

    As Chang E the fairy lady from the sky,

    She moves her dainty shape

    And trails her gown of crape.

    Her virgin love is locked between her brows,

    Which curve like verdant hills

春烟淡和。
相看四目谁轻可!
恁横波,来回顾影不住的眼儿睃。
却怎半枝青梅在手,活似提掇小生一般?

【啼莺序】
他青梅在手诗细哦,
逗春心一点蹉跎。
小生待画饼充饥,
小姐似望梅止渴。
小姐,小姐,未曾开半点幺荷,
含笑处朱唇淡抹,韵情多。
如愁欲语,只少口气儿呵。
小娘子画似崔徽,诗如苏蕙,行书逼真卫夫人。小子虽则典雅,怎到得这小娘子!蓦地相逢,不免步韵一首。[题介]"丹青妙处却天然,不是天仙即地仙。欲傍蟾宫人近远,恰些春在柳梅边。"

【簇御林】
他能绰斡,会写作。
秀入江山人唱和。

With mists of hair from rills.

I gaze at her and she at me:

Up and down, right and left,

Our four eyes yearn to see.

How is it that she carries a twig of green plums in her hand as if she were holding me in her arms?

(*To the tune of Tiyingxu*)

Green plums in hand, she sings her verse,

Disturbing my quiet universe.

I seem to draw a cake to ease my greed;

She seems to look at plums to quench her need.

Oh my dear, my dear,

Her lotus bud of a tiny mouth

And rosy lips that smile

Display a graceful style.

She has a saddening tale to tell,

But lacks the breath to yell.

This fair lady is good at painting, poetry and calligraphy. Learned as I am, I'm no match to her. At this chance encounter, I'll write a poem in the corresponding rhyme.

(*Writes on the scroll*)

"A precious painting shows her genuine self,

A wondrous fair lady if not an elf.

Here comes your spouse who'll share the pillow,

Just as spring dwells in the plum and willow."

(*To the tune of Cuyulin*)

She can paint,

She can write,

Her portrait has the hills and rills in sight.

待小生很很叫他几声:"美人,美人!姐姐,姐姐!"
向真真啼血你知么?
叫的你喷嚏似天花唾。
动凌波,盈盈欲下——不见影儿那。
咳,俺孤单在此,少不得将小娘子画像,早晚玩之、拜之、叫之、赞之。

【尾声】
拾的个人儿先庆贺,
敢柳和梅有些瓜葛?
小姐小姐,
则被你有影无形看杀我。

不须一向恨丹青,
堪把长悬在户庭。
惆怅题诗柳中隐,
添成春醉转难醒。

Let me call out: "Fair lady, fair lady! My dear, my dear!"

    Have you heard me calling you?

    I'll call out till you call back.

    You seem to move your feet anew

    And walk out of the scroll,

    But you are still out of view.

Well, in my solitude, I'll cherish, revere, call and praise her portrait from morning till night.

    (*To the tune of* **Coda**)

    It is my luck to find this portrait of a maid.

    Is she someone I can't evade?

Mistress, mistress!

    Your intangible form will kill me, I'm afraid.

    The painting art is by no means to blame;

    I'll always hang the portrait on the wall.

    I'm puzzled by the verse that hides my name;

    To wake from vernal dream is hard for all.

第二十七出　　魂　游

【挂真儿】
　　[净扮石道姑上]台殿重重春色上。
　　碧雕阑映带银塘。
　　扑地香腾，归天磬响。
　　细展度人经藏。
　　"几年红粉委黄泥，十二峰头月欲低。折得玫瑰花一朵，东风吹上窈娘堤。"俺老道姑看守杜小姐坟庵，三年之上。择取吉日，替他开设道场，超生玉界。早已门外竖立招幡，看有何人来到。

【太平令】
　　[贴扮小道姑，丑扮徒弟上]岭路江乡，
　　一片彩云扶月上。
　　羽衣青鸟闲来往。

Scene Twenty-seven
The Roaming Soul

(*Enter Announcer*)

Sister Stone:

(*To the tune of Guazhener*)

Now that spring arrives at every hall,
The pillars find reflections on the pond.
When smoke of incense coils around the wall
And sounds of death-knells echo in a drawl,
I read the scripture for the World Beyond.
"When flowers fall onto the yellow earth,
The moon will gaze upon the mountain flanks.
I pick a solitary rose in mirth
As the east wind blows o'er river banks."

I've been looking after Miss Du's memorial shrine for over three years now. I've chosen this auspicious day for Taoist rites to savour her soul in the heaven. The savouring banners have been hoisted outside the gate. I'll wait and see who will attend the rites.

(*Enter a young nun and a novice*)

Young Nun:

(*To the tune of Taipingling*)

Above the hills and rills,
The moon ascends the rainbow.
A nun and a novice come and go.

Novice:

[丑]天晚，梅花观歇了罢。
[贴]南枝外有鹊炉香。
小道姑乃韶阳郡碧云庵主是也，游方到此。见他庄严幡引，榜示道场，恰好登坛，共成好事。[见介]
[贴]"大罗天上柳烟含，
[净]你毛节朱幡倚石龛。
[贴]见向溪山求住处，
[净]好哩，你半垂檀袖学通参。"小姑姑从何而至？
[贴]从韶阳郡来，暂此借宿。
[净]东头房儿，有个岭南柳相公养病。则下厢房可矣。
[贴]多谢了。敢问今夕道场，为何而设？

As it's getting late, let's stop over at the Plum Blossom Nunnery.

Young Nun:

The incense smoke leaks from the windowsills.

I am head of the White Cloud Nunnery in Shaoyang County. We have just travelled to this place. As the savouring banners announce the Taoist rites, we're just in time to mount the altar and join in the rites.

(*Greets Sister Stone*)

"*The curling incense floats in the sky;*

Sister Stone:

You bring your wand and banner to the shrine.

Young Nun:

I'd like to find a place where I can lie;

Sister Stone:

Well, in your case,

A worldly nun recites a Taoist line."

Where are you from, young sister?

Young Nun:

I come from Shaoyang County and would like to stop over the night here.

Sister Stone:

You have to put up with the side room because the guestroom has been occupied by a Mr Liu from Lingnan, who is recuperating from his illness.

Young Nun:

Thank you very much. By the way, may I ask the purpose of the evening rites?

Sister Stone:

[净叹介]则为"杜衙小姐去三年,待与招魂上九天"。
[贴]这等呵!"清醮坛场今夜好,敢将香火助真仙。"
[净]这等却好。
[内鸣钟鼓介]
[众]请老师父拈香。
[净]南斗注生真妃,东岳受生夫人殿下。[拈香拜介]

【孝南歌】
钻新火,点妙香。
虔诚为因杜丽娘。
[众拜介]香霭绣幡幢,
细乐风微飏。
仙真呵,
威光无量,
把一点香魂,
早度人天上。

(*Sighs*)

Alas,

"Three years ago Miss Du died here;

We'll send her soul to top celestial sphere."

Young Nun:

I see.

"It's best to hold the Taoist rites tonight;

The incense I burn adds wings to the sprite."

Sister Stone:

That's nice of you.

(*Sound of bells and drums within*)

Young Nun, Novice:

It's time for you to offer the incense.

Sister Stone:

Lady Star of Life and Death, Lady Star of Rebirth,

(*Offers the incense and kowtows*)

(*To the tune of* **Xiaonange**)

I kindle a new fire

To light a pious stick

And offer it for Du Liniang.

Young Nun, Novice:

(*Kowtow*)

Around the banners is the incense dense and thick;

In the breeze the gentle music rings.

Lady Stars,

With your mighty power,

Please send this flower

To the top celestial sphere.

As she still has her span on earth,

怕未尽凡心,
他再作人身想。
做儿郎,做女郎,
愿他永成双。
再休似少年亡。
[净]想起小姐生前爱花而亡,今日折得残梅,安在净瓶供养。[拜神主介]

【前腔】
瓶儿净,春冻阳。
残梅半枝红蜡装。
小姐呵!
你香梦与谁行?
精神忒孤往!
[众]老师兄,你说净瓶像什么,残梅像什么?
[净]这瓶儿空像,
世界包藏。
身似残梅样,
有水无根,
尚作余香想。
[众]小姐,你受此供呵,
教你肌骨凉,
魂魄香。

Please render her a rebirth.

Let her be reborn as a boy,

Let her be reborn as a maid,

Be married with eternal joy

And live long with your aid.

Sister Stone:

I remember that Miss Du died of love for flowers. I've picked a sprig of plum blossoms today and placed it in a purified vase.

(*Kowtows to Du Liniang's memorial tablet*)

(*To the previous tune*)

The purified vase in the room

In early spring sunshine

Holds a sprig of rosy bloom.

Miss Du,

Who is walking with you in your dream?

What a lonely soul with high esteem!

Young Nun, Novice:

Sister, what would you say the purified vase represents? And what does the plum blossom represent?

Sister Stone:

The vase with its void

Holds the world minute.

It's like the bloom of plums,

Which carries water and has no root

But still gives off fragrance acute.

Young Nun, Novice:

Miss Du, the offer you receive here will add

Coolness to your bone

And fragrance to your soul.

肯回阳，
再住这梅花帐？
[内风响介]
[净]奇哉怪哉，冷窣窣一阵风打旋也。
[内鸣钟介]
[众]这晚斋时分，且吃了斋，收拾道场。正是："晓镜抛残无定色，晚钟敲断步虚声。"
[众下]

【水红花】
[魂旦作鬼声，掩袖上]则下得望乡台如梦俏魂灵，
夜荧荧、墓门人静。
[内犬吠，旦惊介]原来是赚花阴小犬吠春星。
冷冥冥，梨花春影。
呀，转过牡丹亭、芍药阑，都荒废尽。爹娘去了三年也。[泣介]
伤感煞断垣荒径。
望中何处也？

If you resume the human role,

Will you return to this selfsame zone?

(*Sound of wind within*)

Sister Stone:

How strange! There arises a blast of chilly whirlwind.

(*Sound of bells and drums within*)

Young Nun, Novice:

It's time for evening meal. Let's go and have meal first, then we'll come back and finish the rites. As the saying goes,

"The morning dispels darkness all along;

The evening bell suspends the holy song."

(*Exeunt all*)

(*Enter Du Liniang, wailing as a ghost and hiding her face with her sleeves*)

Du Liniang:

(*To the tune of Shuihonghua*)

With the Home-gazing Terrace out of sight,

My soul walks in the shimmering night;

Outside the grave-gate is a quiet site.

(*Startled at the sound of barking dogs within*)

With flower-shadows out of sight,

A dog barks in the chilly night;

Pear blossoms foretell a flowery site.

Well, here is the Peony Pavilion, and there is the rose grove. They are both in ruins. It's three years since my parents left this place.

(*Weeps*)

Deserted paths and broken walls are sad.

But what is this place in sight

鬼灯青。

[听介]兀的有人声也啰。

"昔日千金小姐,今日水流花谢。这淹淹惜惜杜陵花,太亏他。生性独行无那,此夜星前一个。生生死死为情多。奈情何!"奴家杜丽娘女魂是也。只为痴情慕色,一梦而亡。凑的十地阎君奉旨裁革,无人发遣,女监三年。喜遇老判,哀怜放假。趁此月明风细,随喜一番。呀,这是书斋后园,怎做了梅花庵观?好伤感人也。

【小桃红】
咱一似断肠人和梦醉初醒。
谁偿咱残生命也。
虽则鬼丛中姊妹不同行,
窣地的把罗衣整。
这影随形,风沉露,
云暗斗,月勾星,
都是我魂游境也。

With a ghostly light?

(*Listens*)

What, human voices nearly make me mad!
"An elegant maiden in the former days,
I'm like a faded flower now.
For such a dainty bloom beyond praise,
Why should I wither on the bough!
Destined to lead a lonely life,
I gaze at stars in vain tonight.
In life or death I yearn to be his wife,
As love gets hold of me too tight."

I'm Du Liniang in the ghost form. I died a dream that made me lovesick. As the Prince of the Tenth Hell was dismissed from office, I was left in the cell for three years with no one to dispatch my case. I'm lucky to meet with a sympathetic old judge and to be allowed to take leave so that I can roam at will in this moonlit night. Why, how is it that the back garden to the study has become the Plum Blossom Nunnery? How distressing!

(*To the tune of* **Xiaotaohong**)

A broken heart awakened from dream,
I wonder who'll bring me to life again.
Although ghosts ne'er travel in a team,
I still put right my garment now and then.
In the shadowy night
When dews settle in the breeze,
The clouds obscure the moonlight,
And stars lie hidden ill at ease,
I wander as I please

到的这花影初更,
[内作丁冬声,旦惊介]一霎价心儿瘆,
原来是弄风铃台殿冬丁。
好一阵香也。

【下山虎】
我则见香烟隐隐,灯火荧荧。
呀,铺了些云霞幰,
不由人打个呓挣。
是那位神灵,原来是东岳夫人,南斗真妃。[作稽首介]仙真仙真,杜丽娘鬼魂稽首。
地投明证明,
好替俺朗朗的超生注生。
再看这青词上,原来就是石道姑在此住持。一坛斋意,度俺生天。道姑道姑,我可也生受你呵。再瞧这净瓶中,咳,便是俺那冢上残梅哩。梅花呵,似俺杜丽娘半开而谢,好伤情也。
则为这断鼓零钟金字经,
叩动俺黄粱境。
俺向这地坏里梅根迸几程,透出些儿影。
[泣介]姑姑们这般至诚,若不留些踪影,怎显的俺鉴知他,就将梅花散在经台之上。

The first drumbeat finds me in a flowery site.

(*Startled at the sound of tinkling bells within*)

What gives me sudden fear

Is the bells that tinkle here.

What a fragrant smell of incense!

(*To the tune of* **Xiashanhu**)

The smoke of incense curls;

The light of lanterns glows.

When I see the holy portraits,

My fear suddenly grows.

Who are those goddesses? Oh, one is Lady Star of Life and Death, and the other is Lady Star of Rebirth.

(*Kowtows*)

Du Liniang in the ghost form kowtows to you Lady Stars.

I've quietly come back to the earth

To pray for my rebirth.

Let me see what are the words of the prayers. Sister Stone is presiding over the rites for my rebirth in the heaven. Sister Stone, I'm deeply indebted to you. In the purified vase is a sprig of plum blossom from my grave. Oh, plum blossom, both you and I are nipped in the bud! How sad it is!

The sound of bells and drums and chants

Has roused me from a dream of mine.

I'll step into the plants

To leave some sign.

(*Weeps*)

If I do not leave some sign, how can the pious nuns know that I appreciate their efforts? Let me scatter some petals of plum blossoms on the shrine.

[撒花介]抵什么一点香销万点情。
想起爹娘何处,春香何处也?呀,那边厢有沉吟叫唤之声,听怎来?
[内叫介]俺的姐姐呵!俺的美人呵!
[旦惊介]谁叫谁也?再听。
[内又叫介]
[旦叹介]

【醉归迟】
　　生和死,孤寒命。
　　有情人叫不出情人应。
　　为什么不唱出你可人名姓?
　　似俺孤魂独趁,
　　待谁来叫唤俺一声。
　　不分明,无倒断,再消停。
　　[内又叫介]
　　[旦]咳,敢边厢什么书生,
　　睡梦里语言胡咥?

【黑蟆令】
　　不由俺无情有情,
　　凑着叫的人三声两声,

(*Scatters the petals*)

My love stays with the petals on the shrine.

Where are my parents and where is Chunxiang? Well, there comes the sound of moaning and calling. Let me listen carefully.

Voice Within:

My dear! My fair lady!

Du Liniang:

(*Startled*)

Who is calling? Whom is he calling? Let me listen again.

(*The voice calls again from within*)

Du Liniang:

(*Sighs*)

(*To the tune of **Zuiguichi***)

Alive and dead,

I'm destined to roam alone.

There's no reply to what you've said;

Why do you just moan?

Lonely tears I shed;

Where is the man of my own?

A voice unknown

Continues to groan.

I'll try to find the tone.

(*The voice calls again from within*)

What is the scholar there,

Whose cries in his sleep fill the air?

(*To the tune of **Heimaling***)

His moans have touched my heart;

Repeated moans and screams

冷惺忪红泪飘零。
呀，怕不是梦人儿梅卿柳卿？
俺记着这花亭水亭，
趁的这风清月清。
则这鬼宿前程，
盼得上三星四星？
待即行寻趁，奈斗转参横，不敢久停呵！

【尾声】
为什么闪摇摇春殿灯？
[内叫介]殿上响动。
[丑虚上望介][又作风起介]
[旦]一弄儿绣幡飘迥，
则这几点落花风是俺杜丽娘身后影。
[旦作鬼声下]
[丑打照面，惊叫介]师父们，快来，快来！
[净、贴惊上]怎生大惊小怪？
[丑]则这灯影荧煌，躲着瞧时，见一位女神仙，袖拂花幡，一闪而去。怕也，怕也！

Make my chilly teardrops start.
Is he the man I met in dreams?
I remember the blooms and streams;
I remember the breeze and moonbeams.
Now that I am a roaming soul,
Can I ever play the bridal role?

I'd like to find out more about it, but as the day is soon to break, I can't linger here any longer.

(*To the tune of Coda*)

Why do the lanterns shimmer in the hall?

Voice Within:

There are noises in the hall.

(*Enter the novice, standing aside and looking around*)
(*Sound of another whirlwind within*)

Du Liniang:

Why do the banners flutter?
This wind is what I leave behind them all.

(*Exit Du Liniang wailing as a ghost, coming face to face with the novice*)

Novice:

(*Cries out in horror*)

Holy sisters, come, come!

(*Enter Sister Stone and Young Nun in a hurry*)

Sister Stone, Young Nun:

What's the matter?

Novice:

When I hid behind the lantern shadows, I saw a goddess flapping the banners with her sleeves and vanishing in a flurry. How terrible! Terrible!

[净]怎生模样?

[丑打手势介]这多高,这多大,俊脸儿,翠翘金凤,红裙绿袄,环珮玎珰,敢是真仙下降?

[净]咳,这便是杜小姐生时样子。敢是他有灵活现。

[贴]呀,你看经台之上,乱糁梅花,奇也,异也!大家再祝赞他一番。

【忆多娇】

[众]风灭了香,

月到廊。

闪闪尸尸魂影儿凉。

花落在春宵情易伤。

愿你早度天堂,早度天堂,

免留滞他乡故乡。

[贴]敢问杜小姐为何病亡?以何缘故而来出现?

【尾声】

[净]休惊恍,

Sister Stone:

What does she look like?

Novice:

(*Gestures*)

About this height, this size, a pretty face with golden headwear, dressed in a red skirt and green coat, clinking with jade ornaments. Isn't she a goddess from the heaven?

Sister Stone:

That's exactly what Miss Du looked like in her lifetime. Hasn't her spirit come to earth?

Young Nun:

Look, the shrine is scattered with petals of plum blossoms. Fantastic! It's really fantastic! Let's chant another hymn for her.

Sister Stone, Young Nun, Novice:

(*To the tune of* **Yiduojiao**)

When the incense has burned up

And corridors are flooded in moonlight,

Appearance of a lonely soul

With scattered petals is a saddening sight.

May you have peace in celestial sphere,

In celestial sphere,

And linger no more in homeland here.

Young Nun:

May I ask how Miss Du died? Why does her spirit come to earth again?

Sister Stone:

(*To the tune of* **Coda**)

Don't be in a fright;

免问当。
收拾起乐器经堂。
你听波,
兀的冷窣窣珮环风还在回廊那边响。

[净]心知不敢辄形相,
[贴]欲话因缘恐断肠。
[丑]若使春风会人意,
[合]也应知有杜兰香。

Don't ask whys!

Let's put away instruments for the rite;

Now, listen,

The tinkling sounds again arise.

Sister Stone:

It's hard to show her genuine stuff,

Young Nun:

Because to tell the truth will make her wail.

Novice:

If the vernal breeze is wise enough,

Sister Stone, Young Nun, Novice:

It should have known the fairy tale.

第二十八出　　幽媾

【夜行船】
　　[生上]瞥下天仙何处也?
　　影空濛似月笼沙。
　　有恨徘徊,
　　无言窨约。
　　早是夕阳西下。
　　"一片红云下太清,如花巧笑玉娉婷。凭谁画出生香面。对俺偏含不语情。"小生自遇春容,日夜想念。这更阑时节,破些工夫,吟其珠玉,玩其精神。倘然梦里相亲,也当春风一度。[展画玩介]呀,你看美人呵,神含欲语,眼注微波。真乃"落霞与孤鹜齐飞,秋水共长天一色"。

【香遍满】
　　晚风吹下,
　　武陵溪边一缕霞,

Scene Twenty-eight
Union with the Ghost

(*Enter Liu Mengmei*)

Liu Mengmei:

(*To the tune of* **Yexingchuan**)
Where is the fairy maid I saw?
She's empty as the moon in mist.
My woe can hardly thaw,
While endless thoughts persist,
The sun has long set in the west.
"A rosy cloud descended from the sky,
Like a flower in broadest smile.
Whose hand has drawn a face so shy,
With loving glances all the while?"

Since I saw the portrait of a loving lady, I've kept thinking of her day and night. In the small hours tonight, I'm spending some time reading her poem and cherishing her portrait. Even if I could meet her in my dream, I would enjoy every minute of it.

(*Unrolls the scroll and cherishes it*)

Oh, what a beauty! She seems to have something to say, and her eyes are eloquent too. As a quotation goes,

"With evening glows the lonely swan would fly;
The autumn waters share the same hue with the sky."

(*To the tune of* **Xiangbianman**)
The evening breeze has brought about
A glow of sunlight from the fairy land —

出落个人儿风韵杀。
净无瑕,
明窗新绛纱。
丹青小画,
又把一幅肝肠挂。
小姐小姐,则被你想杀俺也。

【懒画眉】
轻轻怯怯一个女娇娃,
楚楚臻臻像个宰相衙。
想他春心无那对菱花,
含情自把春容画,
可想到有个拾翠人儿也逗着他?

【二犯梧桐树】
他飞来似月华,
俺拾的愁天大。
常时夜夜对月而眠,这几夜呵,
幽佳,婵娟隐映的光辉杀。
教俺迷留没乱的心嘈杂,
无夜无明怏着他。
若不为擎奇怕涴的丹青亚,
待抱着你影儿横榻。
想来小生定是有缘也。再将他诗句朗诵一番。[念诗介]

【浣纱溪】
拈诗话,

A fairy maid without doubt.

Pure and simple is her claim,

Like the crimson gauze of window-frame.

This portrait of a dainty maid

Has set my heart aflame.

Oh, my dear, how I yearn to see you!

(*To the tune of* **Lanhuamei**)

The maid is delicate and shy,

A daughter from a noble house.

She sits before the mirror with a yearning heart

And draws her portrait with a sigh.

But does she know that

The one who's picked it yearns to be her spouse?

(*To the tune of* **Erfanwutongshu**)

Her moon-shaped visage full of glow

Has brought about a sky of woe.

In the past I could fall asleep facing the moon, but in recent nights

Her radiance is so bright

That I can hardly bear the light.

Disturbed by the thought of her,

I have her on my mind day and night.

But for the fear of spoiling it,

I'll sleep with it at night.

It must be fate that has brought her to me. Let me read the poem again.

(*Reads the poem*)

(*To the tune of* **Huanshaxi**)

These lines she wrote

对会家。
柳和梅有分儿些。
他春心迸出湖山罅,
飞上烟绡萼绿华。
则是礼拜他便了。
[拈香拜介]俟倖杀,
对他脸晕眉痕心上掐,
有情人不在天涯。
小生客居,怎勾姐姐风月中片时相会也。

【刘泼帽】
恨单条不惹的双魂化,
做个画屏中倚玉兼葭。
小姐呵,你耳朵儿云鬓月侵芽,
可知他一些些都听的俺伤情话?

【秋夜月】
堪笑咱,说的来如戏耍。
他海天秋月云端挂,
烟空翠影遥山抹。
只许他伴人清暇,
怎教人佻达。

【东瓯令】
俺如念咒,似说法。
石也要点头,天雨花。

For her future mate —

For willow and plum remote.

From the lakeside hills comes the fairy soul,

Who lands on the scroll.

Whoever she is, I'll pay homage to her.

(*Lights the incense and kowtows*)

It gives me pain

To have your image deep in my brain.

Your lover is here, expecting in vain.

During my stopover here, how can I have a brief rendezvous with you?

(*To the tune of Liupomao*)

One scroll does not contain a loving pair;

I wish I were a reed by your side.

My dear,

As your ears are covered by your hair,

Can you hear the sorrow I confide?

(*To the tune of Qiuyeyue*)

I am a fool indeed

To daydream like a child.

You are the moon above the clouds;

You are the mist above the wild.

You may amuse the crowds,

But not to be beguiled.

(*To the tune of Dongouling*)

It is a magic spell I read;

It is a prayer I said.

A stone would nod its head;

A rain of blooms would spread.

怎虔诚不降的仙娥下?
是不肯轻行踏。
[内作风起,生按住画介]待留仙怕杀风儿刮,
粘嵌着锦边牙。
怕刮损他,再寻个高手临他一幅儿。

【金莲子】
闲啧牙,
怎能够他威光水月生临榻?
怕有处相逢他自家,
则问他许多情,
与春风画意再无差。
再把灯剔起细看他一会。[照介]

【隔尾】
敢人世上似这天真多则假。
[内作风吹灯介]
[生]好一阵冷风袭人也。
险些儿误丹青风影落灯花。
罢了,则索睡掩纱窗去梦他。[打睡介]
[魂旦上]"泉下长眠梦不成。一生余得许多情。魂

But why won't you descend?

It is too hard for you to come ahead.

(*Sound of wind within. Liu Mengmei places his hand on the portrait*)

For fear the portrait be blown away,

I'll hold it under sway.

In case the portrait is torn apart by the wind, I'll find a skilled painter to make a copy of it.

(*To the tune of **Jinlianzi***)

Just imagine

How I can bring you to my bed!

If I could meet you face to face,

I'd hold you in embrace,

To prove what you have said.

I'll trim the wick to have a better look at you.

(*Holds the lamp to the portrait*)

(*To the tune of **Quasi-coda***)

A human fairy oft involves a scheme.

(*Sound of wind within, nearly blowing out the lamp*)

What a chilly blast!

The portrait nearly caught on fire.

Well, think no more about the portrait.

I'll shut the window and meet her in my dream.

(*Dozes off*)

(*Enter Du Liniang in the ghost form*)

Du Liniang:

"My dream left unfulfilled in my eternal sleep,

I cherish human love profound and deep.

When the portrait guides me in the moon,

随月下丹青引,人在风前叹息声。"妾身杜丽娘鬼魂是也。为花园一梦,想念而终。当时自画春容,埋于太湖石下。题有"他年得傍蟾宫客,不在梅边在柳边"。谁想魂游观中几晚,听见东房之内,一个书生高声低叫:"俺的姐姐,俺的美人。"那声音哀楚,动俺心魂。悄然蓦入他房中,则见高挂起一轴小画。细玩之,便是奴家遗下春容。后面和诗一首,观其名字,则岭南柳梦梅也。梅边柳边,岂非前定乎!因而告过了冥府判君,趁此良宵,完其前梦。想起来好苦也。

【朝天懒】
怕的是粉冷香销泣绛纱,
又到的高唐馆玩月华。
猛回头羞飒髻儿鬇,
自擎拿。
呀,前面是他房头了。
怕桃源路径行来诧,
再得俄旋试认他。

I hear a man sigh in a woeful tune."

I'm Du Liniang in the ghost form. I pined away for a dream in the garden. Before I died, I drew a self-portrait and buried it under a Taihu rock. On the portrait is the inscription

　　　"Her future spouse who shares the pillow
　　　Will be found by the plum or willow."

When my soul roamed the nunnery these nights, I heard him calling in the guestroom: "Oh my dear, my fair lady!" The sad voice touched my heart. When I glided into his room, I saw a tiny scroll hanging on the wall. When I looked more closely, I recognised that it was the portrait I left behind. Below my inscriptions, he wrote a poem in the corresponding rhyme. The signature is Liu Mengmei from Lingnan. While *Liu* means willow and *mei* means plum, isn't it predestined that he is the man to be found "by the plum or willow"? Therefore, I asked for leave from the Infernal Judge to fulfil the dream at this pretty night. Alas, how I have suffered!

　　　(*To the tune of* **Chaotianlan**)
　　　A faded beauty in ghost form,
　　　I fear it's second dreamland love affair.
　　　As I'm abashed and got my curls dishevelled,
　　　Let me arrange my hair.

Well, here I am at his room.

　　　Lest I make the wrong tour,
　　　I'll wait and make sure.

Liu Mengmei:

　　　(*Recites the poem in his sleep*)
　　　"Her future spouse who shares the pillow
　　　Will be found by the plum or willow."

[生睡中念诗介]"他年若傍蟾宫客,不在梅边在柳边。"我的姐姐呵。

[旦][听打悲介]

【前腔】
是他叫唤的伤情咱泪雨麻,
把我残诗句没争差。
难道还未睡呵?[瞧介][生又叫介]
[旦]他原来睡屏中作念猛嗟牙。
省喧哗,
我待敲弹翠竹窗棂下。
[生作惊醒,叫"姐姐"介]
[旦悲介]待展香魂去近他。
[生]呀,户外敲竹之声,是风是人?
[旦]有人。
[生]这咱时节有人,敢是老姑姑送茶来?免劳了。

Oh my dear!

Du Liniang:

> (*Listens and weeps*)
>
> (*To the previous tune*)
>
> I shed a flood of tears to hear his call,
>
> While my verse lines echo in the hall.

Is he still lying awake?

> (*Looks into the room while Liu Mengmei talks again in his sleep*)
>
> He talks to himself in his sleep.

Wait!

I'll tap at window-frames and peep.

Liu Mengmei:

> (*Wakes up with a startle*)

My dear!

Du Liniang:

> (*Sadly*)
>
> I shall go forth and meet my mate.

Liu Mengmei:

I seem to hear a tapping at the bamboo frames. Is it the wind or someone there?

Du Liniang:

Here I am.

Liu Mengmei:

Someone's at the door. Are you Sister Stone bringing tea? It's so kind of you, but I don't want any tea now.

Du Liniang:

I'm not Sister Stone.

Liu Mengmei:

[旦]不是。

[生]敢是游方的小姑姑么?

[旦]不是。

[生]好怪,好怪,又不是小姑姑。再有谁?待我启门而看。[生开门看介]

【玩仙灯】

呀,何处一娇娃,

艳非常使人惊诧。

[旦作笑闪入]

[生急掩门]

[旦敛衽整容见介]秀才万福。

[生]小娘子到来,敢问尊前何处,因何黉夜至此?

[旦]秀才,你猜来。

【红衲袄】

[生]莫不是莽张骞犯了你星汉槎,

莫不是小梁清夜走天曹罚?

[旦]这都是天上仙人,怎得到此。

[生]是人家彩凤暗随鸦?

Are you the travelling Young Sister?

Du Liniang:

No, I'm not.

Liu Mengmei:

Strange, it's strange. She's not the Young Nun, either. Who else can it be? Let me open the door and have a look.

(*Opens the door to have a look*)

(*To the tune of Wanxiandeng*)

Oh,

A beauty stands before me,

A beauty rare to see.

(*Du Liniang smiles and slips into the room. Liu Mengmei closes the door in haste*)

Du Liniang:

(*Adjusts her hair and dress, and then greets Liu Mengmei*)

Blessing to you, sir.

Liu Mengmei:

May I ask, young lady, where you are from and why you come at this late hour?

Du Liniang:

Will you have a guess, Sir?

Liu Mengmei:

(*To the tune of Hongnaao*)

Are you the Weaving Star in the sky?

Are you the Fairy Waitress coming by?

Du Liniang:

How can the heavenly immortals come here?

Liu Mengmei:

Are you a phoenix following the crow?

[旦摇头介]
[生]敢甚处里绿杨曾击马?
[旦]不曾一面。
[生]若不是认陶潜眼挫的花,
敢则是走临邛道数儿差?
[旦]非差。
[生]想是求灯的?可是你夜行无烛也,
因此上待要红袖分灯向碧纱?

【前腔】
[旦]俺不为度仙香空散花,
也不为读书灯闲濡蜡。
俺不似赵飞卿旧有瑕,
也不似卓文君新守寡。
秀才呵,你也曾随蝶梦迷花下。
[生想介]是当初曾梦来。
[旦]俺因此上弄莺簧赴柳衙。
若问俺妆台何处也,不远哩,
刚则在宋玉东邻第几家。

(*Du Liniang shakes her head*)

Are you an old acquaintance to see me now?

Du Liniang:

We've never seen each other before.

Liu Mengmei:

Have you mistaken me for someone else?

Have you lost your way to the hotels?

Du Liniang:

No, I haven't lost my way.

Liu Mengmei:

Are you here to borrow a lamp?

Is it because you walk at night

That you come here for the candlelight?

Du Liniang:

(*To the previous tune*)

I have not come to send you bloom,

Nor read books in your room.

I'm not Zhao Feiyan who had a sad fate

Nor Zhuo Wenjun who lost her mate.

Dear Sir,

Have you had a dream of love and hate?

Liu Mengmei:

(*Tries to recall*)

Yes, I have.

Du Liniang:

That's why I come here all the way.

If you ask me where I live, I'd say

In the neighbourhood where beauties stay.

Liu Mengmei:

[生作想介]是了。曾后花园转西,夕阳时节,见小娘子走动哩。
[旦]便是了。
[生]家下有谁?

【宜春令】
[旦]斜阳外,芳草涯,
再无人有伶仃的爹妈。
奴年二八,没包弹风藏叶里花。
为春归惹动嗟呀,
瞥见你风神俊雅。
无他,
待和你剪烛临风,
西窗闲话。
[生背介]奇哉,奇哉,人间有此艳色!夜半无故而遇明月之珠,怎生发付!

【前腔】
他惊人艳,绝世佳。
闪一笑风流银蜡。
月明如乍,
问今夕何年星汉槎?

Yes, I see. When I was turning west in the back garden at dusk, I saw a fair lady walking in the distance.

Du Liniang:

That's me.

Liu Mengmei:

Who lives with you in your family?

Du Liniang:

(*To the tune of Yichunling*)

In the west

Where grows the grass,

With lonely parents lives the lass.

At sixteen years of age,

I'm like a flower in the vase.

When I took a stroll in ebbing spring,

I stole a glimpse of your handsome face.

Here I am

To sit by the candlelight

And chat with you all night.

Liu Mengmei:

(*Aside*)

Fantastic! Fantastic! What a rare beauty in the world! Now that I've chanced upon a pearl of a young lady, what am I to do?

(*To the previous tune*)

Amazing beauty,

Rare beauty bright,

Her smile outshines the candlelight.

By looking at the brilliant moon,

I wonder what day is today.

金钗客寒夜来家,
玉天仙人间下榻。
[背介]知他,知他是甚宅眷的孩儿,
这迎门调法?
待小生再问他。[回介]小娘子黉夜下顾小生,敢是梦也?
[旦笑介]不是梦,当真哩。还怕秀才未肯容纳。
[生]则怕未真。果然美人见爱,小生喜出望外。何敢却乎?
[旦]这等真个盼着你了。

【耍鲍老】
幽谷寒涯,
你为俺催花连夜发。
俺全然未嫁,
你个中知察,
拘惜的好人家。
牡丹亭,娇恰恰;
湖山畔,羞答答;
读书窗,淅喇喇。

A graceful maid should have come to me!

A fairy maid should have come to stay!

(*Aside*)

Yet,

Yet who is this naughty maid

That comes to me to play?

I'll ask her a few more questions.

(*To Du Liniang*)

Am I dreaming now that I see you in the deep of night?

Du Liniang:

(*Smiles*)

No, you're not dreaming. I'm my true self, but I'm afraid you won't accept me.

Liu Mengmei:

I'm still afraid it's not real. If you are really fond of me, I shall be too glad to accept your love. How can I say no?

Du Liniang:

In this case, my dream has come true.

(*To the tune of* **Shuabaolao**)

In the peaceful vale of love,

You brought my heart to bloom at night.

Since then no other men have come to sight;

And you're the one who knows the reason why:

I am a daughter graceful and polite.

At the Peony Pavilion,

We were tender toward each other.

By the lakeside hills,

We felt bashful with each other.

Near the window-frames,

良夜省陪茶，
清风明月知无价。
【滴滴金】
[生]俺惊魂化，
睡醒时凉月些些。
陡地荣华，
敢则是梦中巫峡？
亏杀你走花阴不害些儿怕，
点苍苔不溜些儿滑，
背萱亲不受些儿吓，
认书生不着些儿差。
你看斗儿斜，花儿亚，
如此夜深花睡罢。
笑咖咖，吟哈哈，
风月无加。
把他艳软香娇做意儿耍，
下的亏他？
便亏他则半霎。
[旦]妾有一言相恳，望郎恕罪。
[生笑介]贤卿有话，但说无妨。

We sat silent facing each other.

We shared the night at ease

And knew the price of moon and breeze.

Liu Mengmei:

(*To the tune of Didijin*)

When I wake up with a start,

I see the cool moon gleam.

But is this sudden bliss

A love affair in dream?

Oh, my dear, it is inconceivable that

You dread not when you cross the shade,

You slip not when you tread on the moss,

You fear not when you shun your parents,

You err not when you come to my aid.

Look,

The dipper is aslant;

The petals fold;

The flowers slumber in the cold.

We shall laugh

And sing

In the moon and breeze of spring.

You are tender; you are coy.

How can I let you down?

For every minute, we shall enjoy.

Du Liniang:

I have one request to make. Will you please listen to me?

Liu Mengmei:

Go ahead, please.

Du Liniang:

[旦]妾千金之躯,一旦付与郎矣,勿负奴心。每夜得共枕席,平生之愿足矣。
[生笑介]贤卿有心恋于小生,小生岂敢忘于贤卿乎?
[旦]还有一言。未至鸡鸣,放奴回去。秀才休送,以避晓风。
[生]这都领命。只问姐姐贵姓芳名?

【意不尽】
[旦叹介]少不得花有根元玉有芽,
待说时惹的风声大。
[生]以后准望贤卿逐夜而来。
[旦]秀才,且和俺点勘春风这第一花。

[生]浩态狂香昔未逢,
[旦]月斜楼上五更钟。
[旦]朝云夜入无行处,
[生]神女知来第几峰?

Once you have me, body and flesh, heart and soul, please never give me up. My lifelong desire is fulfilled if only we share the pillow night after night.

Liu Mengmei:

Now that you devote yourself to me, how can I ever forget you?

Du Liniang:

I have one more word to tell you: please let me go before the cockcrow. You don't have to see me off because the morning breeze is chilly.

Liu Mengmei:

I'll do what you tell me, but may I ask your name?

Du Liniang:

(*With a sigh*)

(*To the tune of Yibujin*)

Though each thing has its root and form,

My name may stir up a roaring storm.

Liu Mengmei:

I hope that you'll come every night.

Du Liniang:

My dear sir,

Let's make this first night sweet and warm.

Liu Mengmei:

I spend the night with beauty never seen;

Du Liniang:

The moon goes west before the night-time ends.

The morning clouds come from unknown ravine;

Liu Mengmei:

Who knows from where the fairy maid descends?

大中华文库
汉英对照

LIBRARY OF CHINESE CLASSICS
Chinese-English

牡丹亭
The Poeny Pavilion
II

［明］汤显祖　著
汪榕培　英译
徐朔方　杨笑梅　点校

Written by **Tang Xianzu**
Translated by **Wang Rongpei**
Punctuated and Revised by **Xu Shuofang and Yang Xiaomei**

湖南人民出版社
Hunan People's Publishing House
外文出版社
Foreign Languages Press

目 录

第二十九出 旁 疑	454
第三十出 欢 挠	466
第三十一出 缮 备	484
第三十二出 冥 誓	494
第三十三出 秘 议	528
第三十四出 诇 药	544
第三十五出 回 生	552
第三十六出 婚 走	568
第三十七出 骇 变	596
第三十八出 淮 警	604
第三十九出 如 杭	612
第四十出 仆 侦	622
第四十一出 耽 试	640

CONTENTS

Scene Twenty-nine   455
The Nun's Suspicion

Scene Thirty   467
Disrupting the Love Affair

Scene Thirty-one   485
Preparing for War

Scene Thirty-two   495
Vowing between Man and Ghost

Scene Thirty-three   529
Clandestine Schemes

Scene Thirty-four   545
Asking for Medicine

Scene Thirty-five   553
Returning to Life

Scene Thirty-six   569
Wedding and Departure

Scene Thirty-seven   597
The Pedagogue's Alarm

Scene Thirty-eight   605
The Invasion

Scene Thirty-nine   613
Sojourn in Lin'an

Scene Forty   623
Looking for His Master

Scene Forty-one   641
Late for the Examination

第四十二出 移　镇	662
第四十三出 御　淮	676
第四十四出 急　难	698
第四十五出 寇　间	712
第四十六出 折　寇	728
第四十七出 围　释	744
第四十八出 遇　母	780
第四十九出 淮　泊	806
第五十出 闹　宴	824
第五十一出 榜　下	850
第五十二出 索　元	864
第五十三出 硬　拷	880
第五十四出 闻　喜	918
第五十五出 圆　驾	938

Scene Forty-two   663
Military Transfer

Scene Forty-three   677
Military Defence

Scene Forty-four   699
Concern for Her Parents

Scene Forty-five   713
The Bandits' Wily Scheme

Scene Forty-six   729
Outwitting the Bandits

Scene Forty-seven   745
Lifting the Siege

Scene Forty-eight   781
Reunion with Her Mother

Scene Forty-nine   807
Sojourn near the Huai River

Scene Fifty   825
Spoiling the Banquet

Scene Fifty-one   851
Announcing the Results

Scene Fifty-two   865
Searching for Liu Mengmei

Scene Fifty-three   881
Interrogating Liu Mengmei

Scene Fifty-four   919
Learning the Good News

Scene Fifty-five   939
Happy Reunion at Court

第二十九出　　旁　疑

【步步娇】

[净扮老道姑上]女冠儿生来出家相。

无对向、没生长。

守着三清像，

换水添香，

钟鸣鼓响。

赤紧的是那走方娘，

弄虚花扯闲帐？

"世事难拼一个信，人情常带三分疑。"杜老爷为小姐创下这座梅花观，着俺看守三年。水清石见，无半点瑕疵。止因陈教授老狗，引下个岭南柳秀才，东房养病。前几日到后花园回来，悠悠漾漾的，着鬼着魅一般，俺已疑惑了。凑着个韶阳小道姑，年方念八，颇有风情，到此云游，几日不去。

Scene Twenty-nine
The Nun's Suspicion

(*Enter Sister Stone*)

Sister Stone:

(*To the tune of* **Bubujiao**)

I have been born to be a nun,

Without a spouse,

Without a son.

I tend the shrine of gods in heaven and hell,

Adding water and joss-sticks to the shrine,

Beating drums and striking the bell.

But now I must watch this roaming nun,

Who has lewd looks and a wagging tongue.

"There is not any genuine trust on earth;

Suspicion proves to be a thing of worth."

Since Prefect Du established this Plum Blossom Nunnery, I have been looking after it for three years. Everything has been in good order and above suspicion, except for the young scholar Liu Mengmei from Lingnan. He was brought here by the old scamp Mr Chen and was put up in the eastern guestroom for recovery from illness. When he came back from the back garden a few days ago, he seemed to be in a trance, as if he were haunted by ghosts. I began to have suspicions at once. It happens that a young nun from Shaoyang travelled to this place and has stayed here for a few days. Twenty-eight years of age, she has an attractive face. At night I hear people chatter

夜来柳秀才房里，唧唧哝哝，听的似女儿声息。敢是小道姑瞒着我去瞧那秀才，秀才逆来顺受了。俺且待他来，打觑他一番。

【前腔】
[贴扮小道姑上]俺女冠儿俏的仙真样。
论举止都停当，
则一点情抛漾。
步斗风前，
吹笙月上。
[叹介]古来仙女定成双，
恁生来寒乞相？[见介]
[贴]"常无欲以观其妙，
[净]常有欲以观其窍。"小姑姑你昨夜游方，游到柳秀才房儿里去。是窍，是妙？
[贴]老姑姑这话怎的起？谁曾见来？
[净]俺见来。

【剔银灯】
你出家人芙蓉淡妆，
翦一片湘云鹤氅。
玉冠儿斜插笑生香，

in Mr Liu's room and it seems that there is a female voice. I guess that the young nun is visiting him behind my back and Mr Liu has accepted her offer. I'll try to find out the truth when she comes back.

(*Enter Young Nun*)

Young Nun:

(*To the previous tune*)

A nun as pretty as a fairy maid,

I'm well behaved,

Although my sweetness would not fade.

I've worshipped gods and prayed

And hoped to turn into a fairy maid.

(*Sighs*)

A fairy maid will have her mate,

But why should I be in this wretched state?

(*Greets Sister Stone*)

"Remain dispassionate to watch the soul;

Sister Stone:

Remain passionate to watch the body hole."

Young sister, did you roam to the young scholar's room last night to watch his soul or his hole?

Young Nun:

What are you driving at, old sister? Who saw me going there?

Sister Stone:

I did.

(*To the tune of Tiyindeng*)

As a nun, you paint your face

And wear a simple Taoist cloak.

With adorned hair you smile from place to place,

出落的十分情况。
　　斟量，敢则向书生夜窗，
　　迤逗的幽辉半床？
　　[贴]向那个书生？老姑姑这话敢不中哩。
【前腔】
　　俺虽然年青试妆，
　　洗凡心冰壶月朗。
　　你怎生剥落的人轻相？
　　比似你半老的佳人停当！
　　[净]倒栽起俺来。
　　[贴]你端详，
　　这女贞观傍，
　　可放着个书生话长？
　　[净]哎也，难道俺与书生有账！这梅花观，你是云游道婆，他是云游秀才，你住的，偏他住不的？则是往常秀才夜静高眠，则你到观中，那秀才夜半开门，唧唧哝哝的。不共你说话，共谁来？扯你道录司告去。[扯介]
　　[贴]便去。你将前官香火院，停宿外方游棍。难道

So appealing to the folk.

I can imagine

How you went to the scholar's room

And shared the bed with him in the gloom.

Young Nun:

Which scholar do you mean? You're simply talking nonsense.

(*To the previous tune*)

Although I am still young,

I have a crystal heart.

You accuse me with a vicious tongue

But I have played a better part!

Sister Stone:

You are turning the slander on me!

Young Nun:

Just consider

How there can be a scholar's face

In this sacred Taoist place.

Sister Stone:

Alas, are you alluding that I have an affair with the young scholar? In this Plum Blossom Nunnery, you stop over as a travelling nun and he stops over as a travelling scholar. Why can I put you up but not him? He used to sleep well all through the night; however, since you came here, he has opened his door at night and whispered all night. Who is he whispering to but you? I'll bring the case against you in the Taoist court.

(*Grabs at Young Nun*)

Young Nun:

Off we go! You put up a wandering vagabond in the nunnery established by the former prefect. Do you think they'll easily

偏放过你?[扯介]

【一封书】
[末上]闲步白云除,
问柳先生何处居?
扣梅花院主。
[见扯介]呀,怎两个姑姑争施主?
玄牝同门道可道,
怎不韫椟而藏姑待姑?
俺知道你是大姑他是小姑,
嫁的个彭郎港口无?
[净]先生不知。听的柳秀才半夜开门,不住的唧哝。俺好意儿问这小姑:"敢是你共柳秀才讲话哩?"这小姑则答应着"谁共秀才讲话来",便罢;倒嘴骨弄的说俺养着个秀才。陈先生,凭你说,谁引这秀才来?扯他道录司明白去。俺是石的。
[贴]难道俺是水的?
[末]禁声,坏了柳秀才体面。俺劝你,

let you go?

(*Grabs at Sister Stone*)

(*Enter Chen Zuiliang*)

Chen Zuiliang:

(*To the tune of* **Yifengshu**)

I go to the nunnery alone

To meet the young scholar Liu

And visit Sister Stone.

(*Sees the two nuns grabbing at each other*)

Oh,

How can two nuns fight for a single man?

Both disciples of Tao,

Why don't you quietly spend your life span?

You are older and she is younger now,

Who are you seeking after in your clan?

Sister Stone:

Let me tell you, Mr Chen. I heard the scholar open his door at night and whisper all the time. When I asked the young nun politely, "Have you chatted with him", it was all right that she answered, "Who has chatted with him?" It was too much for her to say that I kept a scholar under my roof. Tell us, Mr Chen, who brought him into my nunnery! Take her to the Taoist court to get the truth out of her. I'm Sister Stone, with a heart of stone.

Young Nun:

Do you mean to say that I am as frivolous as water?

Chen Zuiliang:

Shut up, both of you! You are ruining the reputation of Mr Liu. Now, listen to me.

【前腔】
　　教你姑徐徐。
　　撒月招风实也虚？
　　早则是者也之乎，
　　那柳下先生君子儒，
　　到道录司牒你去俗还俗，
　　敢儒流们笑你姑不姑。
　　[贴]正是不雅相。
　　[末]好把冠子儿扶水云梳，
　　裂了这仙衣四五铢。
　　[净]便依说，开手罢。陈先生吃个斋去。
　　[末]待柳秀才在时又来。
【尾声】
　　清绝处，再踟蹰。
　　[泪介]咳，糁东风穷泪扑疏疏。
　　道姑，杜小姐坟儿可上去？
　　[净]雨哩。
　　[末叹介]则恨的锁春寒这几点杜鹃花下雨。[下]

(*To the previous tune*)

Do not draw conclusions in haste.

Are you sure you know the truth?

A man of lofty taste,

Mr Liu is an honest youth.

If the court should know you are not chaste,

You'll be dispelled and sneered for sooth.

Young Nun:

Indeed we'll make a show.

Chen Zuiliang:

Arrange your hairpins and comb your hair;

Your cloak has gone through wear and tear.

Sister Stone:

All right, let's forget about it. Mr Chen, let's go and have a vegetarian dinner.

Chen Zuiliang:

No, thanks. I'll come again when Mr Liu is in.

(*To the tune of* **Coda**)

In this holy place,

I lag my pace.

(*Weeps*)

Alas,

Against the wind I shed large drops of tear.

Sister Stone, shall we go to Miss Du's grave?

Sister Stone:

It's raining.

Chen Zuiliang:

(*With a sigh*)

How I hate the rainfall here!

[净、贴吊场]
[净]陈老儿去了。小姑姑好噱。
[贴]和你再打听谁和秀才说话来。

[净]烟水何曾息世机!
[贴]高情雅淡世间稀。
[净]陇山鹦鹉能言语,
[贴]乱向金笼说是非。

(*Exit Chen Zuiliang, leaving Sister Stone and Young Nun behind*)

Sister Stone:

Mr Chen is gone and you don't have to worry now.

Young Nun:

Let's try to find out who's been chatting with the young scholar.

Sister Stone:

The Taoist nuns have never shunned the world!

Young Nun:

Seldom do they behave like a sage.

Sister Stone:

When parrots learn to say the human word,

Young Nun:

They start to quarrel with the golden cage.

第三十出　　欢　挠

【捣练子】
　　[生上]听漏下半更多,
　　月影向中那。
　　恁时节夜香烧罢么?
　　"一点猩红一点金,十个春纤十个针。只因世上美人面,改尽人间君子心。"俺柳梦梅是个读书君子,一味志诚。止因北上南安,凑着东邻西子。嫣然一笑,遂成暮雨之来;未是五更,便逐晓风而去。今宵有约,未知迟早。正是:"金莲若肯移三寸,银烛先教刻五分。"则一件,姐姐若到,要精神对付他。偷眲一会,有何不可。[睡介]

Scene Thirty
Disrupting the Love Affair

(*Enter Liu Mengmei*)

Liu Mengmei:

(*To the tune of Daolianzi*)

When it is in the deep of night,

The moon moves to the zenith.

Is the joss-stick burning bright?

"Her finger-nails are painted scarlet-red,

On fingers slender as the bamboo-shoots.

With a pretty maiden on my bed,

I am completely stricken deaf and mute."

As a diligent student, I've been devoted to studies. When I reached Nan'an on my way north to the capital, I met a fair lady from the neighbourhood. Her sweet smile has brought about a series of rendezvous. She is gone with the wind before the day breaks. We'll have a date tonight, but I'm not sure when she will come. As the poem goes,

"Before her tiny feet would move with grace,

The candle has been thus burned down apace."

The point is, I must be fresh and energetic to meet her, and so why not take a nap now!

(*Takes a nap*)

(*Enter Du Liniang in the ghost form*)

Du Liniang:

(*To the tune of Chengrenxin*)

【称人心】
　　[魂旦上]冥途挣挫,
　　要死却心儿无那。
　　也则为俺那人儿忒可,
　　教他闷房头守着闲灯火。
　　[入门介]呀,他端然睡瞌,
　　恁春寒也不把绣衾来摸。
　　多应他祗候着我。
　　待叫醒他。秀才,秀才!
　　[生醒介]姐姐,失敬也。[起揖介]
　　[生]待整衣罗,
　　远远相迎个。
　　这二更天风露多,
　　还则怕夜深花睡么?
　　[旦]秀才,俺那里长夜好难过,
　　缱着你无眠清坐。
　　[生]姐姐,你来的脚踪儿恁轻,是怎的?
　　[旦]"自然无迹又无尘,
　　[生]白日寻思夜梦频。
　　[旦]行到窗前知未寝,

>   I suffer in the nether world,
>
>   But would not die a second death.
>
>   I have the scholar in my mind,
>
>   Who waits for me with bated breath.
>
>   (*Moves into Liu Mengmei's room*)
>
> Oh,
>
>   He slumbers on a low settee,
>
>   Without a quilt to shun spring cold.
>
>   There he lies and waits for me.
>
> Let me wake him up. Scholar, scholar!

Liu Mengmei:

>   (*Wakes up*)
>
>   Oh. It's you, my young lady! I'm sorry.
>
>   (*Rises to his feet and bows*)
>
>   I should have been well dressed
>
>   And gone to meet you.
>
>   But haven't the wind and dew
>
>   Put nocturnal flowers to rest?

Du Liniang:

>   In my place the night is long and deep,
>
>   But thoughts of you deprived me of my sleep.

Liu Mengmei:

>   My young lady, how is it that your steps are so quiet?

Du Liniang:

>   "*Of course I leave no trace and stir no dust;*

Liu Mengmei:

>   *I long for you by day and dream by night.*

Du Liniang:

>   *Through the windows I find you sit awake;*

[生]一心惟待月夫人。"姐姐，今夜来的迟些。

【绣带儿】
　　[旦]镇消停，
　　不是俺闲情忒慢俄。
　　那些儿忘却俺欢哥。
　　夜香残，回避了尊亲。
　　绣床偎收拾起生活，停脱。
　　顺风儿斜将金佩拖，
　　紧摘离百忙的淡妆明抹。
　　[生]费你高情，则良夜无酒奈何？
　　[旦]都忘了。俺携酒一壶，花果二色，在楯栏之上，取来消遣。[旦取酒、果、花上]
　　[生]生受了。是甚果？
　　[旦]青梅数粒。
　　[生]这花？

Liu Mengmei:

I'm waiting for you to come in sight."

Tonight you're later that usual, my young lady.

Du Liniang:

(*To the tune of Xiudaier*)

Don't be annoyed, please.

I do not want to come so late;

I've always kept you in my heart.

Only when the evening incense was lit,

From my parents could I depart.

I leant against my bed

And laid my needlework down.

At once I came here in the breeze,

Without making up or changing my gown.

Liu Mengmei:

Thank you for your kindness. But how are we to spend this wonderful night without wine?

Du Liniang:

I nearly forget that I've brought a kettle of wine and some fruit and flower. They are left on the corridor. I'll get them for you.

(*Fetches the wine, fruit and flower*)

Liu Mengmei:

Thank you very much. What's the fruit you've brought?

Du Liniang:

Some green plums.

Liu Mengmei:

And what's the flower?

Du Liniang:

[旦]美人蕉。

[生]梅子酸似俺秀才，蕉花红似俺姐姐。串饮一杯。[共杯饮介]

【白练序】

[旦]金荷、斟香糯。

[生]你酝酿春心玉液波。

拼微酡，

东风外翠香红酡。

[旦]也摘不下奇花果，

这一点蕉花和梅豆呵，

君知么，爱的人全风韵，

花有根科。

【醉太平】

[生]细哦，

这子儿花朵，

似美人憔悴，

酸子情多。

喜蕉心暗展，

一夜梅犀点污。

如何？

酒潮微晕笑生涡。

It's canna.

Liu Mengmei:

The green plum is as sour as I, and the canna is as red as you.

Let's share a cup of wine.

(*Liu Mengmei and Du Liniang drink from the same cup*)

Du Liniang:

(*To the tune of **Bailianxu***)

Fill in the golden cup

With fragrant wine.

Liu Mengmei:

The wine you brewed

Brings a flush to your cheeks

As the east wind makes the blooms ashine.

Du Liniang:

No other flower or fruit

Is better than canna or plum,

For, you know,

The kernel of fruit is fine,

The flower has its root.

Liu Mengmei:

(*To the tune of **Zuitaiping***)

What's more,

The canna flower

Is like a fragile maid,

While the plum kernel like a learned man.

When canna's pistil is displayed,

The plum petal lures into her span.

What comes next?

With a smile and flush upon your face,

待嗬着脸恣情的呜喓，
些儿个，翠偃了情波，
润红蕉点，
香生梅唾。

【白练序】
　　[旦]活泼、死腾那，
这是第一所人间风月窝。
昨宵个微芒暗影轻罗，
把势儿忒显豁。
为什么人到幽期话转多？
　　[生]好睡也。
　　[旦]好月也。
消停坐，
不妒色嫦娥，
和俺人三个。

【醉太平】
　　[生]无多，花影阿那。
劝奴奴睡也，
睡也奴哥。
春宵美满，
一霎暮钟敲破。

You will be showered with my kiss.

Very soon,

You'll shut your eyes with grace,

And, in your scarlet spot,

Accept the green-plum juice.

Du Liniang:

(*To the tune of Bailianxu*)

I pant,

And heave

In this paradise of love on earth.

Behind the window screen,

We'll make love in the eve;

Why do we speak so many words?

Liu Mengmei:

It's time to go to bed.

Du Liniang:

Let's gaze at the moon.

Sit here for a while

And share the pretty scene

With the moon-land fairy queen.

Liu Mengmei:

(*To the tune of Zuitaiping*)

Leave the fairy queen alone.

In the flower shade,

Let's go to bed,

My pretty maid.

The charming vernal night

Will fly away, I am afraid.

My dear,

娇娥、似前宵雨云羞怯颤声讹，
敢今夜翠颦轻可。
睡则那，
把腻乳微搓，
酥胸汗帖，
细腰春锁。
[净、贴悄上]
[贴]"道可道，可知道？名可名，可闻名？"
[生、旦笑介]
[贴]老姑姑，你听秀才房里有人。这不是俺小姑姑了。
[净作听介]是女人声，快敲门去。
[敲门介]
[生]是谁？
[净]老道姑送茶。
[生]夜深了。
[净]相公房里有客哩。

You were too shy last night;

Tonight you'll be all right.

When we're in bed,

I'll feel your creamy breast,

Embrace your sweaty chest

And hold your waist tight.

(*Enter Sister Stone and Young Nun stealthily*)

Young Nun:

"Tao can be defined as Tao,

But are you aware of Tao?

Names can be used for its name,

But are you aware of its name?"

(*Liu Mengmei and Du Liniang laugh heartily*)

Young Nun:

Listen, Sister Stone, someone's talking in the scholar's room. Now you know it's not me.

Sister Stone:

(*Listens attentively*)

There's a woman's voice. Go and knock at the door.

(*Young Nun knocks at the door*)

Liu Mengmei:

Who's at the door?

Sister Stone:

It's me, Sister Stone, to bring you some tea.

Liu Mengmei:

It's too late for tea now.

Sister Stone:

You seem to have a guest with you.

Liu Mengmei:

[生]没有。
[净]女客哩。
[生、旦慌介]怎好?
[净急敲门介]相公,快开门。地方巡警,免的声扬哩。
[生慌介]怎了,怎了!
[旦笑介]不妨,俺是邻家女子,道姑不肯干休时,便与他一个勾引的罪名儿。

【隔尾】
便开呵须撒和,
隔纱窗怎守的到参儿趖!
柳郎,则管松了门儿。
俺影着这一幅美人图那边躲。
[生开门,旦作躲,生将身遮旦,净、贴闯进笑介]喜也。
[净]什么喜?
[净前看,生身拦介]

No, I haven't.

Sister Stone:

Yes, you have a lady guest.

Liu Mengmei, Du Liniang:

(*In a panic*)

What's to be done?

Sister Stone:

(*Bangs on the door*)

Be quick, sir. Open the door. The patrolmen are coming. I don't want any trouble.

Liu Mengmei:

(*At a loss*)

What shall I do! What shall I do!

Du Liniang:

(*Smiles*)

Never mind. I'm from the neighbourhood. If they won't let you go, you can accuse them of seduction.

(*To the tune of* **Quasi-coda**)

If they want you to open the door, they have to be polite;

Beside the windows, can they stand the whole night?

Dear Mr Liu, just unbolt the door.

I'll hide behind the beauty scroll to stand out of sight.

Sister Stone, Young Nun:

(*Rush in, giggling, as Liu Mengmei opens the door and shields Du Liniang, who hides behind him*)

Congratulations!

Liu Mengmei:

What for?

(*Sister Stone tries to look over Liu Mengmei's shoulder. Liu*

【滚遍】
　　[净、贴]这更天一点锣，
　　仙院重门阖。
　　何处娇娥？
　　怕惹的干柴火。
　　[生]你便打睃，
　　有甚着科？
　　是床儿里窝？
　　箱儿里那？
　　袖儿里阁？
　　[净、贴向前，生拦不住，内作风起，旦闪下介]
　　[生]昏了灯也。
　　[净]分明一个影儿，只这轴美女图在此。古画成精了么？

【前腔】
　　画屏人踏歌，
　　曾许你书生和。
　　不是妖魔，
　　甚影儿望风躲？
　　相公，这是什么画？
　　[生]妙娑婆，

Mengmei blocks her way)

Sister Stone, Young Nun:

(*To the tune of Gunbian*)

Hour by hour the night will pass;

The nunnery's gate is closed tight.

From where comes the pretty lass,

Who stirs the man at night?

Liu Mengmei:

Just look ahead!

Do you indeed believe

That you'll find something on the bed?

Or in the trunk?

Or up my sleeve?

(*Sister Stone and Young Nun push forward. Liu Mengmei fails to keep them back. Sound of wind within. Du Liniang slips offstage*)

Liu Mengmei:

You nearly blew out the lamp.

Sister Stone:

I saw someone's shadow a moment ago, but now there is only the beauty scroll on the wall. Was the painting enchanted?

(*To the previous tune*)

The beauty on the scroll would dance and sing

To form a pair with you.

If it were not demon or something,

Why should it flee while the wind blew?

What painting is this, sir?

Liu Mengmei:

It is a work of art

秀才家随行的香火。
俺寂静里暗祈求,
你莽吃喝。
[净]是了。不说不知,俺前晚听见相公房内啾啾唧唧,疑惑是这小姑姑。俺如今明白了。相公,权留小姑姑伴话。
[生]请了。

【尾声】
[贴]动不动道录司官了私和。
[生]则欺负俺不分外的书生欺别个!
姑姑,这多半觉美鼾鼾,
则被你奚落杀了我。
[净、贴下]
[生笑介]一天好事,两个瓦剌姑,扫兴,扫兴。那美人呵,好吃惊也!

应陪秉烛夜深游,
恼乱春风卒未休。
大姑山远小姑出,
更凭飞梦到瀛洲。

To bless me all along the way.

I worship it from the bottom of my heart,

But you disturb me when I pray.

Sister Stone:

Oh, that's it. I never thought of it. When I heard someone murmuring in your room, I suspected that it was this young nun. Now I see. Excuse me, Sir, for I'll have a word with her.

Liu Mengmei:

Please.

Young Nun:

(*To the tune of Coda*)

You want to drag me to the Taoist court!

Liu Mengmei:

And give an honest man a bad report!

Sister Stone, by what you did,

My sweet dream tonight is cut short.

(*Exeunt Sister Stone and Young Nun*)

Liu Mengmei:

(*Laughs*)

My sweet rendezvous is ruined by these two nasty nuns! What a distress! How they have startled my beauty!

I should escort you in the night,

But spring breeze brings woes hand in hand.

When rolling mountains come in sight,

My dream has borne me to the fairyland.

第三十一出　　缮　备

【番卜算】

[贴扮文官，净扮武官上]边海一边江，
隔不断胡尘涨。
维扬新筑两城墙，
酾酒临江上。
请了。俺们扬州府文武官僚是也。安抚杜老大人，为因李全骚扰地方，加筑外罗城一座。今日落成开宴，杜老大人早到也。

【前腔】

[众拥外上]三千客两行，
百二关重壮。
[文武迎介]
[外]维扬风景世无双，
直上层楼望。
[见介]
[众]"北门卧护要耆英。

Scene Thirty-one
Preparing for War

(*Enter an official and an officer*)

Official, Officer:

(*To the tune of* **Fanbusuan**)

The Yangtze flows, the sea roars,

Yet rebel armies are malign.

Yangzhou has reinforced its walls;

We toast the river with our wine.

How do you do! We are the official and officer of the Yangzhou Prefecture. As Li Quan is making harassment in this area, Envoy Du has ordered us to build an outer city wall. Today we're going to hold a banquet to celebrate the completion of the outer wall. Here comes Envoy Du.

(*Enter Du Bao, followed by subordinates*)

Subordinates:

(*To the previous tune*)

Three thousand followers line the hall;

Our strength is doubled by the wall.

(*The official and officer welcome Du Bao*)

Du Bao:

Yangzhou commands sights ever seen;

Let's climb the tower for a better scene.

Subordinates:

(*Greet Du Bao*)

"To guard the gate we need a warrior old and bold;

[外]恨少胸中十万兵。
[众]天借金山为底柱。
[外]身当铁瓮作长城。"扬州表里重城,不日成就。皆文武诸公士民之力。
[众]此皆老安抚远略奇谋。属宫窃在下风,敢献一杯,效古人城隅之宴。
[外]正好。且向新楼一望。[望介]壮哉,城也!真乃:"江北无双堑,淮南第一楼。"
[众]请进酒。

【山花子】
[众]贺层城顿插云霄敞,
雉飞腾映压寒江。
据表里山河一方,
控长淮万里金汤。
[合]敌楼高窥临女墙,
临风酾酒旌旄扬。
乍想起琼花当年吹暗香,

Du Bao:

I wish I were a warrior crowning all.

Subordinates:

The heaven sets a hill as our stronghold;

Du Bao:

I'll guard the city as an iron wall."

The swift completion of the Yangzhou outer wall is the result of the joint efforts of the officials, officers and civilians.

Subordinates:

You have made all the plans while we have just followed your instructions. Will you accept our toast as a time-honoured tradition?

Du Bao:

Excellent! Now let's have a look around the gate tower.

(*Looks around*)

What a magnificent wall! It is truly

"The strongest city in the north;

The topmost tower in Huainan."

Subordinates:

A toast to you!

(*To the tune of Shanhuazi*)

Cheers to the towering wall,

That has a bird's eye view of streams.

A safeguard to us all,

It is indeed supreme.

All:

On watchtowers above the wall,

We sprinkle wine beside the banners.

When we think of past glories,

几点新亭,
无限沧桑。
[外]前面高起如霜似雪四五十堆,是何山也?
[众]都是各场所积之盐,众商人中纳。
[外]商人何在?
[末、老旦扮商人上]"占种海田高白玉,掀翻盐井横黄金。"商人见。
[外]商人么,则怕早晚要动支兵粮,攒紧上纳。

【前腔】
这盐呵,是银山雪障连天晃,
海煎成夏草秋粮。
平看取盐花灶场,
尽支排中纳边商。
[合前]

Our mournful teardrops fall,

For the world has changed its manners.

Du Bao:

What are those forty or fifty snowy mounds that rise in the distance?

Subordinates:

They are salt piles stored in the yards to be paid to the merchants.

Du Bao:

Where are the merchants?

(*Enter two merchants*)

Two Merchants:

"The jades from brines are piled and sold;

The salt has thus become pure gold."

We merchants pay our respect to you.

Du Bao:

Merchants, as I'm afraid that provisions will be needed here, please bring them in as soon as possible.

(*To the previous tune*)

The salt piles stand as snowy mounds,

In exchange for fodder and grain.

The salt stored on the spacious grounds

Will soon become the merchants' gains.

All:

On watchtowers above the wall,

We sprinkle wine beside the banners.

When we think of past glories,

Our mournful teardrops fall,

For the world has changed its manners.

[外]酒罢了。喜的广有兵粮,则要众文武关防如法。

【舞霓裳】
　　[众]文武官僚立边疆,
　　立边疆。
　　休坏了这农桑,
　　士工商。
　　[合]敢大金家早晚来无状,
　　打贴起炮箭旗枪。
　　听边声风沙迭荡,
　　猛惊起,
　　见蟠花战袍旧边将。

【红绣鞋】
　　[众]吉日祭赛城隍,
　　城隍。
　　归神谢土安康,
　　安康。
　　祭旗纛,
　　犒军装。
　　阵头儿,
　　谁抵当?
　　箭眼里,
　　好遮藏。

Du Bao:
>Now, so much for the sprinkling of wine. I'm glad that we have abundant provisions in store, but I still hope that you must be on the alert to guard the frontiers.

Subordinates:
>(*To the tune of Wunishang*)
>We are the frontier guards,
>The frontier guards,
>Protecting farms and fields,
>Protecting people in the yards.

All:
>Should the Jins dare to invade the land,
>We'll greet them with our bows and guns.
>When war-cries roll along the border,
>At your command,
>All the soldiers are brave ones.

Subordinates:
>(*To the tune of Hongxiuxie*)
>We offer sacrifice to the city god,
>The city god,
>We thank the heaven for our peace,
>For our peace.
>Let us salute the army flags
>And get our weapons piece by piece.
>When battles start,
>Who will fight with pride?
>Behind the battlements,
>Our archers hide.

Du Bao:

【尾声】
[外]按三韬把六出旗门放,
文和武肃静端详。
则等待海西头动边烽那一声炮儿响。

夹城云暖下霓旌,
千里崤函一梦劳。
不意新城连嶂起,
夜来冲斗气何高。

(*To the tune of* **Coda**)

When I deploy the troops,

All of you must take good care

To wait for battle summons there.

With battle flags flying on the wall,

We'll crash the enemy's daydream.

The outer walls are strong and tall,

Guarded by a valiant team.

第三十二出　冥　誓

【月云高】
[生上]暮云金阙，
风幡淡摇拽。
但听的钟声绝，
早则是心儿热。
纸帐书生，
有分盒兰麝。
咱时还早。
荡花阴，
单则把月痕遮。
[整灯介]溜风光，
稳护着灯儿烨。
[笑介]"好书读易尽，佳人期未来。"前夕美人到此，并不提防，姑姑搅攘。今宵趁他未来之时，先到云堂之上攀话一回，免生疑惑。
[作掩门行介]此处留人户半斜，

Scene Thirty-two
Vowing between Man and Ghost

(*Enter Liu Mengmei*)

Liu Mengmei:
(*To the tune of* **Yueyungao**)
When gilded roofs are shadowed by the cloud,
The prayer banners flutter in the breeze.
The evening bells no longer ring aloud,
And I begin to feel so ill at ease.
A scholar as poor as can be,
I have a pretty maid who loves me.
The time is early yet.
When flowers tremble in a gale,
The moonlight dots the garden trail.
(*Shields the lantern*)
When I roam along the garden trail,
I shield the lantern from the gale.
(*Smiles*)
"It's easier to finish learned books
Than wait for maid with pretty looks."

As I did not take any precautions when my fair lady came last night, our rendezvous was disrupted by the nuns. Before she comes tonight, I'll go and chat for a while with the nuns, lest suspicion should arise again.

(*Leaves the door ajar and walks along*)
I leave the door ajar for my beloved one.

天呵,
俺那有心期在那些。[下]

【前腔】
[魂旦上]孤神害怯,
佩环风定夜。
[惊介]则道是人行影,
原来是云偷月。
[到介]这是柳郎书舍了。呀,柳郎何处也?
闪闪幽斋,
弄影灯明灭。
魂再艳,
灯油接;
情一点,
灯头结。
[叹介] 奴家和柳郎幽期,除是人不知,鬼都知道。
[泣介]竹影寺风声怎的遮,
黄泉路夫妻怎当赊?
"待说何曾说,如噤不奈噤。把持花下意,犹恐梦

Oh heavens,

What mood do I have to chat with the nun?

(*Exit*)

(*Enter Du Liniang in the ghost form*)

Du Liniang:

(*To the previous tune*)

In lonely fear I ran

When my pendants rang in a tinkling tune.

(*Taken aback*)

I thought it was the shadow of a man,

But it was a cloud drifting past the moon.

(*Reaches the door*)

Here I am at Mr Liu's study, but where is he now?

The lantern quivers in the gloom,

Adding dimness to the room

As the oil

Ignites the lantern flame,

So the wick

Ignites my loving claim.

(*Sighs*)

My rendezvous with Mr Liu is kept unknown to the mortals but not the ghosts.

(*Weeps*)

As grapevine always stretches fast,

Who knows how long our rendezvous can last?

"*From my mouth comes hardly a word;*

On my brows comes hardly a beam.

I'd like to taste the pleasure in this world,

But fear that it happens only in a dream."

中身。"奴家虽登鬼录,未损人身。阳禄将回,阴数已尽。前日为柳郎而死,今日为柳郎而生。夫妇分缘,去来明白。今宵不说,只管人鬼混缠到甚时节?只怕说时柳郎那一惊呵,也避不得了。正是:"夜传人鬼三分话,早定夫妻百岁恩。"

【懒画眉】

　　[生上]画阑风摆竹横斜。

　　[内作鸟声惊介]惊鸦闪落在残红榭。

　　呀,门儿开也,

　　玉天仙光降了紫云车。

　　[旦出迎介]柳郎来也。

　　[生揖介] 姐姐来也。

　　[旦]剔灯花这咱望郎爷。

　　[生]直恁的志诚亲姐姐。

　　[旦]秀才,等你不来,俺集下了唐诗一首。

Although I've entered the nether world, I still keep my body intact. I'll soon leave the nether world and return to the human world. I died for Mr Liu and shall return to life for Mr Liu. It is our fate to be man and wife; therefore, if I don't tell him about it tonight, what good will come of a rendezvous between man and ghost? I'm afraid that my story will give him a shock, but that's my only choice. It is true to say that

"A ghostly story that he hears

Will fix the marriage of a hundred years."

(*Enter Liu Mengmei*)

Liu Mengmei:

(*To the tune of* **Lanhuamei**)

The bamboo wavers in the breeze;

(*Sound of startled birds within*)

The crows are startled in the trees.

Oh, my door is now opened.

A fairy has arrived at ease.

(*Du Liniang comes out of the door to greet him*)

Du Liniang:

So you're back.

Liu Mengmei:

(*Makes a bow to Du Liniang*)

So you've come.

Du Liniang:

I trimmed the wick while I waited here;

Liu Mengmei:

You are indeed true to me, my dear.

Du Liniang:

While I was waiting for you, sir, I made up a quatrain by col-

[生]洗耳。

[旦念介]"拟托良媒亦自伤，月寒山色两苍苍。不知谁唱春归曲？又向人间魅阮郎。"

[生]姐姐高才。

[旦]柳郎，这更深何处来也？

[生]昨夜被姑姑败兴，俺乘你未来之时，去姑姑房头看了他动静，好来迎接你。不想姐姐今夜来恁早哩。

[旦]盼不到月儿上也。

【太师引】

[生]叹书生何幸遇仙提揭，
比人间更志诚亲切。
乍温存笑眼生花，
正渐入欢肠啖蔗。
前夜那姑姑呵，
恨无端风雨把春抄截。
姐姐呵，
误了你半宵周折，
累了你好回惊怯。

lecting lines from the Tang poets.

Liu Mengmei:

I'll be pleased to hear it.

Du Liniang:

> "I need someone to tell my love
>
> While the cold moon shines above.
>
> When from somewhere the dirges ring,
>
> I yearn for the man of by-gone spring."

Liu Mengmei:

You're indeed a gifted poet.

Du Liniang:

Sir, where have you been in the small hours?

Liu Mengmei:

As we were disturbed last night by the nuns, I visited them before your arrival to make sure that they would not suspect us. I didn't expect that you come so early.

Du Liniang:

I can hardly wait till the moon rises.

Liu Mengmei:

(*To the tune of Taishiyin*)

What a bliss that I have this maid,

So kind and faithful to a man like me.

Her tender eyes that I can't evade

Enchant me degree by degree.

What a pity that the nuns last night

Disturbed us while we were in glee.

My dear sister,

The nuns distressed your mind

And brought you such a fright.

不嗔嫌，
一径的把断红重接。

【锁寒窗】
[旦]是不提防他来的阵嗻，
吓的个魂儿收不迭。
仗云摇月躲，
画影人遮。
则没揣的涩道边儿，
闪人一跌。
自生成不惯这磨灭。
险些些，
风声扬播到俺家爷，
先吃了俺狠尊慈痛决。
[生]姐姐费心。因何错爱小生至此？
[旦]爱的你一品人才。
[生]姐姐敢定了人家？

【太师引】
[旦]并不曾受人家红定回鸾帖。
[生]喜个甚样人家？
[旦]但得个秀才郎情倾意惬。
[生]小生到是个有情的。

If you leave the woes behind,

We'll start the game again tonight.

Du Liniang:

(*To the tune of Suohanchuang*)

Their visit caught me unaware

And scared me out of my wits.

When the moon is hidden in the air,

I stood behind the scroll and quit.

I nearly stumbled on the trail,

As I had never been so scared.

If Dad should hear about the tale,

I won't easily be spared.

Liu Mengmei:

I'm sorry for the trouble I've brought you, but am I indeed worthy of your love?

Du Liniang:

I love you because you are the man of men.

Liu Mengmei:

May I ask whether you have been engaged, my dear?

Du Liniang:

(*To the tune of Taishiyin*)

No one has offered me his hand.

Liu Mengmei:

What kind of husband would you like to have?

Du Liniang:

A loving scholar is what I demand.

Liu Mengmei:

I do have a loving heart.

Du Liniang:

[旦]是看上你年少多情,
迤逗俺睡魂难贴。
[生]姐姐,嫁了小生罢。
[旦]怕你岭南归客路途赊,
是做小伏低难说。
[生]小生未曾有妻。
[旦笑介]少什么旧家根叶,
着俺异乡花草填接?
敢问秀才,堂上有人么?
[生]先君官为朝散,先母曾封县君。
[旦]这等是衙内了。怎恁婚迟?

【锁寒窗】
[生]恨孤单飘零岁月,
但寻常稔色谁沾藉?
那有个相如在客,
肯驾香车?
萧史无家,
便同瑶阙?
似你千金笑等闲抛泄,

A scholar with a love so deep,

You distract me in my sleep.

Liu Mengmei:

Be my wife, my dear.

Du Liniang:

While from Lingnan you roam,

I don't know whether you have a wife at home.

Liu Mengmei:

I'm not married yet.

Du Liniang:

(*Smiles*)

You have deep roots in the native land,

Why should you offer me your hand?

Will you tell me something about your parents?

Liu Mengmei:

My late father served as a minister in the court and my late mother was entitled Lady of the County.

Du Liniang:

In that case, you are from an official's family. How is it that you are not married yet?

Liu Mengmei:

(*To the tune of Suohanchuang*)

Although I live a roaming life,

I will not take a homely wife.

But where's the maid who'd marry

A man like Xiangru who had to roam?

Where's the maid who'd marry

A man like Xiao Shi who had no home?

Your smiles on me are the highest praise,

凭说,
便和伊青春才貌恰争些,
怎做的露水相看仳别!
[旦]秀才有此心,何不请媒相聘?也省的奴家为你担慌受怕。
[生]明早敬造尊庭,拜见令尊令堂,方好问亲于姐姐。
[旦]到俺家来,只好见奴家。要见俺爹娘还早。
[生]这般说,姐姐当真是那样门庭。
[旦笑介]
[生]是怎生来?

【红衫儿】
看他温香艳玉神清绝,
人间迥别。
[旦]不是人间,难道天上?
[生]怎独自夜深行,
边厢少侍妾?
且说个贵表尊名。[旦叹介]

>   And as I'm blessed with smiles from you,
>
>   Although I'm not up to men of ancient days,
>
>   My love will not be like the morning dew.

Du Liniang:

> Since you have a strong love for me, why don't you get a matchmaker for our engagement, so that I don't have to worry about our rendezvous?

Liu Mengmei:

> I'll visit your parents tomorrow morning and ask for your hand.

Du Liniang:

> When you come to my home, you'll only meet me. It's not the time yet for you to meet my parents.

Liu Mengmei:

> Do you mean to say that you are from a distinguished house?
>
>   (*Du Liniang giggles*)

Liu Mengmei:

> What's up on your sleeves?
>
>   (*To the tune of* **Hongshaner**)
>
>   Your beauty of tremendous worth
>
>   Does not belong to mortal earth.

Du Liniang:

> If it does not belong to the mortal earth, does it belong to the heaven?

Liu Mengmei:

>   How can you walk alone in the nightly shade
>
>   Without a servant-maid?
>
>   Will you tell me your name?
>
>   (*Du Liniang sighs*)

Liu Mengmei:

[生背介]他把姓字香沉,
敢怕似飞琼漏泄?
姐姐不肯泄漏姓名,定是天仙了。薄福书生,不敢再陪欢宴。
尽仙姬留意书生,
怕逃不过天曹罚折。

【前腔】
[旦]道奴家天上神仙列,
前生寿折。
[生]不是天上,难道人间?
[旦]便作是私奔,
悄悄何妨说。
[生]不是人间,则是花月之妖。
[旦]正要你掘草寻根,
怕不待勾辰就月。
[生]是怎么说?
[旦欲说又止介]不明白辜负了幽期,
话到尖头又咽。

(*Aside*)

Why does she conceal her name?

Does she enjoy immortal fame?

Since you won't disclose your name, you must be a fairy. As I am not worthy of your trust, I dare not have any rendezvous with you.

For all the love you have for me,

The lord of heaven will not agree.

Du Liniang:

(*To the previous tune*)

You take me as an immortal friend,

But my previous life has come to an end.

Liu Mengmei:

If you are not an immortal, are you a human being?

Du Liniang:

If I can elope with you,

My name should not have been taboo.

Liu Mengmei:

If you are not a human being, are you an elf amid the flowers?

Du Liniang:

I'd like you to dig my root,

But fear to spoil our pursuit.

Liu Mengmei:

What do you mean?

Du Liniang:

(*Hesitates*)

I should have made it clear,

But hesitate with fear.

Liu Mengmei:

[生]姐姐,你"千不说,万不说。直恁的书生不酬决,更向谁边说?
[旦]待要说,如何说?秀才,俺则怕聘则为妻奔则妾,受了盟香说。"
[生]你要小生发愿,定为正妻,便与姐姐拈香去。
【滴溜子】
[生、旦同拜]神天的,神天的,盟香满爇。
柳梦梅,柳梦梅,南安郡舍,
遇了这佳人提挈,作夫妻。
生同室,死同穴。
口不心齐,寿随香灭。

My dear,

"Tell me now;
Tell me how.
If you say no,
Who else should know?

Du Liniang:

I'll tell you now;
I'll tell you how.

Dear Sir,

An elopement is not fair.
I'll tell you if you swear."

Liu Mengmei:

If you want me to swear to marry you, I'll make a vow by burning a joss-stick with you.

(*Kowtows with Du Liniang*)

(*To the tune of Diliuzi*)

Heavens above,
Heavens above,
The incense proves the man.
Liu Mengmei,
Liu Mengmei
Now stays in Nan'an.
I'll have this beauty in life
As my dearest wife.
We'll live to share the room
And die to share the tomb.
If I break my word,
I'll perish from this world.

(*Du Liniang weeps*)

[旦泣介]

[生]怎生吊下泪来？

[旦]感君情重，不觉泪垂。

【闹樊楼】
你秀才郎为客偏情绝，
料不是虚脾把盟誓撒。
哎，话吊在喉咙觑了舌。
嘱东君在意者，
精神打叠。
暂时间奴儿回避趄，
些儿待说，
你敢扑㤺忪害跌。

[生]怎的来？

[旦]秀才，这春容得从何处？

[生]太湖石缝里。

[旦]比奴家容貌争多？

[生看惊介]可怎生一个粉扑儿？

[旦]可知道，奴家便是画中人也。

Liu Mengmei:

How is it that you're weeping now?

Du Liniang:

I'm moved to tears by your strong love.

(*To the tune of* **Naofanlou**)

A scholar with a loving heart

Will never tear his words apart,

Alas,

But my account can hardly start.

Now listen, my dear,

And do not fear.

But I'm afraid when you hear

What I have to say,

You'll stumble and fade away.

Liu Mengmei:

What is it that you have to say?

Du Liniang:

Dear Sir, where did you find the portrait on the wall?

Liu Mengmei:

I found it in a crevice of lakeside rocks.

Du Liniang:

How would you say if you compare me with it?

Liu Mengmei:

(*Compares her with the portrait and gets surprised*)

Why, you look as like as two peas!

Du Liniang:

You know, it's a portrait of me.

Liu Mengmei:

(*Bows to the portrait with folded palms*)

[生合掌谢画介]小生烧的香到哩。姐姐,你好歹表白一些儿。

【啄木犯】

[旦]柳衙内听根节。

杜南安原是俺亲爹。

[生]呀,前任杜老先生升任扬州,怎么丢下小姐?

[旦]你翦了灯。

[生翦灯介]

[旦]翦了灯、余话堪明灭。

[生]且请问芳名,青春多少?

[旦]杜丽娘小字有庚帖,

年华二八,

正是婚时节。

[生]是丽娘小姐,俺的人那!

[旦]衙内,奴家还未是人。

[生]不是人,是鬼?

[旦]是鬼也。

I haven't burnt my incense in vain. My dear, would you tell me more about yourself?

Du Liniang:

(*To the tune of Zhuomufan*)

Now listen, my dear man,

My father was the Prefect of Nan'an.

Liu Mengmei:

Well, the former Prefect of Nan'an has been promoted to Yangzhou, but why are you left behind?

Du Liniang:

Trim the wick, please.

(*Liu Mengmei trims the wick*)

Du Liniang:

Now that the lamp is bright,

I'll bring the truth to light.

Liu Mengmei:

May I ask your name and your age?

Du Liniang:

Du Liniang stands by your side,

Sixteen years of age,

The right time to be a bride.

Liu Mengmei:

Oh, Liniang, my dear sweetheart!

Du Liniang:

Wait, dear Sir, I'm not a mortal being yet.

Liu Mengmei:

If you are not a mortal being, are you a ghost?

Du Liniang:

Yes, I am a ghost.

[生惊介]怕也,怕也。
[旦]靠边些,
听俺消详说。
话在前教伊休害怯,
俺虽则是小鬼头人半截。
[生]姐姐,因何得回阳世而会小生?

【前腔】
[旦]虽则是阴府别,
看一面千金小姐,
是杜南安那些枝叶。
注生妃央及煞回生帖,
化生娘点活了残生劫。
你后生儿醮定俺前生业。
秀才,你许了俺为妻真切,
少不得冷骨头着疼热。
[生]你是俺妻,俺也不害怕了。难道便请起你来?怕似水中捞月,空里拈花。

【三段子】
[旦]俺三光不灭。

Liu Mengmei:

(*Frightened*)

Oh, terrible! Terrible!

Du Liniang:

Stand back, Mr Liu,

And hear my words.

As I told you,

I live between two worlds.

Liu Mengmei:

My dear, how did you manage to return to this world to meet me?

Du Liniang:

(*To the previous tune*)

When I was in the world of hell,

The judge knew that I was from an official's house

And treated me well.

He promised me a second life

And sent me to this world,

As I am fated to be your wife.

Dear Sir,

As you yearn to take me as your wife,

My chilly bones are again warm with life.

Liu Mengmei:

As you are my wife, I have no reason to be afraid, but how can I make sure that you are revived? Would I be just like fishing the moon in the lake or picking the flower in a dream?

Du Liniang:

(*To the tune of **Sanduanzi***)

As my senses still survive,

鬼胡由，还动迷，一灵未歇。
泼残生，堪转折。
秀才可谙经典？
是人非人心不别，
是幻非幻如何说？
虽则似空里拈花，
却不是水中捞月。
[生]捞既然虽死犹生，敢问仙坟何处？
[旦]记取太湖石梅树一株。

【前腔】
爱的是花园后节，
梦孤清，梅花影斜。
熟梅时节，为仁儿，心酸那些。
[生]怕小姐别有走跳处？
[旦叹介]便到九泉无屈折，
幽香一阵昏黄月。
[生]好不冷。

Although a ghost, I can walk like you.

With my spirit still alive,

I shall soon start a life anew.

My dear, are you well versed in classics?

Alive or dead, my heart remains the same;

You hardly know if now you sleep or wake.

You may pick the flower in a dream,

But not fish the moon in the lake.

Liu Mengmei:

Since you are experiencing a living death, where is your burial place?

Du Liniang:

Under a plum tree beside a Taihu rock.

(*To the previous tune*)

In the garden I have stayed

And dreamt alone

Beneath the plum-tree's shade.

When the plums are ripe,

For the man I love,

Large drops of tear I wipe.

Liu Mengmei:

Haven't you found a way out?

Du Liniang:

(*Sighs*)

Even when I've met my doom,

I'm still a fragrant bloom.

Liu Mengmei:

You must have felt very cold.

Du Liniang:

[旦]冻的俺七魄三魂，
　　僵做了三贞七烈。
　　[生]则怕惊了小姐的魂怎好？
【斗双鸡】
　　[旦]花根木节，
　　有一个透人间路穴。
　　俺冷香肌早偎的半热。
　　你怕惊了呵，
　　悄魂飞越，
　　则俺见了你回心心不灭。
　　[生]话长哩。
　　[旦]畅好是一夜夫妻，
　　有的是三生话说。
　　[生]不烦姐姐再三，只俺独力难成。
　　[旦]可与姑姑计议而行。
　　[生]未知深浅，怕一时间攒不彻。
【登小楼】
　　[旦]咨嗟、你为人为彻。

Although my soul is cold,

My faith is as of old.

Liu Mengmei:

Wouldn't I disturb your soul?

Du Liniang:

(*To the tune of Doushuangji*)

The flower roots are in a place

Which leads to the human world,

Where I'm warmed up by your embrace.

If you fear to "disturb my soul",

My soul already flies to you.

Since I saw you for the first time,

Revival has always been in view.

Liu Mengmei:

In that case, it's a long story.

Du Liniang:

To be a couple for a night

Brings about three generation's delight.

Liu Mengmei:

I appreciate your devotion, but I'm afraid I can't do it all by myself.

Du Liniang:

Why don't you talk it over with Sister Stone?

Liu Mengmei:

As I don't know how deep you lie, I'm not sure how long it will take to get through to you.

Du Liniang:

(*To the tune of Dengxiaolou*)

A man who sticks to his aim

俺砌笼棺勾有三尺叠,
你点刚锹和俺一谜掘。
就里阴风泻泻,
则隔的阳世些些。[内鸡鸣介]

【鲍老催】
咳,长眠人一向眠长夜,
则道鸡鸣枕空设。
今夜呵,梦回远塞荒鸡咽,
觉人间风味别。
晓风明灭,
子规声容易吹残月。
三分话才做一分说。

【耍鲍老】
俺丁丁列列,
吐出在丁香舌。
你拆了俺丁香结,
须粉碎俺丁香节。
休残慢,须急节。
俺的幽情难尽说。
[内风起介]则这一蓊风动灵衣去了也。
[旦急下]

Is a man worthy of his name.

If you dig three feet deep,

You'll reach where I lie asleep.

You'll feel the chilly breeze down there,

Some distance from the open air.

(*Sound of cockcrow within*)

(*To the tune of Baolaocui*)

Alas,

For eternal sleep in eternal night,

The cockcrow does not bring daylight.

But tonight,

When cockcrow breaks my dream,

I know the human world is supreme.

Now that the morning breeze dies out in the south

And the moon sets amid cuckoo-songs,

Less than half of my words pass my mouth.

(*To the tune of Shuabaolao*)

Bit by bit,

I've bared my heart.

Since you know my inner part,

You must save my outer part.

Lose no time;

Make haste;

I've told you my story from the start.

(*Sound of a gale within*)

With the gale I have to depart.

(*Exit in a hurry*)

Liu Mengmei:

(*Astonished*)

[生惊痴介]奇哉，奇哉！柳梦梅做了杜太守的女婿，敢是梦也？待俺来回想一番。他名字杜丽娘，年华二八，死葬后园梅树之下。啐，分明是人道交感，有精有血。怎生杜小姐颠倒自己说是鬼？

[旦又上介]衙内还在此？

[生]小姐怎又回来？

[旦]奴家还有丁宁。你既以俺为妻，可急视之，不宜自误。如或不然，妾事已露，不敢再来相陪。愿郎留心，勿使可惜。妾若不得复生，必痛恨君于九泉之下矣。

【尾声】

[旦跪介]柳衙内你便是俺再生爷。

[生跪扶起介]

[旦]一点心怜念妾，

不着俺黄泉恨你，

你只骂的俺一句鬼随邪。

[旦作鬼声下，回顾介]

[生吊场，低语介]柳梦梅着鬼了！他说的恁般分明，恁般凄切，是无是有，只得依言而行。和姑姑商量去。

Absurd! Absurd! I've become the son-in-law of Prefect Du. Am I in a dream? I'll recall what's happened. Her name is Du Liniang, aged sixteen, buried beneath a plum tree in the back garden. Pooh, she's alive and kicking, with flesh and blood. Why on earth did she say that she was a ghost?

(*Re-enter Du Liniang*)

Du Liniang:

You're still here, dear Sir?

Liu Mengmei:

Why are you back again?

Du Liniang:

I have another word with you. If you take me as your wife, please be quick to act. Otherwise, this is our last rendezvous, for I've revealed my secret to you. See to it that you do not lose the opportunity. If I cannot come to life again, I'll bear you hatred in the nether world.

(*Kneels on the ground*)

(*To the tune of Coda*)

You can give me a second life.

(*Liu Mengmei kneels to help her to her feet*)

Have pity on your wife.

If you do not want me to hate you in the nether world,

Make an oath and you're out of the strife.

(*Exit with a ghostly wail, casting a final glance*)

Liu Mengmei:

(*Whispers softly to himself*)

I'm haunted. However, her words ring loud and sincere in my ears. Be it real or not, I must follow her instructions. I'll go and talk it over with Sister Stone.

梦来何处更为云？
惆怅金泥簇蝶裙。
欲访孤坟谁引至？
有人传示紫阳君。

What's better than the dreamland in the room?
The fairy lady makes me moan alone.
Who on earth will guide me to the tomb?
Someone says that it is Sister Stone.

第三十三出　秘　议

【绕池游】
[净上]芙蓉冠岐,
短发难簪系。
一炉香鸣钟叩齿。
"风微台殿响笙簧。空翠冷霓裳。池畔藕花深处,清切夜闻香。　人易老,事多妨,梦难长。一点深情,三分浅土,半壁斜阳。"俺这梅花观,为着杜小姐而建。当初杜老爷分付陈教授看管。三年之内,则见他收取祭租,并不常川行走。便是杜老爷去后,谎了一府州县士民人等许多分子,起了个生祠。昨日老身打从祠前过,猪屎也有,人屎也有。陈最良,陈最良,你可也叫人扫刮一遭儿。

Scene Thirty-three
Clandestine Schemes

(*Enter Sister Stone*)

Sister Stone:

(*To the tune of* **Raochiyou**)

In a lotus cloak,

I wear my hair so short.

Amid the smoke and bells, I invoke.

"*The empty hall is humming in the breeze*

While I sit alone under verdant trees.

With the lotus pond at sight,

I smell the scent at night.

The man will soon grow old;

The scheme is uncontrolled;

The dream can hardly hold.

The love, howe'er profound,

Is buried underground,

With sunshine on the mound."

This Plum Blossom Nunnery was built in memory of Miss Du. Prefect Du entrusted it in the charge of Tutor Chen, who has collected the land rent for the past three years but seldom minded the business. After Prefect Du's departure, Tutor Chen raised donations to build a memorial hall for him. But when I passed by the memorial hall yesterday, I saw shit and dung littering the ground. Chen Zuiliang, Chen Zuiliang, why don't you get someone cleaning the hall? As a contrast, I've kept

到是杜小姐神位前,日逐添香换水,何等庄严清净。正是:"天下少信掉书子,世外有情持素人。"

【前腔】

[生上]幽期密意,

不是人间世。

待声扬徘徊了半日。

[见介]

[生]"落花香覆紫金堂。

[净]你年少看花敢自伤?

[生]弄玉不来人换世。

[净]麻姑一去海生桑。"

[生]老姑姑,小生自到仙居,不曾瞻礼宝殿。今日愿求一观。

[净]是礼。相引前行。

[行到介]

[净]高处玉天金阙,下面东岳夫人,南斗真妃。

Miss Du's shrine clean and tidy, offering incense and changing sacrificial water every day. It's true to say,

> "Don't trust Confucian scholars now;
> Better trust disciples of Tao."

(*Enter Liu Mengmei*)

Liu Mengmei:

(*To the previous tune*)

With a ghost I date,

A spiritual mate.

I'd like to talk, but hesitate.

(*Greets Sister Stone*)

"The fallen petals are fragrant in the hall;

Sister Stone:

Have the petals disturbed your heart?

Liu Mengmei:

The fairy maiden makes a distant call;

Sister Stone:

The human world has made another start."

Liu Mengmei:

Sister Stone, I've lived in your nunnery for quite some time, but I've never visited the main hall yet. Will you show me around today?

Sister Stone:

No problem. Go after me, please.

(*They reach the main hall*)

Sister Stone:

High above stands the Jade Emperor, and on either side stand Lady of Mount Tai and Lady of the Southern Dipper.

(*The bell rings within*)

[内钟鸣,生拜介]"中天积翠玉台遥,上帝高居绛节朝。遂有冯夷来击鼓,始知秦女善吹箫。"好一座宝殿哩。怎生左边这牌位上写着"杜小姐神王",是那位女王?

[净]是没人题主哩。杜小姐。

[生]杜小姐为谁?

【五更转】

[净]你说这红梅院,因何置?

是杜参知前所为。

丽娘原是他香闺女,

十八而亡,就此攒瘗。

他爷呵,升任急,失题主,空牌位。

[生]谁祭扫他?

[净]好墓田,留下有碑记。

Liu Mengmei:

> (*Kowtows*)
>
> "High above in the sky,
>
> The emperor's strength and power pervade.
>
> When River God is beating drums,
>
> We get to know the fairy maid."

What a magnificent hall! On the memorial tablet on the left is the inscription "The Spiri of Miss Du". What's the meaning of "spiri"?

Sister Stone:

To complete the service, we need someone to add the final letter. It's "The Spirit of Miss Du".

Liu Mengmei:

And who is this Miss Du?

Sister Stone:

> (*To the tune of* **Wugengzhuan**)
>
> I'll tell you
>
> For whom this nunnery is built.
>
> It has been built by Prefect Du.
>
> Liniang, his daughter fair and dear,
>
> Who died young,
>
> Is buried here.
>
> On his departure for his latest post,
>
> He left the inscription incomplete
>
> And left alone the ghost.

Liu Mengmei:

Who's taking care of the graveyard and the shrine?

Sister Stone:

> She has land attached to her grave,

偏他没头主儿，年年寒食。

[生哭介]这等说起来，杜小姐是俺娇妻呵。

[净惊介]秀才当真么？

[生]千真万真。

[净]这等，知他那日生，那日死了？

【前腔】

[生]俺未知他生，焉知死？

死多年、生此时。

[净]几时得他死信？

[生]这是俺朝闻夕死了可人矣。

[净]是夫妻，应你奉事香火。

[生]则怕俺未能事人，

With inscriptions to make her name last.

As her kith and kin are far away,

For years she has to make a fast.

Liu Mengmei:

(*Weeps*)

Judging from what you've said, Miss Du must be my dear wife.

Sister Stone:

(*Astonished*)

Are you telling the truth, Mr Liu?

Liu Mengmei:

The truth, nothing but the truth.

Sister Stone:

Then you know the date of her birth and the date of her death?

Liu Mengmei:

(*To the previous tune*)

As I don't know the date of her birth,

How can I know the date of her death?

I only know she has had a lengthy death

And will soon have a rebirth.

Sister Stone:

When did you hear of her death?

Liu Mengmei:

I heard of her in the morning

And she died in the evening.

Sister Stone:

If she's your wife, it's your duty to make offerings to her.

Liu Mengmei:

As I haven't looked after her alive,

焉能事鬼？

[净]既是秀才娘子，可曾会他来？

[生]便是这红梅院，

做楚阳台，

偏倍了你。

[净]是那一夜？

[生]是前宵你们不做美。

[净惊介]秀才着鬼了。难道，难道。

[生]你不信时，显个神通你看。取笔来点的他主儿会动。

[净]有这事？笔在此。

[生点介]看俺点石为人，

靠夫作主。

你瞧，你瞧。

[净惊介]奇哉，奇哉。主儿真个会动也。小姐呵！

【前腔】

则道墓门梅，

How can I look after her after death?

Sister Stone:

Since you've married her, have you ever met her?

Liu Mengmei:

The plum blossom here

Is our nuptial room,

Behind your eye and ear.

Sister Stone:

When was that?

Liu Mengmei:

The night before when you spoilt our cheer.

Sister Stone:

(*Astonished*)

You are haunted. Incredible! Incredible!

Liu Mengmei:

If you don't believe me, fetch a brush-pen. When I complete the word "spirit", the memorial tablet will stir.

Sister Stone:

Is that possible? Here is a brush-pen.

Liu Mengmei:

(*Completes the word*)

I'll give you life,

My dear, dear wife.

Look, look!

Sister Stone:

Fantastic! Fantastic! The tablet is stirring! Oh, my young mistress!

(*To the previous tune*)

I thought that the plum before the tomb

立着个没字碑，
原来柳客神缠住在香炉里。
秀才，既是你妻，
鼓盆歌、庐墓三年礼。
[生]还要请他起来。
[净]你直恁神通，敢阎罗是你？
[生]少些人夫用。
[净]你当夫，他为人，堪使鬼。
[生]你也帮一锹儿。
[净]大明律：开棺见尸，不分首从皆斩哩。
你宋书生是看不着皇明例，
不比寻常，穿篱挖壁。
[生]这个不妨，是小姐自家主见。

【前腔】
是泉下人，央及你。

Served to protect you,

But Mr Liu has been the bloom.

Mr Liu, since she's your wife, you'd better

Build a hut beside her tomb

And live there as your room.

Liu Mengmei:

I'm going to bring her to life.

Sister Stone:

Do you have the spell

Endowed by the Price of Hell?

Liu Mengmei:

I need some labourers to help me.

Sister Stone:

You need a wife,

She needs a life

And ghosts help with your strife.

Liu Mengmei:

I need your help too.

Sister Stone:

According to the present law, grave-robbers are to be beheaded, be he the instigator or the accomplice.

A scholar from the dynasty of Song

Is unaware of the present law:

To rob a grave is wrong.

Liu Mengmei:

It doesn't matter to realise Miss Du's own wishes.

(*To the previous tune*)

It's she down in the hell,

Who asks you to give aid.

个中人、谁似伊。
[净]既是小姐分付，也待我择个日子。
[看介]恰好明日乙酉，可以开坟。
[生]喜金鸡玉犬非牛日，
则待寻个人儿，开山力士。
[净]俺有个侄儿癞头鼋可用。只怕事发之时怎处？
[生]但回生，免声息，停商议。
可有偷香窃玉劫坟贼？
还一事，小姐倘然回生，要些定魂汤药。
[净]陈教授开张药铺。只说前日小姑姑，党了凶煞，求药安魂。
[生]烦你快去也。
这七级浮屠，岂同儿戏。

Who knows so well

As the pretty maid?

Sister Stone:

As I'm carrying out Miss Du's order, I'll try to find an auspicious date.

(*Consults the almanac*)

It happens that tomorrow is an auspicious day to dig the grave.

Liu Mengmei:

Tomorrow is an auspicious day,

But I still need a robust man

To dig the clay.

Sister Stone:

My nephew by the name of Scabby Turtle will be at your service, but what if people should know about it?

Liu Mengmei:

Once we bring her to life,

We'll keep our mouth shut tight

About my dearest wife.

Who needs a corpse in the broad daylight?

One thing more: when Miss Du comes to life again, she must need some herbs to relieve her mind.

Sister Stone:

Tutor Chen keeps a pharmacy. We'll just say that the wandering young nun has run against an evil spirit and that she needs some herbs to calm down.

Liu Mengmei:

Will you please go and get the medicine at once?

To save a life today

Is no child's play!

[净]湿云如梦雨如尘,
[生]初访城西李少君。
[净]行到窈娘身没处,
[生]手披荒草看孤坟。

Sister Stone:

    Amid the mist and raindrops from the skies,

Liu Mengmei:

    I'll go to visit that magician's cave.

Sister Stone:

    Not far from where the pretty maiden lies,

Liu Mengmei:

    I tread the withered grass to watch her grave.

第三十四出　　诇　药

[末上]"积年儒学理粗通，书箧成精变药笼。家童唤俺老员外，街坊唤俺老郎中。"俺陈最良失馆，依然开药铺。看今日有甚人来？

【女冠子】

[净上]人间天上，
道理都难讲。
梦中虚诳，
更有人儿思量泉壤。
陈先生利市哩。
[末]老姑姑到来。
[净]好铺面！这"儒医"二字杜太爷赠的。好"道地药材"！这两块土中甚用？

Scene Thirty-four
Asking for Medicine

(*Enter Chen Zuiliang*)

Chen Zuiliang:

"Confucian learning shows its effect:
I'm now a doctor all admire.
The servants greet me with respect
While neighbours call a doctor squire."

Since I lost my tutor's position, I've kept a pharmacy for a living. I wonder what customer is coming today.

(*Enter Sister Stone*)

Sister Stone:

(*To the tune of Nüguanzi*)

Be it in heaven or on earth,
Good sense is difficult to find.
From dreams a fancy comes in birth;
From Hell a lover comes to mind.
Good luck to your business, Mr Chen.

Chen Zuiliang:

How do you do, Sister Stone.

Sister Stone:

What a fine store you've kept! The inscription "Confucian Doctor" must have been written by Prefect Du. The inscription on the signboard "Choicest Herbs" is well said, but what's the use of these two clods of earth?

Chen Zuiliang:

[末]是寡妇床头土。男子汉有鬼怪之疾，清水调服良。

[净]这布片儿何用？

[末]是壮男子的裤裆。妇人有鬼怪之病，烧灰吃了效。

[净]这等，俺贫道床头三尺土，敢换先生五寸裆？

[末]怕你不十分寡。

[净]啐，你敢也不十分壮。

[末]罢了，来意何事？

[净]不瞒你说，前日小道姑呵！

【黄莺儿】
年少不提防，
赛江神，归夜忙。

[末]着手了？

[净]知他着甚闲空旷？

It comes from beneath the widow's bed. If a man is haunted, just resolve some earth in water and have him drink it. It's very effective.

Sister Stone:

Then what's the use of this rag?

Chen Zuiliang:

It comes from the crotch of a strong man's pants. If a woman is haunted, just burn them to ashes and have her eat it. It's also very effective.

Sister Stone:

In that case, what about exchanging the earth from beneath my bed to the crotch from your pants?

Chen Zuiliang:

I'm afraid you're not much of a widow.

Sister Stone:

Phew! I'm afraid you're not strong enough.

Chen Zuiliang:

Well, forget about it. What can I do for you?

Sister Stone:

To tell you the truth, I've come for the young nun who the day before yesterday

(*To the tune of* **Huangyinger**)

Did not take sufficient care

And late at night

Came back from the fair.

Chen Zuiliang:

Was she in trouble?

Sister Stone:

Who knows in which wild wasteland

被凶神煞党。
年灾月殃，
瞑然一去无回向。
[末]欠老成哩！
[净]细端详，
你医王手段敢对的住活阎王。
[末]是活的，死的？
[净]死几日了。
[末]死人有口吃药？也罢，便是这烧裆散，用热酒调服下。

【前腔】
海上有仙方，
这伟男儿深裤裆。
[净]则这种药，俺那里自有。
[末]则怕姑姑记不起谁阳壮。
翦裁寸方，烧灰酒娘，
敲开齿缝把些儿放。
不寻常，安魂定魄，赛过反精香。

She was caught by some evil turn.

At the ghostly command,

Her soul departed, never to return.

Chen Zuiliang:

How careless she was!

Sister Stone:

You can do your job well

To save her from the living Hell.

Chen Zuiliang:

Is she dead or alive?

Sister Stone:

She's been dead for a couple of days.

Chen Zuiliang:

Can the dead nun take medicine? At any rate, burn this rag of pants and have her take it with warm wine.

(*To the previous tune*)

A magic medicine I grant:

The crotch of strong man's pants.

Sister Stone:

If that's the medicine, I have some in my place.

Chen Zuiliang:

Perhaps you don't know which is fine.

Just cut a little piece,

Burn and mix it with sweet wine.

Then force it down between her teeth.

The medicine retrieves her soul

In a unique way

And plays a magic role.

Sister Stone:

[净]谢了。

[末]还随女伴赛江神,
[净]争奈多情足病身。
[末]严洞幽深门尽锁,
[净]隔花催唤女医人。

Thanks a lot.

Chen Zuiliang:
    She went to markets with her friends,

Sister Stone:
    But fell ill for her dearest love.

Chen Zuiliang:
    As caves are closed when her life ends,

Sister Stone:
    She needs a helping hand above.

第三十五出　　回　生

【字字双】

[丑扮疙童，持锹上]猪尿泡疙疸偌卢胡，没裤。

铧锹儿入的土花疏，没骨。

活小娘不要去做鬼婆夫，没路。

偷坟贼拿到做个地官符，没趣。

[笑介]自家梅花观主家癞头鼋便是。观主受了柳秀才之托，和杜小姐启坟。好笑，好笑，说杜小姐要和他这里重做夫妻。管他人话鬼话，带了些黄钱，挂在这太湖石上，点起香来。

【出队子】

[净携酒同生上]玉人何处，玉人何处？

近墓西风老绿芜。

Scene Thirty-five
Returning to Life

(*Enter Scabby Turtle*)

Scabby Turtle:

(*To the tune of Zizishuang*)
I have a swine's bladder like a gourd —
A scabby head.
My spade will dig into something soft —
The soil bed.
The scholar wants a ghost of a wife —
How can they wed?
A grave-digger will be buried alive —
What a dread!

(*With a laugh*)

I'm Scabby Turtle, nephew of the head of the Plum Blossom Nunnery. She has agreed to help Mr Liu to open up Miss Du's grave. What a funny thing that he says Miss Du would like to be his wife again. Well, that's none of my business. I've brought some yellow paper to burn. I'll put it on the Taihu rocks and then light some incense.

(*Enter Sister Stone, carrying some wine, and Liu Mengmei*)

Sister Stone:

(*To the tune of Chuduizi*)
Where is the pretty lass?
Where is the pretty lass?
Beside her tomb grows luxuriant grass.

《竹枝歌》唱的女郎苏，
杜鹃声啼过锦江无？
一窨愁残，三生梦余。
[生]老姑姑，已到后园。只见半亭瓦砾，满地荆榛。绣带重寻，袅袅藤花夜合；罗裙欲认，青青蔓草春长。则记的太湖石边，是俺拾画之处。依稀似梦，恍惚如亡。怎生是好？
[净]秀才不要忙，梅树下堆儿是了。
[生]小姐，好伤感人也。[哭介]
[丑]哭甚的。趁时节了。[烧纸介]
[生拜介]巡山使者，当山土地，显圣显灵。
【啄木鹂】
开山纸草面上铺。
烟罩山前红地炉。
[丑]敢太岁头上动土？

Now that love-songs ring around,

Has cuckoo's song reached her native town?

With woe in her grave,

In her dreams she would still frown.

Liu Mengmei:

Here we are at the back garden, Sister Stone. Alas, the pavilion has nearly tumbled down, with thorns and brambles all around. Miss Du's sash-trails have been covered with vines and flowers while her skirt-traces have been overgrown with verdant grass. I only remember the Taihu rocks, where I picked up the portrait, but everything is vague and obscure as if in a dream. What can I do about it?

Sister Stone:

Take it easy, Mr Liu. Here it is, the mound beneath the plum tree.

Liu Mengmei:

Oh, dear Miss Du! What a great sorrow you've brought me!

(*Weeps*)

Scabby Turtle:

It's no use weeping at this time. Let's get to work.

(*Burns the yellow paper*)

Liu Mengmei:

(*Kowtows*)

God of Hills and God of Earth, please show your divine power!

(*To the tune of Zhuomuli*)

The yellow paper burns beside the grove

And lights a fire just like a stove.

Scabby Turtle:

How dare you dig the earth upon this seat

向小姐脚跟挖窟。
[生]土地公公，今日开山，专为请起杜丽娘。不要你死的，要个活的。
你为神正直应无妒，
俺阳神触煞俱无虑。
要他风神笑语都无二，
便做着你土地公公女嫁吾。
呀，春在小梅株。
好破土哩。

【前腔】
[丑、净锹土介]这三和土一谜钽。
小姐呵，
半尺孤坟你在这的无？
[生]你们十分小心。[看介]到棺了。
[丑作惊丢锹介]到官没活的了。
[生摇手介]禁声。
[内旦作哎哟介]
[众惊介]活鬼做声了。

And build a tunnel to her feet?

Liu Mengmei:

God of Earth, I dig the grave today in order to bring Du Liniang to life again. I don't want her dead, but I want her alive.

You are a god upright and fair,

And so we do our job without care.

If it should become widely known,

I'll say I've wed the daughter of your own.

Oh, how the plum blossoms in the spring air!

It's time to dig the earth!

Scabby Turtle, Sister Stone:

(*Dig the earth*)

(*To the previous tune*)

Let's dig the earth, dig the earth.

Are you here, Miss Du, to have a rebirth?

Liu Mengmei:

Handle with care!

(*Watches the digging*)

Here's the coffin!

Scabby Turtle:

(*Throws away the spade in alarm*)

The cop? We're finished.

Liu Mengmei:

(*Waves his hands*)

Shut up!

(*Du Liniang moans within, which frightens all*)

Sister Stone, Scabby Turtle:

The living ghost is making a noise!

Liu Mengmei:

[生]休惊了小姐。
[众蹲向鬼门，开棺介]
[净]原来钉头锈断，子口登开，小姐敢别处送云雨去了。
[内哎哟介]
[生见旦扶介]
[生]咳，小姐端然在此。异香袭人，幽姿如故。天也，
你看正面上那些儿尘渍，
斜空处没半米虮蜉。
则他暖幽香四片斑斓木，
润芳姿半榻黄泉路，
养花身五色燕支土。
[扶旦软鞞介]
[生]俺为你款款偎将睡脸扶，
休损了口中珠。
[旦作呕出水银介]
[丑]一块花银，二十分多重，赏了癞头罢。
[生]此乃小姐龙含凤吐之精，小生当奉为世宝。你们别有酬犒。
[旦开眼叹介]
[净]小姐开眼哩。

Don't frighten Miss Du!

(*The three of them squat, facing the entrance, and open the coffin*)

Sister Stone:

Oh, the nails have rusted away and the joints are loose. Miss Du must be making love somewhere.

(*Moaning sounds within*)

Liu Mengmei:

(*Sees Du Liniang and goes to support her*)

Hurrah, Miss Du is here, with heavenly fragrance and former beauty! Oh, my heaven, look!

There's dirt on the coffin lid,

But not a single ant is in the grave.

The fragrant planks have sheltered her

On her way to the nether world,

For her to lie at ease in the cave.

(*Supports Du Liniang, who leans limply on him*)

I'll hold her sleeping head with care,

Lest I hurt the funeral stone there.

(*Du Liniang vomits quicksilver from her mouth*)

Scabby Turtle:

A piece of silver! Well, it's heavy enough. Will you give me as a gift?

Liu Mengmei:

This is her crystallisation of the dragon and the phoenix for me to keep as heirloom. You'll get some other reward.

(*Du Liniang opens her eyes and sighs*)

Sister Stone:

Miss Du has opened her eyes.

[生]天开眼了。小姐呵!
【金蕉叶】
　　[旦]是真是虚?
　　劣梦魂猛然惊遽。
　　[作掩眼介]避三光业眼难舒,
　　怕一弄儿巧风吹去。
　　[生]怕风怎么好?
　　[净扶旦介]且在这牡丹亭内进还魂丹,秀才翦裆。
　　[生翦介]
　　[丑]待俺凑些加味还魂散。
　　[生]不消了。快快热酒来。
【莺啼序】
　　[调酒灌介]玉喉咙半点灵酥。
　　[旦吐介]
　　[生]哎也,
　　怎生呵落在胸脯。
　　姐姐再进些,
　　才吃下三个多半口还无。

Liu Mengmei:
>The heaven has opened its eyes! My dear!

Du Liniang:
>(*To the tune of Jinjiaoye*)
>
>Is it real or illusory
>
>That I awake from a nightmare?
>
>(*Covers her eyes*)
>
>I fear the light might vanish with the wind
>
>As that is too much for me to bear.

Liu Mengmei:
>She fears the wind. What's to be done?

Sister Stone:
>(*Supports Du Liniang*)
>
>Why not take the magic medicine in the Peony Pavilion. Mr Liu, please cut the man's pants-crotch.
>
>(*Liu Mengmei cuts the pants*)

Scabby Turtle:
>Let me add some stronger smell to it.

Liu Mengmei:
>Away with your smell. Warm some wine for me, please. Be quick.
>
>(*Mixes the medicine with the wine and feeds it into Du Liniang's mouth*)
>
>(*To the tune of Yingtixu*)
>
>Drink the medicine and you are blessed.
>
>(*Du Liniang vomits*)
>
>Why do you vomit it on your chest?
>
>Take some more, Miss Du.
>
>You've only taken three tiny sips.

[观介]好了，好了！
喜春生颜面肌肤。
[旦观介]这些都是谁？
敢是些无端道途，
弄的俺不着坟墓？
[生]我便是柳梦梅。
[旦]眇朦觑，
怕不是梅边柳边人数。
[生]有这道姑为证。
[净]小姐可认得道姑么？
[旦看不语介]

【前腔】
[净]你乍回头记不起俺这姑姑。
[生]可记得这后花园？
[旦不语介]
[净]是了，你梦境模糊。
[旦]只那个是柳郎？

(*Keeps a close look at her face*)

Wonderful! Wonderful!

Now she's looking her best.

Du Liniang:

(*Looks around*)

Who are these people around?

Look how you scoundrels behave!

Are you robbing me of my grave?

Liu Mengmei:

I'm Liu Mengmei.

Du Liniang:

As for the moment I'm blind and numb,

I'm not sure if you are the man beside the plum.

Liu Mengmei:

Sister Stone will be the witness.

Sister Stone:

Can you recognise me, Miss Du?

(*Du Liniang looks but does not speak*)

Sister Stone:

(*To the previous tune*)

How is it that you can't recall me?

Liu Mengmei:

Do you remember the back garden?

(*Du Liniang does not speak*)

Sister Stone:

I've got it.

She's still in a dream and cannot see.

Du Liniang:

Are you Mr Liu?

［生应，旦作认介］咳，柳郎真信人也。
亏杀你拨草寻蛇，
亏杀你守株待兔。
棺中宝玩收存，诸余抛散池塘里去。
［众］呸！
［丢去棺物介］向人间别画个葫芦。水边头洗除凶物。
［众］亏了小姐整整睡这三年。
［旦］流年度，
怕春色三分，
一分尘土。
［生］小姐，此处风露，不可久停。好处将息去。
【尾声】
死工夫救了你活地狱，
七香汤莹了美食相扶。
［旦］扶往那里去？
［净］梅花观内。

(*Shows signs of recognition when Liu Mengmei replies yes*)

You've kept your word, Mr Liu.

I thank you for your pains

And now you have your gains.

Take the jewellery from the coffin and throw the rest into the lake.

Liu Mengmei, Sister Stone, Scabby Turtle:

Phew!

(*Throw away the coffin*)

Du Liniang:

I'll start my human life anew

When the evil coffin flows out of view.

Liu Mengmei, Sister Stone, Scabby Turtle:

What hard time for you to sleep for three years!

Du Liniang:

The flowing time

In the grave

Has wasted my prime.

Liu Mengmei:

My dear, it's windy and wet here. Let's find a better place for you to have a good rest.

(*To the tune of* **Coda**)

My efforts have saved you from hell;

A bath and dinner will make you well.

Du Liniang:

Where are you leading me?

Sister Stone:

To the Plum Blossom Nunnery.

Du Liniang:

［旦］可知道洗棺尘,
都是这高唐观中雨。

［生］天赐燕支一抹腮,
［旦］随君此去出泉台。
［净］俺来穿穴非无意,
［生］愿结灵姻愧短才。

You know, acts of love

Will drive away the spell.

Liu Mengmei:

The heaven has bestowed you pretty cheeks;

Du Liniang:

With your help I've left the nether creeks.

Sister Stone:

We haven't dug the pit as vain attempt;

Liu Mengmei:

Don't refuse my hand with contempt.

第三十六出　　婚　走

【意难忘】
　　[净扶旦上]
　　[旦]如笑如呆,
　　叹情丝不断,
　　梦境重开。
　　[净]你惊香辞地府,
　　与槎出天台。
　　[旦]姑姑,
　　俺强挣作,软哈哈,
　　重娇养起这嫩孩孩。
　　[合]尚疑猜,
　　怕如烟入抱,
　　似影投怀。
　　[旦]"蛾眉秋恨满三霜,梦余荒冢斜阳。土花零落旧罗裳,睡损红妆。

Scene Thirty-six
Wedding and Departure

(*Enter Du Liniang, supported by Sister Stone*)

Du Liniang:

(*To the tune of Yinanwang*)

I smile, I stare;

In the web of love,

The dreamland is always there.

Sister Stone:

Far, far away from hell and curse,

You left the nether world in your hearse.

Du Liniang:

Sister Stone,

I'm trying hard to raise

My feeble legs,

But to recover needs a lot of days.

Du Liniang, Sister Stone:

There is still doubt

Whether this will end up in smoke

Or shadow that dies out.

Du Liniang:

"For three years in the deepest gloom,

My dream still lingers in the lonely tomb.

With fallen petals on my skirt,

My rosy cheeks are covered with dirt.

Sister Stone:

[净]风定彩云犹怯，火传金炧重香。如神如鬼费端详，除是高唐。"

[旦]姑姑，奴家死去三年。为钟情一点，幽契重生。皆亏柳郎和姑姑信心提救。又以美酒香酥，时时将养。数日之间，稍觉精神旺相。

[净]好了，秀才三回五次，央俺成亲哩。

[旦]姑姑，这事还早。扬州问过了老相公、老夫人，请个媒人方好。

[净]好消停的话儿。这也由你。则问小姐前生事可记得些么？

【胜如花】
[旦]前生事，
曾记怀。
为伤春病害，
困春游梦境难捱。
写春容那人儿拾在。
那劳承、那般顶戴，
似盼天仙盼的眼哈，
似叫观音叫的口歪。

Although the wind might start anew
And incense fragrance might ensue,
She puzzles deities down and above
With her ardent love."

Du Liniang:

Sister Stone, I was away from this world for three years, but ardent love has brought me back to this world again. I owe my second life to you and Mr Liu. Your delicious food and meticulous care have given me fresh energy within a few days.

Sister Stone:

That's nice. Mr Liu has asked me time and again to prepare for your wedding.

Du Liniang:

Sister Stone, it's not the right time yet. I have to go to Yangzhou and ask Dad and Mom to find a matchmaker.

Sister Stone:

What a trite idea! But it's up to you to decide. By the way, do you still remember what happened before you died?

Du Liniang:

(*To the tune of* **Shengruhua**)

What happened then
I've always kept in mind.
I took a stroll when I felt bored
And for my vernal dream I pined.
When the scholar picked up my portrait,
He was so earnest
And tried hard to find.
He was so eager to meet me
That he looked as if dumb and blind.

[净]俺也听见些。则小姐泉下怎生得知?
[旦]虽则尘埋,
把耳轮儿热坏。
感一片志诚无奈,
死淋侵走上阳台,
活森沙走出这泉台。
[净]秀才来哩。
【生查子】
[生上]艳质久尘埋,
又挣出这烟花界。
你看他含笑插金钗,
摆动那长裙带。
[见介]丽娘妻。[旦羞介]
[生]姐姐,俺地窟里扶卿做玉真。
[旦]重生胜过父娘亲。
[生]便好今宵成配偶。
[旦]懵腾还自少精神。

Sister Stone:

I've heard something about it, but how do you get to know?

Du Liniang:

Although I was buried in earth,

I was moved by his words.

For his devoting heart,

I left the nether world

And came back brisk and smart.

Sister Stone:

Here comes the young scholar.

(*Enter Liu Mengmei*)

Liu Mengmei:

(*To the tune of* ***Shengchazi***)

Buried for years in earth,

She gained a second birth.

See how she smiles with pins on her head

And how her sash trails when she walks ahead.

(*Greets Du Liniang*)

Oh, my dear wife!

(*Du Liniang is abashed*)

Liu Mengmei:

My dear, it's me who helped you out of the grave.

Du Liniang:

I owe more to you than to my parents.

Liu Mengmei:

Let's get married this very night.

Du Liniang:

I still feel dizzy and weak.

Sister Stone:

[净]起前说精神旺相,则瞒着秀才。

[旦]秀才可记的古书云:"必待父母之命,媒妁之言。"

[生]日前虽不是钻穴相窥,早则钻坟而入了。小姐今日又会起书来。

[旦]秀才,比前不同。前夕鬼也,今日人也。鬼可虚情,人须实礼。听奴道来:

【胜如花】

青台闭,白日开。

[拜介]秀才呵,

受的俺三生礼拜,

待成亲少个官媒。

[泣介]结盏的要高堂人在。

[生]成了亲,访令尊令堂,有惊天之喜。要媒人,道姑便是。

[旦]秀才忙待怎的?

也曾落几个黄昏陪待。

You just said that you were full of fresh energy. She's not telling the truth, Mr Liu.

Du Liniang:

Mr Liu, you must know the quotation from *Mencius*: "Await the injunctions from the parents and the discussions of the go-betweens."

Liu Mengmei:

The other day I did not "make holes and crevices in order to catch sight of you", to quote the same book, but I did dig the grave. And now you are quoting from the classics!

Du Liniang:

There's a world of difference. I was a ghost then, and I am a maiden now. A ghost can ignore the ethic codes, but a maiden can't. Listen to me:

(*To the tune of* **Shengruhua**)

Gone is the night;

The day is bright.

(*Kowtows to Liu Mengmei*)

Mr Liu,

With deep respect I kowtow to you,

But a matchmaker is needed too.

(*Weeps*)

My parents must be on the site.

Liu Mengmei:

When we visit your parents after we get married, they will be overjoyed. Sister Stone will be the matchmaker.

Du Liniang:

What's the hurry, Mr Liu?

I've waited upon you night by night.

[生]今夕何夕？
[旦]直恁的急色秀才。
[生]小姐捣鬼。
[旦笑介]秀才捣鬼。
不是俺鬼奴台妆妖作乖。
[生]为甚？
[旦羞介]半死来回，
怕的雨云惊骇。
有的是这人儿活在，
但将息俺半载身材。
[背介]但消停俺半刻情怀。
【不是路】
[末上]深院闲阶，
花影萧萧转翠苔。
[扣门介]人谁在？
是陈生探望柳君来。
[众惊介]

Liu Mengmei:
> But what special night is this?

Du Liniang:
> You're lustful, right?

Liu Mengmei:
> You are being naughty!

Du Liniang:
> (*Smiles*)
> You are being naughty!
> Not that I make a pretentious show,

Liu Mengmei:
> But what?

Du Liniang:
> (*Abashed*)
> But that I'm just back to life,
> Not fit to make love, you know.
> Here I stand before you,
> Give me time to rest;
> (*Aside*)
> Of course I love you best.
> (*Enter Chen Zuiliang*)

Chen Zuiliang:
> (*To the tune of Bushilu*)
> In the vacant yard,
> The flower and moss are wet with dew.
> (*Knocks at the door*)
> Is anyone in?
> I've come to visit Mr Liu.
> (*Liu Mengmei, Du Liniang and Sister Stone are startled*)

[生]陈先生来了,怎好?
[旦]姑姑,俺回避去。[下]
[末]忒奇哉,
怎女儿声息纱窗外,
硬抵门儿应不开?[又扣门介]
[生]是谁?
[末]陈最良。
[开门见介]
[生]承车盖,
俺衣冠未整因迟待。
[末]有些惊怪。
[生]有何惊怪?

【前腔】
[末]不是天台,
怎风度娇音隔院猜?
[净上]原来陈斋长到来。

Liu Mengmei:

Tutor Chen is at the door. What shall we do?

Du Liniang:

Sister Stone, I'd better withdraw.

(*Exit with Sister Stone*)

Chen Zuiliang:

It's strange to me

That I hear a girl's voice

While the door is closed fast.

(*Knocks at the door again*)

Liu Mengmei:

Who is it?

Chen Zuiliang:

It's me, Chen Zuiliang.

Liu Mengmei:

(*Opens the door and greets Chen Zuiliang*)

Your visit honours me all the more;

I'm sorry to be late to open the door.

Chen Zuiliang:

There's something unusual here.

Liu Mengmei:

What is unusual here?

Chen Zuiliang:

(*To the previous tune*)

But for the fairyland,

Where comes the gentle voice offhand?

(*Enter Sister Stone*)

Sister Stone:

Oh, it's you, Tutor Chen.

[生]陈先生说里面妇娘声息,则是老姑姑。
[净]是了,
长生会,
莲花观里一个小姑来。
[末]便是前日的小姑么?
[净]另是一众。
[末]好哩,这梅花观一发兴哩。也是杜小姐冥福所致。因此径来相约,明午整个小盒儿同柳兄往坟上随喜去。暂告辞了。
无闲会,
今朝有约明朝在,
酒滴青娥墓上回。
[生]承拖带,
这姑姑点不出个茶儿待。
即来回拜。
[末]慢来回拜。[下]
[生]喜的陈先生去了,请小姐有话。

Liu Mengmei:

The gentle voice inside is from Sister Stone.

Sister Stone:

Oh I see what you mean.

What you hear

Comes from a young nun who comes here.

Chen Zuiliang:

Is she the young nun who came the other day?

Sister Stone:

It's another nun.

Chen Zuiliang:

Well, the Plum Blossom Nunnery is thriving, thanks to the blessing from Miss Du. I've come to invite Mr Liu to make offerings to Miss Du's tomb tomorrow at noontime. See you tomorrow.

That's why I've come to your room.

So that's settled for tomorrow —

We'll sprinkle the wine on her tomb.

Liu Mengmei:

Thank you for inviting me;

Sorry we haven't prepared tea.

I'll pay a return visit soon.

Chen Zuiliang:

See you soon.

(*Exit*)

Liu Mengmei:

Well, Mr Chen's gone at last. Please ask Miss Du to come for a chat.

(*Enter Du Liniang*)

[旦上介]

[净]怎了,怎了?陈先生明日要上小姐坟去。事露之时,一来小姐有妖冶之名,二来公相无闺阃之教,三来秀才坐迷惑之讥,四来老身招发掘之罪。如何是了?

[旦]老姑姑,待怎生好?

[净]小姐,这柳秀才待往临安取应。不如曲成亲事,叫童儿寻只赣船,夤夜开去,以灭其踪。意下何如?

[旦]这也罢了。

[净]有酒在此。你二人拜告天地。

[拜,把酒介]

【榴花泣】

[生]三生一会,

人世两和谐。

承合卺,送金杯。

比墓田春酒这新醅,

才酸转人面桃腮。

Sister Stone:

What's to be done? What's to be done? Mr Chen will go to Miss Du's tomb tomorrow. If our act is known to the public, firstly, Miss Du will be accused of witchcraft; secondly, Prefect Du will be accused of lacking family discipline; thirdly, Mr Liu will be ridiculed for his bewilderment; fourthly, I'll be accused of grave-robbing. What can we do about it?

Du Liniang:

What is the way out then, Sister Stone?

Sister Stone:

Miss Du, as Mr Liu is going to Lin'an for the imperial examination, why don't you just get married, have Scabby Turtle find a boat and sail off this very night so that no one will know anything about it? What's your opinion?

Du Liniang:

That's the only choice.

Sister Stone:

The wine is ready and you two just kowtow to the heaven and the earth.

(*Liu Mengmei and Du Liniang kowtow, each holding a cup of wine in hand*)

Liu Mengmei:

(*To the tune of Liuhuaqi*)

It's really something rare

For us to be a pair.

In the golden cup,

The wine is for us to share.

The wine is of good taste

And makes your cheeks rosy and fair.

[旦悲介]伤春便埋,
似中山醉梦三年在。
只一件来,
看伊家龙凤姿容,
怎配俺这土木形骸!
[生]那有此话!

【前腔】
相逢无路,
良夜肯疑猜?
眠一柳,当了三槐。
杜兰香真个在读书斋,
则柳耆卿不是仙才。
[旦叹介]幽姿暗怀,
被元阳鼓的这阴无赖。
柳郎,奴家依然还是女身。
[生]已经数度幽期,玉体岂能无损?
[旦]那是魂,这才是正身陪奉。
伴情哥则是游魂,
女儿身依旧含胎。

Du Liniang:

>(*In sorrow*)
>
>I died of vernal sorrow
>
>And slept for three long years.
>
>One thing still worries me now:
>
>How can I be your match,
>
>Back from the nether spheres?

Liu Mengmei:

>Don't talk like that!
>
>(*To the previous tune*)
>
>I'm fortunate to meet you on the way;
>
>How can I have doubt on our wedding day?
>
>To share the bed with you
>
>Is worth all that I pursue.
>
>You are a lady of good name,
>
>But I am not a man of far-reaching fame.

Du Liniang:

>(*Sighs*)
>
>In the intercourse,
>
>I was tempted by his manly force.
>
>Mr Liu, I'm still a virgin.

Liu Mengmei:

>We've made love several times. How can you remain a virgin?

Du Liniang:

>You met my spirit at that time. Now I'm standing before you in my real self.
>
>You touched my spirit for sure
>
>While my real self is a virgin pure.

[外扮舟子歌上]春娘爱上酒家子楼,不怕归迟总弗子愁。推道那家娘子睡,且留教住要梳子头。
[又歌]不论秋菊和那春子个花,个个能嗒空肚子茶。无事莫教频入子库,一名闲物他也要些子些。
[丑扮疙童上介]船,船,船,临安去。
[外]来,来,来。[摆船介]
[丑]门外船便,相公篆下小姐班。
[净辞介]相公、小姐,小心去了。
[生]小姐无人伏侍,烦老姑姑一行,得了官时相报。

(*Enter Boatman*)

Boatman:

(*Singing a ditty*)

The maid is fond of tavern house,

And never comes back late with care.

She says the master's spouse

Needs her help to comb the hair.

(*Singing another ditty*)

For maids by this name or that name,

Each can drink a pot of tea.

They steal from the storehouse without shame,

Taking everything for free.

(*Enter Scabby Turtle*)

Scabby Turtle:

Boatman! Boatman! Boatman! There're passengers to Lin'an!

Boatman:

Coming, coming, I'm coming.

(*Rows his boat toward the bank*)

Scabby Turtle:

The boat has arrived. Mr Liu, please help Miss Du on board.

Sister Stone:

(*Says farewell to Liu Mengmei and Du Liniang*)

Take care, Mr Liu and Miss Du.

Liu Mengmei:

There's no one to wait on my wife. Would you come with us, Sister Stone? I'll requite your kindness when I obtain an official position.

Sister Stone:

［净］俺不曾收拾。

［背介］事发相连，走为上计。［回介］也罢，相公赏侄儿什么，着他和俺收拾房头，俺伴小姐同去。

［丑］使得。

［生］便赏他这件衣服。

［解衣介］

［丑］谢了，事发谁当？

［生］则推不知便了。

［丑］这等请了。"秃厮儿堪充道伴，女冠子权当梅香。"［下］

【急板令】

　　［众上船介］别南安孤帆夜开，

　　走临安把双飞路排。

　　［旦悲介］

　　［生］因何吊下泪来？

I haven't got my belongings yet.

(*Aside*)

If the story is known to the public, I'll be punished. Flight is the best policy.

(*Turn to Liu Mengmei*)

All right. Mr Liu, please give my nephew something and ask him to take care of the nunnery. I'll go with you.

Scabby Turtle:

Agreed.

Liu Mengmei:

I'll give him this robe.

(*Takes off his robe and gives it to Scabby Turtle*)

Scabby Turtle:

Thanks. Who will take the blame if the story leaks out?

Liu Mengmei:

Just say you don't know.

Scabby Turtle:

Bye-bye, then.

"A scabby boy gives the nun some aid
While Taoist nun becomes the servant maid."

(*Exit*)

Liu Mengmei, Du Liniang, Sister Stone:

(*Board the boat*)

(*To the tune of **Jibanling***)

By night we sail off Nan'an,

On our way toward Lin'an.

(*Du Liniang weeps*)

Liu Mengmei:

Why are you weeping now?

[旦]叹从此天涯，从此天涯。
叹三年此居，三年此埋。
死不能归，活了才回。
[合]问今夕何夕？
此来、魂脉脉，
意哈哈。

【前腔】[生]似倩女返魂到来，
采芙蓉回生并载。
[旦叹介]
[生]为何又吊下泪来？
[旦]想独自谁挨，独自谁挨？
翠黯香囊，泥渍金钗。
怕天上人间，心事难谐。[合前]

Du Liniang:

> We'll start to roam;
>
> We'll start to roam.
>
> I lived here for three years;
>
> I lay dead here for three years.
>
> When I was dead, I was away from home;
>
> Now that I've revived, I'm going home.

Liu Mengmei, Du Liniang, Sister Stone:

> What special night is this?
>
> From this very night,
>
> The bliss is
>
> That a couple unite.

Liu Mengmei:

> (*To the previous tune*)
>
> A beauty has regained her soul,
>
> As well as her female role.
>
> (*Du Liniang sighs*)

> Why are you weeping again?

Du Liniang:

> I was so helpless, so alone.
>
> I was so helpless, so alone.
>
> My perfume sachet was lost in grass;
>
> On my golden pin, dust has grown.
>
> I feared that between two worlds,
>
> Our hearts could hardly be known.

Liu Mengmei, Du Liniang, Sister Stone:

> What special night is this?
>
> From this very night,
>
> The bliss is

[净]夜深了,叫停船。你两人睡罢。
[生]风月舟中,新婚佳趣,其乐何如!

【一撮棹】
蓝桥驿,
把溱河桥风月筛。
[旦]柳郎,今日方知有人间之乐也。
七星版三星照,两星排。
今夜呵,把身子儿带,情儿迈,意儿挨。
[净]你过河衣带紧,请宽怀。
[生]眉横黛,
小船儿禁重载?
这欢眠自在,
抵多少吓魂台。

【尾声】
情根一点是无生债。
[旦]叹孤坟何处是俺望夫台?

That a couple unite.

Sister Stone:

As the night is deep, I'll tell the boatman to moor the boat and you two can have some sleep.

Liu Mengmei:

The breeze, the moon, the boat — all have added joy to our wedding night.

(*To the tune of* Yicuozhao)

With a fairy maid as my wife,

I've now brought love to life.

Du Liniang:

My dear, only now do I understand the joy of the human world!

The love between the ghost and man

Was where the wedding began.

Tonight,

We have attained our goal;

I'll serve you body and soul.

Sister Stone:

You've fastened your belt in the breeze;

It's time to make yourself at ease.

Liu Mengmei:

With your heavy woe,

Can the boat bear the weight?

To bed we shall go

And your terror will abate.

(*To the tune of* Coda)

Our love is bound with mortal life;

Du Liniang:

With persistent love I become your wife.

柳郎呵,
俺和你死里淘生情似海。

[生]偷去须从月下移,
[净]好风偏似送佳期。
[旦]傍人不识扁舟意,
[净]惟有新人子细知。

Mr Liu,

> We've gone through a life-and-death strife.

Liu Mengmei:

> **We take flight under the shining moon,**

Sister Stone:

> **With gentle breeze to whisper soon.**

Du Liniang:

> **Who knows what happens on the boat?**

Sister Stone:

> **On the water true love sails afloat.**

第三十七出　骇　变

[末上]"风吹不动顶垂丝,吟背春城出草迟。毕竟百年浑是梦,夜来风雨葬西施。"俺陈最良。只因感激杜太守,为他看顾小姐坟茔。昨日约了柳秀才到坟上望去,不免走一遭。[行介]"严扉不掩云长在,院径无媒草自深。"待俺叫门。[叫介]呀,往常门儿重重掩上,今日都开在此。待俺参了圣。[看菩萨介]咳,冷清清没香没灯的。呀,怎不见了杜小姐牌位?待俺问一声老姑姑。[叫三声介]俗家去了。待俺叫柳兄问他。[叫介]柳朋友![又叫介]柳先生!一发不应了。[看

Scene Thirty-seven
The Pedagogue's Alarm

(*Enter Chen Zuiliang*)

Chen Zuiliang:
"My hair is unstirred in the gentle breeze;
I take a stroll out in late spring at ease.
As hundred years elapse in endless dreams,
The nightly storm has sent the blooms to streams."

I, Chen Zuiliang, am looking after Miss Du's tomb out of my gratitude for Prefect Du. Yesterday I invited Mr Liu to visit Miss Du's tomb with me. It's time to go now.

(*Walks on*)

"The gate is open and enwrapped in clouds;
The yard is overgrown with grass in crowds."

Let me call at the gate.

(*Calls aloud*)

Oh, the gate used to be closely shut, but today it's left open. I'll pay respects to the Bodhisattva.

(*Looks around the statue*)

Why, there's neither lamp nor incense today. And where's Miss Du's memorial tablet? I'll ask Sister Stone about it.

(*Calls three times*)

She's out. Let me ask Mr Liu.

(*Calls aloud*)

Mr Liu, my friend!

(*Calls again*)

介]嗄,柳秀才去了。医好了病,来不参,去不辞。没行止,没行止!待俺西房瞧瞧。咳哟,道姑也搬去了。磬儿,锅儿,床席,一些都不见了。怪哉![想介]是了。日前小道姑有话,昨日又听的小道姑声息,其中必有柳梦梅勾搭事情。一夜去了。没行止,没行止!由他,由他。到后园看小姐坟去。[行介]

【懒画眉】
园深径侧老苍苔,
那几所月榭风亭久不开。
当时曾此葬金钗。
[望介]呀,旧坟高高儿的,如今平下来了也。缘何不见坟儿在?
敢是狐兔穿空倒塌来?
这太湖石,只左边靠动了些,梅树依然。
[惊介]咳呀,小姐坟被劫了也。

Mr Liu! Still no response.

(*Looks around*)

Oh, Mr Liu is gone. I cured him of his disease, but he has never said a word of gratitude, not even saying good-bye when he left. It's a shame! It's a shame! Let me look at the living-room in the west wing. Ah, Sister Stone is gone, too. The bells, the pots and the mattress are all gone. How strange!

(*Meditates*)

I've got it. There have been some rumours about a young nun, and I heard voices of a young nun again yesterday. There must be something between Mr Liu and the young nun and they must have eloped last night. It's a shame! It's a shame! Forget about it! Forget about it! Let me go to the back garden and have a look at Miss Du's tomb.

(*Walks on*)

(*To the tune of* **Lanhuamei**)

The moss is thick along the garden trail

While the pavilions are lying waste.

Here we bury the beauty and here we wail.

(*Stares around*)

Oh, the high mound has been levelled.

What's happened to the grave?

Has it collapsed into the cave?

The Taihu rocks have been moved to the left and the plum trees are still there.

(*Alarmed*)

Alas! Miss Du's tomb has been robbed!

(*Cries out*)

Oh, heavens! Miss Du!

【朝天子】
[放声哭介]小姐，天呵！
是什么发冢无情短倖材？
他有多少金珠葬在打眼来。
小姐，你若早有人家，也搬回去了。
则为玉镜台无分照泉台。
好孤哉！
怕蛇钻骨，
树穿骸。
不提防这灾。
知道了，柳梦梅岭南人，惯了劫坟。将棺材放在近所，截了一角为记，要人取赎。这贼意思，止不过说杜老先生闻知，定来取赎。想那棺材，只在左近埋下了。待俺寻看。[见介]咳呀，这草窝里不是硃漆板头？这不是大锈钉？开了去。天，小姐骨殖丢在那里？[望介]那池塘里浮着一片棺材。是了，小姐尸骨抛在池里去了。狠心的贼也！

【普天乐】
问天天，
你怎把他昆池碎劫无余在？
又不欠观音锁骨连环债，
怎丢他水月魂骸？
乱红衣暗泣莲腮，

(*To the tune of Chaotianzi*)

What heartless scoundrel has robbed the grave?

How much gold has he found in the cave?

Miss Du, if you had been married, your body would have been buried in your husband's ancestral cemetery.

    Without a spouse of her own,

    She died and lay alone.

    I feared that snakes and roots

    Might disturb her bone,

    But did not expect a man with heart of stone.

That's it. Liu Mengmei is from Lingnan, and grave-robbing must be something common there. He must have hidden the coffin in a nearby place and cut off a corner as a demand for ransom money. He must have expected Prefect Du to pay the money when he learns about it. The coffin must have been buried somewhere near. Let me search for it.

(*Discovers the coffin*)

Oh, isn't it the coffin-head in the grass? Isn't it the rusted coffin-nail? The coffin has been broken open. Oh, heavens! Where are Miss Du's remains?

(*Looks around*)

A coffin plank is floating on the pond. Yes, Miss Du's remains must have been thrown into the pond. What a brutal robber!

(*To the tune of Putianle*)

    Oh heavens! How can you bear

    To see her remains be thrown away?

    She does not owe anyone a debt;

    Why should her remains be thrown in water and decay?

    The lotus would have shed tears,

似黑月重抛业海。
待车干池水，捞起他骨殖来。
怕浪淘沙碎玉难分派。
到不如当初水葬无猜。
贼眼脑生来毒害，
那些个怜香惜玉，
致命图财！
先师云："虎兕出于柙，龟玉毁于椟中，典守者不得辞其责。"俺如今先去禀了南安府缉拿。星夜往淮扬，报知杜老先生去。

【尾声】
石虔婆他古弄里金珠曾见来。
柳梦梅，
他做得个破周书汲冢才。
小姐呵，
你道他为甚么向金盖银墙做打家贼？

丘坟发掘当官路，
春草茫茫墓亦无。
致汝无辜由俺罪，
狂眠恣饮是凶徒。

For her remains to be thrown into evil spheres.
When the pond is drained to recover her remains,
  Her scattered bones would look the worst.
  How I wish that she were buried in water at first!
  The robber is a brute of a man;
  How can he care for the fair maiden
  When he wants to grab whatever he can!
Confucius said, "When a tiger or a rhinoceros gets out of a cage, or tortoise-shell or jade is damaged in a box, the keeper cannot escape the blame." I'll first report it to the Nan'an prefectural office for them to apprehend the grave-robber, and then leave for Huaiyang this very night to report to Envoy Du.

  (*To the tune of* **Coda**)
  Sister Stone knew the jewels in the cave;
  Mr Liu ventured to dig the grave.
  Miss Du, can you see why
  Like a housebreaker they behave?
  When he dug the grave to gain his aim,
  The mound was levelled with shame.
  Although it's not my fault to bring the harm,
  The robber drunkard is to blame.

第三十八出　　淮　警

【霜天晓角】

[净引众上]英雄出众，
鼓噪红旗动。
三年绣甲锦蒙茸，
弹剑把雕鞍斜鞚。

"贼子豪雄是李全，忠心赤胆向胡天。靴尖踢倒长天堑，却笑江南土不坚。"俺溜金王奉大金之命，骚扰江淮三年。打听大金家兵粮凑集，将次南征，教俺淮扬开路，不免请出贼房计议。中军快请。

[众叫介]大王叫箭坊。

[老旦扮军人持箭上]箭坊俱已造完。

Scene Thirty-eight
The Invasion

(*Enter Li Quan with his men*)

Li Quan:

(*To the tune of* **Shuangtianxiaojiao**)

A hero rises above all;
The drums and banners are the battle-call.
For three years in a coat of mail,
I've joined in battles big and small.
"Here I stand, the bravest chieftain Li Quan,
For the alien emperor I'll do whatever I can.
My troops will sweep across the Yangtze River,
To stun the cowards of the southern clan."

At the behest of the great Jin dynasty, I, Gilded Prince, have been making trouble in the area between the Yangtze River and the Huaihe River for three years. Reports have it that the great Jin dynasty has amassed sufficient troops and supplies for a southward expedition and that I am ordered to make advances on the Huaiyang area. I'd better discuss with my wife. Attendants, call for my spouse.

Attendants:

(*Call out*)

His Highness calls for his louse.

(*Enter a soldier with arrows*)

Soldier:

I've got arrows to shoot the louse.

[净笑恼介]狗才怎么说?

[老旦]大王说,请出箭坊计议。

[净]胡说!俺自请杨娘娘,是你箭坊?

[老旦]杨娘娘是大王箭坊,小的也是箭坊。

[净喝介]

【前腔】

[丑上]帐莲深拥,

压寨的阴谋重。

[见介]大王兴也!

你夜来鏖战好粗雄。

困的俺垓心没缝。

大王夫,俺睡倦了。请俺甚事商量?

[净]闻得金主南侵,教俺攻打淮扬,以便征进。思想扬州有杜安抚镇守,急切难攻。如何是好?

Li Quan:

(*Scolds with amusement*)

What did you say, son of a bitch?

Soldier:

Your Highness just said that you want to shoot the louse.

Li Quan:

Nonsense! I called for my spouse Lady Yang, not to shoot a louse.

Soldier:

Your Highness will discuss with your spouse and I'll shoot my louse.

(*Exit, amid shouts from Li Quan*)

(*Enter Lady Yang*)

Lady Yang:

(*To the previous tune*)

In the inner tent,

The chieftain's wife is a brilliant portent.

(*Salutes Li Quan*)

Prosperity to Your Highness!

How fierce your assault was last night,

Which wore me out with great delight.

My chieftain husband, I had been so exhausted that I was nearly torn out of bed. What is it that you'd like to discuss with me?

Li Quan:

Reports have it that the Jin emperor will be on a southward expedition and that I am ordered to invade Huaiyang so as to clear his way of advance. I'm afraid that Yangzhou is guarded by Envoy Du and is not an easy prey for us. What's the best

[丑]依奴家所见,先围了淮安,杜安抚定然赴救。俺分兵扬州,断其声援,于中取事。
[净]高,高!娘娘这计,李全要怕了你。
[丑]你那一宗儿不怕了奴家!
[净]罢了。未封王号时,俺是个怕老婆的强盗,封王之后,也要做怕老婆的王。
[丑]着了。快起兵去攻打淮城。

【锦上花】
　　[净]拨转磨旗峰,
　　促紧先锋。
　　千兵摆列,
　　万马奔冲。
　　鼓通通,鼓通通,
　　噪的那淮扬动。

policy?

Lady Yang:

As far as I can see, you'd better besiege Huai'an first so that Envoy Du will come to its rescue. Then I'll lead some of our troops to attack Yangzhou so as to cut his provisions. At that time the ball is in our hands.

Li Quan:

Marvellous idea! Marvellous idea! On hearing this scheme, I am stricken with awe myself.

Lady Yang:

And when were you not stricken with awe?

Li Quan:

Quite right. Before I was made a prince, I had been a henpecked robber; since I was made a prince, I have been a henpecked prince.

Lady Yang:

Stop your nonsense. Now order the troops to set off to Huai'an at once.

Li Quan:

(*To the tune of Jinshanghua*)

When I move my troops,

I've sent the vanguard groups.

Onward march, men of valiant deeds!

Onward gallop, my brave steeds!

Beat the drum!

Beat the drum!

Huaiyang will be deaf and numb!

All:

(*To the previous tune*)

【前腔】
　　[众]军中母大虫，
　　绰有威风。
　　连环阵势，
　　烟粉牢笼。
　　哈哄哄，哈哄哄，
　　哄的淮扬动。
　　[丑]溜金王听俺分付：军到处，不许你抢占半名妇女。如违，定以军法从事。
　　[净]不敢。

　　[丑]日暮风沙古战场，
　　[净]军营人学内家妆。
　　[众]如今领帅红旗下，
　　[众]擘破云鬟金凤凰。

> We have a tigress that would roar,
>
> Whom we regard with awe.
>
> She makes her plan;
>
> She controls her man.
>
> Laugh with cheer!
>
> Laugh with cheer!
>
> Huaiyang will tremble with fear!

Lady Yang:

> Gilded Prince, now take my orders! Wherever your troops go, leave women alone! If you violate my order, you'll be punished in a court-martial.

Li Quan:

> I won't violate your order.

Lady Yang:

> **On the stormy field of ancient warfare,**

Li Quan:

> **The warriors imitate a woman's wear.**

All:

> **Beneath the scarlet battle-flag,**
>
> **We honour golden brooches on her hair.**

第三十九出　　如　杭

【唐多令】
[生上]海月未尘埋,
[旦上]新妆倚镜台。
[生]卷钱塘风色破书斋。
[旦]夫!昨夜天香云外吹,
桂子月中开。
[生]"夫妻客旅闷难开,
[旦]待唤提壶酒一杯。
[生]江上怒潮千丈雪,
[旦]好似禹门平地一声雷。"
[生]俺和你夫妻相随,到了临安京都地面。赁下一所空房,可以理会书史。争奈试期尚远,客思转

Scene Thirty-nine
Sojourn in Lin'an

(*Enter Liu Mengmei*)

Liu Mengmei:

(*To the tune of Tangduoling*)

The mirror is clean and clear,

(*Enter Du Liniang*)

Du Liniang:

In my new dress I appear.

Liu Mengmei:

I see the Qiantang sights from my room.

Du Liniang:

My dear husband,

A fragrance came from the sky last night —

The laurel on the moon in bloom.

Liu Mengmei:

"Long trips are boring for the man and wife;

Du Liniang:

A cup of wine will add pleasure to your life.

Liu Mengmei:

The Qiantang bore is surging like the snow;

Du Liniang:

They foretell good tidings heavens bestow."

Liu Mengmei:

We have travelled together to the capital of Lin'an. Now that we've rented an empty house, I should be able to study the

深。如何是好?

[旦]早上分付姑姑,买酒一壶,少解夫君之闷,尚未见回。

[生]生受了,娘子。一向不曾话及:当初只说你是西邻女子,谁知感动幽冥,匆匆成其夫妇。一路而来,到今不曾请教。小姐可是见小生于道院西头?因何诗句上"不是梅边是柳边",就指定了小生姓名?这灵通委是怎的?

[旦笑介]柳郎,俺说见你于道院西头是假。我前生呵!

【江儿水】

偶和你后花园曾梦来,

擎一朵柳丝儿要俺把诗篇赛。

奴正题咏间,便和你牡丹亭上去了。

[生笑介]可好哩?

classics and histories. However, as the date for the imperial examination is still far off, I'm growing more and more homesick. How can I cheer up?

Du Liniang:

This morning I asked Sister Stone to buy a kettle of wine to relieve your melancholy. She's not back yet.

Liu Mengmei:

Thank you for your kindness, my dear. There's still one thing we haven't talked about. When we first met each other, you said that you were from the neighbourhood. Who knows that the nether-world prince was moved and we were married in haste! Throughout the journey I've never asked this question. Did you first see me in the west wing of the nunnery? How could you allude to my name in the poem "Will be found by the plum or willow"? How did you come across this magical idea?

Du Liniang:

(*Smiles*)

Mr Liu, it is sheer fabrication to say that I first saw you in the west wing of the nunnery. In my previous life,

(*To the tune of Jiangershui*)

I chanced to meet you in my garden dream

And wrote poems on the willow theme.

I was just beginning to write the poem when you took me to the Peony Pavilion.

Liu Mengmei:

(*Laughs*)

How did you like it?

Du Liniang:

(*Smiles*)

[旦笑介]咳，正好中间，落花惊醒。此后神情不定，一病奄奄。
这是聪明反被聪明带，
真诚不得真诚在，
冤亲做下这冤亲债。
一点色情难坏，
再世为人，
话做了两头分拍。

【前腔】
[生]是话儿听的都呆答孩。
则俺为情痴信及你人儿在。
还则怕邪淫惹动阴曹怪，
忌亡坟触犯阴阳戒。
分书生领受阴人爱，
勾的你色身无坏。
出土成人，
又看见这帝城风采。
[净提酒上]"路从丹凤城边过。酒向金鱼馆内沽。"呀，相公、小姐不知：俺在江头沽酒，看见各处秀才，都赴选场去了。相公错过天大好事。
[生、旦作忙介]

Alas, while we were enjoying ourselves, petals fell and woke me up. From that time on I was simply sitting on pins and needles and fell seriously ill.

Cleverness may hurt a clever man;

Sincerity does not requite a sincere man;

Predestined love is destined to befall the man.

With profound love for you,

I'm brought back to life again.

That's my story from a different point of view.

Liu Mengmei:

(*To the previous tune*)

Although I am amazed at your strange tale,

My faith tells me to believe in you.

I feared the nether prince would blame our love,

And for grave-digging I would rue.

As I'm destined to have a nether wife,

You have kept your body intact, too.

You'll see the splendour of the capital town

When you start your life anew.

(*Enter Sister Stone with a kettle of wine*)

Sister Stone:

"I walked by the Phoenix Palace and beyond,

Then bought my wine in Goldfish Pond."

Oh, Mr Liu and Miss Du, I've something to tell you. When I was buying the wine by the river, I saw scholars from all over the country going to the examination halls. Don't you miss your chance, Mr Liu!

(*Liu Mengmei and Du Liniang get into a flurry*)

Du Liniang:

[旦]相公只索快行。
[净]这酒便是状元红了。

【小措大】
[旦把酒介]喜的一宵恩爱，
被功名二字惊开。
好开怀这御酒三杯，
放着四婵娟人月在。
立朝马五更门外，
听六街里喧传人气概。
七步才，
蹬上了寒宫八宝台。
沉醉了九重春色，
便看花十里归来。

【前腔】
[生]十年窗下，
遇梅花冻九才开。
夫贵妻荣八字安排。
敢你七香车稳情载，
六宫宣有你朝拜。
五花诰封你非分外。
论四德、似你那三从结愿谐。
二指大泥金报喜。
打一轮皂盖飞来。

You must make haste, my dear.

Sister Stone:

Please let me toast to your success in the examination.

Du Liniang:

(*Holds up a cup of wine*)

(*To the tune of Xiaocuoda*)

The pleasure of one night's love

Is cut short by the two words: fame and name.

Please drink three cups of wine;

I wish that quadruple bliss be to our claim.

You'll stand at palace gate at five o'clock

And hear the bustle in the six streets.

With your talent to write a poem in seven steps,

You'll ascend the eight-treasure terrace for your feats.

With a drink from the royal "ninth sphere",

You'll watch flowers along ten miles of streets.

Liu Mengmei:

(*To the previous tune*)

After ten years of studies,

The plums will bloom in the coldest nine days.

Our fates are fixed by eight points of time—

You'll ride in a carriage of seven fragrant trees,

Have an audience with the queen in her six halls,

And have your title on the five-coloured silk.

A model of four virtues

And three laws of obedience, you'll live well.

When you see my name on golden lists two inches long,

I'll be meeting you on a magnificent carriage.

Du Liniang:

[旦]夫！我记的春容诗句来。

【尾声】
盼今朝得傍你蟾宫客，
你和俺倍精神金阶对策。
高中了，同去访你丈人、丈母呵，
则道俺从地窟里登仙那大喝彩。

[旦]良人的的有奇才，
[净]恐失佳期后命催。
[生]红粉楼中应计日，
[合]遥闻笑语自天来。

My dear, I still remember the poem I wrote on my portrait.

(*To the tune of Coda*)

I shall see you in your best

When you do well in the imperial test.

When you succeed in your examination, we'll go and meet your parents-in-law. They will say that

From hell to heaven I am blessed.

Du Liniang:

My dearest husband is indeed sublime;

Sister Stone:

You must hurry lest you miss your time.

Liu Mengmei:

Forget not to count the days in your bedroom,

Du Liniang, Sister Stone, Liu Mengmei:

From high above there comes joyous chime.

第四十出　仆　侦

【孤飞雁】
　　[净扮郭驼挑担上]世路平消长,
十年事老头儿心上。
柳郎君翰墨人家长。
无营运,单承望,
天生天养,果树成行。
年深树老,把园围抛漾。
你索在何方?好没主量。
凄惶,趁上他身衣口粮。
　　"家人做事兴,全靠主人命。主人不在家,园树不开花。"俺老驼一生依着柳相公种果为生。你说好不古怪:柳相公在家,一株树上摘百十来个果儿;自柳相公去后,一株树上生百十来个虫。便胡乱结

Scene Forty
Looking for His Master

(*Enter Hunchback Guo, carrying his luggage on a shoulder-pole*)

Hunchback Guo:
(*To the tune of Gufeiyan*)
The human life is long and tedious;
I keep decades of life in mind.
My master, Mr Liu, is a learned man,
With no other means of life
Than rely on the orchard trees,
Which nature makes them ripe.
As years go by,
The orchard lies in waste.
Master, where are you?
I have no idea as to what to do.
I do not know
Where to find my revenue.
"The servants do their work well
When their master's there.
When Master says farewell,
The orchard trees are bare."

For all my life I have grown trees for the Lius. Strange to say, when Mr Liu was at home, each tree could bear over a hundred fruits; but since Mr Liu was gone, each tree has born over a hundred worms. For the few fruits on the trees, they

几个儿,小厮们偷个尽。老驼无主,被人欺负。因此发个老狠,体探俺相公过岭北来了,在梅花观养病,直寻到此,早则南安府大封条封了观门。听的边厢人说,道婆为事走了,有个侄儿癞头鼋是小西门住。去寻问他。[行介]"抹过大东路,投至小西门。"[下]

【金钱花】

[丑扮疙童披衣笑上]自小疙辣郎当,郎当。

官司拿俺为姑娘,姑娘。

尽了法,脑皮撞。

得了命,卖了房。

充小厮,串街坊。

"若要人不知,除非己不为。"自家癞头鼋便是。

are all stolen by the boys. With no master to help me, I have been bullied all the time. At last I decided to look for my master. I heard that he had crossed the Five Ridges and was put up in the Plum Blossom Nunnery for illness. I followed him all the way to this place only to find that the city-gate had been sealed by the Nan'an Prefecture. I learned that the nun had fled for some crime and that she had a nephew, Scabby Turtle, who lived near the west city-gate. I'll go and try to find out the whereabouts of my master.

(*Walks on*)

"*Follow the eastern road,*

And reach the western gate."

(*Exit*)

(*Enter Scabby Turtle in Liu Mengmei's robe, laughing*)

Scabby Turtle:

(*To the tune of Jinqianhua*)

I have a scabby head since my boyhood,

Since my boyhood.

I was put in jail for my aunt's sake,

For my aunt's sake.

I was tied

And was tried.

I was released,

But my house was leased.

I run errands in the open air,

From lane to street, from here to there.

"Nobody will know it,

Unless you haven't done it."

I am Scabby Turtle. As there's nobody around, I'll tell you

这无人所在，表白一会。你说姑娘和柳秀才那事干得好，又走得好！只被陈教授那狗才，禀过南安府，拿了俺去。拷问俺："姑娘那里去了？劫了杜小姐坟哩！"你道俺更不聪明，却也颇颇的。则掉着头不做声。那鸟官喝道："马不吊不肥，人不拶不直，把这厮上起脑箍来。"哎也，哎也，好不生疼！原来用刑人先捞了俺一架金钟玉磬，替俺方便，禀说这小厮夹出脑髓来了。那鸟官喝道："捻上来瞧。"瞧了，大鼻子一飐，说道："这小厮真个夹出脑浆来了。"他不知是俺癞头上脓。叫松了刑，着保在外。俺如今有了命，把柳相公送俺这件黑海青穿摆将起来。[唱介]摆摇摇，摆摆摇。没人所在，被俺摆过子桥。

[净向前叫揖介]小官唱喏。

[丑作不回揖，大笑唱介]俺小官子腰闪价，唱不的子

my story. Indeed, my aunt and Mr Liu did a good job and escaped at the right time. After Tutor Chen the rascal reported it to the Nan'an Prefecture, I was put in custody and questioned: "Where's your aunt? Who's robbed the grave?" I was not clever, but I was cunning enough. I hung my head and kept my mouth shut. The damned judge said, "Truss up a horse and it grows; squeeze a man and he talks. Put the head-hoop on that scoundrel's head!" Oops, oops, what a pain! The torturers had got a golden bell and a jade chime out of me, so they did me a favour by reporting to the judge that they had squeezed my brains out of me. The damned judge said, "Take some and show it to me." He looked and said with a wave of his nose, "It's true you've squeezed his brain out of him." As he didn't know that it was the pus from my scabby head, he let me off. And so I was released on bail. Now that my life is preserved, I put on the robe Mr Liu gave me and swagger in the street.

(*Sings*)

Sway and strut,

Strut and sway.

In the empty street,

I swagger on the way.

(*Enter Hunchback Guo*)

Hunchback Guo:

(*Bows to Scabby Turtle*)

How do you do, Sir.

Scabby Turtle:

(*Does not return the bow, but sings with a laugh*)

I've got a pain in my back

And cannot bow.

喏。比似你个驼子唱喏,则当伸子个腰。
[净]这贼种,开口伤人。难道做小官的背偏不驼?
[丑]刮这驼子嘴,偷了你什么?贼?
[净作认丑衣介]别的罢了。则这件衣服,岭南柳相公的,怎在你身上?
[丑]咳呀,难道俺做小官的,就没件干净衣服,便是岭南柳家的?隔这般一道梅花岭,谁见俺偷来?
[净]这衣带上有字。你还不认,叫地方。
[扯丑作怕倒介]罢了,衣服还你去啰。
[净]耍哩!俺正要问一个人。
[丑]谁?
[净]柳秀才那里去了?

For a hunchback,

You are stretching yourself now.

Hunchback Guo:

You thief, you're mouthing dirty words. Have you never bowed?

Scabby Turtle:

I'll slap on your face. What have I stolen from you? Me, a thief?

Hunchback Guo:

(*Inspects Scabby Turtle's robe*)

I don't care about anything else, but how is it that you're wearing a robe that belongs to Mr Liu from Lingnan?

Scabby Turtle:

Well, why can't I have a decent coat or two by myself? When you say that it belongs to the Lius of Lingnan, who has seen me stealing it from across the ridge?

Hunchback Guo:

His name is woven into the ribbon. If you don't tell the truth, I'll call the cop.

(*Tries to grab at Scabby Turtle*)

Scabby Turtle:

(*Frightened, stumbles on the ground*)

All right, I'll give back the robe to you.

Hunchback Guo:

No more kidding! I just want to ask you about someone.

Scabby Turtle:

Who is it?

Hunchback Guo:

Where is Mr Liu, the scholar?

[丑]不知。

[净三问][丑三不知介]

[净]你不说,叫地方去。

[丑]罢了,大路头难好讲话。演武厅去。

[行介]

[净]好个僻静所在。

[丑]咦,柳秀才到有一个。可是你问的不是?你说得像,俺说;你说不像,休想叫地方,便到官司,俺也只是不说。

[净]这小厮到贼。听俺道来:

【尾犯序】

提起柳家郎,

他俊白庞儿,典雅行藏。

[丑]是了。多少年纪?

[净]论仪表看他,三十不上。

Scabby Turtle:

   I don't know.

      (*Hunchback asks the question three times and Scabby Turtle says that he does not know all the time.*)

Hunchback Guo:

   If you won't tell, I'll call the cop.

Scabby Turtle:

   Well, I'll tell you, but it's not convenient to talk in the street. Let's go to the army's training ground.

      (*Scabby Turtle and Hunchback Guo walk on.*)

Hunchback Guo:

   What a quiet place!

Scabby Turtle:

   So there was a Mr Liu, but I don't know whether he's the man you're looking for. If you tell me that he's the right person, I'll tell you; if you can't, I won't tell you even if you call the cop or the judge.

Hunchback Guo:

   How cunning you are! Now listen to me:

      (*To the tune of* **Weifanxu**)

     This Mr Liu

     Has a fair face

     Full of grace.

Scabby Turtle:

   Yes, and what is his age?

Hunchback Guo:

     From his appearance,

     He looks less than thirty.

Scabby Turtle:

[丑]是了。你是他什么人？
[净]他祖上、传留下俺栽花种粮。
自小儿、俺看成他快长。
[丑]原来你是柳大官。你几时别他，知他做出甚事来？
[净]春头别，
跟寻至此，
闻说的不端详。
[丑]这老儿说的一句句着。老儿，若论他做的事，咦！
[丑作扯净耳语][净听不见介]
[丑]呸，左则无人，耍他去。老儿你听着。

【前腔】
他到此病郎当。
逢着个杜太爷衙教小姐的陈秀才，
勾引他养病庵堂，
去后园游赏。
[净]后来？

Yes, and what's your relationship?

Hunchback Guo:

> For years and years in his home,
>
> I've tended flowers and grown the rice.
>
> From his childhood,
>
> I was in his place.

Scabby Turtle:

> So you're his steward. When did you part with him and do you know what he has done?

Hunchback Guo:

> We parted in the spring
>
> And I have traced him all the way here.
>
> As to what he has done,
>
> I am not clear.

Scabby Turtle:

> What this old man says makes sense. Old man, I'll tell you what he has done.
>
> (*Whispers to Hunchback Guo, who cannot hear clearly*)
>
> Phew! As no one is around here, I'll make some fun of him. Old man, now listen.
>
> (*To the previous tune*)
>
> He was ill when he arrived here.
>
> He happened to meet Mr Chen, tutor to the prefect's daughter Miss Du, and
>
> Was tempted to live in the nunnery
>
> And was showed around the back garden.

Hunchback Guo:

> What happened next?

Scabby Turtle:

[丑]一游游到小姐坟儿上。拾得一轴春容,朝思暮想,做出事来。
[净]怎的来?
[丑]秀才家为真当假,
劫坟偷圹。
[净惊介]这却怎了?
[丑]你还不知。被那陈教授禀了官,围住观门。拖番柳秀才,和俺姑娘行了杖。棚琶拶压,不怕不招。点了供纸,解上江西提刑廉访司。问那六案都孔目,这男女应得何罪?六案请了律令,禀复道,但偷坟见尸者,依律一秋。
[净]怎么秋?
[丑作按净头介]这等秋。
[净惊哭介]俺的柳秀才呵!老驼没处投奔了。

When he came across Miss Du's tomb, he picked up a portrait of a young lady. As he was haunted by the portrait day and night, he made some trouble.

Hunchback Guo:

What's the trouble?

Scabby Turtle:

He took it for a genuine maid
And dug the grave.

Hunchback Guo:

(*Surprised*)

What happened next?

Scabby Turtle:

I'll tell you. When Tutor Chen reported it to the prefecture, the cops came and surrounded the nunnery. They arrested, bound up Mr Liu and my aunt, Sister Stone and clamped their fingers. They were forced to confess their crimes and sign their confessions. When they were brought to the provincial prison, the magistrate checked the civil codes as to how they were going to be punished and found out that all the grave-robbers should be silenced.

Hunchback Guo:

What does "silenced" mean?

Scabby Turtle:

(*Presses Hunchback Guo's head as if ready to chop his head*)
It means this!

Hunchback Guo:

(*Astonished and in tears*)

Oh my master, I have nowhere to go.

Scabby Turtle:

[丑笑介]休慌。
后来遇赦了。便是那杜小姐活转来哩。
[净]有这等事!
[丑]活鬼头还做了秀才正房,
俺那死姑娘到做了梅香伴当。
[净]何往?
[丑]临安去,
送他上路,
赏这领旧衣裳。
[净]吓俺一跳。却早喜也!

【尾声】
去临安定是图金榜。
[丑]着了。
[净]俺勒挣着躯腰走帝乡。
[丑]老哥,你路上精细些。
现如今一路里画影图形捕凶党。

[净]寻得仙源访隐沦,
[丑]郡城南下是通津。

(*Laughs*)

Don't worry, please.

Later they were acquitted, and Miss Du came back to life.

Hunchback Guo:

How could that happen!

Scabby Turtle:

The revived ghost became his wife;

My aunt became their servant maid.

Hunchback Guo:

Where are they now?

Scabby Turtle:

They went to Lin'an.

When I saw them off,

He gave me this old robe.

Hunchback Guo:

I was really scared to death, but it turned out to be good news.

(*To the tune of* **Coda**)

He went to Lin'an for imperial exams;

Scabby Turtle:

I see.

Hunchback Guo:

I must be on my way to the capital town.

Scabby Turtle:

Look out on the way, old man, for at this moment

The portraits are posted to hunt them down.

Hunchback Guo:

To search for hermits in the fairy spring,

Scabby Turtle:

Just follow main roads on the western wing.

[净]众中不敢分明说,
[丑]遥想风流第一人。

Hunchback Guo:

> Amid the bustling crowd we cannot talk

Scabby Turtle:

> About a scholar who will see the king.

第四十一出　　耽　试

【凤凰阁】

[净扮苗舜宾引众上]九边烽火咤。
秋水鱼龙怎化?
广寒丹桂吐层花,
谁向云端折下?
[合]殿闱深锁,
取试卷看详回话。

"铸时天匠待英豪,引手何妨一钓鳌?报答春光知有处,文章分得凤凰毛。"下官苗舜宾便是。圣上因俺香山能辨番回宝色,钦取来京典试。因金兵摇动,临轩策士,问和战守三者孰便?各房俱已取中头卷,圣旨着下官详定。想起来看宝易,看文字难。为什么来?俺的眼睛,原是猫儿睛,和碧绿琉

Scene Forty-one
Late for the Examination

(*Enter Miao Shunbin with his attendants*)

Miao Shunbin:

(*To the tune of* **Fenghuangge**)

When border areas are aflame with battle-fire,
How can the scholars fulfil their desire?
When flowers blossom on the bough,
Who will obtain the laurel now?

Miao Shunbin, Attendants:

Tightly close the door
When we mark the score.

Miao Shunbin:

"*Examiners await the gifted man,*
Ready for him to appear.
He can requite the love of spring,
If he writes good essays here."

I am Miao Shunbin. As I did a good job in examining the treasures presented by the foreign merchants, I have been appointed chief examiner in the imperial examinations. In face of the Jin invasion, His Majesty decreed the topic for this year's examination: "Among appeasement, offence and defence, which is the best policy?" Now that top-rank papers have been picked out from examinees in different sections, I am instructed to make the final selection. To my mind, it is easier to judge treasures than to judge essays. The reason is that my eyes are

璃水晶无二。因此一见真宝,眼睛火出。说起文字,俺眼里从来没有。如今却也奉旨无奈,左右,开箱取各房卷子上来。

[众取卷上,净作看介]这试卷好少也。且取天字号三卷,看是何如。第一卷,"诏问:'和战守三者孰便?'""臣谨对:'臣闻国家之和贼,如里老之和事。'"呀,里老和事,和不得,罢;国家事,和不来,怎了?本房拟他状元,好没分晓。且看第二卷,这意思主守。[看介]"臣闻天子之守国,如女子之守身。"也比的小了。再看第三卷,到是主战。[看介]"臣闻南朝之战北,如老阳之战阴。"此语忒奇。但是《周易》有"阴阳交战"之说。——以前主和,被秦太师误了。今日权取主战者第一,主守者第二,主和者第三。其余诸卷,以次而定。

like cat's eyes, no different from green crystals. They will glow when they meet genuine treasures, while they won't glow when they meet words. However, I have to carry out the imperial decree. Attendants, open the cases and hand me the papers.

(*Reads the papers when the attendants have fetched the papers*)

Well, there are not many papers. I'll first have a look at three essays from the first section. The first essay reads, "His Majesty's topic is: Among appeasement, offence and defence, which is the best policy?" "In my opinion, The nation's appeasement with the invaders can be compared to the village elder's settlement of a quarrel." Oh, if the village elder fails to settle a quarrel, nothing serious will happen, but, if the nation fails to appease the invaders, who knows what will happen! There's no reason for me to rank it as the first. The second essay is in favour of defence.

(*Reads*)

"In my opinion, the emperor's defence of his nation can be compared to the virgin's defence of her body." This is an improper comparison. The third essay is in favour of offence.

(*Reads*)

"In my opinion, the southern dynasty's combat with the north can be compared to *yang's* offence on *yin*." It's a fantastic comparison, but there is indeed the saying "*yin* and *yang* in conflict" in *The Book of Changes*. Years ago, Qin Hui's appeasement policy impaired the nation. Now I'll put offence in the first place, defence in the second place, and appeasement in the third place. The other papers will be ranked in the

【一封书】
　　[净]文章五色讹。
　　怕冬烘头脑多。
　　总费他墨磨，
　　笔尖花无一个。
　　恁这里龙门日月开无那，
　　都待要尺水翻成一丈波。
　　却也无奈了，
　　也是浪桃花当一科，
　　池里无鱼可奈何![封卷介]
【神仗儿】
　　[生上]风尘战斗，风尘战斗，
　　奇材辐辏。
　　[丑]秀才来的停当，试期过了。
　　[生]呀，试期过了。文字可进呈么？
　　[丑]不进呈，难道等你？
　　道英雄入彀，恰锁院进呈时候。
　　[生]怕没有状元在里也哥。

same order.

(*To the tune of Yifengshu*)

The essays are of various kinds,

But the scholars make their essays trite.

They try to rack their minds,

But few of them are bright.

The chances are still there,

But slim for those in plight.

I can hardly do anything about it—

The annual test is fair and square,

But not a genius comes in sight.

(*Seals the papers*)

(*Enter Liu Mengmei*)

Liu Mengmei:

(*To the tune of Shenzhanger*)

This is a battling-ground,

A battling-ground

For gifted men from all around.

Attendant:

You come at the right time when the examination is over.

Liu Mengmei:

Alas, the examination is over, but may I present my essay?

Attendant:

No, you can't. Do you suppose that we are waiting for you? It is said that

When scholars gather round,

We close the testing ground.

Liu Mengmei:

But I'm afraid the number-one scholar has not been decided

[丑]不多,有三个了。
[生]万马争先,偏骅骝落后。
你快禀,有个遗才状元求见。
[丑]这是朝房里面。府州县道,告遗才哩。
[生]大哥,你真个不禀?
[哭介]天呵,苗老先赍发俺来献宝。
止不住下和羞,
对重瞳双泪流。
[净听介]掌门的,这什么所在!拿过来。
[丑扯生进介]
[生]告遗才的,望老大人收考。
[净]哎也,圣旨临轩,翰林院封进。谁敢再收?

yet.

Attendant:

Not many, but there are three already.

Liu Mengmei:

In a race of ten thousand steeds,

The topmost one is yet to prove in deeds.

Will you go in at once and announce that a scholar for the make-up examination is at the door?

Attendant:

There's no make-up examination in the imperial court. You can have it in your county or prefecture.

Liu Mengmei:

Are you not going indeed, brother?

(*Weeps*)

Oh, heavens! Mr Miao offered the fare for me to present treasures, but

As I fail to present treasures here,

How can I stop my tear?

Miao Shunbin:

(*Overhears the talk*)

Doorman, who's making a fuss in a solemn place like this? Bring him in.

(*The attendant drags Liu Mengmei in*)

Liu Mengmei:

I've come for the make-up examination. I beg you to give me a try.

Miao Shunbin:

Now that His Majesty has decreed the topic and the examination hall has been locked, who dares to accept you?

[生哭介]生员从岭南万里带家口而来。无路可投,愿触金阶而死。
[生起触阶,丑止介]
[净背介]这秀才像是柳生,真乃南海遗珠也。
[回介]秀才上来。可有卷子?
[生]卷子备有。
[净]这等,姑准收考,一视同仁。
[生跪介]千载奇遇。
[净念题介]"圣旨:'问汝多士,近闻金兵犯境,惟有和战守三策。其便何如?'"
[生叩头介]领圣旨。[起介]

Liu Mengmei:

(*Weeps*)

I've come all the way from Lingnan with my family. As I have no way out, I'll bump my head at the steps and die in front of you at once.

(*Tries to bump his head but is stopped by the attendant*)

Miao Shunbin:

(*Aside*)

This scholar looks like the Mr Liu I met before. He's a pearl of a man from the South Sea.

(*Turns to Liu Mengmei*)

Come forward, young scholar. Do you have the paper to write your answers?

Liu Mengmei:

Yes, I have.

Miao Shunbin:

Well, you are admitted to enter the examination and will be judged on the same footing as the other scholars.

Liu Mengmei:

(*Kneels*)

Once in a blue moon am I bestowed such a favour.

(*Reads the topic*)

"His Majesty decrees the topic: In face of the Jin invasion, which is the best policy, among appeasement, offence and defence?"

(*Kowtows*)

I've got the imperial topic.

(*Rises to his feet*)

Attendant:

[丑]东席舍去。[生写策介]

[净再将前卷细看介]头卷主战,二卷主守,三卷主和。主和的怕不中圣意。

[生交卷,净看介]呀,风檐寸晷,立扫千言。可敬,可敬。俺急忙难看。只说和战守三件,你主那一件儿?

[生]生员也无偏主。可战可守而后能和。如医用药,战为表,守为里,和在表里之间。

[净]高见,高见。则当今事势何如?

【马蹄花】

[生]当今呵,

宝驾迟留,

则道西湖昼锦游。

Go to the eastern section.

(*Liu Mengmei writes*)

Miao Shunbin:

(*Reads the three papers again*)

The first essay is in favour of appeasement, the second essay is in favour of defence, and the third is in favour of offence. I'm afraid that His Majesty won't like the idea of appeasement.

(*Liu Mengmei hands in his paper*)

Miao Shunbin:

(*Reads the paper*)

He's written a thousand words in the twinkling of an eye. Marvellous, marvellous! As I can't finish your paper in a glance, just tell me briefly what policy you are in favour of: appeasement, offence, or defence.

Liu Mengmei:

I'm not in favour of any particular policy. Either offence or defence will do, and then appeasement will also do. It's like a doctor prescribing the medicine. Offence can be used to cure outward symptoms, defence can be used to cure inward symptoms, and appeasement can be used to harmonise the two.

Miao Shunbin:

A wonderful idea! Simply wonderful! What do you think of the present situation?

Liu Mengmei:

(*To the tune of* **Matihua**)

His Majesty
>   Remains here
>   By the scenic West Lake,

为三秋桂子,
十里荷香,
一段边愁。
则愿的"吴山立马"那人休。
俺燕云唾手何时就?
若止是和呵,
小朝廷羞杀江南。
便战守呵,
请銮舆略近神州。
[净]秀才言之有理。
【前腔】
圣主垂旒,
想泣玉遗珠一网收。
对策者千余人,
那些不知时务,未晓天心,怎做儒流。
似你呵,
三分话点破帝王忧,
万言策检尽乾坤漏。
[生]小生岭南之士。
[净低介]知道了。
你钓竿儿拂绰了珊瑚,

> Where autumn cassias bloom
>
> And lotus flowers perfume,
>
> Mixed with worries for border war's sake.
>
> I hope that
>
> > The alien king should cease to expand,
> >
> > So that we can recover the lost land.
>
> If we adhere to appeasement,
>
> > The court will bear the shame henceforth;
> >
> > If we adhere to offence or defence,
> >
> > The court should move to the north.

Miao Shunbin:

Your comments are reasonable.

> (*To the previous tune*)
>
> His Majesty on the throne
>
> Would like to retrieve the lost zone.
>
> Over a thousand candidates have come to attend the imperial examination, but
>
> > Few understand the times
> >
> > Or know the imperial care;
> >
> > How can they be worthy scholars there?
>
> It is you alone that
>
> > Have come to the point
> >
> > And exhausted the urgent affair.

Liu Mengmei:

I'm from Lingnan.

Miao Shunbin:

> (*In a low voice*)

I know.

> From a scholar you have hoped to rise

敢今番着了鳌头。
秀才,午门外候旨。
[生应出,背介]这试官却是苗老大人。嫌疑之际,不敢相认。"且当青镜明开眼,惟愿朱衣暗点头。"
[生下]
[净]试卷俱已详定。左右跟随进呈去。[行介]"丝纶阁下文章静,钟鼓楼中刻漏长。"呀,那里鼓响?
[内急擂鼓介]
[丑]是枢密府楼前边报鼓。
[内马嘶介]
[净]边报警急。怎了,怎了?
[外扮老枢密上]"花萼夹城通御气。芙蓉小苑入边愁。"
[见介]

And will be awarded the first prize.

Scholar, wait outside the palace gate for the imperial decree.

Liu Mengmei:

(*Responds and retreats, aside*)

This examiner is Envoy Miao, but to avoid suspicion I have to keep my mouth shut.

"Outside the gate I'll wait for the decree;

I only hope the envoy will choose me."

(*Exit*)

Miao Shunbin:

I've finished marking all the papers. Attendants, make way to the court and I'll make a report to His Majesty.

(*Walks on, followed by the attendants*)

"It's quiet when I send in the report

While time draws on inside the court."

Well, where comes the beating of drums?

(*Rapid drum-beating within*)

Attendant:

The drum-beating comes from the War Ministry to announce the border conflict.

(*Neighing of horses within*)

Miao Shunbin:

There are urgent reports from the border-area. What's happened? What's happened?

(*Enter the elderly War Minister*)

War Minister:

"A walled alley leads to the court;

From War Ministry comes the war report."

(*Miao Shunbin and War Minister greet each other*)

[净]老先生奏边事而来?
[外]便是。先生为进卷而来?
[净]正是。
[外]今日之事,以缓急为先后,僭了。
[外叩头奏事介]掌管天下兵马知枢密院事臣谨奏俺主。
[内宣介]所奏何事?

【滴溜子】
[外]金人的、金人的风闻入寇。
[内]谁是先锋?
[外]李全的、李全的前来战斗。
[内]到什么地方了?
[外]报到了淮扬左右。
[内]何人可以调度?

Miao Shunbin:

Are you going to report the border conflict, sir?

War Minister:

Yes. Are you here to report the examination results?

Miao Shunbin:

Yes.

War Minister:

As my business is more urgent today, I have to report first. Excuse me.

(*Kowtows and reports*)

The War Minister is now reporting to Your Majesty.

Voice Within:

What do you want to report?

War Minister:

(*To the tune of Diliuzi*)

The Jin invaders,

The Jin invaders are launching an attack.

Voice Within:

Who is the vanguard?

War Minister:

Li Quan,

Li Quan is taking the lead.

Voice Within:

Where are they now?

War Minister:

It's said they've reached Huaiyang.

Voice Within:

Whom shall we dispatch for the defence?

War Minister:

[外]有杜宝现为淮扬安抚。
怕边关早晚休，要星忙厮救。
[净叩头奏事介]臣看卷官苗舜宾谨奏俺主。

【前腔】
临轩的、临轩的文章看就，
呈御览、呈御览定其卷首。
黄道日，传胪祗候。
众多官在殿头，
把琼林宴备久。
[内]奏事官午门外伺候。
[外、净同起介]
[净]老先生，听的金兵为何而动？
[外]适才不敢奏知。金主此行，单为来抢占西湖美景。
[净]痴鞑子，西湖是俺大家受用的。若抢了西湖去，这杭州通没用了。

Du Bao is now the Envoy of Huaiyang, but

As they cannot hold on for a long time,

We must send more troops at once.

Miao Shunbin:

(*Kowtows and reports*)

The imperial examiner Miao Shunbin is now reporting to Your Majesty.

(*To the previous tune*)

The papers,

The papers have been scored.

Your Majesty,

Your Majesty shall select the best.

It's an auspicious day

To proclaim the results.

Officials are waiting at the palace gate

For the celebration feast.

Voice Within:

Both of you, wait at the palace gate.

(*War Minister and Miao Shunbin rise to their feet*)

Miao Shunbin:

Do you know why the Jins launch the invasion, Sir?

War Minister:

I dared not mention it just now. The Jin emperor has come to grab the scenic area near the West Lake.

Miao Shunbin:

Those crazy aliens! The West Lake is for us to enjoy. If they should occupy the West Lake, the capital town Hangzhou would be useless for us.

Voice Within:

[内宣介]听旨：朕惟治天下，有缓有急，乃武乃文。今淮扬危急，便着安抚杜宝前去迎敌。不可有迟。其传胪一事，待干戈宁辑，偃武修文。可谕知多士。叩头。
[外、净叩头呼"万岁"起介]

[外]泽国江山入战图，
[净]曳裾终日盛文儒。
[外]多才自有云霄望，
[净]其奈边防重武夫。

Now listen to my decree: In my reign over the world, there are things urgent and less urgent and I should consider the military affairs as well as the civil affairs. Now that the Huaiyang areas are in danger, I order Envoy Du Bao to lose no time in fighting against the enemy. As to the proclamation of the examination results, it will be postponed to a time when the military actions are over and then we shall consider these civil affairs. My decree is to be made known to the public. Kowtow!

(*War Minister and Miao Shunbin kowtow, shout "Long live the emperor" and then rise to their feet*)

War Minister:

When national war affairs now prolong,

Miao Shunbin:

The scholars stick to reading all day long.

War Minister:

The gifted man expects brilliant success,

Miao Shunbin:

But border conflicts need scholars less.

第四十二出　移　镇

【夜游朝】

[外扮杜安抚引众上]西风扬子津头树,
望长淮渺渺愁予。
枕障江南,钩连塞北。
如此江山几处?
"砧声又报一年秋。江水去悠悠。塞草中原何处?一雁过淮楼。天下事,鬓边愁,付东流。不分吾家小杜,清时醉梦扬州。"自家淮扬安抚使杜宝。自到扬州三载,虽则李全骚扰,喜得大势平安。昨日打听边兵要来,下官十分忧虑。可奈夫人不解事,偏将亡女絮伤心。

Scene Forty-two
Military Transfer

(*Enter Du Bao, followed by attendants*)

Du Bao:

(*To the tune of* **Yeyouchao**)

When west winds shake the river trees,
The flowing waters make me ill at ease.
In shielding the south
Against the north,
Is there any better place?
"*The sound to pound the winter coat*
Dies with river waters that flow remote.
Where does the native country lie?
A wild goose flies past the tower of Huai.
The state affairs
That fill me with woe
Eastward flow.
I envy my ancestor poet Du,
Who dreamt with Yangzhou in view."

I'm Du Bao, Envoy of the Huaiyang area. Since I came here three years ago, Li Quan has been making disturbances but I've controlled the overall situation. When I learned yesterday that the invading troops were coming from the frontiers, I was deeply worried. However, my wife knew nothing about this and kept weeping for our departed daughter.

(*Enter Zhen, followed by Chunxiang*)

【似娘儿】
[老旦引贴上]夫主掣兵符，
也相从燕幙栖迟，
[叹介]画屏风外秦淮树。
看两点金焦，十分眉恨，片影江湖。
[老旦]相公万福。
[外]夫人免礼。
[老旦]相公:"几年别下南安路，春去秋来朝复暮。
[外]空怀锦水故乡情，不见扬州行乐处。
[老旦]你摩挲老剑评今古，那个英雄闲处住?
[泪介]
[合]忘忧恨自少宜男，泪洒岭云江外树。"
[老旦]相公，我提起亡女，你便无言。岂知俺心中

Zhen:

> (*To the tune of Sinianger*)
>
> My lord commands the army here,
>
> And brings me closer to the frontier.
>
> (*Sighs*)
>
> I see the Qinhuai trees beyond the screen,
>
> With Jin Hill and Jiao Isle in sight.
>
> I knit my brow
>
> At the sight that looms bright.
>
> Blessings on you, my lord.

Du Bao:

> Sit down, please, my lady.

Zhen:

> My lord,
>
> > "Ever since we left Nan'an,
> >
> > Several years have gone by.

Du Bao:

> > We vainly long for the native land
> >
> > While in Yangzhou pleasure is a far cry.

Zhen:

> > If you strike your sword and search,
> >
> > Is there an idle hero that meets your eye?
>
> (*Weeps*)

Du Bao, Zhen:

> > With no son to relieve our woe,
> >
> > Away from home we weep and sigh."

Zhen:

> You always keep silent whenever I mention our departed daughter. But can you imagine how sad I am? On the one hand, I'm

愁恨！一来为苦伤女儿，二来为全无子息。待趁在扬州寻下一房，与相公传后。尊意何如？

[外]使不得，部民之女哩。

[老旦]这等，过江金陵女儿可好？

[外]当今王事匆匆，何心及此。

[老旦]苦杀俺丽娘儿也！[哭介]

[净扮报子上]"诏从日月威光远，兵洗江淮杀气高。"禀老爷，有朝报。

[外起看报介]枢密院一本，为边兵寇淮事。奉圣旨：便着淮扬安抚使杜宝，刻日渡淮。不许迟误。钦此。呀，兵机紧急，圣旨森严。夫人，俺同你移镇淮安，就此起程也。

[丑扮驿丞上]"羽檄从参赞，牙签报驿程。"禀老爷，

sad for our departed daughter; on the other hand, I'm sad for the lack of an heir. I'll look for a concubine to bear a son for you. What do you think about it?

Du Bao:

No, that won't do. I can't take a concubine from my jurisdiction.

Zhen:

Then, how about having one from Jinling across the Yangtze?

Du Bao:

As I'm busy with my official business, how can I find the time for such things?

Zhen:

Oh, Liniang, my poor daughter!

(*Weeps*)

(*Enter Messenger A*)

Messenger A:

"*The imperial decree sheds its brilliant light*
To heighten spirits of warriors in their fight."

Your Excellency, here are instructions from the imperial court.

Du Bao:

(*Stands up and reads the instructions*)

Instructions from the War Ministry, concerning the invasions on the Huaiyang area. His Majesty decrees: "Envoy Du Bao of the Huaiyang areas is to be transferred to Huai'an without delay." With urgent military affairs comes this stern decree. My lady, we must set off for Huai'an at once.

(*Enter the stationmaster*)

Stationmaster:

"*The plumed letters are sent pile by pile;*

船只齐备。

[内鼓吹介][上船介][内禀"合属官吏候送",外分付"起去"介]

[外]夫人,又是一江秋色也。

【长拍】

　　天意秋初,天意秋初,金风微度,

　　城阙外画桥烟树。

　　看初收泼火,嫩凉生,微雨沾裾。

　　移画舸浸蓬壶。

　　报潮生风气肃,

　　浪花飞吐,

　　点点白鸥飞近渡。

　　风定也,落日摇帆映绿蒲,

　　白云秋窣的鸣箫鼓。

　　何处菱歌,唤起江湖?

[外]呀,岸上跑马的什么人?

The time is counted mile by mile."

Your Excellency, the ship is ready.

(*Sound of drums and pipes within. Du Bao, Zhen and their attendants board the ship.*)

Voice within:

All the local officials are here to see you off.

Du Bao:

Thank you, good-bye.

(*To Zhen*)

My lady, the river is again in its autumn best.

(*To the tune of Changpai*)

Autumn's just arrived,

Autumn's just arrived.

Here comes the gentle breeze

Over the painted bridge and misty trees.

The summer heat no longer hurts

And coolness starts to leave its trace

As a drizzle moistens our skirts.

Our ship is sailing in the scene of fairyland,

With rising tides, a chilling wind,

The spraying waves

And white gulls near at hand.

The wind has lulled, and at sunset

The ship's reflection quivers on the water

While sounds of drums and pipes rise to the clouds.

From where comes the country song

That draws me away from the madding crowds?

Look, who's galloping on the bank toward us?

(*Enter Messenger B on horseback*)

【不是路】
　　[末扮报子，跑马上]马上传呼，慢橹停船看羽书。
　　[外]怎的来?
　　[末]那淮安府，李全将次逞狂图。
　　[外]可发兵守御么?
　　[末]怎支吾?星飞调度凭安抚。
　　则怕这水路里耽延，你还走旱途。
　　[外]休惊惧。
　　夫人，吾当走马红亭路;
　　你转船归去、转船归去。
　　[老旦]咳，后面报马又到哩。
【前腔】
　　[丑扮报子上]万骑胡奴，
　　他要斩断长淮塞五湖。

Messenger B:

> (*To the tune of Bushilu*)
>
> I call out on horseback
>
> To anchor ships for plumed letters.

Du Bao:

> What does the letter say?

Messenger B:

> The Prefecture of Huai'an
>
> Is invaded by Li Quan.

Du Bao:

> Shall I send reinforcements?

Messenger B:

> How can they withstand the foe?
>
> You must deploy the troops tonight.
>
> As it's too slow to go by water,
>
> You'd better go by land to join the fight.

Du Bao:

> Do not fear,
>
> My lady,
>
> I'll go by land.
>
> You just turn back,
>
> Turn back.

Zhen:

> Well, another messenger's coming.
>
> (*Enter Messenger C*)

Messenger C:

> (*To the previous tune*)
>
> Ten thousand rebels on horseback
>
> Threaten to grab our native lands.

老爷快行,休迟误。
小的先去也。
怕围城缓急要降胡。[下]
[老旦哭介]待何如?
你星霜满鬓当戎虏,
似这烽火连天各路衢。
[外]真愁促,
怕扬州隔断无归路。
再和你相逢何处、相逢何处?
夫人,就此告辞了。扬州定然有警,可径走临安。
【短拍】
老影分飞,老影分飞,
似参军杜甫,
把山妻泣向天隅。
[老旦哭介]无女一身孤,
乱军中别了夫主。
[合]有什么命夫命妇,
都是些鳏寡孤独!

Please make haste, Your Excellency.

Do not delay,

I must take leave at once.

For fear that Huai'an will fall into rebels' hands.

(*Exit*)

Zhen:

(*Weeps*)

What will you do?

You'll fight the foes when your hair is grey,

When battle cries arise all along the way.

Du Bao:

What worries me

Is that the way to Yangzhou is cut off.

In that case, where shall we meet again,

Where shall we meet again?

I'm leaving now, my lady. If Yangzhou is in danger, you can go to Lin'an directly.

(*To the tune of Duanpai*)

The ageing man and wife depart,

The ageing man and wife depart,

Just as the poet Du Fu

Separated with his wife with a weeping heart.

Zhen:

(*Weeps*)

When my child is no more,

I must now send my lord to war!

Du Bao, Zhen:

Man and wife with rank and title

Are without child or spouse.

生和死，图的个梦和书。

【尾声】

[老旦]老残生两下里自支吾。

[外]俺做的是这地头军府。

[老旦]老爷也，珍重你这满眼兵戈一腐儒。[外下]

[老旦叹介]天呵，看扬州兵火满道。春香，和你径走临安去也。

隋堤风物已凄凉，
楚汉宁教作战场。
闺阁不知戎马事，
双双相趁下残阳。

Life and death

Come in dreams and word of mouth.

Zhen:

(*To the tune of Coda*)

I have to take my fate in my own hand;

Du Bao:

In this area I take command.

Zhen:

Take care, my lord,

Of your men and your own life.

(*Exit Du Bao*)

Zhen:

(*Sighs*)

Oh heavens! As Yangzhou seems to be aflame with battle fire, Chunxiang, let's go to Lin'an directly.

Bleak are the sights upon the canal dike;
The riversides are battlefields alike.
Ignorant of sounds of spear and gun,
We flee along the route of setting sun.

第四十三出　　御　淮

【六幺令】
　　[外引生、末、众扮军人上]西风扬噪，
漫腾腾杀气兵妖。
望黄淮秋卷浪云高。
排雁阵，展《龙韬》，
断重围杀过河阳道。
[外]走乏了！众军士，前面何处？
[众]淮城近了。
[外望介]天呵！"剩得江山一半，又被胡笳吹断。
[众]秋草旧长营，血风腥。
[外]听得猿啼鹤怨，泪湿征袍如汗。

Scene Forty-three
Military Defence

(*Enter Du Bao, followed by attendants in battle array*)

Du Bao, Attendants:

(*To the tune of* **Liuyaoling**)

With the wild west wind

Spreads the clamour of the battle cry,

While tides are surging to the sky.

The army is deployed

And tactics are employed

To have the foes destroyed.

Du Bao:

I'm exhausted by the march. Attendants, where are we now?

Attendants:

The city of Huai'an comes in sight.

Du Bao:

(*Looks ahead*)

Oh heavens!

"The remaining native lands

Will fall into alien hands.

Attendants:

The ancient battlefield

Smells of sanguine sword and shield.

Du Bao:

I hear the soldiers moan and groan,

With tears soaked to the bone.

[众]老爷呵!无泪向天倾,且前征。"
[外]众三军,俺的儿,你看咫尺淮城,兵势危急。俺们一边舍死先冲入城,一面奏请朝廷添兵救助。三军听吾号令,鼓勇而行。
[众哭应介]谨如军令。
【四边静】
　　[行介]坐鞍心把定中军号,
　　四面旌旗绕。
　　旗开日影摇,
　　尘迷日光小。
　　[合]胡兵气骄,
　　南兵路遥。
　　血晕几重围,
　　孤城怎生料!
　　[外]前面寇兵截路,冲杀前去。[合下]

Attendants:

Your Excellency,

It's not the time for tears;

We'll march and do away with fears."

Du Bao:

My men, my sons! Look, Huaiyang is near in sight and in imminent danger. Let's set death aside and break into the city. At the same time, I'll ask for reinforcement from the court. Now follow my command: beat the drums and advance!

Attendants:

(*In tears*)

Yes, advance!

Du Bao:

(*Walks on*)

(*To the tune of* **Sibianjing**)

I sit on the saddle and give command,

With banners on every hand.

The banners flutter left and right

And dim the sunlight.

Du Bao, Attendants:

The alien troops are full of pride;

The southern troops have had a tiring ride.

Besieged and bathed in blood,

What will happen to this town on our side?

Du Bao:

The alien bandits have blocked the way. Break our way through the enemy troops!

(*Exeunt all*)

(*Enter Li Quan, followed by his men and Lady Yang, yelling*)

【前腔】
[净引丑、贴扮众军喊上]李将军射雁穿心落,
豹子翻身嚼。
单尖宝灯挑,
把追风腻旗儿袅。
[合前]
[净笑介]你看俺溜金王手下,雄兵万余,把淮阴城围了七周遭。好不紧也!
[内擂鼓喊介]
[净]呀,前路兵风,想是杜安抚来到。分兵一千,迎杀前去。[虚下]
[外、众唱"合前"上,净众上打话,单战介]
[净叫众摆长阵拦路介]
[外叫"众军,冲围杀进城去"介]

Li Quan:

> (*To the previous tune*)
>
> I can shoot at the heart of flying geese;
>
> I can mount galloping steed.
>
> When I prick with my stirrup,
>
> My pennants flutter in the breeze.

Li Quan, Lady Yang, Soldiers:

> The alien troops are full of pride;
>
> The southern troops have had a tiring ride.
>
> Besieged and bathed in blood,
>
> What will happen to this town on our side?

Li Quan:

> (*Laughs*)

With my ten thousand soldiers, I've besieged the city with seven rings of troops. I think it's tight enough!

(*Drums and shouts within*)

Well, there are troops ahead. It must be Envoy Du and his men. I'll bring a thousand men to fight against him.

(*Li Quan, Lady Yang and soldiers go to the rear of the stage*)

(*Re-enter Du Bao and his attendants*)

Du Bao, Attendants:

> The alien troops are full of pride;
>
> The southern troops have had a tiring ride.
>
> Surrounded and bathed in blood,
>
> What will happen to this town on our side?

(*Li Quan, Lady Yang, Soldiers turn back to fight with Du Bao and his attendants. Li Quan and Du Bao fight. Li Quan and his men form a line to block the way. Du Bao calls on his men to break through and fight their way into the city*)

[净]呀，杜家兵冲入围城去了。且由他。吃尽粮草，自然投降也。

[合前][下]

【番卜算】

[老旦、末扮文官上]镇日阵云飘，
闪却乌纱帽。

[净、丑扮武官上]

[净]长枪大剑把河桥。

[丑]鼓角如龙叫。

[见介]请了。

[老旦]"枕淮楼，临海际。

[末]杀气腾天震地。

[丑]闻炮鼓，使人惊。插天飞不成。

Li Quan:

Alas, Du Bao and his men have fought their way into the city. Let them go. When their provisions come to an end, they will surrender in due time.

Li Quan, Lady Yang, Soldiers:

The alien troops are full of pride;

The southern troops have had a tiring ride.

Besieged and bathed in blood,

What will happen to this town on our side?

(*Exeunt*)

(*Enter two officials*)

Official A, Official B:

(*To the tune of* **Fanbusuan**)

The battle storm that swirls all day

Almost blows our official hats away.

(*Enter two officers*)

Officer A:

I guard the bridge with spear and sword;

Officer B:

The drums and horns sound like the dragon's roar.

(*The officials and the officers exchange greetings*)

Official A:

"Beside the river of Huai,

Not far from the sea,

Official B:

The battle cries resound in the sky.

Officer B:

The drums and guns

Terrify me.

[净]匣中剑,腰间箭,领取背城一战。
[合]愁地道,怕天冲。几时来杜公?"
[老旦]俺们是淮安府行军司马,和这参谋,都是文官。遭此贼兵围紧,久已迎接安抚杜老大人,还不见到。敢问二位留守将军,有何计策?
[丑]依在下所见,降了他罢。
[末]怎说这话?
[丑]不降,走为上计。
[老旦]走的一个,走不的十个。
[丑]这般说,俺小奶奶那一口放那里?
[净]锁放大柜子里。
[丑]钥匙哩?

I wish I could put on wings and flee.

Officer A:

With our swords,

With our arrows,

We'll fight to the last.

Officials, Officers:

We fear the tunnels;

We fear the armoured carts.

When shall we see Envoy Du?"

Official A:

We are officials in the Huai'an Prefecture. Besieged by the enemy troops, we've been waiting for Envoy Du for a long time, but he has not arrived yet. May I ask you generals for some advice?

Officer B:

In my opinion, we'd better surrender.

Official A:

How can you talk like this?

Officer B:

If we don't surrender, we'd better take escape.

Official A:

One out of ten can escape at the best.

Officer B:

In that case, what shall I do with my wife?

Official A:

Lock her in the wardrobe.

Officer B:

Where shall I put the key?

Officer A:

[净]放俺处。李全不来,替你托妻寄子。

[丑]李全来哩?

[净]替你出妻献子。

[丑]好朋友,好朋友!

[内擂鼓喊介]

[生扮报子上]报,报,报。正南一枝兵马,破围而来。杜老爷到也。

[众]快开城门迎接去。"天地日流血,朝廷谁请缨。"

[众并下]

【金钱花】

[外引众上]连天杀气萧条,萧条。

连城围了周遭,周遭。

风喇喇,阵旗飘。

叫开城,下吊桥。

Leave it to me. If Li Quan does not come, I'll take care of your wife and your son.

Officer B:

What if Li Quan comes?

Officer A:

I'll present them to him for you.

Officer B:

You're a friend in need! A friend indeed!

(*Drums and shouts within*)

(*Enter Messenger*)

Messenger:

Report, report, report! An army from the south has broken through the enemy lines. Envoy Du is coming!

Officials, Officers:

Let's open the city gate at once and meet His Excellency.

"*Blood is shedding day and night;*

Who's come to join the fight?"

(*Exeunt*)

(*Enter Du Bao, followed by attendants*)

Du Bao:

(*To the tune of* ***Jinqianhua***)

The battle cries soar to the sky,

To the sky.

The town is tightly besieged,

Tightly besieged.

The wind whistles;

The banners flutter.

Open the city gate

And let down the drawbridge!

[老旦等上]

[合]文和武,索迎着。

[老旦等跪介]文武官属,迎接老大人。

[外]起来,敌楼相见。

[老旦等应,起下]

【前腔】

[外]胡尘染惹征袍,征袍。

血花风腥宝刀,宝刀。

[内擂鼓介]淮安鼓,扬州箫。

摆鸾旗,登丽谯。

[合]排衙了,列功曹。[到介]

[贴扮办事官上]禀老爷升堂。

【粉蝶儿引】

[外]万里寄龙韬,

(*Enter the officials and the officers*)

Officials, Officers:

(*Kowtow*)

The local officials and officers are here to welcome Your Excellency.

Du Bao:

Stand up, please. I'll meet you in the city tower.

(*The officials and the officers respond, rise and exeunt*)

Du Bao:

(*To the previous tune*)

The dust has soiled my battle-robe,

My battle-robe.

The blood has stained my treasured sword,

My treasured sword.

(*Drums within*)

Amid Huai'an drums

And Yangzhou flutes,

I hoist the flag

And mount the city tower.

Du Bao, Attendants:

Meet in the hall

And talk to all.

(*Reach the city tower*)

(*Enter Clerk*)

Clerk:

Please take the chair, Your Excellency.

Du Bao:

(*To the tune of* **Fendieeryin**)

Miles and miles the troops go,

那得戍楼清啸？

[贴报门介]文武官属进。

[老旦等参见介]孤城累卵，方当万死之危；开府弄丸，来赴两家之难。凡俺官僚，礼当拜谢。

[外]兵锋四起，劳苦诸公，皆老夫迟慢之罪，只长揖便了。

[众应起揖介]

[外]看来此贼颇有兵机。放俺入城，其中有计。

[众]不过穿地道，起云梯，下官粗知备御。

[外]怕的是锁城之法耳。

[丑]敢问何谓锁城？是里面锁，外面锁？外面锁，锁住了溜金王；若里面锁，连下官都锁住了。

[外]不提起罢了。城中兵几何？

But how can I expel the foe?

Clerk:

(*Announces*)

Officials and officers, come in please.

(*Enter the officials and the officers*)

Officials, Officers:

(*Kneel to greet Du Bao*)

Our besieged city is in imminent danger. Your Excellency, an excellent warrior, has come to our rescue. The local officials and officers are most grateful to you.

Du Bao:

As I am slow in coming, you have suffered from all the trouble in the battles. Therefore, please accept my deep bow.

(*The officials and the officers respond, rise and return a bow*)

Du Bao:

It seems to me that this Li Quan is good at martial arts. He must be playing a trick by letting me break into the city.

Officials, Officers:

He will rely on no more than digging the tunnels or raising the ladders. We know something as to take precautions.

Du Bao:

I'm afraid he's trying to block the city.

Officer B:

May I ask what it means? Is he going to block from the inside or from the outside? To block from the outside, they'll block Gilded Prince out; to block from the inside, they block me in too.

Du Bao:

Forget about it for the moment. How many troops are there in

［净］一万三千。
［外］粮草几何？
［末］可支半年。
［外］文武同心，救援可待。
［内擂鼓喊介］
［生扮报子上］报，报，李全兵紧围了。
［外长叹介］这贼好无理也。

【划锹儿】
兵多食广禁围绕，
则要你文班武职两和调。
［众］巡城彻昏晓，
这军民苦劳。
［内喊介］［泣介］
［合］那兵风正号，
俺军声静悄。

the city?

Officer A:

Thirteen thousand troops.

Du Bao:

What are the provisions in the city?

Official B:

The provisions will last us half a year.

Du Bao:

As long as all the officials and officers are of one mind, we can hold out and wait for the reinforcement.

(*Drums and shouts within*)

(*Enter Messenger*)

Messenger:

Report, report! Li Quan's troops are closer to the city.

Du Bao:

(*With a long sigh*)

What a rascal!

(*To the tune of* **Chanqiaoer**)

With ample men and grain we can hold out,

But all of you must fight in one mind.

Officials, Officers:

We'll keep watch day and night,

With all our efforts combined.

(*Yells within*)

All:

(*Weep*)

Amid the alien yells,

Our silent hatred swells.

Du Bao:

[外拜天,众扶同拜介]泪洒孤城,把苍天暗祷。

【前腔】
　　[众]危楼百尺堪长啸,
　　筹边两字寄英豪。
　　[外]江淮未应小,
　　君侯佩刀。
　　[合前]
　　[外]从今日起,文官守城,武官出城,随机策应。
　　[丑]则怕大金家兵来了。
　　[外]金兵呵!

【尾声】
　　他看头势而来不定交,
　　休先倒折了赵家旗号。
　　便来呵,
　　也少不得死里求生那一着敲。

　　[净]日日风吹虏骑尘,

(*Kowtows to heavens while officials and officers join him*)

With our tears rolling down the wall,

We pray that heavens bless us all.

Officials, Officers:

(*To the previous tune*)

A good commander can expel the foes;

To guard the frontier depends on the heroes.

Du Bao:

As Yangzhou and Huaiyang are strategic parts,

We have to take arms with all our hearts.

All:

Amid the alien yells,

Our silent hatred swells.

Du Bao:

From now on, the officials shall defend the city walls while the officers shall go out to fight. You must support each other as the situation demands.

Officer B:

But I'm afraid the main forces of the Jins will come soon.

Du Bao:

As to the Jins,

(*To the tune of* **Coda**)

It's hard to say whether the Jins will come by now,

But you should not smear the banners of Zhao.

Even if they should come,

To fight to the end is our solemn vow.

Officer A:

The aliens run riot day by day,

Officer B:

[丑]三千犀甲拥朱轮。
[外]胸中别有安边计,
[众]莫遣功名属别人。

With three thousand troops on the way.

Du Bao:

I have my scheme to quell the foe,

Officials, Officers:

A feat that will always stay.

第四十四出　急　难

【菊花新】
[旦上]晓妆台圆梦鹊声高,
闲把金钗带笑敲。
博山秋影摇,
盼泥金俺明香暗焦。
"鬼魂求出世,贫落望登科。夫荣妻贵显,凝盼事如何?"俺杜丽娘跟随柳郎科试,偶逢天子招贤,只这些时还迟喜报。正是:"长安咫尺如千里,夫婿迢遥第一人。"

【出队子】
[生上]词场凑巧,
无奈兵戈起祸苗。
盼泥金赚杀玉多娇,
他待地窟里随人上九霄。

Scene Forty-four
Concern for Her Parents

(*Enter Du Liniang*)

Du Liniang:

    (*To the tune of* **Juhuaxin**)

    When magpies greet me for my happy dream,

    I tap my golden hairpins with a smile.

    The incense smoke coils in autumn breeze

    And makes me anxious for news all the while.

    "A ghost expects to gain a second life;

    A wretched scholar hopes to gain fame.

    An honoured husband makes a glorious wife,

    I do hope he indeed achieves his name."

I've come with my husband Mr Liu to attend the imperial examination. It happens to be the right time for His Majesty to select talented scholars, but the announcement has not been made yet. It is true to say,

    "*The court is a distant place to seek fame;*

    Will my husband gain his name?"

    (*Enter Liu Mengmei*)

Liu Mengmei:

    (*To the tune of* **Chuduizi**)

    I was lucky in the imperial exam,

    But news of war destroyed my dream.

    Awaiting news of my success at home,

    My wife expects the rise of my esteem.

一脉离魂,江云暮潮。
[见介]
[旦]柳郎,你回来了。望你高车昼锦,为何徒步而回?
[生]听俺道来:
【瓦盆儿】
去迟科试,
收场锁院散群豪。
[旦]咳,原来去迟了。
[生]喜逢着旧知交。
[旦]可曾补上?
[生]亏他满船明月又把去珠淘。
[旦喜介]好了。放榜未?
[生]恰正在奏龙楼,
开凤榜,
蹊跷……
[旦]怎生蹊跷?

Like a homeless soul,

She is adrift with the stream.

(*Greets Du Liniang*)

Du Liniang:

I'm glad you're back at last, Mr Liu. I expected you to come back in a grand carriage, but how is it that you come back on foot?

Liu Mengmei:

Now, listen to my explanation.

(*To the tune of* **Wapener**)

As I was late for the exam,

The gate was locked and scholars gone.

Du Liniang:

Oh, so you were late.

Liu Mengmei:

I happened to meet someone I knew.

Du Liniang:

Did he allow you to make up for the exam?

Liu Mengmei:

He picked me as another pearl that shone.

Du Liniang:

(*Delighted*)

Wonderful! Have you learned of the results?

Liu Mengmei:

When we waited outside the palace gate

For the announcement,

It happened...

Du Liniang:

What happened?

[生]你不知大金家兵起,杀过淮扬来了。
忙喇煞细柳营,权将杏苑抛,
刚则迟误了你夫人花诰。
[旦]迟也不争几时。则问你,淮扬地方,便是俺爹爹管辖之处了?
[生]便是。
[旦哭介]天也,俺的爹娘怎了![泣介]
[生]直恁的活擦擦、痛生生,
肠断了。
比如你在泉路里可心焦?
[旦]罢了。奴有一言,未忍启齿。
[生]但说不妨。
[旦]柳郎,放榜之期尚远,欲烦你淮扬打听爹娘消耗,未审许否?

Liu Mengmei:

Don't you know that the Jins are sending their armies to the Huaiyang area?

As the troops are busy with the war affair,

The scholars' business is put aside

And thus you are delayed to get your share.

Du Liniang:

It doesn't matter to be delayed for some time. By the way, you just mentioned Huaiyang. Is it the area where my father takes command?

Liu Mengmei:

Yes, it is.

Du Liniang:

(*In tears*)

Oh heavens, what's happened to my parents?

(*Weeps*)

Liu Mengmei:

You are nearly mad,

So sad

And depressed.

In the hell were you so distressed?

Du Liniang:

Forget about it. But there's something I hesitate to say.

Liu Mengmei:

Go on.

Du Liniang:

Mr Liu, as we have to wait a long time for the announcement, will you be kind enough to go to Huaiyang and try to find out about my parents?

[生]谨依尊命。奈放小姐不下。
　　[旦]不妨，奴家自会支吾。
　　[生]这等就此起程了。
【榴花泣】
　　[旦]白云亲舍，
俺孤影旧梅梢。
道香魂恁寂寥，
怎知魂向你柳枝销。
维扬千里，
长是一灵飘。
回生事少，
爹娘呵！听的俺活在人间惊一跳。
平白地凤婿过门，
好似半青天鹊影成桥。
【前腔】
　　[生]俺且行且止，
两处系心苗。
要留旅店伴多娇……
　　[旦]有姑姑为伴。
　　[生]阴人难伴你这冷长宵。

Liu Mengmei:

I'll be willing to, but I'm reluctant to leave you here.

Du Liniang:

Don't worry. I'll take care of myself.

Liu Mengmei:

Then, I'll be leaving in an instant.

Du Liniang:

(*To the tune of Liuhuaqi*)

My parents lived below the distant clouds

While I was buried under the plum tree.

Away from the crowds,

My soul was bent on thee.

Between Huaiyang and here,

My soul wandered to and fro.

I'm afraid they will be filled with fear,

Oh, Dad and Mom,

As resurrection is something they hardly know.

How can they expect a son-in-law,

Who marries their deceased daughter and comes to their door!

Liu Mengmei:

(*To the previous tune*)

To go or not to go,

I'm in two minds.

My desires to stay with me dear wife grow.

Du Liniang:

I have Sister Stone to keep me company.

Liu Mengmei:

A nun won't help you spend the long cold night;

把心儿不定，还怕你旧魂飘。
[旦]再不飘了。
[生]俺文高中高，
怕一时榜下归难到。
[旦泣介]俺爹娘呵！
[生]你念双亲舍的离情，
俺为半子怎惜攀高。
小姐，卑人拜见岳翁岳母，起头便问及回生之事了。

【渔家灯】
[旦叹介]说的来似怪如妖，
怕爹爹执古妆乔。
[想介]有了，将奴春容带在身傍。
但见了一幅春容，
少不的问俺两下根苗。
[生]问时怎生打话？
[旦]则说是天曹，
偶然注定的姻缘到，

>   I'm afraid you'll change your mind
>
>   And wander again like a sprite.

Du Liniang:

>   I won't.

Liu Mengmei:

>   In the exam I wrote the best essay;
>
>   I'm afraid I'll miss the announcement day.

Du Liniang:

>   (*Weeps*)
>
>   Oh, Dad and Mom!

Liu Mengmei:

>   In view of your deep love for your parents,
>
>   I'm ready to meet them as a son-in-law.

My dear, as soon as I meet your parents, the first thing they'll mention is how you came back to life again.

Du Liniang:

>   (*Sighs*)
>
>   (*To the tune of* **Yujiadeng**)
>
>   As it seems to be a fantastic tale,
>
>   My dad might not believe what you say.
>
>   (*Ponders for a moment*)

Well, I have an idea. Bring my portrait with you.

>   When they see my portrait,
>
>   They'll ask about you and me right away.

Liu Mengmei:

What shall I say then?

Du Liniang:

>   You just say that it's our fate
>
>   To be man and wife

蓦踏着墓坟开了。
[生]说你先到俺书斋才好。
[旦羞介]休乔，这话教人笑。
略说与梅香贼牢。

【前腔】
[生]俺满意儿待驸马过门，
和你离魂女同归气高。
谁承望探高亲去傍干戈，
怕寒儒欠整衣毛。
[旦]女婿老成些不妨。则途路孤恓，使奴挂念。
[生]秋霄，云横雁字斜阳道，
向秦淮夜泊魂销。
[旦]夫，你去时冷落些，回来报中状元呵……
[生]名标，大拜门喧笑，
抵多少驸马还朝。

And you opened the grave for me.

Liu Mengmei:

I should say you came to my study first.

Du Liniang:

I don't agree.

You'll make them laugh at me,

But you can hint at it to Chunxiang.

Liu Mengmei:

(*To the previous tune*)

I hoped to go with you in carriage and four

And see them as a man of renown;

But now I'll go in times of war

And wear a shabby gown.

Du Liniang:

It doesn't matter for a son-in-law plainly to be dressed. I'm only worrying about your lonely trip.

Liu Mengmei:

At autumn dusk,

The wild geese are on a returning flight.

On Qinhuai River I'll spend the lonely night.

Du Liniang:

My lord, this might be a lonely trip, but when you come back ranking first in the imperial examination...

Liu Mengmei:

What a splendour then!

It'll make a grand show

When I meet them again.

(*Enter Sister Stone*)

Sister Stone:

[净上]"雨伞晴兼雨，春容秋复春。"包袱雨伞在此。

【尾声】
[拜别介]
[旦]秀才郎探的个门楣着。
[生]报重生这欢声不小。
[旦]柳郎，那里平安了便回，
休只顾的月明桥上听吹箫。

[生]不为经时谒丈人，
[旦]囊无一物献尊亲。
[生]马蹄渐入扬州路，
[旦]两地各伤无限神。

"*As the umbrella shelters sun and rain,*
So the portrait endures autumn and spring."

Here's the parcel and umbrella for you.

(*Liu Mengmei and Du Liniang take leave of each other*)

Du Liniang:

(*To the tune of* **Coda**)

You're going to the family of Du;

Liu Mengmei:

At the news of your revival, great joy will ensue.

Du Liniang:

Mr Liu, come back as soon as things are settled there.

Don't let the Yangzhou music detain you.

Liu Mengmei:

To Du's family a scholar will go,

Du Liniang:

Without a precious gift to show.

Liu Mengmei:

On the lonely trip to Yangzhou,

Du Liniang:

Both man and wife are filled with woe.

第四十五出　　寇　间

【包子令】
　　[老旦、外扮贼兵巡哨上]大王原是小喽啰,喽啰。
娘娘原是小旗婆,旗婆。
立下个草朝忒快活,
亏心又去抢山河。
[合]转巡罗,山前山后一声锣。
兄弟,大王爷攻打淮城,要个人见杜安抚打话。大路头影儿没一个,小路头寻去。[唱前合下]

Scene Forty-five
The Bandits' Wily Scheme

(*Enter two bandit sentries, patrolling here and there*)

Sentry A:

(*To the tune of Baoziling*)

Our prince came from the rank and file,

The rank and file.

His wife was once a female courier,

A female courier.

Not content with their rule on the mount,

They start to grab more land on no account.

Sentry A, Sentry B:

Up and down the hill we're on patrol;

We strike the gongs to play our role.

Sentry A:

Brother, our prince is besieging the city of Huai'an and he wants to find someone to bring a message to Envoy Du. As there's not a single shadow on the highway, let's turn to the byways.

Sentry A, Sentry B:

Up and down the hill we're on patrol,

We strike the gongs to play our role.

(*Exeunt*)

(*Enter Chen Zuiliang, bearing an umbrella and a parcel*)

Chen Zuiliang:

(*To the tune of Zhumating*)

【驻马听】
[末雨伞、包袱上]家舍南安,
有道为生新失馆。
要腰缠十万,
教学千年,
方才满贯。
俺陈最良为报杜小姐之事,扬州见杜安抚大人。谁知他淮安被围,教俺没前没后。大路上不敢行走,抄从小路而去。
学先师传食走胡旋,
怯书生避寇遭涂炭。
你看树影凋残,
猿啼虎啸教人叹。
[老、外上]"明知山有虎,故向虎边行。"乌汉那里去?[拿介]
[末]饶命,大王。
[外]还有个大王哩。
[末]天,天怎了!正是:"乌鸦喜鹊同行,吉凶全然未保。"

I used to teach in Nan'an,
But I've lost my position there.
If I want to be a millionaire,
I have to teach a thousand years.
To get my share.

I, Chen Zuiliang, am on my way to Yangzhou to report to Envoy Du on Miss Du's affairs. But who knows that he's besieged in Huai'an with the result that I have nowhere to turn to. As it's too dangerous on the highway, I'll go along the byways.

Like Confucius who wandered here and there,
I am a scholar who lives in worry and care.
When tree shadows meet my eye,
The wails of apes and tigers make me sigh.

(*Enter the two bandit sentries*)

Sentry A:

"*Aware of tigers in the hill,
He goes to the den with a stubborn will.*"
Where are you going, old guy?

(*The sentries catch hold of Chen Zuiliang*)

Chen Zuiliang:

Mercy on me, rebel king!

Sentry B:

There's another king here!

Chen Zuiliang:

On, heavens! As the saying goes,
"*With crows and magpies in the sky,
Who knows if I'll live or die!*"

(*Exit Chen Zuiliang with the sentries*)

[并下]

【普贤歌】

[净、丑众上]莽乾坤生俺贼儿顽,
谁道贼人胆里单!
南朝俺不蛮,
北朝俺不番。
甚天公有处安排俺?
[净]娘娘,俺和你围了淮安许时,只是不下。要得个人去淮安打话,兼看杜安抚动定如何。则眼下无人可使哩。
[丑]必得杜老儿亲信之人,将计就计,方才可行。

【粉蝶儿】

[外绑末上]没路走羊肠,
天、天呵,撞入这屠门怎放![见介]
[外]禀大王,拿的个南朝汉子在此。
[净]是个老儿。何方人氏?作何生理?
[末]听禀:

(*Enter Li Quan, followed by Lady Yang and his men*)

Li Quan:

(*To the tune of Puxiange*)

When I become a bandit head,

Who says that I'm full of dread?

Although I'm alien to the south

And foreign to the north,

The heaven has reserved my bed.

My lady, we've besieged Huai'an for quite some time, but haven't conquered it yet. We'd better find someone to bring a message there and find out what Envoy Du is up to. But I have no idea as to whom to send.

Lady Yang:

The man must know old Envoy Du well and can cope with the situation.

(*Enter Chen Zuiliang, tied up and led by Sentry B*)

Chen Zuiliang:

(*To the tune of Fendieer*)

I got caught on the byway;

Oh, heavens!

In the butcher's house what could I say?

Sentry B:

(*Greets Li Quan*)

My lord, we've captured a man from the south.

Li Quan:

Well, it's an old guy. Where are you from? What is your trade?

Chen Zuiliang:

Now, listen,

(*To the tune of Dayagu*)

【大迓鼓】
　　　　生员陈最良，
　　　　南安人氏，访旧淮扬。
[净]访谁？
[末]便是杜安抚。
他后堂曾设扶风帐。
[丑]你原来他衙中教学。几个学生？
[末]则他甄氏夫人，单生下一女。
女书生年少亡。
[丑]还有何人？
[末]义女春香，夫人伴房。
[丑笑背介]一向不知杜老家中事体。今日得知，吾有计矣。[回介]这腐儒，且带在辕门外去。
[众应，押末下介]
[丑]大王，奴家有了一计。昨日杀了几个妇人，可于中取出首级二颗。则说杜家老小，回至扬州，被

I, Chen Zuiliang,

A scholar from Nan'an,

Am going to visit a friend in Huaiyang.

Li Quan:

Who is it?

Chen Zuiliang:

It's Envoy Du.

I used to teach in his home.

Lady Yang:

So you were a tutor in his home. How many pupils did you teach?

Chen Zuiliang:

His wife Lady Zhen gave birth to a single daughter.

Dead and gone was his daughter Du Liniang.

Lady Yang:

Who else is there in his family?

Chen Zuiliang:

His adopted daughter,

A former maid by the name of Chunxiang.

Lady Yang:

(*Sniggers aside*)

I've never heard about old Du's family affairs. Now that I get to know of it, I've a scheme ready.

(*To the attendants*)

Take this pedant outside the camp.

(*The attendants respond and take Chen Zuiliang off stage*)

My lord, I've conceived a scheme. As we killed some women yesterday, we can pick out two heads and say that they are the heads of Du's womenfolk, presented by my men and killed

俺手下杀了。献首在此。故意苏放那腐儒，传示杜老。杜老心寒，必无守城之意矣。
[净]高见，高见。
[净起低声分付介]叫中军。
[生扮上]
[净]俺请那腐儒讲话中间，你可将昨日杀的妇人首级二颗来献，则说是杜安抚夫人甄氏和他使女春香。牢记着。
[生应下]
[净]左右，再拿秀才来见。
[众押末上介]
[末]饶命，大王。
[净]你是个细作，不可轻饶。
[丑]劝大王松了他，听他讲些兵法到好。
[净]也罢。依娘娘说，松了他。
[众放末缚介]

on their way back to Yangzhou. Then we'll let the pedant go and pass the word to old Du. Overcome by grief, he will lose his heart in defending the city.

Li Quan:

A good idea! A good idea!

(*Rises to his feet and speaks in a low voice*)

Call my adjutant.

(*Enter the adjutant*)

Li Quan:

(*To the adjutant*)

When I speak with the pedant, you just come in to present two heads of the women killed yesterday and say that they are the heads of Lady Zhen and her maid Chunxiang. Do as I tell you.

(*Exit the adjutant after a response*)

Li Quan:

Now bring the pedant in.

(*Enter Chen Zuiliang, escorted by the attendants*)

Chen Zuiliang:

Mercy on me, my lord!

Li Quan:

I won't spare a spy of your sort.

Lady Yang:

Won't you unbind him and let him speak something on the art of war, my lord?

Li Quan:

In that case, do as you say and let him loose.

(*The attendants let loose of Chen Zuiliang*)

Chen Zuiliang:

(*Kowtows*)

[末叩头介]叩谢大王、娘娘不杀之恩。

[净]起来,讲些兵法俺听。

[末]卫灵公问陈于孔子,孔子不对。说道:"吾未见好德如好色者也。"

[净]这是怎么说?

[末]则因彼时卫灵公有个夫人南子同座,先师所以怕得讲话。

[净]他夫人是南子,俺这娘娘是妇人。

[内擂鼓,生扮报子上介]报,报,报!扬州路上兵马,杀了杜安抚家小,径来献首级讨赏。

[净看介]则怕是假的。

[生]千真万真。夫人甄氏,这使女叫做春香。

Thank you, my lord and my lady, for sparing me my life.

Li Quan:

Stand up and say something about the art of war.

Chen Zuiliang:

When Duke Ling of Wei asked Confucius about the deployment of troops, Confucius refused to answer the question but said, "I've never met anyone whose desire for virtue is as strong as his sexual desire."

Li Quan:

What does he mean?

Chen Zuiliang:

As Duke Ling's wife was present, Confucius would not like to speak.

Li Quan:

His wife's name Nanzi sounded like a man's, but my wife is a woman.

(*Drums within*)

(*Enter the messenger*)

Messenger:

Report, report! Our troops to Yangzhou killed the womenfolk of Envoy Du. They've come to present the heads for a reward.

Li Quan:

(*Looks carefully at the heads*)

I'm afraid they are not the heads of Envoy Du's womenfolk.

Messenger:

They are as true as can be. His wife is Lady Zhen, and his maid is Chunxiang.

Chen Zuiliang:

[末做看认,惊哭介]天呵,真个是老夫人和春香也。
[净]咦,腐儒啼哭什么!还要打破淮城,杀杜老儿去。
[末]饶了罢,大王。
[净]要饶他,除非献了这座淮安城罢。
[末]这等容生员去传示大王虎威,立取回报。
[丑]大王恕你一刀,腐儒快走。
[内擂鼓发喊,开门介][末作怕介]

【尾声】
　　显威风、记的这溜金王。
[净、丑]你去说与杜安抚呵,
着什么耀武扬威早纳降。
俺实实的要展江山、非是谎。[下]

(*Looks at the heads and wails in astonishment*)

Oh heavens! This is Lady Zhen's head and that is Chunxiang's head!

Li Quan:

Tush, none of your wailing, old pedant! We'll soon break through the city of Huai'an to kill old Du as well.

Chen Zuiliang:

Please have mercy on him, my lord!

Li Quan:

I won't spare him unless he gives up the city of Huai'an.

Chen Zuiliang:

Will you please let me bring your words to him and report to you in no time?

Lady Yang:

If you want to save your neck, old pedant, get out of here at once!

(*Drums and shouts within. The gate is opened*)

Chen Zuiliang:

(*In terror*)

(*To the tune of* **Coda**)

The mighty Gilded Prince

Will always linger on my mind.

Li Quan, Lady Yang:

Go and tell Envoy Du

To surrender and leave his airs behind.

We're bound to grab more land,

With manoeuvres well designed.

(*Exeunt*)

Chen Zuiliang:

[末打躬送介]

[吊场]活强盗,活强盗。杀了杜老夫人、春香。不免城中报去。

海神东过恶风回,
日暮沙场飞作灰。
今日山翁旧宾主,
与人头上拂尘埃。

(*Bows to see them off*)

Sheer robbers and bandits! They've killed Lady Zhen and Chunxiang. I'll bring the news to Huai'an.

The sea god blows an ill wind to the east

And swirls dusts when the sun sets in the west.

The present envoy is my former host,

Who'll honour me as his distinguished guest.

第四十六出　　折寇

【破阵子】
[外戎装佩剑，引众上]接济风云阵势，
侵寻岁月边陲。
[内擂鼓喊介]
[外叹介]你看虎咆般炮石连雷碎，
雁翅似刀轮密雪施。
李全，李全，你待要霸江山、吾在此。
"谁能谈笑解重围？万里胡天鸟不飞。今日海门南畔事，满头霜雪为兵机。"我杜宝自到淮扬，即遭兵乱。孤城一片，困此重围。只索调度兵粮，飞扬金鼓。生还无日，死守由天。潜坐敌楼之中，追想

Scene Forty-six
Outwitting the Bandits

(*Enter Du Bao, fully armoured and bearing a sword, followed by his attendants*)

Du Bao:

(*To the tune of Pozhenzi*)

In various formations I deploy the troop;

To guard the frontiers I shall never stoop.

(*Drums and shouts within*)

Du Bao:

(*With a sigh*)

Like thunder the cannons roared;

Like whirling snow flashes the sword.

Li Quan, Li Quan,

To grab the land,

You have to grab it from my hand.

"Who can break through the siege in tease?

In the northern sky not a single bird flees.

Since rebels started skirmish in despair,

The worries for the war have greyed my hair."

Since I, Du Bao, arrived in Huai'an, I have been involved in a warfare. The city has been completely isolated and heavily besieged. As I can do nothing but manage the provisions and keep up the morale, I cherish no hope of returning alive and entrust the survival of the city to the heavens. Now that I sit upon the city tower, I cannot but think of the fall of the former

靖康而后。中原一望,万事伤心。

【玉桂枝】
问天何意:
有三光不辨华夷,
把腥膻吹换人间,
这望中原做了黄沙片地?
[恼介]猛冲冠怒起,猛冲冠怒起,
是谁弄的,江山如是?
[叹介]中原已矣,
关河困,心事违。
也则愿保扬州,济淮水。
俺看李全贼数万之众,破此何难?进退迟疑,其间有故。
俺有一计可救围,
恨无人与游说。
[内擂鼓介]
[净扮报子上]"羽檄场中无雁到,鬼门关上有人来。"好笑,城围的铁桶似紧,有秀才来打秋风,则索报

capital and grieve at the sight of the lost territory.

(*To the tune of* **Yuguizhi**)

Oh heavens, what do you mean

By showing favour to the alien tribe?

The stink of mutton is hard to describe;

The desert sands are here to be seen.

(*Annoyed*)

How my anger rises!

How my anger rises!

Who is to blame

To bring our land to shame?

(*Sighs*)

Our central plains are in alien hands at last!

Entrapped in siege

And devoid of hope,

I'll still defend Yangzhou

And Huai River in my scope.

With tens of thousands of troops, I don't think it difficult for Li Quan to break our defence. There must be some reason for him to be hesitating.

To break the siege I have a plan,

But I fail to find a suitable man.

(*Drums within*)

(*Enter a messenger*)

Messenger:

"*On the battlefield no wild geese dwell,*

But a man has come from Hell."

Funny indeed that a scholar has penetrated the siege and come to pay tribute to his patron. I'll make a report all the same.

去。禀老爷：有个故人相访。

[外]敢是奸细？

[净]说是江右南安府陈秀才。

[外]这迂儒怎生飞的进来？快请见。

【浣溪沙】

[末上]摆旌旗，添景致，

又不是闹元宵鼓炮齐飞。

杜老爷在那里？

[外出笑迎介]忽闻的千里故人谁？

[叹介]原来是先生到此。教俺惊垂泪。

[末]老公相头通白了。

[合]白首相看俺与伊，三年一见愁眉。

[拜介]

Your Excellency, a former acquaintance of yours is at the gate.

Du Bao:

Would he be a spy?

Messenger:

He says that he's Mr Chen, a scholar from Nan'an Prefecture in the south.

Du Bao:

How can a pedant like him break through the siege? Show him in at once.

(*Enter Chen Zuiliang*)

Chen Zuiliang:

(*To the tune of* **Huanxisha**)

The battle-flags provide a good display.

It's not the Lantern Festival now,

But firecrackers crackle away.

Where is Lord Du?

Du Bao:

(*Comes out to welcome Chen Zuiliang with a smile*)

Which distant friend appears?

(*Sighs*)

Oh, it's you, Mr Chen.

Your arrival startles me into tears.

Chen Zuiliang:

Your hair has turned completely grey, Lord Du.

Du Bao, Chen Zuiliang:

Two worried grey-heads

Meet again after three years.

(*They greet each other*)

Chen Zuiliang:

[末]"头白乘驴悬布囊,
[外]故人相见忆山阳。
[末]横塘一别千余里,
[外]却认并州作故乡。"
[末]恭念公相,又苦伤老夫人回扬州,被贼兵所算了。
[外惊介]怎知道?
[末]生员在贼营中,眼同验过老夫人首级,和春香都杀了。
[外哭介]天呵!痛杀俺也!

【玉桂枝】
相夫登第,
表贤名甄氏吾妻。
称皇宣一品夫人,
又待伴俺立双忠烈女。
想贤妻在日,想贤妻在日,
凄然垂泪,俨然冠帔。

"A donkey ride is hard for a grey-head;

Du Bao:

This meeting makes me think of olden days.

Chen Zuiliang:

With a thousand li and more to tread,

Du Bao:

I now take Nan'an for my native place."

Chen Zuiliang:

Lord Du, you always linger on my mind, but I do feel sorry that Lady Zhen on her way back to Yangzhou was captured and killed by the bandits.

Du Bao:

(*Startled*)

How did you get to know it?

Chen Zuiliang:

I saw with my own eyes her head in the bandit camp; Chunxiang has been killed as well.

Du Bao:

(*Wails*)

Oh heavens! How my heart pains!

(*To the tune of* **Yuguizhi**)

You have shared my name and fame,

My lady, my dearest wife!

You deserve the highest claim,

A worthy mate all through your life.

When I recall our marital years,

Our marital years,

You seem to stand before me

And my eyes are filled with tears.

[外哭倒，众扶介]
[末]我的老夫人，老夫人怎了！你将官们也大家哭一声儿么？
[众哭介]老夫人呵！
[外作恼拭泪介]呀，好没来由！夫人是朝廷命妇，骂贼而死，理所当然。我怎为他乱了方寸，灰了军心？
身为将，怎顾的私？
任恓惶，百无悔。
陈先生，溜金王还有话么？
[末]不好说得，他还要杀老先生。
[外]咳，他杀俺甚意儿？
俺杀他全为国。
[末]依了生员，两下都不要杀。[做扯外耳语介]那溜金王要这座淮安城。
[外]喋声！那贼营中是一个座位，是两个座位？

(*Faints as he wails and is helped to his feet by the attendants*)

Chen Zuiliang:

Oh respectful lady, respectful lady! How can you come to this! Join me in weeping, officers and officials!

All:

Oh, respectful lady!

Du Bao:

(*Wipes off his tears in irritation*)

Well, I shouldn't have acted like this! My wife is a lady of an honoured title. It befits her to die cursing the enemy. How can I lose control of my temper and cause disturbance among my men?

As the commander,

I'll do away with my private woe.

Come what may,

I'll sustain the blow.

What did the Gilded Prince say, Mr Chen?

Chen Zuiliang:

His words are beyond mentioning. He said that he'd kill you.

Du Bao:

Oops!

Why does he want to take my life?

I'll kill him for the national strife.

Chen Zuiliang:

In my opinion, there's no sense in all the killings.

(*Whispers in Du Bao's ears*)

The Gilded Prince intends to occupy the city of Huai'an.

Du Bao:

Shut up! Tell me whether there's one seat or two seats in his

[末]他和妻子连席而坐。
[外笑介]这等,吾解此围必矣。先生竟为何来?
[末]老先生不问,几乎忘了。为小姐坟儿被盗,径来相报。
[外惊介]天呵!冢中枯骨,与贼何仇?都则为那些宝玩害了也。贼是谁?
[末]老公相去后,道姑招了个岭南游棍柳梦梅为伴。见物起心,一夜劫坟逃去。尸骨丢在池水中。因此不远千里而告。
[外叹介]女坟被发,夫人遭难。正是:"未归三尺土,难保百年身。既归三尺土,难保百年坟。"也索罢了,则可惜先生一片好心。

camp?

Chen Zuiliang:

He sits side by side with his wife.

Du Bao:

(*Laughs*)

In that case, I'm sure that I can lift this siege. But may I ask why you came all the way here?

Chen Zuiliang:

If you hadn't reminded me, I nearly forgot about it. I've come all way to report to you that your daughter's grave was robbed.

Du Bao:

(*Taken aback*)

Oh, heavens! Her dried bones in the grave couldn't have offended the robbers. They must have come for the buried treasures. Who were the robbers?

Chen Zuiliang:

After you had left, the nun took in a vagabond from Lingnan, Liu Mengmei, as her companion. With greed for the treasures, they robbed the grave and escaped by the night, casting her remains in the pond. That's why I went all the way to report to you.

Du Bao:

(*With a sigh*)

My daughter's grave was robbed and my wife was killed. As the saying goes,

"*It's hard to live a safe life*

Before you are buried.

It's harder still to keep a safe grave

After you are buried."

There's nothing we can do about it. But I must thank you all

[末]生员拜别老公相后,一发贫薄了。
[外叹介]军中仓卒,无以为情。我把一大功劳,先生干去。
[末]愿效劳。
[外]我久写下咫尺之书,要李全解散三军之众。余无可使,烦公一行。左右,取过书仪来。倘说得李全降顺,便可归奏朝廷,自有个出身之处。
[杂取书礼介]"儒生三寸舌,将军一纸书。"书仪在此。
[末]途费谨领。送书一事,其实怕人。
[外]不妨。

【榴花泣】
兵如铁桶,
一使在其中。
将折简、去和戎。
陈先生,

the same for your kindness.

Chen Zuiliang:

Since you left me, my life has gone from bad to worse.

Du Bao:

As I'm now in the camp, I've got no gift for you. However, I'll give you a chance to do some service.

Chen Zuiliang:

I'm ready at your service.

Du Bao:

I've written a short letter to demand Li Quan to dismiss his army, but I haven't found a suitable messenger yet. Will you go on the errand? Attendants, fetch the letter. If you can persuade Li Quan into surrender, I'll report your meritorious deeds to the court and you will be offered a position.

Attendant:

(*Brings in the letter and money*)

"*The scholar wags his tongue;*
The general writes his letter."

Here's the letter and the travel fare.

Chen Zuiliang:

Thank you for the money, but this errand is risky indeed.

Du Bao:

Set your heart at ease.

(*To the tune of Liuhuaqi*)

Through the tightest blockade

The scholar will go.

With a letter from me,

He will appease the foe.

Mr Chen,

你志诚打的贼儿通。
虽然寇盗奸雄,
他也相机而动。
[末]恐游说非书生之事。
[外]看他开围放你来,其意可知。
你这书生正好做传书用。
[末]仗恩台一字长城,
借寒儒八面威风。[内鼓吹介]

【尾声】
戍楼羌笛话匆匆。
事成呵,你归去朝廷沾寸宠,
这纸书敢则是保障江淮第一封。

[外]隔河征战几归人?
[末]五马临流待幕宾。
[外]劳动先生远相访,
[末]恩波自会惜枯鳞。

I'm sure you'll convince the foe,

For, wicked as they are,

They'll change with the ebb and flow.

Chen Zuiliang:

Scholars are not good at appeasement.

Du Bao:

You know, as he let you through the blockade, he had his ulterior motives.

To bring the message, you are the suitable man.

Chen Zuiliang:

With your letter to defeat the foe,

I'll be as dignified as I can.

(*Drums and bugles within*)

Du Bao:

(*To the tune of* **Coda**)

On the watchtower our meeting is brief.

When you succeed,

You'll be an honoured man.

This letter will bring

Safety to the city of Huai'an.

Du Bao:

Few soldiers come back from the battlefield

Chen Zuiliang:

When the prefect comes to meet his men.

Du Bao:

Your mission will foretell a bumper yield;

Chen Zuiliang:

I hope I'll be lucky in the bandit den.

第四十七出　　围　释

【出队子】

[贴扮通事上]一天之下,
南北分开两事家。
中间放着个蓼儿洼,
明助着番家打汉家。
通事中间,拨嘴撩牙。

事有足诧,理有必然。自家溜金王麾下一名通事便是。好笑,好笑,俺大王助金围宋,攻打淮城。谁知北朝暗地差人去到南朝讲话!正是:"暂通禽兽语,终是犬羊心。"[下]

【双劝酒】

[净引众上]横江虎牙,
插天鹰架。
擂鼓扬旗,
冲车甲马。

Scene Forty-seven
Lifting the Siege

(*Enter the interpreter*)

Interpreter:

(*To the tune of Chuduizi*)

Under the selfsame sky,

A war begins between north and south.

A bandit gang lies in between,

Helping the aliens fight the Hans.

As an interpreter,

I meddle with disputes with my mouth.

Where there is a dispute, there is a root. I am an interpreter under Gilded Prince. It's ridiculous that our chieftain should assist the Jins to besiege the Hans and attack the city of Huai'an while the Jins sent secret envoys to negotiate with the southerners. The saying is true indeed,

"Even if you speak the words of the beast,

You don't understand them in the least."

(*Exit*)

(*Enter Li Quan followed by his men*)

Li Quan:

(*To the tune of Shuangquanjiu*)

Across the river camps lie

While towering racks rise to the sky.

Amid sounding drums and waving flags,

Our armoured steeds and vehicles ally.

把座锦城墙、围的阵云花。

杜安抚、你有翅难加。

自家溜金王。攻打淮城，日久未下。外势虽然虎踞，中心未免狐疑。一来怕南朝大兵兼程策应，二来怕北朝见责委任无功：真个进退两难。待娘娘到来计议。

[丑上]"驱兵捉将蚩尤女，捏鬼妆神豹子妻。"大王，你可听见大金家有人南朝打话，回到俺营门之外了？

[净]有这事？

[老旦扮番将带刀骑马上]

【北夜行船】

大北里宣差传站马，

虎头牌滴溜的分花。

[外扮马夫赶上介]滑了，滑了。

[老旦]那古里谁家？跑番了拽喇。

We have besieged the town,

Ready to bring it down.

Envoy Du,

Even if you have wings, we'll catch you.

I am the Gilded Prince. For days we've been attacking the city of Huai'an, but without success. I put up a fierce appearance, but I'm filled with doubts within my heart. On the one hand, I'm afraid that there will be reinforcements from the south; on the other hand, I'm afraid that there will be reprimands from the north. Caught in a dilemma, I'm waiting for my lady for consultation.

(*Enter Lady Yang*)

Lady Yang:

"*I'm a demon through thick and thin,*

A leopard in woman's skin."

My lord, have you heard that the Jins' messenger to the south is back at the gate of our camps?

Li Quan:

Is that possible?

(*Enter the Jin General on horseback, sword in hand*)

Jin General:

(*To the tune of* **Beiyexingchuan**)

I'm envoy from the north,

With a passport shedding the light forth.

(*Enter the groom, chasing after him*)

Groom:

Slippery! The ground is slippery!

Jin General:

Whose camp is this,

怎生呵，大营盘没个人儿答煞。

[外大叫介]溜金爷，北朝天使到来。[下]

[净、丑作慌介]快叫通事请进。

[贴上，接跪介]溜金王患病了。请那颜进。

[老旦]可才、可才道句儿克卜喇。

[下马，上坐介]都儿都儿。

[净问贴介]怎么说？

[贴]恼了。

[净、丑举手，老旦做恼不回介][指净介]铁力温都答喇。

With soldiers running here and there?
Why is it
That no one comes to give me any care?

Groom:

(*Shouts*)

Your Highness Gilded Prince, the envoy from the north is at the gate.

(*Exit*)

Li Quan, Lady Yang:

(*In a panic*)

Send for the interpreter at once.

(*Enter the interpreter*)

Interpreter:

(*Kneels to welcome the Jin general*)

The Gilded Prince is too ill to meet you at the gate. Come in please, General!

Jin General:

kubla kubla...

(*Dismounts and takes the main seat*)

durr durr...

Li Quan:

(*To the interpreter*)

What did he say?

Interpreter:

He's angry.

(*Li Quan and Lady Yang raise their hands in salutation, but the Jin General ignores them in anger*)

Jin General:

(*Points at Li Quan*)

[净问贴介]怎说？
[贴]不敢说，要杀了。
[净]却怎了？
[老旦做看丑笑介]忽伶忽伶。
[丑问贴介]
[贴]叹娘娘生的妙。
[老旦]克老克老。
[贴]说走渴了。
[老旦手足做忙介]兀该打剌。
[贴]叫马乳酒。
[老旦]约儿兀只。
[贴]要烧羊肉。

tieli wendo dala...

Li Quan:

(*To the interpreter*)

What did he say?

Interpreter:

I'm afraid to repeat — he wants to kill you.

Li Quan:

For what?

Jin General:

(*Stares at Lady Yang and grins*)

hulin hulin...

(*Lady Yang asks the interpreter*)

Interpreter:

He admires your good looks.

Jin General:

kulo kulo...

Interpreter:

He says he's thirsty after the long journey.

Jin General:

(*Waves his hands and feet*)

ergai dala...

Interpreter:

He wants horse-milk wine.

Jin General:

yorr erchi...

Interpreter:

He wants baked mutton.

Li Quan:

(*Aloud*)

[净叫介]快取羊肉、乳酒来。

[外持酒肉上]

[老旦洒酒，取刀割羊肉吃，笑，将羊油手擦胸介]一六兀剌的。

[贴]不恼了，说有礼体。

[老旦作醉介]锁陀八，锁陀八。

[贴]说醉了。

[老旦作看丑介]倒喇倒喇。

[丑笑介]怎说?

[贴]要娘娘唱个曲儿。

[丑]使得。

【北清江引】

呀，哑观音觑着个番答辣，

胡芦提笑哈。

兀那是都麻，

请将来岸答。

Get him the mutton and milk wine. Be quick!

(*Enter the attendant with mutton and wine*)

Jin General:

(*Drinks by himself, slices the mutton and eats it, laughs, wipes his greasy hands on his chest*)

Yelu erlada...

Interpreter:

He's not angry now. He says you've done the right thing.

Jin General:

(*Drunk*)

sodoba sodoba...

Interpreter:

He says he's drunk.

Jin General:

(*Stares at Lady Yang*)

dola dola...

Lady Yang:

(*Smiles*)

What did he say?

Interpreter:

He wants you to sing a song.

Lady Yang:

No problem.

(*To the tune of* **Beiqingjiangyin**)

Ha,

The dumb Bodhisattva Guanyin meets a foreign guy,

And smiles with her face awry.

General from the north,

You're welcome to come by.

撞门儿一句咬儿只不毛古唎。
通事，我斟一杯酒，你送与他。
[贴作送酒介]阿阿儿该力。
[丑]通事，说什么？
[贴]小的禀娘娘送酒。
[丑]着了。
[老旦作醉，看丑介]孛知，孛知。
[贴]又央娘娘舞一回。
[丑]使得，取我梨花枪过来。

【前腔】
[持枪舞介]冷梨花点点风儿刮，
裊得腰身乍。
胡旋儿打一车，
花门折一花。
把一个睃啜老那颜风势煞。
[老旦反背，拍袖笑倒介]忽伶忽伶。
[贴扶起老旦介]

We greet you with a loud cry.

Interpreter, I'll pour a cup of wine and you'll hand it over to him.

Interpreter:

(*Hands over the wine*)

arar galie...

Lady Yang:

What did you say?

Interpreter:

I said that you poured the wine for him.

Lady Yang:

Right.

Jin General:

(*Stares at Lady Yang in a drunken state*)

boch boch...

Interpreter:

He asks you to dance for him.

Lady Yang:

No problem. Get my pear-blossom spear.

(*To the previous tune*)

As I twist my pretty waist

And wield the spear like a whirl,

There flies a shower of cold pear blooms.

I show the foreign guy

A shower of pear blooms.

Jin General:

(*Turns aside, flaps his sleeves and collapses with laughter*)

hulin hulin...

(*Lady Yang helps Jin General to his feet*)

[老旦摆手倒地介]阿来不来。
[贴]这便是唱喏,叫唱一直。
[老旦笑点头招丑介]哈噉哈噉。
[贴]要问娘娘。
[丑笑介]问什么?
[老旦扯丑轻说介]哈噉兀该毛克喇,毛克喇。
[丑笑问贴介]怎说?
[贴作摇头介]问娘娘讨件东西。
[丑笑介]讨什么?
[贴]通事不敢说。
[老旦笑倒介]古鲁古鲁。

Jin General:

(*Waves his hands and collapses on the ground*)

ala bulai...

Interpreter:

He's encoring. He wants you to sing another song.

Jin General:

(*Laughs and nods to Lady Yang for her to come nearer*)

hasa hasa...

Interpreter:

He wants to ask you a question.

Lady Yang:

What did he want to ask?

Jin General:

(*Pulls Lady Yang by the sleeve and whispers*)

hasa erge hairkela, hairkela...

Lady Yang:

(*To the interpreter with a smile*)

What did he say?

Interpreter:

(*Shakes his head*)

He begged something from you.

Lady Yang:

(*Smiles*)

What is it?

Interpreter:

I dare not repeat his words.

Jin General:

(*Collapses with laughter*)

gulu gulu...

[净背叫贴问介]他要娘娘什么东西?古鲁古鲁不住的。
[贴]这件东西,是要不得的。便要时,则怕娘娘不舍的。便是娘娘舍的,大王也不舍的。便大王舍的,小的也不舍的。
[净]甚东西,直恁舍不的?
[贴]他这话到明,哈㘄兀该毛克喇,要娘娘有毛的所在。
[净作恼介]气也,气也。这臊子好大胆,快取枪来。
[净作持花枪赶杀介]
[贴扶醉老旦走,老旦提酒壶叫"古鲁古鲁"架住枪介]

【北尾】
[净]你那醋葫芦指望把梨花架,
臊奴,铁围墙敢靠定你大金家。
[搠倒老旦介]则踹着你那几茎儿苦嘴的赤支砂,
把那咽腥臊的噢子儿生搭杀。

Li Quan:

>(*Aside, to the interpreter*)

>What did he want from Lady Yang, by *gulu-gulu* all the time?

Interpreter:

>As for this, he should not have wanted. Even if he wants it, Her Ladyship would not give him. Even if she will give him, Your Highness would not allow her. Even if you will allow her, I would not hand it over to him.

Li Quan:

>What is so precious?

Interpreter:

>His words are clear enough: *hasa erge hairkela...* He wants Her Ladyship's hairy private parts.

Li Quan:

>(*Annoyed*)

>What a shame! What a shame! That son of a barbarian bitch! Get me the spear!

>(*Dashes at Jin General with a spear in his hand*)

Jin General:

>(*Fends off the spear with his wine jar*)

>*gulu gulu...*

Li Quan:

>(*To the tune of Beiwei*)

>How can you fend off my spear with a jar?
>You son of a barbarian bitch,
>>What do you aliens think we are!

>(*Pushes Jin General to the ground*)

>I'll pull your scarlet beard;
>I'll choke you and have you speared.

[丑扯住净，放老旦介]

[老旦]曳喇曳喇哈哩。[指净介]力娄吉丁母剌失，力娄吉丁母剌失。

[作闪袖走下介]

[净]气杀我也。那曳喇哈的什么？

[贴]叫引马的去。

[净]怎指着我力娄吉丁母剌失？

[贴]这要奏过他主儿，叫人来相杀。

[净作恼介]

[丑]老大王，你可也当着不着的。

[净]啐，着了你那毛克喇哩。

[丑]便许他在那里，你却也忒捻酸。

[净不语介]正是我一时风火性。大金家得知，这溜金王到有些欠稳。

[丑]便是番使南朝而回，未必其中有话。

(*Lady Yang grasps Li Quan and lets Jin General go*)

Jin General:

yela yelaha...

(*Points at Li Quan*)

lilo chiding chiding mulash, lilo chiding mulash...

(*Exit with a flap of his sleeves*)

Li Quan:

What a shame! What did he mean by *yelaha*?

Interpreter:

He's calling for the groom.

Li Quan:

Why does he point at me, shouting *lilo chiding mulash* ...?

Interpreter:

He's going to report this to his emperor and ask him to send troops to kill you.

(*Li Quan is enraged*)

Lady Yang:

My lord, it's not the time for you to fly into a rage.

Li Quan:

Oops, he wants your *hairkela*!

Lady Yang:

What if he gets it? You're too jealous.

Li Quan:

(*After a pause*)

I was being outrageous. When the Jin emperor learns about it, my position as Gilded Prince is shaky enough.

Lady Yang:

As this alien envoy has just returned from the south, there must be some bargain between the south and the north.

［净］娘娘高见何如？

［丑］容奴家措思。

［内擂鼓介］

［贴扮报子上］报，报，报！前日放去的秀才，从淮城中单马飞来。道有紧急，投见大王。

［丑］恰好，着他进来。

【缕缕金】［末上］无之奈，可如何！

书生承将令，强喽啰。

［内喊，末惊跌介］一声金炮响，将人跌蹉。

可怜，可怜！

密札札干戈，

其间放着我。

［贴唱门介］生员进。

Li Quan:

What's your suggestion?

Lady Yang:

Let me think it over.

(*Drums within*)

(*Enter the messenger*)

Messenger:

Report, report, report! The scholar we released the other day has galloped back alone on horseback from Huai'an. He says that he's got an urgent message for Your Highness.

Lady Yang:

He's here at the right time. Show him in.

(*Enter Chen Zuiliang*)

Chen Zuiliang:

(*To the tune of Lülüjin*)

On an errand beyond my power,

I have to wait and see.

A military mission fits the soldier

Better than a scholar like me.

(*Stumbles when he hears the yells within*)

At the sound of cannon roar,

I stumble on the ground.

Dear me, dear me,

I try to find my way,

With swords and spears around.

Messenger:

(*Announces*)

Here comes the scholar.

Chen Zuiliang:

[末见介]万死一生生员陈最良百拜大王殿下,娘娘殿下。

[净]杜安抚献了城池?

[末]城池不为希罕,敬来献一座王位与大王。

[净]寡人久已为王了。

[末]正是官上加官,职上添职。杜安抚有书呈上。

[净看书介]"通家生杜宝顿首李王麾下"。

[问末介]秀才,我与杜安抚有何通家?

[末]汉朝有个李、杜至交,唐朝也有个李、杜契友,因此杜安抚斗胆称个通家。

[净]这老儿好意思。书有何言?

【一封书】

[读书介]"闻君事外朝,

(*Greets Li Quan and Lady Yang*)

The scholar Chen Zuiliang, after a narrow escape, bows a hundred times to Your Highness and Your Ladyship.

Li Quan:

Has Envoy Du surrendered his city?

Chen Zuiliang:

A city is nothing, compared with the kingship he has to offer you.

Li Quan:

I have been a king since long ago.

Chen Zuiliang:

He's offering you more titles and honours. Here's his letter to you.

Li Quan:

(*Reads the letter*)

"Family friend Du Bao shows his respect to His Highness, Prince Li." Scholar, what family connections do I have with Envoy Du?

Chen Zuiliang:

In the Han dynasty, there were two bosom friends named Li Gu and Du Qiao; in the Tang dynasty, there were also two bosom friends named Li Bai and Du Fu. Therefore, Envoy Du ventures to say that you were family friends.

Li Quan:

The old guy's clever enough. Let me see what he's got to say.

(*Reads the letter*)

(*To the tune of* **Yifengshu**)

"I hear that you serve the alien king,

虎狼心，难定交。
肯回心圣朝，
保富贵，全忠孝。
平梁取采须收好，
背暗投明带早超。
凭陆贾，
说庄跻。
颙望麾慈即鉴昭。"
[笑介]这书劝我降宋，其实难从。"外密启一通，奉呈尊闻夫人。"
[笑介]杜安抚也畏敬娘娘哩。
[丑]你念我听。
[净看书介]"通家生杜宝敛衽杨老娘娘帐前。"咳也，杜安抚与娘娘，又通家起来。
[末]大王通得去，娘娘也通得去。
[净]也通得去。只汉子不该说敛衽。

Who is as fierce as wolf and tiger;

Such friendship can hardly last.

If you turn to serve the court of Song,

You'll have abundant wealth

And be promoted fast.

Keep your crown

And turn over a new leaf.

As I try to persuade you

To stop the strife,

Please take my words in full belief."

(*Laughs*)

This letter is trying to persuade me to turn to the court of Song, but I can hardly follow his advice. "Enclosed is a private letter to Her Ladyship."

(*Laughs*)

Envoy Du has learned to show his respect to you, my lady.

Lady Yang:

Read it for me.

Li Quan:

"Family friend Du Bao pays homage to Her Ladyship, Lady Yang." Well, Envoy Du is building family connections with Lady Yang, too.

Chen Zuiliang:

As he's a family friend of yours, so he's a family friend of hers.

Li Quan:

There's some sense in it, but he should not say "pay homage" to a lady.

Chen Zuiliang:

[末]娘娘肯敛衽而朝，安抚敢不敛衽而拜！
[丑]说的好。细念我听。
[净念书介]"通家生杜宝敛衽杨老娘娘帐前：远闻金朝封贵夫为溜金王，并无封号及于夫人。此何礼也？杜宝久已保奏大宋，勒封夫人为讨金娘之职。伏惟妆次鉴纳。不宣。"好也，到先替娘娘讨了恩典哩。
[丑]陈秀才，封我讨金娘娘，难道要我征讨大金家不成？
[末]受了封诰后，但是娘娘要金子，都来宋朝取用。因此叫做讨金娘娘。
[丑]这等是你宋朝美意。
[末]不说娘娘，便是卫灵公夫人，也说宋朝之美。
[丑]依你说。我冠儿上金子，成色要高。我是带盔儿的娘子。近时人家首饰浑脱，就一个盔儿，要你南朝照样打造一付送我。

If Her Ladyship is willing to pay homage to the court, why shouldn't the envoy pay homage to her?

Lady Yang:

Well said. Now read on!

Li Quan:

(*Reads the letter*)

"Family friend Du Bao pays homage to Her Ladyship, Lady Yang. It is said that your husband has been entitled Gilded Prince by the dynasty of Jin, but that you have not been entitled. I have reported to our emperor to entitle you as Anti-Jin Princess. I hope Your Ladyship will accept the offer with pleasure. With best regards." He's so considerate as to gain some imperial favour for you!

Lady Yang:

Mr Chen, does he want me to fight the Jins by conferring me the title Anti-Jin Princess?

Chen Zuiliang:

When you accept the offer, you can get gold from the dynasty of Song whenever you need it. That's why you're entitled Anti-Jin Princess.

Lady Yang:

I must thank the kindness from your emperor.

Chen Zuiliang:

Everybody is singing praise of Song.

Lady Yang:

I take your words for granted. I need a helmet of purest gold. As I am a woman general, I only wear a helmet without jewellery. I'd like to have a helmet in the southern style.

Chen Zuiliang:

[末]都在陈最良身上。
[净]你只顾讨金讨金,把我这溜金王,溜在那里?
[丑]连你也做了讨金王罢。
[净]谢承了。
[末叩头介]则怕大王、娘娘退悔。
[丑]俺主意定了。便写下降表,赍发秀才回奏南朝去。

【前腔】
[净]归依大宋朝,
怕金家成祸苗。
[丑]秀才,你担承这遭,
要黄金须任讨。
[末]大王,你鄱阳湖磬响收心早,
娘娘,你黑海岸回头星宿高。
[合]便休兵,随听招。

I'll get it for you.

Li Quan:

You only care about gold, gold. What about me, Gilded Prince?

Lady Yang:

Then, you'll be Anti-Jin Prince.

Li Quan:

I accept the title with pleasure.

Chen Zuiliang:

(*Kowtows*)

I'm afraid that Your Highness and Your Ladyship will change your minds.

Lady Yang:

I've fixed my mind. We'll write a petition for surrender and ask you to bring it to the southern court.

Li Quan:

(*To the previous tune*)

When we turn to the court of Song,

Our relations with Jin will go wrong.

Lady Yang:

Mr Chen,

It's your task indeed

For me to get all the gold.

Chen Zuiliang:

Your Highness,

Conversion gives you peace of mind

Your Ladyship,

And brings you bliss of every kind.

Chen Zuiliang, Li Quan, Lady Yang:

Withdraw the troops

免的名标在叛贼条。

[净]秀才，公馆留饭。星夜草表送行。

[举手送末，拜别介]

【尾声】

[净]咱比李山儿何足道，
这杨令婆委实高。
[末]带了你这一纸降书，
管取那赵官家欢笑倒。

[末下][净、丑吊场]

[净]娘娘，则为失了一边金，得了两条王。人要一个王不能勾，俺领下两个王号。岂不乐哉！

[丑]不要慌，还有第三个王号。

[净]什么王号？

[丑]叫做齐肩一字王。

[净]怎么？

And obey the royal call

Lest our names be cursed by all.

Li Quan:

Mr Chen, have dinner in the guesthouse. We'll draft a petition of surrender by night and see you off tomorrow morning.

(*Raises his right hand as a gesture of farewell. Chen Zuiliang bows his farewell*)

Li Quan:

(*To the tune of* **Coda**)

While I am but a skeleton,

My wife carries the day.

Chen Zuiliang:

With your petition of surrender,

Our emperor will be happy and gay.

(*Exit Chen Zuiliang, leaving Li Quan and Lady Yang on the stage*)

Li Quan:

My lady, by deserting Jin, we've got two princely titles. For most people, one princely title is unattainable, but we've got two. Aren't we lucky!

Lady Yang:

Wait, we'll have a third title.

Li Quan:

What's the third title?

Lady Yang:

Headless Prince.

Li Quan:

What do you mean?

Lady Yang:

[丑]杀哩。
[净]随顺他,又杀什么?
[丑]你俺两人作这大贼,全仗金鞑子威势。如今反了面,南朝拿你何难。
[净作恼介]哎哟,俺有万夫不当之勇,何惧南朝!
[丑]你真是个楚霸王,不到乌江不止。
[净]胡说!便作俺做楚霸王,要你做虞美人,定不把赵康王占了你去。
[丑]罢,你也做楚霸王不成,奴家的虞美人也做不成。换了题目做。
[净]什么题目?
[丑]范蠡载西施。
[净]五湖在那里?——去做海贼便了。

We'll be beheaded.

Li Quan:

Now that we've surrendered, why should they kill us?

Lady Yang:

We became chieftains because we had Jins at our back. Now that we have no one to turn to, the southern court can easily capture us.

Li Quan:

(*Annoyed*)

Alas! I'm strong enough to fight ten thousand men; why should I be afraid of the southern court?

Lady Yang:

You are but another Xiang Yu, who would not admit defeat until he reached the Wujiang River.

Li Quan:

Nonsense! Even if I were Xiang Yu and you were Beauty Yu, I would not submit you to the southern court.

Lady Yang:

Well, you are not Xiang Yu and I'm not Beauty Yu. Let's find another way out.

Li Quan:

What way out?

Lady Yang:

We'll be like Fan Li sailing with Xi Shi.

Li Quan:

Where are the Five Lakes where they sailed? — You mean we'll go out to sea and be pirates?

Lady Yang:

(*Gives commands*)

[丑作分付介]众三军,俺已降顺了南朝。暂解淮围,海上伺候去。

[众应介]解围了。

[内鼓介]船只齐备了,禀大王起行。

[众行介]

【江头送别】
　　淮扬外,淮扬外,海波摇动。
　　东风劲,东风劲,锦帆吹送。
　　夺取蓬莱为巢洞,
　　鳌背上立着旗峰。

【前腔】
　　顺天道,顺天道,放些儿闲空。
　　招安后,招安后,再交兵言重。
　　险做了为金家伤炎宋。
　　权袖手,做个混海痴龙。

Men in the camps, we've surrendered to the southern court.

We'll lift the siege on Huai'an and then go out to sea!

Attendants:

(*In response*)

The siege is lifted.

(*Drums within*)

The ships are ready. Your Highness, it's time to set off.

(*All embark the imaginary ships and walk around the stage*)

Li Quan:

(*To the tune of **Jiangtousongbie***)

Beyond Huaiyang,

Beyond Huaiyang,

The sea surges wave on wave.

With the east wind,

With the east wind,

The sails go to the sea.

We'll build our camps near the Penglai cave,

And raise our flags on ancient debris.

Lady Yang:

(*To the previous tune*)

Follow heavenly ways,

Follow heavenly ways,

We'll live an easy life.

When we submit,

When we submit,

We'll do away with war.

We nearly hurt the Song court in the strife

But now we'll brave the sea with awe.

Attendants:

[众]禀大王娘娘,出海了。
[净]且下了营,天明进发。

[净]干戈未定各为君,
[丑]龙斗雌雄势已分。
[净]独把一麾江海去,
[众]莫将弓箭射官军。

Your Highness, Your Ladyship, we are out at sea.

Li Quan:

Lay anchor for the night. We'll set sail at dawn.

Each fights the war for his own lord

Lady Yang:

Until one side has gained the field.

Li Quan:

I lead the troops to sea on board,

All:

No longer wielding sword or shield.

第四十八出 遇 母

【十二时】
[旦上]不住的相思鬼,
把前身退悔。
土臭全消,
肉香新长。
嫁寒儒客店里孤栖。
[净上]又着他攀高谒贵。
[旦]"寂寞秋窗冷簟纹,
[净]明珰玉枕旧香尘,
[旦]断潮归去梦郎频。
[净]桃树巧逢前度客,
[旦]翠烟真是再来人,
[合]月高风定影随身。"

Scene Forty-eight
Reunion with Her Mother

(*Enter Du Liniang*)

Du Liniang:

(*To the tune of Shiershi*)

My unconquerable love

Restored me to life.

Freed from the smell of earth,

New flesh grows in the world above.

I stay at an inn as a lonely wife.

(*Enter Sister Stone*)

Sister Stone:

You've pushed your man into the worldly strife.

Du Liniang:

"When bamboo mattress is left in the cold

Sister Stone:

And dust remains upon the pillowcase,

Du Liniang:

My man comes in my dreamland as of old.

Sister Stone:

Since the scholar met you in new bloom,

Du Liniang:

The yearning maid has come to life again,

Du Liniang, Sister Stone:

But has to stay by herself in her room."

Du Liniang:

[旦]姑姑，奴家喜得重生，嫁了柳郎。只道一举成名，回去拜访爹娘。谁知朝廷为着淮南兵乱，开榜稽迟。我爹娘正在围城之内，只得赍发柳郎往寻消耗，撇下奴家钱塘客店。你看那江声月色，凄怆人也。
[净]小姐，比你黄泉之下，景致争多。
[旦]这不在话下。

【针线厢】
虽则是荒村店江声月色，
但说着坟窝里前生今世，
则这破门帘乱撒星光内，
煞强似洞天黑地。
姑姑呵，三不归父母如何的？
七件事儿夫家靠谁？
心悠曳，不死不活，
睡梦里为个人儿。
[净]似小姐的罕有。

【前腔】
伴着你半间灵位，
又守见你一房夫婿。

Sister Stone, I was lucky to regain my life and get married to Mr Liu. I hoped that he would pass the imperial examination and that we could visit my parents at home. It happened that the announcement of results was postponed because of the disturbances in Huainan. As my parents are in the besieged city, I've sent Mr Liu to find out what has happened to them and I'm thus left alone at an inn by the Qiantang River. How melancholy the moon looks and the river moans!

Sister Stone:

This sight is much more lovely than what you saw in the netherworld.

Du Liniang:

Of course it is.

(*To the tune of Zhenxianxiang*)

Although I dwell in a lonely village inn,

Compared with years of burial in the tomb,

The broken door and ragged blinds

Are heavens to me in my room.

Sister Stone,

How about life with my parents far away?

How about life with my man day by day?

In a trance, I seem

To live between life and death—

I have only one man in my dream.

Sister Stone:

Few have had your experience.

(*To the previous tune*)

I kept your memorial tablet in the house

And waited for you to see your spouse.

[旦]姑姑,那夜搜寻秀才,知我闪在那里?
[净]则道画帧儿怎放的个人回避,
做的事瞒神唬鬼。
[旦]昏黑了,
你看月儿黑黑的星儿晦,
萤火青青似鬼火吹。
[旦]好上灯了。
[净]没油,
黑坐地,三花两焰,
留的你照解罗衣。
[旦]夜长难睡,还向主家借些油去。
[净]你院子里坐坐,咱去借来。"合着油瓶盖,踏碎玉莲蓬。"[下]

[旦玩月叹介]

Du Liniang:

Sister Stone, do you know where I hid myself when you called on the scholar the other night?

Sister Stone:

To hide behind the painting shade

Is a baffling trick by a maid.

Du Liniang:

It's getting dark.

Sister Stone:

The moon and stars are obscure in the skies;

The fireflies glitter like the devil eyes.

Du Liniang:

It's time to light the lamp.

Sister Stone:

We've run out of oil.

Let's sit in the dark

And save the last drop of oil

For you to doff your dress in sparks.

Du Liniang:

I cannot go to sleep in the long night. You'd better go and borrow some oil from the landlord.

Sister Stone:

You just sit in the courtyard while I'll go and borrow some oil.

"When I go for the oil,

My tiny feet will toil."

(*Exit*)

(*Du Liniang gazes at the moon and sighs*)

(*Enter Zhen and Chunxiang, travelling on the way*)

Zhen:

【月儿高】
[老旦、贴行路上]江北生兵乱,
江南走多半。
不载香车稳,
跋的鞋鞓断。
夫主兵权,
望天涯生死如何判。
前呼后拥,一个春香伴。
凤髻消除,打不上扬州纂。
上岸了到临安。
趁黄昏黑影林峦,
生忔察的难投馆。
[贴]且喜到临安了。
[老旦]咳,万死一逃生,得到临安府。俺女娘无处投,长路多孤苦。
[贴]前面像是个半开门儿,蓦了进去。
[老旦进介]呀,门房空静,内可有人?
[旦]谁?

(*To the tune of Yueergao*)

When war starts in the north,

We have to wander in the south.

As I have to go on foot,

I wear out my shoes away from my house.

My lord commands the army,

With his life oft in ordeals.

I have no one to go with me

But Chunxiang at my heels.

I have no time to do my hair,

Not even in the common Yangzhou style.

Now that we've arrived in Lin'an,

In the gloomy forest near the hills,

Where can I put up for the while?

Chunxiang:

Thank heavens! We've arrived in Lin'an at last.

Zhen:

Alas,

"It is a narrow escape

That we have reached Lin'an.

Where can we take refuge?

On the road we haven't met a man."

Chunxiang:

The gate ahead seems to be ajar. Let's get in.

Zhen:

(*Steps into the house*)

It seems to be an empty house. Is there anybody in here?

Du Liniang:

Who is it?

[贴]是个女人声息。待打叫一声开门。

【不是路】
[旦惊介]斜倚雕阑,
何处娇音唤启关?
[老旦]行程晚,
女娘们借住霎儿间。
[旦]听他言,
声音不似男儿汉,
待自起开门月下看。[见介]
[旦]是一位女娘,请里坐。
[老旦]相提盼,
人间天上行方便。
[旦]趋迎迟慢,趋迎迟慢。
[打照面介]
[老旦作惊介]

【前腔】
破屋颓椽,
姐姐呵,

Chunxiang:

It's a woman's voice. I'll ask her to open the inner door.

Du Liniang:

(*Taken aback*)

(*To the tune of Bushilu*)

When I lean on the porch,

Who's calling at the door in a voice so soft and light?

Zhen:

As we have travelled late,

We ask you to put us up for the night.

Du Liniang:

Judging from the voice,

They are not men;

I'll open the door and have a look in the moonlight.

(*Du Liniang and Zhen greet each other*)

Du Liniang:

Oh, it's a lady. Come in and sit down please.

Zhen:

A helping hand is of great worth,

Both in the heaven and on earth.

Du Liniang:

Sorry to have kept you waiting;

Sorry to have kept you waiting.

(*Du Liniang and Zhen look at each other*)

Zhen:

(*In surprise*)

(*To the previous tune*)

In this dilapidated site,

Young lady,

你怎独坐无人灯不燃?
[旦]这闲庭院,
玩清光长送过这月儿圆。
[老旦背叫贴]春香,这像谁来?
[贴惊介]不敢说,好像小姐。
[老旦]你快瞧房儿里面,还有甚人?若没有人,敢是鬼也?[贴下]
[旦背]这位女娘,好像我母亲,那丫头好像春香。
[作回问介]敢问老夫人,何方而来?
[老旦叹介]自淮安,
我相公是淮扬安抚、遭兵难,
我避虏逃生到此间。
[旦背介]是我母亲了,我可认他?

Why do you sit alone without a light?

Du Liniang:

In this empty court,

I watch the moon as a sport.

Zhen:

(*Aside, to Chunxiang*)

Chunxiang, whom do you think this lady looks like?

Chunxiang:

(*Alarmed*)

I dare not say it. She looks like Miss Du.

Zhen:

Give a quick look inside the room to see if anyone else is there.

If no one else is inside the room, she must be a ghost!

(*Exit Chunxiang*)

Du Liniang:

(*Aside*)

This lady looks like my mother and her maid looks like Chunxiang.

(*To Zhen*)

May I ask where you are from?

Zhen:

(*Sighs*)

I'm from Huai'an;

My husband is the Envoy of Huai'an.

To escape from the war,

I've travelled a long way and come to your door.

Du Liniang:

(*Aside*)

She must be my mother, but how shall I present myself?

[贴慌上,背语老旦介]一所空房子,通没个人影儿。是鬼,是鬼!
[老旦作怕介]
[旦]听他说起,是我的娘也。
[旦向前哭娘介]
[老旦作避介]敢是我女孩儿?怠慢了你,你活现了。春香,有随身纸钱,快丢,快丢。
[贴丢纸钱介]
[旦]儿不是鬼。
[老旦]不是鬼,我叫你三声,要你应我一声高如一声。
[做三叫三应,声渐低介]
[老旦]是鬼也。
[旦]娘,你女儿有话讲。
[老旦]则略靠远,
冷淋侵一阵风儿旋,
这般活现。

(*Enter Chunxiang in a panic*)

Chunxiang:

(*Aside, to Zhen*)

It's an empty house with no one around. She must be a ghost, a ghost!

(*Zhen trembles with fear*)

Du Liniang:

From what she's said, she must be my mother.

(*Throws herself in Zhen's bosom and cries*)

Mom, Mom!

Zhen:

(*Tries to move away*)

Are you my daughter? I must have neglected your offerings and you appear before me in the human form! Chunxiang, get some sacrificial money and scatter it! Scatter the money!

(*Chunxiang scatters the sacrificial money*)

Du Liniang:

I'm not a ghost.

Zhen:

If you are not a ghost, answer my three calls with increasing voice!

(*Calls three times and Du Liniang answers three times, but each time in a weaker voice*)

You must be a ghost!

Du Liniang:

Mom, please listen to me.

Zhen:

Please keep away,

For a chilly wind does blow

From where you stay.

[旦]那些活现?

[旦扯老旦作怕介]儿,手恁般冷。

[贴叩头介]小姐,休要捻了春香。

[老旦]儿,不曾广超度你,是你父亲古执。

[旦哭介]娘,你这等怕,女孩儿死不放娘去了。

【前腔】

[净持灯上]门户牢拴,

为什空堂人语喧?

[灯照地介]这青苔院,

怎生吹落纸黄钱?

[贴]夫人,来的不是道姑?

[老旦]可是。

Du Liniang:

What comes from where I stay?

(*Pulls at Zhen*)

Zhen:

(*In fear*)

Your hands are cold, my child.

Chunxiang:

(*Kowtows*)

Please don't hurt me, Mistress.

Zhen:

We should have held a ceremony to transcend your soul but for the objection from your father.

Du Liniang:

(*Wails*)

Why should you be in such fear, Mom? I won't let you go at any event.

(*Enter Sister Stone*)

Sister Stone:

(*To the previous tune*)

Before I left, I closed the door,

But how come from the yard all the roar?

(*Lowers the lamp to light the ground*)

How is it that I've found

Sacrificial money on the ground?

Chunxiang:

Isn't it Sister Stone coming, Madam?

Zhen:

Yes, it is.

Sister Stone:

[净惊介]呀,老夫人和春香那里来?这般大惊小怪。
看他打盘旋,
那夫人呵,怕漆灯无焰将身远。
小姐,恨不得幽室生辉得近前。
[旦]姑姑快来,奶奶害怕。
[贴]这姑姑敢也是个鬼?
[净扯老旦,照旦介]休疑惮。
移灯就月端详遍,
可是当年人面?
[合]是当年人面。
[老旦抱旦泣介]儿呵,便是鬼,娘也舍不的去了。

【前腔】
肠断三年,
怎坠海明珠去复旋?
[旦]爹娘面,阴司里怜念把魂还。

(*Surprised*)

Where are you from, Madam and Chunxiang? Why are you making such a fuss? Look,

    How they move about in fear—

The old mistress

    Would like to leave a ghost from the grave;

The young mistress

    Would like to get the light and draw near.

Du Liniang:

Come over quickly, Sister Stone! My mom is greatly terrified.

Chunxiang:

Isn't the nun also a ghost?

Sister Stone:

(*Grasps Zhen by the sleeve and holds up the lamp to Du Liniang*)

Too much of your ado!

Have a close look in the light.

Isn't this the face you knew?

Zhen, Chunxiang:

This is the face we knew.

Zhen:

(*Embraces Du Liniang and weeps*)

I won't tear myself away from you, my child, even if you are a ghost.

(*To the previous tune*)

My heart has broken for three years,

But how did you leave the nether-world spheres?

Du Liniang:

Out of respect for Dad and Mom,

[贴]小姐，你怎生出的坟来？
[旦]好难言。
[老旦]是怎生来？
[旦]则感的是东岳大恩眷，
托梦一个书生把墓踹穿。
[老旦]书生何方人氏？
[旦]是岭南柳梦梅。
[贴]怪哉，当真有个柳和梅。
[老旦]怎同他来此？
[旦]他来科选。
[老旦]这等是个好秀才，快请相见。
[旦]我央他看淮扬动静去把爹娘探，
因此上独眠深院，独眠深院。

The nether judge released me from the hell.

Chunxiang:

How did you manage to get out of your grave, young mistress?

Du Liniang:

It's a story hard to tell.

Zhen:

How did you manage it?

Du Liniang:

Thanks to the Goddess of Mount Tai,

A scholar got the inspiration from a dream to dig my grave.

Zhen:

Where is the scholar's native place?

Du Liniang:

The scholar Liu Mengmei is from Lingnan.

Chunxiang:

What a coincidence! His name indeed carries the willow *liu* and plum *mei*!

Zhen:

Why did he bring you here?

Du Liniang:

He's here to take the imperial test.

Zhen:

Then he must be a nice scholar. Ask him to meet us.

Du Liniang:

I asked him to meet you in Huaiyang.

Therefore,

Here I stay alone;

Here I stay alone.

Zhen:

[老旦背与贴语介]有这等事?
[贴]便是,难道有这样出跳的鬼?
[老旦回泣介]我的儿呵!

【番山虎】
则道你烈性上青天,
端坐在西方九品莲,
不道三年鬼窟里重相见。
哭得我手麻肠寸断,
心枯泪点穿。
梦魂沉乱,
我神情倒颠。
看时儿立地,
叫时娘各天。
怕你茶饭无浇奠,
牛羊侵墓田。
[合]今夕何年?今夕何年?
咦,还怕这相逢梦边。

【前腔】
[旦泣介]你抛儿浅土,
骨冷难眠。
吃不尽爷娘饭,
江南寒食天。

(*Aside, to Chunxiang*)

How is it possible!

Chunxiang:

I think so, for how can there be such a pretty ghost?

Zhen:

(*Turns back to Du Liniang and weeps*)

(*To the tune of* ***Fanshanhu***)

I thought that you had soared to the sky,

Seated on the lotus in the western spheres,

But I didn't expect to meet you again in three years.

I cried till my limbs were numb

And my eyes were dry.

My dream would be haunted;

My thoughts would fly.

I was afraid that

You would lack food and drink;

In your graveyard cattle would saunter by.

All:

What night indeed is this?

What night indeed is this?

Oh,

We fear that this reunion is a lie.

Du Liniang:

(*Weeps*)

(*To the previous tune*)

You put me in a grave that was shallow,

Where bones lay cold and sleep came slow.

I got your food and drink,

Offered on Festival for the Ghost.

可也不想有今日,
也道不起从前。
似这般糊突谜,
甚时明白也天!
鬼不要,
人不嫌,
不是前生断,
今生怎得连!
[合前]
[老旦]老姑姑,也亏你守着我儿。
【前腔】
[净]近的话不堪提咽,
早森森地心疏体寒。
空和他做七做中元,
怎知他成双成爱眷?
[低与老旦介]我捉鬼拿奸,
知他影戏儿做的恁活现?
[合]这样奇缘,这样奇缘,
打当了轮回一遍。

I had no hope for the future;

The past terrified me the most.

This is a confounding puzzle,

Only heavens will ever know.

I'm no longer a ghost;

I've come back from down below.

If I had not cut off the nether tie,

How can I have you close by?

All:

What night indeed is this?

What night indeed is this?

Oh,

We fear that this reunion is a lie.

Zhen:

Sister Stone, thank you for watching over my child.

Sister Stone:

(*To the previous tune*)

Never mention the past three years,

For they make me shudder all the time.

I observed all the rites for her;

Who knows she had a love affair sublime!

(*Whispers to Zhen.*)

I tried to find out about the love affair,

But she played tricks on me all the time.

All:

Miraculous love!

Miraculous love!

Her soul made love on earth above!

Chunxiang:

【前腔】
　　[贴]论魂离倩女是有,
　　知他三年外灵骸怎全?
　　则恨他同棺椁、少个郎官,
　　谁想他为院君这宅院。
　　小姐呵,你做的相思鬼穿,
　　你从夫意专。
　　那一日春香不铺其孝筵,
　　那节儿夫人不哀哉醮荐?
　　早知道你撇离了阴司,跟了人上船!
　　[合前]
【尾声】
　　[老旦]感得化生女显活在灯前面。
　　则你的亲爹,
　　他在贼子窝中没信传。
　　[旦]娘放心,有我那信行的人儿,
　　他穴地通天,打听的远。

　　想象精灵欲见难,
　　碧桃何处便骖鸾?
　　莫道非人身不暖,
　　菱花初晓镜光寒。

(*To the previous tune*)

I've heard about souls that stroll,

Who cannot keep their bodies whole.

A pity that they had no tomb-mates

To love them heart and soul.

My mistress alone has attained her goal.

Young mistress,

Your love is obstinate,

And now you've had your mate.

I offered food and drink for you every day;

Your mom never forgot the memorial date.

Who knows that you have changed your fate

And is sailing with your mate!

All:

Miraculous love!

Miraculous love!

Her soul made love on earth above!

Zhen:

(*To the tune of Coda*)

Thank heavens that you've come back to life,

But your dad is still entangled in the military strife.

Du Liniang:

Don't worry, Mom. My faithful man will

Probe high and low

To find the news for his wife.

Imaginary sprites are hard to meet;

Where in the heaven flies the blossom sweet?

Don't say that only mortals have some warmth;

The morning mirror is like a chilly sheet.

第四十九出　　淮　泊

【三登乐】

[生包袱、雨伞上]有路难投,
禁得这乱离时候!
走孤寒落叶知秋。
为娇妻思岳丈,
探听扬州。
又谁料他困守淮扬,
索奔前答救。

"那能得计访情亲?浊水污泥清路尘。自恨为儒逢世难,却怜无事是家贫。"俺柳梦梅阳世寒儒,蒙杜小姐阴司热宠,得为夫妇,相随赴科。且喜殿试撺过卷子,又被边报耽误榜期。因此小姐呵,闻说他尊翁淮扬兵急,叫俺沿路上体访安危。亲赍一幅春容,敬报再生之喜。虽则如此,客路贫难,诸凡

Scene Forty-nine
Sojourn near the Huai River

(*Enter Liu Mengmei with a bundle and an umbrella*)
Liu Mengmei:
    (*To the tune of* **Sandengle**)
    There is no easy road
    In times of war.
    At the sight of fallen leaves,
    The traveller sees the coming fall.
    As my wife worries about her father,
    I'm on my way to Yangzhou.
    When I know he's besieged in Huai'an,
    To his rescue I must go.
    "*How can I go and see my kin?*
    I have to go through thick and thin.
    For a scholar in times of distress,
    Poverty will throw him in a mess."

As I, Liu Mengmei in the human world, was loved by Du Liniang in the nether world, we became man and wife. We went together to Lin'an to enter the imperial examination. I was lucky enough to have my belated paper accepted, but the border conflict delayed the announcement of the results. As soon as my wife heard that her father was besieged in Huaiyang, she asked me to seek information on the way. Therefore, I set off with her self-portrait to report the news of her resurrection. My only means to cover the travel expenses is

路费之资，尽出圹中之物。其间零碎宝玩，急切典卖不来。有些成器金银，土气销熔有限。兼且小生看书之眼，并不认的等子星儿。一路上赚骗无多，逐日里支分有尽。得到扬州地面，恰好岳丈大人移镇淮城。贼兵阻路，不敢前进。且喜因循解散，不免迤逦数程。

【锦缠道】
　　早则要、醉扬州寻杜牧，
　　梦三生花月楼，
　　怎知他长淮去休！
　　那里有缠十万顺天风、跨鹤闲游！
　　则索傍渔樵寻食宿、败荷衰柳，
　　添一抹五湖秋。
　　那秋意儿有许多迤逗！
　　咱功名事未酬，
　　冷落我断肠闺秀。
　　堪回首？
　　算江南江北有十分愁。
一路行来，且喜看见了插天高的淮城，城下一带清长淮水。那城楼之上，还挂有丈六阔的军门旗号。大吹大擂，想是日晚掩门了。且寻小店歇宿。

the jewellery unearthed from her tomb. Some little articles are not easy to sell or pawn on the spot, and some vessels of precious metal are of little weight. What's more, I'm a scholar who does not know much about the scales. The little cash I have is spent on my daily expenses on the way. Now that I have reached Yangzhou, I hear that my father-in-law has been transferred to defend the city of Huai'an. As the bandit troops have blocked the way, I dare not move on. However, the bandit troops seem to be dispersing and so I'm moving forward again.

(*To the tune of* **Jinchandao**)
I cherished the hope that in Yangzhou
I would drink as much as I can
And relish in the song and dance,
But who knows that Envoy Du has gone to Huai'an.
I have no fortune
To take a pleasure ride on a crane.
I have to live with the rustic folk,
With sight of decayed lotus and willow
Scattered on the autumn plain.
What melancholy thoughts when I roam!
I have to wait for my fame and name,
And leave my dear wife at home.

Well, forget about it!

Woeful thoughts are a shame!

After a long journey, the towering city-wall of Huai'an comes in sight at last! Around the city wall flows the clear Huai River; above the wall-tower floats the sixteen-feet military streamer. Amid drums and bugles, the city gate is closed. I'll try to find

[丑上]"多挽白水江湖酒,少赚黄边风月钱。"秀才投宿么?

[生进店介]

[丑]要果酒,案酒?

[生]天性不饮。

[丑]柴米是要的?

[生]吃倒算。

[丑]算倒吃。

[生]花银五分在此。

[丑]高银散碎些,待我称一称。[称介,作惊叫介]银子走了。[寻介]

[生]怎的大惊小怪?

[丑]秀才,银子地缝里走了。你看碎珠儿。

[生]这等还有几块在这里。

an inn to put up for the night.

(*Enter the innkeeper*)

Innkeeper:

"Add a lot of water to the wine;

Don't earn money in indecent line."

Do you need a room for the night, Sir?

(*Liu Mengmei enters the inn*)

Will you have wine with nuts and fruits or with dishes?

Liu Mengmei:

I never drink wine.

Innkeeper:

Will you have some food?

Liu Mengmei:

I'll pay after I eat.

Innkeeper:

No, you'll pay before you eat.

Liu Mengmei:

Here are some scraps of silver.

Innkeeper:

What scraps! I'd better weigh them.

(*Weighs and calls out in surprise*)

The silver's gone.

Liu Mengmei:

Why all the fuss?

Innkeeper:

Sir, your silver has disappeared in the floor cracks. Look at the tiny drops!

Liu Mengmei:

I've some more for you.

[丑接银又走,三度介]呀,秀才原来会使水银?

[生]因何是水银?[背介]是了,是小姐殡敛之时,水银在口。龙含土成珠而上天,鬼含汞成丹而出世,理之然也。此乃见风而化。原初小姐死,水银也死;如今小姐活,水银也活了。则可惜这神奇之物,世人不知。

[回介]也罢了。店主人,你将我花银都消散去了,如今一厘也无。这本书是我平日看的,准酒一壶。

[丑]书破了。

[生]贴你一枝笔,

[丑]笔开花了。

[生]此中使客往来,你可也听见"读书破万卷"?

Innkeeper:

(*Takes the silver and it vanishes again. The same happens a third time*)

Oh, you're giving me quicksilver!

Liu Mengmei:

Why do you call it quicksilver?

(*Aside*)

I've got it. It must be the quicksilver my love held in her mouth at the burial. "The dragon soars to the sky when the earth in its mouth turns into pearls; the ghost resurrects to the human world when the quicksilver in its mouth turns into pellets." It conforms to the natural course of events that these things are gone with the wind. When my love died, the quicksilver was dead; when my love comes to life again, the quicksilver becomes alive. It's a pity that the common people do not understand these miraculous things.

(*Turns to the Innkeeper*)

Well, Sir, you've squandered all my silver and I have no more left. Here is a book I read every day. It's worth a flask of wine.

Innkeeper:

The book is too worn and torn.

Liu Mengmei:

Here is a brush-pen to go with it.

Innkeeper:

The pen is battered.

Liu Mengmei:

From your numerous customers, haven't you ever heard of Du Fu's line "Wear out ten thousand books"?

[丑]不听见。
[生]可听见"梦笔吐千花"？
[丑]不听见。

【皂罗袍】
　　[生作笑介]可笑一场闲话，
　　破诗书万卷，
　　笔蕊千花。
　　是我差了，这原不是换酒的东西。
　　[丑笑介]"神仙留玉佩，卿相解金貂。"
　　[生]你说金貂玉佩，那里来的？
　　有朝货与帝王家，
　　金貂玉佩书无价。
　　你还不知道，便是千金小姐，依然嫁他。
　　一朝臣宰，端然拜他。

Innkeeper:

　　No, I haven't.

Liu Mengmei:

　　Haven't you ever heard of Li Bai's line "Dream of a pen that bears a thousand blooms"?

Innkeeper:

　　No, I haven't.

Liu Mengmei:

　　　(*With a giggle*)

　　　(*To the tune of Zaoluopao*)

　　　It would be fun that he assumes

　　　He'll "*wear out ten thousand books*"

　　　And "*dream of a pen that bears a thousand blooms*".

　　　I'm wrong to swap these things for wine.

Innkeeper:

　　　(*Smiles*)

　　　"An immortal leaves his jade pendant;

　　　A minister gives his golden plate."

Liu Mengmei:

　　Where do you think these jade pendants and golden plates come from?

　　　When a scholar serves the royal court,

　　　His intelligence will be considered great.

　　You probably don't know that

　　　A maid of noble birth

　　　Will marry him;

　　　A minister of lofty worth

　　　Will visit him.

Innkeeper:

[丑]要他则甚?
[生]读书人把笔安天下。
[生]不要书，不要笔，这把雨伞可好?
[丑]天下雨哩。
[生]明日不走了。
[丑]饿死在这里?
[生笑介]你认的淮扬杜安抚么?
[丑]谁不认的!明日吃太平宴哩。
[生]则我便是他女婿来探望他。
[丑惊介]喜是相公说的早，杜老爷多早发下请书了。
[生]请书那里?
[丑]和相公瞧去。
[丑请生行介]待小人背褡袱雨伞。[行介]

What do they want of him?

Liu Mengmei:

With his pen, a scholar quells the earth.

If you don't want my book or brush-pen, how about the umbrella?

Innkeeper:

You're asking for rain!

Liu Mengmei:

I won't leave tomorrow.

Innkeeper:

Do you want to starve yourself to death here?

Liu Mengmei:

(*Smiles*)

Do you know Envoy Du in this Huaiyang area?

Innkeeper:

Oh, who doesn't know him? A Banquet of Peace will be held tomorrow.

Liu Mengmei:

I'm his son-in-law to pay a visit to him.

Innkeeper:

(*Startled*)

I'm lucky that you mention this early. Envoy Du has sent you a letter of invitation.

Liu Mengmei:

Where's the letter?

Innkeeper:

We'll go and read it.

(*Shows the way for Liu Mengmei*)

I'll carry the bundle and umbrella for you.

[生]请书那里?

[丑]兀的不是!

[生]这是告示居民的。

[丑]便是。你瞧!

【前腔】

"禁为闲游奸诈。"

杜老爷是巴上生的:

"自三巴到此,万里为家。

不教子侄到官衙,

从无女婿亲闲杂。"

这句单指你相公:

"若有假充行骗,地方禀拿。"

下面说小的了:

"扶同歇宿,罪连主家。

为此须至关防者。

右示通知。建炎三十二年五月日示。"你看后面安抚司杜大花押。上面盖着一颗"钦差安抚淮扬等处地方提督军务安抚司使之印",鲜明紫粉。相公,相公,你在此消停,小人告回了。"各人自扫门前

(*Goes with Liu Mengmei*)

Liu Mengmei:

Where's the letter?

Innkeeper:

There it is!

Liu Mengmei:

This is an official notice.

Innkeeper:

So it is. Just look!

(*To the previous tune*)

"Prohibition on Vagabonds and Impostors".

Envoy Du is from Sichuan:

"I came here from Sichuan,

Ten thousand li away from my hometown.

I have neither kin by my side

Nor son-in-law around."

This sentence is meant for you, Sir:

"Put him to jail

If any swindler should be found."

The next sentence is for me:

"The host will also be published

If he takes in the swindler within his door.

Let this notice be known to all."

"That's all for the notice. The fifth day of the fifth month, the thirty-second year of Jianyan, Song dynasty." Look at the signature of Envoy Du at the end, with the glaring seal of "Imperial Envoy and Commander-in-Chief to the Huaiyang Region". Take your time, sir, and I'll be off now.

"Each one sweeps the snow from his own doorstep

雪，休管他家屋上霜。"［下］

［生哭介］我的妻，你怎知丈夫到此凄惶无地也。

［作望介］呀，前面房子门上有大金字，咱投宿去。

［看介］四个字："漂母之祠。"怎生叫做漂母之祠？

［看介］原来壁上有题："昔贤怀一饭，此事已千秋。"是了，乃前朝淮阴侯韩信之恩人也。我想起来，那韩信是个假齐王，尚然有人一饭，俺柳梦梅是个真秀才，要杯冷酒不能够！像这漂母，俺拜他一千拜。

【莺皂袍】

［拜介］垂钓楚天涯，

瘦王孙，遇漂纱。

楚重瞳较比这秋波瞎。

太史公表他，

And heeds not the frost on his neighbour's roof."
　　(*Exit*)

Liu Mengmei:

　　(*Weeps*)

My dear wife, do you know that I'm in such a wretched state here?

　　(*Looks around*)

Well, there's a house ahead with big golden characters. I'll try to find shelter there.

　　(*Looks*)

The characters read: "Memorial Hall to Mother Washer". Why is this called "Memorial Hall to Mother Washer"?

　　(*Looks*)

There is an inscription on the wall:

　　"The ancient sage keeps a meal in heart;

　　For a thousand years it lives in works of art."

Yes, I see. This memorial hall was built in honour of Marquis of Huaiyin Han Xin's benefactress, Mother Washer. Just think that Han Xin was a sham-king of Qi and could still be fed by a woman; I am a genuine scholar but no one will provide me with a cup of cold wine. I'll bow a thousand times to Mother Washer.

　　(*Bows*)

　　(*To the tune of* ***Yingzaopao***)

　　When he fished in the land of Chu,

　　Han Xin, the hungry gentleman, met Mother Washer.

　　Compared with her,

　　Xiang Yu the Conqueror was blind to virtue.

　　She was praised by the great historian Sima Qian

淮安府祭他，
甫能够一饭千金价。
看古来妇女多有俏眼儿：
文公乞食，僖妻礼他；
昭关乞食，相逢浣纱。
凤尖头叩首三千下。
起更了，廊下一宿。早去伺候开门。没水梳洗。[看介]好了，下雨哩。

旧事无人可共论，
只应漂母识王孙。
辕门拜手儒衣弊，
莫使沾濡有泪痕。

And honoured in the Prefecture of Huai'an.

Therefore, a meal is of immense value.

It seems that women always have better vision.

When Duke Wen of Jin went begging,

Lady Xi gave him food.

When Wu Zixu went begging,

A washing woman did all she could.

I'll give three thousand kowtows to those who did good. Now goes the first night watch-beat. I'll put up for the night in the corridor and get up early tomorrow morning to enter the city gate. But there's no water to wash my face...

(*Looks around*)

Wonderful, it's raining now.

None in the past could be compared

To Mother Washer with discerning eyes.

When I bow before official gates,

I will control myself when tears arise.

第五十出　　闹　宴

【梁州令】
　　[外引丑众上]长淮千骑雁行秋，
浪卷云浮。
思乡泪国倚层楼。
[合]看机遘，逢奏凯，且迟留。
"万里封侯岐路，几两英雄草屦。秋城鼓角催，老将来。烽火平安昨夜，梦醒家山泪下。兵戈未许归，意徘徊。"我杜宝身为安抚，时值兵冲。围绝救援，贻书解散。李寇既去，金兵不来。中间善后事宜，且自看详停当。分付中军门外伺候。

Scene Fifty
Spoiling the Banquet

(*Enter Du Bao, followed by gatekeeper and attendants*)

Du Bao:

(*To the tune of* **Liangzhouling**)

A thousand steeds gallop along the Huai,

While wild geese flock across the cloudy sky.

Thoughts of homeland make me weep and sigh.

All:

With good cheer,

We've won the day,

But now we still stay here.

Du Bao:

"The road to peerage is tough and rough;

The hardship I've never had enough.

Amid sounds of drums and bugles bold,

I'm growing old.

When peace arrived amid cheers,

I dreamed of home and woke in tears.

The war has kept me from home,

Bringing endless thoughts on the roam."

As Envoy for Appeasement, I have been caught in the warfare. I broke through the blockade line to save the city and lifted the siege by a letter. Li Quan's bandits are gone and Jin troops are not coming yet. During this interval, I have to deal with a lot of aftermath. Attendants, wait for my orders outside

［众下］

［丑把门介］

［外叹介］虽有存城之欢，实切亡妻之痛。［泪介］我的夫人呵，昨已单本题请他的身后恩典，兼求赐假西归。未知旨意如何？正是："功名富贵草头露，骨肉团圆锦上花。"［看文书介］

【金蕉叶】

　　［生破衣巾携春容上］穷愁客愁，
　　正摇落雁飞时候。
　　［整容介］帽儿光整顿从头，
　　还则怕未分明的门楣认否？
　　［丑喝介］什么人行走？
　　［生］是杜老爷女婿拜见。

the gate.

(*Exeunt attendants*)

(*The gatekeeper stands on guard at the gate*)

Du Bao:

I'm glad that the city has been preserved, but I'm in deep woe that my wife died.

(*In tears*)

My dear wife, I sent a memorial to the court yesterday, asking for an honoured funeral for you and asking for leave to send your remains to Sichuan. For the moment, I don't know yet what the imperial decree will be. It is true to say,

"*Fame and wealth is but the dew*

While family union is extra hue."

(*Reads the documents*)

(*Enter Liu Mengmei in ragged clothes, carrying Du Liniang's self-portrait in his sleeves*)

Liu Mengmei:

(*To the tune of Jinjiaoye*)

Poverty and weariness fill me with dismay,

In addition to the autumn decay.

(*Straightens his clothes*)

I straighten my cap and gown,

Not sure whether I'll be accepted today.

Gatekeeper:

(*In a harsh voice*)

Who's coming outside?

Liu Mengmei:

Envoy Du's son-in-law asks for admittance.

Gatekeeper:

[丑]当真？
[生]秀才无假。
[丑进禀介]
[外]关防明白了。[问丑介]那人材怎的？
[丑]也不怎的。袖着一幅画儿。
[外笑介]是个画师。则说老爷军务不闲便了。
[丑见生介]老爷军务不闲。请自在。
[生]叫我自在，自在不成人了。
[丑]等你去，成人不自在。
[生]老爷可拜客去么？
[丑]今日文武官僚吃太平宴，牌簿都缴了。
[生]大哥，怎么叫做太平宴？

Are you serious?

Liu Mengmei:

A scholar never tells falsehoods.

(*The gatekeeper comes to report*)

Du Bao:

I've made it clear in the official notice.

(*To the gatekeeper*)

How does he look like?

Gatekeeper:

Just so so. He carries a scroll of painting in his sleeves.

Du Bao:

(*Smiles*)

So he's a painter. Tell him that I'm occupied with military affairs.

Gatekeeper:

(*To Liu Mengmei*)

His Excellency is occupied with military affairs. You are free to go anywhere else.

Liu Mengmei:

If I'm free to go anywhere else, I'll be nobody.

Gatekeeper:

If you are somebody, you'll not be free to go anywhere.

Liu Mengmei:

Is His Excellency going out for a visit?

Gatekeeper:

All the officials and officers will be attending the Banquet of Peace. No appointments will be made today.

Liu Mengmei:

What is the Banquet of Peace?

[丑]这是各边方年例。则今年退了贼,筵宴盛些。席上有金花树,银台盘,长尺头,大元宝,无数的。你是老爷女婿,背几个去。

[生]原来如此。则怕进见之时,考一首《太平宴诗》,或是《军中凯歌》,或是《淮清颂》,急切怎好?且在这班房里等着打想一篇,正是"有备无患"。

[丑]秀才还不走,文武官员来也。

[生下]

【梁州令】

[末扮文官上]长淮望断塞垣秋,

喜兵甲潜收。

贺升平、歌颂许吾流。

[净扮武官上]兼文武,

陪将相,

宴公侯。

请了。

Gatekeeper:

It's an annual banquet in the border area. As we've dispelled the bandits this year, the banquet is more sumptuous. On the banquet there are gold-flower trees, silver plates, bolts of silk, silver ingot, and gifts of all sorts. If you are Envoy Du's son-in-law, you may bring some home.

Liu Mengmei:

Yes, I see. I'm afraid when I meet him, what if he should ask me to improvise such poems as *"On the Banquet of Peace"*, *"Song of Triumph"* or *"Ode to the Pacific Huai"*. I'd better prepare a poem or two while I wait in the gatekeeper's room. As the proverb goes, "Better prepared, less embarrassment."

Gatekeeper:

Will you step aside, sir? The officials and officers are coming.

(*Exit Liu Mengmei*)

(*Enter Official*)

Official:

(*To the tune of* **Liangzhouling**)

When autumn arrives at the river Huai,

We're glad that arms are laid by.

It's time for us to sing praise

Of peace with the best phrase.

(*Enter Officer*)

Officer:

Officials and officers,

Generals and ministers,

Enjoy the dishes on the trays.

How do you do!

[末]今日我文武官属太平宴,水陆务须华盛,歌舞都要整齐。

[末、净见介]圣天子万灵拥辅,老君侯八面威风。寇兵销咫尺之书,军礼设太平之宴。谨已完备,望乞俯容。

[外]军功虽卑末难当,年例有诸公怎废?难言奏凯,聊用舒怀。

[内鼓吹介]

[丑持酒上]"黄石兵书三寸舌,清河雪酒五加皮。"酒到。

【梁州序】

[外浇酒介]天开江左,
地冲淮右。
气色夜连刁斗。
[末、净进酒介]长城一线,
何来得御君侯!
喜平销战气,不动征旗,

Official:
> At the Banquet of Peace for the officials and officers, we've seen to it that aquatic food and land produce are sumptuous and that song and dance are splendid.

Official, Officer:
> (*Greet Du Bao*)
>
> Under the rule of His Majesty who is beloved by all his subjects, Your Excellency has inspired awe from all sides. As the bandits have been dispersed with a mere letter from you, we've prepared a Banquet of Peace in the army tradition. Now that everything is ready, would you please join the banquet?
>
> (*Drums and pipes within*)

Gatekeeper:
> "The book on arts of war enhances eloquence;
> The Qinghe River sweetens cortex wine."
>
> The wine, please.

Du Bao:
> (*Sprays the wine*)
> (*To the tune of Liangzhouxu*)
> To the north of the Yangtze,
> To the south of the Huai,
> The beats of night watch ring in the sky.

Official, Officer:
> (*Offer a toast*)
> What an honour for the frontier area
> To welcome Your Excellency here!
> To our great joy,
> Without fighting a single battle,

一纸书回寇。
那堪羌笛里望神州!
这是万里筹边第一楼。
[合]乘塞草,秋风候,
太平筵上如淮酒,
尽慷慨,为君寿。

【前腔】
[外]吾皇福厚。
群才策凑,
半壁围城坚守。
[末、净]分明军令,杯前借箸题筹。
[外]我题书与李全夫妇呵,
也是燕支却虏,
夜月吹篪,
一字连环透。
不然无救也怎生休!
不是天心不聚头。
[合前]

The war clouds are dispersed
With a mere letter of persuasion.
The alien horns are cursed
On the first tower against invasion.

All:

When autumn winds
Sweep the border weeds,
We drink to our hearts' content.
For your meritorious deeds,
Let's drink to your health in the tent.

Du Bao:

(*To the previous tune*)
As His Majesty is amply blessed,
With our unanimous efforts,
The besieged city is no longer distressed.

Official, Officer:

Your commands are strict and stern;
Your tactics are hard to learn.

Du Bao:

With my letter to Li Quan and his wife,
I used the old trick of bribing the wife
And playing mournful alien tunes—
A word is as sharp as knife.
Without outside help, we would have no way;
It is the heaven that blesses us today.

All:

When autumn winds
Sweep the border weeds,
We drink to our hearts' content.

[内擂鼓介]

[老旦扮报子上]"金貂并入三公府。锦帐谁当万里城?"报老爷奏本已下,奉有圣旨,不准致仕。钦取老爷还朝,同平章军国大事。老夫人追赠一品贞烈夫人。

[末、净]平章乃宰相之职,君侯出将入相,官属不胜欣仰。

【前腔】

[末、净送酒介]揽貂蝉岁月淹留,
庆龙虎风云辐辏。
君侯此一去呵,
看洗兵河汉,
接天高手。
偏好桂花时节,
天香随马,
箫鼓鸣清昼。
到长安宫阙里报高秋,
可也河上砧声忆旧游?

[合前]

For your meritorious deeds,

Let's drink to your health in the tent.

(*Drums within*)

(*Enter Messenger*)

Messenger:

"The gifts and titles from the imperial court,

Are given to him who valiantly fought."

Your Excellency, the imperial decree has it that you are not allowed to retire. You are to return to the capital and be promoted to the position of Grand Chancellor. Her Ladyship has been conferred the posthumous title of first-rank Virtuous Lady.

Official, Officer:

Grand Chancellor is equal in rank to the prime minister. As your subordinates, we're overjoyed to hear that Your Excellency has been a minister of the highest rank.

(*Offer wine to Du Bao*)

(*To the previous tune*)

For years and years you will have high renown,

When you serve His Majesty in the capital town.

After your departure,

We'll lay aside arms of any sort,

When you serve in the court.

The fragrance of osmanthus bloom

Will accompany your steed;

Amid flutes and drums, by night you'll speed.

When you serve in the palace,

Will you remember the place where you succeed?

All:

When autumn winds

［外］诸公皆高才壮岁，自致封侯。如杜宝者，白首还朝，何足道哉！

【前腔】
　　每日价看镜登楼，
　　泪沾衣浑不如旧。
　　似江山如此，
　　光阴难又。
　　猛把吴钩看了，
　　阑干拍遍，
　　落日重回首。
　　此去呵，
　　恨南归草草也寄东流，
　　[举手介]你可也明月同谁啸庾楼？
　　[合前]
　　[生上]"腹稿已吟就，名单还未通。"[见丑介]大哥

>   Sweep the border weeds,
>
>   We drink to our hearts' content.
>
>   For your meritorious deeds,
>
>   Let's drink to your health in the tent.

Du Bao:

>   Talented and in the prime of your life, you are destined to attain peerage. As for me, I return to the capital in grey hair. It's nothing worth mentioning.
>
>   (*To the previous tune*)
>
>   When I look at the mirror every day,
>
>   I weep because old times won't stay.
>
>   The landscapes change;
>
>   The times change.
>
>   I caress my sword;
>
>   I tap the rails in melancholy tune,
>
>   Only to raise my head to see the moon.
>
> When I leave this time,
>
>   My feat will go with the eastward stream,
>
>   (*Raises his hands in salutation*)
>
>   But with whom will you sing under the moon?

All:

>   When autumn winds
>
>   Sweep the border weeds,
>
>   We drink to our hearts' content.
>
>   For your meritorious deeds,
>
>   Let's drink to your health in the tent.
>
>   (*Enter Liu Mengmei*)

Liu Mengmei:

>   "With a poem ready at the gate,

替我再一禀。

[丑]老爷正吃太平宴。

[生]我太平宴诗也想完一首了,太平宴还未完。

[丑]谁叫你想来?

[生]大哥,俺是嫡亲女婿,没奈何禀一禀。

[丑进禀介]禀老爷,那个嫡亲女婿没奈何禀见。

[外]好打!

[丑出作恼,推生走介]

[生]"老丈人高宴未终,咱半子礼当恭候。"[下]

[旦、贴扮女乐上]"壮士军前半死生,美人帐下能歌舞。"营妓们叩头。

【节节高】

辕门箫鼓啾,阵云收。

To see the envoy, I have yet to wait."

　　(*Greets the gatekeeper*)

Will you announce for me again, Sir?

Gatekeeper:

　　His Excellency is still at the Banquet of Peace.

Liu Mengmei:

　　I've composed a poem on the Banquet of Peace, but the banquet itself is not over yet.

Gatekeeper:

　　Who told you to compose the poem?

Liu Mengmei:

　　As I'm his son-in-law, Sir, will you announce for me?

Gatekeeper:

　　(*To Du Bao*)

　　Your Excellency, your son-in-law is at the door.

Du Bao:

　　You're asking for a spanking!

Liu Mengmei:

　　(*As the gatekeeper angrily pushes him*)

　　"The envoy is still at the fete;

　　His son-in-law has to wait."

　　(*Exit*)

　　(*Enter two singing girls*)

Singing Girls:

　　"On the battlefield the warriors die when they advance;

　　In the camp, the beauties sing and dance."

　　We camp-girls are kowtowing to you.

　　(*To the tune of* ***Jiejiegao***)

　　The flutes and drums resound in the camp

君恩可借淮扬寇?
貂插首,玉垂腰,金佩肘。
马敲金镫也秋风骤,
展沙堤笑拂朝天袖。
[合]但卷取江山献君王,
看玉京迎驾把笙歌奏。
[生上]"欲穷千里目,更上一层楼。"想歌阑宴罢,小生饥困了。不免冲席而进。
[丑拦介]饿鬼不羞?
[生恼介]你是老爷跟马贱人,敢辱我乘龙贵婿?打不的你。[生打丑介]
[外问介]军门外谁敢喧嚷?

When battle clouds disappear.

Can His Excellency remain here?

With a marten hat on your head,

A belt of jade on your waist

And a gold seal in your hand,

You'll gallop in the autumn breeze

And walk on a road covered with sand.

All:

As you have defended the motherland,

You'll be welcomed by the musical band.

(*Enter Liu Mengmei*)

Liu Mengmei:

"You can enjoy a grander sight

By climbing to a greater height."

Well, I suppose the songs have ended and the banquet is over by now. As I'm too hungry and tired, I have to force my way in.

Gatekeeper:

(*Tries to stop Liu Mengmei*)

Don't you feel the shame, you hungry devil?

Liu Mengmei:

(*Annoyed*)

How dare you a humble groom insult the son-in-law of an honoured lord? I'll give you a beating.

(*Beats the gatekeeper*)

Du Bao:

(*Calls out*)

Who's making such a noise outside the camp?

Gatekeeper:

[丑]是早上嫡亲女婿叫做没奈何的,破衣、破帽、破褡袄、破雨伞,手里拿一幅破画儿,说他饿的荒了,要来冲席。但劝的都打,连打了九个半,则剩下小的这半个脸儿。
[外恼介]可恶。本院自有禁约,何处寒酸,敢来胡赖?
[末、净]此生委系乘龙,属官礼当攀凤。
[外]一发中他计了。叫中军官暂时拿下那光棍。逢州换驿,递解到临安监候者。
[老旦扮中军官应介][出缚生介]
[生]冤哉,我的妻呵!"因贪弄玉为秦赘,且戴儒冠学楚囚。"[下]
[外]诸公不知。老夫因国难分张,心痛如割。又放着这等一个无名子来聒噪人,愈生伤感。
[末、净]老夫人受有国恩,名标烈史。兰玉自有,不必虑怀。叫乐人进酒。

It's that son-in-law who came this morning, with a tattered gown, a battered hat, a ragged bundle, a broken umbrella and a torn portrait. He says that he's so hungry and tired that he has to force his way in. He beats whoever wants to stop him. He's beaten nine and a half men — only half of my face is spared.

Du Bao:

(Angry)

What a shame! I've issued an official notice of prohibition. Where comes the wretched guy, making all the disturbances?

Official, Officer:

If he's really your son-in-law, we'll be honoured to meet him.

Du Bao:

You've been tricked! Tell the adjutant to arrest the scoundrel, send him by the postal route to Lin'an and put him to jail.

(*Enter Adjutant, shouting assent and tying Liu Mengmei up*)

Liu Mengmei:

Injustice! Oh, my dear wife!

"Coming to Huai'an for my dear wife,

I, a Confucian scholar, is put up in jail."

(*Exit*)

Du Bao:

You know, my heart breaks as my family breaks in the war. I'm all the more grieved when this vagabond makes all the trouble.

Official, Officer:

Her Ladyship has been conferred a posthumous title; her name has been recorded in the honourable list. You will have an heir in the future. So don't be grieved. Tell the singing girls to pour

【前腔】

[末、净]江南好宦游。

急难休,

樽前且进平安酒。

看福寿有,子女悠,夫人又。

[外]径醉矣。

[旦、贴作扶介]

[外泪介]闪英雄泪渍盈盈袖,

伤心不为悲秋瘦。

[合前]

[外]诸公请了。老夫归朝念切,即便起程。

[内鼓乐介]

【尾声】

明日离亭一杯酒。

[末、净]则无奈丹青圣主求。

[外笑介]怕画的上麒麟人白首。

the wine.

> (*To the previous tune*)
>
> In the south you'll have a better career.
>
> Now that the urgency is over,
>
> Please have a drink with good cheer.
>
> You'll enjoy a long and prosperous life,
>
> And have numerous heirs
>
> When you marry a second wife.

Du Bao:

> I've got drunk.
>
> (*Supported by singing girls*)
>
> (*Weeps*)
>
> I shed a hero's tears on beauties' sleeves,
>
> But never for autumns a hero grieves.

All:

> As you have defended the motherland,
>
> You'll be welcomed by the musical band.

Du Bao:

> I must say farewell to you now. As I'm eager to go to the capital city, I must set off at once.
>
> (*Drums within*)
>
> (*To the tune of Coda*)
>
> Tomorrow we'll drink a cup of parting wine.

Official, Officer:

> We hope to see your portrait in the Hall of Fame,

Du Bao:

> (*Laughs*)
>
> But only portraits of grey heads are in line.

Du Bao:

[外]万里沙西寇已平,
[末]东归衔命见双旌。
[净]塞鸿过尽残阳里,
[众]淮水长怜似镜清。

    When bandits have been conquered in the west,

Official:

    You go back to the court with flags abreast.

Officer:

    When wild geese fly across the sunset glow,

All:

    Quietly flows the Huai with your name impressed.

第五十一出　　榜　下

[老旦、丑扮将军持瓜、锤上]"凤舞龙飞作帝京，巍峨宫殿羽林兵。天门欲放传胪喜，江路新传奏凯声。"请了。圣驾升殿，在此祗候。

【北点绛唇】

[外扮老枢密上]整点朝纲，

运筹边饷，

山河壮。

[净扮苗舜宾上]翰苑文章，

显豁的升平象。

请了，恭喜李全纳款，皆老枢密调度之功也。

[外]正此引奏。前日先生看定状元试卷，蒙圣旨武

Scene Fifty-one
Announcing the Results

(*Enter two generals of palace guards, carrying the Imperial Squash and Mallet respectively*)

Generals:

"*The dragon and phoenix symbolise the crown,*
With palace guards patrolling up and down.
When results for imperial test are announced,
News of triumph spreads the capital town."

How do you do! His Majesty is going to give an audience. Let's wait in attendance.

(*Enter the aged War Minister*)

War Minister:

(*To the tune of* **Beidianjiangchun**)

I manage state affairs firm and fast

And raise funds for the border provisions.

Our country will forever last.

(*Enter Miao Shunbin*)

Miao Shunbin:

The scholars' essays

Sing praise of prosperity unsurpassed.

How do you do! Congratulations on the surrender of Li Quan and his gang. It all owes to your excellent maneuver.

War Minister:

I'm here to report this to His Majesty. When you fixed the number one candidate for the imperial examination the other

偃文修，今其时矣。
[净]正此题请。呀，一个老秀才走将来。好怪,好怪!
[末破衣巾捧表上]"先师孔夫子，未得见周王。本朝圣天子，得睹我陈最良。"非小可也。
[见外、净介]生员陈最良告揖。
[净惊介]又是遗才告考么?
[末]不敢，生员是这枢密老大人门下引奏的。
[外]则这生员，是杜安抚叫他招安了李全，便中带有降表。故此引见。

day, His Majesty decreed that the results would be announced when the war ended. It's high time for the announcement.

Miao Shunbin:

I'm here to submit my memorial to His Majesty. Well, here comes an old scholar. Strange, what has he to do here?

(*Enter Chen Zuiliang in shabby clothes, holding a memorial in his hand*)

Chen Zuiliang:

"*Confucius, far and wide his name rang,*
Never met the emperor of his day,
But the emperor of today
Will meet me, Chen Zuiliang."

That's something unusual.

(*Greets Miao Shunbin and War Minister*)

Your student Chen Zuiliang pays respect to you.

Miao Shunbin:

(*Surprised*)

Are you another student who missed the imperial examination?

Chen Zuiliang:

No, I'm not. I'm brought here by the War Minister for an audience.

War Minister:

Oh, he is the student whom Envoy Du sent to appease Li Quan. He's carried Li Quan's petition for surrender with him. That's why I brought him for the audience.

(*Drums within*)

Voice Within:

(*Solemnly*)

[内响鼓,唱介]奏事官上御道。

[外前跪,引末后跪、叩头介]

[外]掌管天下兵马知枢密院事臣谨奏:恭贺吾主,圣德天威。淮寇来降,金兵不动。有淮扬安抚臣杜宝,敬遣南安府学生员臣陈最良奏事,带有李全降表进呈。微臣不胜欢忭!

[内介]杜宝招安李全一事,就着生员陈最良详奏。

[外]万岁![起介]

[末]带表生员臣陈最良谨奏:

【驻云飞】
淮海维扬,
万里江山气脉长。
那安抚机谋壮,
矫诏从宽荡。
嗏,李贼快迎降,
他表文封上。
金主闻知,
不敢兵南向。

Those who have memorials to His Majesty, come to the royal court!

(*War Minister kneels at the front, with Chen Zuiliang at his heels, and kowtows*)

War Minister:

Your Majesty's War Minister in charge of all forces begs to report with congratulations that Your Majesty's heavenly virtue and earthly power have brought the Huai bandits to submission and halted the Jin troops. Du Bao, Envoy to Huaiyang, has dispatched Chen Zuiliang, student in the official school of Nan'an Prefecture, to report on this and submit Li Quan's petition for surrender. That's all I have to report.

Voice Within:

Let Chen Zuiliang make a detailed report on Du Bao's appeasement of Li Quan.

War Minister:

Long live the emperor!

(*Rises to his feet*)

Chen Zuiliang:

The letter carrier, student Chen Zuiliang, begs to report.

(*To the tune of Zhuyunfei*)

In the area from Yangtze to Huai,

Plains and mountains lie.

Envoy Du devised

A royal pardon and made him surprised.

Ha,

The bandit Li Quan surrendered at once

And wrote a petition for surrender as a good chance.

When the Jin emperor heard about it,

他则好看花到洛阳,
咱取次擒胡到汴梁。
[内介]奏事的午门候旨。
[末]万岁![起介]
[净跪介]前廷试看详文字官臣苗舜宾谨奏:
【前腔】
殿策贤良,
榜下诸生候久长。
乱定人欢畅,
文运天开放。
嗏,文字已看详,
胪传须唱。
莫遣夔龙,
久滞风云望。
早是蟾宫桂有香,
御酒封题菊半黄。
[内介]午门外候旨。
[净]万岁![起行介]今当榜期,这些寒儒,却也候久。

He dared not advance.

He could only reach Luoyang,

And we shall soon defeat him in Bianliang.

Voice Within:

Wait for the imperial decree outside the palace gate.

Chen Zuiliang:

Long live the emperor!

(*Rises to his feet*)

Miao Shunbin:

(*On his knees*)

Miao Shunbin, Your Majesty's Chief Examiner to the last imperial examination, begs to report.

(*To the previous tune*)

The scholars who took the imperial test

Are waiting for Your Majesty's behest.

Now that war has come to an end,

It's time for scholars to contend.

Ha,

Now that papers have been carefully marked,

It's time to announce the results.

We shall not keep the talented men

Waiting like dragons in the den.

The laurels are waiting for their owners;

The chrysanthemum wine is waiting for the winners.

Voice Within:

Wait for the imperial decree outside the palace gate.

Miao Shunbin:

Long live the emperor!

(*Rises to his feet and moves aside*)

[外笑介]则这陈秀才夹带一篇海贼文字,到中得快。
[内介]圣旨已到,跪听宣读。"朕闻李全贼平,金兵回避。甚喜,甚喜。此乃杜宝大功也。杜宝已前有旨,钦取回京。陈最良有奔走口舌之才,可充黄门奏事官,赐其冠带。其殿试进士,于中柳梦梅可以状元。金瓜仪从,杏苑赴宴。谢恩。"
[众呼"万岁"起介]
[众扮杂取冠带上]"黄门旧是黉门客,蓝袍新作紫袍仙。"
[末作换冠服介]二位老先生,告揖。
[外、净贺介]恭喜,恭喜。明日便借重新黄门唱榜了。

The results for the imperial examination will be announced today. These poor scholars have waited long enough.

War Minister:

(*Sneers*)

By smuggling a pirate's letter, this Mr Chen does not have to wait long.

Voice Within:

On your knees to listen to the imperial decree: "I am very, very pleased to learn of the appeasement of bandit Li Quan and the withdrawal of the Jin troops. These are the meritorious deeds of Du Bao, of whose return to the capital has been made clear in my previous decree. For his eloquence, Chen Zuiliang is appointed Palace Announcer at the palace gate, with due attire of hat and belt. Among all the candidates for this imperial examination, Liu Mengmei has been selected as the Number-one Scholar. He will attend the royal banquet, escorted by Imperial Squash and other guards of honour." Give thanks to the imperial decree.

(*All shout "Long live the emperor" and rise to their feet*)

(*Enter attendants with hat and belt*)

Attendants:

"When a student wins renown,

A purple robe replaces his blue gown."

Chen Zuiliang:

(*Changes clothes*)

Thank you very much, Your Excellencies.

War Minister, Miao Shunbin:

Congratulations, congratulations to you. Tomorrow we'll have a new announcer at the palace gate to make announcements.

[末]适间宣旨,状元柳梦梅何处人?
[净]岭南人,此生遭际的奇异。
[外]有甚奇异?
[净]其日试卷看详已定,将次进呈。恰好此生午门外放声大哭,告收遗才。原来为搬家小到京迟误。学生权收他在附卷进呈,不想点中状元。
[外]原来有此![末背想介]听来敢便是那个、那个柳梦梅?他那有家小?是了,和老道姑做一家儿。[回介]不瞒老先生,这柳梦梅也和晚生有旧。
[外、净]一发可喜可贺了。

[净]榜题金字射朝晖,
[外]独奏边机出殿迟。

Chen Zuiliang:

Where is Liu Mengmei, the Number-one Scholar proclaimed in the imperial decree, from?

Miao Shunbin:

He's from Lingnan. His experience is quite unusual.

War Minister:

How is it unusual?

Miao Shunbin:

When I finished marking the papers the other day and was about to submit the results to His Majesty, this scholar wailed loudly outside the palace gate and begged for a make-up examination. It happened that he missed the examination because he had moved his family to the capital. I included his paper in an appendix to my list and he, out of everybody's expectation, was selected as the Number-one Scholar.

War Minister:

How remarkable!

Chen Zuiliang:

(*Aside, to himself*)

It sounds like that Liu Mengmei I knew! Does he have a "family"? He must have married that old nun!

(*To War Minister and Miao Shunbin*)

To tell you the truth, I knew this Liu Mengmei.

War Minister, Miao Shunbin:

Another congratulation to you!

Miao Shunbin:

The gilded names of candidates shine bright;

War Minister:

The border conflict makes a long report.

［末］莫道官忙身老大，
［合］曾经卓立在丹墀。

Chen Zuiliang:

> Don't blame the official for displaying might;

All:

> He has a high position at the court.

第五十二出　索　元

【吴小四】
[净扮郭驼伞、包上]天九万,路三千。
月余程,抵半年。
破虱装衣担压肩,
压的头脐匾又圆,
挖喇察龟儿爬上天。
谢天,老驼到了临安。京城地面,好不繁华。则不知柳秀才去向,俺且往天街上瞧去。呀,一伙臭军踢秃秃走来,且自回避。正是:"不因渔父引,怎得见波涛!"[下]

【六幺令】
[老旦、丑扮军校旗、锣上]朝门榜遍,
怎生状元柳梦梅不见?
又不是黄巢下第题诗赸。

Scene Fifty-two
Searching for Liu Mengmei

(*Enter Hunchback Guo, carrying a bundle and an umbrella*)

Hunchback Guo:

(*To the tune of* Wuxiaosi)

Ninety thousand *li* by air

Or three thousand *li* by land is by no means near.

A month's journey

Takes me half a year.

The bundle of lousy clothes weighs on me

And makes my body awry;

I crawl like a turtle to the sky.

Thank heavens, I've reached Lin'an at last. The capital city is full of hustle and bustle. As I don't know where Mr Liu is, I'll try to look for him in the main street. Well, here comes a troop of dirty soldiers. I'd better step out of their way. As the saying goes,

"But for the fisherman to lead the way,

How can I see the billows in the bay?"

(*Exit*)

(*Enter two sergeants, with flags and gongs*)

Sergeants:

(*To the tune of* Liuyaoling)

We've put posters on every gate,

But where's the Number-one Scholar Liu Mengmei?

He can't be a rebel sneaking away.

排门的问，刻期宣，
再因循敢淹答了杏园公宴。

[老旦笑介]好笑，好笑，大宋国一场怪事。你道差不差？中了状元干鳖煞。你道奇不奇？中了状元啰喤唏。你道兴不兴？中了状元胡厮跄。你道山不山？中了状元一道烟。天下人古怪，不像岭南人。你瞧这驾牌上，"钦点状元岭南柳梦梅，年二十七岁，身中材，面白色。"这等明明道着，却普天下找不出这人？敢家去哩。亡化哩，睡觉哩？则淹了琼林宴席面儿。

[丑]哥，人山人海，那里淘气去？俺们把一位带了儒巾吃宴去。正身出来，算还他席面钱。

[老旦]使不得，羽林卫宴老军替得，琼林宴进士替不得。他要杏苑题诗。

[丑]哥，看见几个状元题诗哩。依你说叫去。[行叫

We go from door to door

Without delay,

Lest he miss the honourable day.

Sergeant A:

How funny it is! How funny it is! Something strange has happened in our country. Isn't it unbelievable that the Number-one Scholar makes light of his career! Isn't it incredible that the Number-one Scholar brings so much trouble! Isn't it unthinkable that the Number-one Scholar walks away without notice! Isn't it inconceivable that the Number-one Scholar disappears like a coil of smoke! Men from Lingnan are the oddity of oddities. Just look at the placard. It reads, "Wanted: Liu Mengmei, the Number-one Scholar by imperial decree, born in Lingnan, aged twenty-seven, of middle height, with a pale face." The descriptions are clear, but the man is nowhere to be found! Has he gone home, or passed away, or gone to sleep? He'll miss the palace banquet for him.

Sergeant B:

Brother, how can we pick him out in an ocean of people? Why don't we grab a Confucian scholar and bring him to the banquet? If the real person shows up, we'll pay him for the banquet he missed.

Sergeant A:

That won't do. It will do to find a substitute for a banquet of our Palace Guards, but it won't do to find a substitute for a banquet of scholars. The Number-one Scholar will have to compose a poem in the palace.

Sergeant B:

Brother, how many Number-one Scholars are heard of com-

介]状元柳梦梅那里?

[叫三次介]

[老旦]长安东西十二门,大街都无人应,小胡同叫去。

[丑]这苏木胡同有个海南会馆。叫地方问去。[叫介]

[内应介]老长官贵干?

[老旦、丑]天大事,你在睡梦哩!听分付。

【香柳娘】

问新科状元,问新科状元。

[内]何处人?

[众]广南乡贯。

[内]是何名姓?

[众]柳梦梅面白无巴缱。

posing impromptu poems? Well, I'll do as you like and continue to call out.

(*Walks and calls out*)

Where're you, Number-one Scholar Liu Mengmei?

(*Calls out three times*)

Sergeant A:

No one answers at the twelve city gates and through all the main streets. Let's call out in the side lanes.

Sergeant B:

There's a Hainan Regional Guild in Sumu Lane. Let's ask the community chief.

(*Calls out*)

Community Chief's Voice Within:

What can I do for you, sirs?

Sergeants:

An earth-shaking event has happened and you are still sleeping! Now listen,

(*To the tune of Xiangliuniang*)

We ask you about the new Number-one Scholar;

We ask you about the new Number-one Scholar.

Community Chief's Voice Within:

Where's he from?

Sergeants:

He's from Guangnan.

Community Chief's Voice Within:

What's his name?

Sergeants:

Liu Mengmei with a pale face without spots.

Community Chief's Voice Within:

[内]谁寻他来?
[众]是当今驾传,是当今驾传。
要得柳如烟,
才开杏花宴。
[内]俺这一带铺子都没有,则瓦市王大姐家歇着个番鬼。
[众]这等,去,去,去。
[合]柳梦梅也天,柳梦梅也天。
好几个盘旋,
影儿不见。[下]
[贴扮妓上]"残莺何事不知秋?日日悲看水独流。便从巴峡穿巫峡,错把杭州作汴州。"奴家王大姐是也。开个门户在此。天,一个孤老不见,几个长官撞的来。
[老旦、丑上]王大姐喜哩。柳状元在你家。

Who's searching for him?

Sergeants:

> The present emperor;
>
> The present emperor.
>
> When the man is found,
>
> The palace banquet will be held.

Community Chief's Voice Within:

> The man of your description is nowhere to be found around here, but there's a southerner staying in Sister Wang's place in the marketplace.

Sergeants:

> Well, let's go, let's go.
>
> Ah Liu Mengmei,
>
> Ah Liu Mengmei!
>
> We've searched several rounds,
>
> But he's nowhere to be found.
>
> (*Exeunt*)
>
> (*Enter Sister Wang, a harlot*)

Sister Wang:

> *"Why doesn't a harlot know of her age?*
>
> *She only grieves o'er flowing rivers in her cage.*
>
> *While gorge by gorge the river flows down,*
>
> *She mistakes Hangzhou for the capital town."*
>
> I'm Sister Wang, opening a little brothel here. Oh heavens, there's not a visitor today, but here come two sergeants.
>
> (*Enter the two sergeants*)

Sergeants:

> Congratulations, Sister Wang. The Number-one Scholar Liu is in your house.

［贴］什么柳状元？

［众］番鬼哩。

［贴］不知道。

［众］地方报哩。

【前腔】笑花牵柳眠，笑花牵柳眠。

［贴］昨日有个鸡，不着裤去了。

［众］原来十分形现。

敢柳遮花映做葫芦缠。

有状元么？

［贴］则有个状匾。

［丑］房儿里状匾去。［进房搜介］

［众诨，贴走下介］

［众］找烟花状元，找烟花状元。

热赶在谁边，

Sister Wang:

What Number-one Scholar Liu?

Sergeants:

A southerner.

Sister Wang:

I don't know him.

Sergeants:

The community chief gives the information.

(*To the previous tune*)

A scholar sleeps with a flower of a girl;

A scholar sleeps with a flower of a girl.

Sister Wang:

A visitor came yesterday and he went off before he got his pants on.

Sergeants:

Well said, well said,

The man slipped off from your bed!

Is the Number-one Scholar in?

Sister Wang:

I've only got a scalar.

Sergeant B:

Let's go and get the scalar.

(*The sergeants go into the house and search, molesting*)

(*Exit Sister Wang, running away when she is molested by the sergeants*)

Sergeants:

We seek for the amorous Number-one Scholar;

We seek for the amorous Number-one Scholar.

He's on which pillow

毛臊打教遍。
去罢。
[合前][下]

【前腔】
[净拐杖上]到长安日边，到长安日边，
果然风宪，
九街三市排场遍。
柳相公呵，
他行踪杳然，他行踪杳然。
有了俏家缘，
风声儿落谁店？
少不的大道上行走。
那柳梦梅也天！
[老旦、丑上]柳梦梅也天！
好几个盘旋，
影儿不见。
[丑作撞跌净，净叫介]跌死人，跌死人！

　　　　To idle away his sorrow?

　　Let's go.

　　　　Ah Liu Mengmei,

　　　　Ah Liu Mengmei!

　　　　We've searched several rounds,

　　　　But he's nowhere to be found.

　　　　(*Exeunt*)

　　　　(*Enter Hunchback Guo, leaning on a stick*)

Hunchback Guo:

　　　　(*To the previous tune*)

　　　　Here I am in the capital town;

　　　　Here I am in the capital town.

　　　　It's a city for the elite,

　　　　With marketplaces and crowded streets.

　　Oh, Mr Liu,

　　　　You've left no trace;

　　　　You've left no trace.

　　　　With a pretty wife on your side,

　　　　Where on earth will you hide?

　　I've no way out than walking on the streets.

　　　　Ah Liu Mengmei!

　　　　(*Enter the two sergeants*)

Sergeants:

　　　　Ah Liu Mengmei!

　　　　We've searched several rounds,

　　　　But he's nowhere to be found.

Hunchback Guo:

　　　　(*Yells when Sergeant B bumps into him*)

　　　　You're killing me! You're killing me!

[丑作拿净介]俺们叫柳梦梅,你也叫柳梦梅。则拿你官里去。

[净叩头介]是了,梅花观的事发了。小的不知情。

[众笑介]定说你知情!是他什么人?

[净]听禀:老儿呵!

【前腔】

替他家种园,替他家种园,

远来探看。

[众作忙]可寻着他哩?

[净]猛红尘透不出东君面。

[众]你定然知他去向。

[净]长官可怜,则听是他到南安,其余不知。

[众]好笑,好笑!他到这临安应试,得中状元了。

Sergeant B:

(*Catches hold of Hunchback Guo*)

We're calling Liu Mengmei and you're also calling Liu Mengmei. We'll put you in jail!

Hunchback Guo:

(*Kowtows*)

Oh, I see. It must be for the Plum Blossom Nunnery affairs. I know nothing about it.

Sergeants:

(*Laugh*)

You must know something! What's your relationship with him?

Hunchback Guo:

I'll tell you everything.

(*To the previous tune*)

I tended the garden for him;

I tended the garden for him.

I've walked all the way to see him.

Sergeants:

(*Anxious to know*)

Have you found him?

Hunchback Guo:

There's nowhere to find him.

Sergeants:

You must know his whereabouts.

Hunchback Guo:

Pity on me. I only know that he's been to Nan'an.

Sergeants:

Funny, funny indeed! He's been here in Lin'an to enter the imperial examination and has become the Number-one Scholar.

[净惊喜介]他中了状元,他中了状元!
踏的菜园穿,
攀花上林苑。
长官,他中了状元,怕没处寻他!
[众]便是哩。
[合前]
[众]也罢,饶你这老儿,协同寻他去。

[老旦]一第由来是出身,
[丑]五更风水失龙鳞。
[净]红尘望断长安陌,
[合]只在他乡何处人?

Hunchback Guo:

    (*Surprised and overjoyed*)

    He's become the Number-one Scholar;

    He's become the Number-one Scholar.

    He came from the vegetable garden

    To make his way to the royal garden.

Now that he's the Number-one Scholar, he can't get lost!

Sergeants:

    We agree.

Hunchback Guo, Sergeants:

    Ah Liu Mengmei,

    Ah Liu Mengmei!

    We've searched several rounds,

    But he's nowhere to be found.

Sergeants:

    Well, we'll spare you this time but you'll search for him with us.

Sergeant A:

    After he won the imperial test,

Sergeant B:

    He lets the honour slip out of his hand.

Hunchback Guo:

    Along the road of dust and sand,

Sergeants, Hunchback Guo:

    Where can he be in this strange land?

第五十三出　　硬　拷

【风入松慢】
[生上]无端雀角土牢中。
是什么孔雀屏风?
一杯水饭东床用,
草床头绣褥芙蓉。
天呵,系颈的是定昏店,赤绳羁凤;
领解的是蓝桥驿,配递乘龙。
"梦到江南身旅羁,包羞忍耻是男儿。自家妻父犹如此,若问傍人那得知!"俺柳梦梅因领杜小姐言命,去淮扬谒见杜安抚。他在众官面前,怕俺寒儒薄相,故意不行识认,递解临安。想他将次下马,提审之时,见了春容,不容不认。只是眼下凄惶也。
[净扮狱官,丑扮狱卒持棍上]"试唤皋陶鬼,方知狱吏

Scene Fifty-three
Interrogating Liu Mengmei

(*Enter Liu Mengmei*)

Liu Mengmei:

(*To the tune of* **Fengrusongman**)

I'm jailed for not a single reason at all;

Is this due treatment for a son-in-law?

All I've got is a bowl of porridge

And a mattress of straw.

Oh heavens!

All the way I've come

To see my father-in-law,

But who knows that he should put to jail

His very son-in-law!

"To be detained here in a foreign place,

A gentleman must learn to bear disgrace.

If my father-in-law acts like this,

Who else would understand the case?"

I, Liu Mengmei, followed Miss Du's words to go to Huaiyang and meet Envoy Du. I was sent to jail in Lin'an, because he was not willing to accept me as his son-in-law before his subordinates. I think that he will have to accept me when he comes to question me and sees the self-portrait of his daughter. For the time being, however, I'm in a wretched situation.

(*Enter the warden, followed by a jailer holding a rod in his hand*)

尊。"咄！淮安府解来囚徒那里？

[生见举手介]

[净]见面钱？

[生]少有。

[丑]入监油？

[生]也无。

[净恼介]哎呀，一件也没有，大胆来举手。[打介]

[生]不要打，尽行装检去便了。

[丑检介]这个酸鬼，一条破被单，裹一轴小画儿。

[看画介]

[丑]是轴观音，送奶奶供养去。

[生]都与你去，则留下轴画儿。

Warden:

"When you have the prison god in sight,

You'll know the warden's might."

Well, where's the prisoner from Huai'an?

(*On hearing these words, Liu Mengmei raises his hands*)

What do you have for a gift for our first meeting?

Liu Mengmei:

I've got nothing to give you.

Jailer:

What about your entrance fee?

Liu Mengmei:

I've got nothing to give you, either.

Warden:

(*Annoyed*)

Then, how you dare to raise your hands when you've got nothing for us!

(*Beats Liu Mengmei*)

Liu Mengmei:

Oh, please don't! You can take whatever you find in my bundle!

Jailer:

(*Searches Liu Mengmei's bundle*)

What a wretched devil! He's only got a torn bed-sheet and a small scroll of painting.

(*Looks at the portrait*)

It's a portrait of Bodhisattva Guanyin. I'll give it to my grandma.

Liu Mengmei:

Take everything except the scroll.

(*The jailer tries to grab the scroll from Liu Mengmei's hands*)

[丑作抢画，生扯介]
[末扮公差上]"僵杀乘龙婿，冤遭下马威。"狱官那里？
[丑揖介]原来平章府祗候哥。
[末票示介]平章府提取送解犯人一名，及随身行李赴审。
[丑]人犯在此，行李一些也无。
[生]都是这狱官搬去了。
[末]搬了几件？拿狗官平章府去。
[丑、净慌叩头介]则这轴画、被单儿。
[末]这狗官！还了秀才，快起解去。
[净、丑应介][押生行介]老相公，你便行动些儿。
"略知孔子三分礼，不犯萧何六尺条。"[下]

(*Enter the bailiff*)

Bailiff:

"The son-in-law is put in jail,

Where he suffers from blackmail."

Where's the warden?

Jailer:

(*Bows his salutation*)

So you're from the Grand Chancellor's office.

Bailiff:

(*Shows the warrant*)

Orders from the Grand Chancellor to fetch a prisoner for interrogation. He'll bring all his belongings with him.

Jailer:

The prisoner's here, but he's got no belongings.

Liu Mengmei:

He's taken away everything.

Bailiff:

What did he take? I'll bring the jailers to the Grand Chancellor's office.

Jailer, Warden:

(*Kowtow*)

All he's got is a scroll of painting and a bed-sheet.

Bailiff:

Give them back to the scholar, you dirty dogs, and bring him to the Grand Chancellor's office.

Warden, Jailer:

(*Respond and escort Liu Mengmei*)

Will you start moving, Sir?

"If you learn the Confucian rites with awe,

【唐多令】
　　[外引众上]玉带蟒袍红，
新参近九重。
耿秋光长剑倚崆峒。
归到把平章印总，
浑不是黑头公。
"秋来力尽破重围。入掌银台护紫微。回头却叹浮生事，长向东风有是非。"自家杜平章。因淮扬平寇，叨蒙圣恩，超迁相位。前日有个棍徒，假充门婿。已着递解临安府监候。今日不免取来细审一番。
[净、丑押生上]
[杂扮门官唱门介]临安府解犯人进。[见介]
[生]岳丈大人拜揖。
[外坐笑介]
[生]人将礼乐为先。
[众大呼喝介]
[生长叹介]

You will not violate the law."

(*Exeunt all*)

(*Enter Du Bao, followed by attendants*)

Du Bao:

(*To the tune of* **Tangduoling**)

In a crimson robe girdled by a belt of jade,

I'm promoted to serve in the court.

I stand with a sword of shining blade.

Now I take the Grand Chancellor's post,

But my hair has greyed.

"Now that I've quelled the autumn strife,

I'm thus promoted to the highest post.

When I look back at my eventful life,

I've suffered more than I can boast."

I'm Du Bao, the Grand Chancellor. As I've quelled the bandits in Huaiyang, I've been promoted by His Majesty to the position of Grand Chancellor. But a vagabond came the other day and pretended to be my son-in-law, and so I had him put in jail in Lin'an. Today I'm going to interrogate him.

(*Enter Liu Mengmei, escorted by the warden and the jailer*)

Doorman:

(*Announces*)

Here comes the prisoner from the Lin'an Prefecture!

Liu Mengmei:

(*Bows*)

My respect to you, father-in-law.

(*Du Bao remains seated and laughs*)

Man should put courtesy and music in the first place.

(*Sighs when attendants shout at him*)

【新水令】
　　则这怯书生剑气吐长虹，
　　原来丞相府十分尊重，
　　声息儿忒汹涌。
　　咱礼数缺通融，
　　曲曲躬躬；
　　他那里半抬身全不动。
　　[外]寒酸，你是那色人数？犯了法，在相府阶前不跪！
　　[生]生员岭南柳梦梅，乃老大人女婿。
　　[外]呀，我女已亡故三年。不说到纳采下茶，便是指腹裁襟，一些没有。何曾得有个女婿来？可笑，可恨！祗候们与我拿下。
　　[生]谁敢拿！
【步步娇】
　　[外]我有女无郎，
　　早把他青年送。
　　划口儿轻调哄。
　　便做是我远房门婿呵，
　　你岭南，吾蜀中，
　　牛马风遥，甚处里丝萝共？

(*To the tune of **Xinshuiling***)

A scholar has to learn more

When he enters a noble house

And faces the deafening roar.

However I bowed,

However I show courtesy,

He sat motionless and proud.

Du Bao:

Wretched pedant, what do you think you are? As an offender of the law, why aren't you on your knees before me?

Liu Mengmei:

I'm Liu Mengmei, a scholar from Lingnan. I'm your son-in-law!

Du Bao:

My daughter has been dead for three years. She had neither accepted betrothal gifts, nor been engaged before her birth or in her childhood. How can I have a son-in-law? How ridiculous! How disgraceful! Attendants, have him tightly bound!

Liu Mengmei:

Who dares to bind me!

Du Bao:

(*To the tune of **Bubujiao***)

I have no son, but have a daughter,

Who died young.

How can I believe your wagging tongue?

You cannot even wed my distant niece—

As you come from Lingnan

While I come from Sichuan,

We are so far away

敢一棍儿走秋风!
指说关亲、骗的军民动。
[生]你这样女婿,眠书雪案,立榜云霄,自家行止用不尽,定要秋风老大人?
[外]还强嘴!搜他裹袱里,定有假雕书印,并赃拿贼。
[丑开袱介]破布单一条,画观音一幅。
[外看画惊介]呀,见赃了。这是我女孩儿春容。你可到南安,认的石道姑么?
[生]认的。
[外]认的个陈教授么?
[生]认的。
[外]天眼恢恢,原来劫坟贼便是你。左右采下打。

That you cannot meet anyone from my clan.

You go begging here and there;

By claiming to be my relative,

You're trying to stir up some smoke in the air.

Liu Mengmei:

As your son-in-law, I study hard day and night, summer and winter, so that I can rank high in the imperial examination. As I'm talented enough to sustain myself, why should I beg from you?

Du Bao:

How dare you talk back! Now search his bundle to see whether he has some forged letters or seals. These evidences will be enough to put him in jail.

Jailer:

(*Unwraps the bundle*)

He's got a torn bed-sheet and a portrait of Bodhisattva Guanyin.

Du Bao:

(*Astonished to see the portrait*)

Now I've got you at last! This is my daughter's self-portrait. Did you go to Nan'an and meet Sister Stone?

Liu Mengmei:

Yes, I did.

Du Bao:

Did you meet Tutor Chen?

Liu Mengmei:

Yes, I did.

Du Bao:

Oh, the heaven is like an enormous net and its meshes allow no escape. So it's you who robbed the grave! Attendants,

[生]谁敢打?

[外]这贼快招来。

[生]谁是贼?老大人拿贼见赃,不曾捉奸见床来。

【折桂令】

你道证明师一轴春容。

[外]春容分明是殉葬的。

[生]可知道是苍苔石缝,迸坼了云踪?

[外]快招来。

[生]我一谜的承供,

供的是开棺见喜,挡煞逢凶。

[外]圹中还有玉鱼、金碗。

[生]有金碗呵,两口儿同匙受用;

玉鱼呵,和我九泉下比目和同。

[外]还有哩。

take him away and give him a sound flogging!

Liu Mengmei:

Who dares to beat me!

Du Bao:

Then make confessions, you wretched thief!

Liu Mengmei:

Whom are you calling a thief? You should catch the thief red-handed and catch the lovers in bed.

(*To the tune of Zheguiling*)

You take the portrait as the evidence.

Du Bao:

The portrait was buried in my daughter's grave.

Liu Mengmei:

Don't you know that rocks might crack

And reveal the portrait at the back?

Du Bao:

Make confessions at once!

Liu Mengmei:

This is all I have to say—

I opened the grave to save your daughter,

But I myself have fallen a prey.

Du Bao:

There was also a jade fish and a gold bowl buried in the grave.

Liu Mengmei:

The gold bowl is

For man and wife to share;

The jade fish is

To swim with me as a pair.

Du Bao:

［生］玉碾的玲珑，金锁的玎珰。
［外］都是那道姑。
［生］则那石姑姑他识趣拿奸纵，
却不似你杜爷爷逞拿贼威风。
［外］他明明招了。叫令史取过一张坚厚官绵纸，写下亲供："犯人一名柳梦梅，开棺劫财者斩。"写完，发与那死囚，于斩字下押个花字。会成一宗文卷，放在那里。
［贴扮吏取供纸上］禀老爷定个斩字。
［外写介］
［贴叫生押花字］
［生不伏介］
［外］你看这吃敲才！

【江儿水】
眼脑儿天生贼，
心机使的凶。
还不画花？
［生］谁惯来。

Did you get anything else?

Liu Mengmei:

A roller made of jade

And a lock made of gold.

Du Bao:

Sister Stone is to blame.

Liu Mengmei:

Sister Stone let the lovers go without grief

While Your Excellency makes much ado about a thief.

Du Bao:

As he's made his confession, secretary, take a piece of official paper and write on it his confession and the verdict: "The criminal Liu Mengmei is sentenced to death because he opened the coffin and robbed its contents." When the document is completed, let the criminal sign his name under the word "death" and then keep the document in the files.

(*Enter the secretary with a piece of official paper*)

Secretary:

Would Your Excellency indict the sentence here?

(*Du Bao writes. The secretary forces Liu Mengmei to sign. Liu Mengmei refuses*)

Du Bao:

The thief is asking for a sound beating.

(*To the tune of Jiangershui*)

You're born with eyes of a thief,

Doing evils without grief.

Do you still refuse to sign?

Liu Mengmei:

I've never done anything wrong.

［外］你纸笔砚墨则好招详用。
［生］生员又不犯奸盗。
［外］你奸盗诈伪机谋中。
［生］因令爱之故。
［外］你精奇古怪虚头弄。
［生］令爱现在。
［外］现在么，
把他玉骨抛残心痛。
［生］抛在那里？
［外］后苑池中，
月冷断魂波动。
［生］谁见来？
［外］陈教授来报知。
［生］生员为小姐费心，除了天知地知，陈最良那得知！
【雁儿落】
　　我为他礼春容、叫的凶，

Du Bao:

    With ink and paper you should confess.

Liu Mengmei:

    I've committed neither theft nor adultery.

Du Bao:

    You've committed theft and adultery to excess.

Liu Mengmei:

    What I did was for your daughter's sake.

Du Bao:

    Deceit and trickery are in your veins.

Liu Mengmei:

    Your daughter is now...

Du Bao:

    You scattered my daughter's remains.

Liu Mengmei:

    Where did I scatter her remains?

Du Bao:

    In the garden lake,

    Where the chilly waves shiver for her sake.

Liu Mengmei:

    Who's the witness?

Du Bao:

    Tutor Chen has told me everything.

Liu Mengmei:

    Only heaven and earth know my efforts for Miss Du. How can Tutor Chen know?

    (*To the tune of* ***Yanerluo***)

    For Miss Du,

        I worshipped her portrait

我为他展幽期、耽怕恐,
我为他点神香、开墓封,
我为他唾灵丹、活心孔,
我为他偎熨的体酥融,
我为他洗发的神清莹,
我为他度情肠、款款通,
我为他启玉肱、轻轻送,
我为他软温香、把阳气攻,
我为他抢性命、把阴程迸。
神通,医的他女孩儿能活动。
通也么通,到如今风月两无功。

    And called her name aloud.
For Miss Du,
    I had rendezvous with her
    And lived in fear but still avowed.
For Miss Du,
    I burned the sacred incense
    And opened up her grave.
For Miss Du,
    I took the quicksilver from her mouth
    And revived her from the cave.
For Miss Du,
    I warmed her with my flesh
    And made her come back to life.
For Miss Du,
    I gave her a sense of love
    And made her my dear wife.
For Miss Du,
    I raised her arms
    And stretched them up and down.
For Miss Du,
    I thawed her heart
    And made her alive and well.
For Miss Du,
    I saved her life
    From the darkest hell.
    As a wonder of love,
    I have relieved her pain.
    Wonder or not,
    I've saved her life, but loved in vain.

[外]这贼都说的是什么话?着鬼了。左右,取桃条打他,长流水喷他。

[丑取桃条上]"要的门无鬼,先教园有桃。"桃条在此。

[外]高吊起打。

[众吊起生,作打介]

[生叫痛,转动,众诨、打鬼介,喷水介]

[净扮郭驼拐杖同老旦、贴扮军校持金瓜上]"天上人间忙不忙?开科失却状元郎。"一向找寻柳梦梅,今日再寻不见,打老驼。

[净]难道要老驼赔?买酒你吃,叫去罢。[叫介]状元柳梦梅那里?

[外听介]

[众叫下]

[外问丑介]

Du Bao:

What nonsense is he talking about? He must have been haunted by the ghosts. Attendants, fetch the peach canes to flog him and fetch the water to spurt over him.

Jailer:

(*Goes off stage and enters again with peach canes*)

"To drive away the ghost,

Grow peach trees for the host."

Here are the peach canes.

Du Bao:

Hang him up and flog him!

(*The attendants hang Liu Mengmei up and flog him. As Liu Mengmei cries and twists in pain, the attendants mimic a show of dispelling the ghost and spurting the water*)

(*Enter Hunchback Guo, with Sergeants A and B carrying Imperial Squashes*)

Sergeants A and B:

"The heaven and earth is in chaos all around;

The Number-one Scholar is nowhere to be found."

We've been looking for Liu Mengmei all these days. If we can't find him today, we'll give this hunchback a sound beating.

Hunchback Guo:

Am I to blame? I'll buy some wine for you, but let's go on with our search now.

(*Shouts*)

Where are you, Number-one Scholar Liu Mengmei?

(*Du Bao listens. Hunchback Guo and the sergeants go on with their shouting when they exit. Du Bao asks the jailer*)

［丑］不见了新科状元，圣旨着沿街寻叫。
［生］大哥，开榜哩。状元谁？
［外恼介］这贼闲管，掌嘴，掌嘴。
［丑掌生嘴介］
［生叫冤屈介］
［老旦、贴、净依前上］"但闻丞相府，不见状元郎。"咦，平章府打喧闹哩。［听介］
［净］里面声息，像有俺家相公哩！
［众进介］
［净向前见哭介］吊起的是我家相公也！
［生］列位救我。
［净］谁打相公来？

Jailer:

As the Number-one Scholar is missing, His Majesty decrees that they search for him by shouting along the streets.

Liu Mengmei:

Have the results for the imperial examination been announced, Sir? Who's the Number-one Scholar?

Du Bao:

(*Annoyed*)

It's none of your business. Attendants, slap his face! Slap his face!

(*Liu Mengmei protests when the jailer slaps him on the face*)
(*Re-enter Hunchback Guo with Sergeants A and B carrying Imperial Squashes*)

Sergeants A and B:

"From the chancellor's house comes a noisy sound,
But the Number-one Scholar is still nowhere to be found."

Well, what's the row from the Grand Chancellor's house?

(*Listen to the row*)

Hunchback Guo:

My master's voice seems to come from within.

(*Hunchback Guo and the sergeants enter Du Bao's house*)

Hunchback Guo:

(*Bursts into tears when he sees Liu Mengmei*)

Why do you hang up my master?

Liu Mengmei:

Help! Help!

Hunchback Guo:

Who has ordered to beat you?

[生]是这平章。

[净将拐杖打外介]拚老命打这平章。

[外恼介]谁敢无礼?

[老旦、贴]驾上的,来寻状元柳梦梅。

[生]大哥,柳梦梅便是小生。

[净向前解生,外扯净跌介]

[生]你是老驼,因何至此?

[净]俺一径来寻相公,喜的中了状元。

[生]真个的!快向钱塘门外报与杜小姐知道。

[老旦、贴]找着了状元,俺们也报知黄门官奏去。

"未去朝天子,先来激相公。"[下]

Liu Mengmei:
   The Grand Chancellor.

Hunchback Guo:
   (*Waves his stick to strike at Du Bao*)
   I'll risk my life to strike at the Grand Chancellor.

Du Bao:
   (*Irritated*)
   Dare you!

Sergeants A and B:
   By the imperial decree, we're searching for the Number-one Scholar Liu Mengmei.

Liu Mengmei:
   I'm Liu Mengmei, Sir!
   (*When Hunchback Guo goes forward to release Liu Mengmei, Du Bao tries to pull him but stumbles*)

Liu Mengmei:
   Oh, you're Hunchback Guo! How come that you are here?

Hunchback Guo:
   I've been looking for you all the way here. I'm overjoyed that you have become the Number-one Scholar.

Liu Mengmei:
   Really! Go quickly outside the Qiantang Gate and tell Miss Du about it.

Sergeants A and B:
   Since we've found the Number-one Scholar, we'll report the news to the Palace Announcer.
   "Before the imperial audience,
   He has trouble with the chancellor."
   (*Exeunt Sergeants A and B, and Hunchback Guo*)

[外]一路的光棍去了。正好拷问这厮，左右再与俺吊将起。

[生]待俺分诉些，难道状元是假得的？

[外]凡为状元者，有登科录为证。你有何据？则是吊了打便了。

[生叫苦介]

[净扮苗舜宾引老旦，贴扮堂候官，捧冠袍带上]"踏破草鞋无觅处，得来全不费工夫。"老公相住手，有登科录在此。

【侥侥犯】

[净]则他是御笔亲标第一红，
柳梦梅为梁栋。

[外]敢不是他？

[净]是晚生本房取中的。

[生]是苗老师哩，救门生一救！

[净笑介]你高吊起文章钜公，

Du Bao:
>Now that these vagabonds are gone, I'll go on with my interrogation. Attendants, hang up this fellow again.

Liu Mengmei:
>Please listen to me. How can I feign to be the Number-one Scholar?

Du Bao:
>The Number-one Scholar must have his name registered in the list. Can you show me the list? Attendants, just hang him up and give him a sound flogging!
>
>(*Liu Mengmei protests*)
>
>(*Enter Miao Shunbin, followed by two officers carrying the official head-dress, robe and belt*)

Miao Shunbin:
>"You may wear out straw shoes and search in vain,
>But find the man by chance with little pain."
>
>Your Excellency, please stop! Here's the list.
>
>(*To the tune of Jiaojiaofan*)
>
>As the most successful candidate,
>Liu Mengmei is a pillar of the state.

Du Bao:
>I'm afraid he's not the right person.

Miao Shunbin:
>I'm his examiner myself.

Liu Mengmei:
>Oh, honourable Master Miao! Help me!

Miao Shunbin:
>(*Smiles*)
>You're hanging up a man of high seating

打桃枝受用。
告过老公相,军校,快请状元下吊。
[贴放,生叫"疼煞"介]
[净]可怜,可怜!
是斯文倒吃尽斯文痛,
无情棒打多情种。
[生]他是我丈人。
[净]原来是倚太山压卵欺鸾凤。
[老旦]状元悬梁、刺股。
[净]罢了,一领宫袍遮盖去。
[外]什么宫袍,扯了他!

【收江南】
[外扯住冠服介]
[生]呀,你敢抗皇宣骂敕封,
早裂绽我御袍红。
似人家女婿呵,
拜门也似乘龙。
偏我帽光光走空,
你桃夭夭煞风。
[老旦替生冠服插花介]

And giving him a sound beating.

That's the whole story, Your Excellency. Officers, release the Number-one Scholar at once.

(*Officer B releases Liu Mengmei, who groans with pain*)

Miao Shunbin:

Poor fellow! Poor fellow!

A scholar suffers from pains

From ruthless canes.

Liu Mengmei:

He's my father-in-law.

Miao Shunbin:

The father-in-law has put you to ordains.

Officer A:

The Number-one Scholar has to suffer somehow.

Miao Shunbin:

Forget about it. Now give him the official garments.

Du Bao:

Give him the official garments? Tear up the garments!

(*Tries to tear up the official garments*)

Liu Mengmei:

(*To the tune of Shoujiangnan*)

You defy royal orders to the excess

If you tear up the official dress.

The first visit by a son-in-law

Should be honoured all the more.

But you won't listen to what I explain

And put me to the cane.

(*Officer A helps Liu Mengmei with his official garments and puts a flower on his robe*)

[生]老平章,
好看我插宫花帽压君恩重。
[外]柳梦梅怕不是他。果是他,便童生应试,也要候案。怎生殿试了,不候榜开,来淮扬胡撞?
[生]老平章是不知,为因李全兵乱,放榜稽迟。令爱闻得老平章有兵寇之事,着我一来上门,二来报他再生之喜,三来扶助你为官。好意成恶意,今日可是你女婿了?
[外]谁认你女婿来!

【园林好】
[净、众]嗔怪你会平章的老相公,
不刮目破窑中吕蒙。
忒做作、前辈们性重。
[笑介]敢折倒你丈人峰?
[外]悔不将劫坟贼监候奏请为是。

Liu Mengmei:

Your Excellency,

Just see what great honour I obtain.

Du Bao:

I'm afraid that he's not the right Liu Mengmei. If he were, he should have waited for the announcement after he took the imperial examination. How is it that he roamed to Huaiyang instead of waiting for the announcement in the capital?

Liu Mengmei:

You don't know the whole story, Your Excellency. The announcement was postponed because Li Quan started an insurrection. On hearing that you were engaged in the battle against the bandits, your daughter told me to present myself to you, to inform you of her revival and to offer my service to you. My good intentions have been ill returned. Now, will you accept me as your son-in-law?

Du Bao:

I won't!

Miao Shunbin, Attendants:

(*To the tune of* **Yuanlinhao**)

You are to blame

For your contempt for a scholar poorly dressed.

Like elderly men,

You put on airs to a guest.

(*Laugh*)

You have an honourable son-in-law at your behest.

Du Bao:

I regret that I didn't keep him in jail until death sentence for this grave robber is confirmed.

【沽美酒】
　　[生笑介]你这孔夫子,把公冶长陷缧绁中。
　　我柳盗跖打地洞向鸳鸯冢。
　　有日呵,把燮理阴阳问相公,
　　耍无语对春风。
　　则待列笙歌画堂中,
　　抢丝鞭御街拦纵。
　　把穷柳毅赔笑在龙宫,
　　你老夫差失敬了韩重。
　　我呵,人雄气雄,
　　老平章深躬浅躬,
　　请状元升东转东。
　　呀,那时节才提破了牡丹亭杜鹃残梦。
　　老平章请了,你女婿赴宴去也。
【北尾】
　　你险把司天台失陷了文星空,
　　把一个有对付的玉洁冰清烈火烘。
　　咱想有今日呵,
　　越显的俺玩花柳的女郎能,
　　则要你那打桃条的相公懂。[下]
　　[外吊场]异哉,异哉!还是贼,还是鬼?堂候官,去请那新黄门陈老爷到来商议。

Liu Mengmei:

>(*Laughs*)
>
>(*To the tune of Gumeijiu*)
>
>You put me in jail
>
>Because I dug your daughter's grave.
>
>As Grand Chancellor,
>
>You can't answer for how you behave.
>
>I thought I would be welcomed in the hall
>
>And would ride through the street,
>
>But instead of good reception,
>
>A rude father-in-law I meet.
>
>When I become a man of esteem,
>
>You will bow and scrape
>
>And treat me as an honoured guest —
>
>Only then shall I realise my long-cherished dream.

I must take my leave now, Your Excellency. I'm going to the palace dinner.

>(*To the tune of Beiwei*)
>
>You nearly murdered the Number-one Scholar
>
>By inflicting upon him all the pains.

When I think of the glory I receive today,

>I do admire my wife's gifts
>
>And my father-in-law's canes.
>
>(*Exeunt Liu Mengmei, Miao Shunbin, and Officers*)

Du Bao:

How queer! Queer indeed! Is he a thief or a ghost? Attendant, go and ask the Palace Announcer to come over for consultations.

Attendant:

[丑]知道了。"谒者有如鬼,状元还似人。"[下]
[末扮陈黄门上]"官运精神老不眠,早朝三下听鸣鞭。多沾圣主随朝米,不受村童学俸钱。"
自家陈最良。因奏捷,圣恩可怜,钦授黄门。此皆杜老相公抬举之恩,敬此趋谢。
[丑上见介]正来相请,少待通报。[进报见介]
[外笑介]可喜,可喜!"昔为陈白屋,今作老黄门。"
[末]"新恩无报效,旧恨有还魂。"适间老先生三

Yes, I see.

> "The Palace Announcer looks like a ghost
> While the Number-one Scholar looks like a man."

(*Exit*)

(*Enter Chen Zuiliang, as the Palace Announcer*)

Chen Zuiliang:

> "Now that I serve in the royal court,
> I start my service with great joy.
> Now that the emperor gives me food of every sort,
> I no longer teach any rustic boy."

I am Chen Zuiliang. I've been appointed Palace Announcer because His Majesty was pleased with the news of victory I brought. I must owe everything to the patronage of Envoy Du, and therefore I'm going to his place to express my gratitude.

(*Re-enter the attendant*)

Attendant:

(*Greets Chen Zuiliang*)

I'm on my way to invite you. Please wait and I'll report your arrival.

(*Comes in to report. Du Bao and Chen Zuiliang greet each other*)

Du Bao:

(*Smiles*)

Congratulations! Congratulations to you!

> "The former wretched teacher
> Has become the Palace Announcer."

Chen Zuiliang:

> "New favours can hardly be repaid,
> But old grief can easily fade."

喜临门：一喜官居宰辅，二喜小姐活在人间，三喜女婿中了状元。
[外]陈先生教的好女学生，成精作怪哩！
[末]老相公葫芦提认了罢。
[外]先生差矣！此乃妖孽之事。为大臣的，必须奏闻灭除为是。
[末]果有此意，容晚生登时奏上取旨何如？
[外]正合吾意。

[外]夜读沧州怪亦听，
[末]可关妖气暗文星。
[外]谁人断得人间事？
[末]神镜高悬照百灵。

I've just heard that you are blessed by triple happiness: your promotion to the position of Grand Chancellor, your daughter's revival and your son-in-law becoming the Number-one Scholar.

Du Bao:

You've tutored such a good pupil that she's become a sprite!

Chen Zuiliang:

Why don't you accept what she is?

Du Bao:

You are wrong. For witchcraft like this, a minister must report it to His Majesty and have it exterminated.

Chen Zuiliang:

If that's your intention, shall I report to His Majesty at once and ask for his decree?

Du Bao:

That suits me very well.

A monster listens when I read at night;

Chen Zuiliang:

It is ill clouds that blur the starry sight.

Du Bao:

Who is able to judge the human affairs?

Chen Zuiliang:

The sacred mirror overhead shines bright.

第五十四出　闻　喜

【绕池游】

[贴上]露寒清怯,
金井吹梧叶,
转不断辘轳情劫。
咳,俺小姐为梦见书生,感病而亡,已经三年。老爷与老夫人,时时痛他孤魂无靠。谁知小姐到活活的跟着个穷秀才,寄居钱塘江上。母子重逢。真乃天上人间,怪怪奇奇,何事不有!今日小姐分付安排绣床,温习针指。小姐早来到也。

【绕红楼】

[旦上]秋过了平分日易斜,
恨辞梁燕语周遮。
人去空江,身依客舍,
无计七香车。
"秋风吹冷破窗纱,夫婿扬州不到家。玉指泪弹江

Scene Fifty-four
Learning the Good News

(*Enter Chunxiang*)

Chunxiang:

(*To the tune of* **Raochiyou**)

When autumn dew glitters cold,

The parasol leaves fall into the well.

Love's karma rotates heaven and hell.

Well, Miss Du died of lovesickness three years ago for a scholar who appeared in her dream. My master and my lady have been grieved over her solitary spirit. Who knows that she's revived and stayed with a poor scholar by the Qiantang River? Now she has been reunited with her mother. It's true indeed that nothing is impossible in the heaven and on earth. Today Miss Du told me to prepare for the embroidery table for her to do some needlework again. And here she comes.

(*Enter Du Liniang*)

Du Liniang:

(*To the tune of* **Raohonglou**)

At early sunset when autumn was half way through,

The swallows chirped and my sorrow grew.

Since my man sailed away,

In a hotel I've stayed.

I've waited, but seen no carriage in view.

"When chilly autumn winds pierce the window,

My husband is still in Yangzhou.

北草，金针闲刺岭南花。"春香，我同柳郎至此，即赴试闱。虎榜未开，扬州兵乱。我星夜赍发柳郎，打听爹娘消息。且喜老萱堂不意而逢，则老相公未知下落。想柳郎刻下可到，料今番榜上高题。须先翦下罗衣，衬其光彩。

[贴]绣床停当，请自尊裁。

[旦裁衣介]裁下了，便待缝将起来。[缝介]

[贴]小姐，俺淡口儿闲嗑，你和柳郎梦里、阴司里，两下光景何如？

【罗江怨】

[旦]春园梦一些，
到阴司里有转折。
梦中逗的影儿别，
阴司较追的情儿切。
[贴]还魂时像怎的？
[旦]似梦重醒，猛回头放教跌。

While tears drop on the northern grass,
From my needles southern flowers grow."

Chunxiang, as soon as I came here with Mr Liu, he entered the imperial examination. Before the announcement was made, an insurrection broke out in Yangzhou. I asked Mr Liu to set off by night and to find out what happened to my parents. To my great joy, I happened to meet my mother here, but I haven't got any news of my father yet. Mr Liu is expected to arrive at any time and I'm sure that his name will be on the top list. I'll make him a new garment for this grand occasion.

Chunxiang:

The embroidery table is ready at your disposal.

Du Liniang:

(*Cuts out the garment*)

Now that the cutting is done, I'll start sewing.

(*Sews the garment*)

Chunxiang:

Mistress, may I venture to ask what it was like in your dream and in the nether world?

Du Liniang:

(*To the tune of **Luojiangyuan***)

A sweet dream in the spring

Became real love in the nether world.

While two shadows parted in the dream,

We stuck together in the nether world.

Chunxiang:

How did you feel like when you were revived?

Du Liniang:

As from a dream I came around,

[贴]阴司可也有好耍子处?
[旦]一般儿轮回路,驾香车,
爱河边题红叶。
便则到鬼门关逐夜的望秋月。

【前腔】
[贴]你风姿恁惹邪,
情肠害劣。
小姐,你香魂逗出了梦儿蝶,
把亲娘肠断了影中蛇。
不道燕冢荒斜,
再立起鸳鸯舍。
则问你会书斋灯怎遮?
送情杯酒怎赊?
取喜时,也要那破头梢一泡血。
[旦]蠢丫头,幽欢之时,彼此如梦,问他则甚!呀,
奶奶来的恁忙也!

I looked back and fell to the ground.

Chunxiang:

Were there any places of interest in the nether world?

Du Liniang:

There were samsara roads

For perfumed carts,

Amorous rivers for love odes

And nether gates for broken hearts.

Chunxiang:

(*To the previous tune*)

Your beauty allures the man;

Your passion torments the man.

Mistress,

While your soul wandered in a dream,

Your mother shed tears like a stream.

Now that your tomb lies in waste,

You build your nest in graceful taste.

I'd like to ask

How you managed to hide behind the light

And how you bought the wine at night.

I'm afraid when you made love for the first time,

Your virgin blood must have come in sight.

Du Liniang:

You silly girl! I seemed to be in a dream when we made love. There is no sense for you to ask such questions. Look, my mother is coming in a hurry.

(*Enter Zhen in a hurry*)

Zhen:

(*To the tune of Wanxiandeng*)

【玩仙灯】
　　[老旦慌上]人语闹吱嚷,
听风声,
似是女孩儿关节。
儿,听见外厢喧嚷,新科状元是岭南柳梦梅。
[旦]有这等事!
【前腔】
　　[净忙走上]旗影儿走龙蛇,
甚宣差,教来近者!
[见介]奶奶、小姐,驾上人来。俺看门去也![下]
【入赚】
　　[外、丑扮军校持黄旗上]深巷门斜,
抓不出状元门第也。
这是了。[敲门介]
[老旦]声息儿恁忡忡!
把门儿偷瞥。
[启门,校冲开介]
[老旦]那衙门来的?

There is noise from the street;

It's my daughter they seem to greet.

My child, from what I've heard from the street, I can gather that the latest Number-one Scholar is Liu Mengmei from Lingnan.

Du Liniang:

Is that so?

(*Enter Sister Stone in quick steps*)

Sister Stone:

(*To the previous tune*)

Holding flags amid the roar,

Who are the messengers

That approach our door?

(*Greets Zhen and Du Liniang*)

Madam and Mistress, the imperial messengers are coming. I'll go and wait at the door.

(*Exit*)

(*Enter two sergeants, with imperial flags*)

Sergeants:

(*To the tune of Ruzhuan*)

Among the shabby houses in the narrow lane,

We look for the scholar's home in vain.

This might be the one.

(*Knock at the door*)

Zhen:

Terrified by the deafening roar,

I'll peep through the door.

(*Opens the door. The sergeants burst in*)

Which office are you from?

[校]星飞不迭。
你看这旗，看这旗影儿头势别。
是黄门官把圣旨教传泄。
[老旦叫介]儿，原来是传圣旨的。
[旦上]斗胆相询，金榜何时揭？
可有柳梦梅名字高头列？
[校]他中了状元。
[旦]真个中了状元？
[校]则他中状元，急节里遭磨灭。
[旦惊介]是怎生？
[校]往淮扬触犯了杜参爷，
扭回京把他做劫坟茔的贼决。
[老旦]我儿，谢天谢地，老爷平安回京了。他那知

Sergeants:

We come here as quick as can be.

Look at the flags,

Look at the supreme flags.

The Palace Announcer sends us to pass the decree.

Zhen:

(*Calls aloud*)

My child, they've come to pass the imperial decree.

Du Liniang:

(*Steps forward*)

May I venture to ask

When the results will be announced?

Is Liu Mengmei on top of the list?

Sergeants:

He's the Number-one Scholar.

Du Liniang:

Is that so?

Sergeants:

Although he's on top of the list,

His misdemeanor can hardly be dismissed.

Du Liniang:

(*Taken aback*)

What happened to him?

Sergeants:

In Huaiyang he offended Lord Du

As grave-robbing was a taboo.

Zhen:

Thank heavens, my child! Your father has arrived in the capital safe and sound. Of course he won't believe that you're

世间有此重生之事。
[旦]这却怎了?
[校]正高吊起猛桃条细抽掣,
被官里人抢去游街歇。
[旦]恰好哩。
[校]平章他势大,动本了。说劫坟之贼,不可以作状元。
[旦]状元可也辨一本儿?
[校]状元也有本。
那平章奏他恶茶白赖把阴人窃。
那状元呵,他说头带魁罡不受邪。
便是万岁爷听了成痴呆。
[旦]后来?
[校]侥幸有个陈黄门,是平章爷的故人。奏准,要平章、状元和小姐三人,驾前勘对,方取圣裁。

revived.

Du Liniang:

What happened to him next?

Sergeants:

When the flogging was not yet complete,

He was rescued and paraded through the street.

Du Liniang:

So he was rescued at the right time.

Sergeants:

But the Grand Chancellor was in a position to submit a memorial to His Majesty, saying that a grave-robber was not entitled to be the Number-one Scholar.

Du Liniang:

Did the Number-one Scholar submit a memorial to defend himself?

Sergeants:

Yes, he did.

The Grand Chancellor accused him of robbing the grave;

The Number-one Scholar argued that he was brave.

His Majesty did not know how to behave.

Du Liniang:

And then?

Sergeants:

It happened that the Palace Announcer, Mr Chen, was an old friend of the Grand Chancellor. He suggested that the Grand Chancellor, the Number-one Scholar and you, Miss Du appear before the throne at the same time so that His Majesty might make his judgement.

Zhen:

[老旦]呀,陈黄门是谁?
[校]是陈最良,他说南安教授曾官舍。因此杜平章抬举他掌朝班、通御谒。
[老旦]一发诧异哩。
[校]便是他着俺们来宣旨。分付你家一更梳洗,二鼓吃饭,三鼓穿衣,四更走动。到得五更三点彻,响玎珰翠佩,那是朝时节。
[旦]独自个怕人。
[校]怕则么!平章宰相你亲爷,状元妻妾。俺去了。
[旦]再说些去。
[校]明朝金阙,讨你幅撞门红去了也。[下]

Well, who is that Palace Announcer Chen?

Sergeants:

His name is Chen Zuiliang,

Who said that he once taught in Nan'an.

Therefore,

The Grand Chancellor recommended him

To be the palace announcer.

Zhen:

Amazing indeed!

Sergeants:

It's him who sent us to bring you the imperial decree. Miss Du is to make up at the first watch-beat, have breakfast at the second watch-beat, get dressed at the third watch-beat and set out at the fourth watch-beat.

Till the fifth watch-beat you'll wait

And in tinkling ornaments,

You'll enter the palace gate.

Du Liniang:

I'm afraid to go alone.

Sergeants:

What is there to be afraid of?

You're the daughter of the Grand Chancellor

And wife of the Number-one Scholar.

We'll be leaving now.

Du Liniang:

Tell me something more before you leave.

Sergeants:

Tomorrow at the court,

Please give us tips of some sort.

[旦]娘,爹爹高升,柳郎高中,
小旗儿报捷,
又是平安帖。
把神天叩谢,神天叩谢。

【滴溜子】
[拜介]当日的、当日的梅根柳叶,
无明路、无明路曾把游魂再叠。
果应梦、花园后摺。
甫能够迸到头,抢了捷。
鬼趣里因缘,人间判贴。

【前腔】
[老旦]虽则是、虽则是希奇事业,
可甚的、可甚的惊劳驾帖?
他道你、是花妖害怯,

(*Exeunt*)

Du Liniang:

Mom, Dad has been promoted and Mr Liu has become the Number-one Scholar.

The sergeants have brought the good news

Of their safety and success.

Let's thank heavens!

Let's thank heavens!

(*They kowtow*)

Du Liniang:

(*To the tune of* **Diliuzi**)

Years ago,

Years ago we got acquainted at the plum and willow;

Outside the nether gate,

Outside the nether gate my soul met my mate.

My dream came true

At the garden behind our house.

In this way finally comes the day

For the success of my spouse.

The match in the nether world

Awaits the judge of human world.

Zhen:

(*To the previous tune*)

Although we say,

Although we say things have gone astray,

Is there any need,

Is there any need for imperial decrees indeed?

You are thought

To be disturbed in your cave

看承的柳抱怀做花下劫。
你那爹爹呵,
没得个符儿再把花神召摄。

【尾声】
女儿,紧簪束扬尘舞蹈摇花颊。
[旦]叫我奏个什么来?
[老旦]有了你活人硬证无虚胁。
[旦]少不的万岁君王听臣妾。
[净扮郭驼上]"要问鼋鼍窟,还过乌鹊桥。"两日再寻个钱塘门不着。正好撞着老军,说知夫人下处。抖擞了进去。[见介]
[老旦]你是谁?
[净]状元家里的老驼,特来恭喜。

>While Liu Mengmei is thought
>
>To have robbed a grave.
>
>But your father
>
>>Has no magic powers
>>
>>To summon the god of flowers.

Zhen:

>(*To the tune of Coda*)
>
>My child,
>
>>Get prepared to present yourself at court.

Du Liniang:

>What shall I say to His Majesty?

Zhen:

>>Your presence alone will clarify the day;

Du Liniang:

>His Majesty will listen to what I have to say.
>
>(*Enter Hunchback Guo*)

Hunchback Guo:

>"*To find the turtle's cave,*
>
>*You have to cross the magpies' bridge.*"
>
>I've looked for the Qiantang Gate for two days, but in vain. I was lucky enough to meet an old sergeant, who told me Miss Du's address. Now I'll venture to enter her house.
>
>(*Greets Zhen and Du Liniang*)

Zhen:

>Who are you?

Hunchback Guo:

>I'm Hunchback Guo, serving in the Number-one Scholar's house. I've come to offer my congratulations.

Du Liniang:

[旦]辛苦，你可见状元么？
[净]俺往平章府抢下了状元，要夫人去见朝也。

[老旦]往事闲征梦欲分，
[旦]今晨忽见下天门。
[净]分明为报精灵辈，
[旦]淡扫蛾眉朝至尊。

Thank you for your congratulations. Have you seen the Number-one Scholar?

Hunchback Guo:

It was I who rescued him in the Grand Chancellor's office. He sent me to bring you to the palace.

Zhen:

The bygone dreams will come to light;

Du Liniang:

Today the sky appears to be so bright.

Hunchback Guo:

To gratify the deep love of the sprite,

Du Liniang:

I'll see His Majesty in all his might.

第五十五出　　圆　驾

[净、丑扮将军持金瓜上]"日月光天德，山河壮帝居。"万岁爷升朝，在此直殿。

【北点绛唇】

[末上]宝殿云开，

御炉烟霭，

乾坤泰。

[回身拜介]日影金阶，

早唱道黄门拜。

"鸾凤旌旗拂晓陈，传闻阙下降丝纶。兴王会净妖氛气，不问苍生问鬼神。"自家大宋朝新除授一个老黄门陈最良是也。下官原是南安府饱学秀才。因柳梦梅发了杜平章小姐之墓，径往扬州报知。平章念旧，着俺说平李寇，告捷效劳，蒙圣恩钦赐黄门

Scene Fifty-five
Happy Reunion at Court

(*Enter two generals of palace guards, carrying the Imperial Squashes*)

Generals:

"The sun and moon set forth heaven's feat;
The hills and rills consolidate the royal seat."

When His Majesty gives an audience, we stand on duty here.

(*Enter Chen Zuiliang*)

Chen Zuiliang:

(*To the tune of* **Beidianjiangchun**)

The palace towers above the clouds
And incense coils to the skies.
Eternal peace blesses the crowds.

(*Turns to the emperor and kowtows*)

When the sun shines over the stairs,
I kowtow and then rise.

"When phoenix banners flap in the morning breeze,
His Majesty issues his decrees.
In order to sweep away the monstrous airs,
He relies on gods and ghosts to appease."

I'm old Chen Zuiliang, newly-appointed Palace Announcer in the Great Song Dynasty. I was a learned scholar in the Nan'an Prefecture. As Liu Mengmei robbed Miss Du's grave, I brought the news to Yangzhou. For old times' sake, the Grand Chancellor sent me to appease the bandit Li Quan. When I com-

奏事之职。不想平章回朝，恰遇柳生投见。当时拿下，递解临安府监候。却说柳生先曾挥过卷子，中了状元。找寻之间，恰好状元吊在杜府拷问。当被驾前官校人等冲破府门，抢了状元，上马而去，到也罢了。又听的说俺那女学生杜小姐也返魂在京。平章听说女儿成了个色精，一发恼激。央俺题奏一本，为诛除妖贼事。中间劾奏柳梦梅系劫坟之贼，其妖魂托名亡女，不可不诛。杜老先生此奏，却是名正言顺。随后柳生也奏一本，为辨明心迹事。都奉有圣旨："朕览所奏，幽隐奇特。必须返魂之女，面驾敷陈。取旨定夺。"老夫又恐怕真是杜小姐返魂，私着官校传旨与他。五更朝见。正是："三生石上看来去，万岁台前辨假真。"道犹未了，平章、状元早到。

pleted my task, I was assigned the position of Palace Announcer. It happened that on his way to the capital, the Grand Chancellor received a visit by Liu Mengmei, who was arrested at once and sent to prison in Lin'an. The story was that Mr Liu had entered the imperial examination and was selected as the Number-one Scholar. When people were looking for him, he was being flogged and interrogated in Lord Du's office. The sergeants broke into the office to rescue him and carried him away on horseback. That was part of the story. It was said that my pupil Miss Du was revived and took a residence in the capital. To his greater annoyance, the Grand Chancellor heard that his daughter had become a wanton sprite. He told me to write a memorial to His Majesty for the extermination of evil spirits. Liu Mengmei was accused of grave-robbing and releasing an evil sprite which took on the name of his daughter; therefore, Liu Mengmei must be executed at once. Lord Du's memorial was justified, but Mr Liu also sent in a memorial in his own defence. There came the imperial decree, saying, "Due to the unusual mysticism as narrated in your memorials, the revived girl must appear in an audience so that I can make the final judgement. " As I was afraid that Miss Du had indeed revived, I privately sent two sergeants to tell her of the imperial decree for her to appear before the throne at the fifth watch-beat tomorrow morning. As the saying goes,

"*The past and present are shown on the Eternal Rock;*
Truth and falsehood are judged at the imperial court."

Before I can finish my monologue, here come the Grand Chancellor and the Number-one Scholar.

【前腔】

[外、生幞头、袍、笏同上介]

[外]有恨妆排,无明耽带,真奇怪。

[生]哑谜难猜,今上亲裁划。

岳丈大人拜揖。

[外]谁是你岳丈!

[生]平章老先生拜揖。

[外]谁和你平章?

[生笑介]古诗云:"梅雪争春未肯降,骚人阁笔费平章。"今日梦梅争辩之时,少不的要老平章阁笔。

[外]你罪人咬文哩。

[生]小生何罪?老平章是罪人。

[外]俺有平李全大功,当得何罪?

(*Enter Du Bao and Liu Mengmei, dressed in official hats and robes, each holding a memorial tablet*)

Du Bao:

    (*To the previous tune*)

    I hate to face confrontation at court

    For no apparent reason at all.

    It's a case of peculiar sort.

Liu Mengmei:

    To solve the riddle,

    I wait for His Majesty's call.

    My respect to you, father-in-law!

Du Bao:

    None of your father-in-laws here!

Liu Mengmei:

    My respect to you, Grand Chancellor!

Du Bao:

    None of your Grand Chancellors here!

Liu Mengmei:

    (*Laughs*)

    As an old poem goes,

        "When snow and plum blossom vie to win spring grace,

        The poet lays down his pen to settle the case."

    When I defend myself today, you'll have to lay down your pen.

Du Bao:

    You are a criminal, but you are still playing with words now.

Liu Mengmei:

    What am I guilty of? In fact you are a criminal.

Du Bao:

    I've done meritorious deeds for the country by quelling the

[生]朝廷不知,你那里平的个李全,则平的个"李半"。
[外]怎生止平的个"李半"?
[生笑介]你则哄的个杨妈妈退兵,怎哄的全!
[外恼作扯生介]谁说?和你官里讲去。
[末作慌出见介]午门之外,谁敢喧哗![见介]原来是杜老先生。这是新状元。放手,放手。
[外放生介]
[末]状元何事激恼了老平章?
[外]他骂俺罪人,俺得何罪?
[生]你说无罪,便是处分令爱一事,也有三大罪。
[外]那三罪?

bandit Li Quan. What am I guilty of?

Liu Mengmei:

The court is unaware of the fact that you haven't quelled Li Quan, but quelled his better half.

Du Bao:

What do you mean by saying that?

Liu Mengmei:

(*Sneers*)

You have tricked his wife into withdrawing the troops. This is not a complete victory.

Du Bao:

(*Grasps at Liu Mengmei in annoyance*)

Who told you that? Let's argue before the throne.

Chen Zuiliang:

(*Rushes toward Du Bao and Liu Mengmei*)

Who's making such a roar outside the royal palace?

(*Greets Du Bao and Liu Mengmei*)

Oh, it's Lord Du. This is the new Number-one Scholar. Please let him off! Please let him off!

(*Du Bao lets off Liu Mengmei*)

How is it that he has offended you?

Du Bao:

He calls me a criminal. What am I guilty of?

Liu Mengmei:

How can you say that you are not guilty? You have at least committed three errors concerning your daughter.

Du Bao:

What are the errors?

Liu Mengmei:

［生］太守纵女游春，一罪。
［外］是了。
［生］女死不奔丧，私建庵观，二罪。
［外］罢了。
［生］嫌贫逐婿，刁打钦赐状元，可不三大罪？
［末笑介］状元以前也罪过些。看下官面分，和了罢。
［生］黄门大人，与学生有何面分？
［末笑介］状元不知，尊夫人请俺上学来。
［生］敢是鬼请先生？
［末］状元忘旧了。
［生认介］老黄门可是南安陈斋长？

First, as a prefect, you allowed your daughter to go on a spring stroll.

Du Bao:

That's true.

Liu Mengmei:

Second, after your daughter died, you didn't send her remains to her native town to be buried in your ancestral cemetery, but set up a private nunnery instead.

Du Bao:

There's something in what you said.

Liu Mengmei:

Third, in addition to dispelling your son-in-law because he is poor, you put a Number-one Scholar to tortures.

Chen Zuiliang:

(*Laughs*)

Mr Liu, you have your errors to blame too. Just listen to me and make peace between you.

Liu Mengmei:

What have I to do with you?

Chen Zuiliang:

(*Laughs*)

Probably you don't know that I used to be your wife's tutor.

Liu Mengmei:

Are you a tutor for the ghosts?

Chen Zuiliang:

Have you forgotten your old friend, Mr Liu?

Liu Mengmei:

(*Recognises Chen Zuiliang*)

Are you Tutor Chen from Nan'an?

[末]惶恐,惶恐。

[生]呀,先生,俺于你分上不薄,如何妄报俺为贼?做门馆报事不真;则怕做了黄门,也奏事不以实。

[末笑]今日奏事实了。远望尊夫人将到,二公先行叩头礼。

[内唱礼介]奏事官齐班。

[外、生同进叩头介]

[外]臣杜宝见。

[生]臣柳梦梅见。

[末]平身。

[外、生立左右介]

[旦上]"丽娘本是泉下女,重瞻天日向丹墀。"

【黄钟北醉花阴】

　　平铺着金殿琉璃翠鸳瓦,

　　响鸣梢半天儿刮剌。

Chen Zuiliang:

That's me! That's me!

Liu Mengmei:

Oh, Mr Chen, we were on good terms, but why did you say that I was a robber? You didn't tell the truth when you were a tutor, and I'm afraid you will not tell the truth now that you become the Palace Announcer.

Chen Zuiliang:

(*Laughs*)

I'm telling the truth today. I see Miss Du approaching in the distance. Both of you, kowtow to His Majesty first.

Voice Within:

(*Solemnly*)

Those who want to make reports, stand in your places.

(*Du Bao and Liu Mengmei kowtow*)

Du Bao:

Your Majesty's humble servant Du Bao kowtows.

Liu Mengmei:

Your Majesty's humble servant Liu Mengmei kowtows.

Chen Zuiliang:

Rise to your feet.

(*Du Bao and Liu Mengmei stand on separate sides*)

(*Enter Du Liniang*)

Du Liniang:

"Du Liniang, once a ghost,

Will have His Majesty as her host."

(*To the tune of* **Huangzhongbeizuihuayin**)

Inside the palace with glazed tiles,

The ceremonial whip calls for silence.

［净、丑喝介］甚的妇人冲上御阶?拿了!

［旦惊介］似这般狰狞汉,叫喳喳。

在阎浮殿见了些青面獠牙,

也不似今番怕。

［末］前面来的是女学生杜小姐么?

［旦］来的黄门官像陈教授,叫他一声:"陈师父,陈师父!"

［末应介］是也。

［旦］陈师父喜哩!

［末］学生,你做鬼,怕不惊驾?

［旦］噤声。再休提探花鬼乔作衙,

则说状元妻来面驾。

［净、丑下］

Generals:

> (*Shout*)
>
> Who is that woman stepping on the palace stairs? Have her arrested!

Du Liniang:

> (*Frightened*)
>
> The ugly guards
>
> Are shouting at me.
>
> In the nether world,
>
> > The fierce demons
> >
> > Are not so frightening to see.

Chen Zuiliang:

> Is my pupil Miss Du coming?

Du Liniang:

> The Palace Announcer coming to me seems to be Tutor Chen. Let me call out to him—Tutor Chen! Tutor Chen!

Chen Zuiliang:

> (*Responds*)
>
> Here I am.

Du Liniang:

> Congratulations to you, Tutor Chen!

Chen Zuiliang:

> Miss Du, since you are a ghost, I'm afraid you'll give a shock to His Majesty.

Du Liniang:

> None of your nonsense!
>
> > Don't say that I've just come back to life;
> >
> > Here I am as Number-one Scholar's wife.
>
> (*Exeunt the two generals*)

［内］奏事人扬尘舞蹈。

［旦作舞蹈、呼"万岁，万岁"介］

［内］平身。

［旦起］

［内］听旨：杜丽娘是真是假，就着伊父杜宝，状元柳梦梅，出班识认。

［生觑旦作悲介］俺的丽娘妻也。

［外觑旦，作恼介］鬼也些真个一模二样，大胆，大胆！［作回身跪奏介］臣杜宝谨奏：臣女亡已三年，此女酷似，此必花妖狐媚，假托而成。俺王听启：

【南画眉序】
臣女没年多，
道理阴阳岂重活？
愿吾皇向金阶一打，
立见妖魔。

Voice Within:

Kowtow to His Majesty!

Du Liniang:

(*Kowtows*)

Long live the emperor! Long live the emperor!

Voice Within:

Rise to your feet.

(*Du Liniang rises to her feet*)

Now listen to the imperial decree: Du Bao and Liu Mengmei, step forward to see whether this is the genuine Du Liniang.

Liu Mengmei:

(*Gazes at Du Liniang and shows signs of woe*)

Oh Liniang, my dear wife!

Du Bao:

(*Gazes at Du Liniang and shows signs of annoyance*)

The ghost looks exactly like my late daughter. Sheer witchcraft! Sheer witchcraft!

(*Turns back to face the throne and makes his report*)

Your humble servant Du Bao begs to report. My daughter died three years ago, but this woman looks exactly like her. It must be a flower sprite or a fox sprite assuming the human form. This is what I have to say:

(*To the tune of **Nanhuameixu***)

As my daughter has been dead for years,

How can she come back to life again?

If you strike her with a cane,

Her demonic form soon appears.

Liu Mengmei:

(*Weeps*)

[生作泣]好狠心的父亲!
[跪奏介]他做五雷般严父的规模,
则待要一下里把声名煞抹。[起介]
[合]便阎罗包老难弹破,
除取旨前来撒和。
[内]听旨:朕闻人行有影,鬼形怕镜。定时台上有秦朝照胆镜。黄门官,可同杜丽娘照镜。看花阴之下,有无踪影回奏。
[末应,同旦对镜介]女学生是人是鬼?

【北喜迁莺】
　　[旦]人和鬼教怎生酬答?
形和影现托着面菱花。
[末]镜无改面,委系人身。再向花街取影而奏。[行看影介]
[旦]波查。花阴这答,

What a stone-hearted father!

(*Kowtows to the emperor and makes his report*)

As her father, he pretends to be stern;

It's a good fame he wants to earn.

(*Rises to his feet*)

Du Bao, Liu Mengmei:

Neither nether nor human judge can settle the case;

Only Your Majesty will decide with grace.

Voice Within:

Now listen to the imperial decree: "I've heard that men cast shadows while ghosts dread the mirrors. On the Time Platform there is a Penetrating Mirror from the Qin dynasty. Palace Announcer, bring Du Liniang to the mirror and then take her along the flower tracks to see whether she leaves a shadow. When you've followed my instructions, report the results to me."

Chen Zuiliang:

(*Assents and then leads Du Liniang to the mirror*)

Are you a human being or a ghost, Miss Du?

Du Liniang:

(*To the tune of* **Beixiqianying**)

How can I say whether I am a ghost?

The mirror will soon tell the truth.

Chen Zuiliang:

As you have your exact image in the mirror, you prove to be a human being. Now let's go along the flower tracks and see if you cast a shadow. Then I'll report the results to His Majesty.

(*Walks and inspects her shadow*)

Du Liniang:

Oh, dear me!

一般儿莲步回鸾印浅沙。
[末奏]杜丽娘有踪有影,的系人身。
[内]听旨:丽娘既系人身,可将前亡后化事情奏上。
[旦]万岁!臣妾二八年华,自画春容一幅。曾于柳外梅边,梦见这生。妾因感病而亡。葬于后园梅树之下。后来果有这生,姓柳名梦梅,拾取春容,朝夕挂念。臣妾因此出现成亲。
[悲介]哎哟,凄惶煞!
这底是前亡后化,
抵多少阴错阳差。
[内]听旨:柳状元质证,丽娘所言真假?因何预名梦梅?
[生打躬呼"万岁"介]

Along the flower tracks,

I leave my footprints to see.

Chen Zuiliang:

(*Reports to the emperor*)

Du Liniang has an image and a shadow, therefore she is a human being.

Voice Within:

Now listen to the imperial decree: "Du Liniang, as you are human, tell me your experience of death and revival."

Du Liniang:

Your Majesty, I drew a self-portrait when I was sixteen years old. I once saw in my dream a scholar beside a plum tree beyond the willow trees. After I died of lovesickness for him, I was buried under a plum tree in the back garden. It happened that a scholar by the name of Liu Mengmei found my self-portrait and kept yearning for me day and night. That's why I came back to this world and married him.

(*Sadly*)

Oh how sad!

My revival after death

Implied all the mishaps I had.

Voice Within:

Now listen to the imperial decree: "Liu Mengmei, come forward and testify whether Du Liniang has told the truth. Why are you named Mengmei, which literally means 'dreaming of plums'?"

Liu Mengmei:

(*Bows*)

Long live the emperor!

【南画眉序】
　　臣南海泛丝萝,
　　梦向娇姿折梅萼。
　　果登程取试,养病南柯。
　　因借居南安府红梅院中,游其后苑,拾得丽娘春容。因而感此真魂,成其人道。
　　[外跪介]此人欺诳陛下,兼且点污臣之女也。论臣女呵,
　　便死葬向水口廉贞,
　　肯和生人做山头撮合!
　　[合]便阎罗包老难弹破,
　　除取旨前来撒和。
　　[内]听旨:朕闻有云:"不待父母之命,媒妁之言,则国人父母皆贱之。"杜丽娘自媒自婚,有何主见?
　　[旦泣介]万岁!臣妾受了柳梦梅再活之恩。
【北出队子】
　　真乃是无媒而嫁。

(*To the tune of* **Nanhuameixu**)

When I sought marriage across the southern sea,

I met a girl by the plum tree when the dream began.

On my way to take the imperial exam,

I fell ill and was detained in Nan'an.

As a result, I stayed at the Plum Blossom Nunnery in Nan'an Prefecture. When I took a stroll in the back garden, I found the self-portrait of Du Liniang. Miss Du was so moved by my affection for her that she resumed her human form.

Du Bao:

(*Kneels*)

He is cheating Your Majesty and slandering my daughter as well. As for my daughter,

She'd rather sink in the river and lie there

Than have an illicit affair!

Du Bao, Liu Mengmei:

Neither nether nor human judge can settle the case;

Only Your Majesty will decide with grace.

Voice Within:

Now listen to the imperial decree: "As the saying goes, 'Illicit love without the consent of parents and the introduction of matchmakers is despised by the parents and the people all over the country.' Du Liniang, how can you justify yourself?"

Du Liniang:

(*Weeps*)

Your Majesty, I owe my second life to Liu Mengmei.

(*To the tune of* **Beichuduizi**)

I won't use the word "illicit affair".

Du Bao:

[外]谁保亲？
[旦]保亲的是母丧门。
[外]送亲的？
[旦]送亲的是女夜叉。
[外]这等胡为！
[生]这是阴阳配合正理。
[外]正理，正理！花你那蛮儿一点红嘴哩！
[生]老平章，你骂俺岭南人吃槟榔，其实柳梦梅唇红齿白。
[旦]喋声。眼前活立着个女孩儿，亲爷不认。到做鬼三年，有个柳梦梅认亲。
则你这辣生生回阳附子较争些，
为什么翠呆呆下气的槟榔俊煞了他？
爹爹，你不认呵，有娘在。
[指鬼门]现放着实丕丕贝母开谈亲阿妈。
[老旦上]多早晚女儿还在面驾。老身踹入正阳门叫

Who was your matchmaker?

Du Liniang:

Our matchmaker was the Funeral Star above.

Du Bao:

Who were your wedding attendants?

Du Liniang:

They were the nether-world sprites.

Du Bao:

Sheer nonsense!

Liu Mengmei:

It's a perfect match of heaven and hell.

Du Bao:

Perfect! Perfect lies from your scarlet lips!

Liu Mengmei:

Sir, you are mocking at southerners chewing betel nuts, but I was born with scarlet lips and white teeth.

Du Liniang:

No arguments! A daughter alive and kicking is ignored by her father while a ghost for three years was married by Liu Mengmei.

You cannot revive your daughter;

Why are you reviling at my man?

Dad, if you refuse to accept me, Mom has accepted me.

(*Points at the entrance*)

The one to persuade you is my mother.

(*Enter Zhen*)

Zhen:

Why is my daughter kept so long in the palace? I'll enter the palace gate to plead for her.

冤去也。

[进见跪伏介]万岁爷,杜平章妻一品夫人甄氏见驾。

[外、末惊介]那里来的?真个是俺夫人哩。

[外跪介]臣杜宝启,臣妻已死扬州乱贼之手,臣已奏请恩旨褒封。此必妖鬼捏作母子一路,白日欺天。[起介]

[生]这个婆婆,是不曾认的他。

[内]听旨:甄氏既死于贼手,何得临安母子同居?

[老旦]万岁![起介]

【南滴溜子】

  [老旦]扬州路、扬州路遭兵劫夺,

  只得向、只得向长安住托。

  不想到钱塘夜过,

  黑撞着丽娘儿魂似脱。

  少不的子母肝肠,死同生活。

(*Steps into the palace and kneels on the ground*)

Your Majesty, the first-rank Lady Zhen, wife of Grand Chancellor Du Bao, presents herself before the throne.

(*Du Bao and Chen Zuiliang are surprised*)

Du Bao:

Where are you from? You're my wife, aren't you?

(*Kneels to the emperor*)

I beg to report that my wife died at the hands of the bandits in Yangzhou. I have applied for posthumous honours for her from Your Majesty. The mother and daughter must have been some devilish incarnation to fraud Your Majesty in the broad daylight.

(*Rises to his feet*)

Liu Mengmei:

I've never seen this lady before.

Voice Within:

Now listen to the imperial decree: "Since Zhen has been killed by the bandits, how can she live with her daughter in Lin'an?"

Zhen:

Your Majesty,

(*To the tune of* **Nandiliuzi**)

On my way to Yangzhou,

On my way to Yangzhou I encountered the bandits.

I had to,

I had to seek shelter in Lin'an.

One night beside the river Qiantang,

As blood is thicker than water,

I happened to meet the likeness of Liniang.

We have lived together as mother and daughter.

Voice Within:

［内］听甄氏所奏，其女重生无疑。则他阴司三载，多有因果之事。假如前辈做君王臣宰不臻的，可有的发付他？从直奏来。

［旦］这话不题罢了，提起都有。

［末］女学生，"子不语怪"。比如阳世府部州县，尚然磨刷卷宗，他那里有甚会案处！

【北刮地风】

［旦］呀，那阴司一桩桩文簿查，

使不着你猾律拿喳。

是君王有半副迎魂驾，

臣和宰玉锁金枷。

［末］女学生，没对证。似这般说，秦桧老太师在阴司里可受的？

［旦］也知道些。说他的受用呵，那秦太师他一进门，

忐楞楞的黑心锤敢捣了千下，

浙另另的紫筋肝剁作三花。

According to what you said, your daughter must have been revived. As she lived in the nether world for three years, she must have learned much about karma. What were the punishments for kings and ministers who neglected their duties? Tell me exactly what you know.

Du Liniang:

Better forget about it, but there are indeed many people under punishment.

Chen Zuiliang:

My pupil, "Confucius never talked about things grotesque." In the human world the archives of the prefectures and counties are checked from time to time, but how can similar things be done in the nether world?

Du Liniang:

(*To the tune of Beiguadifeng*)
All the cases are clearly recorded in the nether world,
With no room for a denying word.
The kings are honoured as of old
While ministers are fettered with jade and gold.

Chen Zuiliang:

My pupil, there is no evidence for what you said. If that were the case, would Premier Qin Hui have suffered in the nether world?

Du Liniang:

I know something about him. To speak about his sufferings, as soon as he entered the nether world,
A hammer crushed his black heart
And a knife cut his liver into three parts.

All:

[众惊介]为甚剁作三花?
[旦]道他一花儿为大宋,一花为金朝,一花儿为长舌妻。
[末]这等长舌夫人有何受用?
[旦]若说秦夫人的受用,一到了阴司,捋去了凤冠霞帔,赤体精光。跳出个牛头夜叉,只一对七八寸长指弧儿,轻轻的把那撒道儿搭,长舌揸。
[末]为甚?
[旦]听的是东窗事发。
[外]鬼说也。且问你,鬼乜邪,人间私奔,自有条法。阴司可有?
[旦]有的是。柳梦梅七十条,爹爹发落过了,女儿阴司收赎。
桃条打,罪名加,
做尊官勾管了帘下。
则道是没真场风流罪过些。

(*Terrified*)

Why was his liver cut into three parts?

Du Liniang:

Because he served one part for the Great Song Dynasty, another part for the Jin Dynasty, and a third part for his wife with a wagging tongue.

Chen Zuiliang:

What were his wife's sufferings?

Du Liniang:

To speak about her sufferings, as soon as she entered the nether world, she was stripped of her coronets and robes until she was naked. An ox-headed sprite jumped forward to clutch at her throat with nails seven or eight inches long.

Her wagging tongue was torn out by the sprite.

Chen Zuiliang:

Why should she suffer so much?

Du Liniang:

Because her tricks had come to light.

Du Bao:

Sheer nonsense! Little devil, I'll ask you one question: In the human world there are punishments for elopement. Are there similar punishments in the nether world?

Du Liniang:

Yes, there are plenty. Liu Mengmei was flogged seventy strokes, which you administered by yourself, while I was detained in the nether world for three years.

Mr Liu was flogged,

Blamed,

And put under arrest

有什么饶不过这娇滴滴的女孩家。

[内]听旨:朕细听杜丽娘所奏,重生无疑。就着黄门官押送午门外,父子夫妻相认,归第成亲。

[众呼"万岁"行介]

[老旦]恭喜相公高转了。

[外]怎想夫人无恙!

[旦哭介]我的爹呵!

[外不理介]青天白日,小鬼头远些,远些!陈先生,如今连柳梦梅俺也疑将起来,则怕也是个鬼。

[末笑介]是踢斗鬼。

[老旦喜介]今日见了状元女婿,女儿再生,二十分

For our love affair.

Why don't you let us go now that we have confessed?

Voice Within:

Now listen to the imperial decree: "According to what Du Liniang said, she must have been revived. Palace Announcer, take her outside the palace gate so that the parents and daughter, man and wife can be reunited. When they return home, a formal wedding ceremony should be held."

All:

Long live the emperor!

(*Walk around the stage.*)

Zhen:

My lord, congratulations on your promotions!

Du Bao:

My lady, I didn't expect that you had a narrow escape.

Du Liniang:

(*Weeps*)

Dad!

Du Bao:

(*Ignores Du Liniang*)

You little devil had better stay away from broad daylight. Mr Chen, now I am beginning to suspect that Liu Mengmei is a devil too.

Chen Zuiliang:

(*Laughs*)

He's a devil of a literary star.

Zhen:

(*Elated*)

It's a double happiness to meet my Number-one Scholar son-

喜也。状元,先认了你丈母罢。

[生揖介]丈母光临,做女婿的有失迎待,罪之重也。

[旦]官人恭喜,贺喜。

[生]谁报你来?

[旦]到得陈师父传旨来。

[生]受你老子的气也。

[末]状元,认了丈人翁罢。

[生]则认的十地阎君为岳丈。

[末]状元,听俺分劝一言。

【南滴滴金】
你夫妻赶着了轮回磨,
便君王使的个随风柁,
那平章怕不做赔钱货。
到不如娘共女,翁和婿,明交割。

[生]老黄门,俺是个贼犯。

in-law and see my revived daughter. Come on, Number-one Scholar, greet your mother-in-law first.

Liu Mengmei:

(*Makes a bow*)

I'm sorry that I didn't greet you earlier.

Du Liniang:

Congratulations on your success, Mr Liu.

Liu Mengmei:

Who told you about it?

Du Liniang:

Tutor Chen brought me the imperial decree.

Liu Mengmei:

I was ill-treated by your father.

Chen Zuiliang:

Mr Liu, greet your father-in-law.

Liu Mengmei:

I'd rather have the nether-world king as my father-in-law!

Chen Zuiliang:

Listen to me, Mr Liu,

(*To the tune of* **Nandidijin**)

As man and wife you have suffered your share

But the emperor is almighty and fair.

The Grand Chancellor has to marry his daughter.

It's better for mother and daughter,

Father-in-law and son-in-law,

To make a deal then and there.

Liu Mengmei:

Mr Chen, I'm a convicted robber.

Chen Zuiliang:

[末笑介]你得便宜人，偏会撒科。
　　则道你偷天把桂影那，
　　不争多先偷了地窟里花枝朵。
　　[旦叹介]陈师父，你不教俺后花园游去，怎看上这攀桂客来？
　　[外]鬼乜邪，怕没门当户对，看上柳梦梅什么来！
【北四门子】
　　[旦笑介]是看上他戴乌纱象简朝衣挂，
　　笑、笑、笑，笑的来眼媚花。
　　爹娘，人间白日里高结彩楼，招不出个官婿。你女儿睡梦里、鬼窟里选着个状元郎，还说门当户对！
　　则你个杜杜陵惯把女孩儿吓，
　　那柳柳州他可也门户风华。
　　爹爹，认了女孩儿罢。
　　[外]离异了柳梦梅，回去认你。

(*Laughs*)

You are lucky enough,

But you still want to take advantage.

When you were expected to win the imperial test,

You stole a flower of a girl lying at rest.

Du Liniang:

(*Sighs*)

If you had not allowed me to take a stroll in the back garden, how could I have met this scholar?

Du Bao:

Little devil, since Liu Mengmei is from a family inferior to ours, what is it that makes you love him so much?

Du Liniang:

(*Smiles*)

(*To the tune of* **Beisimenzi**)

I love his hat and robe in official style,

And so I smile and smile and smile.

Dad and Mom, in the human world people fail to pick a son-in-law in high position even if they build high platforms to attract wooers; in the nether world, in my dream, I picked a Number-one Scholar. How can you say that his family background is inferior to ours?

You are from the honoured family of Du

While he is from the honoured family of Liu.

Dad, please accept me as your daughter!

Du Bao:

I'll accept you as my daughter back at home if you do away with Liu Mengmei.

Du Liniang:

[旦]叫俺回杜家，趄了柳衙。
便作你杜鹃花，也叫不转子规红泪洒。
[哭介]哎哟，见了俺前生的爹，即世嬷，
颠不剌俏魂灵立化。
[旦作闷倒介]
[外惊介]俺的丽娘儿！
[末作望介]怎那老道姑来也？连春香也活在？好笑，好笑！我在贼营里瞧甚来？

【南鲍老催】
[净扮石姑同贴上]官前定夺，官前定夺。
[打望介]原来一众官员在此。怎的起状元、小姐嘴骨都站一边？
[净]眼见他乔公案断的错，
听了那乔教学的嘴儿嗑。
[末]春香贤弟也来了。这姑姑是贼。

If you want me to go back to the family of Du

And leave the family of Liu,

All my life I'll weep and hate you.

(*Weeps*)

Alas,

In front of my previous-world father

And present-world mother,

My soul will wander farther.

(*Faints*)

Du Bao:

(*Taken aback*)

Oh Liniang, my child!

Chen Zuiliang:

(*Looks ahead*)

How does it happen that Sister Stone is coming and Chunxiang is still alive? Ridiculous, ridiculous! What did I see in the bandit camp?

(*Enter Sister Stone with Chunxiang*)

Sister Stone:

(*To the tune of* **Nanbaolaocui**)

The case is settled before the throne;

The case is settled before the throne.

(*Looks around*)

How is it that Mr Liu and Miss Du are standing there with pursed lips?

Lord Du makes a judgement of the worst sort;

Tutor Chen makes a speech of the worst sort.

Chen Zuiliang:

Here comes Chunxiang! This nun is a robber!

[净]啐,陈教化,谁是贼?你报老夫人死哩,春香死哩!做的个纸棺材,舌锹拨。
[向生介]柳相公喜也。
[生]姑姑喜也。这丫头那里见俺来?
[贴]你和小姐牡丹亭做梦时有俺在。
[生]好活人活证。
[净、贴]鬼团圆不想到真和合,
鬼揶揄不想做人生活。
老相公,你便是鬼三台,费评跋。
[净、贴并下]
[末]朝门之下,人钦鬼伏之所,谁敢不从!少不得小姐劝状元认了平章,成其大事。
[旦作笑劝生介]柳郎,拜了丈人罢!
[生不伏介]

Sister Stone:

>Oops! Beggar Chen, who do you say is a robber? You made the false report that the lady was dead and Chunxiang was dead.
>
>>You put them in a paper coffin
>>
>>And buried them with your tongue.
>
>(*To Liu Mengmei*)
>
>Congratulations, Mr Liu!

Liu Mengmei:

>Congratulations, Sister Stone! But where is it that I once saw this servant maid?

Chunxiang:

>I was in the dream you and Miss Du experienced.

Liu Mengmei:

>So you're a living witness.

Sister Stone, Chunxiang:

>>Who knows that ghostly union may turn true!
>>
>>Who knows that ghostly love may renew!
>
>Lord Du,
>
>>Even if you rule over the nether world,
>>
>>You will find the case absurd.
>
>(*Exeunt Sister Stone and Chunxiang*)

Chen Zuiliang:

>In front of the palace gate, both men and ghosts will have to show submission. Miss Du, it's up to you to persuade Mr Liu into greeting his father-in-law for everybody's benefit.

Du Liniang:

>(*Smiles and tries to persuade Liu Mengmei*)
>
>My dear, just greet your father-in-law with a bow!
>
>(*Liu Mengmei is reluctant to do so*)

【北水仙子】

[旦]呀呀呀，你好差。

[扯生手、按生肩介]好好好，点着你玉带腰身把玉手叉。

[生]几百个桃条!

[旦]拜、拜、拜，拜荆条曾下马。

[扯外介][旦]扯、扯、扯，做泰山倒了架。

[指生介]他、他、他，点黄钱聘了咱。

俺、俺、俺，逗寒食吃了他茶。

[指末介]你、你、你，待求官、报信则把口皮喳。

[指生介]是是是，是他开棺见椁渞除罢。

[指外介]爹爹爹，你可也骂够了咱这鬼乜邪。

Du Liniang:

    (*To the tune of **Beishuixianzi***)

    Oh, oh, oh,

    You are making a show.

    (*Pulls at Liu Mengmei's hand and presses his shoulder*)

    Now, now, now,

    By pressing your shoulder, I'll force you to bow.

Liu Mengmei:

    I won't forget the flogging!

Du Liniang:

    Bow, bow, bow,

    Ancient kings were flogged anyhow.

    (*Pulls at Du Bao*)

    Pull, pull, pull,

    The father-in-law has to be cool.

    (*Points at Liu Mengmei*)

    He, he, he,

    He burnt paper money to marry me.

    I, I, I,

    I accepted the offer from this guy.

    (*Points at Chen Zuiliang*)

    You, you, you,

    You have indeed made much ado.

    (*Points at Liu Mengmei*)

    True, true, true,

    You opened my coffin to bring my corpse to view.

    (*Points at Du Bao*)

    Dad, dad, dad,

    Your swearing is indeed bad.

［丑扮韩子才冠带捧诏上］圣旨已到，跪听宣读。"据奏奇异，敕赐团圆。平章杜宝，进阶一品。妻甄氏，封淮阴郡夫人。状元柳梦梅，除授翰林院学士。妻杜丽娘，封阳和县君。就着鸿胪官韩子才送归宅院。"叩头谢恩。
［丑见介］状元恭喜了。
［生］呀，是韩子才兄。何以得此？
［丑］自别了尊兄，蒙本府起送先儒之后，到京考中鸿胪之职，故此得会。
［生］一发奇异了。
［末］原来韩老先也是旧朋友。［行介］

(*Enter Han Zicai in official robe, holding the imperial decree in his hands*)

Han Zicai:

Here comes the imperial decree. Kneel and listen: "In regards to the extraordinary story, I hereby decree that the family be reunited. Grand Chancellor Du Bao is promoted to the topmost rank. His wife Lady Zhen is granted the title Lady of Huaiyang Prefecture. The Number-one Scholar Liu Mengmei is appointed member of the Imperial Academy. His wife Du Liniang is granted the title Lady of Yanghe County. Master of Ceremony Han Zicai is to accompany them to their residence." Kowtow and thank the imperial grace.

(*Greets Liu Mengmei*)

Congratulations to you, Number-one Scholar.

Liu Mengmei:

Oh, it's you, Mr Han Zicai! How did you become Master of Ceremony?

Han Zicai:

After I saw you off, the prefect showed special favour to me as the descendant of a renowned family by offering financial aid for me to enter the imperial examination in the capital. I passed the examination and was appointed Master of Ceremony. That's why we have the chance to meet here.

Liu Mengmei:

It's all too fantastic!

Chen Zuiliang:

So Mr Han is also an old friend of ours.

(*Walks around the stage*)

All:

【南双声子】
　　[众]姻缘诧，姻缘诧，
　　阴人梦黄泉下。
　　福分大，福分大，
　　周堂内是这朝门下。
　　齐见驾，齐见驾，
　　真喜洽，真喜洽。
　　领阳间诰敕，
　　去阴司销假。
【北尾】
　　[生]从今后把牡丹亭梦影双描画。
　　[旦]亏杀你南枝挨暖俺北枝花。
　　则普天下做鬼的有情谁似咱！

　　杜陵寒食草青青，
　　羯鼓声高众乐停。
　　更恨香魂不相遇，
　　春肠遥断牡丹亭。

　　千愁万恨过花时，
　　人去人来酒一卮。
　　唱尽新词欢不见，
　　数声啼鸟上花枝。

(*To the tune of* **Nanshuangshengzi**)

How absurd!

How absurd!

The match began with a dream in the nether world.

How fortunate!

How fortunate!

The wedding takes place in front of the palace gate.

What the emperor has to say,

What the emperor has to say

Makes everybody happy and gay,

Makes everybody happy and gay.

By imperial decree,

From the nether world Miss Du is set free.

Liu Mengmei:

(*To the tune of* **Beiwei**)

From now on,

We shall enjoy the Peony-Pavilion dream.

Du Liniang:

Thanks to your tender care,

My ghostly love becomes supreme!

When verdant grass grows on the vernal sand,

The Jin drums resound across the land.

The yearning soul regrets to miss her mate;

The Peony Pavilion sees her woeful trait.

While ladies weep and sigh as blooms decline,

Men come and go to drink a cup of wine.

All raptures vanish when the curtain falls;

From blooming twigs a charming birdsong drawls.

ABOUT THE TRANSLATOR

Wang Rongpei was born in Shanghai on June 28, 1942. He got his BA from Shanghai University of Foreign Languages in 1964 and MA from Fudan University in 1967. He is Professor of English and has been President of Dalian University of Foreign Languages since 1985. He has made great achievements in English education, and in the research and translation of Chinese classics. His main translations include *Laozi, Zhuangzi, Book of Changes, The Book of Poetry, 300 Early Chinese Poems, The Complete Poems of Tao Yuanming, The Peony Pavilion*, etc.

图书在版编目(CIP)数据

牡丹亭／(明)汤显祖著；汪榕培英译．－长沙：湖南人民出版社，2000.12
(大中华文库)
ISBN 7-5438-2534-1

Ⅰ.牡... Ⅱ.①汤... ②汪... Ⅲ.汉英对照，戏剧
Ⅳ.H319.4:Ⅰ

中国版本图书馆CIP数据核字(2000)第19650号

组稿编辑：尹飞舟
责任编辑：戴 茵 曹伟明
审 校：路旦俊

大中华文库

牡丹亭

[明] 汤显祖 著

汪榕培 英译

本书版权由上海外语教育出版社提供

ⓒ2000 湖南人民出版社

出版发行者：
湖南人民出版社
（湖南长沙银盆南路78号）
邮政编码410006
外文出版社
（中国北京百万庄大街24号）
邮政编码100037
http://www.flp.com.cn

制版、排版者：
湖南省新华印刷三厂（湖南新华精品印务有限公司）

印制者：
深圳当纳利旭日印刷有限公司印刷

开本：960×640 1/16(精装) 印张：66.5 印数：1-3000
2000年第1版第1次印刷
（汉英）
ISBN 7-5438-2534-1/Ⅰ·320
定价：135.00元（全2卷）

版权所有　　盗版必究